Devil in the Detail

Leo McNeir

enigma
publishing

Also by Leo McNeir

Getaway with Murder

Death in Little Venice

Kiss and Tell

and published by enigma publishing

enigma publishing
PO Box 1901, Milton Keynes, MK19 6DN

First published 2004
© Leo McNeir 2004

A CIP record for this book is available from the British Library.

ISBN 0 9531742 2 0

Typesetting and cover design by *specialist* publishing services ltd, Milton Keynes

Printed in Great Britain by The Baskerville Press, Salisbury, Wiltshire

Leo McNeir is a linguist and lexicographer and has edited eight dictionaries in fifteen languages in the past decade, the standard works in their field.

Devil in the Detail is his fourth novel, following the successful publication of *Getaway with Murder* (2000), *Death in Little Venice* (2001) and *Kiss and Tell* (2003).

He lives with cookery writer Cassandra McNeir and their cat, Mog, in a three hundred year old cottage in a Northamptonshire village.

They have four children between them and a narrowboat on the Grand Union Canal.

Dedication

For Tessa and Johnny ...
the usual suspects

For Berwyn ...
who knows all about details

and for Roy
in loving memory

Prologue

He was walking quickly along the towpath when he spotted the pub and stopped in his tracks. It was on the *other* side of the canal from where he now stood … the *wrong* side, as far as he was concerned. Hesitating, he looked back down the towpath. There was a bridge not far behind him. Presumably, if he crossed over at that point he would be able to walk round the houses that backed onto the water and find his way to the pub along the road leading to its car park. That would probably involve a lengthy detour, and he was already late. The phone call had delayed him.

There was no one in sight to ask for help. He stood thinking for a few seconds, a fine-looking man over six feet tall, with broad shoulders and slim build. Like many black athletes and sportsmen, he wore his hair close-cut so that his head was almost shaved.

Somewhere at the back of his mind he had the notion there was an alternative way to go. Looking behind him he saw steps leading down the bank and remembered Marnie talking about a pedestrian tunnel at Cosgrove under the Grand Union. Cautiously on the bumpy surface, he descended and found the entrance.

It looked as if it had been built for children, or even *by* children, and it brought a smile to his face. Everything about it seemed eccentric, from its irregular outline to its undulating walls. From outside he saw how the roof lining dipped in the middle and knew he would have to walk its length bent forward to avoid hitting his head. He could understand why Anne had said it was her favourite tunnel on the whole waterways network.

They had sat out that evening a few weeks earlier, the whole group, making plans for the summer, Estelle, Marnie, Anne, Serena, Ralph, Dorothy, George, Margaret, Ronny and the others. He pictured each of their faces in turn as they sat drinking chilled wine in the warmth of the evening while the stars gradually came out. On one face in particular his mind dwelt. Ducking his head to enter the tunnel, he revisited the scene, lit by the flares they had stuck in the ground when the light had begun to fade into dusk.

He had barely gone five paces when someone came into the tunnel from the opposite end, and he felt self-conscious; they would feel threatened at the sight of a powerfully-built black man in such a confined area, especially in these difficult times. But the person coming towards him seemed unconcerned, and he began to move over, ready to stand aside to let them pass more easily.

As he stopped, recognition dawned on him, and he was now no longer surprised that the on-comer had no hesitation in advancing towards him. The smile was already returning to his lips.

Talk of the devil, he thought.

1

Looking back later on the strange and terrible events of that long hot summer, Marnie judged that this was the moment when she had the first inkling that things were going badly wrong.

Life had started to settle down to a busy but enjoyable pattern. She had begun feeling that all the changes she had brought into her existence were paying off. The struggle to establish herself with a new business in a new place, a new home and new relationships had reached a plateau from which she could look to the way ahead with confidence.

That morning she had left the office for a routine meeting with her biggest client with words of warning in her mind ... there's something you ought to know for your journey ... you could have problems.

Now, sitting at the traffic lights in Leicester she stared at the scene unfolding before her with incredulity. How could this be happening on a pleasant summer's day in the heart of England? While she waited, not daring to move for fear of drawing attention to herself and inviting trouble – potentially very big trouble – she scrolled back through her memory to try to work out when the series of events that had led her here first started.

The last moment of normality – if anything connected with her sister approached the normal – was when Beth had phoned about her plans for the summer. If only Marnie had taken up her sister's suggestion, everything would have turned out differently, for good and for ill.

Yes, she decided, the starting point was that phone call.

2

"You *cannot* be *serious!*"

It was Marnie's sister, Beth. She always had a tendency to sound like John McEnroe when faced with what she would regard as the wilder eccentricities of her younger sister.

"What did I say?" Marnie retorted into the phone.

"You said you weren't going to take a summer holiday. Marnie, you *need* a break, especially after all your hard work over the past year ... not to mention ... well, all the things that have happened to you recently."

"I told you I was staying here – in this *rural paradise* – for the summer. I can relax here while everyone else is away. What's so strange about that? Don't answer that. Tell me about your holiday plans, instead."

"And that's another thing you always do."

"What?" she said wearily.

"Change the subject as soon as I pin you down in an argument."

"Do I?"

"And you do that, too."

"Now what?"

"You aren't going to tell me you're not aware that you start answering a question with another question?"

"Are you sure about that?"

"*Marnie!*"

"Sorry. Only joking. But seriously, do tell me about your holiday. Where did you say you were going?"

"Phuket."

"I'll pretend you didn't say that."

"You're trying to wind me up, Marnie ... and that's a *very* old joke."

"I thought you said *you forget.*"

"You know perfectly well I said *Phuket.*" She pronounced it Foo-kett. "You also know it's in the south of Thailand. It'll be idyllic. We're staying in a gorgeous hotel. One of Paul's colleagues stayed there last year on a stopover from San Francisco. Actually, it's more like a chalet with its own patio under the palm trees, almost on the beach. I can't wait."

"You'll hate the crowds."

"*Crowds?* Marnie, the place is famous for its seclusion. Our next-door neighbours will be hermit crabs."

"No. I meant the crowds at Gatwick airport. That's what summer's all about. Your next-door neighbours will be irate tourists complaining about the delays to their flights – and yours – as the air traffic controllers can't squeeze all the planes into the sky, while the baggage-handlers go on strike. It's the Great British Summer Holiday Rush."

"Would there be a touch of jealousy creeping in here, by any chance?" said Beth.

"Why would I be jealous?"

"There you go again ... a question on top of a question." Before Marnie could reply, Beth added, "Don't even think about it."

"Beth, I have no reason to be jealous. I'm sure you'll have a great time and it'll be perfect. For you and Paul. Me, I'm happy to stay here. This is a beautiful place. They've promised a long hot summer, and I'll be able to go for trips on my boat on the lovely Grand Union Canal. Who could ask for more than that?"

"Well, yes, that's very nice too, and I can see why ... wait a minute. Aren't you forgetting something? *Sally Ann* is in fact *my* boat ... Paul's and mine. It seems to have escaped your notice that you haven't yet paid us for her."

"Of course. Fair comment. Anyway, this chalet ... does it have cooking facilities or do you get all your meals at the hotel?"

"The chalet? Oh, it's got absolutely *everything*. We thought some of the time we'd – *Marnie!*"

Ten minutes later, she was still smiling at the thought of her conversation with Beth when Anne walked into the office carrying a tray. She had been doing her regular morning round in the yard, handing out mugs of tea and coffee to the builders working on the renovation of the former Glebe Farm. Without pausing, she walked across to the kitchen area at the back of the large open-plan space and filled the kettle. She looked over at Marnie.

"You've been speaking to Beth, haven't you?"

"Anne with an 'e', I swear you're psychic. How else could you know that?"

Anne poured hot water into the cafetière. "Easy, really. First, I was the one who gave you the message to ring her just before I went out on site." She enjoyed using the proper term. "And second, you usually have that amused expression on your face after you've been chatting with her. You wound her up, didn't you?"

Marnie stood up and went to look out of the window into the yard. "Yes, but she enjoys it. And she deserved it ... telling me all about her exotic holiday trip to Thailand."

"When are they going?"

"Next week. Paul's finished all his exam marking, and they want a break before he gets on with his research project. They're coming back via California so he can join in a seminar at Stamford University."

"You're not jealous," said Anne.

"Course not. I love my life ... wouldn't want to change a thing. Travel's great, but at the moment ..." She made a gesture with her hand, encompassing the farm complex, the office, their environment, everything around them.

"I know. I feel the same. Though I would like to do some travelling. I've only been abroad once, to France. We went camping. It was great. That was before dad was made redundant the first time. Since then ..." She made the same gesture with her hand.

"Actually," Marnie said. "I think we might be in line for a job in Italy."

She walked back to her desk and picked up a letter from the pile of correspondence. It had been sent by Philip Everett, senior partner in the firm in London where Marnie had worked for nine years, most of them as head of the interior design group.

"*Italy?*"

"Yeah. Philip has asked if we could look at this renovation project in Umbria."

Anne brought the mugs of coffee and stood beside Marnie to read the letter. They were both about the same height: Marnie five foot seven, Anne an inch shorter. Marnie was in her early thirties but looked younger. She had dark hair that had been cut close to her head after treatment for an almost fatal head injury the year before, but was now growing back to her preferred shoulder-length style. With a clear complexion and brown eyes, she had the kind of slim outline that looked good in jeans.

Anne was seventeen, and 'slim' would have been an understatement. A tramp of their acquaintance had once described her as a 'skinny bint with no tits' and, although her figure was developing as she grew to maturity, no one would yet have called him an out-and-out liar. On a good day she looked as pale as bone china, with light blonde hair cut ultra-short and bright blue eyes. A fortnight earlier she had passed her driving test at the first attempt, and the examiner had remarked that she looked far too young to be at the wheel of a car, but he could not fault her ability as a driver.

Marnie pointed at Philip's letter. "I think there's a catch here. Look at the last paragraph."

Anne read it out. "*The job was to be handled by one of our team in the office, but she has had a few problems lately, and it would help matters if she could do the work under your guidance. Need any staff up there? Give me a ring and we'll discuss.*"

"See what I mean?" said Marnie.

"You think Philip wants you to take her on as well as the job?"

"I wonder." She sat down and reached for the phone. "Let's find out."

Philip was out at a site meeting. His secretary promised he would ring Marnie back later in the day. She put the phone down and glanced through the letter again.

"Oh well," she said. "It'll keep."

• • • • •

Work on the renovation of Glebe Farm was going well. True, they had experienced some delays with the supply of materials, but that was normal on any construction project, especially where it was necessary to match finishes with an early eighteenth century building. The farmhouse stood on one side of the yard, built of cream limestone under a slate roof, with stone-mullioned windows, two on each side of the central front door. The proportions were good, giving the house a simple elegance, and it presided over the complex with a calm authority.

To the left of the elevation were attached three cottages, forming a terrace that made up the second side of the square. They were built of the same stone, but with timber window frames painted white. Their front doors were a glossy deep blue, and each bore a number in solid brass: one, two and three. Number one, furthest from the farmhouse, had been rented since the previous September by a newly-married couple, Jill and Alex Burton, who were in a state of blissful happiness with their marriage, their home and the universe in general. Apart from contributing a steady flow of income, they were a friendly presence at the farm and helped by feeding Dolly, Marnie's sturdy black cat, when business required Marnie and Anne to be absent.

That Tuesday afternoon, Marnie was making her regular inspection tour with Bob, the foreman. Anne took notes as they walked from room to room. The petty snags experienced in cottage number one had been quickly eradicated, and number two was virtually ready for occupation.

Marnie closed the door behind them as they turned towards number three. "It's looking good, Bob ... great. There's just that kitchen door to be eased and anyone could move in tomorrow."

The foreman smiled.

"And there's the slatted shelving to go in the airing cupboard in the bathroom," Anne added.

The smile faltered. "Ah, yes. Don't know how we missed that, me dook."

Anne checked her list. "And the dodgy thermostat on the radiator in bedroom three."

Bob's smile vanished. "Er ..."

"They've promised the replacement ASAP," Anne reminded him.

"Don't you worry. We'll get on to it as soon as it arrives."

"OK. It's on my desk, actually ... came this morning. I'll let you have it when we've finished."

Marnie concealed a smile as she opened the door to number three and led the way inside. They went from room to room, and Anne was surprised how few notes she had to take. In the third bedroom, the last to be inspected, Marnie looked down from the window into the yard.

As if muttering to herself, she said, "Clean up the yard, finish those setts and pavers, put in a few tubs of plants, and the place'll look quite presentable."

Bob joined her and looked out. "If it was me, me dook ..." he said tentatively.

"Go on."

"Well, I'd put the gravel down round the paved areas … make it look lighter … and we could shift the mixer and the gennie round the back of the farmhouse, so's you wouldn't know they were there."

"It wouldn't be inconvenient for you and the men?"

"Not really. We'd just get in from the back. And if it was me …"

"Bob, it is you. Just tell me."

"Well, I'd get a coat of paint on the front door, and you'd never know the whole place wasn't ready."

"True. But I wouldn't want to make it difficult for you to get on with the job."

"It wouldn't."

Anne said, "Marnie's being tactful. She means she doesn't want you and the others scratching new paint on her nice front door."

Bob laughed. "You're the guv'nor, Marnie, but she's the one we have to watch out for!"

Marnie grinned. "You're right … appearances can be deceptive."

She turned and looked through the window, imagining the yard cleared of clutter. The pile of gravel would be gone, and the equipment would be out of sight. The paving would be hosed down. No more dust. Excellent. She looked across the yard to the barn that she and Anne used as their workplace, the *office barn*. Its door was slid back to reveal glazing like a shopfront, slightly tinted, that turned their otherwise windowless space into a bright and pleasant working environment. When the doors were closed, the building looked like a normal stone barn, in keeping with the farmyard.

"If you're sure, Bob … let's go for it."

"Righto. Are you moving in here now, Marnie, into number three? Is that the plan?"

"That's the idea. But to be honest, I've had so much on my mind, I hadn't given it much thought lately. The main thing is that we get number two completed. Grace is coming down to have a look round later on today. She won't be disappointed."

• • • • •

Shortly before four o'clock, Anne set off up the field track to the village. It was one of her favourite times of the day, her trip to the post-box and then on to the shop for any provisions they might need. It brought the opportunity to see other people from the village, including the children as they came out of primary school. Anne was a popular member of the community. She had been feared dead not long before, and had played a major part in solving an ancient murder mystery the previous year, almost at the cost of her own life. The children liked her because she and Marnie had once organised a visit for them to *Sally Ann*, complete with boat trip and a spectacular tea party.

On that afternoon the routine was varied. Anne met a car bumping its way down the sloping track over hardened ruts in the ground. It stopped beside her, and a smiling face looked out as the driver's window slid open.

"Hi, Grace. Marnie's expecting you."

"Is it finished?"

"Good as. Just one or two small adjustments, and you can move in."

"Brilliant! We can't wait."

"I think you'll be pleased."

"*Pleased*? We'll be *blissful*. Bye! See you later."

Anne was smiling as she continued on her way. *Blissful*, she thought. That was exactly how Jill and Alex had described themselves soon after they moved in. Anne was delighted. All Marnie's plans were coming to fruition just as she had hoped. It was going to be a *blissful* summer.

• • • • •

Grace parked beside Marnie's Land Rover Discovery at the back of the office barn, and wondered if she and Will would need a four-wheel-drive when they lived at Glebe Farm. *When they lived at Glebe Farm!* The idea thrilled her, and even the thought that there was no proper road down over the field could not diminish her enthusiasm. She stood momentarily by the barn and looked across at the cottages nestling together, the stone facade glowing in the afternoon sun. *Grace Parchman*, she thought, *you are a lucky girl.*

She had grown up in the village and had often heard her father, landlord of the pub, *The Two Roses*, bemoan the fact that there were no houses within the price range of young people. Now, Marnie's developments brought the prospect of affordable homes. True, they were for rent not for purchase, but most young couples wanted somewhere to make a start, and were not looking for a home for the rest of their lives. This was a better beginning than they had ever expected.

One of the builders was tipping gravel from a wheelbarrow outside cottage number one, and the uncluttered yard seemed bigger than when she had last visited, just a week earlier. It was starting to look like somewhere to live rather than a building site. Grace knocked on the office door and went in to find Marnie speaking on the phone.

With a hand over the mouthpiece, Marnie held up a keyring. "Grace, hi. If you'd like to go over, I'll join you shortly. Won't be long."

Grace was only too happy to have the house to herself and she headed for the blue door with the shiny brass number two gleaming on the new paint. Marnie went back to her phone call. At the other end, the secretary announced that she was putting her through to Philip Everett.

"I'm intrigued about this job in Italy, Phil. Am I right in thinking there's a catch?"

"You have a suspicious mind, Marnie. And yes ... there is a catch. But it's not obligatory, just an idea I had."

"Are you asking me to supervise the work or take it on? That's not clear from your letter. And who's this member of staff with problems?"

"Answers are: yes, yes and you don't know her. In that order."

"Come on, then. Spill the beans. What am I letting myself in for?"

"Briefly, one of our clients has bought a villa in Umbria and wants it restored. You'd love it: sixteenth century, stone, painted ceilings, murals, galleried upstairs, the works. The structure's pretty sound, but the inside needs a complete makeover. Just your kind of thing."

"When do I fly out?"

"Exactly."

"And the catch?"

"Estelle."

"*Estelle?*"

"Very promising designer. Reminds me of you when you were starting here: lots of ideas and flare, enthusiastic, very hard-working."

"You never said those things when I was asking for a rise."

"Damn right!"

"But?" said Marnie. "I can sense a *but* creeping in here."

"Yes. Take all her qualities – *your* qualities – and exaggerate them just a little. What do you get?"

"If the answer's not Superwoman, I give in."

"You get a great worker with real talent ... and a tendency to get obsessive about things."

"And you think I might be able to help her?"

"To tell you the truth, Marnie, I just don't know. But I had this idea that if she got out of the office and had the chance to work alongside someone else with her kind of talent, but a more balanced approach ... I dunno ... I thought it might calm her down."

"Not quite."

"Not keen? Pity, she's really –"

"I didn't mean that, Phil. I meant ... that isn't the whole picture. You're keeping something from me, aren't you? What else is there?"

Philip laughed and replied with a Japanese accent. "You one sharp cookie for a *gaijin*."

"So?"

"She's had a bad time just lately. Usual thing ... long-term relationship ... boyfriend decided to end it ... she went to pieces."

"When was this?"

"Couple of months ago."

"And she's still cut up about it?"

"She took it very badly. They'd been living together for four years or so ..."

"By coincidence," said Marnie, "about the same length of time Simon and I'd been married when we split up."

"Well, yes."

"And you remembered how I went to pieces at the time and you thought I'd be a suitable nursemaid."

"I remembered how you got through, Marnie ... forced yourself to go on, even when I knew how painful your life was."

"I can't say I'm overjoyed about this, Phil. I love the idea of getting the job in Italy – sounds great. But having those strings attached ... playing the agony aunt ... I don't know."

"No strings, Marnie. I'm offering you the job anyway. To be honest, the client asked for you personally. You did their house in Notting Hill a few years back. The Estelle thing was an afterthought on my part."

"How'd you see it working?"

"That rather depended on you. If Estelle had a break from the office ... pastures new – literally in your case – perhaps she'd get things in perspective ... put herself back together again."

"I found the team in the office a great support when I was having problems. Perhaps you're underestimating them."

"I don't think so. There's a ... a further side to this."

"Meaning?"

"You went into a shell, Marnie ... went quiet ... threw yourself into the work."

"It's how I coped."

"Estelle's been ... different. She went off the rails ... partying, drinking too much, throwing herself at men ..."

"Including you?"

"No."

"So you're jealous?"

"I'm being serious."

"I know. Look ... what if I came down and met her ... just to talk about the job? We could take it from there."

"That'd be great."

"But I can't promise anything ... not until I've had a chance to meet her."

"When can you come?"

• • • • •

Marnie and Anne prepared supper in the galley, managing despite the confined space on *Sally Ann*, to keep out of each other's way. Anne was slicing red peppers, spring onions, sugar-snap peas and carrots, while Marnie scooped out the pips from two melons. A pan of noodles was bubbling beside them.

Marnie wiped her hands on a towel and opened a bottle of red wine. "OK. Ralph can arrive when he likes. We're ready. Need any help with those?"

"Nope. All done. When will he be back?"

"That's in the hands of the gods or – more precisely – the traffic on the Oxford ring-road. Any time now, I expect."

Marnie was draining the noodles when Anne called into the cabin from laying the table on the stern deck. "Here's Ralph!"

Through the galley window she caught sight of a tall figure in a light grey suit moving quickly. Marnie saw his hand rise to greet Anne and heard him call out before he turned towards his boat that was moored by the canal at right angles to *Sally Ann* in her docking area.

Ralph was on sabbatical from All Saints College, Oxford. A professor of economics, he had been using the time to write his latest book on the 'tiger economies' of the Far East. For the past year he had lived on his boat, where he had installed all the facilities he needed for writing. In contrast to the ageing and homely lines of *Sally Ann*, his boat was sleek, a deep sage green with the name *Thyrsis* emblazoned in gold lettering on the sides. Anne had compared it irreverently to the colours of a Harrods carrier bag. In recent months Ralph had been arranging to leave his college to concentrate full-time on research, writing and consultancy, while acquiring the title and status of visiting professor.

Ralph was an acknowledged expert in his field. In his mid-forties, he had built up an international reputation through his writing and lecturing. A widower for several years, he was convinced he owed much of his recent success to Marnie. She had first met him at a difficult time in his life. Now, he was back on course, they were what Anne described as an *item*, and were planning to marry.

Anne came through to the galley in search of cutlery and glasses. "Ralph said he'd be five minutes ... just wants to change out of his suit."

It was a lie. And Marnie knew it.

• • • • •

Ralph often professed he had learnt much from Marnie, though she always refuted it. But one skill she had taught him was the art of opening champagne bottles without spilling the wine or spraying everyone within range like racing drivers on the podium.

It had been true that he wanted to change into casual clothes, but he had omitted to tell Anne that the real reason he had gone direct to *Thyrsis* was to retrieve the Veuve Clicquot that he had put in the fridge that morning before leaving for his meetings. Now, as Marnie and Anne sat at the table on the stern deck of *Sally Ann* in the warmth of the evening sun, he stood and removed the gold cap and wire cage from the bottle. Holding it tilted at forty-five degrees, he fastened his grip round the cork and carefully twisted the base of the bottle till the cork eased its way out with a satisfyingly loud *pop!* Vapour like smoke from a gun barrel swirled out, but not a drop was lost.

"For one so talented," said Marnie, "you look remarkably pleased with yourself at accomplishing such a simple act. Or do you have something special to tell us?"

"*Special?*" Ralph repeated casually. "I don't know what you mean."

"Of course not," Anne chimed in. "Everyone has champagne to celebrate Tuesdays. It's a well-known fact."

Ralph smiled at them. "It's a fair cop, guv. Today *is* rather special. The University Senate has approved my appointment as Visiting Professor."

"I thought that was just a formality," said Marnie.

"Yes, but it's nice to have it confirmed officially. And that's not all. My publisher has accepted the new book, my colleague at Yale has finalised my lecture tour of the States and Canada, and the BBC has asked me to do a three-programme series on television in the autumn."

"*Wow!*" Marnie exclaimed.

"Quite. The letters were all in my pigeon hole when I got in to college this morning."

Anne was beaming. "This is a real Red Letter Day."

Ralph poured the champagne into flutes. Marnie looked on benignly.

Anne frowned. "Wait a minute, Ralph. You said you'd put the champagne in the fridge this morning."

"That's right."

"Which was before you went to college."

"Of course."

"I know you're a genius and all that, but how could you know those letters would be waiting for you?"

"I didn't. In fact, the celebration has nothing to do with any of *my* news. That was just a coincidence."

Marnie laughed.

"I don't get it," Anne said.

Marnie stood up, holding her glass. "Come on." She stepped ashore and gestured to Anne to go with her. Ralph handed her a glass of champagne and followed.

"What's going on?" Anne asked.

Ralph took her arm. "You'll see."

They walked through the spinney where dappled light and shade made patterns on them as they passed. All the while, Anne asked what they were doing and where they were going, and received only non-committal replies. Arriving at the end of the barn where Marnie kept her cars, Ralph pointed across at the cottages, just visible round the side of the office barn. Anne stared at them.

"What am I looking for? They seem no different to how they were when we left an hour ago."

"Perhaps you're looking the wrong way," said Marnie. "Try turning round."

Anne shook her head in bewilderment. "I don't get this at –"

She stopped in mid-sentence. In front of her, parked at the side of the barn was a car, a Mini, red with a white roof, shiny as new. Two features immediately caught her eye. The first was a pink bow attached to the top of the radio aerial. The second was a large black cat curled up on the bonnet. Anne understood immediately.

"It's a new perch for Dolly," she said.

"Correct," said Ralph.

Marnie added, "And when Dolly doesn't need it, you can use it for its secondary purpose and drive around in it."

Anne turned to Ralph, solemnly handed him her glass and performed a cartwheel. When she had completed the manoeuvre, Ralph gave her back the glass and Marnie gave her an envelope.

"I can really use it?" Anne said, her eyes sparkling.

"It's yours," Marnie said. "Those are the documents. It's taxed, insured, and the tank's full. It's two years old, low mileage. A present from both of us."

Anne handed her glass to Ralph and fell flat on her back on the ground, eyes closed. Dead. The cat sat up and yawned.

• • • • •

Supper was delayed that evening while a test drive took place over the field track and through the village. Sadly for Anne, no one was on the street to witness the passage of the gleaming red Mini with her at the wheel, but that did nothing to dampen her enthusiasm. Returning to base, she found it fitted perfectly into the garage barn alongside Marnie's Discovery and her pre-war MG sports car.

During supper Anne interrogated Marnie and Ralph on how they had come to buy the Mini, and when she protested that they really, but *really*, should not have done so, Marnie told her that it in no way compensated for all the work Anne had done on a minimal wage. Anne had the good sense not to hog the whole conversation on such an important day for Ralph, though he was happy just to fill in a few more details.

Eventually Marnie said, "Well, I've got some news, too. Philip wants me to supervise a project in Italy."

"Wonderful. Whereabouts?" said Ralph.

"Umbria."

"Whereabouts is that?" Anne asked.

"Other side of Tuscany."

"I'll drive you down if you like," Anne said nonchalantly, trying to adopt the heavy eyelids of Marlene Dietrich while fiddling with her car keys on the table.

"I'll bear it in mind."

"Good. A Mini would be just right. Remember that film, *The Italian Job*? Minis were the stars."

"This job," said Marnie, "would be more mundane ... but there is a catch."

"What kind of catch?" said Ralph.

"Phil wants me to supervise a designer from his office on the project. For 'supervise', read 'play nursemaid to'."

She outlined her conversation with Philip. Ralph listened attentively.

Anne asked, "Will she be coming to work here then?"

"That all depends on my talking it over with Philip ... and Estelle, of course. I'm going to see them the day after tomorrow."

• • • • •

After they had cleared the table, Anne excused herself, saying she wanted an early night tucked up with a good book. When asked what she was reading, she held up the instruction manual for the Mini.

Marnie and Ralph walked over to *Thyrsis*, with its efficient modern shower and more spacious interior, where they slept.

Marnie said, "You didn't say much when I explained about the Estelle proposition. Were you lost in thought about your budding television career?" She prodded him gently in the ribs.

"Actually ..." He opened the hatch in the middle of the boat and went down the steps. "I was wondering how this arrangement with Estelle would work. You've got a good routine with Anne, but it's all based on you as the designer. Were you wanting to take on staff at this stage?"

Marnie followed him down and pulled the hatch closed behind her. "That's one of my questions for Philip. I get the impression he'd still be employing her, and she'd just assist me on that one job."

"It will all depend on the details," Ralph said. "Typical of Philip to try and help sort out her life."

"Yes. He always means well, and I do trust him ..."

Ralph drew the curtains over the portholes and switched on the lights. "But?"

They walked along to the sleeping cabin. Marnie sat on the bed looking thoughtful. "There are so many imponderables."

"You have some misgivings about Estelle?"

"It's just ... we've made such a good start, Anne and I. We're a team. I don't want to introduce a discordant note that might spoil the atmosphere we've built up at Glebe Farm." Marnie kicked off her shoes. "Do you want to shower first?"

"Why don't we share?"

She smiled up at Ralph. "I didn't realise you were so environmentally-minded. It's very public-spirited to want to save water like that."

"My thoughts exactly."

Ralph ran the shower for a minute to warm up the cubicle while they undressed. They climbed in together and began squeezing shower gel over each other.

"There's not a lot of room in here," Marnie observed.

Ralph worked the gel on his hands into a lather. "What's the bad news?"

3

Marnie caught an express for London after the commuter rush had finished and sat by the window watching the canal that threaded the same route as the railway. She regarded the canal network as a kind of linear village, or like a series of desert trails from oasis to oasis, travelled by nomads who were her neighbours. The newspaper on her lap lay unopened.

The proposal from Philip Everett had been troubling her, an intrusion into the world she had built around herself and Anne – and to an increasing extent, Ralph – since leaving London. She had no desire to expand Walker and Co in the way Philip had developed Everett Parker Associates. She just wanted to work freelance. Somewhere in that idea she hoped there would be a long-term place for Anne.

What made her feel uncomfortable was knowing she could not reject Philip's request to help a colleague with a problem. Two years earlier he had offered Marnie a sabbatical, and she had borrowed *Sally Ann*, travelling the waterways for the summer. Now here she was successfully established in the country. Philip had given her his blessing when she left the firm, and had put projects her way, including her biggest client, Willards Brewery. Anne called them the *staple diet* of Walker and Co.

Marnie resolved to meet Estelle with an open mind and a positive spirit. Looking out of the window, she was astonished to find that the train was pulling into Euston station. She had arrived.

• • • • •

Marnie studied the file of photographs. Philip, sitting opposite her at the low table by the window in his office, finished the remains of his coffee.

"This is quite a place," she said without looking up. "I was expecting a kind of farmhouse."

Philip shook his head. "Used to be the manor, home of the local aristo ... quite a big landowner at one time."

"I thought you said it was sixteenth century."

"It is, mainly."

"These vaulted cellars look ancient."

"Yeah. The original house was medieval. The cellars are all that remains of it. I'll let Estelle fill you in on the details ... if you want to go down that track, that is."

Marnie put the file on the table. "The least I can do is meet her. She can brief me ... talk about the project. Has she come up with any ideas?"

"A few, I think. We only got the photos on Monday."

"Fair enough."

"I don't want you to feel under any pressure about this, Marnie."

"That's all right. Tell me how you see it working out ... where she'd be based, who pays her salary ... expenses ... practical matters."

"Up to you ... I'm open-minded. She'd stay on the payroll here. The project would cover travel costs, plus your fees and expenses, of course. Usual rates. But I'd like her to have a break from the office. I think it might help."

"Presumably, she's able to work from home?"

"That might be one solution."

"Where does she live?"

"Barnet."

"Right side of London for getting to us. Or perhaps she'd be better not working in isolation? Personally I wouldn't mind that, but not everyone's the same."

"You can judge when you meet her. It depends on the two of you. I'm out for the rest of today. I'll call you this evening to see how you got on."

"OK. Let's meet."

• • • • •

Estelle opened the briefcase and began spreading photographs on the boardroom table, while Marnie watched her. She had expected someone nervous or at least serious, but Estelle seemed totally at ease. She was petite, about five foot two, with dark auburn hair and grey-blue eyes, light make-up discreetly applied. Dressed in a pale grey silk shirt over black trousers, she looked business-like.

Her handshake had been firm and cool, her smile friendly. If she had any apprehensions about working with Marnie, she did not show them. On entering the boardroom she had at once opened the window, complaining about the fug.

Marnie looked down at the photos. "Great place, this."

"Oh, it's *fabulous*. Have you been there?"

"Umbria? No. Been to Tuscany a few times. You?"

"I've been through it. Absolutely *gorgeous*."

"Phil said you had some ideas about the job."

Estelle opened her briefcase and began extracting sketches and notes for every room. She set them out in the middle of the table, fitting them together to show the whole of the ground floor. Next, she lined the photographs up beside the corresponding rooms. Within a minute most of the table was invisible under paper.

Marnie blinked. "These are good. Who did the plans ... Philip?"

"No. I just drew them myself. The owner had a list of room sizes plus the photos. I thought it'd be useful." She pointed to a site plan. "North is that way, and there's a line of cypresses here in the grounds to mask the afternoon sun on this terrace."

"Right."

"I've got some preliminary ideas about how we might handle this."

Estelle opened a folder to reveal page after page of schemes, room by room, with samples of fabrics and furnishing materials. As she laid them out, she gave a running commentary, explaining how the design fitted together and what furniture was to go in each room.

Marnie was incredulous. "I must've misunderstood. I thought you only had the photos on Monday."

"That's right."

"And you've done all this in the past few days?"

"Not quite. They phoned us last week ... I went round to see them on Friday. You know the Gunns, of course, Marcia and Terry. I think they were disappointed when I turned up. You see, they really asked for you. I told them I was your assistant."

"Yeah. We got on OK when I did their Notting Hill place."

"It's brilliant, Marnie. And they *absolutely* love it. That's why they wanted you again."

Marnie picked up one of the sketches. "I think they'll like these colours. They go for bold. You've made a good choice. How long were you there?"

"Ooh ... an hour maybe."

"And you did all this after one meeting?"

"I got them to describe the house as they saw it, showed them pictures of Italian villas, asked them about their tastes, what they wanted ..." She shrugged.

"I'm impressed."

• • • • •

"Philip, I was impressed."

Marnie was sitting at her desk in the office barn that evening, going through the day's post and Anne's list of messages when Philip rang.

"Good."

"Had you seen what she'd done since meeting the clients?"

"A few of her sketches."

"She's produced a *whole scheme* ... wall finishes, curtains, fabrics for furniture. Extraordinary."

He laughed. "So you're telling me you're superfluous!"

"Well ... she's made a great start. I must say I wouldn't have done so much myself at this stage, not without a site visit. But I couldn't fault her ideas."

"And you reckon you could work together?"

"Don't see why not."

"And on the personal level? How did lunch go?"

• • • • •

Estelle turned the Golf into the street round the corner from the pool of Little Venice and pulled up opposite the pub. The car was blocking the rear garage of one of the houses overlooking the water. She switched off the engine.

"You're going to leave it here?" said Marnie.

"Sure. The house is empty. No one's going to want this space today. The builders have been in there for weeks doing it up. There's nobody around now."

"All London's a building site," Marnie muttered, getting out of the car.

"That's good for people like us," said Estelle cheerfully. "If they can afford us."

They sat with sandwiches and spritzers at a table by the window where they could see the car. The walls around them were covered in pictures of boats, drawings, paintings and photographs, some of them very old.

"So what's it like having your own firm, Marnie?"

"To call me a firm is an exaggeration. I really work as a freelance designer."

"There's just you?"

"I have an assistant – she'd call herself my *apprentice*. Her name's Anne. She's seventeen … about to start doing A-levels at college … wants to be a designer … is going to be a designer."

"How does she fit in with your work?"

"She runs the office, deals with admin, keeps everything ticking over smoothly. We go through the designs, and she gives her ideas. She's got a lot of promise."

"You live together?"

The question took Marnie by surprise, and Estelle noticed.

"Sorry. I just meant –"

"She has a little place of her own, the loft over the office. I'm living on the boat for the time being … until the main house is ready."

"You live alone, then."

"Not exactly. My partner's around for much of the time. He travels quite a bit … has a base in Oxford. He's an academic. How about you?"

Her eyes clouded. "Philip's probably told you about my … relationship."

"He mentioned that you'd split up. I'm sorry."

"Don't be," Estelle said brightly. "Things are much better now."

"Good."

"I've … met someone."

"I see."

"You're probably thinking it's some kind of rebound thing, but –"

"I wouldn't make any hasty judgments," said Marnie. "In fact, I wouldn't make any judgments at all."

Estelle tossed her head. "Well, if you did, you'd probably be right. But I think it's almost like fate."

She sipped her spritzer. Marnie said nothing.

"I met him at the gym where I work out. He's a fitness freak, like me. Only he's more like a real athlete … weight training, serious time on the rowing machine, in the pool."

"So he invited you out for a five mile jog?"

Estelle laughed. "I'd never keep up!" She became serious. "I think he's the most wonderful person I've ever met."

• • • • •

Marnie doodled a heart on a pad as she spoke to Philip. "You didn't mention that she was in a new relationship."

"A *new* …? I had no idea. It must be *very* new."

"A couple of weeks, apparently."

"I really didn't –"

"Not the kind of thing you put up on the office notice board," Marnie said. "Not if you want any kind of privacy."

"I suppose not. And she's really keen ... it's serious?"

"Understatement. Expressions about sliced bread spring to mind. Tell me Phil, is she always like this?"

A pause. "You mean, OTT?"

"That's what I mean."

"She does have a reputation for having ... let's say, *enthusiasms*. Does it put you off?"

"No. Actually, I liked her. She's got character ... a mind of her own. I found her enthusiasm infectious. And she certainly works hard."

"Some people thought she was obsessive ... too obsessive, if that's possible ... got too involved in the projects ... in *everything* really."

"That's not rare," said Marnie. "Anyway, as her employer you should be pleased. You can't blame someone for being keen on her work."

"So ... we have a deal?"

"Why not?"

4

It was late morning on Saturday when the VW Golf came to a halt in the farmyard and Estelle climbed out. Marnie was working in the office barn and she reached the door to find Estelle standing in the middle of the yard taking in the view.

"*Wow*, Marnie! This is some *cool* place. No wonder you gave up your job at Everett Parker. *No contest!*"

Marnie walked over, smiling and offering a hand, but Estelle kissed her on both cheeks and dived back into the car. She pulled out a huge bunch of flowers and a bottle of sparkling wine.

"Not real champagne, I'm afraid, but it's a good Aussie. I think you'll find it drinkable. Watch out for the lilies – that pollen can leave a stain. Are you going to show me round? It looks terrific. Is that your office?"

Marnie laughed. "Do you ever stop for breath, or is that just a misuse of time?"

"Sorry. I get carried away. Calm down, Estelle! Right. I'm calm."

"Would you like the conducted tour first?" said Marnie. "Or shall we go to the boat?"

"Up to you. But since we're here ..."

Marnie showed her round and was surprised that apart from murmurs of approval and interest, Estelle remained quiet throughout most of the tour, letting Marnie explain the layout, her development programme, her plans for the future. Standing in the front bedroom of the unrestored farmhouse, Estelle looked down on the cobbled yard that had been freshly swept and hosed.

"Mistress of all you survey," she muttered quietly. "You must be really proud."

Marnie shrugged. "To tell you the truth, Estelle, I have so much to do, I never think about it like that. I just get on with the job and hope it turns out right. So far, so good."

"If all this belonged to me, I'd be so over the moon, I'd go around in a daze half the time. It's *wonderful*. And just think ... when it's completed, you'll actually be *living* here, so it's not just a gorgeous scheme for someone else to enjoy; *you* get the benefits, too."

"It sounds good when you put it like that."

"Come on, Marnie. Show me the rest of the place. I'm *dying* to see your boat."

Marnie was closing the front door behind them when the sound of an approaching car made them look towards the field track. A grey Vauxhall came into the complex and parked at the edge of the yard with a familiarity born of practice.

Estelle said, "I was just thinking you've got loads of space for a car park here for when friends come to call."

"These aren't friends," said Marnie, her expression suddenly serious.

Estelle looked concerned. "Is there a problem?"

"We're about to find out."

Two men walked over. Both were tall and wore dark suits. One slightly built, the other more burly, both in their forties. Detective Chief Inspector Bartlett and Detective Sergeant Marriner were no strangers to Glebe Farm.

"Good morning, Mrs Walker," said Bartlett.

He nodded in the direction of Estelle. Marriner, the older man, smiled briefly.

"Good morning," said Marnie. "This is unexpected. Would you like to come into the office?"

"This is just a short visit."

Marnie had learnt not to say more than was necessary to the police and never to be flippant. Saying the wrong thing had caused her problems with Bartlett in the past. Serious problems.

"What can I do for you?"

"Have you seen any strangers in the area lately ... anyone acting oddly?"

"What sort of strangers do you have in mind, Mr Bartlett? We're rather out of the way down here. Or do you think weirdoes and villains have a natural tendency to congregate at my door?"

"It's nothing personal, Mrs Walker. But you are off the beaten track, that's why we're checking. And you're beside the canal. You might've noticed if there'd been any suspicious characters around."

"I haven't seen anybody here or on the canal who'd answer to that description."

"No odd people at all?"

Marnie shook her head. "The odd boatload of New Age travellers, I suppose, but they're not rare, and they don't do any harm to anyone."

"If you do see anyone, let me know, will you?" He handed her a business card.

"Of course. What am I looking for exactly? Drug dealers, escaped convicts, stalkers, prowlers ...?"

"I don't want to put ideas in your head, Mrs Walker. Just be aware and keep a lookout, if you would."

"Could these people be dangerous?"

"Not to you."

"OK. That's reassuring ... I think."

Bartlett looked around him. "It's come on very nicely here. Is the work finished now?"

"I wish. Some time to go yet." She restrained herself from repeating her old joke that she was thinking of allocating a parking space just for their police car.

"Good morning, then."

As they turned to go, Marriner winked at Marnie, and she smiled back.

After retrieving the flowers and wine from the office barn, the two women headed for the canal. On the way through the spinney, to Marnie's surprise, Estelle linked arms with her and showered her with questions.

"What was all that about? How do you know those two? And how come they know you so well? They seemed to know a lot about you."

"I've had ... let's say, dealings with them before."

"Ah ... That must've been when you were nearly ..."

"Killed, yes."

Estelle squeezed her arm. "Sorry, Marnie, how thoughtless of me. Not the sort of thing you want to remember."

Marnie forced a smile. "Not the sort of thing it's easy to forget."

"So what did they want, do you think?"

"You heard them as well as I did."

"Sure, but they didn't give much away."

"Do they ever?" said Marnie. "Suspicious characters ... odd people ..."

"I didn't like the way he looked at *me* when he said that."

"Perhaps he didn't realise flared jeans were back in fashion."

Estelle laughed. "Still, he didn't seem to think they were dangerous ... not to you, at any rate."

"*Not to me*, no. That was very curious."

"But possibly dangerous to somebody else? Was that what he was implying?"

"I wonder. Not like Bartlett to be enigmatic."

"Perhaps some time you'll find out what he meant."

"I hope not."

They were walking together arm-in-arm like old friends, sharing confidences. Marnie found it hard to believe they had only met for the first time two days before. When they arrived at the docking area, Estelle stopped abruptly.

"Which is your boat? Oh I can see ... it's that one, *Sally Ann*. Marnie, this is so *beautiful* ... so *pastoral*. I never realised canals could be so ... *charming*."

"That's why lots of people spend their holidays on them."

"Yeah, I suppose so. I'd never thought about it. Is this the same canal as the one outside our office window in London?"

"Not strictly speaking. That's the Regent's Canal. This is the Grand Union."

"But they're all joined up? This ultimately leads back to the firm?"

"That's how we got here."

Just then, Anne came out onto the stern deck of *Sally Ann*, carrying a folding chair under each arm. She caught sight of Marnie and Estelle and smiled, stepping from the deck onto the bank where the table was set out with a blue gingham cloth under a huge cream parasol.

Estelle said quietly, "Is that Anne? She's *lovely*. You know ... I'm going to be so happy working here with you two, Marnie. I think it's going to be a real turning point in my life."

· · · · ·

The popping of corks was becoming a habit around *Sally Ann*. It created a festive atmosphere that partly offset the doubts and questions raised by the visit of the two detectives. During lunch, Estelle was as bubbly as the wine she had brought, and Marnie noticed that Ralph and Anne were sitting with smiles permanently switched on. Dolly had retreated to curl up on the hatch.

They left the table in place when they set off for a trip on the boat after lunch. On the stern deck Anne supervised Estelle in her first lesson in driving a narrowboat, while they chatted easily about the organisation of the firm, and Anne told her new colleague about her plans for college and beyond.

There was real summer warmth in the sun, and Marnie sat up front with Ralph in the half shade provided by the cratch roof with the side blinds rolled up. The countryside drifted lazily by, the sound of the engine a faint rumble at the stern. Occasional walkers nodded or waved as *Sally Ann* passed, and Marnie found herself examining them discreetly but more carefully than normal, wondering how to identify a *suspicious character* if she encountered one. She looked at the steerer and crew on every boat they met. Not one was carrying a Kalashnikov assault rifle or even a chainsaw.

They tied up at the foot of the Stoke Bruerne flight of locks and walked half a mile or so to the village where they ate ice creams while looking at the other boats, then mooched about in the museum shop. Estelle bought a miniature Buckby can, gaily painted with roses and scrollwork. It was a relaxed early summer's afternoon, and Marnie slowly forgot DCI Bartlett and his questions. She had her own life to lead and was gradually forming the opinion that Estelle would fit in very well to the operations of Walker and Co.

It was still only mid-afternoon when *Sally Ann* rounded the final bend in the canal, and Anne manoeuvred her expertly into the docking area to applause from Estelle.

"Would there be time for me to see round the village?" she asked, while they finished tying the mooring ropes.

"As much time as you want," said Marnie. "There's no rush. We've got the whole day set aside for your visit."

"That's great. But I can't stay too long. I'm seeing Luther this evening. He's been away all week on a course."

"Oh ... fine."

"You don't mind, do you? Perhaps I should've said earlier."

"Not a bit. No problem. Let's show you the bright lights of Knightly St John."

Ralph said, "Would you think it rude of me if I excused myself from the village tour? I've still got a report to finish."

"He can't stand the pace," said Anne. "Ralph finds Knightly too exciting."

There could be no better time to stroll round an English country village than on an afternoon in early summer. Marnie was growing accustomed to Estelle's tendency towards exaggerated praise for what she liked, but when they walked along the high street, she was more subdued, as she had been on the tour of Glebe Farm. Looking at buildings, her approach was more detached, more professional.

"So Northamptonshire's basically a stone county," she observed.

"That's right," said Marnie. "Mainly limestone down here, sandstone and ironstone through the middle, limestone again at the northern end."

"Like a sandwich," said Anne.

They walked on and reached the gate of the primary school, set back in its playground.

"Very attractive buildings," said Estelle. "How old's the school ... turn of the century?"

Marnie agreed. "Eighteen-ninety something, I think, but modernised inside. We've got to know the head quite well. Margaret Giles. You'll no doubt meet her at some point."

A row of cottages held their attention, with cream-grey stone walls under thatched roofs, every window a different size and shape, front gardens filled with marigolds, delphiniums and lupins. Estelle pointed at the end cottage, its facade almost covered in wisteria.

"That's what I'd call an outbreak of mass wisteria," said Anne.

Estelle squeezed her round the shoulders. "Is it really as dreamy and peaceful here as it looks?" she asked. "Or are there hidden passions behind those lace curtains?"

"I expect they have their moments," Marnie replied with a grin.

Estelle pointed. "Look at the church in relation to the pub, facing each other across the road like that, both made of the same stone, centuries apart. It all fits together beautifully. That's a splendid tower on the church. And why's the pub called *The Two Roses*?"

"Something to do with the Wars of the Roses, I think. Do you know, Anne?"

"Not sure. I'll have to find out."

They had stopped at the church gate. While they were speaking, a curtain moved in one of the upstairs rooms of the pub, and a window opened outwards. A young woman waved across to them.

"Who's that?" Estelle said quietly.

"One of the hidden passions," Marnie whispered.

"Really?"

"Passionate about our cottage number two ... and her future husband, no doubt."

They crossed the road, and Marnie called out, "Hallo, Grace. Lovely day."

"Hi! Didn't want to interrupt your walk, but I'd like a word when you have a moment."

"Problem?"

"No, just some questions about you-can-guess-what."

"A certain cottage, by any chance? This is Estelle. She's going to be working with us. Just up for a visit."

"Well, like I said, Marnie, I don't want to interrupt things ..."

"Don't mind me," said Estelle.

"I can take Estelle on the guided tour if you want to talk," said Anne.

It was agreed. Marnie went into the pub to see Grace; Anne and Estelle continued along the high street.

"There's the village shop," said Anne. "Along with the church, the pub and the school, that completes the essentials."

"You like it here, don't you?"

"*Love* it ... wouldn't want to be anywhere else."

"What about college and A-levels?"

"I can do those in Northampton."

"Is it far?"

"Half an hour. And it's no problem ... not now I have a car."

"A *car*? Crikey! You don't look old enough to have a licence, let alone a car of your own."

Anne laughed. "Marnie and Ralph gave it to me. I think it was Marnie, mainly. You see, I wouldn't accept any wages when we started ... apart from a small amount, like pocket money ... and Marnie says the car is sort of in lieu of that."

"That's why you call yourself her *apprentice*."

"Yes, like in the old days."

"And you have a *loft* over the office? Sounds very ... New York ... or Docklands."

"I'll show you if you like. It's small but very cosy. All mod cons ... CD player, TV, video ... everything I need."

"And later? Will you eventually move into the house with Marnie?"

"We haven't talked about things that far ahead. It depends on Marnie and Ralph."

"You think they might move in together?"

"Oh, yes. They're planning to get married some time."

"I see."

"It's not a secret," Anne added hastily. "But they've got to figure out how it'll work. Their lives are very busy."

"I can understand that. And with Ralph working in Oxford –"

"He's leaving Oxford. He's going to be a visiting professor, but he'll be writing books ... doing lecture tours."

"They'll make an interesting couple. And what about you? Do you have a boyfriend?"

Anne smiled. "Not really ... but there is a boy in the village who's a sort of friend. He'll be going to university in the autumn, though he might take a gap year. What about your plans, Estelle?"

"Oh, you know ... carry on working ... do this project in Italy with Marnie ... think about the future ..."

"Where will you live? Will you be spending much time in Italy? I'm not sure how it's all going to work. Marnie hasn't said much about it yet."

Estelle looked thoughtful. "You're right. We've still got a lot of details to sort out. I'd just thought I could stay at my flat in north London, work mainly from home and commute up to here when I need to ... probably go over to Italy for the odd trip. But now that I'm here ..."

As they were strolling slowly along, a dark green Range Rover pulled up at the kerb outside the shop. A man got out, nearing sixty, heavily built with a bull neck. Even though it was a warm day, he wore a tweed hat and jacket and a tie. The car gleamed like new.

"Hallo, my dear," he called out to Anne. "Splendid day for a walk."

"Hallo, Mr Stubbs. Yes, beautiful."

He walked round the car, raised the hat to reveal a balding head and held out a hand to Estelle. It was like a bear's paw, fingers as thick as sausages, and it enveloped her slim hand as if it were a child's, but he held it gently ... for several seconds.

"This is Estelle. She's going to be working with us on a big project. Estelle, this is Mr Stubbs. He lives just up the road ... in a *lovely* house."

He beamed at the young woman. "You forgot to mention that I'm a good friend of Marnie ... and of you, of course, Anne. Delighted to meet you, Estelle." He released her hand, on the borderline of outstaying his welcome.

"And you, Mr Stubbs."

"Call me George. I must say the village has become a lot brighter since Marnie and Anne moved in; all these attractive young ladies gracing the high street. *Wonderful*. Will you be living at Glebe Farm, Estelle?"

"We've not talked about the details yet. This is my first visit ... exploratory talks and all that."

"Have you come far?"

"From Barnet ... northern edge of London? I was figuring I could probably commute up here by car. It wasn't a bad journey."

George frowned. "This is the weekend. During the week it's *dreadful* on the motorway." He shook his head. "The M1 ... all those lorries. It's no joke."

"Is it really so bad?"

"*Murder*." His eyes flickered fleetingly in Anne's direction. He added hastily. "You could get held up for ages. You'd be much better staying here ... if there's room for you. Of course, it's none of my business; I don't mean to interfere."

"Like I said, we've still got the details to sort out. And thanks for your advice."

George raised his hat again. "I shall look forward to seeing you around." He stepped smartly across the pavement and went into the shop.

"Ugh!" said Estelle under her breath. "Creepy old bloke ... made me want to cringe. What does he do for a living ... teach leering at the local college?"

"Professor of Leering at Oxford," said Anne. "Actually, he has his own business ... he's a butcher."

"I might've known it. I guessed he was into flesh."

Anne laughed, and they walked on. "Oh, don't take any notice of him ... it's just talk. Marnie says it's to do with his age. He's quite nice in some ways ... when you get to know him ... in small doses."

"They're all just talk ... until they do something about it," Estelle said. "Mind you, he had a point there. I'm wondering if commuting's a very practical idea. I just don't see what else I could do ... can't imagine there's anything to rent round here."

Anne became pensive. "Mm ... The cottage is being let to Grace and Will."

"That means they're all taken, does it?"

"All the ones that are ready for occupation ... although ..."

"What?"

"Well ... there's number three ..."

"Aren't you and Marnie moving in there?"

"We were thinking about it."

Estelle's turn to be pensive. "Mm ... No. I can get up and leave home before the traffic gets heavy. It's no problem."

• • • • •

An hour later, Marnie, Ralph and Anne waved Estelle on her way up the field track, heading for the motorway back to London and the arms of her boyfriend. It had all been agreed. Estelle would start work with Walker and Co. in about two weeks, and would stay in cottage number three at Glebe Farm for the period of her attachment. To commemorate the decision, Anne had drawn up a special list of tasks to prepare the way for the move.

As the car went over the brow of the field and out of sight, leaving just a puff of dust in its wake, Marnie put her arm round Ralph's waist and rested her head on his shoulder.

"Weary?" he asked.

"No. Though I must say Estelle does rather have the effect of the proverbial white tornado."

"It does seem a lot quieter now she's gone," Anne said.

"Are you having doubts about her working with you? You have just agreed to let her move in to the cottage."

"No, Ralph." Marnie turned to walk back. "No doubts. I'm sure she'll be fine. She'll be a very stimulating colleague, that's for sure."

He took Marnie's hand as they walked. "And it is just for this contract, isn't it? Or are you thinking of taking her on for longer?"

"Yes ... no ... in that order. There will be room for a second designer if my plans work out, but that won't be for another couple of years yet."

"We should start making plans for that now," Anne joined in. "It's never too early to start."

"What do you have in mind?" Marnie asked, the smile forming in anticipation.

"There's got to be a list involved," Ralph suggested. "Probably a mile long."

"Yes ... and no ... in that order," said Anne, stopping at the door to the office barn. "We need to draw up a list of candidates ... but a short one."

"Good idea," said Marnie. "Go for it."

Anne took her notebook and carefully tore a thin sliver of paper from the bottom of a page. She held it up. It was just big enough for one line of writing. She balanced on one leg and wrote a single name on the strip of paper. She pushed open the door to the office, went in and pinned the paper to the cork noticeboard.

Closing the door behind her, she said, "Now the candidate has just got to do her A-levels and train as a designer, and I'll arrange interviews."

"Has she forgotten something?" said Ralph, turning his head.

"She never forgets anything," said Marnie. "You should know that by now."

"No, no, not Anne ... Estelle. I can hear a car coming back down the track. Listen."

They went to the end of the barn and looked round the corner. The car making its way slowly on the rutted track was not a Golf but a Vauxhall. A grey Vauxhall.

Marnie sighed. "I don't believe it. They must be rounding up the usual suspects. We'll have to give Inspector Bartlett a season ticket."

"Or start charging him rent," said Anne.

Ralph muttered, "I wonder what he wants."

"There's probably been a mass murder. He knows I go in for mass murder."

"Well, we'll soon find out."

"No. I will. You two go back to the boat … put the kettle on for coffee. I want to get this over with quickly. I'll be along in a minute or two."

While waiting for Bartlett, Marnie closed the barn door shutter and turned to lock up the office. It was only when she looked round to face the car that she realised she had been wrong. Instead of two detectives emerging from the Vauxhall, she saw a young Indian couple, who climbed out from the back and stood hesitantly beside it. On the front passenger door a telephone number was printed in clear, bold letters. It was a taxi. The driver's door opened and a third figure appeared, an older, stockier Indian wearing a turban. He leaned on the roof of his taxi, smiled and waved.

"Rajeev, hallo," Marnie called out, walking towards the car. "This is a surprise."

She had several times used his services for ferrying herself, Anne and occasional clients back and forth to the central station in Milton Keynes.

"Hi, Marnie. I've brought you two new clients."

Marnie nodded at the couple and advanced towards them. "On a Saturday afternoon?" They shook hands.

The young man spoke. "We were recommended to you by Mr Dyson at Blackey and Johnson, the estate agents in Towcester."

"Estate agents?"

"He said you had some interesting cottages for sale."

Marnie was puzzled. "Mm … not quite right, I'm afraid. Actually, Mr Dyson is rather jumping the gun. He isn't in fact acting for me, but he won't take no for an answer."

"But you do have cottages that you're putting on the market?"

"I'm sorry, but no. My cottages are for let … and they're already taken."

The young woman said something that Marnie did not hear, and her husband nodded.

"But you said he was jumping the gun. Doesn't that mean he was pushing them too early rather than too late? My wife and I are cash buyers … no chain involved … and our mortgage is agreed."

"Look, I really am sorry, but I don't have any cottages for sale or for let. As you can see, the first one is occupied, the second one's finished and the tenants will be moving in next month. I've just agreed to let the other one."

"So soon?"

"This afternoon, as a matter of fact."

The couple looked disappointed.

Marnie went on, "And you'd need a car to live out here in the country."

"Our car broke down and we had to call the AA. Mr Dyson called a taxi for us and said we could look in here while it's being fixed."

"Oh dear ... not a very fruitful day for you at all. I'm sorry."

The young man shrugged and began climbing back in to the car as his wife spoke quietly to him again. To Marnie's surprise, Rajeev began a torrent of indignant speech in a language that she did not recognise. He seemed to be rebuking the couple, who looked shamefaced in Marnie's direction.

"What's the matter, Rajeev?"

"I told them you weren't like that. If you said you had no houses ... then you had no houses. It was nothing to do with them being Asian."

Marnie blushed with embarrassment. "With being ...? Good god, no. Of *course* not. I'm telling the truth. The cottages really are all let, just as I said. I assure you."

"Thank you for your time," said the young man, getting back into the car.

· · · · ·

Marnie could see Anne and Ralph through the window in the galley on *Sally Ann*. They were putting out cups and saucers. Ralph was pouring water into the coffee pot. It looked very civilised, very English. Except they were on a narrowboat, which gave the scene a faintly exotic appearance. She had been wondering about assumptions as she had walked through the spinney. Having spent most of her life in London, she had grown up in a multi-coloured world surrounded by people of every shade imaginable, who spoke more languages than she could name, and she had regarded it as the norm in her country. She knew that most eating-out in Britain was in Indian restaurants, and the most popular British meal was chicken tikka masala.

Now suddenly she had met young Asians who had suspected her of racial prejudice. It was inconceivable, but they had lumped her in – however loosely – with the Ku Klux Klan!

On reflection, she was glad she had not tried to explain herself by telling them about her good friend Faye Summers, whose father was from Trinidad. She winced at the thought that she might have said, "Some of my best friends are ..." It was too awful to contemplate.

She stepped down into the cabin on *Sally Ann*.

"Out on bail?" said Anne.

· · · · ·

There was moonlight on the water, and Marnie heard the sound of a fish jumping without seeing it in some dark margin of the canal. But she saw the faint wave of ripples that disturbed the smoothness of the surface. She was standing at the stern door on *Thyrsis*, as she often did after taking a shower. Wearing only a thin cotton bathrobe to ward off the cool of the night, she let her thoughts drift back to the Indian couple who were still disturbing her below the surface.

There was a slight sound behind her, and she felt the boat move gently as Ralph came along the corridor, past the shower room, the second sleeping cabin and the engine compartment to join her. He slipped an arm round her waist and kissed her hair. She leaned against him without looking round.

"Perfect," Ralph murmured quietly.

"Mm."

"Or nearly perfect, anyway," he said.

"Why nearly?"

"Because something's bothering you … enough to take the edge off the scenery."

"Am I so transparent?"

"Well, if I can't judge your state of mind by now, it's a sorry state of affairs."

"Because you're a sensitive man?"

"No … because your chin has been trailing on the ground since you came back from meeting the Indian couple."

Marnie laughed. "You're right, of course. It really got to me … the idea that they could think I was prejudiced. *Me!* I'm going to strangle that bloody Dyson. He's no right to interfere in my affairs. I've told him a hundred times I'm not selling the cottages."

"He's probably hoping you'll be tempted by the cash. They'd fetch a good price."

"And he'd earn a good commission. Too bad. I'll phone him tomorrow … tell him to back off. I'm really annoyed he put me in the position of making that nice young couple think they were up against prejudice."

Ralph nuzzled her head. "They probably meet it in various forms a lot of the time. It's no wonder they thought you might not want them to move in."

"I bet if they did come to live here," said Marnie, "the village would make a huge fuss of them. They'd get thoroughly spoilt. And if they had kids … everyone'd be all over them."

Ralph put his other arm round her waist and pulled her closer. "Yes, I wouldn't be at all – *Gosh!* What was that? Did you see it?"

"A flash in the sky?" said Marnie. "Over there …"

They quickly stepped up onto the tiny stern deck – the counter – and peered into the distance over the darkened fields, balancing themselves against the cold steel of the tiller. Over the horizon hovered a pinkish glow, as if someone had suddenly switched on the lights of a big city.

"What direction was it?"

Ralph said, "It must be Northampton way, at a guess. I've never seen anything like that before."

Marnie shuddered. "I have."

5

At breakfast time on Sunday Ralph looked out into the spinney from the galley window on *Sally Ann* where he was laying the table.

"Does Anne know breakfast's ready?"

Marnie was taking rolls from the oven. "Don't worry. I saw her going for her shower when I went to get the papers from the office barn. She's fitted with the same radar system as Dolly … programmed to appear at mealtimes."

Gentle purring sounds were rising from the direction of the cat's feeding bowl by the fridge.

"You know what I mean," said Ralph. "I was just wondering where she is."

"Oh, I can guess where she is. I'm surprised you can't."

Ralph thought about it. "Of course. Silly of me. She's probably polishing inside the hub caps on the Mini."

"Ralph, you can't blame her being excited about having her first car."

"Not a bit. I'm delighted she's so thrilled with it. Everyone gets obsessive about cars when they first have them, I suppose."

"*Obsessive*," Marnie said. "That's the in-word at the moment. That's how Philip described Estelle."

"Huh! I don't think Anne's such an extreme case as Estelle. Mind you, that *would* be difficult."

Marnie put the basket of warm rolls on the table and turned to pick up the coffee pot. "There ... look at that. What did I tell you? Perfect timing."

Through the Venetian blind Ralph saw Anne jogging out of the spinney. She flashed past the window and seconds later burst into the cabin.

"It's OK," said Ralph. "No need to rush. We haven't fed your share to the cat."

"You were right, Marnie," Anne said breathlessly. "It was an explosion."

"Now that's what I call a dramatic entrance."

"An *explosion*," Ralph repeated. "How did you find out?"

"I went back to my room to see if there was anything on the television news ... and there it was. I've videoed it ... you can see it after breakfast."

• • • • •

It was like a scene from an American action movie, a huge explosion, flames and smoke billowing, the hero flinging himself away from the blast, miraculously missed by debris flying in every direction except his. Only here the aftermath was all that could be seen, and there was no hero, just a TV news reporter holding her microphone, with a building blazing in the background. The report had evidently been filmed the previous night soon after the explosion.

Anne adjusted the volume with the remote control. All three of them were perched on Anne's bed in the loft, concentrating intently on the report.

... and it was a miracle that no one was killed or seriously injured by the explosion. The caretaker, Mr Winston Coolidge, had left the premises only minutes earlier after locking the club at the end of the evening.

The image changed to a worried-looking Afro-Caribbean, with balding head and gold-rimmed glasses standing in the street. They had positioned him so that the glow from the fire was reflected in his lenses. A microphone was hovering under his chin.

I shut up as normal and checked everything was all right. We've got alarms and a security camera ... 'cos of the insurance ... and it all seemed OK.

Mr Coolidge, did you specifically check the boilers for the heating system?

I just had a look round like I always do. You don't expect this sort of thing. We're just a social club ... not political or anything.

Have you had threats of any kind?

No ... nothing like that. Never.

Do you get on with the people living in the area?

Sure ... well, we've had one or two complaints about noise ... you know, music, people dancing in the street after coming out late ... but not recently. We've had to be strict because of keeping our licence, you know.

Back to the building. A blackened shell half-hidden in smoke, flames still leaping upwards from window openings, silhouetting fire-fighters and their ladders, lighting up the water covering the ground. The reporter was talking to the presenter at the studio newsdesk.

Yes, the authorities haven't yet issued a formal statement on that, but the senior officer I spoke to a short while ago said he couldn't rule out that the fire had been started deliberately. A statement will be made at a press conference in the morning. Until then, the emergency services don't wish to comment.

The report ended, and Anne switched off the recording.

"And you actually saw it *happen*," she said.

"Though we didn't know it at the time ... not for certain."

"But you suspected it was an explosion, didn't you, Marnie?" said Ralph.

"It took me back to the boat explosion that I saw in London in the winter, only last night's must've been much bigger. I mean, Northampton's fifteen miles away, and we saw the flash from here."

"Do you think it was an accident?" Anne said.

Ralph stood up. "No way of knowing."

"I agree," said Marnie. "But something tells me ..."

6

There was little time to talk about the weekend, that Monday morning. Marnie and Anne moved busily around the office assembling papers and drawings. Willards had invited Marnie to their headquarters in Leicester for a progress review meeting, and Anne checked each item off her list. She was aching to tell Marnie about her drives to home and back the previous day.

No shinier car had ever been seen, and no prouder driver since the first hardy motorist on the highways of Britain, Henry Hewetson, took his Benz for a spin in 1894 – behind his manservant carrying a red flag. For the first time in British history a red flag had heralded a revolution. Now, on a sunny Sunday morning, a bright red Mini had made its way through Knightly St John, revolutionising the life of a budding interior designer. Stopping only briefly to collect Ronny Cope from his house near the church, Anne had driven off to spend the day with her parents, to show them her new possession and introduce her friend. She planned to tell Marnie all about it that evening.

As usual Anne took the call when the phone rang.

"It's Mr Jeffries at Willards, Marnie. Wants a quick word before you leave."

Marnie rolled her eyes. Jeffries was always fussing over trivia. He could get old women a bad name.

"Morning, Neil. I was just about to leave."

"You'll probably think I'm fussing –"

"Heaven forbid."

"Quite. But nonetheless, I think there's something you ought to know for your journey."

"For the journey?"

"I saw diversion signs as I drove into town this morning ... I thought you'd want to know ... to avoid any inconvenience."

Jeffries was a stickler for punctuality.

"I'll keep a lookout. What is it ... roadworks ... gas board digging up a water main?"

"No. There's some sort of ceremony, apparently. It was on the radio. A minister from the Home Office ... opening a community centre or something like that. You could have problems."

"OK, Neil. Thanks for the warning. I'm on my way."

· · · · ·

"I will personally throttle that man, Dyson."

Marnie found herself smiling at the memory of her talk in bed with Ralph that night after the young Indian couple had come to Glebe Farm. He had been indignant that she should have been suspected of racial prejudice, indignant to the point of threatening violence on an estate agent who was, after all, only trying to earn a living in a tough world. *Ralph!* She could never imagine him attacking anyone. Though when she had made the point that he was unlikely to do anything physical in any circumstance, he had done his best to dispel that illusion. She smiled at that memory, too.

Diversion signs sprang up as she reached the city, just like Jeffries had warned her. The problem was that every traffic light on the route was programmed to turn red as she approached, and the diversion meant that there was more traffic than usual.

Muttering under her breath, she accelerated away from the penultimate set of lights. Up ahead she could see pinpricks of red from the next traffic lights and adjusted her speed with the aim of reaching them as they turned to green. That at least would be a source of satisfaction, and she concentrated on getting the speed just right to sail through in triumph. Her judgment was perfect, and with twenty metres to go, the red changed to red and amber.

She was congratulating herself on her skill, when a pedestrian stepped off the kerb and began crossing the road, followed by another and then another. Marnie eased back on the accelerator, muttering again. She gritted her teeth, musing on the prospect of flooring the pedal and scattering the pedestrians like ninepins, when it became clear that the line of jaywalkers was growing.

She shifted her foot to the brake and slowed. And still they came on, an unbroken line walking singly or in groups of two and three, all of them young men. It reminded her of an army on the move, though this column of troops looked more like a band of brigands with more than a passing resemblance to the orcs in a Tolkien novel.

By now the brakes were firmly bringing the car to a halt as the lights changed to green. Marnie thought of hooting to make them move aside, but suspected it would be a waste of effort. This gang was not even glancing at the traffic, but trudged on at a steady pace looking ahead, like an occupying force beyond the reach of normal conventions, sure of their strength and their ability to have their own way. Other drivers around her were similarly watching the procession, silently waiting.

A strange feeling came over her. Later she would look back on that moment as a premonition that events were taking a turn for the worse.

The green lights taunted Marnie as she sat in the Discovery immobilised, looking down at the rebels. Despite the warm weather, they seemed to favour black leather jackets with jeans, and heavy boots laced up their ankles. Their heads were shaved, almost devoid of hair. Light glinted on studs and rings in noses and ears. Their march was a kind of determined slouch with attitude and a dash of swagger thrown in.

And then she realised why thoughts of armies had come into her head. Several of the men were carrying flags over their shoulders. Most were furled, but some hung open. They were black with a diagonal red stripe. Many of the men wore armbands: red with an emblem in black. Marnie strained to study them. The design seemed to be a capital *N*, an italic letter like a bolt of lighting. One man turned his head in passing to scowl at her, and she quickly looked down.

Slowly she eased her right arm back from the steering wheel, finding the lock button on the door with her elbow. She pressed it down gently and heard the sharp click of the central locking mechanism securing all the doors. Her sense of relief lasted only two seconds, as three or four of the skinheads hesitated in their march and looked her way. She felt like a fugitive behind enemy lines, trying not to draw attention to herself. The men tramped on, a battalion of irregulars moving up to the front, needing only the beat of a drum to complete the scene.

Marnie asked herself what was going on. Why the ugly crowd of thugs? Then an image flickered across her mind. *Community centre ...* Neil Jeffries had mentioned the opening of a community centre by a government minister. Could all this be connected with the opening ceremony? *Ridiculous!* But in her mind she saw a pink flash on the horizon in the night sky, television images of burning and devastation, ladders and hoses, an anxious caretaker with fear and flames in his eyes. Perhaps ... She focused again on the now diminishing band of marchers.

There must have been hundreds of them, and the crowd had now passed, followed by a few stragglers hurrying to keep up. With the gear lever in first, Marnie began easing up the clutch, feeling it engage just as the lights turned to amber. And red.

• • • • •

The return journey was easy. The traffic lights seemed to have other things on their mind and were no longer looking out for Marnie, no longer turning red every time she approached. She wondered if they had been demoralised after being ignored by the rag-tag army that had shown them so little respect that morning. There were no more lines of skinheads on the march, and she put them out of her memory.

The meeting had been a doddle, and Marnie was on a high. They had reviewed every project, in preparation for a board meeting that Neil Jeffries would be attending the following week. He described Marnie as a 'safe pair of hands' who never let him down. She had said she hoped he also regarded her as a good designer, and he had waved that aside with a casual – *yes, that as well … the best.*

She made good time and was soon turning off the dual carriageway to take the country road home. It always pleased her when she passed the name board for the village: *Knightly St John – Please drive carefully.* Even though she worked hard and for long hours, she only ever thought of the village as a place of calm, a peaceful haven in a busy world. On the high street she saw George Stubbs coming towards her in his Range Rover, and they raised a hand to each other. How different, she thought, from the anonymous bustle of working in London.

She parked the Discovery in its usual space and climbed out. Anne came hurtling from the office barn. This was not her customary friendly welcome home. She looked worried, annoyed and fearful in equal measures.

"*Marnie!* Thank *goodness.* Where have you *been?*"

"What do you mean? You know where I've been … Willards." She smiled reassuringly. "You ticked me off your list, so it must be all right. What's the matter?"

"I'm not joking, Marnie, I've been worried *sick* … trying to get you on the mobile, but it didn't work."

"Ah … the mobile." She reached into her shoulder bag and pulled it out. "I forgot … had it switched off during the meeting."

"Switched off?" Anne said. "I thought we agreed you'd always have it on in case of an emergency … as a lifeline."

"That's right. But I always switch off when I'm at Willards so that – *emergency?* What *emergency?*"

"My mum rang up. She said … Look … let me show you, then you'll understand."

Marnie followed Anne up the wall-ladder to her attic. Video shows in her room were becoming the latest thing. While Anne fiddled with the VCR, Marnie had a misgiving that this show might be another disaster movie.

"What are we watching?"

Without looking round Anne said, "Lunchtime news on the BBC. I'm just finding the place. I'd wound it back to the start of the tape … won't be a sec."

Anne fast-forwarded to the new sequence. She moved back to sit on the bed, holding the remote out in front of her like a magic wand. The scene changed abruptly and settled down to normal speed.

Police vehicles were lined up facing an angry mob in a street. Black and grey smoke was drifting in clouds like fog. Bottles and bricks were hurtling through the air. Over to one side, a van was burning and a line of policemen in riot gear was slowly moving forward, transparent shields extended to ward off missiles. In the corner of the screen a red box was lit up with the word *LIVE.* As they watched the struggle, a bottle smashed at the feet of one officer and burst into flames. They set the man's trousers alight, making him jump back, while another policeman rushed to smother the fire.

"Watch this next bit," Anne said quickly.

The screen changed to give a view from a camera high up on a building. It was a different part of the city centre. A crowd of rioters, some of them waving flags, was rushing across the street in the shelter of cars and buses. The camera zoomed out. In the background about twenty metres away, a group of riot police was assembling. Some of the skinheads were lining up to block the traffic so that it formed a barrier across both lanes. Pedestrians could be seen fleeing into shops or diving into doorways.

Suddenly, as if by a signal, the rioters hurled petrol bombs towards the police. A dozen or more missiles exploded among them, and while the officers tried to avoid the fire and regroup, they were hit by a volley of stones and bricks. Several of them, concentrating to step round the fires, took direct hits, and one man fell to the ground. It would have been madness to remain where they were, and they withdrew to a side street, the felled man dragged away by two others.

A cheer went up from the mob, who began hammering on the roofs and bodywork of the cars. The occupants could be seen twisting and turning inside, gripped by sheer panic, all of it witnessed by the camera, live on lunchtime television. Immediately, the police came storming out from their protected positions with shields raised, visors lowered, brandishing truncheons, while the sound of sirens could be heard in the distance, growing louder by the second.

"See what I mean?" said Anne.

"Yeah ..." Marnie muttered softly.

The news reporter was back in view, this time standing in front of a fire engine. Behind her, senior police officers were conferring in a small group beside a dark blue van. Beyond them the line of riot police seemed very thin compared with the crowd of demonstrators waving their flags and lobbing more petrol bombs. Everywhere was fire and smoke, mangled vehicles and smashed shop windows. It was an image from hell. And it was taking place in the centre of a British city on a normal working day. Marnie tried to pay attention to what the reporter was saying.

... and a few minutes ago one of the senior police officers told me this was the first time in his experience that a mob of rioters – those were his words – had used ordinary passers-by in vehicles as human shields for camouflage and cover. This was no ordinary mob, he said. They were well organised and co-ordinated, sending one group out as decoys to make the police think they'd be coming from one direction, when the main force in fact came from the other end of the city. This is Caroline Dewar, BBC News, Leicester.

The calm of the television studio was in vivid contrast to the devastation of the city, the city where Marnie had spent the morning, through which she had driven twice that day. No wonder Anne had been anxious. The news presenter was looking worried.

We'll bring you updates on the situation in Leicester later in this bulletin. We also hope to have an interview with Home Office Minister Gray Fordyce, whose opening of the Bharat Community Centre was marred by the violent demonstrations that we have just witnessed.

Anne pressed the button on the remote, and the screen went blank.

"Now do you see why I was *frantic* with worry?"

Marnie reached over and put a hand on Anne's shoulder. "I certainly do."

Anne looked drained. "I thought you might be caught up in all that. You'll think I'm silly to make such a fuss, and I expect you didn't see a thing, but –"

"I did ... I did see ... I saw some of the mob ... those Neanderthals ... when I was on my way into town."

"That's a bit harsh, calling them Neanderthals," said Anne.

"Well they certainly looked sub-human to me."

"No ... I mean it's a bit hard on the Neanderthals."

"Good point."

Anne's eyes widened in realisation. "You actually *saw* them? What did they do?"

"Nothing much. They were just marching along. They held up the traffic."

"*Held up the traffic!*" Anne repeated, eyes wider than ever.

"Not like that," Marnie said hastily. "Just walking along. There were so many we had to stop to let them go by. Obviously the riot came later."

"They shouldn't be *allowed* to do that sort of thing," Anne protested. "Why do the police let them get away with it?"

"Perhaps there's nothing they can do to stop them until a demonstration turns into a battle. People have a right to demonstrate peacefully ... at least I think they do. Anyway, it looks as if the police were out-numbered."

Anne looked determined. "Well I think demonstrations like that should be banned."

Marnie sensed that now was not the time for an objective discussion on civil rights. She said softly, "Sorry to make you worry like that. This rights business is a tricky question. Perhaps it's best if these people do show themselves on the streets and are seen for what they are. Better the devil you know ..."

"I suppose so." Anne sounded unconvinced. "Is that what you really think?"

In her mind Marnie saw again the army on the march, their flags and armbands, their intimidating swagger, their air of menace.

"I'm not so sure."

7

Today was different. Monday, Marnie had driven alone and encountered the army of brigands. On Tuesday morning she rode shotgun in the Mini to Northampton where everything was peaceful as usual. Marnie had given in to Anne's wish to use her car. She was pleased to see how carefully and precisely she drove, each gear change executed smoothly, accelerating and braking steadily. Another safe pair of hands. Today's excitement was a visit to the accountants.

"You sure you're happy about this?" Marnie had asked as they were setting off up the field track.

"Why not? Someone has to do it. It's not all flair and glamour, being an interior designer."

Marnie had laughed. "*Flair and glamour!*" She thought of the hours she spent poring over colour charts, swatches of materials, wallpaper samples. "I'd never thought of it quite like that. Creative, yes. Interesting, sure. But, well ..."

"Well," Anne had said, "the accounts are just as important in their way, and I might as well learn how to do them properly. I'm not letting you keep me while I'm studying, without pulling my weight."

Marnie respected Anne's attitude and was only too glad to let her friend take care of the bookkeeping. Typically, it had been Anne's idea to arrange a meeting with their accountant to make sure she was keeping the books correctly. Now, here they were, driving into town that morning in the shining red Mini. Only one set of traffic lights delayed them and as they waited, the car in neutral, handbrake engaged, Anne at the wheel concentrating, Marnie glanced at the billboard outside a corner newsagents: *New Force Threat to Town.* A frown crossed her face, but before she could interpret the wording, Anne was moving off, asking for directions. They soon turned into a side street of large Victorian houses and pulled up outside the offices of Rothwell Crawford and Company, accountants.

Anne silently pulled on the handbrake. "Great. We're here. No probs."

Marnie smiled. "I've never seen anyone so excited about a visit to their accountants."

"Oh, it's all fun as far as I'm concerned. So much to learn. They don't teach you this kind of thing at school."

• • • • •

Rex Crawford smiled at Anne over the top of his horn-rimmed glasses across the desk. Among his clientele such enthusiasm was rare. It compensated for Marnie's absence at another meeting. He had a soft spot for Marnie.

"I can see why Marnie regards you as a great asset, Anne. If ever you decided you wanted a change from interior design, I think you'd have a great future in accountancy." He laughed gently. "Have I covered all your points?"

Anne looked down at her notebook. In their half hour together she had filled several pages. "You've certainly done that, Mr Crawford."

"Call me Rex. It's a pleasure to meet someone who takes their accounting seriously."

"I wouldn't want to make mistakes and get into trouble with the tax people. You can't be a designer if you're locked up in chains in the Tower of London."

"Ah, but most people who have problems with the taxman haven't committed fraud, Anne. They've just been sloppy in their bookkeeping. You'd never do that because of your attention to detail. That's what counts in the end."

"I've written everything down. I want to make sure I get it right."

"Splendid. You keep the accounts in order and that'll be one less thing to worry about. It'll leave you to get on with the creative side of your job."

"Is that what's meant by *creative accounting?*"

"Ah ... not quite. That's something else ..."

• • • • •

While Anne was being initiated into the mysteries of double-entry accounting, a quarter of a mile away Marnie was sipping pale coffee in a solicitor's office. Her usual solicitor, fellow boat-owner Roger Broadbent, had recently announced that he was going into semi-retirement and was at that time away on a long-promised Caribbean cruise with his wife.

Marnie had found Jennings Plowright Beardman in the yellow pages and she was now sitting opposite Anthony Plowright watching him as he checked over a tenancy agreement. As he read, he gently chided her for not coming to see him sooner to sort out the legal documents for Jill and Alex Burton before they had moved into cottage number one. Marnie had not liked to tell him that she had been immersed in a murder enquiry at the time and had rather more pressing concerns than sorting out a rent book. She consoled herself with the thought that in the country people kept their word whether or not it had been approved by a lawyer. Mr Plowright consoled himself with the thought that Marnie had not caused herself or him any real problems. Yet.

He gave her a wad of papers to read, with copies of the tenancy agreements to discuss and finalise with the Burtons, with Grace and Will and with Estelle.

"Get the tenants to read everything carefully before they sign it. If they have any queries, you can give me a ring."

A momentary embarrassment had occurred when Marnie had confessed that she did not know Estelle's surname. Mr Plowright removed his glasses and looked pensively at Marnie. He spoke slowly.

"You don't actually know the surname of this ... lady ... who is going to be living in your property. I see. How long have you known her?"

"A few days. We've met twice. But how long do landlords normally know new tenants, Mr Plowright?"

"Fair point ... but it is a good idea to know something about them. A name is a good way to start ... as are references, for example."

This conversation was irritating Marnie. She guessed that he would now ask if she had a fresh handkerchief in her bag, if she had put on clean knickers that morning and if she realised he was only trying to protect her interests.

"I am only trying to protect your interests, Mrs Walker."

One out of three, she thought. *Could be worse.* She said, "Estelle comes with impeccable references."

"That's good."

He did not sound altogether convinced.

• • • • •

Rex Crawford gathered together the sample accounts that he had been perusing with Anne. She looked down at the list of questions that she had brought. There was a tick beside each one.

"Have we covered all your queries, Anne?"

"I think so ... unless you have any last words of advice for me?"

"Not really. Just bear in mind that if the tax office can find an error, that opens the door to further enquiries. If they find one thing to query, they'll have the opportunity to query anything. Always check the facts and tie up all the loose ends."

"I won't forget."

Rex stood up and held out his hand. "You'll be all right as long as you always read the small print. That's where all the problems lie ... and the answers to all the questions. Remember the old saying ... *the devil is in the detail* ... and you won't go far wrong."

• • • • •

Marnie checked her watch. Ten minutes to go before their agreed meeting time. She walked briskly up the street and was about to enter the coffee shop when she spotted the Tourist Information Office. It was a good opportunity to pick up some leaflets about summer events.

The office was busy with visitors, and Marnie's attention was taken by a poster showing the Northampton branch of the Grand Union Canal. Making her way towards it, she had to manoeuvre round a small child clutching an ice cream cornet, trying to attract the attention of his mother who was in conversation with an assistant at the counter. He had an ice cream moustache and was slowly chanting *Mummy, mummy* like a mantra. His cornet was tipping over and in a second or two would spill its contents onto the floor. Marnie knelt quickly and touched the little boy's arm. As he turned his gaze towards her, she smiled and moved his hand to keep the ice cream upright. The mother was unaware of this act of charity, and the child also seemed to miss its significance, staring at her blankly, but Marnie was noticed by another assistant who was just walking past.

"The summer playscheme leaflets are over there on the rack," she said, looking down at Marnie, who straightened up to face her.

"Playscheme?"

"The second batch has been delivered. The organiser's just brought them. Weren't you in the other day asking for them ... with your little boy?" She glanced in the direction of the child with the ice cream moustache.

"Er no ... not actually ... it's the first time I've been in here this year. And that isn't my little boy."

"Oh, sorry. But if you do have children, you'll want to see the programme. There's a lot on this summer ... should be good – loads of activities, outings, games – for all ages, right through the holidays. She's done a good job."

"She?"

"The organiser ... Serena McDowell."

Hearing her name mentioned, the organiser looked round and smiled vaguely in Marnie's direction before returning to her conversation with the office manager. She had a striking appearance, and even in that brief moment her manner seemed to exude a dynamic energy. In jeans and a white sweatshirt, she was Afro-Caribbean with straightened hair reminiscent of a Tamla Motown singer, and just as glamorous.

"Is it only for children living in the town?" Marnie asked.

"No. It's open to anyone in the county, but they have to provide their own transport to the community centre in Northampton ... that's where it's based."

Marnie suddenly remembered her meeting with Anne, thanked the assistant, quickly grabbed a few leaflets, including the playscheme, and dashed out.

• • • • •

They settled in a corner of the coffee shop with sandwiches and a Northampton cheesecake for dessert, a wickedness that Marnie permitted herself once or twice a year.

"You don't mind eating here instead of a pub lunch?" she said.

Anne shook her head. "This is fine. I wouldn't drink anything anyway when I'm driving. Pity to lose my licence when its ink hasn't even dried. "

"Quite right," Marnie agreed. "So how did it go with Rex?"

Anne patted her bag. "I've taken *reams* of notes."

"*Quelle surprise.*"

"Don't mock ... you'll be grateful when all your accounts are copper-bottomed. Rex thinks I'd make a good accountant. How did you get on with Mr Plowright?"

"He didn't exactly offer me a partnership. In fact he was rather unimpressed with my grasp of legal matters altogether." She pulled out the wad of papers from her bag. "Look at this lot ... look at the size of the print. I'd need a microscope to go through that. Still, I don't suppose he expects me to read it all."

"Oh but you must, Marnie. I will too, if you like. It's no use sighing. Remember ... *the devil is in the detail*. Rex told me that."

Marnie mumbled something inaudible and chomped on her sandwich. Anne had the good sense not to ask her to repeat it.

• • • • •

"Would it distract you if I put the radio on?" Marnie asked. "We're in time for the one o'clock news."

The Mini was in a stream of traffic heading for the outskirts of town.

"Go ahead," said Anne. "Will you do it? I've got some idiot in a white van trying to climb into the boot."

Marnie reached for the switch. "Ignore him."

"He'll be on the back seat any minute now. We'll be making introductions."

Marnie had a number of interesting tactics that she had learnt over time, but did not want to lead Anne into bad habits so young. "Still ignore him."

The newsreader was in the middle of the headlines, with a report about a drugs raid in Manchester. The next item made Marnie sit up.

The far-right group calling itself New Force has issued a statement condemning police violence during yesterday's demonstrations in Leicester. Leaders of the group stated that they wanted to make a peaceful protest at the opening of the Bharat Centre by Home Office Minister, Gray Fordyce. They claimed that they were prevented from approaching the ceremony and when they tried to move forward, they were attacked by police in full riot gear.

A new oil-field has been identified off the north coast of Scotland ...

Marnie lowered the volume. "Police violence! Huh! The police were *completely* outnumbered. Those thugs were throwing *petrol bombs* at them. I suppose they'll claim they just made them on the spur of the moment when the police attacked them."

"I always carry a petrol bomb or two with me," Anne said cheerfully. "You never know when they might come in handy."

"Quite."

"Actually, I wish I had one now for a certain white van."

Marnie looked over her shoulder. "The driver thinks he's being really clever ... he's grinning like an ape."

"That's unfair to apes," Anne observed. "Oh, listen ... it's that item again."

Marnie turned up the volume.

... but were provoked by what they described as a huge police presence. Faced with a disproportionate response by the police, they had no choice but to defend themselves. We invited New Force to be interviewed on this programme, but they declined to do so. The minister at the centre of the disturbance, Gray Fordyce, described the demonstration as a riot and a disgrace.

"I'm not opposed to freedom of expression, far from it, but I'm appalled at what happened yesterday. The statement put out by this group is a complete travesty and bears no relation whatsoever to the events that took place."

During the demonstration three policemen were injured and taken to hospital, one suffering serious burns to his legs. No arrests were made. The Home Secretary has ordered the Chief Constable to conduct an urgent enquiry into the events.

Marnie switched off the radio, staring ahead. "Those rioters think they can just tell any lies they want."

"Mm."

Marnie glanced at Anne who was concentrating hard, a frown on her face. "Is your van driver still following you?"

"He's halfway up the exhaust pipe."

"OK. Slow down to twenty-five."

"What?"

"Just do it. Now! Twenty-five and hold it steady."

Anne eased back, and the Mini slowed. Seconds later a horn sounded behind them. Close behind them.

"What are we doing, Marnie?"

The road ahead and on the opposite side became clear of traffic.

"Go back up to thirty. Now!"

Anne accelerated at the moment when the horn sounded again. It was a long blast and continued while the van pulled out and charged past, the driver waving his fist as he swerved round them. He spotted the speed camera just as he pulled in front of the Mini and roared ahead. They saw his brake lights flash as the horn stopped blaring, and the driver attempted an emergency stop. But it was too late. He must have been well over the limit when the camera caught him.

"Go right here," Marnie said quickly. "I think we'll go the long way round."

• • • • •

There was silence in the Mini, apart from Marnie giving directions onto the southern ring road. They took the Oxford road and headed out of town. Anne settled down to cruise at a comfortable sixty.

"Marnie, that was cool ... what you did back there ... with the speed camera and the van and all."

"Speed camera?"

"Yes, the speed camera."

"I don't know what you mean. And if I did, I wouldn't condone it. OK?"

"But –"

"No buts. The rule is: never retaliate. Never. Always ignore other people driving badly. *Always.*"

Anne smiled. "Right. There's a lot to learn about, isn't there ... when you're driving a car, I mean. It alters the way you see things. Before I started driving, I hardly noticed cars. I'm much more aware of them now."

"Yes. And you don't want to pick up bad habits."

"*Moi?*" Anne protested. "*You're* the one who came up with the slow-down-speed-up James Bond routine."

"And I was in the wrong. In future ignore everything I tell you to do when you're driving. Everything. Is that understood?"

"Fine."

"Oh, by the way, I want you to stop at the village school on our way home."

"Is that a test, Marnie? Am I supposed to ignore that?"

"Smartarse!"

• • • • •

With perfect timing they arrived in the village before the end of the school lunch break, and Margaret Giles invited them into her office for coffee.

"I'm glad you've called in," she said. "I was going to contact you myself. There's something I wanted to ask you."

"What can we do for you?"

"I was wondering if some of the top juniors could visit *Sally Ann* towards the end of term, as they did last year. The children still talk about it. I think it was the highlight of their year."

"Fine. OK by you, Anne?"

"No probs. I enjoyed it, too."

"Thank you," said Margaret. "The only snag is there isn't much time to organise things before we break up."

"What about Friday afternoon?" Marnie suggested. "Would that fit in?"

"That would be excellent. Now, what can I do for you?"

Marnie took some leaflets from her bag and passed them over.

"I picked these up in town this morning ... wondered if it would be of interest to your pupils. There isn't a bus laid on, but otherwise everything's provided."

Margaret looked at the leaflet. "Mm ... they usually run a holiday playscheme in town. There's a lot on this year ... a good programme. Small charge. Thank you, Marnie. It's the perennial problem ... finding things for the children to do in the summer holidays."

"I can imagine. She's done a good job, the organiser."

"It's a woman?"

"Serena McDowell."

"Oh, yes. Of course."

"You know her?"

"Not personally. She's the Youth Officer for the town. Dynamic ... very ambitious ... wears lots of hats."

Marnie and Anne chorused. "Hats?"

"Metaphorical ones. She's into all sorts of things, or so I gather. Moved up here from London. She chairs CAPE ... that's Community Action for Parents and Education. It used to be called the Northampton Community Parents and Education Group, I think."

"Quite a mouthful," said Marnie.

"Exactly. I think it was Serena McDowell who said you had to have a catchy acronym that people will remember. You can't exist these days without an acronym."

"I'll try and resist the temptation," said Marnie.

"I remember," Margaret continued, "when I was a young teacher in Yorkshire years ago, they were reorganising the schools system, trying to get rid of the eleven plus. The head of my school was a member of a pressure group: Primary Heads Against Grammar Schools. They were known, of course, as ... PHAGS."

"I suppose you got sponsorship from Benson and Hedges," Marnie said with a straight face, aware of a titter coming from Anne.

"Benson and ...? Oh, quite. Actually, they decided to change their name in the end."

"Too much like a smokers' club?" Marnie suggested.

"Oh, no. Rumour has it that they were approached by the ... er, Gay and Lesbian Alliance ... about possible affiliation. It was all very embarrassing at the time."

Anne suddenly made a loud noise somewhere between a splutter and a snort and reached for her coffee.

"Oh dear," said Margaret. "Did your biscuit go down the wrong way?"

Anne croaked. "Something like that."

Marnie avoided looking in Anne's direction, to Anne's great relief, and said, "So do you think some of your pupils might go to the summer scheme, Margaret?"

"I'm sure some will. They all should. It's good for village children to meet town children ... and some from other ethnic backgrounds. Sometimes little village schools can be too cosy, even unworldly."

"I'm sure you're right," said Marnie.

Anne discreetly wiped her mouth with a tissue.

• • • • •

After supper that evening they stayed outside, sitting round the table on the stern deck of *Sally Ann*, enjoying the warmth, raising their glasses to the occasional passing boat. It was around the time of the longest day of the year, and the sun was still slanting through the high branches in the spinney behind them, picking out small flying insects, while the trees and bushes added a fresh tang of early summer to the air. None of them wanted to move for fear of disturbing the atmosphere.

Ralph had listened to Anne's story of her meeting with Rex Crawford and told them of his day in Oxford. The arrangements for his change of status to visiting professor were now finalised and, once his duties as an examiner were completed, he was free to begin his new life.

"No regrets?" asked Marnie.

"None at all." He smiled at her. "Not about anything. It's the right thing to do. I know it is."

"That's how I felt about leaving my secure job in London and starting up here."

"Me too," said Anne. "Though I did worry sometimes that something might come along to spoil it."

Marnie nodded. "We've had enough incidents since we came here to stop us getting complacent, that's for sure."

"You don't strike me as the complacent type," Ralph said.

"Far from it. In fact, to be honest, I've been rather anxious that the whole world could come crashing round our ears, this past day or two."

Anne sat up in her chair. "Why?"

"Watching those scenes of violence on TV ... seeing the thugs marching through Leicester ... that billboard in town this morning. I never did find out what that was about ... forgot to buy a paper."

"What did it say?" Ralph asked.

"Something about a new force threatening the town ... sounded like a science fiction novel by H. G. Wells or Wyndham Lewis."

"New Force, the organisation, presumably," said Ralph. "If that's not a contradiction in terms when referring to a bunch of anarchists."

"Is that what they are ... anarchists?" said Anne.

"Loosely speaking, I suppose. Anarchists, fascists, racists, the far right ... call them what you will."

"But they're highly organised," Marnie joined in. "I saw them. They may have looked like a rabble, but they had a sense of purpose. There was an order there, a queer sort of discipline. They even had flags, armbands ... and a uniform of sorts. Are they linked to a political party, Ralph?"

"Not formally, I think ... not openly, at any rate. They just want to disrupt everything, destabilise society. And of course there's the race angle."

"What do they think they can achieve? Surely, we're too racially integrated these days for them to be able to do that."

"That's what most Germans thought when Hitler and his gang started."

"You think they could be a serious threat?"

"You're still in touch with some of your Jewish friends in London? Ask them their view on what's happening. I had a chat with Guy Fellheimer in college the other day. His parents got out of Germany in '37. He reminded me how fragile the fabric of society can be."

Anne said, "But no one will believe what they say, these New Force people ... will they?"

"Another technique perhaps learned from the Nazis. Did you do that period in history at school, Anne?"

"Yes, but it's not the same now. The Germans were demoralised after the First World War. They felt betrayed, and Hitler put the blame on Jews and foreigners."

"The Big Lie."

"A lie is still a lie," Marnie said. "People were easier to dupe in those days. They didn't have the media. Now, you can see it's a lie just by looking at the television."

"Maybe," said Ralph. "But the media can also make it easier to manipulate opinion."

"How?" said Anne. "Don't they say the camera cannot lie?"

Ralph sipped his coffee. "Let's test that idea, Anne. What do you know about the Bharat Centre?"

"The what?"

"The Bharat Centre."

"That rings a bell," said Marnie. "Got it! It's that centre in Leicester that the minister was opening yesterday."

"That's right. And what can you tell us about it?"

Anne said. "I know ... Bharat means India. I came across the *Mahabharat* – I think that's how you say it – when we were doing Comparative Religions at school."

"Who said education's wasted?" said Marnie. "I didn't know that. I'm impressed."

"So am I," said Ralph. "But what about the centre in Leicester specifically?"

Anne shrugged. "That's it ... must be a cultural centre for Indians. QED."

"And what you know is that there was a riot about it."

Marnie narrowed her eyes. "You're saying that New Force succeeded in drawing all the attention away from the opening of the centre to focus on their protest. But that doesn't make their lies any closer to the truth, Ralph. We could see they caused the trouble. We saw them throwing bricks and petrol bombs."

"But they said it was in self-defence ... provoked by the police. We know that's a lie. But a lot of people will remember the police with helmets, truncheons and riot shields. That's the Big Lie technique ... straight out of the manual of Dr Josef Goebbels, Hitler's Minister of Propaganda: repeat the lie often enough and it starts to take on the mantle of truth. That's the theory."

"A kind of *no smoke without fire* idea," Marnie said. "Well, we've had plenty of both in the last few days."

"Let's hope that's an end to it," said Anne.

"I'd like to agree with you," Ralph said quietly. "But I'm starting to wonder if it could be just the beginning."

8

As far as work was concerned, Marnie had written off Friday afternoon for the school visit, but had planned a full programme for the morning, finalising the design for Willards' newest and biggest hotel on the outskirts of Hemel Hempstead. It was close to the Grand Union, and her design employed mural panels with views of the canal in its earliest days. She had been looking forward to spending an hour or two on her scheme, combining brightness in blues and greens with a bold, dramatic use of space, and had settled down with relish to a creative morning.

But it was not to be. Interruption followed interruption and Anne, normally the most effective watchdog, was faced with enquiries that would not wait and were beyond her experience to handle. Marnie finally abandoned all hope of concentration when the electricity company rang to discuss a new sub-station in the village and the energy needs of the Glebe Farm complex. Muttering under her breath, she had dropped her pen onto the drawing board and taken the call.

But despite her frustrations, the afternoon was, she had to admit, nothing but enjoyable. The sight of the schoolchildren filing past the office barn with Anne at their head was heart-warming, and a marked contrast with the last column she had seen marching that Monday morning in Leicester.

She had realised how glad she was to have the children once again visiting *Sally Ann*, once again watching Anne hand out bright coloured badges marked 'Crew', distributing the question sheets she had prepared for them, giving them their work folders. As before, the children's concentration had been intense and their pleasure palpable during their short cruise up to the Stoke Bruerne flight and back.

This year there was a difference. Ronny Cope had volunteered to help, and was happy to place himself under Anne's orders, assisting with the supervision of the 'crew' and generally making himself useful.

The children had been enthralled by Anne, as their predecessors had been the previous summer, happy to be with this 'big girl' who knew so much about the waterways and made their learning fun. If there was a high point of their visit, it was when Anne produced a cake from the galley at teatime in the shape of a working narrowboat, and they had yelled out as loud as they could when she asked them what type of boat it was. The name *Josher!* echoed across the water and through the trees, and they settled down in high spirits to their picnic on the canal bank.

It was while the group was working its way solidly through sandwiches, biscuits and the Josher-cake, that Marnie became aware of someone approaching from behind them. She had been sitting under the huge cream parasol with Margaret Giles having their own tea a short distance from the school group, and they turned their heads to find Estelle walking out of the spinney towards them.

"What a lovely sight!" she exclaimed. "It's straight out of *Swallows and Amazons* or the *Famous Five*."

Marnie invited her to join them and introduced her to Margaret Giles. Ronny rushed up with a folding safari chair and settled her with a cup of Darjeeling and lemon. He went off to find her a plate.

"I didn't expect you this early, Estelle," said Marnie.

"I mis-judged the traffic ... it wasn't half as bad as I anticipated ... *sailed* past that junction where there's always supposed to be a hold-up. *Brilliant*."

"Well, everything's ready for you. I've had the cottage windows open all day to give it a good airing." She turned to Margaret. "Estelle's moving in today and starting with us on Monday."

"So you're expanding the business," said Margaret. "I'm so glad things are going well."

"Estelle's working with us on a project in Italy."

"In *Italy*? You're going international. That's impressive."

"I'm on loan from the company in London," Estelle said. "Marnie's old firm."

"Will you be staying here long?"

Estelle looked at Marnie and said, "For the summer, I expect. Maybe a little longer, depending on the job."

"Well," said Margaret, "you're coming at a good time. If today's anything to go by, we're in for a long hot summer."

Ronny was coming towards them carrying a tray when a child rushed over from the main group and held out a jar. Breathlessly she said, "Anne says please will you open the honey. The lid's too tight. She can't get it off."

Marnie held out a hand. "Here. Ronny's got his hands full. Let me have a go." She took firm hold of the jar.

Margaret said, "Don't run back with it, Jenny. You should walk. We don't want you having an accident."

"No, Mrs Giles."

Marnie pulled a face. "This is *really* stiff." She strained to turn it, but the jar was solid. "Phew! They must have gorillas in the honey factory to put these lids on." The little girl laughed.

Ronny straightened up from putting the tray down. "Shall I have a go, Marnie?" He rubbed his palms down the sides of his jeans and took hold of the jar, his sturdier fingers taking over from Marnie's slender hands. He frowned, clutching the jar close to his chest. After a few seconds he turned the lid and removed it, screwing it lightly back in place and handing it to the girl. She thanked him and was turning on her heel to race back, when she caught the look in her head teacher's eye and walked away sedately, holding the jar in front of her like a talisman.

"So you're the muscles round here," Estelle said brightly.

"This is Ronny," Marnie said. "He's a friend of Anne's ... and mine too. Thanks, Ronny. Meet Estelle. She's coming to work with us over the summer."

Ronny raised a hand. "Hallo."

"Did you go to Margaret's school, Ronny?"

His face clouded for a second as if he was uncomfortable at being linked with the children.

Margaret stepped in. "He left just before I came here, but I heard a lot about him. You left a reputation behind you, Ronny."

"For his strength?" Estelle asked.

"For all-round ability, actually."

Estelle smiled up at him. "A hunk with brains. That's quite a reputation to have."

Ronny grinned, but he was tired of being put under the microscope and excused himself to return to Anne and her crew. Marnie gave Estelle an old-fashioned look as Ronny walked away and offered her a slice of cake before she could laugh.

Margaret said, "They love these visits. They've been excited for days in anticipation."

"Ronny loves visiting here, too," said Estelle with a twinkle. "But for a different reason, of course. Are they an item, he and Anne?"

"She likes him well enough," said Marnie. "And he's certainly keen on her, but I think they're just friends."

"Keen on you, too," said Estelle. "I noticed the way he looked at you. He was thrilled that he could impress you by getting that jar open."

"And you fed his ego," Marnie observed.

"He's a bright young man," Margaret said. "Good all-rounder. I believe he's going to university. Is that right, Marnie?"

"I think he's taking a gap year, then going on to Leicester to do something in the sciences."

"Leicester?" Estelle chimed in. "I've got a friend who's starting a Master's at Leicester this autumn. I'll have to introduce them."

A burst of laughter erupted from the children, and the women looked up to see Ronny shaking his head, his face wet from a soaking of spray from opening a can of Coke. He held it out at arm's length, the foam oozing over the sides. Anne was quick to pass him a tea towel. Several of the children were rocking with laughter where they sat.

"Do you think someone might've shaken it deliberately?" Marnie asked.

"Wouldn't surprise me," said Margaret. "We'd be hard-pressed to find the culprit in that lot, even if we rounded up the usual suspects."

"They don't look very naughty to me," Estelle said.

"No, they're lovely." Margaret spoke with affection. "I shall miss them after the summer, when they go on to their next school."

The three sat in silence for a few moments watching the children collect together the picnic things under Anne's command. Ronny went round with a black plastic rubbish bag for the debris, and a posse of children carried cups and plates on board *Sally Ann*.

"Yes," Margaret said quietly. "I can see why the scene reminded you of children's literature, Estelle. I know they'll look back on this visit in years to come as a perfect, golden summer's day. I'm sure of it. Thank you so much, Marnie, for making it possible."

"A pleasure."

From the corner of her eye Marnie saw Estelle turn her head to one side and raise a hand to her face, as if wiping away a tear. Just then, Anne's voice rang out.

"Have we got time to do some drawing?"

Margaret looked at her watch. "Fine by me, if it's all right with you, Marnie."

Marnie called out, "Sure, Anne. Go ahead."

The children sat excitedly in a circle, picking up their sketchpads. Anne could be heard saying, "Right. First you can draw *Sally Ann* – or *Thyrsis,* if you want – then I'm going to show you how to draw trees. OK?"

"OK!" they shouted enthusiastically and bent to their task.

Marnie poured more tea for her guests as the children settled down. Estelle broke the silence.

"There's something ... strange about the group."

"*Strange?*" said Margaret. "In what way?"

"I'm not sure." Estelle spoke slowly and softly. "I can't quite put my finger on it."

Marnie said, "I think I know what it is. Look at them all ... all those blonde heads. It struck me when I first visited the school last year. I remember thinking ... *this is Anglo-Saxon England.*"

"And that's odd?" said Margaret. "I mean, it is England ... they are English children. Is that really strange?"

"It can seem so, when you come up from London. It did to me."

"Oh, of course," said Margaret. "I see what you mean. I'd never thought about it like that."

"But didn't you say you taught in Yorkshire?"

"Yes, but it was a village school in the North Riding, not downtown Bradford."

"That's what that surprised me," Estelle agreed. "No black kids ... in fact no one from any other race. And most have got fair hair ... your *Anglo-Saxon England,* as you call it."

"You're quite right," said Margaret. " It's just that it had never struck me as being odd."

. . . . .

The class trekked up the field track after the visit, Anne and Ronny leading the way surrounded by a small cluster of girls chatting amicably, Marnie and Margaret Giles trailing the group by a few metres. The head carried the inevitable file under her arm.

"This seems to be becoming a regular fixture on the school calendar, Marnie. I hope it isn't an imposition."

"It's fine. You and the children are very welcome. You can pencil it in for next year if you want."

"Certainly will, thank you." Margaret cocked her head over towards Glebe Farm, which was gradually disappearing behind the trees down the slope behind them. "Your friend gave me something to think about, Marnie. She's right, of course. It is too easy to lead a sheltered life in a village like this. We're very privileged here, but maybe that isn't the best thing for the children."

"I feel like saying you shouldn't worry about it, Margaret, but after what I saw this week in Leicester, I'm not so sure. What can you do about it?"

"Get the children out more ... into the real world, perhaps ... prepare them better for life."

"More trips out of the classroom?" Marnie suggested.

"That's the idea. Not easy, though. You wouldn't believe how much assessment goes on in primary schools these days. The paperwork's an enormous burden. Then there's the worry about legal problems if a child injures itself while on a trip."

"You'd be held responsible?"

"Got it in one, Marnie. It's so much more complicated than it used to be, even in the time that I've been a teacher. I'm going to look into it, though. Perhaps I'll send a letter to all the parents and sound them out. I could do it when I send copies of the leaflets about the summer scheme."

At the top of the track, Marnie said goodbye to Margaret, and Anne parted company with Ronny and her acolytes. The two of them strolled back, Anne feeling pleased with the afternoon.

"You're quiet, Marnie. Did you enjoy the visit?"

"Yes, of course. Nice kids ... Margaret too. She's worried that the children may be too cut off from some of the realities of life."

Anne laughed. "I thought that was part of the attraction of living in Knightly St John. It's so peaceful here. It's what I like about it. Isn't it why you came, Marnie ... to find a refuge from the modern world?"

Marnie frowned. "Partly, I suppose. But you can't cut yourself off from the world."

"Is something worrying you, Marnie?"

The chimneys and roof of Glebe Farm were coming into view, and the afternoon sunlight was shining on the treetops beyond.

"I've got this strange feeling," Marnie began. She checked herself, anxious not to say anything that might worry Anne. "I don't know ..."

"It was those riots, wasn't it? And seeing the demonstrators on your way to the meeting? It's upset you."

"Probably."

"Do you think they could come here?" Anne asked.

"No," Marnie said firmly. "No. They won't come here, but it's bad enough that they're out there somewhere. Just knowing they exist, spreads their poison everywhere."

· · · · ·

Anne crawled out backwards from under the desk after plugging in Estelle's computer. She pressed switches and heard the machinery quietly whirring into life, saw tiny green lights glowing on the monitor, the printer, the zip drive. Outside on the landing she could hear Marnie explaining the wonders of the bathroom, while Ralph, in charge of the heavier loads, was climbing the cottage stairs with another box of books.

"The system heats the water as you turn on any hot tap," Marnie was saying. "So you've got constant hot water any time you need it, twenty-four seven."

"That's *brilliant!*" Estelle enthused.

In fact, she had not stopped effervescing since walking into her temporary new home. Marnie and Anne had returned from escorting the school group up the track to find Estelle staggering under the weight of a box of computer software manuals. They had summoned Ralph on the mobile and joined in ferrying her possessions out of the Golf into cottage number three. Every bag or box carried a label showing its destination, and the transfer was soon completed.

The cottage smelt like a new beginning with a trace of perfume in the air overlaying the fresh paintwork and new carpeting. When Estelle saw the flowers dotted around the house, Marnie thought she was on the brink of tears. In every room stood small vases containing roses or sweet William, cornflowers or pinks, and Marnie was taken aback when Estelle suddenly turned and hugged her tightly, kissing her warmly on both cheeks.

"Country flowers from a country garden!" she exclaimed. "It's *perfect.*"

"And you're right," said Marnie. "They all come from the garden at the back of the farmhouse. It's so overgrown, they practically qualify as wild flowers."

In the middle of the living room, Estelle sat down on the floor, cross-legged like a child, looking around her.

"You've even put pictures on the walls!"

She scrambled to her feet to inspect them. "Are they original water-colours? They're charming."

"One or two of mine, one or two by Anne."

Estelle shook her head. "It really is like home. I shall never want to leave."

Marnie smiled. "Good."

"But don't worry, Marnie, I'll get out of your hair when the contract's completed. I know I can be a bit overpowering, but this is all so *gorgeous*, I just feel like celebrating."

Anne, who had been standing in the doorway, quietly slipped out while Estelle was admiring one of her paintings over the mantelpiece. Estelle turned to compliment her and assumed she had withdrawn out of modesty. But Anne quickly re-appeared balancing a tray holding a bottle of champagne and four glasses. Behind her, Ralph could be heard coming down the stairs. He took the bottle from the tray that Anne held out to him and began removing the gold foil over the cage holding the cork in place.

"I've put the books on the shelves, Estelle. I've not put them in any order; I'll leave that to you."

"I'm overwhelmed. It's like coming home to a family. And real champagne, too!"

"It was on special offer in Waitrose," Anne volunteered, grinning.

The cork popped, the wine flowed and four glasses were raised and chinked together.

"Welcome, Estelle," said Marnie, and Ralph and Anne echoed the sentiment.

"To my new home ... and my dearest new-old friends," said Estelle, her eyes moist and pink.

Anne set out small bowls of olives, cashews and puri, and they sat sipping contentedly on furniture from Marnie's London flat brought out of storage. Estelle could scarcely believe her good fortune, that her life was changing so much for the better after an unbearably difficult year.

Anne was in heaven, seeing the cottage completed and charming. Drinking champagne in the company of interior designers, her colleagues, she understood perfectly how elated Estelle was feeling. But she wondered if Estelle was going to remain on a perpetual high for the entire duration of her contract with them.

Ralph sat admiring the cottage, wondering if champagne had ever before been consumed there in its long history. He speculated on what miracle Marnie would work on the farmhouse, and how he would feel about it eventually becoming his home.

"If it stays fine tomorrow," Marnie said to Estelle, "We're thinking of going for a trip on *Sally* and having lunch on board. Would you like to join us?"

Estelle made a sad face. "I am sorry ... I've made plans already. I'll be out all day."

"Another time, then," Marnie said. "We can't shift it to Sunday, unfortunately: Ralph's off to a conference in Barcelona, and Anne's going to see her family. There'll be other occasions."

"Oh, yes," said Estelle. "They say we're in for a long hot summer."

Where have I heard that before? Marnie thought.

9

Famous last words, Marnie muttered to herself, looking through the porthole curtain on Saturday morning.

She was standing naked in the sleeping cabin on *Thyrsis*. It was around six-thirty, and in the dull early light of an overcast morning she could see pinpricks covering the whole surface of the canal where a faint drizzle was falling. The trees were dripping on the opposite bank, and the landscape had disappeared in an opaque mist. *So much for the long hot summer ...* She shivered and climbed back under the duvet where Ralph was breathing rhythmically, only the top of his head visible, dark hair on the light blue pillow. She could feel his warmth as she snuggled down beside him. She closed her eyes and breathed in deeply.

But it was no good. After a restless minute or two, Marnie slid silently out of bed, reached for her dressing gown and padded through to the galley. While the kettle was heating on the hob, she had a quick shower and pulled on a sweatshirt and jeans. Ralph was still sleeping, so she closed the galley door, poured a mug of coffee and turned on the radio. Two farmers were talking about the iniquities of the Common Agricultural Policy, and she quickly turned the dial, hoping to find some music on Radio Three or Classic fm. She paused in mid-turn, as the radio seemed to collide with her own thoughts. It was a local station, a young bright female voice saying the words she had been thinking minutes before.

... and it gave them the idea for the song, I believe. It was long before my time. I remember reading that John Lennon saw a poster in America: 'Happiness is a warm gun ... and it's going to be a long hot summer'. I'm not sure if it was advertising guns or promoting race riots, but it led to him writing this song ... one of their many classics ...

Behind her voice the music had begun playing, the sound gradually rising as she completed the intro.

So here are The Beatles with John Lennon leading on 'Happiness is a Warm Gun' from their white album of 1969.

Marnie listened to the ironic words, the bitter humour and beguilingly attractive melody. She raised the mug to her lips, and steam rose past her eyes. She saw in flashback the smoke drifting across the street in Leicester, remembered old newsreel footage from Alabama and Mississippi, fiery crosses set ablaze by the Ku Klux Klan all over the South, innocent people lynched, shot, injured and maimed, victims of hatred and prejudice. Sitting fully clothed in the warm galley, for the second time that morning Marnie shivered.

• • • • •

How wrong can you be? Marnie was musing later that morning, as she brought *Sally Ann* out of the docking area across the canal, turned deftly and brought her into mid-channel, pointing northwards for their trip up to Hanford for lunch. Anne walked steadily back along the gunwale, laid the barge pole on the roof and stepped down onto the stern deck.

The sun was climbing high now, burning off the early cloud cover, leaving a haze on the fields and vapour rising from the wet steelwork of the boats. Everything was glistening and sparkling in strong shimmering light. The very air seemed to be rippling before their eyes. The smell of water and new foliage pervaded everywhere, and Marnie thought it blissful to be alive. She hugged Ralph on impulse, her head pressing against his cheek. He kissed her hair, and Anne smiled with them.

"What's that tune you've been humming?" said Ralph.

"Humming?"

"Yes. You've been humming it on and off all morning."

"Have I?"

"It's a Beatles' song," Anne said. *"Happiness is a Warm Gun."*

"I don't think I know that one," said Ralph.

Marnie disengaged herself to steer *Sally Ann* round a bend. "I heard it on the radio this morning when you were still in bed. It's one of John Lennon's."

"It doesn't sound like John Lennon," Ralph said doubtfully. "The title, I mean."

"Well, he certainly sings it. It's full of irony."

Ralph nodded. "There's a double irony there, when you think about it."

Marnie heard the assassin's gunshots on a New York street. "I'd rather not think about it … and just enjoy the day."

• • • • •

And they did enjoy the day. The countryside looked like a tourist brochure, with sheep and cattle grazing in the fields, trees in the full leaf of high summer and wild flowers at the water's edge. They rubbed sun block on their faces and arms, and Marnie put on a white floppy hat.

Ralph's pleasure was only marred at the thought that he would be going away for a week, flying off to his conference the next day. He perched on the stern rail while Marnie steered and Anne leaned against the hatch. For him Marnie was close to perfection. He watched her at the tiller, balancing lightly on her feet, making constant small adjustments to keep the boat on a straight course. In faded jeans and white T-shirt she looked wonderful, and he could scarcely believe his luck.

And yet … and yet … Tomorrow he would be leaving. Even though it was only for a short while, a wave of anxiety rolled over him at the thought. In the past when he had been away, Marnie had run into dangers that had almost proved fatal. It troubled him that she was now disturbed enough by the rioters she had seen to let that prey on her mind, even to the point of creeping in on her thoughts when she was simply humming a tune. A cloud darkened the horizon of this perfect day.

Suddenly, Anne turned excitedly, showing them a lamb kneeling down to drink in the shallow water of the canal where it skirted a meadow, her face delighted as she pointed towards the bank. Marnie was nodding and saying something that was lost to Ralph in the clanking of the engine. Anne must have caught his expression, for she turned back to look at him, her face questioning, anxious. Ralph quickly changed to a reassuring smile. He stood up and went to stand beside Anne, resting one hand lightly on her shoulder, the other on the warm steel of the boat's roof.

"Are we tying up below the manor as usual for lunch?" he asked her.

"'Spect so," she said, her smile now back in place. "Anywhere along here would be ideal as far as I'm concerned. It's all just perfect, isn't it, Ralph? Absolutely perfect … Oops, I'm starting to sound like Estelle!" She made a funny face and laughed into her hand.

• • • • •

Only a few wisps of high cloud were on hand to witness Anne bringing *Sally Ann* home to base at around six o'clock. All three of the crew were glowing with colour after hours spent in the open air. It had been a lazy afternoon. They had eaten lunch on deck and stayed out sunning themselves and reading magazines before strolling to look at the working boats up at Stoke Bruerne. Back on board, Marnie had slipped into a bikini top and shorts and now looked and felt as if she had been on a Mediterranean holiday.

Ralph went on *Thyrsis* to make a pot of Darjeeling. From force of habit Marnie and Anne had gone through the spinney to check messages in the office barn, and had been surprised to see Estelle's Golf standing in its parking slot.

"That's odd," Marnie muttered.

"I thought she said she'd be out for the whole day," said Anne.

Marnie walked over and touched the bonnet. It was cool. "She's been back a while. I wonder if she's all right."

They split forces, Anne checking the office while Marnie walked over to the cottage. Halfway across the yard she hesitated. Estelle would not thank her for interfering, but if she had come home early feeling unwell, she might be in need of some help. No ... she was entitled to privacy. Marnie did not want to meddle. She turned back to the office, but had only taken two steps when a voice sounded behind her. She looked up to see Estelle hanging out of an upstairs window.

"Hi, Marnie! How's things?"

"Great. You?"

"Sure. Were you looking for me?"

"Well ... I saw you were back and ... We were going to have a cup of tea. Would you care to join us?"

"Wonderful. Give me five minutes."

"We'll be on Ralph's boat. Take your time."

Estelle arrived on *Thyrsis* as Ralph carried the pot through to the saloon. She did not come empty-handed. In a small basket she brought fresh figs and a box of homemade biscuits, round like miniature bagels. Anne put them in dishes and set them out on a low table.

"What are these?" she asked, pointing at the round biscuits. "I've never seen these before."

"Karks," said Estelle. "Try one."

"Karks," Anne repeated, picking up the dish and offering it round.

"Mm ... crispy." Anne licked a crumb from her lips. "A sort of nutty taste."

"They're good," said Marnie. "*Very* good. I don't recognise them, either. Did you make them yourself?"

"Yes," said Estelle. "Don't look so surprised. I'm quite domesticated really."

"Of course. It's just ... well, I never thought of you doing home baking in the kitchen. I had you down as a bright-lights city-girl."

"Sure, but deep down maybe there's a country girl from a *stetl* somewhere below the surface."

Ralph nodded appreciatively at the bowl of karks. "She can come to the surface every day as far as I'm concerned. Did you say a *stetl*?"

"Yes. My family back then were orthodox, my own parents are reform ... and me ... I don't actually practise, but it is my background, my upbringing. Greenwood is just a translation, of course."

"Greenwood?" said Marnie. "I seem to have turned over two pages at once."

"Greenwood ... you know, Marnie ... my name?"

"Ah ... right."

"My grandparents got out of the Sudetenland in the thirties. Their name was Grünwald. When they came to England they changed it. Even though they were Jewish refugees, the last thing they wanted was a German-sounding name ... obviously."

"Understandably," said Marnie. "Now I know what name to put on your tenancy agreement."

"Of course. We ought to do it all properly. Have you had an agreement drawn up?"

"Yes." Marnie made a dismissive gesture. "Sorry to talk business when we're having a day off. I wouldn't like you to think I was a ... *schlemiel*."

Estelle burst out laughing. "You speak *Yiddish*, Marnie? Surely you're not ... Or was your name Walker originally *Valkyrie* or something?"

Amid the laughter, Anne felt she was being left behind in this part of the conversation.

"No," said Marnie. "But I grew up in north London, remember. There's a lot of Yiddish in London slang."

"Of course. Look, let me have the agreement and I'll sign it as soon as you want."

"We'll be having supper at around eight," said Marnie. "If you'd like to join us, I could let you have it to check over."

"I'd love to," said Estelle. "Thanks. I'm sure it'll be fine."

"I'll get the agreement from the office and drop it over to you," said Anne. She smiled at Estelle. "I'm sure you'll find it's ... *kosher*."

●　●　●　●　●

They were sitting in the dining area on *Thyrsis* at the end of supper. On the table stood a cheese board and fruit. Ralph poured the final drops of wine. Outside it was still light, but a cool breeze had driven them on board.

Estelle was asking Ralph about his conference in Spain and his new career as a visiting professor at his Oxford college. She observed it seemed an ideal way of life: foreign travel, stimulating experiences and a good home to return to. And Marnie, of course.

"Ah, but that's the main drawback," said Ralph.

Marnie laughed. "The going or the coming back?"

"I leave you to guess. But seriously, it is the only problem in the package."

"I'm not sure I'd agree," said Estelle.

"The trouble is," Ralph began, looking at Marnie. "When I go away on a trip, a *certain person* has a habit of getting into all sorts of scrapes."

"And you feel you have to be here to protect me from my excesses," said a certain person.

"I wouldn't go quite that far ..."

"Well, no need to worry about a *certain person*," said Estelle. "Anne and I will be here to look after her while you're away."

"That's very consoling, but I'll still miss her."

Estelle reached across the table and patted Ralph's hand. "Oh ... that might not be such a bad thing for a relationship ... absence makes the heart grow fonder, and all that."

"I'd sooner have Ralph around, too, but it can't be helped."

Estelle suddenly sat up straight. "Ah ... that reminds me. There's something I wanted to raise ... something in the tenancy agreement for the cottage."

"Not *kosher*, after all?" said Anne.

"Ye-e-s."

"But?" said Marnie.

Estelle bit her lip. "Perhaps now isn't the right time to talk about business."

"The agreement is only a formality," said Marnie.

"But the devil is in the detail," Anne reminded her quietly.

"If you've spotted a problem, I'm sure we can sort it out," said Marnie. "I thought it was pretty innocuous, just a standard form of wording, but I'm no expert in these things."

Estelle reached down to her bag and brought out the document. She laid it on the table and turned a couple of pages. They could see that one paragraph had been ringed.

"This is it," she said, and began reading extracts.

'Not without the written consent of the Owner to permit any person to sleep, reside or stay at the property...

bla-bla-bla ...

Not to keep any animal at the property.'

"I think that's just a catch-all," said Ralph. "It means the landlord has the right to say *no* to a pit bull terrier and *yes* to a goldfish."

"You want permission to keep a goldfish?" said Marnie, smiling.

"No," Estelle said seriously. "I want a man."

"Tricky," said Marnie, keeping a straight face. "I don't think I can promise one of those as part of the tenancy."

Anne laughed.

Estelle smiled. "Can we start again?"

"You want to share the cottage with someone," said Ralph.

"Yes."

"This is all very sudden," said Marnie.

"I know, but I didn't have a chance to talk to him before today. You don't mind, do you?" Estelle beamed at her. "Say you don't mind, Marnie."

"Well ..." she began.

"Is there a problem?" Estelle asked.

"Sorry ... I don't want to be a wet blanket ..."

Estelle looked downcast. "Oh ..."

"It's just that ... normally I'd want at least to meet someone before committing myself to having them as a tenant."

Estelle suddenly brightened. "Oh, Marnie, you've got absolutely nothing to worry about. Luther's *adorable*. He's the sweetest, nicest person I've ever met. And he's dishy too. You'll really love him, I guarantee it."

"You make him sound like a cross between Snow White and Cary Grant."

Estelle laughed. "More like Albert Einstein and Arnold Schwarzenegger, actually ... with one slight difference."

"Really?"

"Oh, yes. Believe me, Marnie. He's a *wonderful* man. As soon as you meet him, you'll know what I mean. And if you don't like him, I'll tell him he can't stay. That's fair, isn't it?"

Marnie shrugged. "What can I say?"

"Then you agree to meet him?"

"Yes."

"Great. He had a lot of work to finish today. He's very conscientious. That's why I came back early."

"What's the *slight difference*, by the way?" Marnie said.

"How do you mean?"

"You said there was one slight difference with Luther ... compared with Einstein and Schwarzenegger?"

"Oh, yes." Estelle laughed. "He's from Barbados, so he'll even help the ethnic mix of the village. He's *perfect.*"

· · · · ·

It was a perfect early summer's night. The breeze had died down, and stars were shining brilliantly in a clear sky. Marnie looked out only briefly before closing the stern door on *Thyrsis*. She did not want Ralph to say he knew she had something on her mind because she stood gazing out over the water before coming to bed. She walked back to the sleeping cabin in her dressing gown.

"No need to ask if you've got everything packed ready for tomorrow," she said brightly.

Ralph was sitting up in bed reading type-written notes. A folder lay in front of him on the duvet.

"Is it bothering you?" he said.

Marnie did not pretend to misunderstand. "Well ..."

"Can't say I blame you."

"Really?"

"Estelle didn't give you much elbow room, did she?"

Marnie shook her head. "I felt uncomfortable, being confronted with a situation without any warning. What Estelle wants might be fine, but the way she put it, if I object, I'll seem like a tyrant."

"Presumably, if she'd told you about Luther from the outset, you wouldn't have objected?"

"Not if I'd had a chance to see him and agree to the idea. Why should I object?"

"I've been wondering ..." Ralph began. "Did she think you might object, so she introduced it like that to make sure she got her own way? If so, why?"

"I thought of that, too. I was completely wrong-footed. It looked as if I was being difficult, when it was Estelle who was bouncing me into accepting a total stranger, about whom I know nothing."

"If it was a deliberate ploy, I wonder why she tried to out-manoeuvre you."

"Perhaps we're reading too much into it, Ralph. There may be a simple explanation. She said she hadn't had a chance to raise it with him until today. He has been away, after all."

"True."

Marnie nibbled a finger nail. "Actually, if it is a rebound thing ..."

"You think that could bring problems?"

"Other people's relationships ... Who knows? It could be great; it could be just one more complication. After everything we've been through these past few months, I could use some stability."

"Marnie —"

"Don't say you wish you weren't going away tomorrow."

"But —"

"No. Here I am maundering on about something that may not be a real issue at all, when I really ought to be making sure you've done everything you need to do before you go off."

"That's OK. I told you I've got all my things packed."

"That isn't what I had in mind."

Marnie slipped off her dressing gown, took Ralph's papers from his hands, dropped them on the floor and reached up to turn off the lights.

10

Anne had a restless night punctuated by weird dreams. Glebe Farm was being over-run by a motley army of rioters, running in and out of the buildings with flaming torches. She heard screaming in the cottages, saw flames gushing from the windows of the farmhouse. Strange banners were flying on the rooftops. Everywhere a smell of burning timbers. When a detachment of thugs ran towards the barn where her Mini was garaged, she sat up in a sweat, gasping.

Across the attic a pale light was penetrating from the narrow slit that was her only window. Anne blinked a few times, calmed down and took stock of the situation. The bedside clock showed six twenty-nine, and she heard a faint sound of movement outside. She listened, swinging her feet out from under the duvet to find her slippers. There was the crunch of tyres on gravel, the murmur of an engine, a change of gear.

Marnie was setting off to take Ralph to the airport for his early morning flight to Barcelona and would return for a late breakfast. Now, Anne was wide awake. Coffee beckoned, and she went down the wall-ladder to put on the kettle, tugging off her long T-shirt as she stepped into the shower cubicle and began turning under the hot jets.

Minutes later, still clutching her mug, she walked through the spinney towards *Sally Ann* to feed Dolly. It was another peculiar morning, cool and damp, even mistier than yesterday. Moisture was glistening on the trees and bushes, dripping on the bare earth. A fresh leafy smell was in the air. Wishing she had put on a sweatshirt, Anne quickened her pace to keep warm. Dolly was waiting for her with a warbled greeting, and they converged on the galley with a common purpose. So it was that Anne did not at first notice the newcomer.

It was only when she emerged from the cabin onto the stern deck that she saw the boat.

• • • • •

Passing the church and the village school, Marnie raised a hand to her mouth between gear changes and yawned. Ralph glanced across at her.

"You know there really was no need for you to take me to the airport like this, Marnie. It's sweet of you, but I feel guilty at getting you up so early."

"No problem, kind sir."

"Then why are you yawning?"

"I always take a little light exercise in the morning. You should try it; it does you good."

He laughed. "You always have an answer, that's for sure. This mist is odd. It felt more like autumn than early summer when we came out just now."

Marnie flicked a switch and the wiper swished once across the windscreen and back.

"A sudden change of air current. It won't last. Nothing to worry about."

"Good. Let's keep it that way."

Marnie turned onto the narrow road that led up towards the dual carriageway. "Meaning?"

"Meaning no worries," said Ralph. "I want you to have a nice unbroken spell of normality, especially while I'm away."

Marnie yawned again. "Me too. We've got plenty to keep us busy, and I just intend getting my head down and pressing on with the work. And we've got Estelle to help. That should be stimulating."

Ralph nodded. "As long as her boyfriend isn't a problem."

"I'm sure he'll be fine," said Marnie. "I just reacted the way I did because I was taken by surprise. I never did like surprises."

• • • • •

Anne pushed open the double doors on *Sally Ann* to let the cat out and paused on the bottom step below the open hatch, looking out across the canal over the stern deck. There was nothing new or unusual about a boat being moored on the opposite bank, especially in the summer. But this boat was different from anything she had ever seen before, and the mist only seemed to accentuate its strangeness.

Most narrow boats had a pleasing appearance, many of them in colourful liveries. Some had leaded panes of glass and frilly lace curtains; the cottage style. Others were impressive with shining brass and glossy, mirror-like paintwork. Tubs of herbs and flowers on the roof were common, and even small satellite dishes were not unknown. But this boat, cloaked in the mist, exuded a different air. As Anne stared at it, her fascination was tinged with a sense of menace. In the dampness she shivered.

Dolly rubbed her flank against Anne's leg and hopped up onto the deck, where she turned and jumped over the gunwale to land on the bank, setting off on her morning prowl. Anne wanted to return inside the cabin where toast and orange juice were waiting for her, but she was mesmerised by the sight of the new boat that had arrived in the night. Quickly she went below and found Marnie's windproof jacket in the locker. Pulling the zip up to her chin, she went out and walked along the bank to cross the canal by the accommodation bridge about twenty metres from the docking area.

Halfway across, she hesitated and looked up and down the canal before turning her gaze back to the new arrival. There was no one in sight in any direction, no sign of life or movement on the boat itself. From her vantage point, the craft was almost swallowed in the murky air, and it seemed to draw Anne towards it. Convincing herself that no harm could come of an apparently casual stroll past the boat, that no one could take offence at her interest in such an unusual vessel, she continued on her way and walked steadily along the towpath, slowing as she drew nearer.

Closer up, the craft was no less unusual than it had seemed from a distance. It was mainly the colour scheme that set it apart from other boats. The topsides were painted all over in a dark shade of grey like a submarine, in an eggshell finish. The lower half of the hull was matt black. Not quite as long as *Sally Ann* or *Thyrsis*, it was built in the traditional style, with a short cratch well and a tiny counter for the steerer. All its windows were portholes. Pipe fenders of thin black rubber tubing hung down the sides, attached with black rope, and Anne noticed that all the mooring ropes were similarly black.

Reaching the bows, she looked down to read the name, which was stencilled in matt black on a white panel. It looked unfinished, comprising only three letters: *X O 2*. She wondered if it meant something in a code. On the roof lay a pole, boathook and gangplank on supporting brackets near the lum, all painted grey. Anne noticed a cluster of antennae, one short and stubby made of rubber, the other a small black satellite dish. This was the strangest boat Anne had ever encountered, and it both intrigued and repelled her. She could not help admire the bold confidence of the colour scheme, yet it seemed intimidating and threatening.

Slowly she began walking back towards the bridge, certain that the boat was unoccupied. The door was secured with a hefty black padlock. As she passed by, Anne saw that the portholes were obscured by light grey curtains, one of which had not been fully drawn. A tantalising gap just a few centimetres wide could be seen through the glass nearest to where she now came to a halt. She tried not to look suspicious as she checked the towpath again for life. Seeing no one, and feeling sheltered by the mist, she bent forward to peep through the gap.

The problem was, the interior seemed to be as dark as the outside, and only one or two reflections from metal surfaces could be distinguished. Something was blocking her view nearer at hand and, altering her focus to close-up, she made a discovery. Close to the porthole, she was looking at the side of a cupboard or a set of shelves on which a picture was fixed. It was indistinct in the gloom but appeared to be an image, some kind of silvery object. She was surprised to see colour in this otherwise monochrome world, a faint circle of red. With a struggle, she finally made sense of the image and gasped. Staying only long enough to make sure of what she had seen, she straightened up, turned and began hurrying back to the bridge, her mind greatly troubled. In the red circle was the unmistakeable shape of a Nazi swastika.

Anne had reached the parapet when a sound came out of the mist. She paused, and in that moment the sun broke through, lighting up the air around her, as if she was transfixed by a spotlight. The vapour was thinning before her eyes, and into view came a bicycle. It was a comfortably reassuring sight, and for a second or two she expected to see Ronny Cope, a regular visitor on two wheels. But this was not Ronny. Reaching the bridge, the rider slowed to a halt and stood straddling the bike, looking at Anne. It was a young man, slim with blonde hair cut short, wearing a black leather jacket, dark grey jeans and black trainers. The sun was gaining in force, reflecting off the shiny chrome handlebars, flashing into Anne's eyes. She glimpsed a red armband on the newcomer, saw the black swastika emblem, and swallowed hard. She blinked and momentarily glanced sideways towards the boat. The stranger followed her look and returned his gaze to Anne.

"Good morning." His voice was quiet. "I hope I'm not trespassing."

Anne blinked again. The sun was diffusing the light all around them, making the scene ethereal, unworldly. The mist was literally evaporating before her eyes. Involuntarily she looked again at his sleeve, but there was no armband on the black leather. She could see panniers either side of the rear wheel, and the edge of a newspaper emerging from the corner of the flap.

"No." It seemed an inadequate greeting. "I mean, you're not trespassing."

"Good."

Without another word, the stranger lifted one foot onto a pedal, rolled the bike forward and moved off up and over the bridge. As Anne expected, he turned along the towpath and coasted to a halt beside the grey boat. He glanced fleetingly up towards her as he unhooked the panniers, set them down in the cratch well and hoisted the bike onto the roof. Anne went on her way without looking back.

• • • • •

The Discovery pulled off the dual carriageway and took the narrow road that led only to Knightly St John. Marnie enjoyed its high driving position that enabled her to see over the hedgerows.

Arriving home, she braked and turned into the garage barn, watching out for Dolly as she swung into her slot beside the old MG sports car. Beyond it, Anne was running a duster over the Mini, getting it pristine for her trip back to her family for the day. But there was something wrong. Marnie saw it at once. Anne looked up and smiled, but there was something about her bearing that gave Marnie the impression that all was not well. She pushed open the door.

"What's up?"

"Nothing."

"Really nothing?"

Anne dropped the duster into the box of car-cleaning things. "Well ..."

"Have you had breakfast? Got time to talk?"

Anne nodded. "OK."

• • • • •

Anne sat holding her mug of coffee in both hands as usual. Marnie always thought it made her look vulnerable, like a refugee. They were on *Sally Ann* having a belated breakfast, and Anne told Marnie about the strange new boat moored opposite. Crunching a piece of toast, Marnie inclined her head towards the window.

"I agree it certainly looks different, Anne. Whoever chose that colour scheme had an eye for the dramatic. It looks somehow ... military, or I suppose, *naval*."

"All it needs is a conning tower to make it just like a U-boat," said Anne.

"Mm. So what did you see through the porthole?"

"That's just it. It was too dark to make out how it was furnished, but I did get one glimpse of something hanging on the wall. I don't know exactly what I was looking at, but I saw a red circle and inside it ... a swastika."

Her eyes were the size of light bulbs.

"A *swastika?*" Marnie repeated. "Are you sure about that?"

"Pretty sure."

"But not absolutely certain?"

"I didn't dream it up."

"Course not."

Marnie was determined that she would keep her concern to herself and reassure Anne that all was fine.

"You don't think I imagined it, do you?" said Anne. "I can tell you don't. You look so worried."

"Do I?" *So much for my acting skills*, Marnie thought.

"You're thinking about the thugs you saw the other day in Leicester, aren't you?"

"Well ... not actually."

"What then?"

There was no way out.

"It was something Inspector Bartlett said that day he came down."

"What day was that?"

"A short while back. I didn't mention it at the time."

"But you're going to now?"

Marnie sighed. "He came asking if we'd seen any strangers ... *suspicious characters*, he called them. He warned me to be on the lookout."

Anne put on a serious face and deepened her voice. "'Allo, 'allo, 'allo. 'Ave you seen anyone answerin' to the description of a suspicious character in this 'ere vicinity?" She checked herself and looked aghast. "*Blimey!* What am I joking for? I'm scared stiff we're about to be over-run by the Gestapo and murdered in our beds."

Marnie laughed. "Idiot! It's not as bad as that."

"It's all right for you, Marnie. You've already been murdered once. Some of us are novices and ... Oh God. Sorry, Marnie. I shouldn't have said that. It was in *really* poor taste. I am sorry."

"That's OK. I'm only glad you're able to make a joke about it."

"Did Mr Bartlett say what kind of *suspicious characters* he was looking for?"

"No, but he did say they weren't dangerous to us ... whatever that meant."

"He probably thought they'd be our chums. He'd regard the vicar as suspicious if he knew we were friends with her."

Marnie looked at her watch. "Time you were going. You don't want to be late for one of your mum's excellent Sunday lunches."

Anne stood up and began clearing the table.

"Leave that," said Marnie. "I'll do it. I've got loads of time."

"It's not too late to change your mind and come too. Mum always makes enough to feed an army."

"Sure, but I've got things to do. Perhaps next time."

"Are you going to get in touch with Inspector Bartlett, then?"

"What about?"

Anne glanced over at the visitor's boat. "Our suspicious character."

"Why? On the basis of seeing someone with a boat painted in an original colour? I spend my working life trying to devise distinctive colour schemes for people. I'd hardly regard it as a crime. For all we know, he might just be someone with a flair for design."

"A design that includes *swastikas?*"

"You don't think you could be mistaken about that, Anne?"

Anne opened her mouth to speak and closed it abruptly. In her mind she saw again the meeting on the bridge, the mist swirling in the sunshine, the flash of light reflected on the handlebars. "I ..."

"What?"

"I'm not sure ... It's just ... Well, when I saw him on the bridge ... I kind of imagined he was wearing an armband."

"What kind of armband?"

"You know ..."

"Like the Nazis?"

Anne nodded.

"And?"

"He wasn't. I'd just thought he was."

"Not a lot to report to Inspector Bartlett, is there?" said Marnie. "We can't turn him in for saying hallo and wearing black clothes."

"Not really."

"Don't give it another thought. It'll be like all the other boats. I expect he'll be gone by tomorrow."

11

The mystery boat was still on its mooring when they awoke on Monday morning. Marnie had had an early night and had not seen either Anne or Estelle when they returned from their visits. Her last action before going to bed on *Thyrsis* was to peep out after turning off the light in the sleeping cabin and look across the canal at the visitor. The boat was in complete darkness, not a trace of light visible anywhere.

As usual Anne joined Marnie for breakfast, arriving shortly after seven as she was emerging from the shower. As usual she was in good spirits. She went straight to the galley and began laying the table. A minute later Marnie came in, ready to face the day, wearing a cream silk shirt and black trousers.

"How was everything at home?"

"Fine. Mum and dad send love." Anne nodded towards the window. "He's still there."

"No, he's not."

Anne looked out. "Some things I imagined, but that is not a mirage, it's a boat."

Marnie shook her head. "You said *he's still there*. He isn't. He left twenty minutes ago on his bike."

"You saw him?"

"Yes, on my way to the shower. He unhooked the bike from the roof and set off down the towpath."

"Did you get a good look at him? Did you say anything?"

"Anne, I was stark naked. I was hardly going to hang out of the window and wave."

Anne laughed. "Just as well ... he might've fallen in the canal."

"Or got back on the U-boat and trained his periscope in this direction."

"So you *do* think he looked suspicious," said Anne, more serious again.

"Actually, Anne ..." Marnie began, "my impression was ... he looked rather like you."

· · · · ·

This was the first staff meeting involving Estelle, and the three of them sat round Marnie's desk armed with coffee mugs for the usual eight o'clock Monday morning programme review. Dolly presided over business from her customary place under Marnie's desk lamp. Anne had printed off the updated list of projects with notes on progress, and they each studied them briefly before the meeting began.

"Can I start with an extra item?" said Estelle, looking up. There was an eagerness in her voice that Marnie guessed had little to do with target dates for project completions.

"Sure."

"I was just wondering when it would be convenient to introduce Luther. Remember you said you'd be willing to see him, Marnie?"

"Of course. When do you have in mind?" Marnie reached across the desk for her filofax.

"Oh, you won't need that." Estelle smiled, looking very pleased with herself. "He's here already. You could see him whenever suits you."

Marnie continued to reach for the filofax and open it at the current date to conceal her irritation at Estelle once again forcing her hand.

"Does he have plans for the day?"

"He'll come over any time you want." The smile again. "Though I think he's probably in the shower at the moment."

Marnie read through her appointments for the week before replying.

"What about ... suppose he joined us for a snack lunch on *Sally* at around noon? That would give me time to clear the desk and get the week launched, unless it interfered with any other arrangements he had. It would mean he'd be able to get back to London before the worst of the evening traffic, presumably."

A cloud passed over Estelle's features. "Get back to London?" she said quietly.

"I was assuming he had not brought all his possessions for this first meeting," Marnie said in an even tone.

Estelle nodded. "No. Of course not. He just came up so as to be here to meet you for a chat."

"Fine. Lunch, then?"

"Thanks, Marnie. I'll tell him after we've finished here."

"Good. So ... where were we? Let's start, as usual, with Willards ..."

· · · · ·

The call came in soon after ten. Anne was out on site dispensing drinks to the builders, so Marnie picked up the receiver. In the background was the steady throbbing of the cement mixer behind the farmhouse, preparing concrete for the base of the terrace.

"Am I speaking to Marnie Walker?" A woman's voice, pleasant and warm.

"Yes, you are. What can I do for you?"

"Are you aware of the fire at the community centre in Northampton about ten days ago?"

"Certainly."

"My name is Serena McDowell. I'm a member of the centre's management committee. One of our members has given me your name and number. I'd like to meet."

"You're aware that we're interior designers, not architects?"

"Well aware. I was given your details by Dorothy Vane-Henderson of Hanford Hall, who speaks very highly of you. The whole decor of the building needs redesigning after the fire."

"How extensive was the damage to the structure?"

"Not as bad as it might've been. The fire brigade got there fast. Probably best if you took a look for yourself. Would that be possible?"

Marnie found herself reaching for the filofax again. The name Luther stared up at her.

"The sooner the better from your point of view, I expect?"

"Yes. We've got builders in at the moment making everything safe and secure. We want to get the place up and running again as quickly as possible ... show those – the people who torched it – that we're not defeated." A hardness had entered her voice.

"I could meet you there tomorrow. Would ten-thirty be convenient?"

• • • • •

As Anne laid the table for lunch beside *Sally Ann*, she kept looking across the canal to the 'U-boat' moored by the bank opposite *Thyrsis*. The owner had not returned; there was no bike attached to the roof. She heard a faint ringing from inside *Sally Ann*; the timer had sounded for the pizzas, and she heard Marnie open the oven door to inspect them. Anne hopped onto the stern deck and called down into the cabin.

"Are they done?"

"Yes."

"Shall I go and check whether Estelle and her friend are ready?"

"No need," Marnie called back. "They won't be late."

Sure enough, within seconds Estelle emerged from the spinney with Luther. Anne tried not to gape and almost succeeded. She managed to close her mouth before anyone noticed and stepped carefully down onto the bank. Estelle approached holding hands with the most handsome man Anne had ever seen, either in reality or on the cinema screen. Luther looked as good as a Hollywood film star on a well-lit film set on a good day. The words *magnificent specimen* floated into her mind.

At that moment Marnie came out from the boat, smiled at Luther as if he was a normal person from planet Earth and held out a hand. The smile that greeted her was of chalk white teeth, and the hand was as big as if he had been wearing wicket-keeper's gloves. Anne feared for Marnie's safety as her slender hand disappeared into Luther's grip, but it reappeared unscathed, and Marnie was still smiling. When Anne shook hands she was transfixed by dark piercing eyes and was only dimly aware of the warm, firm grip that was no bone-crusher. The introductions were completed, Estelle glowing with satisfaction.

"It's just something quick and simple," Marnie was saying. "I grabbed pizzas from the freezer. Hope that's all right with you."

"That's fine, Marnie. It's really nice of you to offer me lunch at such short notice."

Thank God for that, Anne thought. Luther's voice was slightly high-pitched, so he was not perfect. If he had sounded like James Earl Jones, it would have been unbearable. Anne went below to fetch fruit juice from the fridge. When she returned, Marnie was speaking.

"I thought it'd be best if we stayed off wine as it's so warm and we have work to do today."

"Good idea," said Luther. "Actually, I don't drink alcohol anyway. My usual tipple is diet Coke." He flashed the Colgate grin.

Offering juice, Anne was able to take another look at Luther without staring. He was dressed simply in a white shirt, faded blue jeans and trainers. He moved gracefully like an athlete, pulling back Estelle's chair before sitting beside her. The material stretched over his thigh muscles as he sat down. Anne reckoned he stood well over six feet tall, with broad muscular shoulders, skin the colour of caramel, hair shaved to a stubble. Throughout the meal Estelle remained almost silent, basking in an aura of self-confidence that for once had little need of words.

Marnie seemed anxious not to turn the meal into a kind of interview, and the conversation flowed easily round the table. They talked of Marnie's plans for Glebe Farm. Luther asked about Anne's career. He explained he was starting a Master's degree course at Leicester University in business studies in October and had a great deal of preparatory reading to get through. In his view, somewhere like Glebe Farm would be an ideal place to have peace and quiet for study.

"You didn't notice the cement mixer," Marnie said lightly. "One drawback of Glebe Farm is that it's a building site."

"How do you get away from the sounds when you need quiet, Marnie?" Estelle asked.

"I come down here and work on *Sally Ann* ... or sit out by the water in fine weather at this table under the parasol."

"And Ralph works on *Thyrsis*, doesn't he?" Estelle said.

Marnie saw which way the discussion was going.

"Yes. I'm sure it is possible to find peace and quiet here."

Estelle reached over and put her hand on Luther's. "Ideal," she said quietly. Suddenly changing the conversation, she added, "Did you say you had a meeting at the community centre in Northampton that was fire-bombed, Marnie?"

"Tomorrow morning, yes."

"Mrs Frightfully-Frightfully recommended Marnie to the management committee," said Anne.

Luther grinned. "Who?"

"Mrs Vane-Henderson," said Marnie, "one of our clients. We did a full scheme on her place, Hanford Hall. It's the big house in the next village."

"She's not black is she?" said Estelle.

"No. I think the committee is one of her *Good Works*, capital G, capital W."

"This was a racially motivated attack?" said Luther.

"That's the assumption. I don't think anyone's actually claimed responsibility."

"There's a lot of trouble up here at the moment with far right groups," said Anne. "Marnie saw them in Leicester last week. Oh sorry ... I didn't mean to sound negative."

"That's OK," said Luther. "These things come and go. It may seem odd, but I've never encountered racism personally in my life."

"Luther can take care of himself," said Estelle, resting her hand on a powerful shoulder.

"You look as if you could take care of most things," Marnie said to Luther.

For a second, Estelle's smile dropped before returning, broader than ever.

• • • • •

Marnie and Anne walked slowly through the trees towards the canal at the end of a productive day. Estelle had taken Luther to the station to catch a train back to London. Marnie could still picture him swinging his overnight bag onto the back seat of the Golf before waving as he climbed into the passenger seat, every movement fluent and easy. Estelle was trying – and failing – not to look like the cat that has wandered into the kitchen to find a whole salmon laid out on a platter.

Estelle had wandered over to have a quiet word with Marnie as Anne was setting off to the post-box at four.

"So," she said, perching on the corner of Marnie's desk. "What did you think of Luther?"

"He's very nice."

"And you don't mind him coming to stay with me?"

"I'm sure he'll fit in very well. He can stay as long as you're here working with us."

Estelle leapt from the desk, raised both hands in the air and spun round like a top.

"*Great!*"

For a second, it seemed to Marnie a curiously adolescent reaction, and she looked on bemused. Estelle stopped, grabbed Marnie by the arms, kissed her on the cheek and bounded out of the office.

When Anne returned from the post, Estelle was starting off up the field track on her way to the station with Luther, and Marnie told her of their conversation, omitting to mention the effect it had had on Estelle. By the end of their working day around seven o'clock, Estelle had not returned.

"You're quiet, Marnie," said Anne.

"Am I? It's been a busy day, and I've got a lot done ... considering."

"Are you glad you've got Estelle sorted out?"

"Sorted out?"

"You know ... with her boyfriend. *The hunk.*" She grinned.

"I suppose so. Yes, it is good to have that settled. I don't think he'll be a problem. He seems a very steady type ... sensible. I'm sure he'll ..." Her voice petered out.

"Be a calming influence?" Anne suggested.

Marnie smiled. "Something like that."

"But it's all change, isn't it?" said Anne. "I mean, is it like you imagined when you first decided to come here and make a new start?"

"Not exactly. I thought I was going to be working on my own, if you remember, Anne. Then a certain person inveigled her way in on the act …"

Anne linked arms with Marnie. "And you've never regretted it once! So change isn't necessarily a bad thing."

They were emerging from the spinney, turning from their usual path towards *Sally Ann* where supper awaited. Both were smiling, arm in arm.

"No," said Marnie. "Change isn't a bad thing. Of course it isn't."

As they passed *Thyrsis*, the dark grey shape of the new boat on the visitors' moorings came into view across the water. A bicycle could be seen attached to the roof, and the 'pigeon box' flaps were raised for ventilation. The hatch at the steerer's end had been pushed open.

Marnie's expression became more serious. "It's just … there seems to be a lot of it about right now."

• • • • •

There was a clear sky that night and, after taking her shower, Marnie pulled on a T-shirt and pants and went through the routine of shutting the windows and hatches on *Thyrsis*. Her last task was to lock the stern doors, and she looked out as usual down the canal. It was mirror-smooth in the moonlight. She recalled her conversation with Anne about change. She had no problem accepting new situations, new challenges. They could make life stimulating. But sometimes … She leaned out and gazed across the water at the visiting boat with its strange colour scheme.

Her thoughts were interrupted by a warbling from the sleeping cabin. She skipped back along the corridor and dived in to grab the phone from the shelf. As she expected, it was Ralph. He filled her in on the conference and seemed to be having an interesting time. For her part Marnie told him about Estelle and Luther.

"And you really are happy about the arrangement, Marnie? You don't feel you've been bounced into it?"

"Oh, I've certainly been bounced into it, but with any luck Luther will prove to be a stable influence. I was only worried about Estelle and possible rebound problems. Luther's fine."

"Good. That's settled, then. What about the unrest? Any more developments there?"

"I haven't heard of any more riots or fire bombings. Things must be getting dull round here."

"And the strange characters that Bartlett warned you about?"

"No. I don't think …" She fell silent.

"Hallo? Marnie?"

"Still here."

"I thought the line went dead. Is everything all right?"

"Strange characters, you said."

"And?"

Marnie thought for a moment. "It's probably nothing …"

"What is?"

"I'm probably way off beam, but … well, there's a boat come to moor opposite *Thyrsis*. It arrived yesterday, or at least it was there when we got up in the morning. It had come in the night."

"In what way is it strange?"

"It's painted all over in dark grey ... like a submarine, and all the detailing is black."

"Could be just primer or undercoat," Ralph suggested.

"It's not that kind of paint job. This is really well finished. It looks ... well, somehow *menacing*."

"What are the people like? Have you seen them?"

"Just one, a man, quite young. I think he's on the boat by himself. He wears black and grey as well."

"Along with half his generation," Ralph observed. "A lot of my students look like that."

"Sure. But that wasn't all. The timing seems ... I don't know ... somehow more than just fortuitous."

"Marnie, why would anyone want to keep an eye on you or Glebe Farm? It doesn't add up."

"Well ... if it's about racism ... we often have taxis coming down here with clients. The drivers are mainly Asian. And there was that young couple the other day. They were Indian. We could be the only people who have that kind of connection in the village. Maybe there's a link there?"

"No." Ralph sounded emphatic. "A lot of the local taxi drivers are Asian, I grant you, but that would hardly get you singled out for attention. I really don't see any cause for concern if that's all that's bothering you."

"What about ... swastikas? Should that bother me?" Marnie bit her lip. She had not meant to go on about this at such length.

"*Swastikas*? Where have you seen swastikas?"

"I haven't, not personally. But Anne thinks she saw one in the grey boat across the canal."

"She's been on board?"

"No. Through the porthole."

"*Thinks she saw one?* What does that mean?"

"Just that. She looked in and saw one in a picture on the wall."

"What was the picture?"

"She couldn't tell. It was too unclear."

"So on that basis, you think there are Nazis – or one at least – keeping you under surveillance from across the canal on the grounds that you're a regular customer of Asian cab drivers ... is that right?"

Marnie laughed. "Well ... since you put it like that ... Yes, of course, it's absurd."

"I think so." Ralph chuckled.

"I think it's time I went to sleep."

"Good idea. I don't think you have anything to worry about."

"No. You've reassured me, Ralph. Thanks."

"It's the conference dinner tomorrow evening; I'll ring you afterwards. Good night, darling. Sleep well."

After she disconnected, Marnie remembered that she had meant to tell Ralph about the project at the West Indian community centre. On balance, she was glad she had forgotten to mention it.

12

An acrid smell hung in the air, sour and gritty, leaving a bitter taste in the mouth. Marnie walked from room to room, treading carefully on the uneven floor where lino had burned and buckled. What furniture might have stood here, had all been cleared out. Knowing the kind of devastation to expect, she had arrived wearing jeans, a sweatshirt and walking shoes.

The room nearest to the entrance hall of the community centre had a large chunk of its external wall missing and had been boarded up, with scaffolding inserted like pit-props to keep the building stable. It had taken the full force of the blast when the gas tank exploded.

The rooms were dark where the window spaces had been filled in, and emergency lighting threw a harsh glare over the interior. Looking up, there were places where Marnie could see through charred gaps in the ceiling. Beside her, Serena McDowell walked in silence leaving Marnie free to take in the extent of the fire damage and assess what had to be done. She too was dressed for the occasion in jeans, cotton sweater and boots, but her version of practical clothing had something of the designer label about it. At times when Marnie glanced at Serena, she saw anger inscribed in her features. She also saw determination.

"This was quite a blast," said Marnie.

Serena nodded. "It was seen by people almost twenty miles away, apparently. Can you imagine that?"

"I can. I was one of them. We saw it in Knightly St John where I live."

"Did you really?" said Serena. "I heard the explosion from the other side of town. Do you know what the fire officer said to me? He said it was *lucky* we had the explosion when we did. Can you believe that?"

"What did he mean?"

"At that time of night there was no traffic to hold up the fire engines. The fire station's less than a mile from here. And the size of the explosion was so great it alerted people straight away. If that's *lucky*, then I suppose we were."

"Plus no one from the centre was hurt or killed," Marnie added. "It's not much consolation, but things could've been much worse."

Serena stepped out into the hall and looked up at the ceiling. All the surfaces were smeared with a greasy black coating. "Lucky," she muttered.

Marnie decided it was time to get on with the business. "What were these smaller rooms used for?"

"The general office ... manager's office ... two meeting rooms."

Serena pointed as she spoke. Marnie made notes and rough sketches on her pad.

"Ideally I'd like plans of the building if you've got them."

Serena walked over to the corner of the room.

"The filing cabinets were about here, where I'm standing."

"I see." Marnie walked to the doorway leading into the main hall and scanned the building. "Right. I'll come over with Anne and a tape measure. We'll do a rough survey and produce our own drawings."

"Will that add a lot to the costs?"

"Some," said Marnie. "We'll have to talk about the budget in detail. We usually work with architects on a percentage basis plus materials as part of the overall tender. I can see this might be different ..."

"I'm not expecting you to work for nothing, Marnie. Is it OK if I call you Marnie?"

"Sure. What I meant was, if the building's just going to be reinstated as it was, you might want me to work out some schemes and give you some comparative estimates. Our work would then be on a fixed-price basis depending on how much time we put in on the job."

Serena frowned. "OK. This is all very new to me. Dorothy Vane-Henderson said you were totally reliable, as well as being a great designer. I'm in your hands."

Marnie smiled. "Don't worry, we can keep to a budget. I'll work something out. And I'll make sure we stay within the agreed amounts. When you're a small outfit like us, you earn your good reputation by delivering within budget and on time."

"That's my main worry."

"You're insured, aren't you?"

"Yes. But it's the timing that's the biggest problem."

Marnie had spent much of her working life dealing with people who took ages to make up their minds, only to demand that the work be completed immediately. She had not marked Serena down as that type of person.

"What sort of timing did you have in mind?" Marnie asked.

"You know we're running a big activity programme for schoolkids this summer? It starts at the beginning of the holidays ... in just over two weeks. We were planning to run everything from here." Her voice matched her expression.

"Oh boy," said Marnie.

"How long to get all this restored?" Serena spread her arms wide.

"You won't be running anything here inside six months ... maybe more. And that's if everything runs smoothly. Who's your architect?"

"Dunno. We kind of hoped –"

"Forget it. You need an architect to supervise everything. There's a lot to co-ordinate in a job like this. It's harder than new building, believe me."

Serena clenched her fists and pursed her lips. "Got any bright ideas, Marnie?"

"Let's carry on with the grand tour."

They made their way up to the first floor, Marnie noting that the stairs were concrete and relatively unscathed. The upper areas were smaller than downstairs because the hall extended to the full height of the building. Apart from some holes in the floors, the main problem on the higher level was smoke damage. From a landing Marnie looked down into the hall.

"This was a school at one time?"

"Yes, for infants. It closed some years ago. The numbers went down ... they moved the kids to another school half a mile away."

Marnie walked silently down the stairs and turned to face Serena at the bottom.

"That might be a way out ... or at least a start. It's worth a try."

"I don't follow," said Serena.

"You bought this building from the council?"

"It's leased from the education authority. Ninety-nine years at a peppercorn rent. I've no idea what that means."

"They'll have plans in their files. That'll save time ... and money. Also, they'll know the private architects who handle school projects."

"Right. We should've thought of that." Serena shrugged. "Too many things on our minds."

"Think it over," said Marnie.

"I just did."

"What kept you?" She smiled.

"I was working out who's the best person to talk to the education people about plans and architects and that kind of thing ... someone who talks their language."

"You've got someone in mind already?"

Serena looked Marnie straight in the eyes without blinking.

· · · · ·

Anne received a call from Marnie at twelve. She would be staying in Northampton for the afternoon and wanted to check how things were going at base. They discussed the morning's phone messages and then hung up. Anne went out into the yard and called up to Estelle's study window to see if she wanted to be included in a sandwich lunch. The farmyard intercom, simple but effective. Opening the window, Estelle thanked her but declined; she rarely stopped in the middle of the day, at least not for food. She laughed and closed the window.

Anne always stopped for food in the middle of the day. Dolly sidled up alongside her, and they walked together through the trees to *Sally Ann*, where Anne succumbed to the cat's unspoken request and they both had a snack lunch. Anne took a sandwich of tuna and mayonnaise with salad onto the stern deck. The rest of the tuna was gradually disappearing from a saucer near the fridge in the galley.

It was warmer than Anne expected, and she put up the parasol. While she ate, Dolly came out on deck and curled up on the hatch at the edge of the shade. Anne kicked off her shoes and felt the deck warming her feet, unable to imagine anything better than her life in the whole world. And yet there was one false note and, try as she might to position herself to look the other way, Anne could not ignore the presence of the dark boat on the opposite bank. It seemed to hum an ominous tune from over the water.

When she had finished eating, she sat with a glass of sparkling water contemplating the strange boat. Had she really seen a swastika inside it? Or was it put there by her imagination? She had told herself it looked like a U-boat, so she imagined the rest. It was maddening to think that it was moored just a short way away with the answers to her questions hidden on board. As she looked at it, a simple plan came into her mind. Why not have another look? The bike was missing, so the owner was out. It would be easy to take a stroll on the towpath and peep in when no one was around.

Before she could change her mind, Anne was over the bridge and sauntering along the path towards the dark grey shape. For a *U-boat*, she found its lines rather pleasing. Close up, she made a sideways inspection of the portholes and was disappointed to see that the one she had used the previous day was now almost completely closed off by its curtain. Looking both ways up and down the towpath like a child being taught kerb drill, Anne slunk up to the boat and examined the porthole. She pressed her face against the glass and squinted. It took a few seconds for her eyes to grow accustomed to the dimness of the interior, and she was just starting to focus when a sudden sound made her jump. It was her worst fear.

Coming along the towpath on his bike, dressed entirely in black, in contrast with his blonde hair, was the owner of the boat. *Damn!* There was no way he could mistake what she was doing there. For an instant Anne tried to look as if she was preparing to tie her shoe lace – she was wearing slip-ons – or was using the glass as a mirror to adjust her hair. There was nothing for it but to own up and face the consequences. Given that she was convinced she was spying on a neo-Nazi, she had misgivings about what form those consequences might take. Images of fire-bombs and rioting skinheads raced through her mind.

The stranger reached the stern of his boat, stopped the bike and scowled at her. An odd expression, but she was definitely not welcome.

"I –" she began.

The far-right-neo-Nazi-fascist-thug heaved his bike onto the counter without another glance in Anne's direction, undid the padlock on the stern door and went down into the cabin, leaving Anne standing beside the boat, her mouth ajar. Without hesitation she turned and walked quickly back towards the bridge, breathing heavily with relief.

• • • • •

"I'm sure I've met you somewhere before, Marnie. Is that possible?"

They were sitting in a coffee-house in the town centre where they had gone for a sandwich.

"In the tourist information office," said Marnie. "You'd just gone in to deliver the leaflets about your summer playscheme. They were well produced … very attractive for children."

"You took one? You've got kids?"

"I took several. I don't have children myself, but I thought they might be of interest to the school in our village."

"Were they interested?"

"Yes. I think you might have some customers, provided they can organise transport."

"And provided we can organise a building. Nice of you to help us, Marnie. We're going to need all the help we can get this summer."

"Why this summer in particular? Are there special circumstances?"

"You bet!"

Serena lowered her voice, her eyes sweeping the interior of the coffee-house. Most of the clientele were middle-aged women in summer dresses and cardigans, out for a day's shopping in the county town. Not an obvious hotbed of intrigue. Unless they were clones of Miss Marple.

"You've seen the community centre, Marnie. You saw the explosion from miles away. You've stood in the ruins of what was left after the fire."

Serena had a graphic way of speaking that seemed out of place in downtown Northampton. Marnie felt like a bit player in a *film noir*.

"You think there's going to be more trouble … that it might affect the summer playscheme?"

The two ideas seemed incongruous. Fire bombs and a playscheme. Serena remained serious.

"I'm not kidding, Marnie. And I'm not exaggerating, either." Her voice was still low. "We hear things on the grapevine."

"What sort of things?"

"You know there was a race riot in Leicester the other day?"

"I was there."

For once Serena's unshakeable composure and confidence were shaken. Her eyes widened.

"You were there at the riot?" Her voice was suddenly louder.

Several heads craned in their direction before politely turning away. Marnie knew that every set of ears in the establishment would now be tuned to full volume and maximum range.

"I was on my way to a meeting," she said quietly. "I saw the thugs heading into the centre of the city."

"Did you see the news coverage on TV?"

"Yes."

"Then you know what we're up against."

"But I can't imagine those people would want to attack *children*."

"That's not the point." Serena leaned forward. "Marnie, you may be a trendy designer, but you have a lot to learn about life on the streets."

• • • • •

Anne found concentration difficult. She was longing for Marnie to return so she could talk about her close encounter. It kept playing back in her thoughts like a videotape on a loop. The sudden arrival, her confusion and sense of guilt, the fair hair against the black clothes, the look on his face. *Why was it strange, his expression?* she asked herself. He had every right to be hostile. *But was he hostile?*

The more she thought about it, the more she felt the need to clarify exactly what she had seen. Now she was wanting Marnie not to come back for a while, not until she was sure of the facts. She replayed the mental videotape. There he was coming towards her. He was frowning. Definitely. But when she looked closely she recalled that his eyes did not seem to be focused on her or even on the surface of the towpath. It was as if he was looking nowhere. And his appearance. The light-coloured hair and the fair skin. No wonder Marnie thought he looked like her. And yet … She zoomed in on his face. *What was it about him?*

His frown turned into a scowl. *Or was it a grimace?* Anne tried to interpret the scene in another way. *What if it was a grimace? Why should it be?* She had no illusions about her looks, but she knew she was not unpleasant. There was no reason to pull a face.

Another possibility crossed her mind. She froze the image and concentrated on his face, or more particularly on his skin. Pale, like her own. She knew pale, saw it whenever she looked in a mirror, but this was of a different order. She looked closely. This could have been sickly pale. *That would make sense.* The eyes as he approached were not on her, or on where he was going, but looking into some inner, hurting place, perhaps.

The grimace could have come from *pain*. The unwillingness to talk or even acknowledge her presence. The hasty disappearance on board ... without securing his bike. And the reason he was there at all. Wherever he went during the day – to work or college – he had returned early ... *perhaps he was unwell. Yes!*

Now Anne wanted Marnie back. She wanted her advice on what to do. Looking up at the clock, she realised she had been sitting for half an hour mulling things over. She knew she ought to be dealing with the invoices that had to go out that afternoon. She also knew she could definitely not settle now.

Fingering the mobile, outside looking up the field track, there was no sign of the Discovery. Anne hesitated to ring Marnie when she was in a meeting or distract her attention when she might be driving. She took a decision on the spot and hurried through the spinney, over the bridge and back along the towpath, telling herself all the way not to slow down or question her course of action. Her breathing was rapid by the time she reached the boat.

It was exactly as it looked when she had left it. The bike was resting against the tiller, the stern door open, curtains drawn. Anne took a breath and put one foot on the counter, canting her head in at the doorway.

"Hallo," she called softly. No reply, no sound of movement. "Hallo." Nothing.

She picked up the bike and was surprised how light it was. The handlebars were straight, the tyres knobbly. The frame was yellow decorated with black pawprints, and the name *Muddy Fox*, also in black. A mountain bike. She lifted it onto the roof and set it down carefully.

"Hallo." This time a little louder. Still no response.

Anne knew she should leave at that point, but curiosity gave her a nudge in the back. Frowning, she began to step down into the cabin, wriggling through the narrow inner door and down the steps. For a few seconds she stood still without breathing and listened. She was standing beside the bathroom. Its sliding door was half open, and a faint musky smell seeped out, a masculine aroma, not unpleasant.

With a sinking feeling in her stomach, she pulled open the next door and found herself in the sleeping cabin. It was in semi-darkness, and it took a few moments for her eyes to adjust. She gasped when she realised there was a shape on the bed. *Anne with an 'e' – what the devil are you doing here?!* The young man was lying on his front, sprawled diagonally, fully dressed and asleep. Now was the time to turn and leave. Anne had no doubts about that, but was surprised at herself, remaining motionless where she stood. She listened to him breathing, a slow panting like a wounded animal.

Anne had suffered occasional migraines and knew the signs. He was lucky he could sleep, but she knew what he would be going through, the troubled dreams, the waking pain, the searing thirst and the misery of loneliness with no one to help. Perhaps like some, he might even be temporarily blind.

Beyond the sleeping cabin, through the partly open door, somewhere in the darkened boat, there would be a galley. Using all her reserves of courage, Anne stepped forward into the next space. Here, it was as dim as the cabin she was leaving, with the curtains closed, and only porthole-sized windows. She strained to see clearly ahead. This was the galley that led on to the other open-plan areas. Searching in cupboards, she took out a glass, eased open the door of the fridge and found a bottle of mineral water. She filled the glass and returned the bottle to its place.

It was as she turned back to the sleeping compartment that memory collided with curiosity. Her eyes had become accustomed to the dimness, and she looked from the galley towards the front of the cabin. Ahead was a dining area with built-in seating and table, and beyond that seemed to be a workspace with desk and storage. She scanned the walls for the cupboard beside the porthole where she thought she had seen the swastika and found it there, almost beside where she was standing.

It was a shelving unit, black-lacquered side panels on steel supports. Two shelves held crockery in neat rows. On the third, the top shelf, three cameras were carefully displayed all at the same angle, equidistant from each other, like exhibits in a gallery. Anne moved forward for a closer look. They were compact, black bodies with steel protrusions and switches. On the lens covers she read the maker's name: *Leica*. She knew it as a famous company from Germany. They were shining and free of dust as if lovingly tended. Her eyes travelled to the side of the unit nearest to the porthole. There were three photographs attached to the end panel, one above the other, invisibly mounted. They were colour photographs but with a monochrome tint, three racing cars, all very old, all silver, each standing on black tarmac, as if posing for their portraits. It was the middle photo that attracted her attention. There, on the driver's headrest, defined in a red circle, was the infamous shape. She had not been deceived; it was a swastika.

Anne wondered if one of the cameras on the top shelf had taken the photographs of the racing cars. They were probably of much the same age, from the 1930s. The cabin now had a quite definite look about it. Yes, it was as purposeful to her eyes as the interior of a submarine. Black, grey, metallic. A *U-boat*. Everything very orderly. Time to go.

She tip-toed into the sleeping cabin, put the glass of water on the shelf over the bed, its occupant still unconscious, and left without making a sound.

• • • • •

"We've run playschemes for the past few years, each one getting more ambitious ... more activities, more outings. But this year, it's gonna be different ... a whole new ball game."

"You're going in for more sports?" said Marnie.

Serena spluttered and started laughing. "Not literally ball games!"

"Of course not." Marnie felt foolish. "I know that doesn't actually mean games with balls, I simply –"

Serena snorted and had to put a hand over her mouth to control the spasm of laughter that threatened to overwhelm her. It was a while before she could speak again.

"You're making it worse, Marnie."

"*Me?* You're the one talking balls."

This time they both erupted and decided they had to leave the coffee house and get out on the street. They walked along to their cars, shoulders touching, both grinning, feeling like schoolgirls. Another new friend perhaps, Marnie was thinking. When they reached the Discovery, Serena suddenly became more serious. She leaned against the front wing.

"That's the first time I've laughed in over a week."

"You've not had a lot to laugh about," said Marnie. "Tell me more about your playscheme."

"For a start, it's not a playscheme as such any more. When we began, the idea was just to run a sort of crèche for a few days during the summer holidays to give the little ones a chance to meet other kids and play together and help mums who were working or just needed a break."

"You have children?"

"Two. Charlie and Joseph. Charlie's the girl, she's five-and-a-half. Joey's four. I began the group with some other young mums, mostly Afro-Caribs, but not all. Now we have all races, though the West Indian group is still the biggest. We've got white kids, Chinese, Vietnamese, a few Turks, even Indians and Pakistanis. Now that says a lot about how well it's been going. We have high standards, and people recognise that."

"And the age range?"

"All ages … mainly primary school kids, some younger secondary. Say, seven to eleven or twelve. This year there'll be more than ever, and I reckon we'll have them up to thirteen or maybe fourteen."

Marnie shook her head. "I had no idea it was like that. I imagined organised games and a few outings."

"You saw the leaflet."

"Sure, but it didn't mention the scale of the operation. And how do you staff all this?"

"Ah … That's one of the worries. If it grows again like it has before, we'll be needing a bigger team. The council's offered to help with some youth workers, but if we haven't got proper premises …"

"I'll start ringing them as soon as I get back to the office." Marnie took out her car keys. "One thing you haven't told me, Serena. Why so big this year? What's so special?"

"Haven't you figured it out, Marnie?" She gestured with her hand. "Can we get in the car for a minute?"

Once they were seated, Serena continued.

"I told you we heard there was going to be trouble from the race thugs. Word has reached us that they're trying to whip up riots here, just like in Leicester. It's this latest outfit, New Force. They're all over this part of the country, spreading down here from cells – yes, that's what they call them – mainly in the big Midland cities."

"And you plan to get the kids out of the way in case New Force make trouble?"

"Partly. Also to stop the young ones causing any trouble themselves."

"Why should they?"

"Because we know they're going to be provoked. They'll be a target, the young black and Asian kids. And if they retaliate – which would be understandable – they'll be in the thick of any trouble. New Force will blame them for causing it and its consequences. I know it must sound far-fetched to you, Marnie, but –"

"No, no, it doesn't. I saw what happened in Leicester. The New Force people blamed the police for causing all the trouble. *Police brutality*, attacking a lawful, peaceful demonstration ... that's what they said."

"Huh! Well, that's what we're up against here."

"You think your playscheme can make that much difference? I don't mean to sound discouraging, but ... how many kids can you handle?"

"We're expecting hundreds."

"Every day, right through the summer holidays?"

"You got it."

Serena opened the car door and swung her legs out.

"Good luck, Serena. It's a huge task ... a lot to do."

"Thanks for your support, Marnie. I appreciate it."

"You're welcome. I'll give you all the help I can."

"I'll certainly need it ... keeping all those balls in the air."

Their laughter rang out, and both were smiling as they went their separate ways.

· · · · ·

Anne was on her way back from the post run when she was overtaken by Marnie near the end of the field track. She walked round to the garage barn, and they met as Marnie was climbing out of the Discovery. Anne began asking how the meetings had gone, especially the talk with Serena McDowell. Passing the Golf, Marnie asked if Anne had seen Estelle that day, and Anne told her of their brief exchange just before lunch. They reached the door to the office barn, and Anne had difficulty turning the key in the mortise lock.

"What's the matter?" said Marnie.

"Dunno. It doesn't want to turn."

"Shall I have a go?"

Anne stood aside, and Marnie took hold of the key.

"Jammed," she muttered and twisted it both ways. "Ah ..."

The lock clicked, Marnie turned the key again and twisted the doorknob. The door swung inwards.

"How did you do that, Marnie?"

"Easy. It was already unlocked."

Anne looked puzzled. "It can't have been. I always lock it when I leave the office unattended."

They stepped inside cautiously and closed the door behind them.

"Well, it was certainly unlocked. Maybe just this once you ..." Marnie stopped beside her desk. "What's this?"

Anne followed her and looked down at a large bunch of flowers on the blotter. Glancing across the room, she saw another bunch on her own desk, and when she went to examine it, she found a tin of luxury cat food beside it.

"The burglars round here haven't quite grasped the principle of breaking and entering, I think, Marnie."

Marnie walked over to Anne's desk.

"Cat burglars, obviously," she observed.

They grinned at each other, and Anne went to find vases under the sink.

"How mysterious."

"Oh, I don't think so, Anne. This really is elementary."

"I wondered if Ralph had come home earlier than planned."

"Not Ralph. I think you'll find Estelle is no longer living alone in her cottage. That's why she was late coming back last night. She drove down to Barnet to collect Luther's things."

Anne recalled her conversation. *I rarely stop in the middle of the day, at least not for food.* She could hear laughter in the voice. All became clear.

"I'll just go across and thank them for the flowers," said Marnie. "I'd better see if there's anything they're wanting by way of furniture. I might need to get them a bigger bed. That one's only four feet wide."

"I doubt they'll have noticed," Anne muttered.

• • • • •

For the first evening in their new home, Estelle and Luther went out to explore the fleshpots of Northampton. Marnie had been too busy handling phone calls and correspondence when she had returned to the office to be able to talk about Serena, and Anne had to wait until supper time to ask about their meeting.

Marnie outlined her discussion in the community centre and described the scene to Anne while they waited for garlic bread to finish baking in the oven. When they sat down to begin supper, Marnie asked Anne how her day had gone. As Anne began outlining her visit to the *U-boat*, Marnie's piece of bread stopped on its way to her mouth.

"You did *what*?"

Anne grinned. "You sounded just like Beth then."

"You really went *on the boat*, when the owner was *in his sleeping cabin* and you *had a good look round*? I can hardly believe it."

"To be honest, Marnie, nor could I. In fact, I don't know how I had the nerve to do it, but I was so curious, I had to see what it was like. It's quite stylish and –"

"Anne, I don't care if it was decorated like the *QE2* ... you should not have gone on that boat. Don't you remember what Inspector Bartlett said about suspicious characters in the area?"

"He was unconscious, Marnie. The worst he could've done was tell me to get out."

"And come looking for you later, when he was feeling well again."

"Ah ... yes, I suppose so. I guess it was a crazy thing to do."

Marnie reached across the table and touched her hand.

"You're not stupid, Anne," she said softly. "And I'd trust your judgment in practically any situation ... apart from those where you've almost got yourself killed, of course ..."

"Fair enough."

"Right. But I think you can see why that wasn't a good idea, can't you?"

"Because it could have led to trouble," said Anne.

"And?"

"What I saw means he probably is a Nazi ... or at least a sympathiser?"

"Got it in one."

"So what do we do about it? Should we contact Inspector Bartlett and tell him we might have one of his weirdoes camping out on our doorstep?"

Marnie shrugged. "I suppose we ought to ... though apart from one photograph and the fact that he likes black clothes ..."

They began eating in silence. Marnie was worried about alerting the police to a possible felon, and shopping a fellow boater to the authorities without any evidence of wrongdoing on his part. Anne's thoughts were tempered by her sympathy for someone probably suffering with a migraine, while she merrily trespassed on his boat uninvited, even if her motives were good. Partly good, she admitted to herself, as she recalled that it was curiosity that had led here on.

"What proof do we have that he's not perfectly straight?" said Marnie.

"His boat looks unusual, he rides a mountain bike and he has a picture of an old racing car on the wall. Not exactly criminal, is it?"

"No," said Marnie. "It isn't."

"And he's got a collection of cameras."

"*Cameras*? That's not criminal either ... unless they're stolen property."

"He's got them on display on a shelf."

"Oh? Are they special in some way?"

"It says *Leica* on the front. They look quite old."

"If they're genuine, they could be valuable," said Marnie. "Old Leicas are worth hundreds in reasonable condition."

"I think they're just his collection," said Anne.

"So ... all other considerations aside – about the right to personal privacy, and such – there's nothing whatever to link him with the far right people causing mayhem on the streets."

"Except he turns up when the police are warning about suspicious characters," Anne replied. "He's in a boat painted like no other boat we've ever seen, the interior looks like something out of *The Spy in Black*, we're surrounded by thugs causing race riots and bombing buildings, and he's got a swastika as a decoration on the wall."

Marnie frowned. "You think there's a link?"

"You think it's a coincidence?"

"Now *you're* sounding like *me*," said Marnie. "That's a bad sign. Ask Beth."

13

"Hallo." No response. Marnie raised the volume a touch. "Hallo, Anne. Are you receiving me, over?"

Across the office Anne's head jerked up. "What? Oh, sorry, Marnie ... I was thinking of something."

"You've done more thinking this morning than Einstein did in a week."

"It's these, er ... invoices ... I've got to sort them out and –"

Marnie waved papers. "I've got them here. I took them from your desk for checking half an hour ago. They're all done."

Anne sighed. She had been in a near trance since their day had begun and now, with the builders' breaktime rapidly approaching, she was still unfocused. Marnie knew the reason why.

At breakfast time they had been listening as usual to the BBC *Today* programme when a report was made on a series of incidents that had happened in the night. In several parts of the country, shops owned by Asians had had their windows broken, and some had been sprayed with graffiti. The newsdesk was making the connection that these were not coincidences or unrelated occurrences.

Anne had asked Marnie if they could look at the morning news programme on television to see the damage for themselves, and reluctantly she had agreed. Reluctantly because she did not want Anne to become more worried than she was already. They had finished breakfast at the double and gone back to Anne's room. They were in time to see the reports coming in from around the country. It made the lead story of the day. A map came up on the screen and, one by one, coloured dots were added to show where the attacks had taken place. From Burnley to Bristol, Preston to Portsmouth, Leeds to London, there were dozens of incidents.

The BBC's home affairs editor stood across the street from a corner shop in north London and gave his report, microphone in hand.

Neighbours heard the sound of glass being smashed at around two o'clock this morning and heard a motorcycle roar away. Looking out, they saw that the front window of the shop had been shattered. Nothing was taken. This was not a robbery but deliberate vandalism.

It appears to have been part of a pattern in all parts of the country. Earlier I spoke with Commander Austin Walters of the Metropolitan Police who confirmed that the authorities are treating this as a co-ordinated operation. In his view this was centrally planned, but probably carried out locally by regional groups. He would not comment on the suggestion that it had been led by the far right organisation, New Force, but other police chiefs have stated that it bears all the hallmarks of their style of concerted action.

They had waited for the regional news report to see if local shops had been targeted. Marnie was dreading the possibility that someone might have gone back to finish off the community centre in Northampton. But the sole victim that night had been a shop in a suburb of the town. The reporter suggested that a local agent had staged this attack in liaison with the group that had organised the rioting in Leicester, referring to this person as *Mr. X*. The only difference compared with the London incident had been that no one had heard any vehicle speeding away after the shattering of the window. The reporter speculated that the attacker had used a silent means of transport, possibly a bicycle, to vanish into the night, possibly escaping over rough terrain nearby.

It was at that point that they realised they had not looked to see if the stranger's boat was still moored across from *Thyrsis*. While Marnie got the office underway, Anne jogged back through the trees, returning minutes later to report that the *U-boat* was still in position, but the mountain bike had gone.

Anne decided she had to shake off her pre-occupations and went to fill the kettle. While she was putting the builders' mugs on a tray, Estelle walked in carrying a file of papers. Behind her, Luther put his head round the door, called a hurried greeting and left. Estelle put the file on Marnie's desk.

"Whenever you're ready, Marnie, I've done a design for the whole place. Voilà!"

Marnie sat back in her chair. "You don't waste time, do you?"

"Onward and upward." Estelle beamed. Then her gaze fell on Anne. "Hey, what's the matter?"

Anne looked flustered. "What do you mean?"

"I get the impression you're not a happy bunny."

"We're both feeling a bit disturbed by the reports on the news," said Marnie. "The attacks on the Asian shops ... coming so soon after the riots in Leicester and the fire bomb in Northampton ... well, you know ..."

"Sure. I understand. We saw the TV news. But life has to go on. Luther couldn't put off going to Leicester because there are some nasties there."

"*Nazis?*" said Anne.

"Nasty people." Estelle enunciated it slowly. "We can't just play into the hands of the bad guys. That way, they win. If people had stood up to the fascists, my grandparents' generation wouldn't have been exterminated."

"Would you like coffee?" Marnie tried to veer away from the holocaust for Anne's sake.

"If you've got time to let me go through my scheme," said Estelle, settling on the corner of the desk.

"You're on."

"Great. And before I forget, would you and Anne be free to come to our housewarming party this evening?"

• • • • •

They both knew they were going to do it as soon as they walked back through the spinney for lunch and saw that the mountain bike was still absent from the roof of the *U-boat*. Marnie and Anne exchanged glances on reaching *Sally Ann*'s docking area. Anne's raised eyebrow was met by an imperceptible nod.

Standing on the towpath, Marnie suggested that Anne keep watch while she inspected the porthole. Anne trotted back to take up station on the bridge, giving her a clear view for half a mile along the path in both directions. She signalled to Marnie with a thumbs-up worthy of a Battle of Britain Spitfire pilot.

Marnie advanced quickly towards the boat, aiming for the second porthole from the bows. Anne saw her staring at it, but knew from Marnie's expression that she could not see in. Marnie did a quick inspection of all the path-side portholes, shook her head and hurried back to the bridge.

"No luck?"

"No. He's pulled the curtain right over ... couldn't see a thing. Perhaps *Kapitän X* wants to guard his privacy."

"Is that what you think, Marnie? That he could be the *Mr X* they talked about on the news ... the one masterminding the action round here?"

"Slip of the tongue," said Marnie. "Come on, before he gets back and X marks the spot where he catches us spying on him."

When they reached the shelter of the spinney Marnie said, "I still don't think I can contact Bartlett about our mystery visitor. We really haven't got enough proof of anything. There might be a perfectly innocent explanation for the swastika. We might just look foolish."

"I know. I've been thinking about it as well."

"Non-stop, as I seem to recall."

"Well, yes. Anyway, I was thinking that when Richard – my brother – was younger, he used to make model aeroplanes, little plastic ones from kits of parts."

"Did he hang them from the ceiling?"

"No. Mum said they gathered dust. But dad put up some shelves, and he had them lined up in rows. He used to paint them and put labels on the plinths. I remember that some of them had swastikas on … and black-and-white crosses."

"But that didn't make your brother a Nazi sympathiser."

"Course not. He just wanted to collect the whole set, like his friends."

"I bet there's some reason like that," said Marnie reassuringly, putting an arm round Anne's thin shoulders.

"Yeah. You're probably right."

They made their way in silence back to *Sally Ann* for lunch. Anne was feeling marginally better about the U-boat and the mysterious young Kapitän X, seeing in her memory her brother's little plastic fighter-planes in tidy rows. Marnie was less contented, thinking that grown-ups don't have the same reasons for keeping possessions as children do, especially in the limited confines of a narrowboat.

• • • • •

Marnie changed for the housewarming into a summer dress, for it promised to be a warm evening. Grabbing a bottle of Aussie sparkling wine from the fridge on *Thyrsis*, she headed back to the office barn to meet Anne, who had driven to the nearest garden centre to buy Estelle and Luther a plant. Marnie pushed open the office door and called up the loft ladder.

"Anybody home?"

"I'll be right down."

Seconds later Anne climbed down the ladder wearing black trousers and a magenta silk top.

"Do you think this is OTT, Marnie? I don't seem to have many things suitable for evening wear."

"You look great. We'll have to have a shopping session, when we can find the time, to get you a few more bits and pieces."

"No way. You spoil me as it is."

They were outside and Marnie was locking the office door, when Anne said, "I meant to ask if you'd told Ralph about the project at the community centre, and about the U-boat and what did he think of it all."

"Only about the centre. I didn't think it a good idea to tell him you'd been trespassing on a strange man's boat while he was there … and in bed."

"Marnie, it sounds *awful* if you put it like that."

"How would you put it that made it sound better?" Marnie spoke in an even tone.

Anne bit her lip. "I'm amazed I did that, actually. I can't believe it when I look back."

"You're lucky Kapitän X didn't wake up." She saw Anne's expression. "Better not to think about it."

Armed with plant and wine, they turned to cross the farmyard when a sound reached them that made them stop in their tracks. Normally a bicycle would not be a cause of alarm, but hearing the sound of wheels rolling across the gravel behind the barn, they both shared the same thought.

"Uh-oh," Anne muttered softly. "I think we're about to be raided by the Gestapo."

They braced themselves for the arrival of Kapitän X and were greatly surprised, not to say relieved, when round the corner of the barn came Ronny Cope, expertly raising a leg over the saddle of his bike, which he brought to a stop beside them. He looked at them quizzically.

"Hi! What's up? You look like you've seen a ghost."

"That's a cliché," said Anne. "But you're forgiven because you're not who we thought you were."

"That's all very clear," said Ronny. "Are you two going out? You're all dressed up. I was hoping we might've gone for a walk."

"We're going to a party," said Marnie. "The social event of the year."

Ronny hitched himself back on the saddle. "Oh, well ... *on yer bike, Cope.* And don't tell me ... that's another cliché."

He began turning the bike when a voice called out from across the yard.

"Hey, Ronny, wanna come for supper?" Estelle was standing in the doorway of the cottage wearing a long skirt in Indian cotton and a low-cut top. "Are you free?"

He looked down at his jeans and trainers, the Nike sweatshirt.

"I'm not really dressed for the social event of the year."

"You look good to me."

He coloured slightly and stammered. "Well, er, yeah, I, er ... that's ..."

"I should stick to clichés," said Anne. "At least you manage to say something that way."

• • • • •

It was a small gathering. Estelle had invited Jill and Alex from next door in addition to Marnie and Anne. When Ronny again protested that he was gate-crashing, Luther assured him that seven was a lucky number. They had put the dining table and chairs out on the patio at the back of the cottage, and fairy lights had been strung round the edge of the paving, so that they were sitting surrounded by tiny lamps on all sides. Acoustic guitar music wafted out from inside the house. Ronny's unease was soon dissipated when Luther asked if he would like to help him bring out the food, which was an interesting mixture of Mediterranean and Near Eastern.

Estelle was a vivacious hostess and gave the impression of one who was at ease with herself and with life. She seemed to be completely at home in a place that she had known for only a few days and had slept in for only a couple of nights. Anne's plant gift was a patio rose, a pink variety in a rustic pot of terra-cotta, and it was received with effervescent praise and thanks, and kisses on both cheeks. Estelle placed it artistically on the corner of the patio and declared it perfect.

Marnie commended Anne for her choice of present while they were sampling a plate of mini-bagels topped with cream cheese and smoked salmon. They both noticed that Ronny was getting on well with Luther, who seemed to be telling a funny story, and Ronny almost spilled his Rioja when Luther reached his narrative's punch line. Estelle, meanwhile, was grilling Alex and Jill about life in Knightly St John. The conversation was flowing as freely as the wine.

"Is this how you imagined it would be one day?" Anne asked Marnie quietly. "Civilised people living happily, enjoying life in lovely surroundings? Is it how you wanted?"

"I suppose it is. Though I'd never thought about it in that sort of detail. I just wanted people to come and live here in harmony and make a good atmosphere."

"Live in harmony," Anne repeated. "Sounds great to me."

For a second Marnie had a mental flashback to an army of thugs on the move like trolls, and reading her momentary change of expression, Anne saw the U-boat, but this time decorated on the outside with the hooked cross motif from the photograph. They looked at each other, both aware in an instant of intimate telepathy of what the other was thinking. The atmosphere was only broken when Ronny came towards them carrying a bottle of wine to replenish their glasses.

"You seem at home," said Marnie. "I think you've found a friend."

Ronny grinned. "Luther's great. He knows a lot about sport. I think he comes from a really interesting family."

The others gathered round him, holding up their glasses for more wine. In the background, Luther had gone into the house to fetch further plates of food.

"I'll say he does," Estelle chimed in. "But he's very modest about them and about himself. You must have the knack of being a good listener, Ronny. Any woman will tell you it's the greatest quality a man can have ... well, almost the greatest."

They all laughed, including Ronny, though he wondered fleetingly whether the joke was on him. Luther returned carrying a tray holding bowls of hummus, taramosalata and tsatsiki, plus dishes of chopped vegetables for dipping. Everyone took seats round the table, and when Luther asked what was the cause of the laughter, Estelle explained that Ronny had been interested to hear about his family.

"Where do they come from?" said Alex.

"Wood Green, in my case," said Luther. "Though I was actually born in Goodge Street, off the Tottenham Court Road."

More laughter.

"And the rest of the family?"

"West Indies. Barbados."

"Do you play cricket?"

"That's what everybody asks."

"And do you?"

"Well, yes ... in a modest way."

"His dad was a test player," said Ronny. "Go on, Luther, tell us about him ... and the others. And about you."

"I thought this was meant to be a housewarming, not an interview," Luther protested half-heartedly and smiling.

"You can't stop now," said Estelle. "Just give the potted version of the family history. Then we can all admire you and leave you in peace."

"OK. My father played cricket in the 60s and 70s ... and, yes, he played for the West Indies ... moved to England to play for Middlesex. He's still there as a coach, though he's semi-retired now."

"What's his name?" Alex interrupted.

"Greville."

"Not *Greville Curtiss*? I've heard of him. Fast bowler. *Brilliant* player. Didn't he get some sort of record against ... India?"

"Yes ... though it was Pakistan."

"Wow!"

"Luther's a cricketer, too," said Estelle.

"Not in my father's class, though."

"You played for London schools," said Estelle. "At cricket *and* football."

Luther grinned. "You've got to do something to keep warm in England in the winter."

"He played for Tottenham Hotspur," Estelle explained with a note of pride.

"For *Spurs*?" said Ronny. "That's *amazing*."

"Only for the youth team. I had a trial for the senior side, but I wasn't serious enough to go the whole way. You might say I was the black sheep of the family."

Everyone laughed, and Marnie suspected it was a joke he had used before.

"Did the fact that all the others were so sporty put you off?" Anne asked.

"Oh, he can be pretty athletic when he wants to be," said Estelle.

More laughter.

"I mainly wanted to do academic things ... too keen on my studies. My father thinks I lacked the incentive of boys born and raised in the West Indies. Sport was a way up the ladder for him, and to some extent for my brothers and sister."

At that moment Marnie's mobile began ringing in her bag. She reached down and pulled it out, apologising as she stood up and moved into the house, pressing the green button.

"Marnie Walker."

"Marnie, sorry to disturb you in the evening. This is Dorothy Vane-Henderson. Are you watching the television news?"

"Hallo, Mrs Vane-Henderson. No, I'm not."

"Then switch it on now. I'll speak to you later." The line went dead.

There was alarm in her voice that made Marnie rush to the living room and turn on Estelle's TV without stopping to ask permission. The image that came up on the screen looked like a re-run of something she had seen before. Fire-fighters were swarming over a building, flames licking from window frames, ambulances and fire engines in the background. The picture changed as the reporter came on, a young woman speaking into a microphone.

All the signs point to a determined attack aimed at killing or at least injuring the members of the community centre who were in the building clearing up the remains of the debris left behind from the previous fire.

The previous fire! Marnie thought. Could it be?

At the time the bomb went off there were about a dozen people inside the building. Four have been taken to hospital suffering from cuts and burns, with two more being treated for smoke inhalation. Paramedical staff are treating others at the scene and have had to abandon any further attempts to enter the building because of its instability.

Marnie's phone rang again. Another voice, no less alarmed than the first.

"Are you watching the news, Marnie?" It was Serena.

"Yes. Is it the centre in Northampton?"

"Can you see an ambulance in the picture?"

"Yes."

"I'm in it."

"*In it?* Are you injured? Are you all right?"

"Got hit by flying woodwork. I'm OK, though. It's the ones who breathed in the smoke I'm worried about. They got trapped ... lucky to get out ... *damn'* lucky. Oh ... My turn to be patched up. Gotta go. I'll talk to you soon, Marnie. We've gotta nail these bastards." She was gone.

"What's going on?" Estelle was standing in the doorway.

Marnie apologised for her abrupt exit and filled Estelle in on what had happened. The news item had come to an end, and they switched off the television.

"That's where you went yesterday?" said Estelle.

Marnie nodded. "To plan redecoration."

"Won't be much to redecorate, I'd say."

"I'm sorry about having the mobile on, Estelle. I didn't even realise it was in my bag." She smiled ruefully. "A night off ..."

On cue, it warbled again. Estelle excused herself to return to the party, leaving Marnie to take the call. It was Dorothy Vane-Henderson.

"I've phoned the hospital to find out how they are ... the ones admitted with smoke inhalation."

"Any news?"

"Not yet. They're still being treated."

"And the hospital staff probably won't talk to anyone except relatives, I suppose," said Marnie.

"Oh, they'll speak to *me*. I tell them who I am and that these are my people."

"I see." Marnie had a flash of sola topees, ebony servants in white uniforms serving sundowners on the veranda, with a punkah wallah in attendance.

"I don't think we'll be able to do anything about the centre for quite a while now, Marnie. Serena told me you were going to contact the authority about finding an architect and try to get some alternative premises for the summer scheme. I think you can forget the architect for the time being."

"And the summer scheme?"

"I'll phone the Leader of the County Council and tell him we need support."

"You mean the summer scheme will still go ahead?" Marnie failed to keep the note of doubt out of her voice.

"Of course. Why shouldn't it?" Mrs Vane-Henderson did not try to keep the note of determination out of hers.

"Well ... there are thugs out there serious enough about harming the community to stop at nothing, and ..." Marnie's voice petered out. "You're thinking we need some Dunkirk spirit, aren't you, Mrs Vane-Henderson?"

"Of course. It's the only way. It's the British response to any form of hostility."

Marnie went back to the gathering, and all eyes turned towards her on the patio. She reassured everyone that the situation in Northampton was under control. With rapid presence of mind Ronny poured some wine and handed Marnie a glass. She raised it towards her new tenants.

"A toast. To Estelle and Luther. Welcome and every happiness."

"In this haven of tranquillity," Anne added in a stage whisper.

Everyone laughed and drank.

• • • • •

Marnie was sitting up in bed trying to read a design magazine when the mobile rang that night. She expected Ralph, but it was Serena.

"Where are you?"

"They let me come home. I've hardly got a scratch."

"What about the others, the ones taken to casualty?"

"Two have been kept in for observation. They've been on oxygen because of the smoke."

"Do the police know who did this?"

"They won't say anything in public – no evidence – but privately they think it's someone connected with New Force. It's the same type of bomb used on a hall in Coventry last month."

"What's happened to the building?"

"It's a shell. We can forget the redecoration, Marnie. It'll have to be pulled down."

"Who says so?"

"Just guessing."

"You ought to get an expert to look it over."

"That's why I'm ringing."

"You need a proper architect or structural engineer, Serena. I'm not trained in that sort of thing."

"Could you just take a look, though? Then you could talk to an architect on our behalf. You at least speak the right language."

Marnie thought for a few seconds. "I could have a look round ... take some Polaroids, I suppose ... maybe have a word with Philip. Perhaps Estelle could come with me. She's well advanced with her project. She's good on structural things."

"Could you come in the morning?"

"Will they allow us on site so soon after the fire?"

"I'm going."

"OK. I'll be there."

The mobile rang again after a few minutes. Marnie told Ralph about the housewarming party and asked how the conference was going. She had had enough of arson and terrorism for one night and decided not to tell Ralph about the second fire bomb. Minutes after disconnecting she fell into a troubled asleep.

14

Leaving Anne in charge of the office, Marnie set off with Estelle aiming to meet Serena at nine at the community centre. She had rushed to get ready and deliberately avoided listening to the news programmes on the radio. All she wanted was to be on the road and doing something, rather than just hearing what was happening in the outside world. Estelle had been only too ready to go with her to Northampton, and they piled into the Discovery like a plane crew scrambled for action and charged up the field track on their way to the town. It was a beautiful sunny morning.

The traffic was thinning as they drove through the streets, and Marnie pulled into a multi-storey car-park round the corner from the centre. The two women, carrying files and notepads, briskly walked the short distance down the road with the unmistakeable odour of burnt timber pervading the air. Turning into the side street, they were immediately stopped by police tape stretched right across the opening. A uniformed officer approached, eyeing the files and Marnie's camera bag and taking in their business-like appearance.

"Are you from the authority?"

Before Marnie could speak, a car pulled up behind them and Serena's face looked out as the driver's window slid down.

"This is a colleague from the centre management," Marnie said quickly.

"I'm the vice-chair," Serena called out. "Superintendent Harris arranged to meet us here this morning."

The constable looked at Serena for a few seconds and lifted the tape, indicating where to park. Marnie and Estelle followed, and quick introductions were made at the kerbside.

"This may not be easy," said Marnie. "The police are treating this as a crime scene ... obviously ... and they won't want us in the way."

Serena frowned. "But their boss, Harris, said it would be OK to come and have a quick look-see. I wasn't expecting all this."

All this was a cluster of police cars and vans, including an ominous unmarked navy blue van standing to one side.

"There's the Superintendent over there." Serena pointed towards one of the officers conferring with a man in fire brigade uniform near the entrance. "I think I ought to say hallo."

When Harris noticed their arrival he detached himself from the fire officer and came towards them.

"Mrs McDowell, we need to have a word ... in private, please."

He looked serious, even by police standards. Marnie's antennae were twitching.

"These are my colleagues," said Serena. "They need to be present."

"Very well. But this must remain confidential. Can you account for all the people who were here in the building last night? You gave us about a dozen names. Was that a complete list?"

"It was our clearing-up party for last night. So, yes."

"You're certain it contained the names of everybody present ... *everybody* in your group?"

"It wasn't easy to get that many to turn out. There weren't any extras.

Why are you asking me this?"

"You've found a body," Marnie said quietly.

Three pairs of eyes snapped in her direction.

"You are?" Harris was staring at her.

"This is Mrs Walker," said Serena. "She's in charge of the renovation of the building. Is she right?"

Harris breathed in. "Remains have been found in amongst the rubble," he said slowly. "We need to know if it was one of your work-party."

"I told you. All our people are accounted for. I've spoken with the families concerned on the telephone."

"You think you might've found the bomber?" Marnie asked.

"We can't rule anything out at the present time. Please remember this is highly confidential information, ladies. It must not be divulged to anyone at all. In fact to do so could result in serious legal consequences."

"It's not the sort of thing we'd be likely to chat about with our friends," said Estelle.

Marnie spoke again. "I take it we'll not be able to enter any part of the building today, Superintendent."

"I'm afraid not."

"Then I think we should leave. We're only getting in the way here."

"Thank you for your understanding, Mrs ... Did you say Mrs Walker?"

"Yes," said Serena.

Harris's eyes narrowed. "Mrs *Marnie* Walker, by any chance?"

"Yes," said Marnie. To the others she added, "Come on. Let's go."

Leaving the site, Serena said quietly, "Does Harris know you, Marnie?"

"Sort of."

• • • • •

Anne completed the builders' morning drinks round and slotted the tray into its place by the sink. The jar of instant was empty, and she debated with Dolly whether to forego her own mug that morning, but the cat's contented purring as she slurped her milk persuaded Anne that she wanted to do the same. Locking the door behind her, she went through the spinney to fetch the ground coffee and cafetière from *Sally Ann*. She could not resist glancing over at the *U-boat*, and told herself she really ought to stop thinking of it like that.

The dark grey boat still lay at its mooring, the mountain bike absent, all quiet. In the sunshine it looked less menacing, and Anne was crossing the bridge before she knew what she was doing, telling herself she would just check on the porthole curtains, perhaps one last time. It would only take a second or two.

To her surprise, all the curtains on the towpath side were open. She put her face close to the glass of the first one and stared in. With the opposite curtains all drawn it was not easy to see into the cabin, but she managed to make out the details of the built-in furniture, all of it located down the left side of the boat. It occurred to her that the builders had carefully adjusted the underfloor ballast to prevent it from listing heavily on that side. In the front section she could see a workplace, with a laptop computer and other equipment. Further back was the dining area, with fitted benches either side of a table, the upholstery seeming to be a kind of grey tweed material. At the next porthole was the infamous photograph, and it struck Anne as odd that the boat owner should display it on full view where any passer-by could see it. It was almost as if he wanted people to know he had a swastika, as if it was a badge ... or a signal.

Anne straightened and walked along from porthole to porthole, seeing the galley, the sleeping cabin, the bathroom. It was all so well planned, so unified. The latest and most modern boats on the waterways, with all their expertly-fitted joinery and facilities, did not have an ounce of style compared with this. The thought depressed her, and into her head came an old saying, *the devil has the best tunes.*

Reaching the stern, she suddenly noticed that the heavy black padlock was missing from the door. Pondering why this should be, she understood too late the implication. The voice came from behind her, and although it was quiet, it made her jump visibly.

"It was you."

• • • • •

Serena insisted on paying, and they found a table in the corner of the coffee house where they could enjoy a degree of privacy. At first they said nothing. There were so many thoughts spinning through their minds, they hardly knew where to begin. It was Serena who broke the silence.

"How did Harris know you, Marnie? It was like he suddenly recognised you, after not expecting to see you there."

"Marnie has helped the police with an inquiry in the past," said Estelle.

"*Helped?* In what way?"

"Good question," said Marnie. "They probably don't see it that way. I, er ... played a part in solving a kind of mystery last year. The trouble is ... for a while the police thought I was concealing evidence to protect someone. They had me down as a suspect, or at least an accomplice. Then I nearly became a murder victim myself. So I'm not exactly their favourite person. They have, shall we say, mixed emotions about me."

"Phew! I don't know how I missed it in the news. When was this exactly?"

"Mostly during the summer holiday period."

"Ah ... I was in the West Indies. My grandfather died, and I spent two months back home with the family. So ..."

"So I might be something of a liability if you're going to be dealing with the police. I'm *known to them,* as they say."

"But as a murder *victim*, more or less," Serena protested. "They can't hold that against you."

"You were quick on the uptake about the body being found, Marnie," Estelle said admiringly.

"It was the only explanation for all that activity. And I saw a mortuary van in amongst the police cars."

"I think you're going to need help from everyone you can get," Estelle said to Serena. "Especially after last night."

"What about you, Estelle? Can you help?"

"Sure. I'll do what I can, but I'm likely to be going to Italy very soon. That's why I'm up here working with Marnie."

"Well, like you said, after all that happened last night, we're going to have to gather our allies around us."

"It looks as if you might not have to," said Marnie. "If the bomber is the body in the ruins, I mean."

"I'm not talking about that. I mean all the other things."

Marnie looked blank. "What other things?"

Serena and Estelle stared at her.

"Don't you listen to the news on the radio?" said Serena.

"I was too rushed getting ready to come here. I haven't even eaten this morning."

With perfect timing, one of the coffee-house assistants moved among the tables.

"Bacon sandwich?" she called.

Marnie raised a hand and gratefully took delivery of breakfast. Her companions momentarily regretted their decision not to order food with their coffee.

"Tell me what the other things were," Marnie said as she began on the sandwich.

Serena answered. "It was another lot of attacks. More shops had their windows smashed. Asian restaurants, too. Some were sprayed with paint, things like *Go home Pakis, Wogs out!* No one's claimed responsibility, but everyone's thinking it must be this New Force outfit."

Estelle joined in. "The report I heard said they're targeting their victims so well, they must have local co-ordinators in every area. It's just like the Nazi party when they started up in the 30s."

"But they'll be dismissed as bigots and extremists," said Serena. "They won't fool the people in Britain."

"Germany was the country of Beethoven," said Estelle reasonably. "And Bach and Dürer and a whole load of others. Hitler preyed on their fears and used the Big Lie technique."

"Was anyone hurt in these attacks last night?" said Marnie.

"Nothing serious."

"And the police have no leads on who did the damage ... no arrests, no people they want to question?"

"They've not made any announcements to that effect. They don't seem to have any idea."

"Not a single clue," said Serena. "These people are really highly organised."

They drank their coffee, and Marnie finished her sandwich, each pondering the situation that faced them.

"I suppose ..." Estelle began. "Well, I was just thinking. If they were really like the Nazis, they'd start laying blame on sections of the community ... scapegoats."

"They've got no reason to blame us for anything," said Serena. "The centre's just a club. Nobody drinks too much; we're strict about that. Nobody does drugs. In the daytime older folk play bingo."

"My guess is they'll try to provoke the different communities into reacting to these attacks," said Marnie. "Cause rioting on the streets. After a while people will forget who started it all and just see the latest images of violence on their TV screens. There'll be black and Asian youngsters fighting the police."

"And the Big Lie will be used to lay the blame on them?" said Estelle.

"That's why we want to get all the youngsters away over the holidays," said Serena. "It's the one way to keep them out of trouble."

"I think you're right," said Marnie. "It's building up. Everything will come to a head in the summer."

"Why now?" Estelle asked. "Why should they want to cause all this trouble at this particular time?"

Marnie nodded. "That's what's been on my mind. I've been wondering ... could it be they've got a new leader ... someone driving everything along?"

Estelle shrugged. "Leaders are supposed to be charismatic. So why don't we know about him? Why isn't he up front leading?"

"Maybe he's not ready to make an appearance yet," Serena suggested.

"What's he waiting for?"

"We'll have to wait to find out," said Marnie. "But events are definitely building up. And there's another thing ... it's going to get more dangerous from now on."

"How can you be so sure?" Serena asked.

Marnie lowered her voice almost to a whisper. "The stakes are higher. If he really is as sinister as you think ... he's potentially got a martyr."

"How do you work that out?"

"The body in the community centre."

"But that's almost definitely the person who tried to burn the place down," Serena retorted.

"Who says so?"

"The police for one."

"Really? You think they can actually prove that?"

"They can prove if it was a white person," Estelle said, gradually seeing the point Marnie was making. "Even if it's burnt beyond recognition, forensic scientists can do that, but they can't prove anything else. Is that what you mean, Marnie?"

"Who's to say that person hadn't been abducted and died when the building caught fire again?"

"But that's ridiculous! It would be a downright lie!" Serena's eyes were blazing. "Everyone would see that."

"It would be a Big Lie," said Estelle.

• • • • •

It was a gloomy drive back to Glebe Farm. Even the fine weather failed to lift their spirits, and when Marnie rang the office just before setting off, Anne had sounded strangely distant and remote, as if Marnie had said something to offend her.

"What *is* going on?" Marnie muttered. "The whole country seems to be falling apart. What's the matter with people?"

"I think you were right when you wondered if this New Force thing was behind it all," said Estelle. "Luther and I were talking about it last night in bed after ..."

"Listening to the news?" Marnie suggested.

"Yes. Luther's never been worried very much about racism. He thinks prejudice of some sort is everywhere, but it's largely inactive and harmless. He's quite generous about it, in fact. I think he's inspired by Nelson Mandela ... twenty-seven years in prison and he comes out saying he forgives his captors."

"You don't have to be black to be inspired by Nelson Mandela," said Marnie. "Or Christian to be inspired by Desmond Tutu, come to that."

"True. Both charismatic leaders. And if you're right, Marnie, the New Force thing has a leader who's keeping in the shadows till the time's right for him to appear in public. I thought that was an interesting idea."

"It was only a guess. I'm no great shakes at politics. But something or someone seems to be pushing matters along. I saw it for myself on the streets of Leicester. That was an organised army. They had discipline, if you can call it that ... banners, armbands, almost a kind of uniform."

"A *uniform*? What was it like?"

"It was not so much a uniform ... more a style. They had black leather jackets, black or grey jeans and T-shirts, thick boots. They were like renegade bikers ... only without the bikes."

"I'll keep a lookout," said Estelle. "If we see anyone like that, maybe we should tell your police inspector, the one who came down that day I was visiting. What's his name?"

"Detective Chief Inspector Bartlett," Marnie said slowly.

• • • • •

The next surprise of the day came when Marnie grabbed the handle of the door to the office barn and found it locked. She peered in through the tinted plate-glass window and could see that the equipment was working; small lights were glowing on the machines. Catching sight of Bob, the site foreman, Marnie called out.

"Seen Anne anywhere?"

"Not since coffee time this morning, me dook. She came running back through the trees like she was late for something and went in the office. Haven't seen her since. Sorry."

He went back to the farmhouse and, just as Marnie was searching in her bag for a key, she saw movement in the barn, and Anne unlocked the door.

"I thought you sounded odd on the phone," said Marnie stepping inside, putting her bag down on the desk. "What's up? Aren't you feeling well? You look a bit pasty."

She touched Anne's cheek.

"I've done something *really* silly, Marnie."

As she spoke, Anne looked anxiously over Marnie's shoulder towards the door. Marnie placed both hands on Anne's shoulders and looked her in the eyes.

"I'm going to sit you down, make you some coffee and whatever the problem is, we're going to sort it out together."

As usual, Anne sat holding the mug in both hands. Looking at her friend, Marnie wanted to wrap her up and carry her off to a place where she would be safe from anything the world chose to throw at her. The trouble was, she had always thought of Glebe Farm as that place. Anne explained about her visit to the strange boat and being discovered there by the owner.

"What did you say to him?"

"Nothing. I ran like hell. I feel so *stupid*. And he knows I was on his boat ... he just stood there looking at me and he said, *It was you*. That's when I legged it. But he knows I was there trespassing when he was ill. Running off like that was admitting it."

She looked desperate.

"Anne, you didn't really explain to me why it is that you went back to the boat again."

"I felt somehow drawn to the boat. I wanted to check it out and look in again."

"And?"

"The curtains were all open on one side. It was as if he had done it on purpose ... set a trap. And he was there behind me ... waiting."

"I don't think he'd just lie in wait all day, Anne. That must've been a coincidence."

"It can't all be just coincidence, Marnie. Ever since he came here there's been all that race trouble and the fire-bombing, and here he is practically parked in our back garden, in his weird boat, looking like a U-boat *Kapitän*, covered with swastikas, dripping with black leather. That *can't* just be a coincidence, and we haven't done anything about it."

Anne was speaking breathlessly, and Marnie felt the weight of her words as a reproach to her own inactivity.

"You're right. Of course you are, and I should've spoken to Bartlett about him. He told me to watch out for any suspicious-looking characters."

Marnie was surprised by Anne's reaction. She spluttered and laughed.

"What's so funny?"

"That day ... when you first saw him, Marnie, you said you thought he looked like *me*!"

"There you are, then ... definitely dodgy. Seriously though, I'll speak to Bartlett and get him to check out the *Kapitän*. Would you mind if I told Ralph first? He'll be ringing as usual from Barcelona tonight."

"Good idea. I don't suppose the *Kapitän* will come and murder us in our beds."

"I've had another thought," said Marnie. "Did you notice if the boat had a proper licence and a registration number?"

Anne spoke without hesitation. "I didn't look, but I know he'll have one. Just seeing how he keeps the boat, I'm sure he's got all the documentation up-to-date." She smiled. "I expect he writes lists for everything, like me."

"I might've known," said Marnie. "Like I said ... definitely a dodgy character."

• • • • •

Marnie was at her desk talking over the Umbria project with Estelle when the phone rang. Anne was out on her post run, so Marnie took the call. It was a voice from the past. Valerie Paxton, the village school secretary, was phoning on behalf of Margaret Giles. Mrs Paxton had been prominent in the first few months of Marnie's time in Knightly St John as a champion of the then vicar, Randall Hughes. Suspicious of Marnie as a newcomer, Valerie Paxton had not been as welcoming as she might be, and there was a tension in her voice even now.

"Mrs Walker, I've been asked to give you a message from the head."

Marnie reflected that she was the only person in the village who addressed her as *Mrs Walker*, though she accepted it as a feature of school custom and practice.

"A message? Is she away?"

"She's had to go to a meeting at the education office and she's phoned to say it's running late and she'll not be back this afternoon."

"I see."

The silence that followed was so long that Marnie wondered if they had been cut off. She willed herself not to speak and was determined not to show her irritation. She failed on both counts.

"You said you had a message. Presumably you're going to tell me what it is?"

"It's about the ... summer scheme – playscheme – or whatever it's called." Her tone was dismissive. "Because of the trouble with the community centre in town, the parents aren't happy for their children to take part. They want to withdraw. Mrs Giles thinks they should discuss it and has called a meeting for tomorrow after school."

"And I'm invited?"

"Yes. The head wants you to explain what's going on."

"*Me*? Why me?"

"Mrs Giles says you're involved with them and know more about the details than she does. The parents don't feel these people can be relied on to guarantee the safety of their children."

"It's hardly the fault of *these people* if someone else is setting fire to their building." Marnie tried to sound reasonable.

"That's the point. The place seems to be out of control."

Marnie sighed. "What time is it being held?"

"Quarter to four."

"Thank you." Marnie looked at her diary. "I'll be there."

"Good bye."

Dial tone.

· · · · ·

It was going to be a quiet evening. Marnie and Anne had supper on *Sally Ann* and afterwards went up to Anne's room to watch a video, Anne propped up on the bed with pillows, Marnie nestling on the giant beanbag on the floor, leaning back against the bed.

Marnie laughed when Anne produced bags of popcorn, and they settled back to enjoy the film, with Dolly curled up on the duvet behind her head, punctuating the film soundtrack with intermittent bouts of purring.

After the first hour of the video, they had a break while Anne got up and made mugs of hot chocolate. She tried to tempt Dolly into bad habits by offering her a piece of popcorn, but the cat had too much sense, especially when it stuck fleetingly to her nose as she sniffed it amid more laughter. Marnie was glad to put their cares aside for one evening at least and enjoy simple pleasures with friends.

When they parted at the end of the evening, Marnie noticed that Estelle's car was absent and remembered that she and Luther had gone to Leicester to spend the evening with one of Luther's friends from the university. A film plus dinner, she recalled, hoping that they would have as pleasant an evening as her girls' night in.

• • • • •

"What time do you make it?" Estelle yawned as she steered the Golf into a roundabout.

Luther automatically pulled back his cuff to check, but in the darkness he could not see the watch face. He looked down at the instrument panel.

"Eleven forty-four precisely. You're tired."

"I knew it was a mistake to go back to their place for coffee."

"I wouldn't have minded if we'd gone home straight from the restaurant," said Luther. "If you'd only said …"

"I know." She reached across and ran a hand up and down his thigh. "But it was a good film and a good meal … and I didn't want to be a party-pooper. Mind you, I hadn't realised they lived north of the city. It'll be midnight before we get home."

"We can have a lie-in in the morning. No need to rush."

"Mm … That'll be nice." Estelle was almost purring at the thought. "Another advantage of not having to commute to work. Can we get to the motorway from here? It isn't showing up on the road signs."

"Not sure. I expect so. Why not just go into the city? There'll be hardly any traffic and we'll soon pick up directions to the M1."

"Good idea."

• • • • •

Marnie was missing Ralph, realising how she had become accustomed to having him around these days. It was one thing to devise a semi-detached way of life in which they accepted the inevitability of temporary absences, but it had its drawbacks. She really needed him to be there, able to talk through the strange situations confronting her and Anne. There was nothing for it but to make do with late-night conversations that lasted on that particular night – a night that was to be a turning point in so many lives – until the battery on Ralph's mobile ran out.

"Ralph, tell me something. Is the conference going OK? Anything earth-shattering you need to tell me about?"

"Nothing like that, but it's going fine. We had an interesting paper today on the imminent turn-down in the US economy. What's on your mind? Something wrong?"

"I don't want to ignore your news, but I want some advice."

"Go ahead. I'm listening."

Marnie told Ralph about the second fire-bomb attack on the community centre and about the arrival of the strange boat. She explained about Anne going on board yesterday while the owner was there and how he had surprised Anne today into taking flight. She mentioned the swastika emblem that Anne had seen on the car in the photograph.

"The boat's moored opposite *Thyrsis*, and he's still there?"

Marnie was sitting on the bed in the sleeping cabin; she reached over and moved the curtain aside with a finger.

"The boat's there, but it looks as if he's out. The bike isn't in its usual position on the roof."

"OK. And you think the situations are somehow linked … the race problems, the arson attacks and this man turning up?"

"That's how it seems to us, but we may be making a connection that doesn't hold up."

"Is his behaviour in any way suspicious?"

"You don't think the swastika might be a clue to something?" said Marnie.

"There are plenty of people who like those cars, Marnie. Classics from a Golden Age. There was even a British driver in the Mercedes team in those days, and I'm sure he wasn't a political appointment."

"Well, there is another thing … Anne thinks he was lying in wait for her this afternoon."

"Really? How would he know when she was going to be there? I would've expected her to keep away. Didn't you say it was a spur-of-the-moment decision on her part to go and take another look at the boat?"

"Yes. I told her it was probably just coincidental."

"I think you were right. Also, I don't think it was unreasonable to say something to Anne when he caught her snooping on him again. That's how he'll have seen it."

"But he scared the wits out of her."

"You said he only spoke quietly."

"Ye-e-s."

"I'm only giving you an objective opinion, Marnie. On the evidence you've quoted, there doesn't seem to be much cause for suspecting this chap of being some kind of fascist mastermind. Or is there more to it than that, something you haven't told me?"

"No. You're making me have second thoughts. I just wanted to do something to make Anne feel better. But the more I think about it … although …"

"What?"

"There is the boat itself … it does look strange … *menacing* … and it does have an odd name."

"Marnie, your signal's breaking up. I think my battery's fading. Do you want me to phone you when I get back to the hotel? They always eat so late in Spain. What's this odd name?"

"Don't worry about phoning later. I'll probably be asleep. The boat's called X O 2. What do you make of that?"

"X O what?"

"X O 2. Does that make any sense? Does it mean anything to you?"

For the second time that day she was listening to air. She put the mobile on its charger and had one last look out of the window. No bike. Restless, her mind filled with colliding images of flying glass, incendiary bombs and U-boats, she found it impossible to relax and for a long time sat up reading a design magazine. Eventually her eyelids began to droop shut, and she dropped the magazine onto the floor, turned out the light, pulled the duvet up over her shoulders and closed her eyes. It was ten minutes to midnight.

• • • • •

"If we go much further on this road, we'll be out of town heading south."

"Don't worry," said Luther. "It's not far now to our turn-off. I think I recognise this area."

He swivelled his head to read the name of the road. They were in a mixed neighbourhood with shops and restaurants on both sides. Most of the restaurants were from the Indian sub-continent, but that was true of much of Britain, and Luther was becoming less certain of exactly where they were. Nevertheless, he was convinced they were pointing in the right general direction. They were on a wide road, a one-way street with three lanes, travelling down the middle to pass parked cars, and no other traffic in sight.

"Traffic lights up ahead," said Estelle. "There'll probably be a sign. It might be where we turn."

"Could be."

"We'll have plenty of time to check. Marnie says the lights in Leicester are programmed to change to red when they spot a car approaching."

"There's the sign, and you were right. It's our turn. You want to pull over into the right-hand lane." Luther laughed. "And Marnie was right, too."

The lights changed to amber as they drew near. Estelle moved over and braked, bringing the car to a halt at the crossroads with the dual carriageway, ready to turn right. She glanced down at the clock at the very moment when it changed to eleven-fifty. She was strumming her fingers on the top of the steering wheel when suddenly, above the sound of the engine idling, the night erupted with an enormous crash. They both jumped in their seats.

"What the hell –" Luther began, twisting in his seat towards the source of the noise.

"*Christ!*" Estelle gripped the wheel so tightly that her knuckles turned white.

The sound came from the left and slightly behind them. The crashing exploded again. In the streetlights they could see a small group of figures on the pavement. They seemed to be dressed entirely in black, with balaclavas covering their heads, so they looked like macabre puppets. Each one was hurling stones or bricks at a building the size of a large house. Every window was smashed, and glass was showering down onto the pavement. In seconds the assault was over. One of the puppets ran forward gripping a container. He swung it with both hands, forwards and upwards, releasing it at the top of its arc. Liquid flew out through the air to hit the wall high up with a splash, a dark stain spattering a large area and running down the façade like blood from a deep wound.

Estelle and Luther were transfixed in their seats, mesmerised by the spectacle. It was unreal, like a film or a piece of theatre, and nothing in their past experience prepared them with a reaction. Everything was over so quickly that they barely had time to close their mouths before the puppets were leaping into a car parked a short distance behind the action. The car was already screeching away, the puppets slamming their doors, before Estelle and Luther realised it was roaring across the road directly at them.

They gasped as it veered away at the last instant, almost hitting the nose of their car, engine roaring, tyres smoking, blasting across the junction, where the lights were still red, and racing away into the distance. They breathed out audibly and slumped back in their seats.

"Dear God," said Estelle, panting for breath. "What on earth's going on? What do we do now?"

Luther shook himself. "Drive!"

"What? Shouldn't we report this or something? Dial 999?"

"*Drive!*" he yelled. "Just do it!"

Absurdly, Estelle looked up at the traffic lights. They changed to red and amber, and she signalled, put the car in gear and accelerated uncertainly across the junction, turning right. She drove on auto-pilot.

"Are we doing the right thing, Luther? I mean, we witnessed something dreadful happening. We ought to notify the authorities ..."

"Sure. But first we get away from the scene. You'd better put your foot down."

"Why?"

"What if they've thrown a bomb in there? We don't want to be their next victims."

"Oh God, yes!"

"*Damn!*" Luther hit his knee with his fist, making Estelle jump again. "I was so stunned, I didn't get the car's number."

"Never mind. We'll stop down the road and ring 999." Estelle looked in the rear-view mirror. "No bomb so far."

She was looking for a place to pull over when a flash of light in the mirror caught her attention. Momentarily she thought it was a bomb, but a second look told her that a car with a flashing blue light on the roof was overhauling them rapidly. They heard its siren wailing on the night air as it flashed past.

"Looks like someone rang them first," said Luther.

"Yeah. The people living near that house. I wonder why they attacked it."

"It wasn't a house, Estelle. It was a mosque. There was a sign on the wall. That was the target for the paint ... or whatever it was."

"What else could it have been?" she said.

"It looked like blood."

Estelle grimaced. "I'll pull up as soon as I find a side street. We'd better ring the police and report what we saw."

The road made a sweeping curve to the left and as it straightened out, they could see flashing lights ahead. They were the first car to reach the road block, and they generated a high level of excitement. Two policemen wearing flak jackets and carrying guns waved them to the side, pointing their weapons to emphasise their meaning. Others rushed towards them, and one officer shouted that they should get out of the car with their hands in the air. Nothing that they had ever seen in the cinema prepared them for the feeling of having real assault rifles loaded with live ammunition aimed at their chests, with very animated cops screaming orders at them.

15

Marnie felt *Thyrsis* rock as she was swivelling out from under the duvet early next morning. She had had a disturbed night, and it had been a long time before she dropped off. The movement of the boat meant that another craft was travelling past, and she split open the curtains with one finger to see if *X O 2* was leaving. But nothing was passing, and the only boat in sight was the motionless dark grey shape on the opposite bank. She was registering the fact that the bike was still absent from its roof when she heard knocking on the stern door. Grabbing her dressing gown, Marnie went along to investigate. Before she reached the stern she heard a familiar voice.

"Marnie, it's me." There was an urgency in the tone.

She quickened her pace and unlocked the door to let Anne down the steps into the passage. The girl was breathless and looked as if she had dragged on jeans and a sweatshirt in a rush before diving into sandals and running through the spinney.

"Hi, Anne. What's up?"

Anne gathered her breath, hand on chest. "It's on the radio ... there's been more trouble in the night ... someone was killed ... places smashed up ... it's terrible ..."

Marnie held Anne's arms. "Where was this? Try to tell me slowly ... one word at a time will do."

She led Anne through to the saloon and sat her down.

"Put the radio on," Anne gasped. "The news is full of it."

They sat and listened together as report after report came in from all parts of the country and as they listened, each story seemed to be a repeat of the one before. A pattern was emerging of attacks on buildings belonging to ethnic minorities. Mosques were a prime target; dozens of them had had their windows smashed. In some cases, fires had been started, in others, red paint had been thrown inside. Racist slogans had been sprayed on the walls.

Not only mosques had been singled out for attention. Bars frequented by Afro-Caribbeans had been set on fire, youth clubs vandalised, community centres torched, shop windows shattered. Dance halls and discos had been smashed in a series of assaults that bore the outward appearance of spontaneous frenzy. But this was a co-ordinated offensive, and the radio news presenters and commentators were of one mind. It required a high degree of synchronisation across the whole of England.

Accounts by local news reporters from north to south, east to west, repeated the same version of events.

... and the first explosion was heard just before midnight. Neighbours were awakened by a loud blast and saw flames shooting into the sky ...

It was as if the Blitz had started all over again, said Mrs Muriel Wallace, aged seventy-nine, who could remember war-time London. She had just gone to bed when the fire broke out nearby at about ten to twelve ...

An eye-witness who was walking home from a night out with friends saw a car racing away seconds before the windows of a mini-market owned by an Asian family were blown out by a bomb. He noted that the explosion came at exactly ten minutes to midnight ...

"Ten to midnight," Marnie muttered. "That was the time I put my light out."

The broadcast continued with a studio interview involving a Chief Constable and a junior government minister, each trying to sound as if they were taking decisive action to track down the perpetrators. But when the interviewer asked if they knew who was behind the attacks, neither could produce a name with any certainty. The interviewer pressed them on the possibility that the incidents had been organised by New Force, but both seemed reluctant to speculate. When the interview gave way to a discussion with the BBC's home affairs editor, it became clear that no one in authority had a clue about what was happening. No group had claimed responsibility. No word had come from New Force. There was no hint, leak or suggestion about who was planning the strategy or how it was being put into operation.

The report ended with a comment from a retired colonel living, inevitably, in Tunbridge Wells where, inevitably, there had been no disturbances.

I doubt if the British bloody army would be capable of co-ordinating a mass attack on that scale nowadays. It would take someone like Monty to get the thing off the ground. Makes you wonder who's running it. Who's the supremo?

That question was on everybody's lips, but the answer would be a long time in coming.

When the news moved on to other matters, Marnie switched off the radio. Anne was visibly shaken.

"Did you tell Ralph about our visitor and his boat?"

"Well, yes, but before we could get very far, we were cut off. Ralph's battery ran out."

"What did he think? Did he get a chance to say anything?"

Marnie hesitated, wanting to reflect Ralph's reassurance that the stranger was not necessarily part of New Force, but without giving the impression that he was dismissing Anne's overall worries as unfounded.

Anne looked crestfallen. "Did he think I was being stupid?"

"No! Of course not. Ralph knows you better than that."

"But?"

"Not really *but*. It's just that he thought we didn't have much evidence to go on ... hard facts that proved the stranger was connected with the trouble-makers. He was only trying to be objective about it all."

"Before I came to see you, there was some expert on the radio saying that this could only be a combined operation, and there was definitely a mastermind somewhere behind the scenes backed up by what he called 'local commanders'."

"And you think our *Kapitän* might be one of these *local commanders*?" said Marnie.

"Who knows? He's not there now, is he? Did you see when he went off?"

Marnie looked across the canal to where *X O 2* was moored. There was still no mountain bike attached to the roof.

"As far as I know ... he's been out all night."

• • • • •

Marnie was going through the pile of plans on her desk. It was soon after nine and Estelle had not shown up. They had arranged to talk about the Umbria job. She turned in her seat and looked at the upstairs windows of cottage number two. The curtains were drawn.

Without a word to Anne, Marnie stepped out into the courtyard and walked round the side of the barn. Estelle's car was standing in its usual parking space beside Ralph's Volvo. She wandered over to the farmhouse and went through to the rear where Bob and one of his mates were fitting new windows on the ground floor. Staying only long enough to learn that they had not seen Estelle or Luther that morning, Marnie returned to the office. She was opening the door when a voice hailed her.

"Hi Marnie!"

She turned to see Estelle at an upstairs window in her bathrobe.

"Hi. You OK?"

Estelle waggled her head in a so-so gesture. "I'll tell you all about it. Can we put our meeting back to ten o'clock?"

"Sure. Everything all right?"

"Apart from getting arrested at gunpoint last night, everything's fine."

• • • • •

The plans of the villa in Italy lay ignored on the desk. Marnie and Anne listened intently without comment while Estelle told her story. She described seeing the vandals smashing up the mosque and daubing it with paint the colour of blood before roaring away just ahead of them. That explained why the police had become so excited when they found a dark-coloured car caught by their road block only minutes after the attack had been reported. Her description of them being stood up against a wall while armed police trained guns on them at point blank range evoked mutterings of dismay and disbelief.

Marnie leaned across the desk, put a finger under Anne's chin and pushed her mouth shut with a snap.

"How long did they hold you?" said Marnie.

"About forty-five minutes."

"And they seriously thought you were far-right terrorists?" She could not keep the incredulity out of her voice.

"You'd think they took us for Himmler and Goering reincarnated, the fuss they were making! They wanted to know if we either of us had our passports with us."

"Your *passports*?" More incredulity.

"I said: are you kidding? Passports? We've been out for the evening in Leicester. I know they've got a large Asian population, but let's not exaggerate. God, I'm starting to sound like a Yiddisher Mamma!"

Marnie smiled. "I'm amazed you can joke about it. It must have been terrifying for you."

Estelle shrugged. "Well, it was and it wasn't. Sure, it wasn't fun having all those guns aimed at us, but we knew we were innocent, after all. We didn't think they'd really shoot us."

"So what did they do?"

"Searched my bag, found my driving licence and credit cards, searched

Luther's wallet and found the same, plus his university ID card and library ticket." She laughed. "They were really pissed off. There they were thinking they'd got Bonnie and Clyde the urban guerrillas, and they couldn't even breathalyse me … I hadn't touched a drop all evening."

"Even so …" said Marnie.

"Yes, even so, it took them three quarters of an hour before they saw the funny side of it all. By that time, the real vandals were probably safely tucked up in bed under their little Third Reich duvet covers."

"There's a funny side?"

"The whole thing is a joke, Marnie! I mean, look at us … one five foot two inch Jewish woman and one six foot two inch black West Indian. We're neither of us very convincing models of the white Aryan master race, are we? Some disguise!"

Even Anne could see the funny side.

• • • • •

They did their best for the remainder of the day to conduct business as usual. Anne applied herself to keeping the show on the road, providing the builders with refreshment, writing notes on Marnie's and Estelle's designs for later discussion. Marnie strained to focus on the projects in her programme and had a further meeting with Estelle on the Umbria scheme. For all of them it was a struggle.

Marnie left a message on Serena's answerphone, and shortly before noon, when Anne was collecting mugs from the site, Serena returned the call.

"I just got back from the centre."

"I'm not holding my breath for the redecoration job."

"You may be right there, Marnie, but it's not as bad as it looked. The place was just an empty shell, so there wasn't much to ignite, and the fire brigade came quickly, so it didn't burn for long. But that's not why I was going to call you anyway."

"The body?"

"The body. I was talking to this detective who said something to the effect that the scientific people had found that it was a white man, probably in his twenties."

"They can't have had the results back so soon, surely … Wait a minute … white man in his twenties?"

"Not an unreasonable assumption."

"No, I suppose not."

"Anyway, the detective said his boss had been pestering the pathologist for a quick result. I was with him when he got the call. It's funny. You had the same reaction as the detective."

"In what way?"

"He was surprised at the age. He thought it would be someone younger because he was fairly small and slight, probably a teenager. But there was something about the skull made them realise he was a bit older."

"Did he say anything else?"

Serena paused. "Don't think so. Oh, yes … he had fair hair. There were traces, that's all. What a grisly job some people have, Marnie."

"Yeah. Listen, I wanted to let you know there's a meeting here at the school this afternoon. With all this trouble in town, the parents are feeling agitated. The head thinks they're going to pull out of the summer scheme."

"That'd be a shame."

"What can I tell them? They need reassurance. Margaret wants me to speak to them."

"The bombing of the centre was a one-off, Marnie. There was no other trouble in Northampton."

"Some might say a fire bomb – a *second* fire bomb – plus a dead body was bad enough. And you did say trouble-makers could cause disruption during the holidays."

"Which is why we're getting the kids out of town. I'm organising more outings. It's the best way."

"Your budget can run to that?"

"I'm past worrying about budgets. We can deal with that later."

"OK. I'll see what I can do."

"Do you want me to come to the meeting?"

"Can you find the time?"

"What are grandmothers for, Marnie?"

• • • • •

At about the time of Marnie's conversation with Serena, Ralph's working group finished its morning session in Barcelona. The members spilled out of the air-conditioned conference centre into bright sunshine and Mediterranean heat. They had an hour to wait before lunch and decided to split up in search of a drink in the many bars scattered around the main harbour. Ralph walked along the promenade, chatting about monetary policy, in the company of a friend from Copenhagen, a Dane whose two passions in life were beer and running marathons.

They found a table under a parasol on a terrace overlooking the sea and hung their jackets on the backs of their chairs. A waiter came out to take their order.

"*Buenas tardes, señores.*"

"*Buenas tardes,*" Ralph returned the greeting, raising an eyebrow in the direction of his friend. "Do I need to ask, Henning?"

"Beer," said the Dane with a smile.

"*Cerveza,*" said the waiter. He raised two fingers. "*Dos?*"

Ralph nodded. "*Dos, por favor.*"

"*Dos cervezas.*" The waiter repeated the order and withdrew.

Henning returned to their conversation in excellent English, soon realising that Ralph's thoughts were elsewhere.

"Ralph? Have you had enough of monetary theory for one morning?"

"Of course not. I can never get enough of it, Henning."

But his eyes and thoughts were following the waiter as he vanished behind the bar.

• • • • •

Marnie's thoughts were troubled, and it had nothing to do with anxiety about the meeting planned for that afternoon. She knew that if she helped to persuade the parents to let their children take part in the summer playscheme and something terrible happened, she would never forgive herself. Equally importantly, she suspected the community in Knightly St John would never be able to forgive and forget. It would be the end of her dream, and she would have to leave Glebe Farm for ever. But she had made up her mind only to present the facts as she saw them. The parents would have to decide for themselves. She felt that her attitude was selfish, but she was not going to jeopardise everything for a few weeks of activities in the summer holidays.

No. Her thoughts were troubled because she could not tear them away from the idea that the charred body of the young man found in the burnt-out building might have been their neighbour from *X O 2*.

When they broke for a quick sandwich on *Sally Ann*, Marnie and Anne both looked immediately towards the visitor's boat. The mountain bike was still missing from its resting place on the roof.

"I know what you're thinking," Anne said, as they unlocked the stern doors on *Sally Ann*.

"You don't."

Anne was surprised at the firmness of the reply.

"I *don't*? I usually do."

Marnie smiled wryly. "True. But not this time."

"What don't I know? What haven't you told me?" Suspicion.

They walked through to the galley.

"You think I'm wondering whether the *Kapitän* is the local mastermind of this New Force outfit. Right?"

"Yes," Anne said quietly. "But we both think that. So what's different this time?"

Marnie poured a carton of soup into a pan and lit the gas burner. The distinctive smell of butane floated between them, joining the aroma of carrot and coriander. She knelt to light the oven and took the rolls that Anne passed her. Laying them on the rack, she closed the oven door and straightened up.

"I know when you're playing for time, Marnie. It usually means you're wondering whether you can tell me something without me getting worried about it. Right?"

"You're such a know-all, Anne." She smiled. "And you know I feel responsible for you."

"But you know I'll probably only worry more if you don't tell me what's bothering you. I'll imagine all sorts of horrible things."

"OK. Fair enough. While you were out of the office, Serena phoned."

"You told me that. You said she's coming to the meeting at the school."

"Yes. She also told me the police know from the post-mortem that the fire-bomber in the centre was a young man ... in his twenties ... with fair hair."

Anne's eyes strayed to the window. "Ah ... And you were thinking ..."

"He's been gone for a day or two," said Marnie. "He arrived when the trouble was starting. Now he's ... missing."

Anne looked thoughtful. "As in *missing in action*," she muttered. "So that could be the end of the line."

A cloud passed over Marnie's face.

"But you don't think so," said Anne.

"Er ..."

"Go on. Tell me."

Marnie shook her head. "I'm probably being unnecessarily pessimistic … In fact, the more I think about it –"

"Just say it," Anne interrupted.

"Well … if he is – *was* – the local co-ordinator, or whatever it is, then he may have had papers … plans … information. They'll be top secret. New Force would want to recover them."

Anne's eyes were the size of Frisbees.

"And they could come looking for them here," she murmured. "That could be fun."

• • • • •

There was a good turnout for the meeting, and the school hall was full. A few latecomers had to stand at the back. Margaret Giles invited Marnie to join her and the chairman of governors at the desk on the low platform stage, but Marnie preferred to take a seat in the front row where she was joined by Serena, Anne, Estelle and Luther, who had come to give moral support. The chairman of governors was none other than Dorothy Vane-Henderson, who seemed to be a professional committee-person and greeted Serena warmly. She opened proceedings with a few brisk well-chosen words and handed over to Mrs Giles to explain the situation.

As usual, Marnie was impressed by Margaret Giles. She briefly summed up the circumstances surrounding the event. In her view the summer playscheme was a good opportunity for the children of the village to benefit from a programme of events that would enhance the long summer holiday in a positive and enjoyable way. Marnie found her thoughts contrasting the planned programme of destruction organised by New Force, and the more she listened to the head outlining the advantages of the summer scheme, the more convinced she became that it was worth supporting.

Margaret invited Serena to describe the scheme in detail, and she was again impressed. Not only was Serena a good organiser, she was an accomplished speaker. Sensing that the audience did not want a rousing speech, she addressed them in a calm voice, drawing attention to the printed leaflet – she had brought a pile of extra copies – and describing the range of activities in just enough detail to get her points across. She concluded by mentioning the additional outings that were now being arranged. The parents, most of them being the mothers of the children, given the timing of the meeting, seemed to find her approach convincing and reassuring. Resisting the temptation to hog the limelight, Serena ended by saying she would be pleased to answer any questions.

There was the usual silence that follows any invitation to ask questions. Margaret Giles smiled encouragingly at the audience, and a tentative hand rose from the middle of the hall.

"Mrs Graham," Margaret called.

The young mother stood up. "We've all seen the accounts of the fires at the community centre in town. It seems that coloured people are being targeted." She hesitated. "I suppose what I'm saying is … could it be dangerous … will this summer scheme be seen as mainly a programme organised by – and for – the West Indian community?"

Serena began leaning forward as if to stand. For a moment she hesitated, noticing Luther in the front row for the first time. Their eyes locked, and Margaret Giles was on her feet in an instant.

"I think that's the question we've all been asking ourselves, Mrs Graham, and I'm glad you've raised it. The summer scheme does have the advantage that it will give our children the opportunity to mix with children from other backgrounds. A small village school can't normally provide that, and I believe it will be a valuable experience."

"But can the organisers guarantee our children's safety?" another voice called out.

There were murmurs of agreement. Margaret nodded, seeming untroubled by the question.

"I was coming to that point. The fact is that Mrs McDowell ..." She glanced sideways, "... and her management committee, of which our own chairman of governors is a leading member ..." Another glance, "... have arranged supervision by parents, youth workers and volunteers. There will be an excellent ratio of adults to children. I myself will be spending a few days assisting. I can also inform you that Mrs Walker ... Marnie ..." A nod to the front row, "... has made enquiries with the education office that have led to the offer of premises as a base for the scheme. We will have the use of Garfield primary school, close to the town centre, for the whole of the holiday period."

Another hand was raised, and a tall serious woman rose to her feet. She paused before speaking, and the assembly became quiet in anticipation.

"I'm sure we find all that very helpful, Mrs Giles." She looked at the audience around her. There was complete silence. "But I know I'm not the only *parent* wondering whether our *children* are being invited to take part in a kind of ... *social experiment* for the benefit of *townschildren* ..." There were mutterings of assent mixed with murmurs of protest. "... from some *sections* of the community."

Serena looked startled. The volume of sound began to rise rapidly in the hall. From the platform Margaret stepped in to restore order.

"I don't really think that's what we're being invited to do, Mrs Wilkinson." She had to raise her voice to be heard over the hubbub.

The speaker persisted. "We've never been involved in the schemes before, so why now? The simple question is ... should we be entrusting our *children's* safety to these *people* who are in the middle of a *dangerous conflict*? We all saw on TV what happened last night when all over the country ethnic groups were attacked and bombed." Her voice had become shrill as other voices rose on all sides.

Suddenly Estelle was on her feet pointing at the parent, and her voice could be heard above the din.

"Are you saying it was the ethnic communities' fault that they were attacked like the Jews were attacked by the Nazis?"

Mrs Wilkinson retorted. "Are you saying that we should push our own children into the front line, like human shields?"

All over the hall arguments were breaking out. Mrs Wilkinson was not alone in her doubts, but others were appalled by the implication of what she was saying. Marnie suddenly stood to face the audience. A hush began to settle. Estelle sank back onto her seat. Marnie looked at Margaret Giles, who nodded back.

"Ladies and gentlemen," Marnie began. The formality of her tone calmed the situation. She spoke slowly and clearly. "I think we run the risk of losing sight of what is being proposed here. The programme will be based in a school like any other summer scheme, but the children will be going off each day on outings and activities. They'll be away from the school. The scheme will be run by the *whole* community, not a particular section of it. And it will benefit all the children who take part. The charge is small, so anyone can join in. That's all it is. Let's keep things in perspective."

Marnie sat down. From her seat a few rows back, Mrs Wilkinson spoke up again.

"And it's being run by people who are in the front line as targets of aggression."

The tumult was rising again when a loud voice, a man's voice, came from the back of the hall.

"There is a very unfortunate undercurrent to this meeting."

Every head in the hall was turned towards the new speaker. Marnie recognised the voice, but without standing she could not locate him. Anne had also turned, and her expression of curiosity turned to surprise and dismay.

"This discussion is getting out of hand," the man continued. "The plain fact is that the situation is being blown up out of all proportion."

Marnie tried not to wince at the unfortunate turn of phrase. No one else seemed to notice it. The man continued.

"Mrs Walker is quite right. It's a summer holiday scheme. Let's not play into the hands of those individuals who are trying to destabilise our country. We fought wars against fascists. You defeat them by standing up to them." He prodded the air. "We're not pushing our children and grandchildren into a battle zone as human shields. They're just going out to play with other children."

"Aren't you making a rather big assumption?" said Mrs Wilkinson, half rising. "Can we trust these people to look after our children and have the same standards as ourselves?"

"With respect, Sylvia, I think *you* are making the big assumption. You assume that because the scheme is being run by West Indians, it will not be as good as if it was run by people like us." He paused. "Speaking as a West Indian myself – by birth – I can assure you that there is no merit in prejudice."

A frisson of surprise went round the hall. Everyone present paused for reflection before renewed murmurings broke out in every part of the gathering. Surprised expressions were the order of the day. Serena and Luther, who had never met before that day, stared at each other in bewilderment. Estelle laid a hand on Luther's arm. Members of the audience asked their neighbours if they had heard the intervention correctly. The centre of everyone's attention, the man who had spoken up from the back of the hall, was George Stubbs.

Margaret Giles took control, decisively seizing the moment.

"I think we've gone as far as we can today. I'd like to suggest that you all consider the points raised and let me have your enrolment forms by tomorrow morning. Thank you for attending the meeting. Special thanks to

Mrs McDowell and Mrs Vane-Henderson, and to all of you who spoke from the floor. Good afternoon."

As Marnie reached down to pick up her shoulder-bag from beside the chair, Anne grabbed her arm.

"Look at the door at the back," she whispered urgently.

They had to stand, as everyone was on their feet blocking the view. Marnie strained to see.

"What am I looking for?"

Anne rose on tiptoe, steadying herself with a hand on Marnie's shoulder. She looked exasperated and sighed audibly.

"What is it, Anne?"

"He was there ..." She spoke softly. "... the *Kapitän* ... at the back of the hall. He'd come to see what was happening ... like he was spying on us."

"Are you sure?"

"How could I be mistaken? He looked right at me."

Marnie was puzzled. "One mystery solved ... another one arises."

"What do you mean?"

"Well, at least we know he wasn't the body in the ruins. If the body was the fire-bomber, it wasn't our friend from across the cut."

"And the other mystery?"

"Who'd have thought that George Stubbs was a West Indian?"

Serena appeared at Marnie's side.

"You never told me you had a West Indian community in Knightly St John." She was smiling. "Do the pubs stay open in the afternoon around here?"

They left Margaret Giles talking with Dorothy Vane-Henderson on the platform and filed towards the door where George Stubbs could be seen in conversation with Angela Hemingway, the vicar. Marnie found her way blocked by the tall parent who had cast doubt on the playscheme.

"Mrs Walker ..."

"Marnie."

"Marnie, I'm Sylvia Wilkinson. There's something I want to ask you ... and I'm not the only one who needs an answer."

"I think we're going over to the *Two Roses*. Would you like to join us?"

"Thanks, but I can't. I have to get back to collect the children from my mother's. I wanted to ask if you really believe the children will be safe on this playscheme. You've seen the bombed building, you're involved with the community, so I reckon you must have a feel for how things really are."

"Sylvia, I don't have a crystal ball ... and I don't have children of my own. All I can say is I genuinely do not believe anyone would try to harm the children taking part. Skulduggery against a building during the night ... riots against the police ... that's one thing. Attacking children ... no. That I definitely do not believe will happen."

"Well," said Sylvia, "when you put it like that ..." She smiled at Marnie and extended it to Serena and the others before turning to leave.

Before she could move away, Marnie spoke again. "There's something I don't understand. You said I'd been to the building. How did you know that?"

"I saw the photograph in the newspaper. You were talking to a police officer. The report said you were redesigning the building, or something like that."

When they reached the door, George was still talking to Angela. Marnie asked if they wanted to join them for a drink, but Angela said she had to dash to another meeting. Her parting shot was that she would do whatever she could to help. George accepted and beamed at Marnie, pleased to be invited.

Spilling out onto the pavement through the school gate, they bumped into Ronny Cope passing on his bike. He stopped beside them.

"What's this?" he said to Anne.

"We've been to a parents' meeting about the summer playscheme."

"We're going over to the *Two Roses*," said Marnie. "Care to join us? My treat."

The group settled at a table by the window, and George insisted on buying the drinks. Luther went with him to the bar to help carry the glasses.

"What was that about him being a West Indian?" said Serena in a low voice. "Did you know that, Marnie?"

Ronny looked amazed and mouthed *West Indian, Mr Stubbs?* at Anne. She shrugged.

"Unbelievable," said Marnie. "His family have been in these parts since the Middle Ages, probably since the Dark Ages – sorry, no joke intended. How did you think the meeting went, Serena?"

"Not too bad, though I did think at one point – when that tall woman got up – that she was going to be awkward. I'm still not sure about her."

"I don't think she meant to sound as prejudiced as she came over," said Marnie. "She spoke to me at the end, and I think she's just worried about her kids' safety. It's only natural."

"Of course," said Serena. "My own kids' are too young right now, but in a few years' time ..."

"You really think there could be any danger?" said Estelle. "Could you really think of calling it off? I thought it was like a crusade for you."

"Like Marnie said ... it's a summer playscheme, not a matter of principle. If I thought any child could get hurt, I'd walk away tomorrow."

"But you won't," said Marnie. "You see this as one way of protecting the youngsters."

"Yeah. That's right."

George and Luther placed the drinks down on the table and passed them round.

"So you're a West Indian, George?" said Marnie, grinning. "That's a new one on me."

"My father was a young captain in the army and was doing a tour of duty in Jamaica when war broke out. My mother had joined him, stayed on because it was too dangerous to cross the Atlantic unless absolutely necessary, and I came along in the fullness of time."

"But presumably you have a British passport?" said Luther.

"That was quite a saga, I can tell you. I came back to Britain on my mother's passport, of course, at the end of the war, and stayed on it whenever we travelled abroad for holidays. It was quite a long time before I needed one for myself alone, and when I applied, I was told I wasn't entitled to a British passport as a right. *I* was a *Jamaican!*"

"Same as me, then," said Serena, laughing. "We're both Jamaicans!"

Luther roared with laughter. "And as I was born in London, I'm the only true-born Englishman of the three of us!"

"So technically you're still a Jamaican citizen?" Estelle said to George.

"No, but it was a close-run thing. In the end I was able to point out that my family were noted in Debrett's Landed Gentry going back to the 1600s, so I was able to reclaim my birthright. No offence to you two – and I love the land where I was born – but we are what we are, and I'm as English as roast beef and Yorkshire pudding."

They drank a toast to Jamaica and roast beef. As they lowered their glasses, George licked his lips and made an offer.

"Now look here ... if there's anything I can do to help with this summer scheme, let me know. I'm semi-retired these days, so my time's largely my own."

"That's very generous, Mr Stubbs," said Serena.

"George."

"Thank you, George. You make me feel ashamed that I was wavering about it at all."

"Nonsense." He twinkled his most charming smile. Marnie and Anne, who recognised it from past experience, tried not to wince. "Anyway, we Jamaicans must stick together!"

He raised his glass for another toast.

• • • • •

Arriving back at Glebe Farm on foot, Marnie headed for the office barn to round off the day's work, while Estelle and Luther returned to their cottage. Anne noticed that Bob the foreman's car was still on site, and she walked round to the rear of the farmhouse to find him locking the garden door.

"Still here, Bob? You're late. It's well past your bedtime."

"Yeah, well I had to hang on for this delivery." He nodded towards the door. "We had all the pipework and radiators due from Nuneaton ... didn't want them just left outside, so I waited for them to come. Everything's in the house now, safe and sound."

"Can I get you a cup of tea before you go?"

"No thanks, me dook. I'll just be off home."

"Good night, then. See you tomorrow."

She turned to go.

"Did he catch up with you, your boyfriend ... on his bike?"

"My ...? Oh, Ronny, yes." She laughed gently, taking his remark as a joke. "We all went to the pub for a drink after the meeting."

"Right. Nice bikes, those. My eldest's got one."

Anne had never really noticed Ronny's bike. It was just an ordinary tourer in dark green, as far as she recalled. She made a mental note to have a good look at it next time he came down. Bob wiped his hands on his jeans as they walked round the side of the house together.

"Course, there aren't many of them about now ... stopped making Muddy Fox, so I hear. Pity ... they're very good. And I always liked the yellow ones best."

Anne stopped abruptly. "What did you say?"

"They've stopped making –"

"About it being yellow."

"Yellow, that's right. With the name in black and those funny pawprints going up the frame. Always reminds me of Bugs Bunny, somehow."

"Bob, you asked if he'd found me."

The foreman was now looking confused. "And you said he had."

"He came here, then?"

"Getting on for an hour ago, yes. I saw him looking in at the window. I was upstairs in number three, so I called down and told him you'd gone out."

"Did he actually say he was looking for me ... by name?"

Bob thought about it. "Don't think so. I just assumed it was you he was after. He looks more your age, not like one of Marnie's clients. And they don't usually come by bike."

"You didn't think he might have been ... an intruder?"

"Not really. He looked relaxed enough, I'd say. Just like the other lad who comes down here sometimes. He wasn't shifty-looking or anything. Isn't he a friend of yours, Anne?"

"Not exactly ... more an acquaintance."

• • • • •

There was a lot to do in the office. They had lost a sizeable chunk of the afternoon by attending the meeting and going to the pub. Marnie had immersed herself in preparing a presentation for Willards and studying Estelle's revised Umbria design. It would soon be time for her visit to Italy, and Marnie had to resist a growing desire to take off with her for a few days' break.

Faced with Marnie's intense concentration, Anne did not feel she could interrupt to tell her about the conversation with Bob. It was not until they locked the office and turned their faces towards the spinney that Anne mentioned what Bob had said.

"He came looking for you?" said Marnie.

"Seems like it. Bob thought he was a friend of mine ... because he came on a bike." She rolled her eyes.

"I can understand that. When I saw him across the canal, I thought he looked quite young ... slight build ... fair hair."

"Bit worrying, isn't it?" said Anne. "It gave me quite a shock when I saw him lurking at the back of the school hall."

"*Lurking?* Is that how you'd describe it?"

"Don't you think it's odd ... to come after me like that?"

"It was a public meeting." Marnie stopped walking. "Hang on a minute. Let's think this through. Here we are blithely heading towards the boats, not giving a thought to what we might be walking into." She scanned the spinney in all directions. Anne peered through the trees, straining to catch any sound of movement. "What does it mean, that he came looking for you at the office and then followed you to the school meeting?"

"It means I'm shivering up and down my spine, for a start."

Marnie put an arm round Anne's shoulders. "But is there any cause for worrying? There might be a perfectly harmless explanation."

"You don't think being stalked is just a little bit sinister, Marnie?"

"Well, one thing's for sure. We can't stand here in the spinney all night. I suggest we act normally ... go back to the boat and prepare supper. Would you prefer to sleep in the saloon on *Thyrsis* tonight?"

"Why not? That should make it easier for him to wipe us both out in one go," Anne said cheerfully.

Marnie squeezed Anne's shoulder before releasing her grip. It was intended to reassure and comfort. But as they moved off she was thinking how easy it would be for someone with malign intent to smash one of the boat's windows ... someone who had knowledge of making fire bombs. She hoped the same idea had not occurred to Anne.

"What if he lobbed a Molotov cocktail into the cabin?" said Anne quietly. "We wouldn't stand a chance."

Marnie tried not to shudder. "There's no reason why anyone would want to do that." She hoped she sounded convincing.

"Not even our friendly local neo-Nazi-fascist-thug-mastermind who happens to have followed us to a meeting at which we publicly demonstrate our support for the West Indians and their summer scheme?"

Marnie touched Anne's arm as they reached the docking area, and they came to a halt. She put a finger to her lips for silence and gestured to Anne to stay where she was. Advancing towards *Thyrsis*, she was bent forward for concealment behind Ralph's boat, wishing that he was with them. Anne saw her straighten gradually to look over the top of the cabin. Marnie stood upright and beckoned Anne to come forward. Anne advanced like a commando approaching an enemy blockhouse.

"It's all right," said Marnie in her normal voice.

"No bike?" said Anne drawing nearer.

"No boat. He's gone."

• • • • •

They decided that the visitor was either playing out some devilish tactic of withdrawing to a distance to lull them into a false sense of security prior to launching a surprise attack, or he had simply gone on his way. It did not occur to them that there might be a third possibility. By the time they had finished supper, Anne decided that she felt braver and could return to her attic room for the night. Marnie opted for the modern facilities on *Thyrsis* and reflected on the day's events while she turned beneath the hot jets of the electric shower.

That night Ralph had left the post-conference dinner early to phone Marnie from his hotel without fear of being cut off. He had nothing of significance to report and immediately wanted to know what was happening at home. He had read in the papers about attacks and burnings and was in agony to know that Marnie and Anne were safe and well. Marnie tried to sound cheerful.

"Tell me the truth," he said. "I want to know what's going on. From what I read in the Mediterranean edition of the *Guardian*, last night was like a re-run of *Kristallnacht*."

"Of what?"

"It's an ironic name," said Ralph. "It literally means 'Night of Crystal', but that doesn't really convey anything in English."

"It sounds rather ... Romantic," said Marnie, trying to remember whether she had heard of it before.

"It was anything but Romantic. It was the night the Nazis smashed up nearly two hundred synagogues all over Germany and Austria ... November 1938. It was a co-ordinated operation on a huge scale. In Frankfurt alone they destroyed five synagogues each about the size of a cathedral."

"Struth! Last night was bad, but not in that league."

"Give them a chance, Marnie, that might just have been their apprenticeship. *Kristallnacht* had far-reaching consequences."

"Why was it called *Krist*—whatever ... Crystal Night?"

"Because of all the windows that were smashed. There was broken glass everywhere. Was there anything in our part of the country?"

"Estelle and Luther had a run-in with the police last night after witnessing an attack on a mosque in Leicester."

"*They* had a run-in? Why?"

"In the area at the same time, driving away from the scene."

"What happened?"

"Nothing in the end. The police let them go. I'll tell you about it when you're back. But there's worse news ... another fire-bomb attack on the centre in Northampton. They found a body in the ruins ... a white person, they think, probably the arsonist caught out by his own bomb. And guess which is the lucky interior design company briefed to do the restoration?"

"Are you *serious*?"

"Yep. Your next question, knowing you, will be: *Is that wise?* Which means: *Are you a complete barking lunatic?* To which I reply: *I just somehow got drawn into it.*" She paused for breath. "Are you still there, Ralph?"

"Yes. Just resting my vocal cords. I'm glad I'll be coming back at the weekend. Someone's got to keep an eye on you."

"The other good news," said Marnie, "is that I'm also getting involved in a summer playscheme mainly organised by the West Indian community."

"Wonderful! What's it called, *Phoenix?*"

Marnie laughed. "Actually, that's rather good. I'll suggest it to the organisers."

"Is that wise?"

"Perhaps not. But you do have a talent for names."

"Talking of which," he said, "I've been thinking about your mysterious visitor and the name of his boat. Is he still around, by the way?"

"He left this afternoon ... to my great relief. Anne was starting to think he might've been the one behind all the trouble being organised locally."

"Why? What's he been doing?"

"Oh ... all sorts of things, but if I described them, they'd just seem like nothing, like the other night when I told you about him."

"Do you think he's involved with New Force, Marnie ... seriously?"

"I dunno. I think maybe Anne's nerves are getting through to me. Still, no need to worry about him any more. He's gone now."

"That's what I expected you to say."

"That he's gone? Why?"

"The name of the boat." Ralph chuckled.

"*X O 2?*"

"Try saying the *two* in Spanish."

Marnie dredged up her holiday vocabulary, acquired for Mediterranean breaks and visits to her parents who had retired there.

"*Dos?* You mean it's called *X O Dos?*"

"It's possible, don't you think?"

"Where does that get us?" She sounded bewildered.

"Try Greek."

"Bloody hell, Ralph! You're supposed to be the intellectual round here. I'm just good at colours and fabrics."

"If you didn't do Greek at school, Marnie, presumably you've read the Bible."

Marnie was becoming very slightly irritated. It was not like Ralph to play academic games to make her feel inferior.

"The *Bible?* You know I'm an agnostic ... I can't do quotes from the ... Ah ... the Bible ... yes, I get it. At least I think I do. Is it Exodus?"

"It could be. I'm only guessing, but in Greek it's spelt Exo-*dos.*"

"And if you're right, Mister Smarty-pants, I still have to come back to my question. Where does that get us?"

"Perhaps your visitor's had a classical education and is just taking time off. Simple as that. *Exodos* in Greek means the way out. Possible? It doesn't mean he's *not* bound up with the far right, of course."

"Just that he's clever," said Marnie. "Which could make things worse."

"Mm ..." Ralph murmured. "That's a good point. This new organisation obviously isn't run by idiots."

"According to the reports here, there's a mastermind behind it all, running a whole network."

"Does the name Garth Brandon mean anything to you, Marnie?"

"No. Should it? Or is this another round of *University Challenge?*"

16

Next day, Anne was in charge. With Marnie and Estelle setting off early to visit a fabric wholesaler in Birmingham, she would be running the office, the site, the company. And she loved it. Beside her phone she had placed a notepad for messages, a pack of yellow post-it notes and her clip-board. She had checked the paper in the fax and photocopying machines and emptied the waste bins. The decks were cleared for action. Everything was in its proper place, including Dolly, who had taken up station under the desk-lamp.

Anne had walked round to the car with Marnie and Estelle. Happy to be leaving the company in safe hands, Marnie had left no particular instructions. When she climbed into the Discovery, the window slid down.

"We may look in on the community centre in Northampton on the way back if we've time. Serena's trying to contact an architect to get advice about the building. Otherwise I'll keep in touch on the mobile. Expect us back late afternoon."

"All will be fine, Marnie. Have a safe journey."

"Right. Dolly's in charge. See you!" Accelerating off with a wave, Marnie called back, "And make sure you have a proper break at lunchtime. OK?"

In the middle of the morning, Anne shut up shop and set off along the path through the trees to fetch a bottle of milk from *Sally Ann*. Halfway into the spinney, she suddenly had the feeling she was being watched. A flash of movement made her jump, but it was only the cat bounding past. Without slowing, Dolly took off from the ground and leapt up the trunk of a tree, coming to rest on a large bough several feet from its base. Anne wished she could do the same and stood rigidly still, listening and watching. But there was only birdsong and shafts of sunlight probing through the canopy of branches. Slowly she edged forward, step by step until she reached the canal bank.

Her anxiety dissipated when two boats came into view, passing at slow speed. The steerer on the first, an older man with a grey beard, lifted his free hand to greet her. Anne felt the smile pulling at her features as she relaxed and gave him a friendly wave. She hopped on board *Sally Ann*, glancing quickly across the water as the boats were going by. The opposite bank was deserted.

"Beautiful day!" she called out.

The man at the tiller grinned back and inclined his head. They were attractively painted boats, the crews were affable, the sun was shining. What could be better? What could go wrong?

• • • • •

"It's the next junction, I think. Did that last sign say how far it was?"

Estelle jumped. "Er … not sure. I haven't been paying attention to the signs. Have you got a road atlas?"

"Anne usually has it by her when we're travelling anywhere. If it isn't in the door pocket, try the back seat."

Estelle twisted round and began rummaging under the briefcases and plans behind them.

"Got it. Hang on."

They were overtaking a lorry in heavy traffic, moving fast on the motorway, and Marnie strained forward to read another sign.

"Damn! Missed it. Why is it that lorries always get in the way just as you approach a sign?"

Without looking up, Estelle said, "You don't want to go as far as Spaghetti Junction, do you?"

"Definitely not. But then who in their right mind does?"

Estelle laughed. "You know something, Marnie? You're spoilt. You're used to having Anne with you to take care of everything. I bet she has the whole car organised when you go on a trip … atlas, tube of Polo's, paper tissues, tin of fruit sweets … She has a great eye for detail."

After a pause Marnie said, "Yes. I suppose you're right. I lead a sheltered life."

"It's a two-way process, isn't it?" said Estelle, desperately searching for a road sign.

"How do you mean?"

"She looks after you … you try to protect her."

"*Protect* her?"

"Sure. Just now I saw this morning's *Guardian* in your bag on the back seat. There's no way we'll have time to look at it. You took it so she wouldn't read it and get worried, didn't you?"

"Yes." Marnie laughed. "But knowing Anne, she'll probably realise I did that ... and worry even more. She doesn't miss a thing, that girl."

"Nor must we. Our turn's coming up. It's about a mile."

Marnie flicked the indicator switch. "One mile to get into the inside lane. Let's hope the truckers are feeling charitable."

She looked hastily over her shoulder to check the flow of traffic. As she did so, she caught sight of the *Guardian* protruding from her bag. She knew that the main front page photograph showed a group of angry young Muslims standing in front of a mosque with all its windows smashed, daubed in blood-red paint with the word *Pigs*. They were waving their fists at the camera beneath a banner headline: *We'll cut off their heads!*

· · · · ·

Twelve-thirty. On Marnie's desk, Dolly stretched and yawned. Anne did the same. She stood and saluted the cat, who watched her with a steady gaze, blinking slowly.

"Permission to break for proper lunch as ordered by the Admiral, skipper?"

Another yawn. Anne took that as permission granted and switched on the answerphone. She promised herself a sandwich of tinned salmon with the surplus to go in Dolly's bowl on *Sally Ann*. The cat's radar picked up on the unspoken thought, and she followed Anne out, waiting while she locked the office door behind them. They set off together on the path through the trees.

It had been a productive morning with enquiries from two potential new clients. The building works were going smoothly, and Anne was up-to-date with her invoices. She was pulling the boat key from her pocket when a shadow loomed at the edge of her vision. Looking up, she frowned. The shadow was the dark grey boat moored against the towpath across from *Thyrsis*, this time facing in the opposite direction. U-boat *X O 2* had returned.

Anne stared. Why was it back? Where had it been? Why, of all the places on the Grand Union Canal, did the owner want to be at Glebe Farm? There were no facilities here, no water-point, no boatyard. So why here?

Anne wished Marnie was there to talk it over. She wished Marnie was there, full stop. Probably best to get the food from the fridge and take it back to the office. It was as she turned towards *Sally Ann* that Anne saw him. He was on the bridge about twenty metres away, looking down at her with an expression she could not read. From the angle at which he was standing, she realised he was probably straddling his bike. Without a word or a gesture, he hitched himself onto the saddle and pedalled on. Anne knew he would arrive beside her at any moment, but she was powerless to move.

The sound of the bike's knobbly tyres scrunching over the ground reached her before he came into sight. He arrived at an unhurried pace as if he was confident she would not have run away, and pulled up a few metres from *Sally Ann*.

"It was you," he said in a quiet voice. "Wasn't it?"

Anne nodded. She could not speak.

· · · · ·

Marnie left Estelle studying a range of fabrics while she took the call. She found a deserted corner of the warehouse where she could speak quietly. Noting the hushed voice, Serena asked if she was calling at an awkward time.

"No problem," said Marnie. "Are you phoning about the architect?"

"He can meet us any time after two o'clock. He sounded very helpful."

"OK. That should suit us. I'll ring you when we're leaving to fix a time."

"It'll be good to get this sorted out," said Serena.

"Before you go," Marnie began, "I'm thinking of doing a buffet supper this evening. Nothing formal, just a few people from the village. Would you and your husband be free to join us? It'll be nice to meet him."

"I'd love to, Marnie, but we've got something on already, I'm afraid. Let's do it another time."

When they disconnected, Marnie rang the office to tell Anne about her idea for the evening. The answerphone cut in, and she left a message asking her to contact the *few people* and invite them to supper.

"We're going to meet the architect in town, but we'll not be late back. Expect us around four. Can you put three or four bottles of white wine in the fridge and the same number of reds on the bench in the galley. Thanks. See you later. Oh … and you can invite Ronny to come too, if you'd like that."

• • • • •

Anne felt like diving into the canal. The young man who stood in front of her astride his bicycle regarded her with a steady gaze. He was wearing a black T-shirt under a black leather jacket, charcoal grey jeans, black trainers. There was a silence about him, not an awkward adolescent inability to articulate; she could see he was a few years older than she was. It was the calm of an observer, taking in details.

Eventually she spoke.

"How did you know it was me?"

"Who else could it have been?" His tone was without reproach.

"Anyone." She did not sound convincing, or convinced.

"I don't think so."

"So you've come to ask why I did it … to explain myself."

"No. That's … fairly obvious."

Anne's brow creased. "Why then? Why have you come?"

"That's pretty obvious, too."

"Is it?" Anne could think of a dozen reasons, most of them disturbing.

"What are you doing here?" he asked in the same quiet voice.

"I'm allowed to be here. I live here."

"No, I mean … what are doing right now … literally?"

"Having a break … a sandwich. It's my lunchtime. Is that what you meant?"

"You have time to talk?"

Anne remembered that she was facing the man they suspected of being part of a far right movement that was attempting, with some success, to disrupt the whole country. Its campaign of violence and wrecked buildings had cost lives. He disappeared at strategic moments … used Nazi images as decoration … lived on a strange boat.

"Look, I can understand if you're annoyed with me, and I'm sorry for overstepping the mark … trespassing … but I –"

"Could we talk while we eat together?"

"Well, I … I suppose … I don't even know your name."

"Smith," he said.

Anne looked doubtful. He held out his hand.

"Donovan Smith."

· · · · ·

Ralph had found it difficult to concentrate that morning on the talk given by one of the senior economists from the Bundesbank: the benefits to European trade of introducing the euro. Over breakfast he had read several articles in The *Guardian* newspaper – the Mediterranean edition published daily in Marseille – about the new extreme organisation that had whipped up controversy all over Britain in just a few weeks of concerted action. Blacks were becoming suspicious of whites, Muslims wary of skinheads, and Asian shopkeepers had begun boarding up their windows at night. Though no one had harmed them so far, the Jewish community was growing increasingly apprehensive. They had seen it all before.

Leaving the conference hall quickly at the end of the talk, he checked the time and pulled out his mobile. It would be around twelve-thirty in Britain. He hit the buttons for Glebe Farm and heard Anne's voice inviting him to leave a message after the tone. Marnie's mobile was engaged.

He told himself he never used to be like this.

· · · · ·

Anne could barely believe what she was doing. Donovan Smith – was that really a name? – was it really *his* name? – had invited her to look over his boat, and she had accepted. Ever practical, she had offered to make sandwiches for them both, and he had sat in the saloon as she mixed salmon with mayonnaise and sliced a red pepper, while pittas warmed in the oven. He offered chilled apple juice from his own stores on *X O 2*.

They walked across the bridge and along the towpath like students going home from college, Donovan wheeling the bicycle, Anne carrying the pittas wrapped in greaseproof paper and two yellow pears. Neither spoke. It was an uneasy silence for Anne. The bike was heaved onto roof brackets and they stepped down into the cabin. Anne followed as Donovan opened the curtains to the portholes. The light inside the boat was subdued, and he switched on two halogen desk lamps and downlighters built into the ceiling over the work and eating areas.

"Have a seat." He pointed at the unit with its table and benches and squatted beside the fridge.

"Would you mind if I looked around?"

"No."

With someone pottering in the galley and food on the table, the cabin seemed less sinister. Anne went forward to the study area and looked on the shelves. They were crammed with books, some of them old with strange lettering. Gothic print, faded covers. A whole row of these had the same author's name, Klaus Herrmann. She could not understand the titles, but recognised the word *Religion* in some of them. She opened one and found a catalogue number beneath a stamp in black ink. The stamp was an eagle with outstretched wings clutching a swastika in its talons. She quickly closed it and returned it to its place.

There were computer software manuals by the armful and textbooks on technical subjects like special effects and film editing. A handful of crime novels. Service manuals for the boat. A Bible in English. A Bible in German, spelt *Bibel*.

One whole shelf contained books in German, lined up in alphabetical order. She read the names on the spines: von Brauchitsch, von Brentano, Carracciola, Eichendorff, Lang, Novalis, Rosemeyer, Seaman – *Seaman?* – Stück, Uhland. They meant nothing to her. She gasped, hoping that Donovan did not notice, when she saw the last volume of all. It was entitled *Mein Kampf*, and the author was … Adolf Hitler.

Anne had a sudden desire not to be on that boat and was thinking up an excuse involving an urgent appointment that she had forgotten, when Donovan said, in his usual soft voice, "I'm afraid I only have plates made of melamine … and plastic glasses. Not of such good quality as you have on *Sally Ann*."

Hearing him say *Sally Ann* like that made the atmosphere more friendly. But Anne still had the feeling she had been captured by the enemy and was being entertained by a courteous and civilised officer … before being handed over to the Gestapo for interrogation.

Donovan excused himself and walked towards the stern. She heard the sliding door of the bathroom, the running of the tap and the *woomph* as the water heater cut in. While he washed his hands, she moved towards the other shelves near the galley. There were the three Leica cameras she had seen on her first visit, one all black, two black and steel, all old, all shining like new. And there were the racing car photos, only one with the swastika on the headrest. The other two were signed … autographed in faded ink. She could not read the names.

Donovan emerged into the corridor by the bathroom, drying his hands on a grey towel.

"I've put out a fresh towel for you, Anne."

When Anne returned from the bathroom, lunch was set out on the table, and Donovan poured apple juice. They began eating the stuffed pittas.

"These are very good."

Chewing, Anne replied with a nod, realising that she would normally have smiled back. Since the handshake with Donovan she had not smiled once. Picking up the glass, she could feel her heart beating and wondered if Donovan could hear it.

"You said …" She cleared her throat. "You said it was obvious … why I came on your boat that day … and obvious why you came over today."

"Yes. I would've thought so." He bit into his pitta.

"Why do you think I came on the boat?"

He looked at her while he chewed the sandwich. Anne wondered if he was going to reply, or whether he just liked playing games. She also wondered what he would do if she stood up and walked out.

"It's not just about why you came on board," he said eventually.

"What then?"

"You came in because you thought I was ill. It was an act of compassion. That's why you left the glass of water. I'm right."

"Yes. Were you ill?"

"I was exhausted. I'd been up all night."

"Why?"

"You might say I had no choice ... an obligation."

"You make it sound as if you were obeying orders."

A faint smile. "More a question of duty."

"I thought you had a migraine."

"I just needed to rest."

"Then you disappeared."

"Why was that, do you think?"

"Was that pretty obvious too?" said Anne. "Duty called again? More orders?"

"You're trying to turn me into a man of mystery." There was no accusation.

"You're making a fair job of that yourself. And you're the one who asked me to guess."

"True. The reason for my ... disappearance was very mundane. My water tank was running low. I travelled up to the water point at the boatyard."

"Oh ..."

"End of mystery." He drank.

"You also said it was obvious why you came over ... but I'm not sure about that."

"It is obvious. Very obvious. I came to see my guardian angel."

• • • • •

They pulled out of the town centre, and Marnie pointed the Discovery southbound towards the motorway. Estelle sat with her briefcase on her lap, map-reading unnecessary on the home run. She looked at the clock on the dashboard.

"We're bang on time. Do you always work like this, Marnie?"

"Like what?"

"All this ... precision. Everything running like clockwork ... efficient. It's awesome ... really impressive."

"That's an exaggeration. I've got a business to run. I try to run it properly."

"Huh! Don't sell yourself short, Marnie. Most people think they're doing well if they remember to phone in advance to apologise for being late. You and Anne are an unstoppable combination."

"You reckon."

"I do. It's your attention to detail. That's the secret of your success."

Detail, Marnie thought. *I've heard that somewhere before.* She kept her concentration on the traffic, and was overtaking a string of lorries when her mobile rang. Estelle offered to field the call. It was Serena.

"Marnie's driving just now. Can I pass on a message or get her to ring you back?"

"A message will do. Can you just say I could make it for this evening, if the invite is still open."

Estelle quoted her verbatim; Marnie said it was great.

"That's no problem," said Estelle, adding, "Will that be two of you coming … you and your husband?"

"It'll just be me this time. Rod's meeting's been cancelled, so he'll baby-sit for me instead of the other way round."

"That's a pity. We were hoping to see both of you."

"Too short notice for baby-sitters on a Friday. You'll have to manage just with me," Serena said brightly.

"Fine."

• • • • •

When Marnie reached the office there was little time to speak about anything other than urgent phone messages before they had to begin preparations for the evening. Marnie had decided they would eat in the courtyard now that it had paving and tubs of plants and flowers. Estelle and Luther came over to help set out tables and put up lights. Ronny arrived in time to join in and wheeled the barbecue round from one of the other barns. A merry banter sprang up between the group as they worked harmoniously under Anne's general supervision.

They draped one string of fairy lights across the front of the office barn. Another set hung along the façade of the farmhouse, while a third decorated the row of cottages. On the tables they placed lamps with small candles. All this took shape as Marnie moved purposefully about the kitchen in the barn.

When Anne switched the lights on for testing, everybody stopped what they were doing and stood staring around the courtyard. Even in the bright light of early evening, a festive atmosphere instantly descended on Glebe Farm.

"Marnie's amazing," said Luther, shaking his head. "Just look at this place. It's transformed."

Anne was standing beside him. "Yes. Everything she does turns to magic."

"Why tonight?" Estelle asked. "Why not wait until Ralph gets back?"

"That's the way Marnie is," said Anne. "She likes doing things on the spur of the moment … just gets an idea and goes for it."

Luther laughed. "I bet she could be a lot of fun!"

Estelle elbowed him in the ribs. He pretended to double up in pain. Ronny laughed.

"Sorry," said Luther. "But you know what I mean."

"All too clearly," said Estelle grinning.

Marnie emerged from the barn and took in the scene. "That looks good. Right … we need a volunteer to man the barbecue … or *person* the barbecue, if you prefer." No one reacted. "Great. Luther, your offer is accepted."

"In that case, I'm going to get out of these jeans," he said. "That OK with you, Marnie?"

With a half smile she turned to go back into the barn. "Sure. As long as you don't frighten the horses."

• • • • •

There was no risk that their music and chattering voices would disturb any neighbours. They had none. Jill and Alex Burton were there, joined by Margaret Giles and Robert her husband. Estelle introduced Luther, who waved from his position behind the barbecue, now wearing a singlet and cut-down faded denim shorts beneath his apron. George Stubbs and his wife Sheila had seemed to Anne surprising choices as guests, but Marnie wanted them to be included because of George's offer to help with the summer scheme.

Marnie emerged from the office barn in her apron, followed by Anne and Ronny who were bearing trays of salads and dips.

Last to arrive was Serena, looking like a star at a film festival, stunning in cream trousers and top, with bare midriff and gold slingbacks. She had put on make-up and gold ear-rings that gave emphasis to her bone structure. George Stubbs nearly fell backwards over his chair in his rush to stand up and offer her the empty seat beside him, hastily muttering to his wife that he and Serena were the Jamaican contingent. Approaching the table, she glanced at Luther, whose muscles were glowing in the light from the illuminations and the grill, and did a double-take.

"I hope you've got something on under that apron!" She sparkled a brilliant white smile. "Or perhaps I don't!"

Everyone laughed. Luther pretended to tease her by pulling it slightly to one side.

"What will you have to drink?" said Estelle, guiding her to the empty chair.

"Something non-alcoholic. I'm driving ... mustn't get carried away."

"Very wise."

"Are you all right there, Luther, or have you had enough?" Marnie called over.

Luther smiled suggestively.

"You're very frisky this evening," she said. "I only meant did you want to be relieved?"

Serena giggled over the top of her mineral water. "If she asks how long he can keep it up, I swear I'll pass out."

Marnie gave her an old-fashioned, guess-who's-out-without-her-husband look. "Right. I'll just go and inspect Luther's meat, and I think we can begin."

Serena almost choked trying not to squawk. Jill and Alex both tried to keep straight faces and sniggered. George leered but, remembering that his wife was sitting beside him, refocused on his drink. Anne and Ronny, eyes averted, laid out the bowls on the table.

Marnie smiled at everyone and invited them to make a start. "But before we dig in, there's something I just wanted to say. For the carnivores among us, this evening we're grilling Aberdeen Angus steaks, courtesy of George, and organic pork sausages, all from his own company. George and Sheila were of course invited as guests, but arrived laden with these goodies. So it's thanks to you, George, that the supermarket produce that I bought is now residing in the freezer."

The assembled company raised their glasses and cheered. "To George!"

Marnie took her seat and muttered to Anne that the veggie section of the grill was well clear of the rest. Anne mouthed *thank you*.

Clouds were gradually building up, though the evening remained warm, and the only effect of the cloud cover was to increase the impact of the lighting as twilight came down. The smell from the grilling wafted over the party, and everyone was more than ready to eat.

Luther turned all the meat on the barbecue and came to the table, depositing the apron on the ground by his chair. He found himself sitting opposite Serena who beamed at him and poured wine into his glass. In the moment of quiet when everyone turned their attention to their plate, Sheila Stubbs leaned forward and turned to speak to Serena.

"George tells me that you're from Jamaica, too. Which part of the island do you call home?"

"I call Northamptonshire home, Mrs Stubbs. It's the only home I've ever known, really."

"Do call me Sheila."

"Thank you. My grandfather comes from the Montego Bay area – in the north? – and my parents grew up in Kingston. We moved to Britain when I was a baby."

"So I lived there longer than you did," said George. "You still have family in the West Indies, don't you, Luther?"

"Some, mainly uncles and aunts, cousins. Though all my immediate family are over here."

"You were telling us about them the other day," said Ronny encouragingly. He turned to George. "Luther's father played cricket for the West Indies."

"Greville Curtiss," Alex chimed in.

"You're kidding!" said George, astonished. "*The* Greville Curtiss, the great fast bowler … record wickets in a test series? And you're his son?"

"I'd blush if I could," said Luther.

"The whole family's brilliant at sport," said Ronny.

"Perhaps Luther prefers grilling to being grilled," said Marnie.

"It's just …" Luther began. "I wouldn't want to hog the conversation and bore everyone."

"You could give the potted version," Estelle said, resting a slim, pale hand on a muscular, dark shoulder. "Then we'd all leave you in peace … for a while."

Even Marnie, who was not given to fantasising, found herself wondering what it would be like to have a lover such as Luther.

"Don't you have a brother who did something in the Olympics?" said George.

"That's Grover. He's a swimmer. Did the Olympics twice … finalist once. Commonwealth games, too."

"Who else?"

"OK. There's Wesley, the eldest … cricketer for Barbados, but full international at basketball. Then Cy … squash player, youth international. He does karate as a hobby … black belt. My sister Milly played tennis for Barbados. Now she's married, got two kids and she's a P.E. teacher. And then Grover, the Olympic swimmer. That's it."

"We mustn't forget *you*," said Serena.

That would be difficult, Marnie thought.

"He played cricket for Middlesex Colts," Ronny interjected. "And football for Spurs."

"Tottenham Hotspur ... really?" said George.

Luther began to rise, looking over towards the barbecue. The meat was spitting and the coals flaring. "Only for the youth team."

"Still, that's an impressive background," said George. "And a most distinguished family."

Marnie rose to her feet. "You finish your first course, Luther. I'll get the barbecue."

"I was talking too much, I'm afraid."

"I'll do it, Marnie." Ronny grabbed Luther's apron and bounded over to the grill where he began turning over the steaks and sausages. "I think these are ready."

As he spoke, a large flame spouted from the hot coals. Ronny jumped back amid good-natured laughter.

"Take care, Ronny," Estelle called out. "Barbecues can be quite hazardous. They usually separate the men from the boys."

More laughter, though Ronny briefly looked uncertain about which way the joke was running, either with him or on him. Splashes of hot fat had caught his forearms, and he rubbed them quickly before picking up a wooden platter to transfer the meat for bringing to the table. Anne decided she would go to help him and was putting her napkin on the table when she looked up and gasped. Marnie heard her and turned her head towards the barbecue.

In the half light, standing back from the barbecue and visible behind Ronny, his face glowing as the sparks flared up, was Donovan Smith, Kapitän X himself. Realising that he had walked into the midst of a social gathering, he turned and was gone before any of the others had been aware of his presence. Marnie and Anne exchanged glances and, when they looked back towards the grill, it was as if Donovan had never been there.

• • • • •

"Say that name again, Marnie." Ralph sounded intrigued. "Could you just repeat what you said."

Marnie had been explaining about Anne's latest encounter with the stranger and her visit to the odd-looking boat.

"Donovan. That's what he said his name was ... Donovan Smith. Do you think it sounds improbable?"

"What does he look like?"

"Tonight he looked a bit weird. Standing there by the barbecue, with the flames spouting, I had a kind of flashback to film I've seen of the big Nuremberg rally ... faces lit up by torchlight ..."

"But presumably he wasn't goose-stepping around the farmyard this evening."

"Not quite. He must've come round the corner, seen we had guests and left. He only stood there for a second or two."

"You were going to tell me what he looks like."

"Well ... not very tall for a man, perhaps about my height, say five seven, slightly built – same colouring as Anne, fair hair and skin – quite young ... early twenties."

"Good lord ..." Ralph sounded distant. "I wonder ..."

"You think you *know* him?" Marnie was startled.

"When you first told me about the stranger, I wasn't particularly worried that he might be a far-right activist. What bothered me was that he might be a stalker."

"Yes, I wondered about that. But if you'd seen the boat – and with everything else going on here just now – you can understand why I made a different connection."

"You might have been right first time, Marnie."

"*Do* you know him, Ralph?"

"I'll need to think about it, but I may be able to fit a piece into the jigsaw. I need some time. I'll have to dredge around in my memory."

"But how would you know him ... as a student?"

"It's not him that I know, not directly. It's possible that I knew his father. And through him, the boy's grandfather."

"A colleague of yours?"

"Oh, no. We were never colleagues. He was before my time. But if I'm right ... well, let's just say that your vision of the torchlight procession might not've been too far off target. That could well be your Nazi connection ..."

17

Saturday morning and all was quiet at Glebe Farm. Too quiet. When Anne failed to appear for breakfast, Marnie hurried through the spinney to the office barn to investigate. Halfway through, she hesitated. *What if she was late because Ronny had stayed over?* She stopped to think about it. Had she seen Ronny go home? Marnie had left as the final clearing-up was in progress, because Anne had told her to return to *Thyrsis* for Ralph's expected phone-call. Her last sight had been the two of them carrying a table to store in one of the barns. She did not want to breeze in to find Ronny scurrying down the loft ladder with his clothes hastily pulled on ... or worse. This was a dilemma. Would Anne have invited Ronny to stay the night? Were they involved in that way? Did she, Marnie, have a right to an opinion on that subject anyway?

Marnie and Anne had never talked about intimate matters of that sort, nor had Marnie ever felt the need to establish any kind of ground rules. Sure, Anne was in her care with the agreement of her parents, but she treated her like a friend rather than a daughter, and she had always trusted in Anne's judgment. Why not? But what about boyfriends and that side of life? Was Ronny a *boyfriend*? Did Anne regard him as one? Did they ...? Had they ...? Had Anne ever ...?

The solution presented itself in an instant of revelation. *On yer bike, Ronny ...* If Ronny was still there, presumably his bicycle would be parked in the garage barn where he always left it. *Elementary, my dear Walker*, she told herself and headed off to the barns.

There was no bike propped against the wall by the MG. If Ronny had stayed, he was not there now. Turning the key to open the office barn, Marnie had an uneasy feeling. Anne was never late getting up. Could something have happened? What if she was not there? She raced to the foot of the ladder and called up.

"Anne? Are you there?" There was a groan, like an injured animal. "Anne?"

A more prolonged groan. "I'm dead."

"You're ...?" Realisation was dawning.

"Nearly dead," came the muted reply from a face buried in a pillow. "No ... very dead ... stuffed."

"That's what I was wondering."

"Mm?"

"Nothing. Can I come up?"

"Only if you bring a pistol to shoot me ... put me out of my ... ugh ..."

Marnie climbed the ladder. Two feet protruded from the bottom of the duvet ... the back of a head visible on the pillow. Sympathetic as she was – she had been there herself, knew the pain and wretchedness – Marnie could not help smiling.

"Have you taken anything?" she said quietly.

Anne shook her head – *big* mistake – and groaned again. "Lost my cyanide pills."

Marnie descended the ladder, went to the kitchen area and was back in the loft a minute later with two Solpadeine tablets dissolving in a glass of water.

"Still alive?"

"Need a second opinion," Anne murmured.

"Here ... take this."

"Strychnine?"

"Strychnine."

"Good."

Anne lurched onto an elbow, squinted at the liquid and downed it in one.

"Well done. You drank it in one go."

"I had to ... to stop the noise from the bubbles."

"I'm going to leave you in peace for a while. OK? I think you ought to stay in bed this morning. Will you be all right while I go shopping?"

"Dig out my will when you get back."

"Your will?"

"I'm leaving everything to Battersea Dogs' Home."

"Anne, you haven't got anything worth leaving."

"That's OK. I don't like dogs."

•　•　•　•　•

Saturday morning and all was quiet at Glebe Farm, but not quiet enough for Anne. The steady droning of the cement-mixer sounded as if it was located in her left ear. *You'd think people would be more considerate*, she thought, *given that someone's dying here*. She raised her head experimentally two centimetres from the pillow and attempted a focusing shot on the alarm clock. It revealed two things. One, her eyes were working independently of each other. Two, elephants were no longer doing aerobics inside her head. Three things. It was nine-thirty. She lowered her head gently. The cement-mixer was still grinding away, but that was only to be expected. Or was it ...?

Anne tried to remember what day it was. An inspired guess made it

Saturday. Why were the builders on site? She eased her head slowly round to the left, in the direction of the window-slit that looked down on the farmhouse, and found that progress was less good than she had thought. It was as if a black shadow had fallen over her eyesight. At that moment the black shadow moved, and two yellow circles appeared in front of her face.

"Dolly ..." she breathed, while the cat blinked again and continued purring on the pillow beside her.

• • • • •

Marnie swung the Discovery into a parking slot at the supermarket, hoping she had done the right thing in leaving Anne to struggle through the hang-over with a morning of peace and quiet. If she could keep the tablets down, she had a good chance of feeling almost human again quite soon. Marnie's only regret was that she had not been able to report back on Ralph's knowledge of Donovan Smith's family ... and its sinister background.

Grabbing a trolley, she paused at the news-stand to read the headlines. It was a name on the front page of the *Telegraph* that caught her eye. Where had she heard it before? Garth Brandon. It was definitely familiar. She read the caption under a photograph.

BRANDON FOR BRITAIN – Garth Brandon, *Wunderkind* of the far right, gave a press conference in London yesterday to announce his candidature for the European Parliamentary by-election ... in Northampton.

In the photograph Marnie saw a man with hardly a hair on his cranium, dressed in a smart suit. He had an intelligent face, not unpleasant, and was smiling reticently with a knowing twinkle in his eye. Of course! It was Ralph who had mentioned it to her on the phone the other night. What could she recall about him? Nothing. Ralph had just asked if she knew the name. She picked up the paper and began reading the article, but there were only a few lines to the bottom of the page where she was invited to continue the story on page three.

She read enough on the front page to learn that Garth Brandon, sometime Conservative MP, had resigned from the party some years earlier in protest at Mrs Thatcher signing the Maastricht Treaty. *Wow!* Marnie thought. *That must be a first ... someone resigning because they thought Maggie was too left wing!* Mentally Marnie shook herself and read on. Brandon had abandoned a promising career and retired to an obscure post at one of the new universities. He had vanished from public life, but was now emerging from the shadows to be revealed as a leading member – some thought *the* leading member – of the Britain First Party. Some commentators were suggesting a link between the BFP and the organisation ...

How annoying! End of the page. Marnie was aware that she was blocking access to the rack of newspapers and took a step backwards, quickly pulling back the front page. At first she failed to locate the article on Brandon, but while hunting for it, realised that she knew what she was going to find. And she was right. The next words in the continuation piece were ... *New Force.*

Marnie dropped the paper into her trolley and moved on.

• • • • •

So far, so good. Anne had advanced three paces from the office barn without the sky falling on her head. Apart from a slight trembling in the hands, she felt surprisingly together. Standing still in the courtyard, she ran an operations check on her senses and began taking deep breaths. All departments were functioning, she estimated, at around seventy per cent. Appetite was on hold. Thirst on overtime.

She set off slowly. The whole place felt deserted. Glancing at the garage barn, she saw that Estelle's car was missing, and so was the Burtons'. There was only Dolly, keeping a discreet distance, for company. *Fine by me*, Anne thought.

A glass of sparkling water on *Sally Ann* made her burp, and for an awful few seconds disaster loomed, but her luck held. Fearing the ignominy of sea-sickness on a narrowboat, she decided on a breakfast of fresh air. Out on the stern deck, she saw that the Muddy Fox was absent from the roof of *X O 2*, so that was one less complication to bother her.

Breathing in slowly and deeply, Anne stepped ashore and began walking, one foot after the other, towards the bridge. She crossed the canal and turned north, away from the U-boat, making sure that there were no bikes visible along the towpath and no one lurking in the hedgerow. As she walked, the impossible happened. Her head cleared; the unpleasant taste in her mouth evaporated; her eyes began pointing in the same direction; the tremble in her hand abated. Life was worth living again. This called for a list to celebrate. At the top, the first item was a reminder never to drink more than two glasses of wine. Ever. The next two items were the same.

Anne turned for home, amazed to feel a hunger pang. Approaching the bridge, she scanned the path, the moorings and the surrounding fields. All clear. She strode forward, as happy as ever with her lot. She turned onto the bridge to find Donovan Smith lying in wait.

To be fair, he was in fact sitting down. And he seemed to be fixing the chain on his bike, but that did not prevent Anne from feeling ambushed. A momentary dizziness overcame her, and she reached for the parapet. The young man looked up and quickly sprang to his feet.

"Are you all right? You look rather pale."

He reached forward and lightly held her arm.

"No, I'm fine ... I'm fine. You just ... sort of ... surprised me."

"You've got purple marks under your eyes and you're face is the colour of starched linen."

"Thanks. You've made me feel better already."

"I can do better than that," he said.

"That wouldn't be difficult. Trust me."

"How would toast, honey and orange juice grab you?"

• • • • •

On the way out of the supermarket, Marnie stopped to look at the other newspapers on the stand. The *Times* and the *Independent* both ran the Garth Brandon story on the front page. The tabloids were playing safe, with exclusives on breast implants among the stars of various soap operas, a pop singer going into rehab to cure his addiction to amphetamines and a famous football player's confession to a 'sex romp' with a 'television personality'.

She decided to take the broadsheets and queued at the kiosk to buy them, noticing that she was in the minority.

• • • • •

Anne had to admit the toast smelled good. She was back on the U-boat, watching Donovan in the galley from the comfort of the eating unit. He had washed his hands thoroughly before starting on the food, and she had a sneaking suspicion he might be an inveterate list-writer. He bent down to open the fridge and brought out a carton of juice.

"You came to Glebe Farm last night," said Anne. "I was wondering why. And don't tell me it's obvious. I'd just like a straight answer."

Donovan put down the carton, walked swiftly towards her and placed a glass of orange on the table. In doing this, his hand brushed her arm. Anne felt the hairs rise on the back of her neck. She went rigid. He had simply touched her very gently, probably without noticing, but it caused a definite frisson.

"I just wanted to talk to you, that's all," he said quietly.

He spun round and went back to the galley before Anne could react. She thought the colour may have returned to her cheeks.

"What about?" she said, struggling to regain her presence of mind and sound casual.

"Anything. Whatever turns you on." He reflected. "Well, not in the sense of ... you know what I mean."

He set a rack of toast down on the table with a pot of honey and went back for plates. Finally he took the seat opposite and invited her to begin. After a tentative bite, Anne spoke.

"All right. Why don't you tell me about you ... who you are ... why you're here ... what you do?"

"The life story thing? Does it matter?"

"I thought the choice was up to me. You could start by telling me where you go at nights."

Anne realised this was a hazardous direction to take, but she was tired of being in the dark, and her return of strength after the hang-over was restoring her self-confidence.

"Nights?" Bemused.

"You stay out all night sometimes. I've noticed." Her eyes strayed to the shelves containing the cameras and the German books. From where she sat, the car photos were invisible. "I wondered where you went."

"I told you. I have work to do."

"Work? You said it was out of a sense of duty ... or something like that."

"In a way ..." Donovan followed her gaze. "You seem very interested in my possessions. Why is that?"

"I'm not sure. They're not the kinds of things you usually find on a narrowboat ... collections of old cameras. Marnie says even old Leicas are worth hundreds."

Donovan shook his head slowly, smiling faintly. "Not those ones," he said quietly.

"They look all right to me," Anne said generously.

"For those ones, I have the original boxes – even for the extra lenses – and the original leather cases. And the operating manuals ... in the original German. I sometimes think I'm stupid to have them on display like that, but I like them so much. They're part of my family."

Anne looked at them with a new insight. "You mean ...?"

Donovan nodded.

"Not hundreds?" said Anne.

"No."

"How did you ... get them?"

"You nearly asked how did I *come by* them." He smiled. "Simple. I inherited them. They belonged since new to a great-uncle who left them to his son, my uncle, who gave them to me."

"And he was German, your great-uncle?"

"Strictly speaking, he was Czech, though I think he was probably Austrian when he was born – or he might even have been Polish – but anyway, he was an ethnic German ... from the Sudetenland."

"Did he come here to escape from the communists and the Russians?"

Donovan gave this some thought. "Indirectly, I suppose he did. But he didn't get out as such ... he was – shall we say – *rescued* ..." He smiled faintly, "by Hitler ... or by his army, to be precise."

"By...? Really?"

"Well, in as much as –"

He was interrupted by the ringing of a phone from somewhere beyond Anne in the study area. Donovan stood up and went to the desk. Picking up the phone, he gave his name.

"Na, Anna. Guten Morgen."

While listening, he looked towards Anne and mouthed *excuse me a moment*. He spoke briefly in German for a minute or so before disconnecting. When he turned round, he found the cabin empty. A half-eaten piece of toast lay on the plate. Anne had gone.

• • • • •

It was ideal weather for a tootle on *Sally Ann*. But then again, Marnie thought as she drove home down the dual carriageway, it probably wouldn't please Anne to have the boat's diesel engine clattering away beneath her feet, not if she was still suffering with her hang-over. Marnie smiled to herself and began changing plans. She would do some work in the garden at the back of the farmhouse. For *garden*, she thought, read *jungle*. Then she would sit out by the canal with a book. It would be good to have some sort of tan for when Beth and Paul got back from their travels in far-flung places, including the real jungle of Thailand.

Anne might join in for the second part of the plan, unless she felt like staying in the shade for the whole day. One thing was certain: Anne would not be wanting to go near alcohol for a while. Musing on the importance of learning by painful experience, Marnie turned the car off the main road and down to the village.

So it was that, as she motored along the high street, she was more than surprised to see a familiar red Mini parked right outside the pub. In disbelief she slowed to check the number-plate. Her first thought was that Anne had driven up to the shop and could find nowhere nearer to park. But the kerb was clear on the shop side of the street. And if Anne really was in the pub – surely, impossible – why not use its car park? Marnie's brain was telling her the answer as her foot was pressing down on the brake pedal.

She parked opposite the pub and by the time she was halfway across the street, Anne was waving from under a Carlsberg parasol at a table in the garden.

"This I don't believe," said Marnie.

"I needed to be here. I was hoping you'd see the Mini and stop."

"You've become a hardened drinker in one day? What are you on?"

Marnie eyed Anne's glass. It was obviously sparkling mineral water.

"Gin ... neat."

"Good choice for clearing the head. Any other reason you've come?"

"Marnie, I'm almost certain he's a Nazi. He as good as admitted it. Well, at least, he was on the point of admitting it when the phone rang. And he was speaking German – I'm pretty sure it was German – so I legged it ... again." It all came out in a rush.

"Now would be a good time to pause for breath," Marnie said evenly. "Why don't we sit down together and you can tell me all about it ... in a way that I can follow. OK?"

Grace Parchman, the publican's daughter, appeared at the back door. Marnie pointed at Anne's glass and at herself. Grace smiled and went inside. The pub had scarcely been open a few minutes, and they were the only patrons so far. As they went and took their seats, Marnie thought it was time to lighten the atmosphere.

"What's the good of my organising drunken orgies in the privacy of Glebe Farm, if you're going to get us a reputation as alcoholics unanimous?"

"I'm serious, Marnie. He's got me really spooked. I don't like all this Nazi stuff. It gives me the creeps."

Marnie reached over and patted her hand.

"Hey, come on. We can sort it out. Just try to look cheerful for a moment."

Grace came over and put Marnie's glass on the table.

"Thanks. How are the wedding plans going, Grace?"

"Usual hassle, or so I'm told." She beamed. "I don't mind. We just can't wait for the day to arrive when we move in to the cottage. We're so looking forward to it. It'll be great."

"It'll be lovely having you at Glebe Farm." Marnie reached for her bag.

Grace waved it away. "On the house."

"Oh no, really ..." Marnie protested.

But Grace was already turning back to the pub. "Let's not argue on a beautiful day."

Anne watched her go. "She wouldn't be so chirpy if she knew Glebe Farm was about to become the New Force Gestapo headquarters."

Marnie put a finger to her lips, grinning. "Shhh ... Keep your voice down. Anyway, it's not as bad as that."

"You weren't there, Marnie. It was *weird*. You'd think we were on the *Graf Spee* or something."

"Anne, Germany isn't like that now. Get things in perspective. It's a very civilised country. Believe me, I've been there a few times. You'd like it. All that Nazi stuff, as you put it ... it's all history."

"It's certainly *his* history. He told me so. He actually said his family were saved by Hitler and his army."

Marnie frowned. "So Ralph was right …"

"You *knew*? Why didn't you tell me?"

"You wouldn't have thanked me in the middle of your *dying Swan* routine this morning if I'd breezed in and said *Oh, by the way, did you know we've got Hitler's nephew living opposite on the Bismarck?*"

Anne's eyes popped out on stalks. "He's *not!*"

"No, of *course* he's not. I was speaking figuratively."

"Then what was Ralph right about?"

"Some sort of … connection," Marnie said slowly. "That's all I know."

Anne sat back, weighing up the situation. The drawn expression left by the hang-over plus this new worry made her look less than happy. Marnie took a sip of the designer water.

"What should we do?" said Anne in a weary voice. "I can't just keep running away the whole time."

"No. That doesn't solve anything." Marnie looked across at her friend, who had placed all her hopes and dreams for the future in her hands. She downed the water and put the glass firmly on the table. "Come on. I'm damned if I'm going to let anything or anyone spoil our home and our life."

"What are we going to do?"

"Take arms upon a sea of troubles and, by opposing, end them," said Marnie, standing up.

Anne finished her drink and got to her feet. "First we were *Swan Lake*, now we're *Hamlet*. Heroic stuff."

"Exactly." Marnie was making her way rapidly between the tables. "Let's go for it."

Anne followed. "OK," she muttered. "If you say so. But look what happened to Hamlet and the swan …"

• • • • •

Nothing happened to Marnie and Anne. They travelled in convoy down the field track to Glebe Farm, bent on confrontation. For all her anxiety, Anne could not help but admire Marnie's resolve. She had seen this side of her character before and knew she was unstoppable. True, it had nearly got them killed in the past, but it was impressive … if you survived. Marnie drove the Discovery straight into its place in the garage barn. Anne manoeuvred the Mini so that it was facing back towards the track … just in case.

From force of habit they went to the office to check for messages. Marnie was reaching into her shoulder-bag for the key when Anne touched her arm and pointed at the door. A piece of paper was tucked into the frame near the lock. Marnie pulled it out and handed it to Anne.

"It's for you."

Anne shook her head. "You read it."

Marnie unfolded the note. "*Anne – you left before we had a chance to talk. I'll be away in London till tomorrow. Duty calls again. See you, DS.* That's it."

"*Duty calls*," Anne repeated. "Not sure I like the sound of that."

• • • • •

Marnie and Anne stood facing the garden at the rear of the farmhouse armed with a hoe, a fork, a spade and a box of assorted tools, including secateurs and a pair of shears. The vegetation stood as tall as they were and stretched back as far as the end wall. Rumour – and the original sales particulars of the property – had it that this was a walled garden, but Marnie could not recall the last time she had ever seen evidence of that structure.

"Where do we begin, Marnie?"

"Good question." Marnie advanced a few steps and peered into the growth. "I think for ecological and environmental reasons we ought to reconsider."

"You mean …" Anne began, "If we touch this it could be the equivalent of damaging the rainforest?"

Marnie nodded thoughtfully. "There could be as yet undiscovered species of wildlife in there."

"So we don't have to do anything?" said Anne, more brightly.

"Not until the BBC has parachuted David Attenborough in and filmed the complete series."

"Or we could offer it to the SAS for training manoeuvres in jungle warfare," Anne suggested.

"They wouldn't accept it … far too risky."

"So?"

"Plan B," said Marnie.

Minutes later, they had changed from jeans into bikinis and were installed in deckchairs by the canal, spreading sunblock over their exposed surfaces. There was no danger that passing boats would fail to slow down as they went by. For a short time they dozed, soaking up the sunshine, enjoying the birdsong, the holiday smell of the suncream, the occasional burble from a boat slipping past. Peace. From one boatman they had a whistle, that they pretended to ignore.

In a dreamy voice Anne said, "I do like dogs … really."

"I know." Marnie spoke without opening her eyes.

"I just said that as a kind of joke."

"Most commendable … in the circumstances."

Anne yawned and extricated herself from the deckchair. She went on board *Sally Ann* and mixed long drinks of mango juice and sparkling water with ice cubes and a chunk of lime. They settled down with books, magazines and the pile of newspapers that Marnie had bought while shopping.

Marnie came across a magazine article about the renovation of a villa in Tuscany and was turning down the corner of the page as a marker for Estelle, when Anne distracted her.

"Marnie, did you see the article about this bloke Brandon?" She held up the paper.

"Mm?"

"Garth Brandon. He's going to stand in the election … for the European Parliament. It says here he's the candidate for the Britain First Party … and it's in Northampton."

"Yes," said Marnie vaguely. "It's a by-election."

"The BFP is the far right … right?"

"Right."

Anne found herself smiling involuntarily. "Marnie! I'm being serious here. They must be like the political wing of these New Force people ... the far right. That's what it says in the *Independent*."

"Then it must be right," said Marnie.

"Oh, don't start that again." Mock reproof. "It says he was in politics before he went to work at that university."

"He was the golden boy of the right wing of the Tory party, but he resigned when Mrs Thatcher signed the Maastricht Treaty."

"You know about him?"

"Yes," said Marnie. "Not much, but I knew that."

"And you didn't mention him to me? What else are you keeping from me?"

Marnie sat up in her chair. "What do you mean? I didn't know I was supposed to provide a news-clipping service. I bought the papers, didn't I? I've not censored them."

"You know what I mean, Marnie." Anne read on. "Apparently, he's having a meeting of his 'inner circle' in London on Saturday evening. That's tonight ... in Shadwell. Where's that? I've never heard of it."

"Docklands, I think. I'll look it up and give you a map reference if you want."

"Ha ... ha ..." Anne said slowly.

"Well, I wouldn't want to be accused of keeping things from you. As if I'd do such a thing ..."

"You're *always* keeping things from me." Her voice softened. "To protect me, or keep me from worrying."

"Only for your own good, Anne. You're such an old worry-guts."

"Blimey!" Anne's turn to sit up sharply.

"What?"

"Donovan Smith ... *he's* gone to London."

"That's in the *Independent*?"

Anne pulled a face. "No, silly ... his note ... *Duty calls*."

"Anne, London's a pretty big place. He might be seeing any one of eight million people. It's just a coincidence. There's absolutely nothing to worry about."

After a pause Anne said, "Oh, I can think of at least two things to worry about."

"Amaze me," said Marnie.

"First ... we know for sure that Donovan Smith has Nazi connections. Even Ralph says so. Right?"

"Go on."

"And second ... this Garth Brandon. He's standing in the election in Northampton. That means he'll be spending a lot of time up here over the next few weeks. It's an election for the European Parliament, don't forget."

"So?"

"That means it's not just for the town ... he's standing for the whole county. He'll be going to every area. That includes here in the south. He and his supporters will be swarming all over us. And that's not a coincidence. That's a guarantee."

18

Ralph's flight was dead on time. Waiting for him to arrive, Marnie installed herself in a café on the main airport concourse and scoured the Sunday papers for news of any unrest the previous night. There were no reports of riots, attacks or general mayhem. All was quiet. There was no mention of Garth Brandon, the BFP or New Force, except for one brief editorial speculating that perhaps the troubles had fizzled out. Marnie was unconvinced.

When Ralph walked through the arrivals gate pulling his suitcase, they embraced warmly. Marnie commented on Ralph's lack of a suntan. He complimented her on hers. Out in the car park Ralph heaved his bag into the boot, and they headed for home.

"No Anne?"

Marnie steered the Discovery into a roundabout and chose the lane to the motorway. "She decided to visit her folks for the day. And I think she wanted to give us some time to ourselves. So ... tell me all about your conference. Spare no gory details."

Ralph laughed. "I know men are supposed to like nothing more than their own voices, but I don't think I should inflict macro-economic theory on even such a willing listener as you, Marnie."

Marnie smiled. "I am interested in your life, Ralph ... your career."

"I know, and it's marvellous. But just now, it's all the goings-on here that are most important to me."

"OK. So ... Donovan Smith? Did you remember anything more about him?"

"Oh, yes ... I remembered all right. And maybe it's just as well that Anne isn't here."

"It's that bad?"

They had reached the motorway. The traffic was light, and Marnie settled the car into a steady rhythm.

"I can't pretend to have all the details, but I'll tell you what I know. Donovan Smith isn't his full name, it's his surname. I can't remember his first name exactly, but I think it's German ... Klaus, Kurt ... something like that."

"So he is German?"

"Partly. Look, I think I'd better start with his grandparents, Professor Doctor Klaus Herrmann and his wife, Luise. She was a musician, very talented, very beautiful. Back in the twenties – and the thirties for a time – they were stars on the academic scene in Berlin. He was a brilliant anthropology lecturer, great expert on the history of early religions. She specialised in ancient music ... gave recitals on weird instruments. OK so far? Not disturbing your concentration?"

"No, that's fine. You seem to know a lot about them."

"I got that from their son-in-law, but I'll come on to him in a minute."

"Go on with the story, then," said Marnie. "I'm sitting comfortably."

"When the Nazis came to power in 1932, the Minister for Internal Affairs was Heinrich Himmler. He's well-known for setting up the secret state police – the *Gestapo* – but he did lots of other things, too. One of his responsibilities was for policy relating to the purity of the Germanic race – the Aryans and all that kind of thing. You can see where this is leading?"

"Would it lead to an interest in a certain leading anthropologist, by any chance?"

"Precisely. Himmler had big research budgets and was keen to fund anyone who could prove that the Aryans were the master race."

"Professor Herrmann ordered the new Mercedes and a set of strings for his wife's sitar?"

"Actually," said Ralph, "that's where I rather lose the thread. Somewhere along the line they managed to survive the war – the whole family ... I think they had three daughters – and ended up for a time in Sweden. What happened after that I don't know, but some years ago I got to know Bill Donovan Smith."

"Our stranger's father?"

"Yes. He was on a post-doctoral fellowship at All Saints, my college. He'd been a research assistant to Herrmann and studied under him in Germany."

"I can't imagine the East Germans harbouring an ex-Nazi at one of their universities," said Marnie.

"No. He wasn't in Berlin any more. It was some other place ... Göttingen, Gießen, I don't know ... somewhere in West Germany. Anyway, Bill ended up marrying the youngest of the daughters ... Greta, I think was her name. Prof Herrmann was dead by then, and Bill was editing his old research papers for a book. That's how he came to be in Oxford for a while, and how I met him."

"He's not still at All Saints, then?"

"No. He's dead. So's his wife. It was tragic, really. He left All Saints to take up a post at Reading University. A few years later they were visiting South Africa, and on a trip to one of the national parks their bus ran off the road. Half the passengers were killed in the crash, including Bill and Greta. Their son was sitting on the other side from them, and he survived. He must've been about ten or eleven at the time."

"When was that?"

"Something like ten years ago, I think."

"Did you ever meet their son?"

"Once or twice. I vaguely remember him as a rather introverted little boy ... ... very quiet and shy."

"What became of him?"

Ralph shook his head. "I'm really not sure. I did ask at the time, but it was soon after Laura died, and I was less aware of what was happening around me for a while. My recollection is that he went to live with relatives. There the trail ends."

"And it looks as if it's now led to our door," said Marnie. "Or to our canal bank."

• • • • •

Marnie urged Ralph to change out of his travelling clothes while she made ready for lunch. He emerged from *Thyrsis* in slacks and a polo shirt to find the table set up on the waterside, their places laid under the big parasol, with blue and white gingham napkins standing in tall wine glasses. Marnie waved from the galley on *Sally Ann* and came out carrying a bottle.

"You've probably had a surfeit of Spanish wine, so I thought we'd open this."

She handed him a chilled bottle of *Crémant de Bourgogne*, a dry white sparkler from Burgundy. By the time he had opened it with a satisfying *pop*, Marnie was returning with a tray containing a basket of bread and the first course. Ralph stood for a moment surveying the scene.

"This must be very close to perfection." He breathed in deeply, turning his face to the sun. "*A book, a jug of wine and you,*" he quoted.

"Very poetic," said Marnie. "But in fact it's a fantail of avocado, sprinkled with vinaigrette."

"Even better, but it doesn't scan so well ... or perhaps it's just a poor translation from the original Persian."

He walked over and kissed Marnie, holding her close to him for several seconds. When they moved apart they were smiling. Ralph was about to speak when he saw Marnie's smile fade. She was looking over his shoulder.

"What is it?"

"Oh, nothing. Let's not spoil a beautiful day."

She kissed him lightly and turned towards the table, but Ralph did not release her. He looked round.

"Ah yes... the famous U-boat. I'd forgotten about it. Strange to think that Donovan is just over there. When I last saw him he was a little sprog."

"He's not there at the moment."

Marnie led Ralph to the table, and he poured the wine, taking care not to let it foam over the top of the flutes.

"How do you know he's not there?"

"No bike. He's got a mountain bike for getting around locally. It's bright yellow – you can't miss it – and it sits on the roof when he's on board."

"Presumably he can't stay there indefinitely," said Ralph, handing Marnie a glass. "He's only allowed so many days on that section in any year. Perhaps he won't be around to bother us much longer."

"His leaving can't come soon enough for me. He gives Anne the creeps. She's really spooked by him. I've never seen her like that. In fact ..."

"Go on."

"Nothing."

Marnie took a fork of avocado and a sip of wine. Ralph touched her hand.

"In fact what? I didn't realise you were so upset by this. Do you really suspect this young man is involved with the far right ... that he's in some way mixed up with New Force?"

"It's only circumstantial evidence, Ralph. But every time something happens at night, he seems to be away. And all the other signs ... the strange-looking boat, his clothes – like the things I saw the New Force people wearing – and the swastika photo ... you can see why Anne's worried."

They finished the avocado in silence, and when Ralph made to collect their plates, Marnie waved him to remain seated.

"You relax. I've got one or two things to do in the galley ... and you're jetlagged."

Ralph laughed. "About as jetlagged as a visit to Waitrose. Can't I help in the galley?"

"No. You'll be in the way. I won't be a minute."

On board *Sally Ann* Marnie loaded a tray with a salad bowl and dishes containing baked trout and roast peppers. She quickly tossed new potatoes in parsley butter and emptied them into another dish. Outside, all her concentration was on stepping down from the stern deck with the tray intact, and it was only when she looked up with an anticipatory smile that she discovered they had a visitor. Ralph had risen from his seat at the arrival of Donovan Smith.

"I seem to make a habit of walking in on your mealtimes," the visitor observed. "I was hoping to see Anne."

"She's away for the day," said Marnie, putting the tray down on the table.

"I'll leave you in peace, then. Sorry to intrude."

He turned and began walking away.

"Aren't you going to wish us … *Guten Appetit?*" said Ralph.

The young man stopped, and his head snapped round. His expression had changed to wariness and surprise. He scanned the boats with his eyes as if expecting an ambush.

"Why do you say that?" he asked, his body tense. He looked fixedly at Ralph. "Do I know you?"

"I think that's a possibility. I believe your late father may for a time have been a colleague of mine at Oxford."

The visitor considered this and almost imperceptibly nodded, his eyes focusing on his past life.

"You know my name from Anne. When father was at Oxford I was only six years old. A lot has changed since then."

"Would you care to join us for lunch?" said Marnie.

"No, thank you. That would be … I should be going. So … *Guten Appetit*, then."

His head dropped in an embryonic bow, and he was gone. Marnie and Ralph stared after him before addressing themselves to their rapidly cooling meal.

• • • • •

The yellow mountain bike was still in place on the roof of *X O 2*, like a royal standard proclaiming that the owner was in residence, when Anne returned in the early evening. She was in good spirits after a day with her family and regaled Marnie and Ralph with the latest news from the home front. It had been a happy, uncomplicated visit devoid of sinister undertones, and listening to Anne's cheerful narration, Marnie felt reluctant to embroil her again in the cares facing them at Glebe Farm.

The three decided to call in at the office barn, Ralph to put his washing in the machine, Marnie to check for phone messages, Anne to put flowers in vases. Her father had cut her several bunches from the garden. They arrived in front of the barn as Estelle's Golf drew in to the yard. Luther opened the passenger door, waved and reached into the back of the car to bring out a heavy box. Estelle smiled radiantly.

"Hi! Luther thinks I'm crazy to want so many books up here when I'm about to go off to Italy, but I like having them around me. Anyway, I want him to have plenty to occupy him while I'm away ... no excuses that he's bored and needs to wander."

"Shall we review the project in the morning?" said Marnie. "Say, around ten o'clock?"

"Sure. We wondered about going up to the pub for a drink this evening. It seems a villagey thing to do. Feel like joining us?"

Marnie and Ralph exchanged glances. "Fine. Give us a shout when you're ready."

In the barn Ralph was sorting his clothes into the machine when Anne climbed down the loft ladder.

"Anything interesting in the messages department?" she said to Marnie, who was at her desk with a notepad.

Ralph was kneeling facing the machine, and his voice was muffled. "Your friend Donovan came looking for you."

"Oh? When was that?"

Marnie looked anxious. "While we were having lunch."

"He seems to be making a habit of doing that," said Anne.

"That's what he said."

"Did he say anything else?"

"Well ..."

"Anything memorable?" Anne cocked an eyebrow.

"Not really."

Ralph wandered over. "I knew his father, Anne. And I met him when he was a child, not long after I got my fellowship at All Saints."

"Gosh, that's *weird*. You actually *know* him."

"That would be an exaggeration. I saw him a couple of times when he was about six."

"And his father's a colleague of yours?"

"*Was*. His parents are both dead ... a road accident in South Africa about ten years ago."

"Did he say what he was doing here ... or what he wanted?"

"No," said Marnie. "He just said he was hoping to see you."

Anne headed for the door. "Then there's one way to find out. I'll go round while I'm feeling in a good mood. See you later."

· · · · ·

Am I really doing this? Anne was slightly amazed at her own temerity as she walked through the spinney and took the path towards the canal bridge. But it was a fine evening, she had had a good day, and everybody was home at Glebe Farm. The world seemed an ordered place again, and she felt able to get the situation in perspective. Everything had become too intense since the rioting and bombing had started. It was time to clear the air. And Ralph knowing Donovan when he was a child somehow made it easier.

Reaching the bridge, she paused and looked over at *X O 2*, nestling peacefully by the bank. She took a deep breath and walked on, aware of the tracks left by Donovan's bike wheels in the earth.

She had reached the stern of the boat when she heard a door open at the bow end, and Donovan climbed out of the cratch well. Without looking in Anne's direction, he reached up for the bike and swung it to the ground in a smooth motion, flicking a pedal round with one foot, preparing to move off. Her presence caught his eye, and he stopped on the point of mounting.

"Have you come to see me?" he asked. He seemed tense.

"Whenever I come here, you're either coming or going," said Anne.

"And when I go over to your place, you're always eating. You never seem to do anything else."

"So you're off."

"Not for long. I have to pop up to the village. I'll be ten minutes."

"The shop isn't open, you know," Anne pointed out.

"I need the phone box. My mobile's run down."

Anne reached for her pocket, but it was empty. "Sorry. You could use mine, but it's in my room."

"That's OK. Look, I've really gotta go ... er ... why don't you wait for me on board. I honestly won't be long."

"Oh ... I don't –"

"Here!" He thrust his boat keys into her hand and pushed off the bike. "Make yourself at home." He began pedalling, looking back over his shoulder to call out. "You could make coffee if you like. You'll find everything in the galley."

He accelerated, made the turn onto the bridge and disappeared from view.

Am I really doing this? Anne was again amazed, this time at accepting Donovan's invitation to enter his inner sanctum in his absence. It looked the same as before, everything neat and orderly. She stood in the saloon – the study area – and realised that she found the overall effect of the almost monochrome environment strangely satisfying. It had been *designed*. It was all of a piece, a thought-out concept. Donovan had style, she grudgingly admitted to herself.

She walked into the galley area and immediately saw the coffeepot on the workbench, beside a brown ceramic filter, like a broad funnel to stand on the pot. Leaning beside them was a box of Melitta filter papers, and she fitted one in place. All that was missing was the coffee. She filled the kettle and lit the gas. It ignited first time. Systematically she began a hunt through the cupboards that smelled pleasantly of coffee and spices until, under the workbench, she found a box of coffee – *Jakobs echter Filterkaffee aus Berlin*. Rummaging further she found cups and saucers – *Rosenthal Studio-line* – in plain white and spoons with the brand mark WMF on the back. It was like being on holiday in a house in a foreign country. She looked in the food cupboard and found brands she did not recognise: *Dr. Oetker, Bahlsen, Stute*. The fridge was much the same: *Onken, Mildessa, Bärenmarke*. Where did he buy these? Presumably he knew shops in England that sold them. In the bread bin she found a dark rye loaf and read the label: *Schneiderbrot – Paderborn*.

The water was heating, and Anne poured a little into the pot to warm it. While she waited she felt an overwhelming curiosity about these surroundings ... and their owner. Living with Marnie, she was accustomed to having continental food and wine in store, but here virtually everything she could see was foreign. German. She was suddenly struck by an image: Donovan as a little boy, lost, orphaned, all alone, clinging to anything he could find that reminded him of his homeland. His Fatherland.

She went towards the desk. His radio was a *Grundig*, his pencils made by *Staedtler*, his pen a *Pelikan*. It was eerie to find this haven of Germany on an English canal in the heart of the country. The laptop bore the Siemens logo. By now she would have expected nothing else. There were drawers under the desk, and she pulled at them, one by one. All were arranged tidily with stationery in separate compartments. In one was a box of small candles, nightlights. In the bottom drawer was an old tin box, its paint chipped and worn away at the corners. Anne eased off the lid and found herself looking at a collection of medals. One of them was the familiar shape – familiar from countless war films and documentaries – of an Iron Cross. And there, lying further back in the drawer was the strangest shape. Anne pushed the lid back on the box and moved it aside. Perhaps what she saw was nothing more than an odd shadow, a trick of the half-light, her imagination distorting things as it had before. She began to reach towards the back of the drawer.

Just then a clang from above her made Anne slam the drawer shut and leap up. She raced to the galley and poured the water from the pot into the sink, hurriedly spooning two measures of coffee into the filter and pouring hot water from the kettle until it reached the rim.

"That smells good!"

Donovan came in through the cratch door. He seemed changed, more relaxed, at ease in his home, more cheerful perhaps after his phone call.

"I hope I've got the quantity right. I'm not used to filters."

Donovan looked at the pot. "Just let that go through, then pour in as much water as you want. Three top-ups should do it. What do you normally use?"

"A cafetière."

He walked through, past the sitting area into the saloon, looking at the book-shelves. "You found everything you were looking for?"

"No probs."

One drawer was not fully closed, and he pushed it home absent-mindedly with his knee. Anne concentrated on pouring water over the coffee grounds. Donovan took a candle from a shelf and set it down in the middle of the table. It was a nightlight like the ones she had seen in the drawer, resting in a shallow ceramic candle-holder. He opened the top drawer of his desk and took out a lighter, holding it sideways to catch the wick. Anne lifted the filter and looked into the pot before adding one more top-up of water. Donovan took the crockery from the bench and laid the table. Returning to the galley, he crouched at the fridge.

"Do you take milk? I only have evaporated at the moment."

"A little," said Anne, and watched as he took a jug from a cupboard and poured in the milk from a tin. *Bärenmarke*.

She checked the pot and removed the filter, placing it in the sink. Donovan came over and lifted the filter paper out, dropping it into the waste bin under the unit, together with the milk tin. They took their places on opposite sides of the table, and Donovan poured the coffee, the candle-light softening his sharp features.

• • • • •

The four from Glebe Farm decided it was warm enough to sit outside and found a table in the pub garden. Luther insisted on buying the first round and came out with a broad grin, carrying a tray of drinks.

"Nice pub ... very *olde worlde*. I assume it's the real thing."

"Oh, yes," said Ralph. "Not a fibreglass beam in sight."

"Why are you looking so pleased with yourself, Luther?" said Estelle.

"I was just thinking ... they can't have seen many black faces in the bar. I suspect the locals are probably sitting in there trying to work out how much I've devalued their properties by moving into the village." He laughed.

"Yep," said Marnie, joining in. "That's Glebe Farm down the drain."

Ralph raised a finger. "Ah, but wait till they find out about your sporting pedigree ... especially at cricket. They'll start worrying how much you'll have put the rates up. People will be flocking to live here when the word gets round. Cheers."

They raised their glasses.

"I'm surprised you didn't bring Anne along," Estelle observed. "She's never usually out of the picture."

"She has things to do this evening," said Marnie.

"Oh?" Estelle noted Marnie's serious expression.

"Actually ..." Marnie began. "I was wondering about sending her with you to Italy."

"Sure. Is she keen to go?"

"I haven't mentioned it to her yet. It's just an idea."

"OK by me," said Estelle.

"Marnie thinks you need a chaperone," said Luther, grinning. "Good idea."

· · · · ·

It was only early evening and still broad daylight outside, but Anne found the candle-flame homely and comforting. She sensed that Donovan had not lit it to increase the lighting in the cabin, even though it was subdued. It seemed to be his custom. He watched her looking at it.

"Do you find the candle eccentric ... unusual?" he asked.

"No. I like it. Do you always do this?"

He paused. "*Always* isn't the right word. If you mean *always* when I have a visitor, then no, I don't. Because I've never had a visitor on the boat before."

"But you often burn candles?"

"Often, yes. Small ones on the table here, larger ones when I'm working at my desk in the evenings. Church candles are best. They last longest."

"What work do you do?" Anne wanted to resist being drawn into an interrogation, but it seemed inevitable.

"I study."

He stopped there. Anne waited, but he seemed unlikely to go further. Or unwilling. She raised an eyebrow.

"I'm not used to talking about myself," he said.

"Is that a polite way of telling me to mind my own business?"

"Not really. It's just a statement of fact."

"Why do you think I came here this evening? And – more to the point – why did you ask me to stay?"

Donovan considered the questions for a while.

"You've been on the boat a few times now. What do you deduce about its owner?"

Anne stared back at him.

"The owner is ... very orderly ... disciplined ... neat and tidy. There's obviously a German connection, but he doesn't speak English with a German accent. He likes technical things ... obviously computing ... photography ... How's that?"

Donovan shook his head. "That's just the surface. Anyone could work that out."

"His taste for order could be regarded by some as ... obsessive."

"By you, for example?"

"Yes ... but I don't count."

"Why not?"

"Because I'm the same. I bet you write lists for everything."

He smiled. "On target. Go on."

"He has a sense of design ... style. Not trained, I don't think ... instinctive."

"Why do you say that?"

"I don't get the feeling of a broad range beyond this style. This might be his only shot."

"Mm ... That's pretty good. Any more?"

"I don't know enough about people to know if he's insecure ... but I do wonder about that."

"Why?"

"It should be obvious ... as you might say."

"Touché! But you can't just stop there. Why insecure?"

"Perhaps because he surrounds himself with special things from home ... German things ... to carry his home around with him. And he only goes out to contact the world on his own terms. Then he comes back to secrete himself away in this ... secure environment. Is that on target?"

"Who knows? I'd be the last person to be able to judge that. So ... when are you going to say what you really think?"

"I think I've said enough already."

"But there's more there."

"I'm allowed my own private thoughts. I don't have to say everything I think. And to be honest, Donovan – or whatever your first name is – I'm starting to find this game a little bit boring."

His eyes narrowed. "So your professor friend has been talking about me. I wonder what he knows."

"Not much. And he's not a gossip. He told us about your parents ... and I'm sorry about what happened to them ... and to you. But he doesn't know much else. He said your father was a lecturer and your grandfather a famous professor in Germany."

"Did he tell you my grandfather had been denounced ... twice?"

Anne did not reply.

"What did you come to find out, Anne?"

"There's little point in going further ... if you don't like talking about yourself. Mind you, you're not making a bad job of it. We've done nothing but talk about you since I came." She began to get up, but he put his hand on her arm.

"Ask me anything you want ... whatever's on your mind."

"All right. Where do you go when you're out all night? What is this *duty* that takes you away? Why have you come here? What are you mixed up in? How's that for starters?"

Donovan's turn to stare.

"Family matters," he said eventually, his voice very quiet. "After my parents died I went to live with one of my mother's sisters and her husband, my aunt and uncle. They've been very good to me. My uncle is suffering from a terminal illness. When I've been away, I've been at the hospital with my aunt. She needs my support."

"So you've been there for them."

He nodded. "Because they've always been there for me."

Anne had a sinking feeling in her chest, and her eyes began pricking. She blinked and took a few deep breaths to retain her self-control, camouflaging her emotions by sipping coffee.

Equally quietly, she said, "So what about the boat and travelling on the canal?"

"The name of the boat is the clue, though you may not find it very obvious."

"I don't."

"When I bought it, it had an airy-fairy name ... a bit of English whimsy ... *September Mist*, or something like that. It was fitted out in the cosy-cottage style that some people seem to like. I changed everything and fitted her out like a real boat ..."

"We nicknamed it the U-boat," said Anne.

"Yeah. That's good! That was the idea ... something purposeful ... something different."

"And the name?"

"It's a pun on the Greek word *exodos* ... like Exodus in the Bible."

"Why? I don't get it."

"It's my way out. *Exodos* is Greek for the Latin word *exit*."

"I still don't ... ah, yes, I think I do ... You've dropped out. Is that right?"

"Not out of everything."

"No. You're still attached to your family."

"I've just dropped out of a university course. It wasn't right for me, so I decided to take some time off to re-think my direction. My uncle's illness has been another ... complication."

"Yes. I'm sorry. Look ... I think I've encroached a lot on your space this evening. We can talk again some time if you want to ... if you're going to be around much longer."

•　•　•　•　•

The group walked down the field track in the still evening, chatting companionably, with dusk gradually descending on the countryside. Estelle and Luther waved a cheery good-night on their doorstep and went in. Marnie glanced up and saw the light in the window slit of Anne's attic room.

"Ralph, I'd like to pop in and see how Anne is. Do you mind if I follow you back in a few minutes?"

"Sure. You've been thinking about her all evening, haven't you?"

"And I thought I kept it well hidden."

"You did. I'll go and have my shower."

"OK. And if you're in bed before I get back, remember what Mae West said."

"What was that?"

"If I'm late, start without me."

He laughed and set off towards the spinney.

Anne had only just come out of the shower and put on pyjamas when Marnie called up the loft ladder. They sat on the bed, and Anne related her conversation with Donovan.

"So that's what he's been doing."

"I feel such a fool," said Anne. "There I was, suspecting him of being some kind of far-right terrorist or mastermind, when all the time he was up all night sitting by his uncle's bedside in hospital."

"It was a reasonable conclusion, Anne, not foolish at all. Did he say anything about what Ralph called the *Nazi connection?*"

"Not really. I figured I'd been there long enough and I didn't want to pry into his private affairs any more than I had already. It was an uncomfortable kind of conversation. But ..."

"What?"

"Come to think of it ... he did say something about his grandfather – the German professor – being denounced."

"*Denounced?* For what? Who denounced him?"

"I didn't get that far. But I think he said he'd been denounced twice."

On the way back to *Thyrsis* Marnie tried to fit all their thoughts about Donovan into a coherent pattern, like a jigsaw puzzle. Seeing his boat moored on the opposite bank, with lights in its portholes in the gathering darkness, it no longer seemed quite so menacing. But at the back of her mind there were still some unanswered questions niggling away. Why was he hanging round in this area? Could it be a coincidence that the European by-election was taking place with a high-profile far-right candidate? What was Donovan's Nazi connection? After all, he may be a dutiful nephew, but even Hitler had a family. And what was this business about his grand-father being denounced?

Standing on the bank between *Sally Ann* and *Thyrsis*, Marnie breathed in the night air, scented by vegetation and cool water, and made two silent vows. The first, was that she would resolve all the questions about Donovan, and she would do so quickly. The second, was that she would think no more of him that night. Talk of Mae West had put other ideas in her mind.

In the attic room, Anne was sitting up in bed reading magazines, her attention wandering. She was thinking that Donovan was still a mystery, and although he was an interesting character, his convoluted style of conversation was wearying. Marnie had seemed reassuring about him, but Anne knew from past experience that that did not mean she was totally convinced all was well.

When she put the magazines aside and turned out the light, Anne was thinking of what she had held back from Marnie. She justified it to herself on the grounds that she was not entirely devoid of doubts about all that had taken place on *X O 2 – Exodos* – that evening. She had reported most of what had been said, but on one matter she had stayed silent. That shadow in the drawer … if it was a shadow … that was something she had not mentioned. If the chance ever arose again, she would check it out. But as she tried to drift off to sleep, she could not get the image out of her mind. Was it just imagination stoked up by anxiety, or had she really seen it lying there at the back of the drawer, behind the box of medals and the Iron Cross – the unmistakeable shape of a Luger pistol?

19

It was shortly before seven on Monday morning. Marnie blinked a few times and looked over at Ralph, still asleep beside her. She began lifting the duvet to slip out of bed without disturbing him, when the mobile on the shelf above their heads started warbling. Marnie reached up and grabbed it, pressed the green button and rushed out towards the saloon.

"Marnie Walker."

"It's me. Are you listening to the radio?" Anne.

"No, not yet. Why?"

"Turn on the news. It's Garth Brandon. Someone tried to kill him last night!"

"See you!"

Marnie's first reaction was to pull the curtain open to look for the bike on the roof of Donovan's boat. It was there.

"It's a good job no boat's passing." Ralph, standing in the doorway in his dressing gown, smiling.

"Why?"

"Because you're standing at the window in full view of the world, stark naked."

"What? Oh, yes. Can I squeeze past you?"

"Now there's a question for a Monday morning …"

"The question should be – *who was that on the phone and what did they want?*"

Ralph produced Marnie's bathrobe from behind his back and held it out. "OK. I'll ask that instead, but it's much more boring."

Marnie pulled on the bathrobe. "It was Anne. Apparently someone tried to kill Garth Brandon last night."

Ralph looked towards *X O 2.*

"He's there," said Marnie. "Let's put on the news."

For a relatively obscure item about a failed attempt at murder on a minority party candidate in a by-election in which little interest had so far been shown by the media – or anyone else – the story did well to make third place in the news round-up.

… Police in Northampton are investigating an incident in the early hours of this morning, involving Garth Brandon, formerly a junior minister in the government of Margaret Thatcher, now a candidate in the European

*parliamentary by-election for the Britain First Party. Returning from a
meeting in London, Mr Brandon was attacked in his car when it pulled up
at traffic lights in the town centre. It appears that the attacker was armed
with an axe or other heavy weapon which he swung at Mr Brandon,
smashing his car's windscreen. Before the assailant could strike any further
blows, Mr Brandon accelerated away and made his escape. The police are
appealing for witnesses to come forward.*

When Anne arrived for breakfast, Marnie asked if she had heard
anything else.

"Only what you heard after the headlines."

"There'll probably be another report coming up later," said Ralph. He was
right.

*Now, more on that story of the attack on Garth Brandon last night. Our
local reporter, Tricia Roberts, has been speaking with the police. Tricia.*

*Well, Martin, it seems that someone must have been following Garth
Brandon's car, waiting for the opportunity to strike. He was alone at the time
and said he had no intimation that anyone was near him. The attacker
suddenly ran up to the car and tried to pull the door open. Finding it locked,
he took a swing at Mr Brandon with what seems to have been a hand-axe.
He only managed one blow before Mr Brandon was able to drive out of
danger.*

What were conditions like, Tricia?

*It was between one and two o'clock in the morning, and there was no other
traffic about at the time. The incident took place in an area of light industry,
and there seem to have been no witnesses.*

Have you spoken to Garth Brandon?

*No. He drove straight to the central police station to report what had
happened. The police have kept his car in their compound, and he was
driven to a secret location, for obvious reasons.*

Have the police issued a statement?

*Not yet. Our newsdesk received an anonymous call shortly after the attack
took place. I understand the police will be making a statement after
speaking with Mr Brandon again this morning.*

*Thanks, Tricia. We'll return to that story as soon as we have further
information.*

• • • • •

Marnie's feeling of resentment was increasing. All she wanted in life was
to get on with building the business and completing the works to develop
the Glebe Farm complex. It was to be her Utopia – if such a thing was
possible, which she doubted – but the pressures from the outside world, and
all its hideous repercussions, were intruding at every turn. As they opened
the office and tried to settle down to a normal working day, she found it
difficult to concentrate. She made a determined effort, but it was to be in
vain.

"Walker and Co, good morning."

Marnie heard Anne across the room. She had not even been aware of the
phone ringing. A glance at the clock; barely eight-thirty. Probably a
builders' merchant.

"Oh, hi! Do you want to speak to Marnie? ... Sure ... No, it's fine. We're always in the office from quite early. She's right here. Hold on." Anne pressed buttons, and Marnie's phone rang. "It's Serena, Marnie. I think she's in her car on the mobile."

Marnie picked up. "Serena, hi! How are things?"

A sound of traffic noise in the background. "Marnie, can I see you this morning?"

"Of course. Is it urgent?"

"I'm on my way to see Dorothy Vane-Henderson at her house. Could I look in on you?"

Hanford Hall was five minutes from Knightly St John.

"I've got a meeting at ten, but it's internal. I could alter it."

"Are you free now?"

Marnie looked at the pile of letters waiting to be read, the list of jobs and phone calls from Anne, the Umbria design that she wanted to study before seeing Estelle, a new client's brief. She hesitated.

"It's probably inconvenient," said Serena. The disappointment in her voice was clear, even on a mobile in a car.

"No, that's all right. How long will it take you to get here?"

• • • • •

Marnie barely had time to deal with her two most urgent calls and instruct Anne on the rest before Serena swept in. She was wearing a pale grey trouser suit that was meant to look serene. The wearer was not living up to her name. Anne drew up a chair for her and went to put the kettle on.

"What's happened?" said Marnie. "Don't tell me it's the community centre again. There can't be that much left to burn down."

"Worse ... if that's possible. The police have started rounding up young blacks on account of this Garth Brandon thing."

"The usual suspects, presumably?"

"Yeah. It's ridiculous! The whole thing is ridiculous. You heard about it on the news, didn't you?"

"I heard the report on the radio, yes. They said he'd been attacked with an axe ... someone tried to kill him."

Serena was highly agitated. "Who said so?"

Marnie thought about it. "I dunno. The police, wasn't it? I just listened to the report ... got the basic facts."

"Huh!" Serena snorted. "*Facts!* What facts?"

"Like I said ... this business with the axe ... the police ... the car damaged. Serena, why are you here? Has something happened ... something we haven't heard about?"

Serena barely noticed the cup that Anne put on the desk in front of her.

"Good question, Marnie. Doesn't it strike you as odd? Brandon's car is supposedly hit with an axe. Who says it was? The police aren't issuing a statement until they've been able to interview Brandon, right?"

"That's what I heard on the news."

"So if not the police, who told the news people? Think about it. You think they have reporters hanging around Northampton central police station through the night in the hope there might be a story?"

Marnie sat back in her chair. "There must be some explanation. Maybe the police press office contacted the local radio. It's hot news."

"Before the police issued their official statement? You think they'd leak like that? It'd be too easy to trace."

"Serena, I don't know the answer to your questions. I just don't know how these things work."

"No great mystery, Marnie. Brandon – or his gang – have put out a statement. They've grabbed the headlines with this so-called *assassination attempt*. He disappears to a secret place to recover, yeah?"

Marnie thought about it. "And no one can question him or challenge his version of the story. Is that what you're saying? But what about the attack? That must've happened."

Serena raised her hands, palm upwards. "A blow to the windscreen. Who says it was an attempt on his life? He does!" She counted on her fingers. "No witnesses ... no evidence ... no proof. And then the police start arresting suspects." Serena shook her head. "You've got to admit it's pretty neat, Marnie. Brandon gets front page publicity; the public hear that blacks are being treated by the police as suspects – *no smoke without fire*; the Afro-Caribs are outraged ... all for the price of a new windscreen on Brandon's car insurance. Meanwhile, he hides away for a few hours while the story does the rounds unchallenged."

"Doctor Goebbels and the Big Lie technique," said Anne.

"You got it."

"You're really convinced the whole thing is a fabrication?" said Marnie. "The young men picked up by the police ... they'll have alibis? Do they have records of violence?"

"They're pussy cats, Marnie. They swagger about in the baggy trousers and the cool-dude shades, like all kids of their generation ... looking cool ... listening to rap music on their Walkman. And who the hell has an alibi for where they were between one and two in the morning?"

"But presumably there won't be any evidence, so the police will have to let them go."

"Of course, but by then the damage is done. The point is ... what are we going to do about it? How can we fight back?"

"What's all this fighting talk?" Ralph in the doorway.

Anne headed towards the rack of mugs in the kitchen area while Marnie filled him in on the latest news. As she outlined the story, Serena gave little snorts of indignation in the background. The steam was coming out of her ears. Ralph listened attentively without interrupting.

"A cunning plot, my lord," he said quietly when Marnie had finished.

"What do you mean?" Serena looked suddenly wary.

"Just a turn of phrase. The incident is meant to look like a spontaneous outburst, when really it's all carefully planned and premeditated. Is that what you think?"

"Yes, that's exactly what it is. And we've got to find some way of turning it round before people start believing it really did have something to do with the black community. This could ruin all our work, all our plans for the summer. We've got to persuade people that black doesn't mean criminal. We'll have to put out our own statement, try and accentuate the positive."

"By George, this is clever stuff," said Ralph. "Whatever you do, it'll seem as if you're in denial. And this is just for openers. Brandon's election campaign hasn't even got off the ground."

"What did you say, Ralph?" said Marnie, staring.

"Well, it's obvious. It's Brandon's way of getting maximum publicity and wrong-footing the opposition from the word go."

"No. Before that."

"About it being pre-meditated?"

"No. *Just a turn of phrase.* I wonder ..."

Only Anne showed no sign of surprise. Marnie grabbed the mobile as she made for the door, calling out to Ralph that she would be back shortly, telling Serena to ring Dorothy Vane-Henderson and warn her she would be a little late for their meeting, and putting Anne in charge of the office.

Serena remained in her seat, baffled. "What's going on?"

"Not sure," said Anne. "I'll work it out. Meanwhile, Serena, I think you'd be well advised to make that call."

"It was obviously something I said," Ralph muttered. "What do you think, Anne? You can usually read the runes."

Anne craned her neck. "She's over at Estelle's cottage."

Ralph wandered towards the window. He laughed. "She's using the phone. Perhaps the doorbell isn't working."

Serena was totally bemused. "Is it always like this round here? I guess I'd better do as she says."

She reached for the phone.

● ● ● ● ●

Marnie guided the Discovery up the field track, skilfully avoiding the bumps and ruts. Nobody drove that trail as fast or as smoothly as she did. Beside her, Serena held on to the passenger handrail, no wiser than before.

"Marnie, what is going on here? Will you speak to me?"

"Hang on. Gotta concentrate."

"Where are we going?" Serena was clearly agitated. "And what has this got to do with what Ralph said about a cunning plot?"

"Nothing at all. Just a sec."

They halted in the gateway to the field. Marnie looked both ways and began accelerating into the village street.

"Nothing?" said Serena. "But you said –"

"It was when he said *By George* ... that's what made me realise."

"I give up. You're talking in riddles, Marnie."

"Sorry. Not far now."

They drove along the high street, past the church and the pub, on beyond the shop and the cottages set back from the road behind long gardens filled with vegetables and flowers. Marnie pulled in to the drive of a substantial stone farmhouse built at right angles to the road.

"This is where George Stubbs lives," said Marnie. "Trust me. He's our salvation."

"Really?" Serena looked unconvinced. "How?"

"You want the West Indian community to refute Garth Brandon's accusation and – most important – be believed?"

"Of course."

Marnie climbed out and rang the doorbell, beckoning Serena to follow.

They were met at the door by George's wife, Sheila. Inside, the entrance hall was cool and spacious, stone-flagged with an Oriental carpet.

"I hope we're not imposing on George," said Marnie.

"*Imposing?*" Sheila Stubbs looked at the two attractive women standing in her hall and smiled. "He'll think Christmas has come early. Let me lead the way."

The living room was an elegant country mixture of blue and white chintz furnishings and matching curtains, two pairs of French windows looking out onto a terrace and the garden beyond. George appeared from another door and invited them to take a seat. They declined Sheila's offer of refreshment.

"Would you like to speak to George in private?" she said.

"No, not at all," said Marnie.

George beamed. "Well, this is a nice surprise. What can I do for you, ladies?"

● ● ● ● ●

Twenty minutes later George's Range Rover sped up the dual carriageway towards Northampton. At the wheel, he was basking in the presence of the two young women. Beside him, Serena was making another call to Dorothy Vane-Henderson, apologising that a sudden change of plan was making it necessary to delay their meeting yet again. On the back seat, Marnie was engrossed in drafting a text on her laptop computer.

"I say, this is all very exciting," said George. "Certainly livens up a Monday morning, I can tell you."

He felt an irresistible urge to reach across and squeeze Serena's thigh, but he managed to cling doggedly to the wheel with both hands and give almost his full attention to the road.

"Very good of you to help," Marnie said absently, tapping at the keys. "Do you think we should say ... *The West Indian community* or *The Afro-Caribbean community*?"

Serena ended her call. "Why not just say *The black community*? We don't have hang-ups about black these days."

"Might sound funny coming from George," said Marnie.

"Oh yeah. Then *Afro-Caribbean* would be tricky as well. Go for *West Indian* to be safe. That would at least be factually correct in this case."

"Right. OK by you, George?"

"Fine. Whatever you think. I'd paint myself with woad if it'd help."

He chuckled, then had a fleeting vision of Marnie and Serena rubbing him all over with blue dye. Swallowing hard, he gripped the steering wheel tighter and ploughed on.

Marnie continued tapping. "I think we need to say something like ...*emphatically deny any involvement whatsoever in this incident* ... no, *alleged incident*. How's that?"

Serena and George chorused in unison. "Great."

"*And we challenge the accuser to produce any evidence of our implication* ... no ... *and we challenge those who are making these baseless* ... er, *unfounded accusations to produce the slightest proof* ... better?"

"Keep going," said Serena.

"... *that we were in any way connected with this attack*. How am I doing?"

"It's good."

"We don't even know for sure there was an attack," said George.

"Good point." Marnie began tapping again. " ... *this so-called attack, for which no verifiable evidence has to our knowledge been produced*."

"That's better."

"How are you going to end it?" said Serena.

"By calling on the authorities to release all those in custody unless they can prove they were actually involved."

"Bingo!"

· · · · ·

On the steps of the BBC offices in Northampton, Marnie took George aside. She spoke very softly, her face close to his, and had no difficulty in gaining his complete attention.

"Listen, I know this is fun for you, George, and I can see you're enjoying it all, but before we go inside I want to remind you that what we're about to do could have serious consequences ... repercussions. Just take a moment to think about it. I don't want to railroad you into something you might regret later."

"No."

"If you think this could cause you any embarrassment with your family or friends – or your political party – it's not too late to pull out now."

George gripped Marnie's upper arms in his thick hands. He was almost giddy with excitement.

"Serena has given me her word that the accusations are nothing but a pack of lies," he said.

"Absolutely, George. Don't be in any doubt on that score."

"We're not letting these thugs come in and damage our community, Marnie – I mean the *whole* community. Today they're after the West Indians. Tomorrow it'll be anyone who doesn't agree with them. I say we have a go at these bastards now. Let's do it."

Marnie leaned forward and kissed him on the cheek. "You're stopping the blood from circulating in my arms," she muttered.

They pushed open the doors and went in.

· · · · ·

Garth Brandon, immaculately groomed, strode into the central police station shortly before eleven to give his statement of events. He was invited to sit in the reception area. While he waited, thinly concealing his impatience, the duty sergeant handed him a single piece of paper. It was a communiqué issued by the County Constabulary's press office, announcing the release of the 'suspects' on the grounds that a thorough examination of the damaged car had produced no evidence to link them – or anyone else – with the smashed windscreen.

When the noonday edition of the local paper reached the news-stands, the front page contained a report on the smashed windscreen incident and a statement from the West Indian community organisation denying in the most emphatic terms that they were remotely involved in the *so-called alleged unwitnessed attack* on Garth Brandon's car. Beside the report was a photograph of the indignant face of the West Indian denouncing the shabby treatment of his fellow-countrymen. Visible in the background was Serena McDowell, whose fine features made her an elegant associate. The West Indian standing centre-stage in the foreground was George Stubbs.

After a busy morning spent dashing between meetings with the media, Marnie, Serena and George repaired to the coffee-house in the town centre, each clutching a copy of the newspaper. They were looking forward to hearing George's interview for the local radio news and wanted to be back in Knightly St John to catch his television appearances on BBC and ITV regional channels. With luck, he might even manage a few seconds' slot on the national bulletins. Their only slight disappointment was when they went to the police station to hand in their statement for the press office. They had hoped they might run into Brandon to see his discomfiture for themselves, but he was holding back as long as he dared, to give the story a good run before he came out in person to press home the message.

The three conspirators folded their papers and sat back to relax after their exertions.

George was grinning like an ape. "Well, there's a cutting for the family album and no mistake."

He was thrilled that the coffee-house was full of morning shoppers, and he had ostentatiously read his paper so that everyone knew he was on the front page. Being flanked by two eye-catching younger women placed him close to the epicentre of paradise.

"It'll be interesting to see how Brandon reacts," Marnie observed over the top of her cappuccino.

"What do you think he might do?" said Serena.

"One thing's for sure; he didn't have a game plan for this scenario."

George laughed. "You can say that again. The last thing he was expecting was a counter-statement from a West Indian who's white and looks just like a boring old fart straight out of the ranks of the Tory party!"

"That *really* doesn't describe you, George," said Marnie.

"You don't think so, my dear?" Under the table his hand began a sideways movement towards her leg.

"Of course not. You're not *old*."

Serena guffawed. George hesitated, figuring out the implications. Marnie smiled sweetly.

"You think we've got Brandon on the run?" said Serena.

Marnie shrugged. "Only for now. We mustn't get complacent. Who knows what he might try next? We may have won this round, but that could make him more desperate."

"You don't really think he could win the election, do you, Marnie?"

"That isn't his aim. It isn't what this is about."

"No?" Serena frowned. "Then why's he going to all this trouble?"

"I agree," said George. "They're not going to win outright. Brandon knows that. What he'll judge as a success is if he can disrupt lives and cause conflict in the community."

"So we have to block him whenever he tries to do that," said Serena.

"Partly," said Marnie.

"Meaning?"

"If we just react to what he does, he'll always have the initiative. We need some way of countering him pro-actively."

"That's why I adlibbed that bit in my interview, encouraging parents to send their children to your summer scheme," said George. "I wanted to end on a positive note."

"That was brilliant," said Serena.

"Good thinking," said Marnie.

George could hear angels singing. He desperately wanted the two women simultaneously to kiss him on each cheek there and then in full view of everyone. But that only happened in the movies.

• • • • •

In the Range Rover on the journey back to Knightly St John, Serena turned to look at Marnie. "What you were saying in the coffee-shop ... about what Brandon might do ... you really think he might react in some way?"

"Oh, he'll react all right. That's guaranteed."

"How can you be so certain?"

"Because we're playing his game, even using his rules ... play a sneaky trick and time it for maximum advantage. The game now is to try to guess what he'll do next."

"Any ideas about that, Marnie?" said George.

"Well ... he's bound to have a number of plans for *legitimate* action ... things relating to his election campaign ... provocative public meetings, inflammatory speeches, offensive press releases ... everything possible to stir up public opinion, keeping just within the law. But he might also have some dirty tricks up his sleeve."

"He'll have to be careful," said George. "He can't afford to be seen to be personally involved in anything disreputable or violent. We've seen how he thinks with this first stunt. He's tried to portray himself as a victim, putting the blame on the black community."

"He doesn't need to do anything personally," said Marnie. "He's got a whole army of thugs backing him, remember. He can keep his distance from all that and just say it's a symptom of the troubled age we live in ... the whites being compelled to defend themselves from black aggression."

Serena groaned with exasperation. "This is a nightmare. All we've got is a kids' playscheme."

"Not quite," said George. "We've also got a secret weapon."

"We have?"

"Of course. We've got Marnie on our side."

"Huh!" Marnie exclaimed weakly from the back seat. "I don't want to worry you two, but I haven't got a single idea about what to do next."

"There may be something we can do." Serena sounded determined. "We can beef up the programme with more outings ... keep the kids away from potential trouble for as long as we can all summer."

They drove on for a few miles in silence, and George, adjusting the rear-view mirror, could see that the *secret weapon* was lying back against the head-rest with her eyes closed. He kicked himself mentally for putting extra pressure on her. Beside him, Serena was looking out of the window, her expression blank, a small portable grey cloud hovering above her head. He racked his brain to find a master plan that would solve all their problems, but imagination had never been his strong point.

At the familiar sign he turned off the dual carriageway and headed for home, a feeling of anti-climax enveloping the car as he took the country road that led to the village high street.

"George?"

The sudden sound of his name coming from behind made him start. "What is it, Marnie?"

"Can you stop at the school?"

"I was going to take you both to Glebe Farm. It's no trouble."

"To Glebe –? Oh, no … I need a word with Margaret Giles. Are you free this evening, George, early on, say around six o'clock?"

"I think so … probably … I suppose … don't think I've got any plans …"

"What about you, Serena? Would that be difficult with the children?"

"I'd need to check with Rod. Would it be for the whole evening?"

"I haven't thought that far ahead. Tell me, when does the summer scheme actually start? Is it next week?"

"Monday. Why?"

"Monday," Marnie repeated to herself. "Blimey! Oh well …"

The whole school seemed to be in the playground when the Range Rover pulled up outside. There was some sort of competition, with all the children wearing coloured sashes of red, green, blue or yellow. One of the teachers, armed with a whistle, was controlling some kind of relay race that involved running with an enormous inflated beach ball. The noise level was impressive, matching the enthusiasm of the competitors and spectators. Stepping inside the school gate, Marnie waved to attract the attention of the head teacher who was standing near the finish line with the school secretary. Margaret detached herself and came over, accepting Marnie's invitation onto the pavement.

They spoke for a few minutes, Margaret listening carefully. She finally nodded and took her leave with a smile. George insisted that he convey his *ladies* down to Glebe Farm.

• • • • •

Thank goodness for Anne, Marnie thought, as she sat on the platform in the school hall watching the parents and staff trickle in. Walker and Co had been kept operating that day by a girl who was barely seventeen, but who had managed the office, dealt with correspondence and kept the builders happy while she, Marnie, had spent half the day gallivanting and trying to save the world. *Get real, Marnie, you've got a business to run!* Now, there was Anne distributing leaflets to everyone arriving, with a cheerful word for them all.

Beside her on the platform, Serena and Margaret Giles were going through the list of activities planned for the first week of the summer holidays. The typed programme now contained several additions that Serena had marked in pencil with arrows in the margin.

Marnie leaned sideways and spoke softly. "Serena, it may be a little late for raising this, but can you actually afford to provide all these extra trips?

I mean, coaches don't come cheap."

"The question is, Marnie, can we afford not to provide them?"

"That's what Ralph would call a politician's answer." Marnie smiled ruefully. "You haven't got a budget, have you?"

Serena spoke quietly but firmly. "I'd sooner face the consequences of a reprimand or a sacking by the education authority than the possibility of a street war with New Force."

"I wonder if that's what Ralph would call a statesman's answer," said Margaret Giles.

In the body of the hall there was much talk of the front page George Stubbs article and when he walked in, every head turned to follow him as he made his way nonchalantly to the platform, kissed Serena and Marnie on both cheeks and took a seat in the middle of the front row beside Luther and Ralph. Estelle was delayed, waiting for a phone call from Italy, and would arrive when she could.

When the meeting got underway, the head teacher welcomed the company and invited Marnie to *say a few words*. Marnie wasted no time. She explained that a more ambitious programme was now planned for the summer scheme and introduced Serena to go through the arrangements. It was while Serena was talking that Marnie heard running feet outside. From her elevated position on the platform, she had a glimpse through the hall windows of rapid movement in the playground. There was a muffled crash from the front door. Seconds later one of the doors into the hall swung outwards and remained open. Marnie tensed, seeing in the shadows a dark shape, fearing for an instant that someone was going to throw a fire bomb into the gathering.

The audience were oblivious of the action behind them, but Anne, from her seat at the end of the front row, picked up on Marnie's anxiety. She got up quietly and stood at the side as if in readiness to give out more leaflets. Casually, she turned to look in the direction of the entrance, but was badly placed to see through into the lobby. Whoever was there was shielded from her by the door.

On the platform Marnie hoped that no one was aware of her concern. She was alarmed that Anne might go to investigate, but at the moment their eyes met, the door swung shut with a clatter. As unobtrusively as she could, Anne walked calmly to the rear of the hall and slipped quietly out. Marnie's anxiety abated as she glimpsed more high speed movement in the playground. This time she had a clear view of the runner. Sprinting across the tarmac in grey sweatshirt and black jeans was Donovan Smith, who broke stride for an instant to hurl something behind him. To Marnie's relief, there was no explosion, and Anne returned to her seat as if nothing had happened. The only outward difference was that she was carrying a folded newspaper.

· · · · ·

There was the usual milling about at the end of the meeting, with several parents clustered around Serena. A few others were speaking with George, who was relishing his new-found glory. Some latecomers were gathered round Anne, asking for the new programme, and Marnie was collared by Sylvia Wilkinson, the mother she had met at the previous meeting, wanting reassurance about the safety of the summer scheme. The caretaker made his rounds, conspicuously checking that all doors were closed, jangling his keys. The hint was taken, and the participants began drifting towards the exit. Serena was heard laughing, and Marnie turned to see her across the hall with a hand on Luther's shoulder, the two of them sharing a joke that had convulsed them. With her attention diverted, Marnie almost walked into Estelle who swept in, breathless.

"Have I missed everything? *Damn!* I drove up that field like the Safari Rally to get here."

Her eyes scanned the hall. Marnie fixed on her.

"Estelle, when you drove up, did you see anybody in the field?"

"Did I ...? Gosh, *yes*. Some bloody idiot on a bike. I was just pulling out from the yard when I saw him ... bouncing down the track. He turned off before the spinney."

"Did you get a good look at the bike? Was it yellow?"

"Can't be sure. I was in a hurry. Where's Luther?"

"With Ralph over there." Marnie indicated with her head.

Estelle stared. "Then Ralph must have had an operation. Quite a change. It suits him."

Luther was walking slowly across the hall with Serena, the two of them still grinning together, her hand now on his elbow as she spoke confidingly in his ear.

Estelle continued. "So, it all seems to have gone well. Serena looks relaxed about things."

"Yes. The new programme's even more exciting. The kids'll have a lovely time."

"I'm sure they will."

Goodbyes were said outside the door, and parents and teachers hurried away to their commitments. The Glebe Farm contingent gathered to one side.

"How nice of you to come, Estelle." Serena reached forward and touched her arm. "Especially when you won't even be around for the scheme."

"That's fine. I wanted to show solidarity and wish you well."

Like the other parents, Serena said that she too had to rush. She blew everyone a collective kiss and sped across the playground to her car.

"I've also got transport," said Estelle. "Who'd like a lift?"

It was decided that Estelle would take Luther home, and the others would walk. As soon as they were out of the gate, Marnie turned to Anne and pointed at the newspaper.

"What was that about? Did you see Donovan? Did he give you the paper?"

"He just took off. I saw him all right, or at least the smoke coming from his tyres."

"Er ..." Marnie gave her A Look.

"Well, perhaps that was an exaggeration. He was certainly in a hurry. The paper was on the ground outside the door."

"Someone else could have dropped it," Ralph commented.

"When I picked it up it was warm, like it had been in his back pocket. I almost had the feeling ..."

"Go on." Marnie's expression changed to encouragement. She knew what she had seen.

"I dunno ... It was as if he'd left it for me."

She unfolded it to reveal the photograph of George and Serena on the front page. If Donovan had wanted them to know about their statement, he was long out-of-date. Passing a waste bin to collect the detritus that attended the ice cream van in summer, Anne reached out to deposit the paper. Marnie and Ralph had gone three paces when they realised that Anne was no longer with them. They stopped and looked back. She was reading an inside page.

"Anne? We've got a copy of that in the office if you want to read it."

Anne shook her head slowly, but did not look up.

"What is it?" Marnie persisted. "Anne?"

Still holding the paper open, Anne caught them up. There was urgency in her voice.

"This is different. It's a later edition, the final. I noticed the lead story had changed, so I checked it out. And look at this."

She held up the front page. At the end of George's statement was a footnote. *Ex-MP's complaint. Brandon's Manifesto. See page five.* Someone had circled it in black ink. Anne turned to the article. Beside a photograph of Garth Brandon was a short piece in which he criticised the police for *bowing to intimidation from immigrant factions* and releasing all the suspects being held for questioning about the *brutal and unprovoked attack on my life.* He added that this was symptomatic of the way that English society was being backed into a corner. *We can no longer enjoy freedom of speech in our own country for fear that the politically correct lobby will hound us for infringing rules that they – the minority – have imposed on all decent British people. Our natural tolerance and fair-mindedness have been turned against us as a weapon.*

"He doesn't miss a trick, does he?" said Marnie.

"What's that about a manifesto?" Ralph asked.

Anne opened the paper wide. "It's this next part: *The Shadwell Declaration.* It's a bit long to read out."

Ralph looked over Anne's shoulder. "Can you just pick out the main points?"

"He calls it his *Credo* ... er ... immigration controls ... bla-bla-bla ... non-acceptance of asylum-seekers ... pull Britain out of the CAP ..."

"The European Common Agricultural Policy," Ralph commented.

"Uh-huh ... bla-bla-bla ... investment grants and subsidies for UK firms ... *let the Eurocrats try to stop us* ... lottery money to finance low-cost housing." Anne looked up. "That doesn't sound like a bad idea."

"Read on a little further," Ralph muttered.

"Oh ... for people whose grandparents were born in this country. That's a bit different. Five pounds per week extra for pensioners."

"If they were born in Britain?" Marnie asked.

"You've got the idea."

"I'm a fast learner."

Anne read on. "Slash upper tax bands and make the UK a tax haven to encourage enterprise."

"He must still have a lot of rich friends." Ralph did not look as if he was joking.

"And investments," Marnie added.

Anne looked up. "Shall I carry on?"

"I think we've got the picture."

"Hang on ... just a sec ... there's another black circle."

"Five pounds for everyone who votes for Brandon, by any chance?" Marnie's voice was dripping with scorn.

"Ten pounds, actually," Anne muttered. "No, seriously, this bit's about New Force. They're condemning the police for trivialising the attack on Brandon and doing nothing to find his attackers."

"So they've become plural now," Ralph murmured. "What part of their statement has been circled?"

"Apparently they reserve the right to take action – *even pre-emptive action* – against any organisation they suspect of planning to attack them or their values."

"Ah ..." Ralph was sombre.

Marnie grabbed his arm. "What?"

"Tell me, Marnie, is it common knowledge that the summer scheme is going to be based in that school?"

"Garfield Primary? Yes. It was announced in the press a while ago, after the community centre was fire-bombed the second ..." Marnie's voice tailed off. "Oh, God. You don't think ...?"

"Attacking their values," Anne repeated. "Do you think Donovan brought this up for us to see?"

"Strange way of delivering it," said Marnie. "Come on, let's go home."

She linked arms with Ralph and Anne as they set off towards the field track, no doubt in her mind about what Donovan had done.

"Why was it called the Shadwell Declaration?" Anne asked.

"It's that district in Docklands," said Marnie. "It's where Brandon lives in London, isn't it Ralph? Was it his constituency when he was an MP?"

"Yes and no. I believe he has a rather nice house there near the river. But his constituency was in the midlands, if I remember rightly."

"That's not a million miles north of here ... and he has contacts there."

Reaching the field, they went through the gate.

"It was strange ..." Anne began. "An odd way to deliver the news ... but I'm sure that's what Donovan was trying to do. He wanted us to know about this Shadwell thingy."

"The rest to some faint meaning make pretence," Ralph intoned, *"But Shadwell rarely deviates into sense."*

"What's that?" Marnie asked. "Do I take it you aren't greatly impressed by Mr Brandon's manifesto?"

"It's John Dryden, the eighteenth century poet. He came from Northamptonshire, you know. And no ... *impressed* isn't the word. The whole thing is codswallop."

"Dangerous, divisive codswallop," Marnie added.

They fell silent, each thinking of what word they would use to sum up their feelings about Brandon's statement.

Anne folded the newspaper. "When we get back, I'm going to ask Donovan why he came up to the school."

But she did not ask him. When they emerged from the spinney and reached the boats, they looked across to *X O 2*'s mooring. It was empty. Donovan had gone.

20

Tuesday began badly. Marnie was closing the office door behind her when she heard a car coming down the track. Anne saw her expression through the window and came out to join her.

"What's up?"

"That's what's up."

A grey Vauxhall rolled to a halt in its usual place, and two men got out. Chief Inspector Bartlett and Sergeant Marriner. They rarely brought good news.

"What is it this time?" Marnie muttered under her breath.

"Probably looking for more strange characters," Anne whispered.

"I wonder how much time they've got. They could be here all day."

Suppressing a smile, Anne went back into the office. Marnie greeted the detectives.

"Good morning, Mrs Walker. Nice day."

"What can I do for you, gentlemen?"

"Nothing, nothing at all ... unless there's something you want to confess."

"I'll go and chain myself to the wall while you fetch the tongs and thumbscrew."

She regretted it as soon as she had spoken. Marnie had learnt a Golden Rule. Never make jokes with the police. They had a way of having the last laugh.

"Sorry, I'm being facetious." She attempted a smile and added, "Sign of a clear conscience."

"Or the opposite," said Bartlett.

"Shall we start again? If there's nothing I can do for you, presumably someone else can help?"

"We've come to see Miss Estelle Greenwood and Mr Luther Curtiss. I believe they live here. Are they available?"

Marnie raised an arm in the direction of cottage number three. As she did so, an upstairs window opened, and Estelle called out.

"Would you be Mr Bartlett and Mr Marriner? I'll come down and let you in. Hi, Marnie. We're being interviewed about the incident we witnessed in Leicester."

"That was ages ago."

"Just a routine follow-up," Bartlett said crisply.

"Right. I'll leave you to it."

Marnie set off to see Bob the foreman in the farmhouse site, feeling as uncomfortable as always when the local CID were around. Sergeant Marriner nodded at her as she walked past. He spoke quietly.

"We'll be over with the tongs afterwards, Marnie. Nice to have something to look forward to ..."

•　•　•　•　•

It was almost an hour before Marnie spotted Bartlett and Marriner leaving Estelle's cottage and walking to their car. They reversed out of the yard and went on their way.

The detectives had barely been gone a minute when Estelle flitted across the yard to land on the corner of Marnie's desk.

"Are these people *real*?" She gave an exasperated sigh.

"Do I take it you have upheld the noble traditions of Glebe Farm in helping the police with their enquiries ... or not, as the case may be?"

"*Did you take down the car's registration number, Miss Greenwood? I mean ... what kind of dumb-ass question is that?*"

"Interesting reply."

"It was dark, it all happened very quickly and we were jumping out of our skins that it was going to smash into us!"

"But you could identify the make, presumably?"

"Ah ... well ... Cars aren't my strong point ... but I thought it was a Golf like mine. Then again, most cars look the same these days."

"So you were just able to tell them what colour it was."

"Colour?" Estelle looked shamefaced. "Well, you know what it's like under street lights ... but I could tell it was dark ... ish."

"What about Luther? Did he get a sight of it?"

Estelle shrugged. "I think they thought he was worse than me."

"Is that possible?"

"Thanks, Marnie."

"No. I mean ... you couldn't tell them anything. How can it get worse than that?"

"Luther said he thought it was a BMW ... black, or maybe dark blue, with fancy alloy wheels ... and er ... silver wheel arches."

"I don't think I've ever seen a BMW of that design," Marnie mused.

"Marriner said he thought it might've been a trick of the street lighting. Bartlett seemed to think Luther made it up ... trying to be helpful ... about as helpful as if he was describing Chitty-Chitty-Bang-Bang."

A snigger came from the other side of the office. "Sorry," said Anne.

Contemplating the police's star eye-witness, Marnie could understand why Bartlett probably put Glebe Farm in the same category of usefulness as a Black Hole in outer space or the Bermuda Triangle.

The rest of that week became a running battle. It was played out in the modern way, not with armies of thugs marching the streets. That could come later. This battle was fought through the media.

Brandon was quick off the mark with a follow-up statement to his manifesto, stressing the need to look after 'our own people'. Anne cut the item out of the newspaper and began keeping a scrap-book of cuttings. As the campaign wore on it became increasingly useful as a record of what had been said and for planning the next move.

The statement was in the noon edition of the evening paper that Anne had fetched from the shop. She ordered a copy from Molly Appleton every day until further notice. Over a hasty sandwich the three of them scoured the paper, searching for anything relevant to their battle with Brandon, the BFP and New Force.

Anne marked up the articles in felt-tip pen. "That's everything about Brandon in this edition." She spread the page open on Marnie's drawing board.

"Anything interesting from the other candidates?" Ralph asked.

"Various statements about policy matters. They seem to be keeping out of the racial argument."

"That's what I'd expect, but they're worth monitoring in case there's a sudden change in direction."

"Is that likely?" said Marnie.

"If they think Brandon's running away with the election and leaving them behind, they'll feel obliged to join in. He'd like nothing better. It would show he was calling the shots."

"I think I'll keep a separate folder of cuttings about them, then." Anne folded the other pages.

Ralph moved in closer. "So what's he saying?"

Anne began reading aloud. "He says his policies mean no harm to any other people … *but no country in the world could afford not to protect its own national identity.* There's a bit about Norman Tebbitt and the cricket test. He says you can tell who is really assimilated into British life by the country they support in a test match. *Do you cheer for India or for England, Pakistan or the MCC?*" Anne was puzzled. "What's that got to do with anything?"

"He's saying that people who move to Britain should support everything British. It's a simple proposition that everyone can understand … dangerously simple."

"But it's silly, Ralph. Look at Luther and his family. They're completely settled here, but you wouldn't expect them to cheer for England against the West Indies, if only for sentimental reasons."

Marnie put a hand on Anne's shoulder. "Brandon can't fool you with dubious logic, but he'll be trying every trick in the book."

"Then it won't work because we're all jumbled up in Britain."

"That's part of his attack," said Ralph, smiling. "He wants all the blond-haired, blue-eyed English people – like you – to vote against the swarthy foreign intruders."

Anne laughed. "Then he's in for a surprise. My grandpa Price lived in London nearly all his adult life, but he spoke Welsh with his family – except my nan who was English – and always wore his daffodil on Saint David's day."

"Did he watch rugby matches?"

"What do you think?"

Marnie looked at her watch. "So what do we do next, and by when?"

Ralph reached for a notepad. "I think we should draft something straight away, agree it with Serena and fax it to the paper. We might get it in the late edition."

"Saying?"

"We have to refute Brandon's argument. Why not use Anne's example about Welsh rugby? It would do the job and keep us away from the black-and-white racist line."

"OK. I'll ring Serena, make sure we're not cutting across anything she might be doing."

Anne offered Ralph her computer, and the Glebe Farm political machine hummed into action.

• • • • •

They did not wait for the evening paper to be delivered. Anne went up in the Mini to collect it. There was good news and bad news. Their statement made it to page three. It was short and pithy and was printed in full. The problem was on the front page. An opinion poll carried out the previous day showed Brandon's rating up by three points since he arrived in town.

Marnie was distraught. "*Damn!* What's going on?"

Ralph was unperturbed. "Don't worry. These things are just a snapshot. It means no more than that people recognise his name. And don't forget, there's a plus-or-minus tolerance of about five per cent."

"Great. So it could be worse than we think."

Anne set herself the task of monitoring the local news bulletins and had the radio playing quietly on her desk. While Marnie and Ralph prepared supper on *Sally Ann*, she watched the TV news in her attic room. When the BBC's Look East programme came on, and the newsreaders announced a survey of opinion for the European election, Anne phoned through to Marnie and Ralph who scrambled on board *Thyrsis* to catch the item, while Anne set her VCR to record it.

The reporter stood in Northampton's main shopping street asking passers-by what they felt about the 'cricket test'. Opinions were divided, with some thinking it reasonable for 'incomers' to support their 'old country', while others believed they should support the country they had adopted as home. Marnie was just muttering that this was getting nowhere, when the interviewer produced an elderly man in the market square, describing him as a veteran of Dunkirk and the Second World War, a Mr Huw Parry-Thomas.

"You've lived in Northampton for over fifty years now. What do you do, sir, when Wales play England at rugby?"

A smile spread across the old man's face, and he drew himself up to his full height, which was far from impressive, and looked into the camera, speaking with a strong South Wales valleys accent. "I wear my leek with pride."

Ralph clenched his fist. Anne sniffed and wiped a tear from her eye. Marnie wanted to hug him.

21

Brandon was back on the offensive the next day. He started a series of tours round the county, speaking in market squares and village halls, spreading his poison. Leaflets were dropped through every letter-box by an army of supporters, each dressed soberly with neat hair-cuts and clean shoes. It looked like the invasion of the Jehovah's Witnesses. No trace was seen of the thugs associated with New Force. Brandon's banner was a union flag draped over a portable lectern that he used for every speech. His backdrop was a Transit van bearing on its side in big letters the slogan: Put Britain First!

Anne lugged her portable TV down to stand on her desk so that they could watch the news at lunchtime. Anglia ran a report on the election trail, featuring sound bite interviews with the main party candidates. They caught up with Brandon who mysteriously until that moment had been elusive somewhere in the north of the county. His three minutes live in front of the camera stole the show. He delivered a short sharp attack on the European Union.

It has led our country to being run by hordes of unelected, faceless bureaucrats in Brussels who have nothing better to do than put a ban on curved bananas. (Weak smile.) *They want to abolish our favourite chocolate because it doesn't conform to some spurious standards and subsidise inefficient European farmers so that they can dump cheap, low-quality produce on the British market as a means of weakening our economy. It's time Britain woke up, time we took back control of our own lives, our own future.*

All of this was said in a firm but moderate tone talking direct to camera. The interviewer suggested that his line was regarded as extreme by commentators and opponents alike. Brandon smiled condescendingly, replying in the same reasonable tone.

I followed the same line when I was a government minister under Mrs Thatcher. I have never wavered. This is not extremism. It's common sense. I challenge anyone to debate with me in public the question of who can best serve Britain's interests. Let my opponents from the other parties stand up and be counted, and let public opinion decide. I trust the British people and I will accept their judgment.

"Blimey, that's depressing," Marnie muttered.

"He's very persuasive," Anne agreed.

Ralph seemed less impressed. "Old-fashioned rhetoric. None of it original. The wake-up call was Hitler's line: *Deutschland erwache. Trust the people,* was what Thatcher said."

"And she never lost an election," Marnie pointed out.

The TV news bulletin saved the best till last. According to a poll carried out that morning, Brandon had slipped back two points since the last survey. Marnie called it the *Parry-Thomas factor*, but Ralph was more cautious, reminding her about the margin of fluctuation. The differences were too small to be significant.

Marnie seemed unsettled. "I wish we weren't stuck in the middle of all this. I wish Brandon would just go away ... leave us in peace ... take all his nasty thugs with him."

"You could get away," Anne began. "You could have a break in Italy with Estelle, if things are getting you down. I can hold the fort for a few days."

"Oh, Anne ... I didn't really mean ..." Marnie shook herself and sat up straight. "Right. Come on, Marnie. Pull yourself together!" She smiled. "So. What's our next move?"

"We counter-attack as before," said Ralph. "I'll draft another reply."

"It'll be hard countering that performance," Marnie said.

"No. It's easy. We can hit back with a few facts ... there are fewer civil servants in Brussels for the whole of the EU than in one major ministry in London ... every EU country needs the UK to have a strong economy so it can buy and sell in the market place to build a sound Europe ... the curved bananas thing was nothing but a tabloid distortion."

"Pity we can't find Mr Parry-Thomas and wheel him out to say all that. Facts aren't very compelling just by themselves. We need something a bit sexier."

"How about Serena?"

The sound of Luther's voice made them turn sharply. He was in the doorway with Estelle looking up at him.

"Come in," said Marnie. "You may have a point there. She's certainly more striking than George Stubbs."

Anne laughed.

"She's sexy as hell," said Luther. "She'd be ideal."

"I'm not so sure," Estelle interjected. "Would you really want to push her into the spotlight?"

Luther shrugged. "Why not?"

"Well, not to put too fine a point on it … she's black."

"Excuse me?"

"Actually, Estelle may be right there." It was Ralph. "First, we'd be opening up a straight black versus white argument. Brandon would love that. It might not be wise. Also, we could be putting her at risk."

Marnie ran a hand through her hair. "Who, then? Any ideas?"

"What about me? On behalf of the Community Alliance, of course."

Everyone looked at Estelle.

"*You?*" Luther was incredulous.

"Sure. Why not? Aren't I sexy enough?"

"No, it's just …" He looked around as if trying to find inspiration. "I mean … in a way it's not your fight. And you've only just arrived here. Nobody knows you."

"That's my advantage. I'd be hard to track down … just a spokesperson for the community. I'm not on the electoral roll or even in the phone book. And don't forget, I'm about to leave the country for several days."

"No comebacks," said Marnie.

Ralph nodded. "I'll get on with that statement."

· · · · ·

Marnie spent the early part of the afternoon in discussion with Estelle. They went through the Umbria project room by room, while Anne fielded incoming calls and did her best to follow progress on the drawing board. The draft design was ready, and Estelle would visit the house to make sure everything hung together, before putting the scheme to their client. Marnie was delighted with Estelle, her flair, her sense of space, and was telling Estelle what she thought of her work when Anne called across the room.

"Can you take a call from Serena, Marnie?"

Estelle sighed. Marnie recognised it as a hint of impatience.

"Er … can I call her back shortly?" She inclined her head towards Estelle.

"I told her you were in a meeting, but she sounded as if it was urgent."

Estelle nodded, and Marnie went to her desk to pick up. Anne pressed the buttons.

"Hi Serena. How are things?"

"Marnie, is there any chance of a meeting this afternoon?" Her voice was leaden.

"Well …"

"I wouldn't ask if it wasn't serious."

"Of course. What's bothering you?"

"Not on the phone."

Serena's tone left Marnie in no doubt that whatever was on her mind could not wait.

"OK. When do you want to come?"

"Could you come up here ... to Garfield Primary School?"

Marnie paused. "What time?"

"Around four, half past?"

"I'll be there. Shall I bring Ralph?"

"Bring the Seventh Cavalry."

• • • • •

Garfield Primary School was a single-storey red-brick cluster of buildings set in a sea of tarmac playground near the town centre. It was built around 1900 at a time when institutions were meant to last for ever. Headings were carved in stone over the main doorways: Boys, Girls, Infants, Babies.

When the cars drew up to park by the office entrance, the children and teachers had departed. Marnie had mustered a fair squadron of the 'Seventh Cavalry'. In the Discovery she brought Ralph, Anne and Ronny. George Stubbs transported Margaret Giles, Estelle and Luther in the Range Rover. With the military associations of Land Rover and their colour schemes of dark green and Marnie's favourite navy blue, they had a look of 'combined operations' about them.

Serena was standing outside the main entrance to guide them in. She looked cool and business-like in a light blue denim trouser suit, but she did not look happy. They went to the staff room where she had set the chairs in a circle. Once they were all seated, she paused before speaking.

"You've had a death threat," said Ralph.

His quiet tone of voice made the words all the more chilling. Everyone looked at him in surprise. Serena nodded. There was a collective intake of breath.

"When was this?" said Marnie.

"I had a phone call in the office this morning. It was a man."

"Is it possible you might be mistaken?"

"I don't think so."

"Can you remember the exact words he used?"

"I'll never forget them. You want the full version? He said ... *you're dead, you black bitch, you're fucking dead.* That was all he said."

"Not much room for doubt, there." Marnie's voice was almost a whisper. "Quite a shocker."

"Yes."

Margaret Giles began, "Serena, we'd all quite understand –"

"There's no question." Serena cut her off. "I wouldn't have asked you all to come here if I was going to pull out. I've always known this could happen."

"What do you want to do?" Marnie asked.

"We must make sure you don't feature as a figure-head in our actions," said Ralph. "We've already been talking about how we spread the load as far as statements to the press are concerned."

"That's good. But I still want to go on running the summer scheme programme. I'm not giving that up."

"A backroom job," George agreed. "Vital but not in the public eye."

"That's what I was thinking."

"It makes sense. Pity, though. You're prettier than I am."

The group smiled and looked at George with his balding head, bull neck and tweeds.

"Only marginally," said Marnie.

"Thank you, my dear."

During the faint laughter that followed this exchange, Anne leaned over and whispered in Marnie's ear.

"Shall I pop out and get the paper? There's a newsagent on the corner opposite."

Marnie nodded, and Anne quickly left the room as Luther started speaking.

"Don't worry, Serena. Your friends will protect you … day and night if necessary."

"That's one of the things that's worrying me."

"You think we should try and get you police protection?" said Estelle.

"Not that. I think the threat was just meant to frighten me … make me back off. No, it's the other implications that bother me."

"That's why you wanted us to come here," said Ralph. "You're worried about the security of the building."

"Yes. We've seen what New Force did to the community centre. I think they wouldn't hesitate to do the same to this school."

"Does the caretaker live on site?"

"No. Worse luck. He's the other side of town."

"So it's up to us," said Marnie. "Unless we can get the police to keep an eye on the building."

George shook his head. "I doubt they'd have the manpower to mount a guard round the clock. And that's what you need."

"Let's just think about that, George. What do we have to do to make the building secure?"

Ralph opened the bidding. "At the least, ideally, we'd need someone here to raise the alarm if anyone tried to attack the place."

"The school's occupied during the day," said Marnie.

In the background they could hear the sounds of cleaners moving tables and chairs. A vacuum cleaner was humming in some distant corner.

"The head and secretary will probably be around until about five on most days," Margaret observed.

"But not in the school holidays."

"No."

"And not at weekends," Ralph muttered.

"Weekends," Serena repeated. "I'd been thinking we might need to do something starting next week. I was going to get Rod to drive round in the car last thing at night just to check that all was well."

Anne opened the door and returned to her seat beside Ronny, holding the evening edition of the paper. Unobtrusively, she set it on her lap and started scanning it, pen in hand.

Ralph stood up and looked out of the window. "It's a very open site, though it's overlooked on all sides by houses."

George turned in his seat. "We can't rely on someone looking out during the night and happening to spot some villains preparing to throw a petrol bomb."

Ralph sat down. "I just thought it might be a deterrent. I can't see the education authority allowing someone to stay here overnight."

"Who said anything about asking them?" Serena.

"Well, you are an officer of the authority, aren't you, Serena? You're part of the Youth Service."

"Yes, I am. That doesn't mean I have to ask questions when I know the answer will be negative. But it does mean ... I can get access to keys to the building."

"And I have inflatable mattresses and sleeping bags on *Sally Ann*," Marnie added.

"I don't think I've heard any of this," said Margaret Giles, head teacher of one of the authority's schools.

Marnie changed the subject. "Anything in the newspaper, Anne?"

Anne pulled a face. "Barely a mention of our statement ... just a few lines on page seven."

"Anything else?"

Anne held up the front page. It looked as if it had been designed by Josef Goebbels. Under the headline, *BRANDON TARGETS SCROUNGERS*, was a photograph of the BFP candidate standing on the roof of a car, holding a megaphone, addressing a crowd in the middle of Kettering. That afternoon's statement singled out *so-called refugees and asylum-seekers*, who were in reality nothing more than *economic migrants, flooding into our country to line their pockets.*

"What the hell is the paper playing at?" Marnie was indignant. "They can't be on the side of Brandon and his cronies. Whatever happened to balanced reporting?"

"We're up against a sharp cookie," said Ralph. "He pins us down with statements that demand boring factual replies, and while we're dealing with them, he hits the press with sound bites."

"The other parties get coverage on page three." Anne opened the paper. "But it's all defensive ... boring, like Ralph says ... statistics and stuff."

"Brilliant," Serena said bitterly. "That's all we need."

"Do you want the bad news or the worse news?"

Everyone stared at Ronny.

"There's *worse*?" said Marnie.

He nodded. "The bad news is that Brandon has jumped five points in the ratings. The three main parties have all gone down."

"Tell us the worst."

Anne held up the next page. "New Force have lodged an official complaint with the Home Office about a march in Northampton being banned by the police. They say they're being victimised and will not be held responsible for any consequences."

It was breath-exhaling time again.

"New Force," Serena muttered. "My death threat's no coincidence, is it? We can't leave the building empty for the whole weekend."

"This could be dangerous." Margaret Giles looked grim. "What if we did have someone here, and New Force tried to burn the place down? They could be injured ... or worse."

"It's all at ground floor level." Marnie was in planning mode. "There are smoke alarms … extinguishers … fire doors. It's not that risky. All we'd need is someone to be here to call for help if anyone suspicious showed up. We could have two people at a time, one sleeping, the other keeping watch."

George shifted uneasily in his seat. "I've got a committee meeting on Friday evening, and we're going to dinner at my sister's in Warwick on Sunday evening … not back till late."

"Anyone else got commitments?" Marnie asked. "And we realise you can't be involved in this, Margaret. That's understood."

"Damn," Luther murmured. "We've got tickets for Friday night in London."

"We could cancel if you want us to, Marnie," said Estelle. "We were planning to stay at the flat in Barnet and come back Saturday morning."

"No. Stick to your plans," said Marnie. "I wanted to do the first stint anyway, to try it out. I'll do Friday night."

"Me too," said Ralph.

Anne frowned. "Shouldn't someone keep an eye on Glebe Farm?"

"Good point."

"Shall I come with you then, Marnie?"

"That would leave Ralph at home."

"That's fine," he agreed.

"I could come for a night," said Ronny. "Count me in."

Serena smiled at him. "Thank you."

They worked out a roster to share surveillance duties, all of them realising that the stakes had changed. On top of all the riots and bombings, it felt as if they were on a war footing. Marnie, who had faced more than her share of violence over the past year or two, looked at the others as they made their plans, wondering if they understood the pressures that would weigh on them in the weeks ahead. A sense of foreboding gripped her by the throat. She felt a desperate need to lighten the atmosphere.

"Why don't we go for a drink?" she blurted out to her own surprise and the evident astonishment of the others.

"A drink?" Estelle repeated.

"Why not?" Luther flashed a brilliant white smile. "Marnie's right. We need to chill out."

• • • • •

As town centre pubs went, it was pleasant enough with a mock-Victorian cosiness, renowned for brewing its own beer in a small glazed outbuilding at the rear. At that time of the day it was not too busy. They congregated round a table in a corner, a group of strange bedfellows to any casual observer.

Marnie stared into her sparkling water. "We're losing the initiative. Brandon's setting the agenda, and everyone's dancing to his tune."

"And he's popping up everywhere," Margaret added. "He's all over the place, north, south, east, west."

"The human angle … that's the way to get him."

They all looked at Ralph.

"What do you mean?" said Serena. "We don't want to put more people in danger."

"We don't have to. We need ordinary people … like that old Welsh boy and his leek … human faces that give the lie to Brandon's message of hate. He depends on … *them, faceless bureaucrats, anonymous immigrants, foreigners.* Once they're seen as real people, leading normal lives as citizens, workers and neighbours, Brandon's lost his advantage."

"Where do we find these normal people?" Margaret asked.

"Anywhere. Immigrants have served Britain for centuries. Think of the institutions they've kept going. In hospitals they're everything from consultants and nurses to porters and cleaners."

"My nan said her doctors saved her life when she had pneumonia," Anne joined in.

"Where did they come from?"

"India … or maybe Pakistan. I'm not sure which."

"People came from the old empire," said Ralph. "And they often took on jobs that the locals did not want to do. If we can show the human faces, Brandon's lies won't stick."

"You're right, of course." Luther was squeezed in between Serena and Estelle. "Look at the sports stars playing for Britain. Lots of them are black. Even the most ordinary people will have interesting stories to tell. Won't they, Serena?"

"Such as?" said Estelle.

"I bet you've got interesting stories to tell." George was the other side of Serena, doing his best to be squeezed up against her.

"But I don't want to be in the foreground," she protested. "We want the local TV news to show people like your old Welsh guy … a friendly face."

"We've got the picture," said Marnie. They were going over the same ground. It was time to lighten up. "Tell us about your family, Luther."

"Everyone knows about my family."

"No, I mean the ordinary side … how they came to Britain, how they settled in, where they lived."

Luther fell silent for a few reflective moments and then chuckled to himself.

"Come on, Luther." Serena patted his hand encouragingly.

"Well … I was born here and I've never lived anywhere else, but I did hear stories when I was a kid about what it was like when the family came over from Barbados. My dad used to tell me them when I was little."

Serena laughed. "*Little*? I thought you were six feet tall at birth!"

He grinned. "Only just."

"Get on with your story," said Estelle.

"My favourite one was how they bought their houses. People came for a better life and they wanted their own homes, so they formed house clubs. In those days you needed a thousand pounds to put down as a deposit. If you could save fifty pounds a month, in twenty months you had it."

"You had to work hard to do that," said George. "That was good money."

"Oh yes. Everybody worked hard. But that was OK. They came here for a better life and they were prepared to go for it."

"So … house clubs," Marnie reminded him.

"Right. You got a group of twenty families together. Each month, they all put fifty pounds in the pot. Then they drew lots. Whoever won the draw got the pot and they had their deposit. At the worst, you had to wait twenty months, but you had to do that anyway."

"A housing co-operative," said Ralph.

"What if someone defaulted?" George asked.

"They never did."

"What, never?"

"No. You see, they had an insurance policy."

"Good lord," George exclaimed. "That's amazing. I never knew the insurance companies were in the market for that kind of business."

Luther chuckled. "Well no ... It's what you might call ... the *black market*."

"Sorry, I don't follow. You mean it involved some kind of fraud?"

"No. Not that kind of black market. Nobody was actually dishonest, but I don't suppose you could call them whiter than white." He was enjoying his joke.

"Come on, Luther." Marnie sounded impatient in a good-natured way. "What was this insurance policy? Spill the beans."

"It was simple. If anyone thought he'd pull out of the deal, the other nineteen members of the group would go round to where he lived and threaten to cut his legs off." Luther shrugged. "No problem."

Marnie grinned. "And that was the story he told you when he tucked you up in bed at night? Though I suppose it's no worse than Little Red Hiding Hood, when you think about it."

"Did you often have nightmares?" Anne asked.

Serena put an arm round Luther's shoulders, smiling broadly. "That's a good story, Luther." To Estelle she said, "Tell us about your family, how they came here. I bet you have some tales to tell."

Estelle suddenly became serious. "We try not to think about our background. The Holocaust doesn't make for good bedtime story-telling."

She sipped her drink. The air temperature cooled by several degrees.

George cleared his throat. "Look, I haven't said this before, but I think there's a real chance that Brandon could win this election."

"You're not serious?" Marnie studied his face.

"Like a lot of Tories I have to admit I'm something of a Euro-sceptic ... nothing fanatical, but I'd prefer us to run our own show rather than have Britain run from Brussels. I'd never leave the party, but in many ways I sympathised with Brandon's position when he quit."

"So is this difficult for you, George?"

"That's not what I'm saying, and I'll still do everything I can to help the summer scheme. I'm against fascism and prejudice, that's definite. But there is a problem with Brandon and the Tories, and it's why he's chosen to contest this particular seat."

"He thinks he can bomb his way to success," Serena interjected.

"He doesn't need to. His main opponents here are the Tories ... his main targets are middle-of-the-road, middle-income voters. They'll decide the result here."

"Why do you think Brandon can grab their votes?" Marnie asked. "Are you saying they're going to swallow his line ... that they're racists at heart?"

"No. To win, the Tories only have to get out their vote. The trouble is, the party activists are unlikely to give their candidate the whole-hearted support he needs. And why? Because Toby Creswell-Brown – apart from being wishy-washy and as bland as cream paint – once described Brandon as a national hero."

"You're kidding."

George shook his head. "That's why Brandon declared his candidature so late. He wanted to be sure he was up against a man who in normal circumstances would've been a natural ally. The party faithful aren't going to oppose someone they feel could well have been a successor to John Major as Prime Minister."

There was a sombre atmosphere surrounding the conspirators when they emerged from the pub. Pausing on the pavement before heading towards their cars, they did their best to buck themselves up and raise their spirits. It was then that they noticed the changes. The district had been transformed, as if a shower or a flash-flood had come while they were inside. The street had been colour-washed in red, white and blue. Every lamp-post had been decorated. Every tree was covered in posters. Some were in the form of union flags; others carried slogans; yet more had photographs. *Put Britain First!* Garth Brandon was everywhere.

• • • • •

"It's one thing deciding to use ordinary people to get the message across, but how do we make it happen?"

Marnie was tailing George's Range Rover past the medieval Queen Eleanor Cross up the hill out of town towards the main road home.

"When we get back I'll ring the newsdesk at the local radio and TV centres." Ralph turned to look round his headrest. "Anne, can you check the video recordings you made and give me the names of the reporters who covered the incidents."

"Sure. I've still got them on tape."

"What are you going to ask them?" Marnie sounded sceptical.

"I'm going to explain that they won't get any more interviews or statements from the community groups because of the threat of intimidation."

"Will that matter to them?"

"When I tell them about the death threat, I think it might get their attention."

Marnie flashed a glance sideways. "You think that's wise? You wouldn't mention Serena by name?"

"No, but I'll say I'm prepared to be quoted on that if necessary."

"You think that's a good idea?"

"They'd definitely believe Professor Lombard." It was Ronny from the back seat.

Anne looked at him with an expression he could not read. Marnie half turned to speak over her shoulder. "I didn't mean it like that, Ronny. I was thinking it might not be wise for Ralph to stick his head above the parapet with things as they are just now."

"And I was thinking," Ralph began, "what choice do we have? If anyone has a better idea, let's hear it."

The car was filled with silence. Ronny was wishing he could come up with a plan that everyone would think brilliant. Anne was making a mental list of all the things she and Marnie would need for Friday night. Marnie was going over what Ralph had said. *What choice do we have ...* How often had she been faced with that question? she asked herself.

• • • • •

Serena's troubled expression quickly turned to a beaming smile when she opened the front door and a little boy ran along the hallway to meet her, arms outstretched. She reached down to pick him up, and he threw his arms round her neck, squealing with delight.

"Joey, Joey, Joey!" she exclaimed, burying her face in the side of his head, twisting to left and right, back and forth.

The little boy shrieked and stretched his arms to the ceiling. The two of them laughed uproariously until Serena turned her son upside down and lowered him till he was performing a handstand. In the midst of this excitement a face looked out from the living room door.

"Hi mum! I see your master plan of getting Joey tired so that he'd be nice and calm hasn't quite worked out." She smiled and looked down at the infant, who was now trying to walk on his hands.

"No, but it's certainly worked on me." Serena's mother laughed wearily.

"Where's Charlie?"

"She's in here, colouring a picture in her book."

Beside Serena on the hall table the phone began ringing. Serena's mother dashed forward and took hold of Joey's ankles.

"That's probably Mr Murfitt from the education office. He's rung three times already."

While her mother righted Joey and carried him back to the living room, Serena took a deep breath and reached for the phone.

"Serena McDowell."

"Ah, Serena. At last. I've been trying to get hold of you."

"You've got my mobile number, Lee. I always carry it with me."

"We've got a problem." He paused for dramatic effect. "Or at least I think we have. I hope you're going to tell me there's been a misunderstanding."

"Try me."

"You don't know what I'm getting at?"

"I will, when you tell me what it is," Serena replied evenly.

He paused again. Serena joined in. Two could play at that game.

"The school holiday activities programme."

"The summer scheme ... yes."

"We see in the press that it's suddenly mushroomed into a much bigger programme than the one we planned."

"The committee's given more detail than we announced before and –"

"In the press, Serena. I've checked my in-tray and I don't see anything from you raising this with me ... as your line manager."

"I've been delegated to manage this project and take decisions in conjunction with the organising committee –"

"Within the approved budget."

"Right."

"And the committee chairperson tells me she has no knowledge of the financial implications of your new plans."

"She said that?"

"What are the financial implications, Serena? Exactly."

"I don't have the figures in front of me, Lee. I'm standing in the hall at home. I've only just come in from a meeting."

"Of course. It's unreasonable of me to expect that. So shall we discuss it at county hall? Perhaps you'd be good enough to see me tomorrow morning at nine-thirty. Meeting room C, ground floor."

"I don't have my diary open at the moment. I'm not sure what I'm doing –"

"I'm asking you to give this priority, Serena ... as your line manager."

"OK. I'll let you have some figures in the morning."

"Oh, I think we have to do better than that. We need to review the whole question of whether the scheme goes ahead."

"*Goes ahead*? It's been approved by the full council. You have no authority to stop it." Serena was determined to keep the conversation low-key, but could feel her breathing accelerate.

Lee Murfitt's voice was oily-smooth. "That's why the meeting will be attended by the deputy chief education officer and the vice-chair of the education committee."

When the conversation ended, Serena could hear music coming to her from far off. *Happiness is a warm gun.* And she could smell the cordite.

22

Ralph was concerned about Marnie. She was already looking harassed when he left Glebe Farm early that Friday morning and set off for Northampton. She had to keep the Walker and Co show on the road, which meant a day pinned down on the phone with clients and suppliers. Ralph had volunteered to collect leaflets about the revised summer scheme programme and deliver them to local organisers around the town. Anything to keep the pressure off Marnie.

Serena had phoned early to ask if Marnie could make the collection. She had a meeting arranged at the last minute and had no option but to attend. Marnie thought she sounded strained, but when she had asked Serena about this, her question had been dismissed. Marnie was not fooled; something was going on. She had agreed to make the journey before looking at her commitments for the day.

So it was that Ralph's venerable Volvo swung off the by-pass and rolled into a district where Victorian terraced houses nestled in with small workshops and factories. He parked outside the print works and emerged soon afterwards carrying a cardboard box which he laid on the front passenger seat. On the top he placed the typed list of recipients that Serena had faxed over. Using a street map, he worked out a route, numbering each organiser's name.

It all seemed straightforward enough. He drove off towards the first address.

• • • • •

Serena arrived several minutes early and found meeting room C without difficulty. She had been there before for a meeting of the County Youth Service Committee and as she made her way along the corridor, she found herself wondering why they had not simply met in Lee Murfitt's room, or at least in the deputy chief's office.

The door was ajar when she approached and she paused, raising a hand to knock. From inside she caught a few words and stopped, hand in the air like a street performer pretending to be a statue.

... all getting out of hand ... never authorised this level of expenditure ... could be horrendous ...

It was Murfitt, her own head of division. *Thanks for the support, Lee.*

... action do you have in mind? ... could cause ripples at this stage ...

That was Frobisher, the deputy chief education officer. She had only met him once at a public meeting, a tall bony man with huge hands, fond of his pipe, looking like a woodwork teacher. He was close to retirement and had a lifetime's experience at handling difficult issues.

... implications ... could be playing into their hands ... political hot potato ...

A woman's voice. Now what was her name? She was Councillor Rowlett ... or Radlett, something like that, a solicitor's wife from one of the small towns out in the sticks. She had once heard her described as a do-gooder. *Let's hope she is,* Serena thought.

She took a deep breath, squared her elegant shoulders and rapped confidently on the door.

• • • • •

Parking in the town centre was a nightmare. Ralph had to go twice round the block near the market square before he found a solution. A place that he had previously taken for a disabled parking area was revealed as a designated loading bay, the markings legible when a van vacated the space. Persuading himself that he was indeed making a delivery, Ralph backed up to the kerb and took the box with the remaining leaflets. His last stop of the morning.

Ahead of him was a pelican crossing conveniently located almost opposite the entrance to the charity shop that was his destination. It was plastered with notices publicising the summer scheme. They were expecting Ralph and were on red alert to snatch the leaflets from him if he only had a second to stop and sprint across the pavement. He could see a woman in the shop window keeping a lookout and he smiled encouragingly in her direction. Sparkling white teeth in an ebony face returned his smile.

By Sod's Law the traffic lights turned against Ralph as soon as he reached the crossing, halting him at the kerbside. Just then, strains of music floated towards him, growing louder by the second. Round the square came a column of vehicles led by a van topped by loudspeakers. *Rule Britannia* made Ralph think of the last night of the Proms, though he wondered why it was being played in a county town in the middle of the morning. The answer was quickly revealed when he spotted the red, white and blue placards covering the van. As it passed, he saw the slogan in bold letters: *Put Britain First!*

The pelican lights were changing, and only the first two vehicles in the procession made it through. The remainder showed dutiful respect for the law of the land and braked to a halt. The first car at the line also bore loudspeakers, and the front passenger took the opportunity to switch on the microphone and chant his message.

This is Garth Brandon, your Britain First candidate. The BFP is the only party that puts Britain in the driving seat. No more control from Brussels. Vote Brandon on polling day. Put Britain first!

Scowling, Ralph was distracted by the BFP convoy but gathered himself together and hurried across the road. He was met on the pavement by the woman from the charity shop who came out to meet him, a matronly West Indian with a sunny disposition. At that moment her expression was troubled, though she forced a complicitous smile before retreating into the shop with the box of leaflets.

Ralph turned back towards the crossing and, exactly on cue, the lights turned against him. Brandon's car began pulling away. The candidate stared at the shop and its summer scheme notices, glared at the woman clutching the box she had taken from Ralph. For an instant Brandon swivelled his head and looked straight at Ralph. Their eyes locked momentarily, and the car was past.

• • • • •

"I'd like to get this point quite clear." Murfitt sat forward in his chair. The three inquisitors were ranged together on one side of the committee table with a clerk taking notes beside them and Serena alone on the other. "You have arranged for additional outings over and above the ones agreed in your original programme that you put to the Youth Service Committee in March, without reference to any other member of –"

"All right, thank you, Lee. We get the point." Frobisher inclined his head towards Serena. "You're obviously worried about the situation this summer, Mrs McDowell ... Serena. And that has led you to expand the number of trips to be taken by the children. What has caused this extra anxiety on your part?"

"You mean apart from the fire bombing of the community centre ... twice ... the second time with loss of life ... the violent acts of vandalism and destruction going on all over the region ... the racist campaign led by one of the candidates in the European Parliament election ... and the personal threats that some members of our community have received?"

Frobisher pulled a pipe out of his top pocket, plugged it into his mouth and fingered the bowl thoughtfully. "I take that as a rhetorical question but, just for the record, would you like to tell us if there is more?"

Serena looked from one to the other, speaking slowly and clearly. "Word has reached us ... from reliable sources ... that a neo-Nazi organisation is planning to make trouble here during the holidays. They'll probably try to stir up the local non-white population to provoke young people into retaliating. If we can get the kids away as much as possible, it will help prevent that happening."

"And enable children of all races to spend time together doing pleasurable things," added Councillor Mrs Rawlings.

"Exactly. That, more than anything else, is what we're setting out to achieve."

"That's why we voted in committee to approve the plan."

"Yes. Thank you."

"But the fact remains that the extra outings will add a great deal to the cost," Murfitt interjected. "And it will come from a budget heading for which I am responsible."

"How would you reply to that, Serena?" Frobisher waved his pipe vaguely. "Have you calculated the effect? Do you have all the figures?"

"We're within the target."

Murfitt was shaking his head.

"And you have a sufficient number of helpers to comply with the adult-to-child regulations?" said Frobisher.

"More than sufficient. The whole community is supporting this project. We have parents, child-minders, teachers – at least one head teacher – youth workers, business people giving up their time –"

"That's very impressive," said Mrs Rawlings. "And you say they come from all sections of the ..."

Serena smiled. "I can see you want the answer in black and white. Yes, all sections of the community, white, black and Asian."

"Excellent."

"Talking of black and white ..." Murfitt was looking desperate. "Can we talk hard figures, please? Can you guarantee – *unequivocally* – that your extra activities will not cause my budget to be exceeded?"

Serena looked him in the eyes. "Can you guarantee – *unequivocally* – that you will take personal responsibility for the consequences if the summer scheme is curtailed and the streets run with ... what was the famous phrase ... *rivers of blood?*"

She looked pointedly towards the clerk taking notes in short-hand. "I hope you got that down."

• • • • •

Marnie asked Anne to call Estelle over towards the end of the morning. Her phone conversations about the supply of materials had raised some doubts in her mind that she wanted to talk through. Needing to stretch her legs, Anne walked out into the yard and shouted up to Estelle's window. Two minutes later Estelle duly appeared clutching her files and drawings. The three of them settled round Marnie's desk and spent half an hour studying colour charts.

Marnie leaned back from the desk. "That's the first thing you have to do when you arrive ... check the builders' merchants and find out if locally they have exactly the colours that you specify."

Estelle was nodding. "Of course. Maybe I've tried to have everything too perfect too early in the design process."

"I suggest you get onto the clients and find out if they have friends and neighbours in the area who've had their houses renovated. That should give you an idea of how –"

Ralph burst in as they were speaking. "Have you got a radio in here?"

"On my desk," said Anne.

"Local radio's doing a programme on the election. They're just on Creswell-Davies."

Anne was on her feet pursuing Ralph across the room. "Button five is the local Beeb."

Ralph's technical skills were legendary. He stood aside to let Anne switch on and find the station. They waited while the presenter rounded off the report on the Tory candidate.

... seems to be fighting a low-key campaign compared with his other main rivals. This is in marked contrast to his challenger and former party colleague Garth Brandon whose campaign is sweeping the county from top to bottom. Astonishingly, our latest poll reveals that of all the candidates Brandon scores highest for name recognition and knowledge of his policies. His campaign is not so much whistle-stop as whirlwind. We caught up with him a short while ago in Northampton.

Where will you be campaigning tomorrow, Mr Brandon?

Everywhere. We're carrying our message of hope to the four corners of this beautiful county in the heart of England.

How do you reply to those who criticise you for being supported by far-right extremist groups? People say you have the backing of an army of thugs and hooligans.

Propaganda. I welcome followers from every side. No one can accuse me or my party of any illegal activities. The whole point is that we support British tradition and British institutions. We put Britain first.

And you have no links with New Force or any similar militant organisations?

Why should I need them? I am an experienced politician, a former government minister. We are developing a new party to serve this country. You should be asking my rivals about their links with mysterious foreign backers.

Do you have evidence of any such links?

I want to focus on the real issues in my campaign, but I will just say this. Only this morning I discovered that my rivals are being supported by activists who operate in the shadows, part of a European Zionist clique desperate to unsettle our country and put us in the hands of continental bankers and financiers.

What evidence do you have of this?

My own eyes. I now know, for example, that Professor Lombard the economist, who recently gave up his post at Oxford to pursue new directions, is personally involved behind the scenes in this election.

And you believe he's part of this 'European Zionist clique'?

Well, his name's something of a give-away, don't you think? Lots of bankers came here from Italy years ago to escape investigation of their activities. That was a problem then; it's still a problem now. Sooner or later people will listen to me and believe what I say. I hope they do so sooner rather than later for their own sake ... and ours.

That was the last in our reports on the candidates from the main parties. The election is also being contested by the Socialist Workers' Party, the Monster Raving Loony Party, the Curved Bananas Alliance ...

Anne switched off.

Marnie was exasperated. "*Main parties?* I don't believe it! I'd sooner support the curved bananas brigade."

"Huh!" Anne smirked. "They're round the bend."

Marnie stuck out her tongue. "Seriously, though. What's he talking about? How did you come into this, Ralph?"

"He spotted me delivering the leaflets this morning."

"He knew you were helping us?"

"He knew all right. It wasn't hard to work it out."

"And he recognised you?"

"We were students at the same college in Oxford, both doing PPE. Then I was adviser to a sub-committee when he was a junior minister ... and so on."

"The price of fame," said Estelle. "But what was that about European and Zionist? Did your family come from Italy?"

Ralph shrugged. "Lombard ... Lombardy. Who knows? The Lombards have certainly lived in the London area for generations."

"And *Jewish*?"

"Not as far as I know. But I've never really been into genealogy."

"So how can he prove what he says?"

"He doesn't have to. He just has to hint, make his point and then say he wants to get back to the real issues. It's an old trick."

"And he makes you seem really sinister ... lurking in the shadows to undermine the pure English race."

Ralph smiled. "Personified by famous *English* people like Laurence Olivier – is the name Norman or Huguenot? – John Betjeman – is that Dutch or Flemish? – Viscount Montgomery – would that be Norman or Welsh? And don't mention Benjamin Disraeli – hardly a native Briton! Unless Jerusalem really was among those dark Satanic mills ... And he was a favourite of Queen Victoria!"

"Didn't I read that she spoke English with a German accent in her youth?" said Estelle.

"Let's not start on the Royal family." Ralph raised his hands. "There hasn't been an English king since Harold died in 1066."

"So it's all irrelevant," said Marnie.

"It only matters if Brandon can use it to further his twisted cause."

Ralph flopped into a chair. They all sat gloomily in silence.

"I suppose that makes the Women's Institute part of a subversive Zionist conspiracy," Anne observed quietly. "Isn't *Jerusalem* their anthem?"

• • • • •

The clerk paused in her note-taking. Frobisher and Mrs Rawlings were conferring in murmured tones, heads together. Murfitt was looking down at his notes, avoiding eye-contact with Serena, who was waiting demurely, hands resting in her lap, ankles crossed under the chair. Frobisher was the first to speak.

"We need to be clear about where we're going with the summer scheme ... what our options are. You've done a great job in organising everything so far, Serena. We understand your concerns ... but they are largely based on rumours of trouble. And rumours are usually unreliable. Perhaps the programme in its original form would be enough to meet everyone's requirements without running the risk of going over-budget."

"The chief education officer said we must sometimes be prepared to take risks," Serena observed quietly.

"Well ..." Frobisher steepled his long fingers and rested his elbows on the table.

"But nobody really takes risks in local government, do they?" She flickered a smile.

"We have to be realistic, Serena. And we have to try to work within what we're given. Presumably you'd agree that your approved programme is a good one?"

Serena nodded. "Of course."

Councillor Mrs Rawlings joined in. "Perhaps it would be best to try to run it in its original form and review the situation as it progresses. That would seem sensible, wouldn't it?"

"Yes." Serena spoke quietly and reasonably. "I could take the necessary steps to do that ... if you didn't mind facing the consequences."

"Consequences?" said Frobisher. "And what do you mean by *necessary steps?*"

"Oh ... just the administrative procedures to change back to the original programme of activities."

Mrs Rawlings looked reassured. Frobisher's eyes narrowed. Murfitt looked up slowly. Serena continued.

"I'll put out a statement that the programme's being cut back. I'll just have to say that it's to save money ... journalists are bound to ask. Better to be up front about it."

"*Journalists?*" said Frobisher. "I don't think they need to be involved. You can just send out a leaflet to parents."

"Oh but journalists are involved anyway. You see, they're pressing me for an interview ... about my death threat."

"*Your death threat?*"

Frobisher was aghast. Mrs Rawlings raised a hand to her mouth.

"You didn't tell me, as your line manager," Murfitt began, but was silenced by a gesture from Frobisher.

Serena was crestfallen. "It'll look bad for the summer scheme. They'll be making connections between the authority reducing its support at the time when my life's being threatened. The whole thing could become a fiasco faced with such bad publicity."

• • • • •

It would not be the first time that someone had been inspired by the hymn, *Jerusalem*. In Marnie's case inspiration took the form of a rapidly-conceived plan. They would mobilise key organisations in support of the summer scheme. As so often in the past, it had been a comment from Anne that had cleared her thinking and pushed her into action. Hastily concluding the meeting with Estelle, they had brainstormed to compile a list of institutions that made up the backbone of Britain.

Formidable battalions would be urged to fight back against Brandon and his cronies, including the Women's Institute, the Scout Movement, the Townswomen's Guild, the WRVS. Anne had suggested that the latter's Meals-on-Wheels branch might be recruited as a form of flying column, pulling down posters around the county when on their delivery rounds.

Ralph urged caution in trying to get these 'respectable' bodies too overtly politically engaged.

Anne armed herself with the phonebook. As a trial run she called the county federation of the W.I., obtained the number of the local organiser and passed it over to Marnie like ammunition.

"This looks familiar somehow," Marnie muttered as she pressed the buttons on her phone. The call was picked up at the third ring.

"Dorothy Vane-Henderson."

"Oh … it's you." Marnie immediately felt foolish. She should not have been surprised.

"Dorothy Vane-Henderson speaking. Who is this?" The voice was courteous but wary.

"Sorry … er … it's Marnie. I want to talk to you about the W.I."

"We'd love to have you as a member, Marnie. I've often thought about mentioning it, but I assumed you'd be too –"

"No, sorry … look … er … let me explain."

"That would be nice." The voice embodied lilac knitwear and low-heeled shoes by Russell and Bromley.

Marnie outlined the situation with the BFP, the threats of violence, inter-community tension and the problems confronting the summer scheme.

"So that's what we're up against. Can the W.I. help us fight Brandon? We need all the allies we can muster."

"No can do, I'm afraid, Marnie. Our constitution doesn't permit us to do anything political. We're meant to be above – er, outside – all that."

"So there's nothing you can do?" Marnie felt her plan falling to pieces.

"I didn't say that exactly." She went into brisk committee-woman mode. "I need to give it some thought. Leave it with me, Marnie. I'll get back to you."

• • • • •

Ralph's plan back-fired. At the end of the afternoon the three of them went over to Estelle's house to watch the local TV news. The first inkling of how badly things were going was the result of the latest polls. Brandon was top of the list for name recognition for the second day running. In fact, his was the only candidate's name that some respondents could cite.

When the news reporter went out onto the streets, everything went downhill. This time there was no Huw Parry-Thomas figure to steal the show. In a vox-pops presentation edited to maintain objectivity, half the people featured spoke in favour of a live-and-let-live attitude to 'immigrants'; the other half thought Brandon had a point. Perhaps we did need to look after our own interests. More than one interviewee stressed that he was proud to be British. The report gave the impression of an uncertain nation at odds with itself.

"I'll get it."

Anne had the phone in her hand before Marnie or Ralph realised it was ringing. She passed it over to Marnie.

"Hi, Serena. Have you been watching the news?"

"Yeah." She sounded weary. "Not looking good. Still, there is a silver lining round our clouds, thank goodness."

"Really? Someone has assassinated Brandon?"

"Not yet. I'm working on it. Seriously, I had my meeting with the big-wigs this morning. In fact, I've been trying to ring you on and off most of the afternoon."

"It's been a madhouse here. Tell me about your meeting."

"It was more like the Inquisition. There were three of them and they tried to get me to reduce the scheme to its original level."

"You've got to cut it back? But we've sent out all the leaflets and –"

"I said they tried. I managed to persuade them by using my diplomatic skills."

"Really? You have diplomatic skills?"

"Don't sound so sceptical. I can be diplomatic when I need to be."

"Sorry. Of course. What did you say to them?"

"Told them I'd go public that they were putting the screws on me at a time when I was receiving death threats."

"Ah … That's … reasonable. You've obviously missed your true vocation. How did they take it?"

"Very well, really. They've probably regained consciousness by now."

"Well done. So … we go ahead with our plan to post sentries in the school overnight during the weekend?"

"I'll let you have the keys. Who's on duty tonight?"

"I'm taking the first night with Anne."

· · · · ·

The Discovery climbed the slope of the field track, its suspension easing out the bumps. Anne sat beside Marnie with their overnight bags on the back seat.

"Anne, there's something I want to say to you. I've been thinking about the Italian job."

"You don't want me to go on the trip with Estelle."

"How did you work that out?"

"You're thinking you could use me here as your extra pair of hands."

"You're more than that. Estelle has to go … it's her job. But things are getting more complicated here just now. I can't expect Ralph to be available all the time. He has his own pressures, setting up this new career. And it seemed to me –"

"Marnie, you don't have to explain anything. I understand. And you're right. With the business to run and all this summer scheme malarkey, you need me to be around. That's fine."

Marnie drove through the open gateway and turned right towards the centre of the village. The road curved round to the left, straightening past the church and the pub.

"I hope you don't feel too disappointed, missing the trip to Italy."

Anne turned sideways in her seat. "Marnie, I couldn't be disappointed with any part of my life. I'm the luckiest person in the world. I've got my job, my attic and my beautiful car, not to mention *Sally Ann* and you and –"

"What the hell?"

Anne was surprised at Marnie's reaction. She turned to look ahead. At first she thought it was a funeral cortège, a long line of cars driving slowly towards them down the high street led by a black Jaguar, its paintwork highly-polished. Behind it a procession of vehicles stretching back as far as the eye could see. Incongruous among them a large van stood out like a conning tower, twin loudspeakers attached to its roof. As they passed the motorcade it was slowing to a halt, taking up the whole of the street. They could see the slogan emblazoned on the side of the van: *Put Britain First!* At that moment martial music began blaring out from the loudspeakers.

Marnie could scarcely keep her attention on the road, snatching glances at the convoy that had now halted.

"Mr Stubbs won't be very happy." Anne pointed at a caravan like a huge silver cigar tube. "They're blocking his driveway with that Starship Enterprise thing."

Numerous people were pouring from the cars and moving rapidly along the pavement towards the leading Jaguar. Marnie strained in the rear-view mirror, estimating that the front car was parked up by the church. Passing the convoy's tail end, she slowed and reversed into a field entrance beyond the last house.

"I don't like this." Marnie looked at her watch and grabbed the mobile from her belt. She pressed buttons and listened. "*Damn!* Serena's mobile isn't available." She disconnected and sat thinking.

"I could go on in the Mini and get the keys from Serena," Anne intruded into her thoughts. "If you wanted to check out what's going on."

Marnie was wracked with indecision. "I don't like leaving Glebe Farm deserted and Ralph alone on *Thyrsis* with this lot around."

"But you don't want us to be split up, I know," said Anne. "I can at least take our bags to the school and settle in. You can come on later when things have quietened down here."

Marnie nodded slowly and engaged first gear. They cruised cautiously back along the high street. It would be a bad move to run over one of the BFP minions who were swarming everywhere like worker ants. Some were posting leaflets through letter-boxes, others attaching placards to lamp-posts. Many wore rosettes. A few sported baseball caps with tricolour roundels like soldiers of the French Revolution.

"Look at them," Marnie muttered. "Where've they all come from?" She braked as a gang crossed the road in front of her heading into the pub, each clutching a wad of leaflets. "There are dozens of them."

"Does it remind you of the troll army you saw in Leicester that day?" Anne asked.

"Not quite. The *trolls* looked like thugs. These look more like accountants. They're so much better dressed and –"

"Watch out!" Anne shouted. "Sorry. I didn't think you'd seen it."

Marnie had signalled to turn onto the field track, but a car was half blocking the gateway. She hit the brakes, and they rocked in their seats.

"Bloody inconsiderate fool!" Marnie pressed the button and her window rolled down.

At the same time, the door of the car flew open, and the driver made to get out. He looked irate and was half out of the car when he was restrained by his passenger who spoke urgently at him. There was a clear moment of tension inside the car, and the passenger door opened. A face appeared.

"Can I help you?"

"Gently does it," Marnie murmured to herself. She leaned out. "You're blocking the gateway. I need to get through."

The face looked puzzled. "Through here?" Disbelief. He looked round at the field.

"That's right."

More words inside the stranger's car. Both doors closed, the engine started and the driver manoeuvred to make room for them to pass. Marnie raised her hand as she slipped into gear and eased forward.

"That's a pity. I didn't want them to know anyone lived down here. I hope they don't get curious and decide to explore."

Anne made no reply and sat deep in concentration. Marnie glanced at her friend as they motored down the track.

"You all right? No need to be scared. We just have to be cautious."

"I'm not scared. I'm trying to remember something. I can't think ..."

Marnie turned into the garage barn, and they got out. Anne straight away unlocked the Mini and began putting their bags into the back.

"Got your mobile switched on?"

Anne patted her pocket. "Yes. I'll get off, otherwise I'll be late for Serena. See you later."

"Ring me if you have any problems," said Marnie. "In fact ring me anyway to let me know how things are."

"Will do."

Anne leapt in, reversed and drove off up the track, hoping the stranger's car was not back in its place blocking the field entrance. With luck, the two men would be gone. She did not want them to have the impression there was something worth investigating down the hill. She approached slowly, scanning the car for signs of activity. It was empty, and they had left the entrance clear. Anne pulled out and headed through the village.

It had been transformed in the few minutes since the convoy arrived. Red, white and blue placards were attached to every surface. Even the church notice board carried a poster exhorting everyone to vote for Brandon and put Britain first. Taped to the window of the shop was a picture of Brandon, his intense gaze staring out.

At the dual carriageway Anne turned north and settled down to cruise at sixty, her self-imposed limit. She took a few deep breaths, reflecting that her life in the country was anything but dull. Several cars overtook her, two of them BMWs that sped past, locked in their own private race, almost bumper to bumper. *Idiots*, Anne muttered. *It's stupid driving like –* She stopped in mid-thought ... *BMWs*. That car blocking the field entrance had been a BMW. But it looked different from others. They had been concerned with where it was parked. Now, Anne thought about its appearance. Dark bodywork, fancy alloy wheels ... wheel arches rimmed ... shiny steel. Where had she heard that before? *Steel arches ... Luther!*

The Mini was wandering in its lane and Anne refocused attention on driving safely. She steadied the car before letting her thoughts return to the incident in the gateway. The car they had encountered exactly fitted the description of the BMW that Luther had identified at the scene of the mosque attack in Leicester. Perhaps the fancy wheel arches could be ordered as an extra from BMW. Maybe she had just never noticed them before. She began watching the cars that passed her. One or two more

BMWs went by. None of them had the unusual wheel arches. Had that really been the fire-bomber's car in Knightly St John ... parked in the entrance to Glebe Farm?

・・・・・

Marnie jogged through the spinney to tell Ralph about the invasion of the BFP hordes and the change of plan. They agreed that Marnie would take up guard duty in the office and ring Ralph at once if any of Brandon's supporters came down to explore Glebe Farm.

It was like being under siege. The worst part was that she could not see what was happening in the village. She rang Angela Hemingway at the vicarage. No reply. When Molly Appleton answered the phone her voice was troubled.

"It's Marnie."

"Oh, Marnie! Do you know what's going on up here?"

"I saw them. That's why I'm ringing. Are the cars still there?"

"The village is full of them. They're knocking on all the doors."

"Have they been to your house?"

"Yes. Actually, they were quite polite. I thought they were trying to sell the *Watchtower* when I opened the door. Then I saw the rosettes and leaflets and all the cars."

"They didn't threaten you or anything?"

"No, quite the opposite. They were very friendly and courteous ... asked if we'd like to vote for Garth Brandon and start putting the country back on its feet. I told them we'd think about it, and they seemed quite happy. They offered to get Mr Brandon to come and talk to us, but I said we were rather busy, so they thanked us and went away."

"Molly, would you do something for me? Could you ring me when they leave the village? I've got to go into town this evening and I don't want the place to be left empty."

"Certainly, Marnie. That's no problem. Oh, just a mo ..." There was a voice in the background. "Richard's just reminded me ... there was one other thing you ought to know about. They asked if we knew of anyone in the village called Lombard."

"*Lombard?*" Marnie felt goosebumps on her neck.

"That's Ralph's surname, isn't it?"

"What did you tell them?"

"I said there was definitely no one of that name on the electoral roll for the village. That convinced them, I think. And it was true."

"Well done, Molly. Phew! You're a star."

・・・・・

Serena stayed at the school long enough to show Anne which keys worked which locks, and disable the burglar alarm – they would not want Anne's movement setting it off – before dashing back to her family obligations.

There was a small common room on an inside wall with just one tiny window high up. It was ideal as a base. Anne laid out the airbeds and sleeping bags and opened the window to its limit of a few centimetres. She closed the curtain. It was a secure space, and from outside no one could see that it was occupied. There was a cupboard and a small sink in the corner with a kettle. Anne unloaded the box of provisions, coffee, tea, milk, biscuits, a four-pack of croissants, some bars of Kit-Kat.

She grabbed a powerful Maglite torch, checked that the mobile was on and set off on her rounds. The stronghold was secured. She was ready.

• • • • •

It was a night that would long be remembered in Knightly St John – and in the *Two Roses* especially – in more ways than one. No one could recall an evening when the pub was so full and did so much business with so little disorder. Grace Parchman was called in by her father, although it was her night off, to help serve the meals that threatened to overwhelm the kitchen. She was crossing the floor with a tray of drinks when a hush fell upon the company. At a corner table a man had risen to his feet, and everyone in his group that filled the saloon bar became silent. Every customer in the pub stopped talking and looked in his direction. He was dressed in a well-tailored suit, with a striped tie and gold cufflinks. His head was almost completely bald, and there was a twinkle in his eye.

"Landlord, thank you for making us all feel so welcome this evening." Murmurs of agreement. "And apologies to your regular customers for taking up so much space in their local. We're here in the village to canvass support for our party – the Britain First Party – in the European election. But tonight we're off duty and we like to feel we're among friends in this fine English hostelry in your charming village. To compensate your regulars for taking over the pub, I would like to offer a drink to all the customers here this evening. The drinks are on me, Garth Brandon. Have a good evening."

He sat down amid cheers and applause, though Grace noticed they came from Brandon's own supporters. The locals were too busy placing their orders. Back at the bar her father was loading another tray. Pulling a pint, he looked up at Grace.

"Tell Gordon to make sure the order for Brandon, table seven, goes to the top of the list. I'll have this lot ready by the time you get back."

She vanished into the kitchen, where the chef was working feverishly, like a gunnery officer in action on one of Nelson's warships.

• • • • •

Anne checked her watch. Time to report in to Marnie. The call was answered immediately.

"Hi Anne. How are things?"

"All quiet here. I've been all round the building twice. It's quite a pleasant evening."

"Nothing suspicious?"

"Nope. In fact, there are kids playing rounders in the playground. It's nice. I feel like joining in."

"Any sign of the caretaker?"

"Long gone. Serena said he doesn't come back once he's seen the cleaners off the premises."

"You don't sound too worried about things."

"I'm not. But you do. Is Brandon's crowd still down at Knightly?"

"I assume so. Molly's going to let me know when they leave. I'll join you as soon as the coast is clear."

"You know, Marnie, I wonder if we haven't over-reacted a bit. Everything's very quiet in this part of town. It's not like round by that centre that was torched, tucked away in a backwater of old factories. I can see people out walking their dogs, kids playing games. The school's very open and it's overlooked on all sides."

"Maybe. We'll see. Call back in half an hour, OK?"

"Aye aye, skipper."

· · · · ·

Richard Appleton pushed open the door of the *Two Roses* and gaped. He had never seen the pub so crowded. A man at the bar beckoned him to come over, and he eased his way through the crowd.

"What'll you have, Richard?"

"Thanks, Mike, but I'm not staying."

"Don't thank me. It's the bald bloke in the flash suit who's paying ... him over there."

"What's he celebrating ... the relief of Mafeking?"

"VE day, more like. Fancies his chances in the European election. He's a candidate. BFP."

"Right. He's the one who's just redecorated the high street, is he?"

"And made *mine host* Jim Parchman rich, I reckon. If you're not staying for a drink, what are you here for?"

"There's a car across my drive. I can't get in."

Grace overheard him and sidled up.

"Have you got the number of the car, Richard? I'll get dad to make an announcement."

He handed her a slip of paper with the number. Seconds later the landlord called for silence by dimming the lights twice. He read out the number, and a man rose at once. Grace accompanied Richard to the door.

"Sorry about this," said the offending driver in a pleasant tone. "Didn't realise I was blocking your driveway. I'll shift it straight away. We can't offer you a drink first, perhaps?"

"No, it's OK. I have to get home."

"You'll be going back to Northampton, will you?" Grace asked the driver.

"Not tonight. We're off to the deep south, down to Brackley. Early start in the morning. It's a big county ... lot of ground to cover." He winked and pushed open the door.

· · · · ·

Marnie had finally managed to fix her attention on a magazine article on loft conversions in New York when the phone rang. She almost fell off the chair in her scramble to pick up.

"I bet you thought I'd forgotten my promise, Marnie."

Got it in one.

"Course not, Molly. Do I take it the presidential motorcade is moving out?"

"That's right. I thought they were coming to visit you at first, but they were only using the field for turning round. They're all on the move now."

"Thanks, Molly. I'll tag onto the end of the line and follow them back to town."

"OK. Oh no ... wait a minute. They're not going to Northampton. One of them told Richard they were going to Brackley. That's the opposite direction."

"*Brackley*? Why Brackley?"

"Next stop on the grand tour, I suppose."

After finishing the call, Marnie rang Ralph. They agreed there was little point in mounting guard at Garfield Primary school if the enemy were on their way to the other end of the county. Minutes later Anne rang in, exactly on time.

"It's tantalising, Marnie. One of the teams out there really needs my skills with the rounders bat. Pity I can't show myself."

"Ralph and I think you should probably show yourself back here."

"Really? Why's that?"

"Brandon's crowd have headed down to Brackley, apparently. You may have been right about us over-reacting. Probably best to pack up and come home."

"That sounds like a nice idea. I'm always happy to be home."

"Good."

"On the other hand ..."

"What?"

"If it is going to be all quiet on the western front, we could use it as a dummy run ... gain experience for future nights."

"Mmm ..."

"You don't sound very keen, Marnie."

"Well ..."

"I don't mind staying here for tonight if you don't want to come up."

"Oh no ... I wouldn't leave you there alone."

"I'm not the least bit nervous. Honestly, this is a safe neighbourhood. Look, if I get at all worried, I'll just get in the car and drive home. It's right by the back door. And I've got my mobile fully charged."

"I don't know, Anne ... I'm not wild about the idea."

"Let's just try it for one night. Nothing's going to happen. Trust me ... I'm a trainee interior designer."

· · · · ·

Brandon's entourage suspected they were being observed by most of the residents of Knightly St John, and they were pleased. Their high-profile strategy was working. The procession was being watched from behind dozens of pairs of curtains as the black Jaguar led the column along the high street and out of the village. They were also being watched by dozens of photos of Garth Brandon, looking down from every available surface.

Arriving at the main road the cars began filtering out into the thin late evening traffic following the signs pointing south towards Brackley. One after another they turned left and accelerated away, with stickers in their windows proclaiming allegiance to Brandon and the party that would put Britain first.

Towards the end of the line a small group separated itself from the main convoy. They pulled into the right-hand lane at the junction, crossed to the central reservation and swept out onto the northbound carriageway. They were six cars in all, moving rapidly in the direction of Northampton, led by a highly-polished black BMW with shiny steel edging round its wheel arches.

· · · · ·

"I'm not happy about this, Ralph. I know I shan't sleep tonight. The thought of Anne up there in that building by herself ..."

"Would you like me to speak to her ... persuade her to come back?"

They were sitting in Ralph's study on *Thyrsis*. Here all was orderly and controlled, a safe purposeful place designed for reflection and thought. Outside was not a sound as darkness came down, not so much as a breath of wind to ripple the surface of the water.

Marnie shook her head. "I don't know. Part of me just wants to get in the car and go up to fetch her. Another part thinks she ought to be allowed to use her own initiative and take her own decisions. But she is only seventeen."

"Would you have done what she's doing when you were seventeen?"

"Probably."

"And what would your parents have thought?"

"That's just it ... I'm not a parent. But I am responsible for her."

"If you feel like that, perhaps you ought to go and get her. What's holding you back?" He grinned. "You're usually more impetuous ... and more protective where Anne's concerned."

"That's what I keep asking myself. I think it comes down to trust. I can't treat her like a child. I wouldn't want her to think I didn't trust her judgment."

"So what will you do?"

Marnie sighed. "I think for Anne's sake I should let her do what she suggests ... and keep the mobile under my pillow."

· · · · ·

Anne patrolled the school for the umpteenth time. She now knew the name of every teacher from the plate on each door. It astonished her that they were all women, and she wondered if it alienated the boys ... *school is girls' stuff*. She had heard that before. In the darkened building she walked slowly and quietly like a prowling cat, relying on the street lights for illumination, not using her torch. She found the place strangely comforting, its sights and smells bringing back memories of her own primary school. Nothing here caused her anxiety.

On one occasion she visited the loo and from habit went into the girls' toilets. It was in the Infants' block, and she laughed out loud when she pushed open the cubicle door and found the miniature lavatory bowl confronting her. It felt strange to be so close to the ground, and she chuckled even while she was using it.

A car passed in the street across the yard, and she watched it turn out of sight at the corner junction. Two more went by, then another ... and another. She looked at her watch. Just after eleven. The pubs were turning out, perhaps. In the corner of her eye she thought she saw movement outside, but it was only the play of shadows thrown up by another set of headlights. She began moving calmly along the corridor towards a side entrance, the one with the heading *Juniors – Girls* carved in stone above the door.

Anne yawned. Time for bed. She had to be up and out of the premises before six-thirty when the caretaker would arrive to do his own rounds. She mused that technically she was an unauthorised intruder and would have some explaining to do if anyone spotted her and called the police. No probs. Serena and the others would – *what was that?*

Something rattled. Was someone trying the door not five metres from where she was standing? Soundlessly she stepped into a classroom doorway and waited. A year went by. A decade. She remembered to start breathing again. Time to get her bearings. This was the north-east corner. Here the door was closest to the street, which was why she had parked her car there. *Her car! The beloved Mini!*

She strained every nerve to detect any sound, but everything seemed to be – *no!* There it was again. This time she was almost within arm's length of the door. In a Hitchcock film she would see the knob turning and her eyes would bulge like footballs. She could see no knob on the inside, but she certainly did the eyeballs thing.

She crept into the nearest classroom to look out of the window. The panes were too high from the ground, and the bottom row of glazing was frosted and wired for security. Waiting for something to happen was not an option, she told herself. It was not why she was there. Two deep breaths. Shoulders back. Chest out ... such as it was. She began counting to ten, but by the time she reached seven she was on the move.

In seconds she reached the back door. It was wider than normal size with a heavy brass security lock at shoulder height. She put her ear to the join just below the lock. Nothing. Time for tough questions. Had she imagined the sounds? Could it have been the wind rattling the door? A security guard checking? The police?

What would Marnie do? There was little doubt. Deep breaths again. Anne pressed nine-nine-nine on the mobile and fitted it back onto her belt, ready to call at the touch of the send button. She stood the Maglite on its face on the floor and pressed against the lock, turning the knob without a sound. The door opened easily on silent hinges. First just a crack, wide enough for one eye. Nothing. She picked up the heavy steel torch, a reassuring weight in her hand, and pulled the door wider. All was quiet. She risked a head out into the playground to check that her car was in one piece.

The sudden beam of light from a powerful torch outside caught her full in the face, and her heart almost stopped beating.

• • • • •

The ringing of the mobile did not wake Marnie. It was well after eleven but she was not asleep. She grabbed the phone from beside her and pressed the green button.

"What's up, Anne?"

"Oh … oh dear … sorry. I must have …"

It seemed to be a wrong number call, but the voice was familiar.

Marnie cupped her hand round the phone and whispered. "Who is this, please?" She rolled out of bed and stepped along towards the saloon to avoid waking Ralph.

"Well, it's Dorothy Vane-Henderson, but is that you, Marnie? I didn't mean to disturb you."

There was a very curious logic at work here. It was eleven forty-five, and she had made the call.

"What can I do for you, Dorothy?"

"I just wanted to leave a message on your answering machine in the office. I didn't think I'd get through direct."

"That's all right." She felt like adding, *No problem, I'm just lying awake worrying that my best friend might be under attack from murderous fire-bombers.*

"It's about your request for help from the voluntary organisations. I've been ringing round a few friends, and Cathy Izzard came up with a wonderful idea. I've got to go out early tomorrow morning, so I thought I'd let you know so that you could think about it before we speak."

"Thank you."

"What she has in mind is that we organise a summer fete. We could do it in the Garfield school playground and get loads of people to run stalls. You know … bric-a-brac, tombola, home-made preserves, toys –"

"I get the picture, Dorothy. It sounds … an interesting plan." Marnie thought, *Here we are faced with an army of Nazi trolls who defeat riot police in straight combat and our counter-attack is a garden party.*

"You're probably thinking it's a bit tame, but it would bring in all your – what did you call them? – *establishment bodies.* It would show that the *backbone of the country*, I think you said, was on your side. And no one attacks a lady in a cardigan running a cake stall. Think it over. I'll ring you tomorrow afternoon. Bye."

Marnie crept back to the bedroom and slipped in beside Ralph.

"Who was that?" His voice was drowsy.

"Field-Marshall Montgomery and the Eighth Army."

• • • • •

Anne winced. Leaning back against the door to close it, the noise as it slammed shut echoed down the corridors and must have been heard in Helsinki. Donovan Smith stood facing her in the semi-darkness. He pointed at her belt.

"Your phone's glowing. It seems to be active."

Anne reached for it carefully. If she touched the wrong button her three nines would be picked up at the emergency service. The last thing she wanted was to summon the police by accident. She cancelled the call and looked up warily. Perhaps that was not a good idea.

"Why are you here, Donovan? Are you following me?"

"How could I do that?"

"In your BMW, for instance?"

He frowned. "My … BMW?"

"You do have a BMW, don't you? Black and silver?"

Donovan looked guarded, his eyes rapidly checking out the shadowy corridor over Anne's shoulder.

"You seem to know a lot about me all of a sudden."

"So you don't deny it?"

"Deny what ... that I followed you ... or that I have a BMW? The answers are no, I didn't follow you and ... yes, I do have a BMW. But how could you possibly know that? It's in pieces in our garage at home. It fell over last year and one of the rocker covers got cracked. I'm trying to get a spare but 1954 motorcycle parts aren't easy to get hold of, even for a BMW."

Anne's turn to be bewildered. "*Motorcycle?* I meant your *car* ... the one with the chrome wheel arches."

"Chrome *what?*" Donovan's face went blank. "I don't know what you're talking about. I don't have a car."

An exasperated sigh from Anne. "Can we start again? I'm missing something here."

"Anne, do we have to stand in this corridor all night, in the dark?"

It was a reasonable enough question, but it posed a problem. Should see lead him to her 'base camp' or keep him somewhere she could make a getaway if the need arose? But there was nowhere secure and that was not a comforting thought. She led him to the common room, closed the door and turned on the light. They sat facing each other across the room.

Donovan surveyed the scene. The temporary bed, the bag of supplies, books and magazines, a spare torch.

"What are you doing here?" he asked.

"That's my question. You answer first."

"I'm checking out the building. This is where the summer scheme's being held, right?"

"So?"

"When I saw that bit in the paper about taking pre-emptive action, it got me thinking. You've heard of *Ground Force* on the television? I thought maybe this place was next on the list for a makeover by *New Force*."

"And that's why you're here ... really?"

Donovan nodded.

"Why didn't you join in to help us, if you're so keen on lending a hand?"

"I got the feeling you might spend hours in public meetings like that one in the school. I thought I could best help by taking direct action ... doing something practical. And I had to start by getting from Knightly to here. My only transport is a boat and a mountain bike. I knew it'd take ages with all those locks on the Northampton Arm, so I set off at once. Anyway ... I know it's late but I've just arrived and here I am. That's it. Now it's your turn."

"That's what you've been doing since that evening ... travelling up here? We were wrong about you having a U-boat ... it's a *stealth* narrowboat."

Donovan flickered a smile. There was something different about him, Anne realised. Perhaps he had become more determined. But before she could trust him, she had other doubts on her mind.

"No other mystery visits to tell me about? No trips to London, for example?"

Donovan's expression clouded, and she knew she had hit the target.

"Well?"

"My uncle Reinhardt died yesterday morning," Donovan said quietly.

Anne's mouth opened. "Your uncle ... he died?"

"Yeah." Barely audible.

Anne did not realise she had moved until she found herself sitting beside Donovan, putting her arms round him.

"I'm so sorry." She could not trust her voice above a whisper. "Would you like a cup of tea?"

A melancholy smile. "Thanks."

• • • • •

While the kettle boiled, Anne took Donovan on a tour of inspection. They kept well back from any windows and moved silently like shadows on a wall in the patchy darkness. Donovan closely inspected every lock and bolt, noted the location of light switches, checked the viewing angles to the outside.

Anne was surprised when he ducked into a classroom near one of the doors to the playground and returned holding two children's chairs. From the adjacent cleaner's cupboard he produced a metal bucket. He balanced one chair upon the other against the door and carefully set the bucket on top. Anne understood at once and scolded herself inwardly for not having thought of such an alarm system herself.

With no need for words, they went from door to door rigging up similar structures. At the last exit, Donovan turned and looked down the corridor behind them. From the high Victorian windows pale light from the distant street lamps was striping the walls.

He walked towards a classroom and stopped in the doorway looking in. Anne realised what he was planning the moment he dived into the room and came back holding the teacher's chair. He closed the door and fixed the back of the chair under the door knob. Anne did the same in the next class, and they leapfrogged each other from room to room, turning each door into an obstacle. The school had become a fortress.

On impulse, Anne suddenly said, "Donovan, if for any reason we get separated and you need to get into my car –"

"Why should I need to do that?"

"I don't know. Maybe I'm feeling a bit jumpy. It's the red Mini parked outside the door there."

"I'm not going to need to. I wouldn't abandon you if things got ... rough or –"

"Just listen. All I'm saying is – in case you ever need to know – I have a spare set of keys in a metal box under the right front wheel arch."

"Good idea. But I'm not going to –"

"I got the idea from Marnie. She keeps a set of keys in the same place on the Discovery. Just remember."

"OK."

• • • • •

In the sleeping cabin on *Thyrsis* Marnie surprised herself by falling asleep. Ralph stirred and was beginning to turn when the overhead cabin light made him blink. He yawned and hitched himself up onto one elbow, leaning across to look at Marnie. She was lying face down, her head turned away from him, breathing calmly. Beside the pillow she was clasping the mobile, inches from her mouth.

He reached over and gently eased the phone from her grip, stretching up to place it on the shelf above the bed. She did not stir. For some seconds he looked down at her, willing her to have a good night's rest and peaceful dreams. He kissed the back of her head, smelling the clean brown hair, before reaching to turn out the light.

His last thought was for Anne, hoping she too would pass a quiet night.

• • • • •

Clutching mugs of tea, Anne and Donovan resumed their seats in the common room. Donovan sipped in silence, and Anne wondered if he was mentally reviewing their defence arrangements or grieving for his uncle. Trying not to make it look obvious, she observed him through the steam rising from her mug. He had always been quiet in the few times she had been with him, and now it seemed to her that perhaps he was not as sinister as she had imagined. She had found him disconcerting in the way some people feel intimidated by the staring of a cat.

"This tastes good." Donovan raised the mug slightly. "I ran out of fresh milk yesterday ... been using powdered."

Anne thought he sounded like a U-boat captain again. "You're running low on supplies?"

"Some fresh things. I carry enough stores on board to withstand a siege."

"Your ... er ... fortifications are a big improvement. The place feels more secure now."

Donovan made a non-committal murmur. "We stealth narrowboat commanders have our uses. They might give early warning of an intruder ... slow them down a bit. But they could hinder us if we have to get out in a hurry."

Us, Anne thought ... *get out in a hurry* ... There was an implication that she had not previously taken on board. He was assuming that they were sharing guard duty for the night. It was strange to hear him speak like that and even stranger that the idea did not cause her fear or alarm.

"You didn't have time to get any milk because you had to go to London?"

"Right. And when I got back, I had to press on to get here."

"Didn't your aunt want you to stay with her? Oh, sorry ... it's not my business. Forget I said that."

"She has a house full ... family over from Germany. Everything's organised. We've known this was coming for months."

"Are all your family German? Presumably the Smiths must be English. Oh ... there I go again. I don't mean to pry."

"Actually, Anne, perhaps you haven't pried enough. Or perhaps I haven't told you enough about my background. We always seem to get interrupted."

"Well ... you do seem to have quite a lot of it ... *background* ... more than most people. You seem to come from an interesting family ... not exactly ordinary."

Without preamble he began telling his story.

"My grandmother was German, a Prussian from Berlin, minor nobility.

She was a famous beauty in her day, studied music at the *Conservatoire*, gave recitals, began a doctorate in Asian musicology. That's when she met my grandfather. He was a lecturer at the university ... anthropology and early religions."

"When was that?"

"Just after the first world war. Most people think my grandfather was German. He had a German-sounding name – Klaus Herrmann – but in fact he was Dutch. That's why he wasn't conscripted into the German army in 1914. They married, my grandmother gave up her studies, and they started a family. He was young and brilliant; she was talented and beautiful; over time they had three lovely daughters ... blonde, blue-eyed, all of them ... a perfect family. You can probably guess what's coming."

"I'd rather not try."

"The National Socialist German Workers' Party came along. That's its official name in translation. You and the rest of the world know it as the Nazi Party."

"What did your grandparents have to do with it?"

"Nothing whatever! They were *respectable* people ... intellectuals ... internationalists. Many of their circle were Jewish. Many were artists, musicians, writers, philosophers, academics. The Nazis were like *gangsters*, brutal and crude. It's the greatest tragedy in European history that they were able to seize power in one of the most civilised nations on earth."

"Couldn't they stand up to the Nazis? Lots of countries and people did."

"They did in Germany, too. And they got liquidated for trying. Did you ever hear of the Scholls?"

Anne was puzzled by the apparent change of subject. "Wooden sandals? My mum's got a pair ... very noisy."

Donovan suppressed a smile. "Not the sandals. That's Dr Scholl. The ones I meant were a brother and sister ... Hans and Sophie Scholl ... students ... they had a clandestine organisation with some friends ... very idealistic ... it's symbol was a white rose ... they tried to mount a resistance movement ..."

"I don't think I want to know what happened to them, Donovan. I think I've guessed."

"You guessed right ... every one of them ... guillotined."

Anne shuddered. "The white rose," she repeated.

"Yes. *Die weiße Rose* ..." He said it in German and fell silent.

Anne cleared her throat. "So ... what happened to your family?"

"In about 1934, after the Nazis had taken over, they offered big research grants to academics in certain disciplines. My grandfather was then a professor and of great interest to them. He specialised in the migrations of ancient peoples across Asia and Europe. Himmler offered him a huge budget for his research team. At first grandpa was delighted. Then he had a meeting with Himmler at a reception and found out about the conditions: he was to prove the superiority of the Aryan race."

"Just like that?"

"More or less."

"Part of Hitler's Big Lie."

"Exactly." Donovan sounded impressed.

"But it's hard to combat that kind of technique."

Donovan said simply, "You have to fight the enemy with the truth. It's all you can do … otherwise you're as bad as them."

"What did grandpa do?"

"He told Himmler he could not prejudge what his research would uncover."

"Bad move," Anne groaned.

"Yeah … *lead balloon!* A week later one of his colleagues came to see him late at night, told him he was in great danger and had to get away at once, before it was too late. My grandparents thought this was all an exaggeration. Next day they learned that that colleague was killed on his way home, hit by a car that failed to stop."

"*Murdered?*" Anne's eyes did the saucers thing.

"They didn't wait for the coroner's report. That afternoon they cleared their bank account and loaded everything they had into the car, including all grandpa's files from his study. As soon as it grew dark they set off for the coast, caught a ferry to Sweden and disappeared."

"And from Sweden they came to Britain?"

"No. They never came to Britain."

Anne wondered how far she had a right to continue the questioning. "Would you like some more tea?"

"I'd like a shower. Is there one in the school?"

Anne nodded. "In the staff toilets, just here at the end of the corridor. Are you running out of water on the boat?"

"Just being careful. I didn't know when I'd get another chance to fill the tank. I don't suppose you have a spare towel, Anne?"

"You're welcome to use mine. I showered this morning." She paused. "But what about your story?"

"You're not bored by the family history?"

"It's more interesting than mine."

"OK. Sweden. My grandparents had to keep a low profile. If they surfaced, Nazi agents could slaughter them. They had to keep away from universities where grandpa would be known. So they took off for the centre of the country … Sommarland. Up there they rented a small farm. It was the last thing anyone would expect them to do. They worked like slaves for ten years, eking out a bare living. In the long winters grandpa worked on his research as best he could, using the notes he'd brought from Berlin."

"How did they cope with the farming?"

"Badly … practically ruined grandpa's health. After the war he got a job as a representative for an academic publisher. One day in Holland, he called in on a publisher who had handled his previous works. They almost threw him out on the street, said Herrmann had disappeared in a concentration camp years ago … was dead. He explained what had happened to the family, produced his research and eventually they believed him. There and then they gave him an advance for the new book."

"So he didn't have to go back to farming or being a rep? What did he do?"

"The publisher gave him the confidence to return to Germany and try to get back into the academic world. He managed to get a chair at one of the small universities."

"So his story had a happy ending."

"That wasn't the ending. And that's not the most amazing thing. He was actually able to get back his library. The Nazis were nothing if not thorough. They'd catalogued all his books – regarding them as potentially valuable for propaganda – and moved them to a store when war broke out. They later became a collection in a university library, and the authorities were delighted to return them to their owner."

"Brilliant. So that was a happy ending."

"No. Anne, contact with an evil as big as the Nazis doesn't produce happy endings. Everyone was corrupted by them. Everything they touched was contaminated."

"But grandpa – I mean, your grandfather – got his books back and a university job."

"Every one of his books was stamped inside with the eagle and swastika ... a nice memento."

Anne felt her cheeks redden at the memory of seeing the stamp on Donovan's boat and she drank from her mug of tea.

"End of story?" she asked.

"Not quite. Fate saved the strangest till the end. One day grandpa went off to the university in the morning and did not come home. Grandma had no word of him ... for over two years. She naturally assumed that a Nazi had finally got him when he least expected it."

"When was that?"

"1948."

"How *awful*."

"Only it wasn't the Nazis. They'd either been killed off or faded from the scene. No, it was the Americans."

"*What?*"

"They occupied that part of Germany at the time. They were tipped off by a communist sympathiser that Klaus Herrmann had worked for Himmler and gone into hiding to avoid capture. They arrested him and held him without trial, without letting him contact my grandmother. She was left struggling to keep the home together – my mother was at school, her sisters at university – while he languished in a detention centre. When the Americans realised they'd been duped, they released grandpa and later on paid him compensation ... quite generous. One afternoon he just walked down the path and found my grandmother working in the vegetable garden. Can you imagine that?"

"*Blimey!*"

"Yes. Years later my mother came to study in London, met my father, married. Here I am. They both died, as you know, ten years ago. One of her sisters and her husband brought me up. That was my uncle Reinhardt ... who died yesterday."

"What about your grandparents?"

"They both lived to a ripe old age ... died about twenty years ago."

Anne shook her head. "So you're not a Nazi," she muttered.

"*Me?*" He looked astonished. "Is that what you thought?"

"I didn't know ... I ..."

"Anne, I am the last person in the world who could ever be a Nazi. I hate them. *I hate them to death!*"

Anne was startled by the vehemence in his voice. She raised a hand to her mouth.

"Sorry, Anne. I didn't mean to shout at you."

"It's all right. I said I was feeling jumpy. Not your fault."

"It *is* my fault. It's my fault I feel so strongly about them." He stood up quickly. "I think it's time I took that shower."

Anne was glad to have something practical to do. She bent down, rummaged in her bag and dug out the towel.

"I've got some shampoo, too. You can use that like a shower gel."

She was rising from the bag when the noise froze her like a statue. Donovan shot out of the door like a rocket. The clattering of one of the warning buckets was still echoing down the corridor. Anne heard footsteps outside.

"There!" she called to him hoarsely, pointing towards the playground.

Donovan accelerated away, noiselessly on rubber soles. Anne seized the heavy Maglite torch and raced after him, her heart pounding. She jumped in the air to gain a view out of the nearest window and glimpsed two dark figures running across the playground. She reached the door as Donovan was clearing the chairs and bucket.

"What are you going to do?" she whispered.

"Find out who our visitor was."

"*Visitors*," said Anne. "Plural. I saw *two* people running off. Your alarm system must've surprised them. We need to think about what's the best thing to do."

"No time to think. They might've left a present for us on the doorstep. Stand back, Anne."

He grabbed the lock and twisted the handle, pressing against the door to open it as quietly as possible. Anne flattened herself against the wall, trying not to think of fire bombs, gripping the steel torch like a club. Donovan yanked the door open and leapt out. Against her better judgment, Anne followed. The sense of anti-climax rolled over her like a wave.

They stood, scanning the open space, straining their eyes to see into dark corners at the edge of their vision. There was no mysterious package lying in the doorway, no incendiary device, no splash of paint, nothing.

"Keep watch for a minute, Anne."

Donovan knelt down and switched on his torch. Methodically he checked in the corners of the recessed doorway, broadening his search in an arc, the fingers of his free hand probing the tarmac.

"Ah ..." he murmured.

"What?" Anne's voice was a croak. She did not look down.

Donovan stood up holding a piece of crumpled paper. Anne glanced at it and shook her head. A chewing gum wrapper.

"Is that all?"

"Yeah. Let's go back inside. I want to check all the doors."

They reassembled the intruder alarm of chairs and mop-bucket and walked cautiously from door to door, keeping in the shadows down the side of the corridors. Nothing had been disturbed, no windows broken. The incident had not been a diversionary tactic.

In the common room they put down their torches and Donovan peered closely at the paper, holding it under the light. Anne watched him begin to unpeel it with his fingernails. It was tightly folded, a grimy pellet squeezed into a plug the size and shape of a cigarette's filter tip. Donovan teased it apart, and they found themselves looking at a five pound note.

"What do you think –" Anne began.

"I know what this is. At least I have a shrewd idea." He passed it to Anne. "Drug money. Some poor sod has been waiting for his fix. I bet he screwed that up and held it in his clammy little hand, dying to get hold of his crack or whatever it was."

"You know about the drug scene?"

"I'm not blind to what goes on. But I don't have anything to do with it, if you're starting to have doubts about me again. I've not made a career move from Nazi *Gauleiter* to drug dealer, if that's what you're thinking."

"No. Of *course* not." Anne was indignant.

"I think they used the doorway as a meeting place. One of them probably bumped against the door and rocked the chairs so the bucket dropped. Must've given them a hell of a fright."

"What should we do with this?" Anne held up the fiver.

Donovan shrugged. "Donate it to the summer scheme fighting fund? I'm going to wash my hands after handling that. God knows where it's been." He made a face.

Anne looked at the note and grimaced. "Right. Good idea. I'll pop along to the loo."

"Do you want your towel, Anne?"

"No. It's all right. There are paper ones in there."

"I'll wait till you get back before I take that shower."

"No. You go ahead. I'll use the girls' toilets. I know where they are." She grinned. "I've already claimed squatters' rights."

Donovan thought about it, and a smile spread across his face.

• • • • •

Anne washed and dried herself as thoroughly as she could and went back to the common room. She had brought only the most basic nightwear and felt slightly self-conscious walking down the darkened corridor wearing only a T-shirt that stopped several inches above the knee. A crack of light was visible under the door where Donovan was taking his shower. Donovan … no longer a cause of apprehension … or was he?

In the common room she slipped under the cover on the airbed. It was almost midnight but she was alert and wide awake. In fact she felt refreshed and happy, even secure. In Donovan they had gained an ally. She smiled at the thought of a *stealth narrowboat*. The smile was still lingering when Donovan returned with the towel fastened round his waist.

"That's much better. I feel like a new man."

"So do I," said Anne. She grinned. "Well … you know what I mean."

They laughed together.

Marnie was instantly awake. Saturday morning. She reached up and ran her hand along the shelf over the bed till she made contact with the clock. Five to six. Ralph was still sleeping. Her thoughts turned to Anne. She would ring her soon and, needing something to occupy herself, skipped along to the shower to wash her hair. She sniffed the herbal shampoo and poured a measure into her hand.

· · · · ·

Donovan blinked and peered at the clock. Light was filtering in from the tiny window. Five fifty-eight. He turned over and looked at the head on the pillow beside him, leaning across to put his face close to Anne's short blonde hair. She stirred and breathed out with a sigh. Her eyes flickered open, and she gradually brought him into focus.

"What are you doing?" she murmured softly.

"Smelling your hair ... so that I'll remember."

"It's Chanel-Number-Five-Christian-Dior-Yves-Saint-Laurent."

"I guessed as much. They always have it in the girls' loos at this school."

"The girls round here have very high standards."

"You can say that again."

Anne smiled. "You always have an answer for everything."

He kissed her. "That's what my uncle Reinhardt used to say ... *Immer eine Antwort*."

Anne eased herself up onto one elbow. "Why did you say ... *so that you'll remember?*"

"Smells are evocative. I always associate certain smells with certain things."

"For instance?"

"In England the smell of summer is roses. In France, it's melons ... ripe Charentais melons."

"In Germany?"

"*Zwetschgenkuchen* ... plum cake taken from the oven to cool, lightly coated with sour cream."

She became suddenly serious. "I'd never done it before."

"I know. Neither had I."

"Really?"

"Really."

The alarm clock went off, and the moment passed.

· · · · ·

Donovan was putting the chairs and buckets of Fortress Garfield back where they belonged, and Anne was squashing the last of her things into the rucksack when the mobile rang. Six-fifteen exactly.

"Everything's fine here, Marnie. Just about to leave."

Thank goodness! Marnie tried to sound matter-of-fact. "Good. Remember the caretaker's coming early to check the place over, even though it's Saturday."

"I know. Serena persuaded him … used her charms."

"Of course. I'll have breakfast ready for you. Drive carefully."

"Er … Marnie?"

"Yes?"

"I'm feeling a bit peckish. I might just grab something on the way."

Odd. "OK. I'll expect you when I see you. You're sure everything's all right?"

"Oh, yes. Absolutely fine. See you soon."

• • • • •

They threw their things onto the back seat of the Mini and drove off without attracting attention. Anne threaded their way through the Victorian terraces and emerged into the town centre's one-way system. Donovan offered her a choice. She could drop him off if she wanted to get home quickly or come for breakfast on the boat.

In a few minutes they were on board *X O 2* at its mooring beside an attractive park on the River Nene Navigation. Donovan produced a dark rye loaf, butter and honey, and a small tin of evaporated milk. The coffee pot stood on the table between them.

"Donovan? Why did you *walk* to the school and not go on your bike?"

"A Muddy Fox mountain bike … bright yellow? Too conspicuous."

"True. It is rather eye-catching."

"It's a classic. I like classics. But it's not good camouflage."

"Same as your cameras," said Anne. "Leicas are classics, aren't they? Are those ones very old?"

"They belonged to my uncle Reinhardt's father. He was a photo-journalist between the wars. There were quite a few of them before television news came along. Sorry … another history lesson."

"No. Tell me … if you don't think I'm prying."

"He was an ethnic German from the Sudetenland. It's in Czechoslovakia now, you know, but they were Germans by cultural background. He even fought in the German army in the first world war. I've got his medals somewhere."

Anne almost said she knew, but managed to steer him back to his subject. "You were saying he was a photo-journalist?"

"Yes, working on magazines. He used the middle camera at the Olympic Games in Berlin in 1936. That thing was aimed at Hitler, Goering and the rest. Pity it wasn't a cannon." He smiled at the unintentional pun. "With one of the others he took the racing car pictures at the German Grand Prix in 1938."

"You even kept the one with the swastika." It was almost an accusation.

Donovan was still smiling. "Did you know that 'swastika' means 'good fortune'? Ironic, isn't it?"

"He must've been in a privileged position to have taken those photos," Anne said tentatively.

The smile faded. "These are almost the only photos I have from him. He was arrested after filing a report on the so-called *liberation* of the Sudetenland by Hitler the following year. Another irony. That invasion brought my uncle's family out, otherwise they'd have been caught by the Russians."

"What about your uncle's father?"

"No one ever saw him again. His report was never published."

"There must be lots of families that suffered like yours ... loads of horror stories to tell."

"Yes. That's why I want to help with things this summer. You can add my name to your list of volunteers, if you think I could be of use."

As they breakfasted neither spoke about the night they had spent together. But there was now a relaxed atmosphere between them. Donovan stroked Anne's hair when he rose to clear the table, and she reached up momentarily to touch his hand. They washed the dishes together in an easy silence.

When it was time to go, Anne took out her car keys and offered Donovan a lift to a shop where he could get milk. It was a small detour, and both were pleased to be together for a few minutes longer. Anne drove up towards the one-way system and was following the obligatory route when she was overtaken by a fire engine, lights blazing, siren wailing. At a point where the road narrowed, a second fire engine loomed up in her mirrors.

"What do I do now?" she yelled at Donovan.

"Go faster!" he shouted over the noise.

The Mini was an unlikely filling in the sandwich as the three red vehicles wove their way rapidly through the streets in procession. With white knuckles Anne gripped the wheel, knowing she would relive this scene in her dreams for years to come. Thankful that the driver behind her had switched off his siren, she clung on doggedly. And suddenly the ordeal was over. Finding the road blocked by fire engines and cars, she pulled in behind an ambulance and let her pursuer pass. For a moment she rested her head on the steering wheel.

"You did brilliantly, Anne. That was..." Donovan's voice faded.

Anne looked up to see him staring ahead. She followed his gaze. The activity going on around them was centred on a bus depot. The sign on the wall was just legible amid the chaos: Graham White Travel – founded 1933. Jets of water were raining down from hoses mounted on extending ladders. Fire-fighters in yellow helmets were rushing to and fro. The sky was clouding with smoke, some black, some grey. The smell of destruction was seeping into the car.

"This looks like my idea of hell," Anne said. She jumped as a gloved hand rapped against the window. Winding it down she looked up to see a face concealed behind a breathing mask.

"You must leave the area at once," came a man's muffled voice. He pointed back down the street. "Reverse up, turn round and make your way in that direction. Drive slowly on dipped headlights. Understand?"

"But how do I get out? The road's blocked off."

"Go between the houses. You'll come into a back alley. Turn right, follow it to the end. Got it?"

In the background an explosion erupted. Flames and debris flew up into the air from the yard behind the garage wall. One of the ladders rocked in the blast, its occupant clinging on bravely, redirecting the water cannon onto its new target. Anne was aware of the man shouting at her.

"You *must* get out of here. *Now!*"

Anne nodded, summoning all her reserves of willpower to keep calm. The words *cool under fire* were running through her mind. What a hope! Donovan's hand was on her shoulder, and she could feel extra strength flowing into her from his grip. The street was becoming darker by the second as smoke filled the air. The noise from the inferno was growing to a hideous roar.

"Your window!" Donovan shouted.

Anne wound it shut and almost missed the gap between the houses. Thanking providence that she had a Mini and not a Range Rover, she guided the car down the narrow passage and found the alley that ran behind the houses. She blew air from her lips and trundled over the cobbles. Here all was quiet and calm. Nearing the top of the passageway she halted to take her breath. Donovan reached across and hugged her.

· · · · ·

Marnie was just beginning to wonder what had become of Anne when the phone rang.

"Is everything all right? You sound a little ... tense."

"Marnie, you won't believe what's just happened to me."

"Fire away."

"Good guess. On the way back I got sucked in between these fire engines and ended up at the scene. It was the garage belonging to a coach company. Graham White Travel. It was *awful* ... fire ... smoke ... an explosion. I wondered if it might've been another attack."

"I don't think so. There's been nothing on the radio. Don't worry about it. You're OK?"

"I'm fine. And I'm on my way back ... at last."

Only a minute had passed when the phone rang again. It was Serena and she was in high spirits.

"No problems at the school? All OK?"

"I didn't go back. Things got complicated here. Anne did the stint on her own. She insisted ... thought it would be a good test-run. There were no problems."

"Brave girl. Good for her. Though I'm glad you told me now, not last night. I'd have worried about her."

"Quite."

"Listen, Marnie. I just want to let you know how things are going. We seem to be making progress again. I've managed to sign up another coach firm. That means we have all the transport we need for the extra summer scheme outings."

An alarm bell started clanging in Marnie's head. "This is recent?"

"I got the confirmation letter in the post this morning. I was in discussions with them all week, and I thought they weren't going to be able to do it, but they've written to say it's on."

"Serena, does the name Graham White Travel mean anything to you?"

"Oh my God, Marnie, that is so *weird*. You must be psychic. That's the firm I'm talking about."

"Graham White?" Marnie's voice was distant.

"It's a kind of play on words," said Serena. "Their coaches are painted in grey and white. Get it? They're an old local firm and they've ... Marnie, what made you think of them?"

"I'm sorry to tell you this, Serena, but I think I've got some bad news."

• • • • •

Such a pleasant day. It was the usual mixture of sunshine flitting through wispy high clouds. A comfortable temperature. It should have been a relaxing summer lunch with friends, then a trip on the boat. Instead, it would be the usual council of war, the main activity that summer.

Ralph and Anne set up the table in the courtyard as Marnie finished preparing lunch. On any other day it would be a delicious summer medley: chilled asparagus soup with mint leaves, a *salade niçoise* and fresh raspberries with cream; white wine from the Loire valley. Today, Marnie wondered if anyone would taste it.

The table was covered in a cheerful cloth of yellow gingham, with small vases of marigolds. While Ralph was in the office barn's kitchen area chopping sticks of French bread, Marnie inspected the setting, determined at least to sound upbeat.

"This is great, Anne. You've done a marvellous job … you and Ralph. The table goes well with the roses, too."

They were standing in front of the cottages that were glorying in their first season of roses climbing round their doors. Marnie and Anne had planted them in the autumn, and an abundance of bright yellow and pink blooms lit up the yard. Bees were droning softly. The call to sniff the flowers was irresistible, and Marnie inclined her face towards them.

"Mm … *gorgeous*. That is *wonderful*."

"Donovan says roses are *the* smell of summer in England."

"Yes, he's right." Marnie frowned. "Er … when did he say that?"

"What?" Anne stepped across and buried her face in the roses, breathing in long and slowly, her eyes closed. She saw his face close to hers on the pillow. "Oh … some time," she added vaguely. "He's all right, you know … on our side."

"You're sure of that."

"Yes." Anne looked at her watch. "When were you expecting Serena and the others?"

"She should've been here by now."

As if on cue, everyone made their appearance. Estelle and Luther emerged from the cottage. Before they even had time to speak, a car hove into view from the field track, and Serena's Clio pulled up by the farmhouse, followed by George's Range Rover. Last to arrive was Ronny, flicking his leg effortlessly over the saddle as he braked to a halt and rested the bike against the wall of the office barn in one fluid movement.

Amid the general kissing of cheeks Ronny went towards Anne as if he intended to do the same. To his surprise, at the last minute Anne pointed to the office and asked him to bring out an extra chair, turning to adjust the flowers on the table. Ronny at once did as he was asked. Marnie observed them with curiosity. Everyone else huddled round Serena who brandished the lunchtime edition of the local paper.

"There's nothing in it about the Graham White depot fire," she announced.

"Must've happened after they'd gone to press," said Ralph.

George edged up beside Serena and leaned close to read over her shoulder. "What's Brandon up to today?"

Serena folded the paper and held it up. "Guess where he is? The front page."

The headline read: BRANDON SLAMS IMMIGRANTS POLICY.

Ralph shook his head. "For the BFP this is the equivalent of a back-to-basics campaign. What's Brandon saying?"

"He's trying to outgun the right wing, undermine the Tories and steal their votes. As if they weren't bad enough." Beside her, George cleared his throat. "Oh, sorry, George ... no offence."

"None taken, my dear. We're all in the same camp. But I would just like to mention that not all of us Tories are actual fascists."

Serena turned and kissed him on the cheek. "Apology accepted?"

"None needed." George caught the eye of his wife, and his smirk evaporated. "So what does the article say?"

Serena chanted the main points. "Basically, the whole of Europe needs a firm hand on immigration policy ... Britain should lead by example ... stop jobs being taken by so-called refugees and bogus asylum-seekers ... bla-bla-bla ... Tory government not strong enough ... bla-bla-bla ... the usual."

"That's positive proof." Luther spoke for the first time.

Serena pinned him with a stare. "Of what?"

"It proves we must be the cleverest people in the country. We come over here – notice we always *come over here* – even those of us who were born in this country – and succeed in taking over all the jobs while simultaneously living entirely on the dole. That's brilliant."

There was general laughter. George cleared his throat again.

"You don't think ..." he began, as all eyes turned in his direction, "purely playing devil's advocate, you understand ... you don't think that some people might have jobs and ... claim benefits?"

Ralph joined in. "There's no evidence that ethnic communities are more guilty of that than any other section of society, George."

"The figures show quite the opposite actually," said Luther. "Among Afro-Caribbeans there's always been a stigma attached to claiming benefits. Anyway, who wants to come over here – it's a long way to Jamaica – and live on the dole? People came here to make a better life for themselves and give their kids a good future."

George nodded. "Good point. And many people have forgotten – or never knew – that the West Indians came to Britain in response to a call to come and help rebuild the old country after the war. They must've been sorely disappointed at not getting a better welcome when they'd come so far."

"That's all very well," said Serena impatiently, "but it's history. What do we say to refute Brandon's statement?"

"There must be figures on who actually claims unemployment benefit," said Luther.

"No, no." Ralph raised his hands. "Not statistics ... big turn-off. No one believes them, and the papers won't be interested. We have to lead with something positive."

"The summer scheme is all we've got," said Estelle. "It's hardly going to make banner headlines on the front page ... *Summer Playscheme Exclusive*

...KIDS GO ON COACH TRIPS. Big deal."

"What about the fire at the coach depot?" They all looked at Anne. "That was horrible. That should make the front page. Newspapers like *horrible*."

"Trouble is ... it might scare off the other coach operators," said Ralph. "We've got to be careful. It'll depend on whether the police find any evidence. Now, if they arrested someone – someone linked with Brandon or New Force – *that* would be something. But without proof ..."

• • • • •

During that Saturday lunchtime the weather grew steadily brighter in every part of the county, with one exception. In the courtyard of Glebe Farm a single grey cloud hovered about three metres above the table. No one could see it but all felt its presence, Serena more than any of the others.

"Why does it always have to be *us*? Why can't the political parties tackle Brandon and his cronies more effectively? Oh ... sorry to be bitching like this, Marnie. Your food is delicious."

There was a chorus of agreement.

"I share your frustration," said Marnie. "But we all have to do what we can. That's what we're here to talk about."

"We need to focus on the positive," said George. "Keep our morale up."

Serena nodded vigorously. "You're absolutely right. First I'd like to thank Anne for doing last night's guard duty at the school."

Another chorus.

"Tell us, how was it for you?"

"Oh ... er ... it was OK."

"What did you do? How did you organise things? Presumably you didn't just listen to Radio One till eleven and turn out the light?"

"Not quite." Anne paused as if searching her memory. "Well ... I tried to fortify the place."

"*Fortify*? Interesting. Go on."

"I rigged up cleaners' buckets on chairs leaning against the doors to the outside. If anyone tried to push the doors open, the bucket would fall off and make a noise."

"An intruder alarm," said Luther. "That's good."

"And I put chairs under the doorknobs of the classrooms to block them. Not much of a barrier, but enough to hold up anyone trying to get in through the classroom windows ... give me time to raise the alarm."

"*Brilliant!*" said Ronny. "Did you think it all up by yourself?"

"No." For a few seconds she looked flustered.

"One of Marnie's bright ideas?" said Luther.

"No. I ... called in the SAS for advice. We renamed the school Fortress Garfield."

The group laughed, and the atmosphere began to lighten.

"And everything was quiet?" Serena asked.

"Yes."

"Let's hope it stays that way."

"We can't count on that," said Estelle. "Especially after the fire at the coach garage. I've got an idea. Whoever's on duty at the school should have a fire extinguisher with them at all times. One for each person."

"They have extinguishers there already," said Anne. "They're mounted in the corridors."

"But they're big, presumably?"

"Quite big."

"I think you should take small ones ... like the ones you have on the boats ... easy to carry and operate. Any trouble, you could run with them and hit the fire quickly."

"That's a good idea," said Marnie. "I've got a couple of spares on *Sally Ann.*"

"Coming back to the coach garage," Serena broke in. "You actually saw the fire, Anne?"

"Yes."

"How much did you see?"

"Lots of smoke coming over the wall ... an explosion. That's when the fireman told me to get away."

"How did you get out?" George asked.

"We drove up an alleyway behind the houses."

George nodded. "A jitty."

"A what?" said Marnie.

"It's a local word. There's a whole network of back alleys in the old parts of Northampton. Jitties."

Estelle leaned forward. "*We*? Did you say *we*, Anne? I thought you were alone."

Anne stood up and began refilling the glasses with wine. "The Mini and me. Force of habit. More wine, Mr Stubbs?"

While Anne made her way round the table with the wine, they resumed eating.

"So who's on duty tonight?" Serena asked.

Estelle said, "I'm doing it with Marnie."

"You're going off on your trip soon, aren't you?"

"Flying out Monday."

"How long will you be gone?"

"Almost a week."

Luther winked at Anne. "Otherwise I'd be volunteering to do the Sunday night slot with Serena," he said.

"More chilled soup for you, Luther?" Marnie asked pointedly. "You seem to need cooling down." She smiled sweetly.

"Who is doing the Sunday night stint?" said Serena.

Ralph spoke up. "I am."

"Shall I come along as back-up?" said Ronny.

"Thanks, but I don't think there's any need, really."

Luther grinned at Ronny. "I thought you might've been Anne's secret back-up last night."

A wry grin. "No such luck, I'm afraid."

Luther continued. "Nice-looking girl like Anne ... I'd have thought she would've organised a friend to keep her company."

Anne just laughed. Ronny glanced at her over the top of his wine glass. So did Marnie.

• • • • •

The party ended early. Serena went over the programme for the first week and gave everyone a copy. There was no more teasing, no more innuendo. Marnie explained about Dorothy Vane-Henderson's offer to organise a summer fete in support of the scheme. George offered sponsorship for any children who needed help to pay for transport to and from the school. As soon as the meal ended, they all began clearing the table.

Estelle went back to the cottage to collect her overnight bag. Marnie had brought her things to the office barn to put in Anne's rucksack.

Ralph was loading the dish-washer. "You get on, Marnie. I can sort things out here. Got everything you need?"

"I forgot to bring a towel. I'll have to fetch one from the boat."

Anne's rucksack was leaning against the washing machine. With the distraction caused by the depot fire it had been abandoned on her return. Marnie tipped its contents into the washing basket.

"Although I could probably just borrow Anne's. She'll hardly have used it. It won't matter."

"Don't forget your sleeping bag, Marnie."

"No. I left it in the car when I ... that's odd ..."

"What is?"

"This... the rucksack ... it's all damp. Her towel's quite wet."

"She probably had a shower," said Ralph.

"She showered in the morning."

"Perhaps she took another to pass the time."

Marnie ran her hand down the back of the rucksack and looked at her damp palm. Reaching inside, her fingers brushed against something lying in the bottom, a piece of paper. She pulled it out and was surprised to find it was a five-pound note. It had a slight unpleasant odour that made her think of stale feet.

Marnie sniffed the towel. It too had a faint smell ... musky ... almost like ... Just then, Anne came backing through the door with a tray of glasses. Marnie quickly threw the towel into the machine with Anne's T-shirt nightdress and pressed the door shut. She moved away from the machine, dropping the fiver into the in-tray as she passed her desk.

"I'm nearly ready ... just need to fetch a towel. Any sign of Estelle?"

"She's in the yard," said Anne. "Fond farewells to Luther. You'd think she was leaving for the Spanish Civil War."

"Tell her to get in the tank. I'll join her in a minute."

Anne skipped outside.

"What was that about the towel?" Ralph said quietly.

"Oh, nothing. You were probably right. I'd better get going."

When they kissed each other goodbye, Ralph wished her an uneventful night on guard duty with Estelle. As it turned out, his wish was granted.

• • • • •

They were on the road again. Marnie tried not to seem pre-occupied as they travelled north up the dual carriageway, but it was a struggle to keep her mind on driving and not bombard herself with questions. Why was Anne's towel so damp? She had only taken it to have a quick wash before bed. Then there was its smell ... not at all unpleasant, but somehow ... not

Anne. The five-pound note was bizarre ... unwholesome. It looked as if it had been rolled into a kind of pellet. Its dampness probably came from contact with the towel, but as for its smell ...

They were approaching the outskirts of Northampton when Estelle broke into Marnie's thoughts.

"Everything all right?"

"Mm?"

"You're very quiet. I didn't want to intrude on you."

"Sorry. Just going over things in my mind."

"You probably miss not having Anne with you, and her famous checklists."

Marnie laughed. "Poor old Anne. Everyone makes fun of her lists. It all began when she started working with me. She asked a lot of questions and wrote everything down. She was desperate not to get anything wrong."

"And now she's indispensable to you."

"Well ..."

"Oh, I think she is. I must admit I did think at one time it'd be good to stay and work with you, Marnie. But I soon realised you had a great running mate in Anne. She's a very precious friend and partner. I can't see you having room for anyone else in the firm."

Marnie had no wish to discuss her relationships. Time to change the subject. "You and Luther seem to have settled in very well."

"Do you mean into the cottage, the village, or together as an item?"

"All three, I suppose."

"It's certainly a great place to live. And I know it's helped us to gel as a couple."

"I'm glad. At first I did wonder if it was a kind of rebound thing, but you do seem happy together. I can tell it's not just a passing fling."

"No, it's not. Luther's the most important thing ever to have happened in my life. It's forever. If I didn't have Luther, I'd be destroyed."

Although she had spoken quietly, the strength of feeling in Estelle's voice had startled Marnie. They had driven through the town in light traffic and were nearing the school. As they pulled up at the kerb, Estelle reached across and took hold of Marnie's arm.

"You don't know how grateful I am to you, Marnie, for giving me a fresh start. I really meant it when I said I'd love to stay and go on working with you, but I know that isn't possible. I just want to say I don't know what I would've done without you."

There were tears in her eyes, and for a second Marnie felt the emotion from Estelle running into her arm like an energy field. She lightly patted her hand, half expecting high-voltage sparks to fly up.

"Everyone deserves a new start, Estelle. I'm glad to have helped."

Estelle was about to speak, but Marnie got in first.

"Come on, let's get the show on the road ... time to get Fortress Garfield up and running."

24

On Sunday morning Ralph had a reviving breakfast ready for Marnie when she got home, and it was warm enough to eat out on the bank framed on two sides by *Sally Ann* and *Thyrsis*. Single-handedly he produced scrambled eggs and smoked salmon with whole-wheat toast, freshly-squeezed orange juice, homemade preserves (purchased from a Women's Institute stall) and a cafetière of Jamaican Blue Mountain coffee.

When Anne reached the docking area and saw the table spread under the parasol, she went down on one knee in front of Ralph and proposed marriage. Marnie told her to get in the queue. During the meal she gave her report on guard duty; a quiet night with no attempted intrusions and not so much as a drunk throwing up in a doorway.

After breakfast they voted on the plan for the day. R and R won by a unanimous decision. Ralph was elected to fetch the Sunday papers from the shop, and he set off on foot, declaring himself in need of a little exercise. Marnie and Anne chatted happily while they cleared the table and began on the dishes in the galley on *Sally Ann*. Their good mood lasted until Anne switched on the radio and they caught the local news bulletin. That weekend's polls, conducted by the BBC and two national research organisations, agreed on their findings. Garth Brandon and the BFP had edged in front of all the other parties by two clear percentage points. It was a first in the history of British politics.

• • • • •

Ralph's good mood lasted until he reached the high street. He arrived as the bells started ringing to call the faithful to church and he found Molly and Richard Appleton leaving their house which was next door to the shop. With a cheerful greeting they began to walk away when Molly had an afterthought.

"Ralph?" she called back. "Did you see him ... your friend? Did he find you all right?"

"Which friend was that, Molly?" A faint alarm bell sounded.

"He didn't give his name, but I think he must've been from the university ... educated sort of chap ... very smart ... well-mannered."

"When was this?"

"Last night. Didn't he see you? I gave him directions." Her expression froze. "Did I do the wrong thing?"

"Did you say he'd find me on the boat?"

"No, I just told him the way to Glebe Farm. I hope I haven't done something silly."

"Don't worry about it, Molly. I'll check with Luther. He was around last night. Tell me about this man who was asking for me. What did he look like?"

"Thirties, probably ... er ... navy blue jacket, I think ... glasses ... I'm sorry, I'm not very observant."

Ralph thought hard. It was just possible it could have been a colleague from All Saints College. Mark Danvers had family in Rugby and might have looked in while passing on a visit there. He matched the description, such as it was, but it could have been almost anyone.

"Notice anything else about him, Molly?"

She shook her head. "Not really. I only spoke to him for a few seconds. He drove up to the shop when I was changing the postcards on the notice board in the window. He stuck his head round the door. Oh … I did notice his car, though."

"What was it?" Danvers drove a white Peugeot.

"Dunno. I'm not very good at makes of cars. But his was a bit unusual. It was dark … black, I think … with chrome over the wheels … not the actual wheels, you know … the bodywork."

"Chrome wheel arches?"

"That's right. It looked quite smart. I'd remember that car if I saw it again. Would it belong to one of your friends, Ralph?"

"Not as far as I know."

• • • • •

Ralph arrived back to find Marnie on the phone to Randall Hughes. He had been the vicar at Knightly St John and after many differences of opinion with leading members of the community, he had been moved on by the bishop in a controversial appointment as Rural Dean of Brackley. A charismatic figure with strong character, he had remained a friend and kept in touch with Marnie and Ralph. Marnie was chuckling when she disconnected.

"What's he up to now?" Ralph asked.

"Doing his bit for democracy. He's offered to help with the summer scheme if we need him."

"Good for Randall," said Anne who was sitting by the bank in a deckchair.

"And good for us. Also, he's fighting back against Garth Brandon, against what he calls Brandon's *charm offensive*."

"In what way?" said Ralph.

"After the BFP convoy left here the other night they went down to Brackley, if you remember. Apparently, they went through their usual routine … stuck posters of Brandon all over the town centre … *hundreds* of them."

Ralph frowned. "The BFP's got serious resources behind it."

"So has Randall," said Marnie. "He's got his own army."

"The church militant?"

"That's Randall." Marnie grinned. "He's mobilised his … what does he call them? … his *guests*."

One of Randall's initiatives had been to convert a large house in the middle of Brackley, bequeathed to the church, as a hostel. Anne described it as a drop-in centre for drop-outs. It had become popular and housed up to two dozen of the homeless and dispossessed at any given time.

"And?" said Ralph.

"He persuaded them to go round the town pulling down all the posters. Now, you'd never know Brandon's lot had been anywhere near the place."

"How did he manage to get them to do that?"

"He appealed to their higher nature and sense of public spirit."

Ralph looked suspicious. "He did?"

"Offered them a cigarette for every ten posters they brought him."

Anne squawked in the background. "That's terrible! He doesn't allow smoking in his hostel because it's bad for their health ... and now he gives them free fags."

"Randall probably thinks the BFP would be even more harmful to their health. He said the end justified the means."

"I think that was the argument of the Spanish Inquisition," Ralph observed.

"And Hitler," Anne added.

25

This was to be a Big Day. That Monday was the first day of the holidays and the start of the summer playscheme. Although it did not begin officially until enrolments at eleven o'clock, everyone at Glebe Farm was up by six-thirty. Ralph's guard duty during the night had passed without incident and he had returned home before the school caretaker came on site. They planned to meet Serena and the other organisers at the school at nine to put up welcome posters and hang bunting and balloons. Despite their early rising, someone was up before them.

When the phone rang on *Thyrsis*, it was Ralph who took the call.

"Hi, Anne. Do you want to speak to Marnie? She's in the shower just now."

"No. I wanted you, Ralph. I think you'd better see this. Can you come?"

"On my way."

The biggest surprise was not what had been done, but how it had been done without anyone knowing. Ralph surveyed the farm complex and shook his head. Anne stood beside him, frowning. On every door, every window and on most of the walls, the face of Garth Brandon smiled down at them, his slogan exhorting them to put Britain first. The courtyard was a mass of red, white and blue.

"You didn't hear anything?"

"Nope."

"Estelle and Luther were leaving for the airport by six."

"Right."

"When did you first see all this?"

"Just before I rang you. I glanced out as usual from my room to see what the weather was like. And there was his face, everywhere ... Brandon. I can't believe they could've done this without me knowing."

"So between six and six-thirty. Too early for the paperboy to spot them. Too late for the milkman. No farmers likely to see them round here. Clever ... and lucky."

"But why do all this?" said Anne. "They know we'll just take them down ... and no one but us will see them. It's not as if ..." Her voice faded. "It's only intended for us. It's a warning, isn't it? It's saying ... *we know where you live.*"

She saw the fire bomb. It hurtled through her mind, and her imagination fanned the flames. Anne pictured again the buildings of Glebe Farm as they were when she first saw them over a year ago, gutted and abandoned, roof timbers pointing at the sky, charred black, like the ribs of a cremated carcass. She shuddered. There had been too many fires already that summer.

• • • • •

"Come on, everybody, lighten up."

No one had spoken since they set off from Glebe Farm. The atmosphere in Marnie's Discovery would have done justice to a funeral car. She heard Ralph breathe out slowly beside her. Looking in the rear-view mirror she saw Anne's glum expression on the back seat.

Anne caught sight of Marnie's eyes reflected and she immediately snapped into Happy Face. "I wasn't really looking sad, Marnie," she said lightly. "I was struggling with a problem."

"Which one in particular? We have so many to choose from."

"I was trying to remember the words of that Cliff Richard number ... *We're all going on a summer holiday* ... Thought it'd be nice to have a sing-song."

Two grins began spreading in the front seats. Marnie laughed, and Ralph joined in.

"Idiot!" they chorused.

Not wanting to spoil the improved ambience, Marnie tried to keep up the tempo. "Well, at least the summer scheme will now help make things better. If it works as well as Serena hopes, there shouldn't be any trouble with the youngsters over the holidays. They'll be out of the way ... one less thing to worry about."

It bothered Marnie that Ralph said nothing in reply. She had hoped for at least a murmur of agreement, but he sat looking out at the passing scenery as if lost in thought. Anne piped up again from behind.

"It's a great programme for the kids. If I'd been a few years younger, I'd have loved to go on all those visits. It's like lots of holidays rolled into one. And they'll all make loads of new friends. Great."

"That's true," said Marnie. "I've been thinking so much about the political motives behind it all, I was forgetting it's being run for the benefit of the children. They'll have a lovely time. What do you think, Ralph?"

He managed a smile. "I agree. But somehow I can't switch my mind off from the other matters."

Marnie sympathised. "I know. And we can't take our eyes off the ball. No time to relax where Brandon's concerned." She had a flashback to the dozens of posters that were waiting for them to take down on their return home. "At least today the initiative's with us. The summer scheme will be positive news. And once the election's over next week, we can enjoy the rest of the summer."

The early cloud cover began dissipating, and a fine day opened up before them. They drove on in better spirits, unaware that their optimism would evaporate in the noonday sun.

• • • • •

It seemed that everyone had risen early that Monday morning. As Marnie swung the car round the last corner and they saw the school, for one horrible second they thought the BFP had struck here as well. Red, white and blue bunting was strung across the buildings and playground. Balloons of the same colour hung from the walls, and a small crowd of people could be seen on the far side of the yard clustered together by the entrance doors. It would be just like Brandon to organise a BFP rally right here on their all-important first day.

But then they noticed other colours blending in with the traditional British. There were strings of green and yellow and orange, mixing jauntily with the rest. It was almost a cacophony of colour like a boating regatta or a fun fair. The sight of it all was enough to put a smile on their faces. There was nothing threatening about this display. This was a welcome.

They caught sight of Serena in pale blue denims and a brilliant white tank top, and as they drew nearer they could make out a group of helpers under her command wrestling with a sheet. Moments later they began to hoist it up, a banner proclaiming *Kidscene 4 Summer*. Serena stood looking up at the name while photographers took pictures. Her coffee-coloured skin shone against the lightness of her clothing, and anyone could be forgiven for mistaking this for a fashion shoot. Turning, she saw Marnie, Ralph and Anne and beckoned them over. She was radiant.

"Our time has come," she said, kissing her friends warmly and perhaps a trifle theatrically.

"I can see you're on good form," said Marnie.

"I've been planning this for so many months, Marnie. It really matters to me. It is so important."

Ralph put an arm round her shoulders and squeezed. "Congratulations."

Serena laughed. "Thanks. Now all we've got to do is make it work, get the kids enrolled and sent off on their trips, keep up the propaganda ... stop the place from turning into a battleground. Doesn't sound too bad if you say it quickly."

A man and a woman materialised beside them, one toting a camera with a fat lens, the woman armed with a walkman-sized tape recorder and a notebook.

"Just a couple more photos, please, Serena? And I need to check a few facts before we go."

"You're going? What about getting pictures of the kids and their parents? That's the whole idea."

"Jason will come back later when the kids are here. If we're to hit today's deadline, I've got to get the story in straight away."

They led her off without looking back.

"She really is on a high," Marnie said quietly.

Anne tugged her sleeve. "Marnie, don't look now, but Mrs Frightfully-Frightfully is waving at us from over there, by those Land Rovers."

They looked in the direction in which Anne was pointing and saw two military-looking vehicles parked at the end of the playground. Each had a canvas roof behind the cab and a tall radio aerial surmounted by a small pennant. People were climbing out. In the middle of a mass of khaki stood Dorothy Vane-Henderson in full W.I. combat regalia, a floral summer dress and sensible shoes. She began striding towards them, and Marnie had a mental image of her as a schoolgirl sallying out to do battle on the hockey field. It was scary. They began walking towards her.

"What's this?" Ralph said, without moving his lips. "The Eighth Army?"

"I've an idea it's the Seventh Cavalry."

"I thought they usually arrived at the last minute when everything was lost."

"Maybe she knows more than we do."

Anne giggled, raising a hand to shield her eyes against the low morning sun. "Surely those are scouts. Were we expecting them?"

It was too late for an answer. The cavalry commander was upon them.

"Hallo, all. Well, we're here." She beamed.

Marnie smiled back. "Great. Er ... who is here, exactly?"

"Why ... your helpers ... as I promised you ... sort of. These are scouts, of course. They've come as a kind of bonus. We'll still run the fete, as I said we would."

Marnie tried to conceal her bewilderment. "That's marvellous, Dorothy." Over her shoulder she could see concerted activity around the Land Rovers. They really did look military, with black and drab green paint in camouflage pattern. Boys in uniform were unloading boxes and bags and stacking them on the pavement while a man in charge checked everything off on a clipboard. "I thought scouts were supposed to be highly disciplined but not run like the military."

"That's right." Dorothy looked round. "Oh ... you mean the Land Rovers. They belong to Gregory Roberts ... a sort of hobby. He restores them ... they're ex-army."

"Is he ex-army?"

"No, no. He's a personnel manager with a big firm in town. He's also the local scout leader, of course. You can meet him once he's got the unloading sorted out."

"Mrs Vane-Henderson," Marnie began tentatively. "What are the scouts going to do?"

"Didn't I mention that? And do call me Dorothy. They're going to pitch camp and guard the base."

"Make a camp *here* ... in the middle of town ... on a concrete playground ... on a school site?"

"Ye-e-s?" Mrs V-H's one-word answer carried a series of questions along the lines of: *Do you think I don't know what I'm doing? Are we likely to be put off by a small technical difficulty? Do you think I don't know the chairman of this or that committee who can give us permission to do exactly what we want to do?*

Marnie was trying to think of a suitable response when the man-in-charge arrived among them. He was immaculately turned out in khaki shirt and shorts, with long socks, lanyard and numerous insignia, sturdily-built and broad-chested, his considerable height increased by a traditional scouter's hat. He touched its brim politely and greeted Marnie and the others with a confident smile while Dorothy made the introductions.

He addressed Ralph. "Where will the coaches be coming in?"

"Er ... I'm not sure. Marnie's one of the organisers."

Marnie pointed towards the Land Rovers. "They'll be lining up where your ... er ... vehicles are parked and all down that street."

"Then we'd better get signs put up to keep people away. Who'll deal with that?"

"The lady over there with the reporters."

For the first time Marnie noticed the group of scouts that had formed round their leader.

"Stephen, Roger, you hop along and see to that. Take three other boys and start putting up the No Parking signs. Ten metre intervals if they've got enough." The boys vanished. "And where will the children be assembling?"

"Over there by the entrance under the banner."

"Good. We'll pitch camp here, here and here." Gregory indicated the spaces; more boys rushed off.

"You're going to camp here for some time. Is that right?"

"I know what you're thinking, Mrs Walker. But we'll use the school's facilities for water supplies and latrines. We'll patrol the premises and grounds from here. We'll secure the site, don't you worry. And we'll take charge of stewarding when the buses are loading and unloading. We'll need copies of schedules, the full programme and timetables."

Leaving Marnie with no further questions, he marched off towards Serena. Even Anne could think of nothing missing from her list.

"I suppose they'll be all right," Ralph muttered.

"Of course they'll be all right," said Dorothy firmly. Already the playground was alive with efficiency as the scouts lugged their gear into place at the double. "They've been all right for the past hundred years. It's the rest of society that's gone wrong. Baden-Powell saw it clearly. Give young people discipline and there's nothing they can't do." She looked pointedly at Anne's clipboard and lists and smiled at her.

Ralph shrugged. "They'll possibly be up against thugs like New Force and schemers like Brandon's BFP."

"Nothing's going to happen here. In a straight contest between the ideals of BP and the BFP my money's on Greg Roberts's boys every time. You think Brandon wants the publicity that his supporters attacked the Scout Movement? That would be bad news for his lot. No. You're in safe hands."

· · · · ·

With half an hour to go before enrolment, children were already arriving. The scouts were marshalling them into queues at the reception tables, and Serena remarked that she wondered if there was anything left for her to do. At her side the sturdy figure of Scoutmaster Greg Roberts watched over proceedings.

"This should be no problem," he asserted. Suddenly he pointed at one scout at the far end of the playground and made a flapping gesture with his hand. The boy began moving to the left. Greg stopped flapping and raised a finger. The boy stopped. It was like a cricket captain repositioning the fielders for a change of bowler. It made Marnie feel they were under the protection of the British Empire. She could not help smiling.

Serena's mobile trilled, and she moved away, pulling it from her pocket. Anne saw a newsvan pause briefly outside the corner shop across the street.

"The papers have arrived. I'll pop over and get one." She went off at the double.

"Your boys certainly have things under control," said Marnie.

"It'll be a walk in the sun."

"And the sun ... the real one ... it won't bother them, dressed in their uniforms?"

"Not a bit. BP was right. Light cotton clothing, shorts, a hat to shade the eyes and protect the crown. Perfect." He swivelled his head towards Anne who was crossing the road. "Whose is that Discovery parked over there, any idea?"

"It's mine."

"Pleased with it?"

"So far. It's very nice. I've only had it a few months."

"Good little run-around," said Greg.

A coach pulled up and two more turned the corner. Scouts waved them to their places in the line. Greg observed, his eyes in shade under the brim of his hat.

"I think you're right, Marnie. I think we've got things nicely under control."

He was about to be proved wrong. Twice.

Marnie could see Serena switching off her mobile, looking unhappy. She excused herself and walked over.

"What's up, Serena?"

The light had gone out from her eyes, leaving them smouldering. Momentarily Marnie thought she might burst into tears or smash the phone to the ground. The spasm passed, and Serena breathed out steadily before replying.

"I don't know what's the matter with these people. Sometimes I really wonder ..."

"What people?"

"The blacks." There was a bitterness in her voice.

Marnie was shocked. "Who do you mean?"

Serena skewered her with a look and said slowly, "People with dark skins ... you know?"

"But that's our lot." Marnie wondered if she was missing something obvious. "They're the ones on our side, aren't they?"

"You wouldn't think so, Marnie. You wouldn't believe it."

"Try me. I used to be a quick learner."

A long sigh. "It appears that our efforts aren't universally admired by our brothers. There's some bad feeling among the black community. Some people feel the kids are being used as part of a political game."

"They've got a point," said Marnie. "But it's Brandon's game ... to stir up trouble and manipulate public opinion. Don't your critics realise you're trying to get the kids out of the frame?"

"Ah well, Marnie, they don't quite see it like that. They're not so charitable. Some would say I'm pushing black kids into the firing line to further my own political ambitions."

"Do you have political ambitions?"

"Yes."

"But that isn't what all this is about."

"No. My work with the community is where it all started. The more I got involved, the more I realised it's the politicians who have the say in what gets done. Believe me, Marnie, I thought by being a youth officer I could play a part, but I keep finding myself up against other people's priorities ... the councillors ... the senior officers. One day I'll stand for election myself.

Maybe I'll go on to try for Parliament. Everybody knows that's my goal. If I get elected, I'll do a good job. I know I can."

"So some suspect you're using this only as a stepping stone with your own personal agenda."

"Right. And really, it's the other way round. This is what's made me want to go on to other things."

"And the phone call?"

"A friend … huh! … *some friend*. A warning. There could be trouble from some parts of the Afro-Carib community."

"What kind of trouble?"

"Unspecified. But there are some elements you wouldn't want to upset."

Marnie had heard about rival factions, gangsters who had come to Britain from the West Indies to deal in drugs and prostitution. This could be seriously bad news. They would be assailed on all sides if they lost the support of the black community through fear. Greg Roberts's calm assurance suddenly seemed illusory.

She was musing over what might happen to harm the summer scheme when she spotted Anne running across the playground, holding the paper. With Ralph, Dorothy and Greg, Marnie and Serena huddled round Anne who held up the front page. There were no prizes for guessing whose photograph occupied it. Garth Brandon had taken up permanent residence there for as long as they could remember. The surprise was the headline. *They're out to kill me.* Beneath it they read: *Brandon in Death Threat.*

"Well it wasn't me," Serena said through clenched teeth. "The way I feel just now, I'm almost ready to join the BFP." Seeing the quizzical expressions around her, she quickly added, "Joke."

"Do your usual, please, Anne," said Ralph. "Read it out."

"OK. The gist is that Brandon's demanding police protection, believes his life's in danger from what he calls 'extremist elements'." The group groaned collectively. "It says … *In a statement issued from BFP HQ …* bla-bla-bla … *Garth Brandon called on the police authorities to assign officers to protect him after he received an anonymous threatening phone call …*"

"Untraceable and unverifiable, no doubt," Ralph interjected.

Anne continued. "*The BFP Leader and candidate …* bla-bla-bla … *stated that his opponents would stop at nothing to stifle his freedom of speech. Brandon added, 'If I am assassinated the blame will lie squarely with the authorities and the police.'*"

Marnie snorted. "Huh! If he's assassinated by having posters stuffed down his throat, the blame will lie squarely with *me*."

"You don't think this is serious?" said Dorothy.

"It's a stunt. And it's worked. There he is back on the front page. Where are his rivals? Nowhere to be seen. He manipulates the press as easily as if he was running the newspaper."

"What about our article?" said Serena.

"It won't come out till the later edition. You'll probably find it on page eleven between the gardening tips and the lonely hearts ads."

"Oh dear …" Dorothy looked deflated.

"Sorry," said Marnie. "I didn't mean to sound so negative. It's just that every time we think we're going forward, we end up taking two steps back."

Greg raised an arm towards the playground where crowds of children were thronging the enrolment tables, being shepherded into orderly lines by the scouts. "This isn't two steps back, Marnie. Look at them. These kids ought to be on the front page."

Marnie quickly turned to Serena. "Do you have a number for that photographer?"

She reached into her back pocket. "I think he gave me his card."

"Get him back here. People have got to see this."

While Serena used her phone, Marnie and the others watched the disciplined but good-natured crowd control in action. Children holding entry forms were lining up in rows. They were from all races, and their parents made a colourful addition, especially the Asians in flowing saris. Those who had been enrolled were forming into groups around adults who were checking off names on clip-boards. Marnie was just thinking they were like children being evacuated from a war zone when she became aware that someone new had joined them. Standing behind Anne was Donovan Smith.

When everyone turned to look at him he said simply, "I've come to help."

A suppressed scream from Serena drew their attention. She held up the mobile.

"I don't believe this. He says he's been called away urgently … to get a picture of Garth *bloody* Brandon."

"His dead body, I hope," said Marnie bitterly.

"He's at an old people's home visiting war veterans."

Marnie was exasperated. "What about pictures of the other candidates? Where are they?"

"Out putting leaflets through letterboxes, I expect," said Ralph. "Not very sexy … nothing to make a good picture."

"So why an interest in old people all of a sudden?"

"Old people vote in elections. Children don't."

Serena was almost stamping her feet with frustration. "We really need photos of all this to show the world what a success we have in bringing all the communities together to make one."

Without a word, Donovan reached into his bag, took out a camera and moved towards the crowds, squatting and bending as he fired off a film, recording every aspect of the proceedings.

Serena stared after him. "Who's he? What's he doing?"

"Donovan Smith," said Anne. "A friend. I think he's taking the photos you wanted for the paper."

"With *that* old thing? It'd have to be something special to be good enough for the newspaper. That camera looks like a museum piece."

"It's very special. It's a Leica … a classic. That camera once shot Hermann Goering and the top Nazis."

"Pity it couldn't shoot Brandon and do us all a favour."

Marnie grabbed Serena by the arm. "Ring that journalist. Tell her we've got photos. Ask her if they'll develop them or should we get them processed. There's a good camera shop in town where they'll do them in an hour."

"Is this called taking one step forward?" said Greg.

Marnie grimaced. "I hope it's called keeping ahead of the game."

• • • • •

Marnie and the Knightly St John contingent did not wait until all the coaches had departed before leaving for home. Announcing that she had work to do and would return later, she shepherded Ralph and Anne into the car and took off.

It had been a tremendous start to the summer scheme, with hundreds of pre-booked children arriving to take part and dozens more turning up unannounced. All the spare seats had been taken, and one of the reserve coaches had been half-filled with extras. Donovan had used a complete roll of film and gone off on his bike to have it processed at the newspaper's own lab.

They felt a weight in the stomach as they drove down the high street and approached Glebe Farm, knowing that Brandon's posters would be reminding them who was really ahead of the game. Pulling up outside the garage barn, they detected a whiff of smoke in the air. Filled with apprehension they rushed to the courtyard. The scene that awaited them was of total normality. Bob the foreman waved from the top of a ladder. His two workmates were busy humping bags of cement through the farmhouse door.

It was a muffled cry from Anne that made them realise something had changed. "The posters ... they've gone!"

Marnie advanced to centre-stage and called up to the builder. "Bob? Did you take the posters down?"

"Yes, me dook. Figured you wouldn't want them spoiling the look of the place."

Marnie laughed. "You're brilliant!"

"Very true."

"Must've taken you ages."

"Aye, half an hour. Don't worry, we'll make it up at the end of the day ... a bit of unpaid overtime."

Smiling and shaking her head, Marnie walked back towards the office barn. She had an afterthought. "What's that burning?"

"Can't you guess? They were great, them posters. Made a smashing start to the bonfire. We've started burning stuff we cut back in the garden to make room for the terrace. One lot of rubbish deserves another." He laughed at his own joke and began whistling to himself.

26

The Discovery sped up the dual carriageway next morning, its occupants in high spirits. Luther had returned from London the previous night by train and taxi and was in Ralph's seat as Ralph had set off for a meeting in Oxford. The atmosphere in the car was elated. Donovan's pictures had been good, so good that Brandon had to share the front page, and the paper had run a double spread of them in the later editions. Anne had a copy with her on the back seat and was perusing them for the umpteenth time.

"You were right about Donovan's camera, Anne." Marnie looked at her in the mirror. "Those pictures are mega-sharp."

"I know. Donovan says the Leica's a classic ... nothing else quite like it."

"But it's not just the camera," Luther butted in. "That guy knows how to use it. It's not just point-and-shoot with those things. You need to know about exposures, focus, depth of field ... all that stuff."

"Yes. He's very ... *meticulous*."

Luther grinned at her. "And very ... *admired*, by the sound of it."

Anne held up the paper. On the front page a close-up of excited children of three races laughing together occupied half the page and took the sting out of Brandon's grim countenance. He had shrunk to make space for them under the headline, *A Day of Contrasts*. A grumpy middle-aged man alongside an image of hope for the future.

Inside was even better. The centre pages were a double spread of action, with scouts gesturing, kids waving, elegant mothers in colourful saris surrounding a general shot of the whole playground. It was like a scene from an epic movie with a cast of hundreds. The heading was *Kidscene Heading 4 Success* – a special report on Day One by Susie Leigh with photographs by Donovan Smith. The editor had included one shot of Serena – *the brains behind the venture* – but his mind had not been on her brains alone when he made the selection. Donovan had taken the photo from behind and had called to her to look back. It may have been nothing more than a chance exposure, but the rear view with the head and torso turning back to the camera, smiling, was the classic glamour pose, emphasising every curve. The 'council youth officer' looked more like a brown young Marilyn Monroe.

Luther pointed at the picture of Serena. "The boy knows how to get a good shot."

"He must've taken it very quickly," said Anne. "It's not quite in focus in the top corner."

Luther laughed. "I hadn't noticed the top corner. I was rather looking at the bottom."

"Oh God," Marnie chuckled. "He's off again. I'm supposed to be keeping you on the straight and narrow while Estelle's away."

"No problem. Everyone knows I only have eyes for Estelle."

Marnie was grinning. "Then you'd better push them back into their sockets and keep them averted from temptation."

Anne suddenly sat upright. "That's odd ... *very* odd."

"What is?" Marnie called over her shoulder.

"Well ... I was just looking at how sharp the photos were, when I spotted this." She passed the paper forward to Luther, pointing at the edge of the playground scene.

"What am I looking for?"

"There ... that car."

Luther strained to see, his face close to the page. "It's not quite clear enough. I can't tell what make it is."

"Can you see the wheel arches?"

"Not really. They just look shiny ... probably the angle of the sunlight reflecting off the edges."

"You don't think they're trimmed in chrome?"

Marnie was turning into a roundabout at that moment and almost veered into the wrong lane. "*Chrome?*" She corrected her steering. "You think it's that BMW again?"

Luther squinted at the photo. "You could be right, Anne. You're brilliant. I'd never have spotted it."

"That's OK," said Anne. "Your mind was probably on higher things."

"Yes," Marnie joined in. "You were no doubt thinking about Estelle and how she's getting on in Italy."

• • • • •

"Thank God for the scouts!" Serena was looking troubled, pecking out numbers on her mobile.

"What's happened?" Marnie looked anxiously at the crowds of children. A large group was standing with a sprinkling of parents in the centre of the playground. The rest were being marshalled into coach parties by the scouts in their distinctive uniforms and hats.

"That's what's happened." Serena pointed at the central group, raising the phone to her ear. "They just turned up out of nowhere wanting to take part in the ... Hallo? Is that Graham White Travel? Good morning. This is Serena McDowell ..."

Greg Roberts walked over as Serena became engrossed in negotiations.

"Has Serena told you? We've got another thirty-odd kids arrived. They saw the report in the paper and want to enrol ... just like that! Their parents must think we can spirit coaches out of thin air."

"Victims of our own success," Marnie murmured. "Hey look." She turned to Anne. "There's Donovan in the middle of the group, talking to the parents."

"He's been a godsend, your photographer pal. He rounded up all the strays – the newcomers – and got them to stay in a bunch so we could see how many there were. I didn't think we could cope with all those extras, but he said we shouldn't turn anyone away. Now Serena's trying to get another coach."

"She's got to be kidding if she thinks Graham White can supply an extra one," Anne said, revisiting in her mind the blaze at their depot.

Sure enough, Serena was now pressing the buttons for a new number on her phone. Looking up, she shrugged at her friends and began another conversation. This time at least there was something to discuss. Serena was walking in a circle, her free arm out sideways, palm up. She stopped, nodded emphatically, clenched her fist and returned to the others. She reached them at the same time as Donovan Smith converged on the group.

"Success?" said Marnie.

Serena pulled a face. "So-so. The best we're going to get. Enterprise Transport have got an old corporation bus that they roll out for parades and special occasions. We can use it for shorter runs to nearby venues. It'll mean some rescheduling, but I think it'll work out."

"Oh well ... better than nothing," said Marnie.

"Better than anything else possible," Donovan protested.

"What do you mean?"

"I mean ..." Donovan patted the shoulder bag, where he kept his camera. "It's a classic. The kids'll love it and –"

"That's irrelevant," Serena interrupted. "We just need something that will get the kids from A to B. And that's what we've got." She looked fraught.

"Sure, but you've got more than that ... much more. In terms of PR you've got a great photo opportunity."

"Donovan's right," said Marnie. "This could keep the summer scheme story going. We've got to seize opportunities like this if we're to keep Brandon off the front page and the 'hope for the future' idea in people's minds."

Serena put a hand on Donovan's shoulder. "That's a great idea. Sorry ... didn't mean to snap at you. I'm a bit edgy and –"

Before she could finish the sentence, Anne grabbed her arm. "Uh-oh ... are these friends or what?"

All eyes turned towards the street. There were six or seven of them, walking slowly like a pride of lions stalking prey on the veldt, seeking out the weakest in the herd to attack. Young black men. Most were in black T-shirts and jeans. Most had dreadlocks. Some had knitted berets in green, yellow, orange and black. They were not smiling, just ambling along with a loose swagger.

"Chums of yours, Serena?" Greg spoke softly without moving his lips.

"Don't know them." Just as softly.

They were about ten metres away when they were intercepted. It was a flanking movement that they had not anticipated and they wheeled in surprise as Mrs Vane-Henderson barked at them.

"Good morning!"

The heartiness of the greeting made them blink and stop in their tracks.

"And you are?" Her voice practically echoed across the playground.

The group seemed uncertain how to answer this tricky question. They hesitated and their cool began to fade away. There was a collective muttering.

"Er ... like er ... er ..."

"Are you wanting to come on the outings?" She articulated the question as if addressing a tribe of bushmen. Perhaps to her, she was.

The young men looked at each other and began grinning. Serena and the others strode forward. The two groups stood facing each other, a metre apart.

"I'll leave you to it," said Mrs V-H. She smiled benignly at the assembly. "I have to get back to the other children."

Oops, thought Marnie. The word *other* reverberated in the space between them. For some time no one spoke. Then the dreadlock gang fixed their gaze on Greg. Like them, he wore headgear. End of comparison.

"Hey bro," said one of the young blacks. "You're a cool dude. You're lookin' just fine, man ..."

The accent was Jamaica full strength. His friends began grinning and shuffling about. There was muted laughter. The atmosphere was building again and there was no telling which way things would go.

Suddenly Anne took a step forward. "Hi. I'm Anne ... Anne with an 'e'. Nice to meet you. Have you come to join in?"

After a short hesitation. "Hi, Anne ... with an 'e'. Yeah ... we've come to join in. We've got some 'E's, too." Muffled murmurings that could be more laughter.

"You've come to help?" said Serena.

"We've come ... yeah."

"How long can you stay?"

"How long does it go on?"

"All day and ... maybe well into the evening."

"Right."

"You want to help?"

"We've come." They all nodded.

"You can't stay together. We need extra stewards on some of the buses. You'd be travelling around with the kids ... and adults, of course."

"Fine."

"Er ... we have a strict no-smoking policy."

More shuffling. "'S OK," their spokesman said eventually. "We all gotta make sacrifices."

The atmosphere was becoming less tense, though Marnie noticed that Greg was eyeing the new arrivals with lightly-disguised scepticism.

Serena continued. "The main organisation of the kids is being carried out by the scouts. Greg here is their leader."

Dark eyes appraised him. The spokesman said, "Love the gear ... cool geezer. W'ain't got no problem wi' him." The words were slurred together in a rhythmic cadence.

Greg muttered, "Too late to book an interpreter, I suppose."

"How many these scouts you got, man?"

"Pardon?" said Greg.

"How many scouts are there?" said Serena.

"About twenty, plus my assistant and me."

"'S OK. We got enough ganja to go round."

The young blacks laughed. Greg's composure was shattered for several seconds. He stood speechless, mouth hanging open.

"Joke, bro. You'll be just fine, man." Chalk-white teeth flashed in an ebony smile.

"OK." Serena was back in business-like mode again. "We've all got things to do. Greg will take you ... er, no ... perhaps not ... er, Greg has to organise the scouts. This is Luther Curtiss. Luther, will you take them over to the main reception desk and get them allocated to buses? Jackie Brice will know which gaps need to be filled."

"OK, Serena."

One of the other West Indians spoke up. "*Luther Curtiss*? Like ... *Greville* Curtiss?"

"His father," said Anne.

The young man examined Luther from head to foot. "*The* Greville Curtiss who got that test record ... the bowler?"

Luther nodded.

"My ole man said he was the greatest —"

"Later," Serena interjected. "You can talk cricket when we've got more time."

No one took offence. The group waited patiently while Serena gave Luther a final briefing on how she wanted the new volunteers to be deployed. While she was speaking, one of the other young men sidled up to Anne.

"You like reggae?"

"Yeah. Love it."

He reached into his back pocket. For two seconds Anne was sure he was going to slip her a joint. He extended his hand towards her. "Here."

She accepted his offering and found herself looking down at stickers, the kind that fans put in their car windows. The stickers bore the colours of Jamaica, yellow, green, orange and black stripes, and looking up at her she saw the unmistakable face of Bob Marley, with the exhortation to stick together and we'll be all right.

Anne looked at the young man, who was watching her expression. "For me?"

"Yeah. If you like them."

"They're great. Thank you."

She leaned forward and kissed him on the cheek, blonde head meeting black dreadlocks. More shuffling from his friends. It seemed to be the collective reaction to most situations. There was much grinning.

Luther beckoned to the group and they set off across the playground, walking more quickly than before. A few were chatting to Luther as they went. It was not difficult to guess the subject of the conversation. Anne showed Marnie and the others her stickers before tucking them into her back pocket.

Serena breathed out audibly, watching the young men go on their way.

• • • • •

They were starting to get into a routine. After a quick briefing session and the organised chaos as the children arrived in droves, the members of the management team were free for the rest of the day. Marnie was grateful she could return to the office where business was growing steadily. It meant she was free to arrange appointments with prospective clients. It also meant she was free when the phone rang to take a call from Italy.

"Marnie this is *the* most beautiful place in the *whole* world. I'm only sorry you're not here to see it."

"Some time, maybe. I'm glad thing's are going well."

"Ah …" Estelle's tone changed. "Not quite. There is some not-so-good news."

"You've sabotaged the place so you can stay longer. Can't fool me."

"Got it in one … sort of."

"Which bit did I get right?"

"Well … I think I've detected rot of some kind in the cellar. There are some old cupboards down there. I noticed a funny smell and got them moved away from the wall. There are spores … could be dry rot … also some evidence of insect activity."

"Can you get it checked by a surveyor?"

"Actually, there's a very good builder in the area. He's well-known and thorough, does a lot of work in these old properties. Everyone calls him in. His costs are also quite reasonable. He's coming this afternoon to take a look."

"OK. What about the rest of the job?"

"No problem with getting the colours we need. And I've found the most *gorgeous* tiles for the hall and kitchen floors. This builder could lay them. The rot in the cellar's the only negative thing."

"Keep me posted."

• • • • •

Marnie and the others were resigned to this being the summer of disrupted evenings. Whatever else they had to do, it became part of their routine to be at Garfield Primary when the coaches returned. That evening the first to roll in was the extra bus, the old campaigner taken out of retirement to cope with the increased numbers.

It seemed happy enough to be plodding the roads again, and Donovan had been proved right; the kids loved it and had dubbed it Chitty-Chitty-Bang-Bang, some with a slightly more dubious pronunciation than others. Donovan was back on duty with his Leica, shooting the venerable bus from a variety of angles, ending with a posed scene with parents and children standing proudly alongside it. Some of the children were dozing from the journey.

"I hope they give you some sort of credit for these photos," Marnie said, as he wound the film back ready for processing.

"I don't mind ... as long as they do the job. The paper hasn't sent a photographer, so without mine there won't be any shots of the bus for people to see. It'll make a good story backed up by a photo."

In one respect he was right. But in others, completely wrong.

27

It was the third day of the week and the third day of the summer scheme. A handful of new children had appeared and been allocated to coaches. The young West Indians arrived in good time, as they had promised, and the early suspicion of the scouts had dissolved. Serena and her team were beginning to feel relaxed about the scheme, or at least less apprehensive.

Their calm state of mind lasted until the noon edition of the paper hit the streets. In Knightly St John Anne was already at the shop when the newsvan made its delivery.

In Northampton Serena was not the only one to rush to the newsagent at the expected time. The front page was dominated by a story about a missing child and for some seconds her heart stopped beating as she raced through the report, until she found that it had nothing to do with the children attending the summer scheme. A wave of relief mingled with a feeling of guilt washed over her. Anxious as she was about the lost child, she was glad it had nothing to do with *her* kids. It was when she opened the paper and saw page three that the shock hit her.

Under the headline, *Brandon slams playscheme* were three photos. None of them came from the camera of Donovan Smith. The article was short and to the point. Brandon accused Serena McDowell and her 'cohorts' of *handing over the children of the town to a gang of drug-using layabouts to further her own career*. He warned of a backlash from all 'decent people' when they realised what was really going on. This was *the crudest form of social engineering since the hippy days of the swinging sixties when decent standards were thrown out of the window and Britain began the steady slide to its current decline.* It was *no wonder we were ready to hand our country over to the bureaucrats of Brussels – we were already getting plenty of practice at home.*

Serena did not bother turning to the editorial page. She was hitting the buttons on her mobile to rage at the editor for printing such blatant fascist propaganda. If he used the familiar argument that he was accurately reporting a statement from a legitimate candidate in a major election, she was going to stuff those words down his throat.

On the other side of town, Donovan straddled his bike outside the paper shop near the canal. He read the article on page three, studied the photographs and stared into space. There was no credit for the photographer, but he had his suspicions.

Anne regretted not taking her car up to the village shop, and she was breathless by the time she burst through the door of the office barn and slammed the paper down on Marnie's desk. Ralph was waiting, coffee cup in hand, and they looked at the paper together. Dismay spread across their faces.

"Where on *earth* did they get these?" Marnie muttered in disbelief.

"They're not by the paper's own photographer," said Ralph. "Too grainy. This is long-lens stuff."

"It's *dreadful* stuff."

The main shot showed a little girl crying. Her head was turned as if she was looking for help. Behind her stood a group of young black men in black T-shirts and jeans, wearing floppy knitted berets, partly covering their dreadlocks. They appeared to be looming over her in a posture of menace.

Below was a group shot of the young blacks sharing a joke. There was no caption, but the inference was that they were loitering in a gang, up to no good. By coincidence the text beside the photo was about *drug-using layabouts.*

The third shot was in close-up. It showed a young man holding a small girl in his arms, her blonde head set against his black dreadlocks. She seemed to be unconscious. It was unfortunate that the picture appeared just above the continuation of the story about the missing child from the front page.

Marnie put her head in her hands. "Oh boy ..."

"Why's the paper doing this?" Anne was exasperated.

"They're just reporting the news," said Ralph. "Look. It mentions an editorial. See what it says."

Anne found the page, and they read together the editorial entitled, *A Free Press in a Free Democracy*. The editor reminded his readers about their policy of reporting the news fairly and honestly. All candidates had a right to have their views represented, and no candidate in the present European election was better organised in putting over his case than Garth Brandon. But the paper was becoming wary of *coming close to the edge of what was acceptable to society.* Some thought they were making too much of the children's summer scheme, *turning it into a showpiece for radical views.* Readers were reminded that it was just a programme of *outings for children while they were at home for part of the holidays.* Others thought too much attention was being paid to one party, *the party with views that many considered extremist.* The editor called on all the participants to raise their game over the last week of the campaign. He ended by calling for *calm and reason in the interests of democracy.*

· · · · ·

Donovan's mind was in overdrive. How long would the paper go on printing his photos? The summer scheme story could surely not keep running for much longer. Why were the other candidates so useless at handling the media? It was really frustrating having to slog on almost unaided by the very people who ought to be dominating the campaign. Couldn't they see what Brandon was doing?

He came out of an alley near the town centre and pedalled hard, the shoulder bag snug in its rack behind the saddle. The photographic print studio was in a side street off the one-way system, and he left the bike in the entrance. The slides that he took the previous day looked good. He placed them on the customer light-box and ran over them with a magnifying glass. The arrangement with the paper was that he would provide ten shots for them to choose what they wanted. One by one he slipped the best into an envelope, sealed it shut and made for the exit.

In less than two minutes he was jumping from the saddle outside the newspaper offices and running in to hand over the envelope in reception. Back on the bike, he looked over his shoulder to judge when to filter into the flow of traffic. He could be home on board *X O 2* in no more than five or six minutes from here.

Traffic was moderate at that time of the morning, but Donovan was vigilant. He knew how little space many drivers gave to cyclists and trusted no one's judgment but his own. A quick glance all round could prevent an accident.

On a straight run through the shopping area something registered in his mind. He eased back, slowed to a halt and looked across the pavement at a shop window. Flicking back the pedal to launch himself off again, he hastily checked that his bag was held firmly in place behind the saddle and moved away from the kerb. Yes, he thought, there was no doubt about it. He was being followed.

· · · · ·

"Calm down, Mrs McDowell … *please* … Serena, will you just shut up for a minute and listen! You've seen the paper so you ought to know my views are not what you've just described. Why do you think I wrote what I put in the editorial?"

"What are you talking about? I'm protesting about your distortion of the truth and I want to know why you're doing this. This is biased reporting … it's irresponsible and dangerous … it's –"

The editor barked down the phone. "No one accuses me of partiality. In fourteen years as editor I have never once been accused of anything of the sort."

"Then explain why you published what you did. Don't you realise the harm it will do?"

"I did explain. That's what the editorial stated *quite* clearly."

"The … editorial?"

"Of course. So what part of it don't you understand?"

"I'm talking about the report and photos on page three."

There was a pause while Serena and the editor caught their breath.

"You have read the editorial, Mrs McDowell?" His voice was quiet.

"I, er … didn't get that far." No response. "Hallo?"

"I've never yet slammed the phone down on anyone in fourteen years as editor." Icy.

"And you're not going to start with me."

"I should be careful what you say, if I were you. You're on dodgy ground here. You should check your facts before spouting off if you want anyone to take you seriously."

"But I saw that report … those pictures … what do you think your readers will make of them?"

"I respect my readers. That's why I pay them the courtesy of explaining my position from time to time. That's why I wrote the editorial. Too bad you didn't bother to read it."

"But you used those photos …"

"They were part of a story. They're not the only part, and it's not the only story, but some of us believe the electorate is grown-up enough to make up its own mind and judge for itself. We've also used photos sent in by one of your supporters. I've got some of them on my desk now. We'll be running them in the next edition."

"The bus?"

"The bus. Look … I have to use what's there. I don't invent the stories, and everyone wants pictures these days. Words alone are not enough. Your Donovan Smith knows this and he knows how to take a good photo. But don't forget … so does the BFP, and my job is to let people know what's going on."

"And what are the other parties doing?"

"What they always do, of course. But Brandon's lot have put much more effort in with the media. To them this isn't about one election. It's their time in the spotlight."

"But they're *fanatics*," Serena protested. "And you're giving them a platform."

"You're missing the point on both counts, Serena. They're *organised* fanatics … highly organised at playing the system. And they make their *own* platform. I'm a newspaper man not a censor. Look … I'm giving you much more coverage than a summer scheme for kids could expect, right?"

"So you're doing this out of the goodness of your heart. Is that what you're saying? You're doing us a big favour?"

"Let's not get back to shouting. You're getting coverage because you're newsworthy, especially at this time of the year. Also, you're organised too. Your photos are good quality."

"When are you going to give prominence to the other parties and not just the BFP?"

"Things change all the time in the press. We've just heard the PM is coming to add weight to the Tory candidate, and the new leader of the Labour Party is coming in the next few days to support his bloke. They're rolling out their rebranded party … *New Labour*. Could be just up your street, Serena. If you want to get involved in all this campaigning, why don't you just get selected as a candidate? Listen, I've got to go. I've got a newspaper to run."

"Right ... er ... listen ... I was out of line, yelling like that. I should've read the editorial first and –"

"Forget it. Good luck with the summer scheme. We can't go on giving you this level of coverage ... old news, you know ... but I wish you well. And cheer up. That missing child has been found, and we'll be running it as our lead story. Great news, eh?"

"Good news in the paper ... whatever next?"

"Yeah ... and whatever happened to good old British apathy about politics?"

"Before you go ... what did you mean about *especially at this time of year*?"

"The summer holiday period is known to journalists as the *silly season*."

"Why?" said Serena.

"Because nothing happens then. People are thinking of their holidays. At this time any old trivia can get into the news."

"Thanks a bunch."

• • • • •

The Ford Escort is one of the most common cars in Britain, a great buy for small families. Also an ideal car to use for following someone. Donovan registered it because he always watched out for cars of that size. His pet hate was small hatchbacks driven by young men whose main interest in life seemed to be training for the Kamikaze section of the air force.

A maroon Escort, unremarkable, almost invisible.

Donovan had first seen it parked half on the pavement down the road from the newspaper offices. He had spotted it again near the traffic lights in the one-way system and again at a junction when he had automatically checked out the traffic behind him.

When he had stopped to look in the shop window, it had not overtaken. Now, it was lying about fifty metres back. Donovan made a left. It made a left. He turned right at the next lights, all nice and easy, no rush, nothing to give away that he had any idea they were there.

By the guildhall he saw a traffic warden on the corner. He dismounted and asked the way to the market square, knowing he would be directed along a short section of road only for use by buses. He walked the bike through and turned the corner opposite the war memorial. Daring to put his head round the corner, he looked back to see the warden holding up a hand to stop the Escort from driving on that piece of road, pointing up at the restricted-entry sign. He could almost see steam coming through the car's windows.

• • • • •

Calls had been coming in all afternoon. Dorothy Vane-Henderson was *appalled*, wondering to whom she should complain. The hot money was on the Lord Lieutenant of the County, closely followed by the Leader of the County Council, the chairman of the newspaper company and the chairman of the Press Complaints Commission. Marnie was thinking how hard it must be to be so well connected you don't know which of your circle of friends to 'phone first, when she remembered how serious the problem was.

George declared himself *flabbergasted* and proposed a letter to the editor signed by everyone in their group.

Margaret Giles found the report and photographs *very upsetting* and wondered what action they were going to take. She offered to phone the other head teachers to try to organise a petition.

The next three calls were all surprises.

"Hallo, Marnie. It's Mrs Jolly here. How are things with you? I've heard on the wireless that you've got rather a lot on your plate at the moment."

"You can say that again, Mrs Jolly. What did you hear?"

"You've got that dreadful Brandon man campaigning in your county and he's threatening to complain to the Press Complaints Board – or whatever it is – about biased reporting in the newspapers."

"He's *what?*"

"He was interviewed on the news this morning. He said they were pushing politically correct stories with a left-wing bias to discredit his campaign. Would they do such a thing? I thought the press was usually accused of being right wing."

Marnie gasped. "I'm *astonished*, I really am. Brandon's practically dictating the headlines in the local paper every day up here. Rumour has it he's taken out a lease on the front page."

"Well, he's making all sorts of allegations, my dear ... says his life's been threatened, he's been attacked in his car ... what else? ... oh, yes ... the media are biased against him and giving distorted accounts of his speeches, trying to whip up feeling against him ..."

"Huh! This is all lies. Didn't the interviewer challenge him on this?"

"Actually, my dear, the interviewer had quite a hard time getting a word in. Every time she tried to put a question, he just cut across her and started off on his own themes. He wasn't interested in anything but putting out his own propaganda."

"That's Brandon all right. It's really worrying."

"But it's not the most worrying."

"Oh?"

"No. The worst was when they took a microphone out onto the street and asked people what they thought of him and his policies."

"Tell me the worst."

"Most of the people said he was only saying what a lot of ordinary folk believed. Britain was overcrowded and should stop letting foreigners in ... the main parties weren't interested in what mattered to most people, which was security ... er ... oh, yes ... when they were asked about his bullying style with interviewers, some people said it was giving them a dose of their own medicine ... good for him."

"Is that it?"

"I think so. Oh, no ... one man said he admired him for standing up against Mrs Thatcher ... when he resigned from her government at the time of the Maastricht Treaty."

"That's some consolation, I suppose."

"The man thought Mrs Thatcher was far too soft."

"It must've been Genghis Khan."

Marnie had hardly put the phone down when it rang again. The second surprise call came from Donovan Smith.

"Did your photos turn out all right?"

"Yeah. I handed them in this morning. They were fine. Have you seen the early edition of the paper, Marnie?"

"Yes, but I'm hoping they'll use at least one of your photos in the later edition."

"The damage is already done."

"I know, but we just have to keep plodding on."

"What does Serena think about it?"

"I haven't heard from her yet. The phone's been going non-stop."

"OK, I'll get out of your way."

"I didn't mean it like that, Donovan. Will you be at the school this evening? We'll all need to talk."

"I'm not sure."

"Can I hear an engine running in the background?"

"I'm on the boat ... moving out of town."

Her heart sank. "You're not giving up, surely?"

"No, but I have to quit the mooring."

"You've reached the time limit?"

"No. I was ... followed this morning."

"*Followed*? Who by?"

"Two people in a car ... couldn't see them clearly."

"Was it a BMW, black, shiny wheel arches?"

"No. Ford Escort ... maroon ... tatty."

"*Damn!* So they know about your boat?"

"No. I managed to lose them. I went where they couldn't follow in the car ... then I doubled back. But I think it'd be a good idea if I slipped away."

"The *stealth narrowboat*."

"Yeah."

"Be careful. You're rather conspicuous. They could recognise you if they're on the lookout."

"I don't think so. I've put the bike inside and changed into jeans and a light T-shirt. With the baseball cap and shades they won't know me."

"Good. Where will you go?"

"I'll head back in your direction. Expect me when you see me ... or even when you don't."

The third surprise call was as clear as if it came from the next room, which was all the more surprising.

"Beth, hi! How are things in Thailand?"

"Things *were* fine, but we left there over a week ago."

"You're home?"

"We're in San Francisco, California. Paul's seminar at Berkeley, remember? It starts next week."

"Of course it does. So how are you?"

"Great. More to the point, how are you?"

"Fine."

"Despite everything?"

Beth sounded surprised. Marnie was amazed. It was the global village turned into reality, the communications revolution.

"Even from the Pacific coast my big sister can keep tabs on me? Who said the media only dealt in trivia?"

"Right. We've been following what's going on back home."

"You know about what's happening?"

"Sure. Do you realise your heatwave is news over here? It's been hotter in London than in Los Angeles."

Beth waited for a reaction. She knew Marnie would be impressed. But there was no response, at least nothing clear, only a few muffled sounds.

"Marnie? … Are you still there? … Are you coughing, Marnie? Can you hear me?"

Covering the mouthpiece with one hand, Marnie reached across the desk for a tissue to dab her eyes as she rocked in her chair.

• • • • •

There was no call that afternoon from Serena, but Marnie had plenty of other matters to handle and was astonished when Anne told her it was time to get ready to leave for Northampton. She was switching on the answering machine when the phone rang.

"Oh good, I've caught you."

"Estelle. Hi! We're about to set off. How's it going?"

"I've just had the builder here. Not good news, I'm afraid. Structural problems in the cellar; could be bark-boring beetle or wood-boring weevil."

"How serious is it?"

"Not sure yet. We need a more detailed survey."

"You've got it in hand?"

"Yep. But, Marnie, I'll need a day or two longer here to sort it all out."

"Take as long as you need. It's easier *in situ*. When do you want to come back?"

"I'll have things sorted by the weekend. Shall I try and change my flight to Saturday?"

"No. You've got enough on your hands. We'll fix it from here. I'll get Anne to contact the airline."

"She can ring me at the hotel with the flight number … leave a message if I'm out."

"Better if we fax the details, Estelle, less complicated. And you'll need something in writing at the check-in."

"Yes, of course."

"Everything else OK?"

"More than OK. I've been visiting some of the other villas owned by Brits. They are just *gorgeous*. This must be *the most beautiful place in the world*."

"And your builder must be hunky too."

"He is. How did you know that?"

"If you're Italian has come on so well you know words like *bark-boring beetle* and *wood-boring weevil*. That's impressive."

"Talking of hunky blokes …" Estelle began.

"I haven't seen much of Luther today. I've had my head down trying to catch up in the office."

"Odd. I've rung a few times but he's not answering."

"Sorry … haven't surfaced for air today, what with the phone and all the paperwork …"

"How's the summer scheme going?"

"Very well, but it's a struggle ... loads more kids than anticipated ... the usual propaganda war with the BFP ... you can imagine."

"Serena's coping all right?"

"Pretty well. We're all giving her a lot of support."

"I bet."

"Donovan Smith has turned up trumps. His photos have been great ... the paper's been using them."

"Those are *his* photos?"

Marnie was puzzled. "You've seen them?"

"Didn't I tell you? I arranged with Molly Appleton. She's faxing me the articles from the paper each day."

"Why didn't you ask us to do that?"

"You've got more than enough to cope with. The photos this morning were surely not by anyone on our side?"

"No ... that's Brandon's lot. But we hope we'll have one or more of Donovan's in this evening's edition."

"Good. Look, I'm holding you up. You'd better get going. If you see Luther, give him my love ... tell him I hope he's behaving himself."

"We'll take good care of him, don't worry."

"That's not very reassuring!"

Marnie was still smiling when she called Anne in and set her to work dealing with the airline. While Ronny helped her put their bags in the car, she thought of Estelle, capably handling the firm's problems in Italy, Molly Appleton sending daily faxes to Umbria from the shop, Knightly St John, the global village ... whatever next!

• • • • •

They reached the school with only minutes to spare before the first coach was due back. Anne went with Ronny to fetch the newspaper. Marnie crossed the playground to where Serena was talking to some of the other organisers. Serena did not look happy.

"What's the matter?"

"Is it that obvious?"

"Your chin's scraping the floor."

"There's always something to drag you down, even when things are going right."

"Well, this is going right."

"Yes, Marnie, it is. Jackie's just told me we've hit the thousand mark for enrolments."

"A thousand kids! That's marvellous. Congratulations ... but?"

Serena drew Marnie aside and flashed a glance across the playground before speaking in a low voice.

"There's trouble brewing."

"So what's new?"

"Big trouble."

Marnie waited.

"They're planning something ... New Force. It could be like the so-called *disturbances* in Leicester."

"When's it going to happen?"

"Not sure ... but soon. Did you know the Prime Minister's coming to town?"

"No."

"And the Labour and Lib Dem leaders, too. All in the next few days. They'll arrive at short notice for security reasons."

Marnie pursed her lips. "A riot would certainly grab the headlines. How did you find out about this? Brandon send you a printed invitation?"

"One of my neighbours ... her son's on the fringes of that far-right crap ... she's really worried about him ... told me she'd heard him on the phone talking to a friend. New Force are trying to whip up support locally."

"Do you reckon they'll get any?"

"I doubt it, Marnie. Maybe one or two idiots. But the people here aren't like that. I don't think they'd respond to the likes of New Force. They're too decent. I couldn't bear it if they did."

With each passing moment more and more parents were arriving to meet the children from the coaches. The playground and streets were awash with people of all colours and races, mingling together, chatting and smiling. Marnie saw Serena's anxiety etched in her face. She touched her arm.

"Look around us, Serena. This is the kind of demonstration you want to see ... peace and goodwill. I know it sounds trite and corny, but it's true."

Serena looked up. "Yes. They are good people here."

"And you made it all possible, Serena. It was your vision."

The scouts signalled that the first coach was returning. It was the superannuated bus in its old-fashioned livery, and at the sight of it, a cheer went up on all sides. Marnie and Serena set off to meet it.

"Where's your friend with the camera?" Serena was craning her neck. "I'm surprised he's not clicking away."

"He's had to pull out."

"Oh?"

"Just for a while. He was followed this morning."

Serena stopped abruptly. "*What?*"

"It's all right, he eluded them. But he's left town on his boat to keep out of sight."

"On his boat ... he'd be a sitting duck if they found him."

"They won't. He's too sharp for them. Pity about his photos, though. They're a great asset. We'll miss them."

"Not really," said Serena. "Sure, they're an asset, but the editor of the paper as good as told me this morning that our run of press coverage has come to an end. We're not news any more."

Marnie remembered Anne and Ronny going for the paper and she turned to scan the playground, spotting them at the far end. She waved to attract their attention, and they came bounding over, weaving their way through the multitude. Children with smiling faces were descending from the venerable bus, happy and tired. Some were being helped off by the adult stewards. One of the dreadlock brigade emerged with a child on each side holding his hands.

"Well, I never thought I would see that." A lilting accent at Marnie's side. A fine-looking Indian mother smiling at the sight of the young man in dreadlocks laughing with the children surrounding him.

"You're not the only one," said Marnie. "They've surprised us all."

More coaches were pulling in one-by-one to their allotted spaces under Serena's watchful gaze. The scouts were waving them in like flight deck crew on an aircraft carrier. The fleet was coming home to its customary welcome after another successful mission. Anne threaded her way to Marnie with Ronny in her wake. She was breathless.

"Cor ... it's like a football crowd. Where've they all come from?"

"You've checked the paper?" Marnie asked.

Anne's smile gave her the answer. She held it open at page three. Pride of place went to the bus that at that moment was standing in front of them. *Its Finest Hour* ran the headline over the story of the bus with more than a million miles on the clock that had come out of retirement in the town's hour of need. Gone were the photos of the earlier edition.

One of the dreadlocks swaggered up. "Hey, Marnie, did you see the paper this morning, all that sh–" He met the almond eyes of the Indian mother, saw the sari in blue and gold, the dark shining plait of hair. "Er ... those pictures ... made us look like Jack the Ripper or something."

Anne turned the page to show him. His angry expression turned to a grin. "That's more like it." He pointed to himself in one of the photos.

"Yes, what was all that?" said the Indian lady indignantly. "It looked awful."

It was dreadlocks who replied. "That little girl was crying and we went over to see what was up. She'd lost her mum ... seeing her other kid onto a bus. That's all it was. We found the mum ... little girl happy again. That's when we were laughing."

"And the child being carried?" the Indian mother asked.

Dreadlocks shrugged. "Fell asleep on the bus. Charlie didn't want to wake her, gave her to her mum still asleep. No problem."

"Well, *really*. Never mind. These new photos are much better. This is wonderful. My little Gurdeep thinks you're all marvellous ... and very funny. Well done ... and thank you all."

She turned and led her children away.

"Anything about Brandon in the late edition?" Marnie asked Anne.

"Anyone would think you're paranoid," Serena observed in an even tone.

"They'd be right. Is there anything, Anne?"

"Just his usual quote of the day." She read aloud, *"Garth Brandon asks if we really want our children to be in the care of drug-taking aliens."*

Dreadlocks hooted. He had now been joined by some of his friends, who stood round doing their customary shuffle. "That makes us sound like creatures from outer space."

Charlie laughed. "We could offer to grow another head if it keeps him happy."

Another spoke up. "I tried some weed once that made me feel I already had two heads." The others groaned in reproach. He added quickly, "That was before I saw the error of my ways."

He attempted an expression intended to convey probity. Serena hit him with the heavy eyelids.

The group split up to check the coaches as they booked in. No major incidents were reported, no lost children, no accidents, no breakdowns. Everyone knew that sooner or later there would be problems of some sort.

The unforeseen they could handle. It was the nagging worry of dirty tricks that they feared.

Ronny wandered off at Marnie's suggestion to see if he could be of help to Greg Roberts and the scouts. When he had gone, Marnie filled Anne in on Serena's news. She jumped in the air at the thousand enrolments. But the account of the trouble being planned by New Force brought her back to earth.

"That's the last thing we want. Right now we've got strength in numbers, but if we were hit by an army of thugs, I bet most of the mums would leave and not come back."

Marnie agreed. "Like that Sylvia Wilkinson at the school. They'd all panic … and I for one couldn't blame them. I know what a *disturbance* looks like."

"What can we do about it?"

"Not a lot."

"Tell Inspector Bartlett?"

"We don't have any evidence, Anne."

"At least it would alert him."

"I doubt if he finds life too restful just now. No, I think we've just got to keep our heads down and get on with making the best job we can of the summer scheme."

While they were speaking they watched the return of the coaches. As each one emptied, it would pull away, leaving space for others to take over. The scouts were impressive. Marnie raised a hand to shield her eyes from the sun.

"Over there, Anne. Can you see them?"

"What am I looking for? Oh, yes. It's that reporter from the paper … Susie … and the photographer."

"Probably one last fling before they drop our story." *Until a full-scale riot breaks out*, Marnie thought to herself. Scanning the scene, a familiar shape stood out at the other side of the street. "Is that George's Range Rover over there?"

Anne turned to look. "Where? He did say he might be able to … uh-oh …"

"What's up?"

"Marnie." Anne tugged her shirt. "Look. Do you see them?"

"Who?"

"Could this be Serena's *trouble*?"

"I can't see any … ah …"

It looked like a re-run of the arrival of the dreadlocks brigade, only this bunch was white. And menacing. There were five or six of them, in black and grey, jeans and slashed T-shirts, bare arms with thick muscles, tattoos, shaved heads. No smiley faces. They walked with heads bent slightly forward, making a line straight for the organisers' reception desks. Marnie took off to intercept them. Anne accelerated to follow, anxiously looking round for Greg, Ronny, anybody.

The skinheads were bearing down on the desks and had just been seen by the women checking off the names and numbers of coaches. They froze. Parents and children parted like the Red Sea to let the men through. With ten metres to go they suddenly found their way blocked. Two people had taken up station directly in their flight path. Marnie and Anne were near enough to hear what was said.

"Good afternoon." It was a loud voice honed with authority. "Can I help you?"

The skinheads faltered in mid-stride. Before them stood a man of middle age, thick-set and tweedy. He seemed to take up a lot of space. The men stopped.

"Can I help you, gentlemen?"

"Who's running this?"

"I am. My name is George Stubbs. What can I do for you? Oh ... and this is my colleague, the *Reverend* Angela Hemingway. We're the organisers, or at least members of the team."

This caused the gang to hesitate. At the organisers' desks, by chance, the staff on duty that evening were also white.

"We thought this was run by niggers."

"I think you must be mistaken." George raised a hand in the direction of the scouts' encampment, where the union flag fluttered in the light breeze. "Unless you're assuming that I'm a ... *nigger* ... a West Indian, perhaps?" There was a twinkle in his eye.

The crowd that had parted at the arrival of the gang was now regrouping to watch this exchange. Marnie and Anne had halted among the onlookers. George and Angela were doing well and so far did not need back-up.

"You're very welcome to stay, of course," Angela joined in. She sounded earnest. "But all the trips have ended for today. I'll shortly be conducting a prayer meeting, though – for all denominations – if you'd like to wait a while."

Marnie turned. She was already praying. The last thing she wanted was for the reporter and photographer to see this confrontation. It would make real news and a photo opportunity, not just an in-filler.

The gang stood as if nailed to the ground. One or two of them noticed that they were now almost surrounded by a large number of people. That many of them were women with children did not make the spectators appear less hostile.

George took up the running again. "After *prayers* ..." He stressed the word for emphasis. "After prayers, there'll be the ceremony of breaking the flag by the scouts. That's supposed to be at sundown, but we do it a bit earlier ... sort of rounds off the day nicely. Remember you don't salute the flag at the end of the day, just in the morning when it goes up."

"Please feel free to stay," said Angela, absentmindedly fingering her dog collar. "You're most welcome."

There was a silence for some seconds. Make-or-break time, Marnie thought. The problem was, the skinheads did not seem to know how to bow out of the situation. They needed a bolt hole. She half turned towards Anne and spoke in a whisper.

"When I move, go round the crowd telling people to disperse. Do it quietly. Don't let the skinheads see you."

Without further delay, Marnie walked quickly through the crowd to George and Angela.

"Sorry to interrupt your conversation, but we need to check the order of service for prayers." Her voice was loud and businesslike. If Angela was surprised by the question, she did not show it. Marnie continued. "Will this be evensong as usual, vicar?"

She moved closer, her back now turned to the men who were becoming aware that the people around them were drifting away. George joined in the huddle to discuss prayer arrangements, expressing a preference for a choral evensong if they could get the choir to stay on. Angela was fighting to control her features, informing George that the Rural Dean would be attending that evening and he liked nothing more than a choral evensong. As they began moving towards the organisers' desks, they found they were alone. The skinhead mob was walking quickly – but still menacingly – away.

Marnie closed her eyes and breathed out heavily.

"You two were *brilliant* … and brave."

"And trembling," said Angela. She put a hand to her stomach. "Are you all right, George?"

He nodded. "The old pulse is up a bit, but otherwise I'm fine … not bad for a *nigger*."

Anne arrived at speed looking troubled. "Don't look now, but we've got visitors."

Over her shoulder they saw the reporter heading their way. Struggling to keep up, the photographer was switching cameras from his bag.

"Wonderful," said Marnie. "Here we are feeling shell-shocked and the press arrives. Great timing. Talk about star quality …"

"Could've been worse," George said quietly. "Three minutes ago …"

"Star quality," Anne muttered. She was staring into the distance as if lost in her thoughts.

"Just a turn of phrase," said Marnie. "And it's a commodity we don't have … sadly."

"Oh yes we do." Anne walked away until she had passed the reporters and then took off like an Olympic sprinter.

Marnie, Angela and George clamped cheerful expressions onto their faces and greeted the press people.

"Still going strong, then," said Susie Leigh.

Marnie shook hands and introduced her companions. "Oh, yes, thriving. We didn't expect to see you again."

"We were in the area … thought we'd look in," the reporter said breezily.

More likely had a tip-off that there could be trouble, Marnie thought. "Great. Wanting any particular details? I don't think we've got anything new to tell you."

"Have you had any interesting reaction from the locals? We're always on the lookout for the human angle."

"They don't seem to mind us being here," said George.

"No adverse comments … confrontations?"

"Would you expect us to tell you if we had?"

"So you have had some?"

"Look around you," Marnie put in. "A lot of satisfied customers. Not so much as a nose bleed."

Behind them Anne approached with Serena and Luther in tow. She went straight up to Susie Leigh and shook hands.

"Hallo. Have you come for the latest news? It didn't take long to get round, did it?"

"Latest news?" Susie looked surprised. "I thought there wasn't anything to report." She looked sideways at Marnie, who was expressionless.

Anne continued. "Of course not. We weren't going to give Serena's story away."

Serena and Luther shook hands with the reporter and the photographer.

"So ... what's the story?" Susie asked, a hint of incredulity in her voice.

"Oh ... it's nothing really," Serena was the picture of modesty. "It's just ... we've exceeded our target by over two hundred. We haven't announced it yet, but we've now topped one thousand enrolments."

"A thousand ... and you anticipated?

"About seven-fifty."

Susie flipped open her notepad. "You hit that number today?"

"Strictly speaking it was yesterday, but I only got the returns just now. We'll be a few up again, once we've got all today's sheets counted."

Marnie and the others withdrew slightly while Susie asked more questions and the photographer adjusted his camera.

"Thank God for your quick thinking, Anne," Marnie said in a low voice. "Oh ... sorry Angela."

"No problem. I was about to say *amen*. And what about George? Where did you get that idea about prayers and evensong? If I hadn't been so frightened of the skinheads, I'd have been laughing my head off."

"It was the first thing that came to mind. Your dog collar gave me the idea."

Anne said, "I told Serena and Luther what you'd done. They thought it was hilarious."

The photographer called over, waving them forward. "Can you all get together for a group shot?"

"Oh no," Marnie protested. "Just do Serena or the kids. We've had a long day."

He was protesting that he wanted something to catch the eye of the readers when a mother walked over.

"Sorry to interrupt, but can I just ask you, vicar ... what time will evensong be?"

After a short pause, there was a burst of laughter. Angela took the mother aside and did her best to explain the subterfuge, hoping the woman would not feel offended at their reaction to her. Serena took Luther's arm, and he inclined his head towards hers, their heads back, expressions of pure joy and happiness as they laughed together. The camera clicked several times in rapid succession.

The photograph to appear in the newspaper next day would certainly have star quality.

28

The inhabitants at Glebe Farm had settled into a new routine and were now running on autopilot. Up early as usual, breakfast on *Sally Ann*, half an hour in the office to clear the decks of e-mails and urgent messages and then on the road to town. Serena had told Marnie that her 'contingent' need not feel obliged to be at the school for the departure of the coaches, but everyone wanted to be on hand to make sure the scheme was running without a hitch.

Thursday was going to be another hot day, and humidity was rising. The morning was warm with a faint mist on the water under a clear sky. Marnie was walking the short distance from *Thyrsis* to *Sally Ann*, her hair still damp from the shower, when Dolly approached, warbling a greeting, tail up straight. She bent down to run a hand over the thick-pile fur and stroke the black velvet ears. A movement in the spinney caught her eye. Anne was arriving for breakfast. Marnie rose and was about to speak when Anne pointed beyond her. Marnie turned. On the opposite bank, curtains drawn like closed eyelids on a sleeping face, *X O 2* lay at her old mooring.

"When did he get here?" said Anne.

"No idea. First I've seen of him."

Anne held out a piece of paper. "This was tucked into the office door."

Marnie read: *Please waken me. Any chance of a lift into town? D*

"You'd better go over and give him a call. What does he like for breakfast?"

For a second Anne's face was tense as if she suspected a trick question. Then she relaxed and smiled. "Sauerkraut and Wienerschnitzel, I expect."

"Tell him the nearest we've got is muesli."

• • • • •

Every morning it was the same. Hundreds of children and their parents thronged the yard. Every morning brought new arrivals. The clerks at the reception desk issued forms to yet more newcomers wanting places on the outings.

Donovan had reverted to his customary black jeans and T-shirt, but wore a baseball cap and dark glasses. His own preference was for Ray-Ban *aviators* – classics – but he had adopted the new style of wrap-rounds as a disguise, while he unobtrusively roamed the perimeter on the lookout for troublemakers.

The participants were in high spirits, and the area sounded like a school playground at break time. Gradually the coaches arrived, were boarded and departed, with mothers and the occasional father giving last-minute instructions about good behaviour.

The last coach revved its engine and pulled away from the kerb leaving an odour of diesel in the summer air as the only sign that so much transport had been there. Marnie and the Knightly St John contingent were saying their goodbyes when a lone figure trudged towards them across the tarmac. They recognised him as Buzz, one of the West Indian brigade. He looked glum.

"What's up?" said Serena.

He scowled. "Teresa … my little sister … she's been sick."

"How sick?"

He shrugged. "Threw up after my mum went to work. She can't go on her trip."

"Where is she now?"

"I took her to my aunt. She'll have her for the day till my mum gets back."

"Nice of you to come along," said Marnie.

"How old's your sister … Teresa?" Anne asked.

Buzz thought about it. "Nine. And really miffed. It was Alton Towers today."

"You did the right thing, Buzz," said Marnie. "That's not the place to go if you're likely to be sick. Never mind. There'll be other trips for her when she's better."

"Yeah, but I was going with her."

Marnie smiled ruefully. He was probably no more than sixteen. A ringing interrupted their conversation, and Serena pulled the mobile from her bag.

"Oh, hi Pat. Everything all right?"

She listened while the others waited. They heard her mutter, and her expression grew serious.

"Where was this? ... How many were there? ... Going which way ... here?" She held the phone away from her ear, tilting her had back. "No I can't ... oh yes, now I do. Thanks for letting me know, Pat."

As she disconnected, they heard the wail of a police car siren in the distance. All faces turned to Serena.

"It's started."

•　•　•　•　•

They decided to walk into the town centre, discussing the phone call as they went. Their group consisted of Marnie and Ralph, Anne and Donovan, Serena and Luther with Buzz tagging along. *Not quite Seven Samurai,* Donovan had said to Anne under his breath.

"So what did she see?" Marnie asked.

"It's a *he,*" Serena corrected her. "Pat Sullivan ... one of the youth workers. He's on a coach to Warwick Castle. Going west out of town he noticed a line of parked coaches, thinking they might be ours. When he looked carefully he saw they were dropping off very strange people, mostly skinheads, nearly all in black or grey, some carrying flags and banners ... loads of them."

"Did he mention what colour the flags were?"

"He didn't say."

Marnie had seen those banners before, seen the flags and the motley army.

"This is New Force, presumably," said Ralph.

Two police cars roared past, their sirens drowning out Marnie's reply. Serena was reaching for the mobile again, pressing buttons to make a call. They waited while she huddled against a wall, one finger in her ear to shut out traffic noise as she spoke. When she finished, they walked on.

"That was the editor. The Prime Minister's due here some time this morning. He's going to open a new business park, with several European companies involved. Then lunch with the County Council."

"I can guess what the headlines will be tomorrow," Marnie chipped in. "And they won't be about business parks or European companies."

"Let's hope they're not about mayhem on the streets of Northampton," said Serena.

As they walked on in silence, each absorbed in their own thoughts, Anne sidled up to Marnie and spoke quietly.

"Where are we actually going? And what are we going to do when we get there?"

"Good questions. I think we just want to see what's happening. Anybody got a master plan?"

There were no takers. They were now drawing close to the town centre, and there was still nothing to see, but gradually they were becoming aware of something in the air. At first they wondered if it might be the sound of voices chanting.

"It's … drumming." Donovan was inclining his head.

"Yeah." Serena looked at him. "Are you armed, Donovan?"

The question surprised them all, except Donovan. He patted the bag slung over his shoulder.

"All set. I've got a new film in."

"You'll have to be discreet."

"Don't you worry. I'll not risk anyone getting hold of my camera."

• • • • •

The streets were eerie, practically deserted like a western movie, the set empty and expectant waiting for the gunslingers to face each other in a shootout. Marnie and the others made their way towards the drumming. It was clearer now and hung over the town like a pall of smoke. All of them were sweating, only partly from their rapid pace on the hot pavement. Marnie found herself recalling the words, *it's going to be a long hot summer*. She hoped no warm guns would be involved.

Instinct led them up towards the old racecourse and they spilled into the roadway, having the streets virtually to themselves. What little traffic they encountered was travelling away from the centre. More than one of the group was wondering why they were not doing the same.

"Why we goin' this way," said Buzz, "when everybody's going that way? Maybe they know somethin' we don't know."

Serena gave him his reply. "Because this is our fight, our struggle. We have to see it through." Her voice was hard.

Marnie was alarmed. She alone had seen New Force on the march. Only she knew what they were facing.

"I think we may be slightly outnumbered. Perhaps we'd better limit our ambitions to just seeing what's going on … from a distance."

Serena kept looking straight in front. "We need to be close enough to bear witness … to get evidence."

They walked on, and the closer they came to the racecourse, the stronger was Marnie's impression that the sound of drumming and marching was now no longer only ahead of them. Her eyes wandered down each side street that they passed, but still there were no sightings of New Force on the move. A cold hand was gripping her by the throat. She knew that Anne would be sharing the same thoughts. They had both faced violence in the past, both come close to death. Whatever Serena thought she was doing, Marnie had other plans and would not let anyone push their group into close combat with an army of thugs.

Reaching the main road they could now see movement in the distance. The throbbing of drums was everywhere, rolling unimpeded across the flat parkland that had once been a racecourse. They were crossing the street when sirens came wailing from behind them. A police car followed by two ambulances roared up scattering the group. From the lead car an officer shouted at them from the front seat. No one heard his words, but the message was evident. He did not have a high regard for their intelligence.

Marnie reached the opposite pavement with Ralph, Serena and Luther. Anne had retreated to the other side of the road, Donovan and Buzz diving with her. It was time to get out, and Marnie was raising an arm to signal the trio to fall back when Serena gasped. A crowd of demonstrators was marching along some way behind them, waving flags and chanting. At the sight of potential victims a cry went up and the column broke into a run, whooping and spreading out across the full width of the street. The seven were divided now with no chance of regrouping. Marnie watched helplessly as Anne and the other two bolted back down the road from which they had come. Ralph seized her arm and pulled her away. They had no choice but to run for their lives.

· · · · ·

Anne had gone three paces when she realised Buzz was no longer beside her. She braked and turned in one motion. He was standing still, looking back up the road.

"Come on … this way!" she yelled at him. He swayed slightly but did not follow. "What are you *doing*?"

Buzz pointed to the crossroads. "We could hide in there." He pointed to a restored Victorian tram shelter standing on the corner at the edge of the park.

"We'd be trapped." She grabbed at his sleeve and pulled hard. "Come *on* … we're wasting time."

Donovan ran back and took his other arm. They yanked him along and he fell into step. They knew he was scared. They knew they were all scared. The more space they put between themselves and the mob on the main road, the better. Anne was hoping their pursuers would lose interest and continue on their way to join the New Force army on the racecourse. She was worried about Marnie and the others, but knew she had to concentrate on getting out of this situation.

She risked looking back and was relieved to see that the mob was not in pursuit. Suddenly she cannoned into the back of Donovan who had stopped running. He staggered forward. Anne bounced sideways, spinning off the pavement into the gutter. Pain shot up her leg as her ankle twisted.

She grimaced. "What did you do that –"

The reason was all too clear. Advancing towards them was a gang of New Force thugs, about a dozen or so, complete with banners, moving up to join the main body, on the lookout for trouble. They spotted the trio at the same time as Donovan stopped abruptly.

Anne pushed Buzz hard in the chest. "Down there!" she gasped.

They had drawn level with a cobbled lane running between the backs of the old houses. Buzz needed no further encouragement. He began running. Donovan took hold of Anne.

"Are you OK? I'm so sorry. I thought you were running and –"

"No time … later," she gasped. "We gotta go."

She pushed Donovan, and they both set off down the alley, Donovan keeping in step with Anne, his face anxious as she ran limping beside him. Cries from behind told them the gang was in full flight chasing them. They had a head start of about a hundred metres. Down one side of the alleyway cars were parked in a long line. At the first one Anne stopped and steadied herself against its bodywork, her head bowed, one foot raised from the ground.

"It's no good … I can't …" She groaned with pain. "You go on."

"No way!"

"We ain't leavin' you," Buzz agreed.

"Get out of here! They won't –" She stopped as if choked.

"Anne!" Donovan grabbed her arm. "Are you –"

She pointed. The next car in the line was a black BMW … with chromed wheel arches. "My God … look at this … this is the car."

"What car?" Buzz was bewildered.

Anne looked up at the frightened and deeply puzzled face of the black boy. She stared into his dark brown eyes, saw the dreadlocks hanging from the beret, white teeth between full brown lips. Those colours … yellow, green, orange, black … the colours of Jamaica, the colours of reggae. All this flashed through her mind in less than a second. In that moment she formed a plan.

"Buzz, get going! Run and don't look back."

He started to shake his head.

"Don't argue, Buzz! Trust me. Get out of here! See us back at the school tonight. Now run!"

He turned and set off faster than he had ever moved before.

Donovan began taking hold of Anne. "I can probably carry you if –"

Her reply startled him. "Have you got a marker pen?"

"A *what*?"

"A felt tip, anything. Hurry up!"

Her voice was a staccato, edged with pain. She pushed him away. Hurriedly he groped in his bag and produced a black marker. She seized it.

"Get going … *please*, Donovan. I've got a plan … *Just do it!*"

The urgency in her voice made him do as she said. He jogged away from her following in Buzz's footprints. Accelerating, he glanced back over his shoulder, and was concerned to see her moving round the back of the car as if trying to hide from the mob. It was a pathetic effort. A wave of remorse and anxiety flooded over him, but he kept going out of respect for her wishes.

He hated himself with every step he took.

• • • • •

Marnie quickly lost sight of Anne and the other two round a curve in the road they had taken. The four of them were running along the pavement past the houses fronting the racecourse. There was nowhere to hide. The road stretched off into the distance in a continuous terrace with no gaps. Luckily both she and Serena were wearing flat shoes, but they had no chance of outrunning their pursuers. It was just a matter of time.

Far away across the park the massed ranks of New Force were gathering, and through the trees Marnie could see the tiny blue flashing lights of police cars. All the time the air was filled with the throbbing of drums beating. This was surely not the peaceful county town where nothing happened?

Glancing over her shoulder, Marnie could see the frontrunners of the mob rounding the corner. So far they were not gaining ground, seeming to prefer hunting in a pack. With her attention diverted, she caught her foot on the raised edge of a paving slab and tipped forward, stumbling for several paces, only regaining balance when Luther steadied her arm. They kept running. Marnie was desperately trying to devise a plan. But there seemed to be no way out. No white knight was going to appear to smash their pursuers with an invincible sword.

And then from nowhere a half-chance presented itself.

A few metres ahead a front door opened. An old lady came out with a shopping bag and a scarf on her head over white hair. She was pulling the door shut behind her when she caught sight of the four people running along the pavement. Her expression changed to alarm. Flustered and agitated, she began retreating, pushing the door that had already clicked shut. She fumbled with her key in the lock, anxiously scrabbling at the paintwork.

The four halted by the hedge of her small front garden. Marnie called out in a breathless voice.

"Don't be afraid. I'm sorry if we startled you."

"What's going on?" the woman asked, suspicious, her eyes darting from one to the other.

Marnie spoke quickly. "There's a riot. They're coming down the road. We're trying to get away from them. We can't get back to our car."

"*A riot?*" The woman sounded as if she had never heard the word before. "*Here?*"

"Back there … coming this way," said Ralph.

The woman glanced down the road, then turned and opened her door to go inside. She looked at Marnie and Ralph, Serena and Luther.

"I've seen your picture in the papers, haven't I? You'd better come inside."

They bundled in and stood in the hall, waiting. Seconds later the rioters rushed past, their shapes a crazy etching in the frosted glass door panels, wave after wave charging by. The mob's momentum was carrying it along. Marnie prayed that they had lost the scent and did not know which house they had entered, as she leaned back against the wall gazing at their unlikely white knight with her shopping bag.

· · · · ·

"'Ere, look what we've got ourselves." It was a hard, ugly voice.

Anne kept her head down, leaning against the boot of the car, not daring to look up at the assailants who had surrounded her. Others were running past down the lane. She reached down and gripped her ankle, gritting her teeth at the pain that had settled into a continuous sharp ache, throbbing in rhythm with the distant drumbeats.

"Oh yeah," said one of the gang. "Tasty."

"Bit skinny." Another hard voice.

"Who cares when it's free?"

This display of wit brought a peal of rough laughter. Anne rested her forehead against her arm, trembling inside, willing herself to stay calm and do what she had to do. She could hear shouting along the alleyway. At that moment her plan seemed implausible if not totally stupid. But it was all she had. She muttered encouragements to herself and took deep breaths to gather every reserve of strength she could muster.

"What you saying? Hey you … it's you I'm talkin' to."

Anne murmured a reply.

"What? Oi! Speak up, you little tart!"

This time she spoke more clearly. "That black *bastard!*" Her voice was bitter, almost a snarl.

"Eh?"

"Kicked me in the *bloody* ankle." She rubbed the ache with genuine feeling and put her foot down, only to wince at the pain. She breathed audibly, with no need of an acting performance, already wondering if she had broken a bone. She rolled down her sock to reveal a pronounced swelling.

"What you talkin' about?"

"This."

Anne pulled up the bottom of her jeans and moved her foot sideways into view. The skin looked ominously yellow and was bulging more with every passing second.

The thugs stared at it. This was not what they had expected. They were scrolling back through their memories to examine what they had seen in the road. There had been three people, two white, one black, running along together. The girl had jumped into the gutter and then grabbed the black one who ran off. What did it mean?

Anne heard a scream in the distance, a terrified tortured sound. She braced herself to concentrate on the hardest part of her plan. This was the tricky part. And if they knew whose car she was using as a prop … it was not something to contemplate. With two deep breaths, she launched her acting career.

"Black *bastard* … doing this to me." Her tone was heavy with loathing.

"Oh yeah? Don't worry … he'll be taken care of. So what're you doing here?" Suspicion.

"What does it look like?"

Good question. The gang examined their quarry. She was young like them, blonde … very blonde … wearing black jeans and a black T-shirt. Grey trainers. Could she be one of them? Had she been chasing the black kid? What about the other one? He was blonde too. And dressed in black like them.

"Who were you with?" said the alpha male. "That geezer?"

"My brother."

It figured.

"What group?"

This was it, she thought. Anne raised her face to look up at them for the first time. Her stomach turned over; some were holding baseball bats; all looked menacing.

"Just a local lot … not proper New Force … we said we'd join in. There are more of us. But we saw the black kid and went after 'im."

The gang looked stunned. Staring at Anne's pale face and light blue eyes, they were surprised to see the mark on her forehead … a swastika. It was not a real tattoo, but it was big and bold. Unmistakeable.

Suddenly, Anne began to laugh through her pain.

"What's up with you?" said alpha male.

"Your faces for a start. You look like you've seen a ghost."

Two of the gang began moving towards her.

"Ironic, isn't it?"

They hesitated, unaccustomed to such subtleties.

"What?"

"This car I'm leaning on ... ironic. It's a BMC."

"It's a *BMW*, stupid." Alpha male.

"You're the stupid one. It's a BMC, I'm telling you ... look." She jabbed a finger at the rear window. "BMC ... Black Man's Car. That's why it's ironic."

The whole gang moved round to stare at the window.

"Oh yeah," said one of them. "Look at that."

They looked down on the smiling face of the King of Reggae, and the slogan that we should all stick together and we'll be all right. A whole row of colourful stickers lined the bottom of the rear window of the BMW, with yellow, green, orange and black stripes predominating. Bob Marley looked out optimistically towards a future that he would not be sharing.

The violent noise made Anne jump as a baseball bat shattered a side window of the car. Forgetting her injury she turned, trying to back away. The pain from her ankle was agony and she went down on the ground, gasping and breathless. Paying her no attention, the gang scattered looking for missiles. A small pile of bricks standing outside one of the back doors was like a gift from the gods.

Anne rolled to face away from the car which was subjected to a fierce bombardment. Every window was smashed or dented, every panel of bodywork buckled under the barrage of bricks. Showers of glass rained down on her head which she covered with both arms. At least they had turned their attention away from her. For now. She could only hope that this was a demonstration of their belief in her story. The story of Anne the Nazi sympathiser.

She was struck on the shoulder by a brick that bounced off the boot, and she squirmed her way under the body of the van parked behind the BMW. Opening her eyes in her new shelter, she brushed glass out of her hair, reaching down to rub her ankle. It was on fire. She was pulling her feet as far under the overhang as she could when she focused on something in the distance. Her heart missed a beat. The gang of thugs had caught Buzz. He was writhing on the ground under a storm of blows from baseball bats, trying to dodge their attack. Failing. She could hear his cries of terror and pain, and she felt desperate at her own helplessness to go to his aid.

As tears pricked her eyes she suddenly made out another form. Squatting behind a car further down the line was a dark figure, bending and stretching every few seconds in a bizarre ritual. It was Donovan.

Anne knew exactly what he was doing. And she promised herself that if she managed to get out of this situation intact, she would add one more piece of trickery to that morning's performance.

A new sound brought her back to reality, the screech of tyres that filled her with dread. If it was the arrival of Brandon's entourage, they would know the car and she would have the devil to pay. The scuffing of running feet made her freeze. The gang was in flight. Heavier shoes were rushing past, and Anne wriggled out of her shelter to find out what was happening.

She rolled over and heaved herself into a squatting position, balancing on the car's bumper.

The BMW was a total wreck. Hastily she grabbed at the stickers, wrenching them from the remains of the window. She flung them to the ground behind the van, once again accidentally putting weight on her damaged ankle. In pain, she laid her head to rest on the dented boot of the car. With her eyes closed, waiting for the pain to subside, she heard footsteps beside her. Hoping it might be Donovan, she looked up.

"You are?" The voice carried authority.

The man facing her was in police uniform, though not that of the local force.

"Am I glad to see you," she said wearily. "I'm one of the scheme's organisers."

"So I see."

He reached forward and took her by the arm, pulling her towards him. She gave out a cry as her foot met the ground.

"Take it easy!" She groaned. "I've damaged my ankle."

"You should've thought of that before you started. Come on."

He checked her ankle really was injured and, having satisfied himself, supported her along the lane to where two police cars were waiting.

"My friends are down there. Something terrible has –"

"Just come this way."

Anne had to hop to keep up with his pace.

"My friends are down the alleyway. We're trying to stop New Force. We've got valuable evidence –"

"Save it for later."

"You don't understand –"

"No. You're the one who doesn't understand. Now pipe down."

"But I'm on your side. Don't you realise? *We're* running the summer scheme."

"*Our* side?" The policeman snorted. "Our side doesn't wear swastika tattoos, love. You're in the wrong outfit."

He pulled open the car door, put his hand on her head and pushed her onto the back seat. Gripping her injured leg, Anne looked down the alley. The gang of thugs was being chased by the police. Two other officers were bending over a heap lying on the ground. It lay ominously still.

• • • • •

They could not stay there for ever. After the mob had finished going past the house, the four of them felt uncertain and self-conscious, standing in the narrow hallway of a complete stranger.

"Thank you so much, Mrs ..."

"Battams."

"Thank you, Mrs Battams. I don't know what we would've done if you hadn't come out when you did."

"That's all right, dear. Would you all like a cup of tea?"

It was the standard British response to any life-threatening situation. It made Marnie smile, and it almost brought her to tears.

"That's very kind, but I think we ought to be going. We've got to find out what's happened to our friends."

"Are you sure? You're very welcome."

They assured her they had to be on their way, and Marnie made a call on her mobile.

"Starcabs."

"Hallo, Tony. This is Marnie Walker. Can you send a cab to ..." She checked the house number with Mrs Battams. "There are four of us. We need to go to Garfield Primary School."

"No problem, Mrs Walker. Five minutes."

"Who'll be driving?"

"It'll be ... Sarinda."

"Ah, no ... Do you have a white driver on duty?"

"Pardon me?"

"I need it to be a white driver. There are disturbances in town. Sarinda might be ... you know."

"Oh, right. I'll send Colin. He's got the people-carrier."

"Thanks, Tony."

A silver Galaxy with a red star on the side stopped outside the house, and Mrs Battams went out to check that the street was clear. Turning back to the house, she gave a brief thumbs-up, and her surprise guests filed out. They all thanked her as they climbed into the taxi.

"Garfield School, is it?"

"Please."

Crossing the traffic lights at the junction, Marnie noticed a police van parked at the roadside and asked Colin to stop. She jumped out and ran across to find a gang of ruffians being herded in through the back doors. A policewoman was standing beside the van.

"Excuse me. I know you can't tell me anything, but I'm looking for someone who was being chased by ..." She nodded her head towards the ruffians. "People like that lot. It was a girl, blonde hair, thin. Any ideas?"

"Sorry. There was a girl of that appearance, but she was one of these."

"You're sure of that?"

"Certain. Swastika tattooed on her face. Not much doubt."

Marnie felt deflated. "No. Thank you." An afterthought. "You've got her in the van?"

"She was injured. They've taken her to casualty."

Marnie climbed back in the taxi and reported to the others.

"OK?" asked the driver.

"Thanks, Colin."

He was pulling away when Marnie had a sudden idea.

"Can we go via the hospital?"

The others looked at her in surprise.

• • • • •

Donovan was sure they had not spotted him. He dropped the camera into his bag and nestled close against the wheel of the van, in case anyone checked under the parked vehicles.

The thugs split as the police charged them, leaving Buzz where he lay. Donovan swallowed hard. It had taken a superhuman effort to restrain himself from going to his aid when the mob had caught him. He heard the first blow and cry of pain as the baseball bat hit him on the legs to bring him down. After that Buzz had no chance, and Donovan had no chance of helping without suffering the same fate. He felt sick inside but knew he had to do what he could to stay on the offensive.

And where was Anne? What was the plan she devised that had made her send him and Buzz away? What had happened to her? He only had brief moments after hearing the crashes and bangs as the car was vandalised when he could risk darting his head out to shoot, but he was sure she was not in the frame. He had never known such agony.

Squatting down, he pressed himself closer against the wheel, hearing the police return with the captured thugs. One of the officers standing over Buzz was using his radio calling up an ambulance. He ended the call as the others passed.

"How is he?"

The reply pierced Donovan through the heart.

"This one's a goner, I reckon."

In a minute the ambulance turned the corner and bumped its way over the cobbles. The paramedics saw the body on the ground and the police standing over it with heads bowed. They did not see the man lying flat under a nearby old van. They did not hear the camera clicking as they lifted the inert shape onto a trolley, slid it into the ambulance and drove off.

As soon as they had left, Donovan eased himself out, slipped silently along to the end of the lane and bolted in the direction of the newspaper office. Hot tears of anger and regret were burning tracks down his face as he ran. Not for the first time that morning, he hated himself. He hated the thugs, their bigotry and prejudice. Hated them for the murder they had done to that poor harmless frightened boy. But he hated someone else more.

Most of all he hated Brandon. Hated him for everything he stood for, everything he did and caused to be done. Donovan hated Brandon with a deep loathing.

•　•　•　•　•

The policeman had examined Anne's ankle, seen the beads of sweat on her pale face and taken her to hospital with a suspected fracture. She was being booked in when a scream announced the arrival of a victim of stabbing. A man, clutching his stomach that was oozing red, was being led in by another policeman, supported on one side by his girlfriend, the screamer. Behind them two more officers were flanking a man with blood all over his face and hands and on his shirt.

Anne was moved to one side as everyone's attention turned to the walking wounded. She knew that bleeding cases always received priority. In a weak voice she asked if she could sit down; putting a hand to her head she swayed ominously as if about to faint. A seat was found for her, and the officer who had brought her in was needed as the stabbed man tried to renew the fight with his opponent.

While this was a welcome entertainment to most people in the waiting area, a nurse skirted them, giving the action a wide berth. Anne caught her attention.

"I'm afraid I need to go to the loo, but I can't walk very well."

Holding her forehead to conceal the swastika, she revealed her injured ankle. In truth, the pain had now settled to a persistent but only mildly uncomfortable ache.

"Can you stand?" said the nurse.

Head down, Anne pushed herself carefully up from the chair. The nurse took her arm and guided her towards the toilets. From his position across the waiting area the policeman saw Anne being led away by a nurse, presumably for treatment.

Anne insisted she would be able to manage the loo unaided, and the nurse went back to her duties. Anne found she could walk slowly as long as she kept the heel of the damaged foot raised off the ground. The first task was to scrub the swastika off her face, thankful that Donovan's marker pen was water-soluble. She washed her hands, cleaning off the dirt from lying in the road, all the way up to the tops of her arms. She pulled off the black T-shirt, brushed it with her hand, then turned it inside out. Looking cleaner and more presentable, she refocused on her ankle.

Rolling up a trouser leg, she grabbed a handful of paper towels, planted her foot in the sink and turned on the cold tap. The shock took her breath away, but she forced herself to keep the ankle under the flow for a full minute, gasping all the while. She dried it off. A final inspection in the mirror. Still not good enough; there was grit and dirt in her hair.

She used the taps to mix warm water and held her head under the swan's neck, brushing out dirt with her fingertips. A palm-full of handwash from the tip-up dispenser served as shampoo. She rinsed off, pressing her wet hair flat with more paper towels and mouthing *because you're worth it* to her reflection in the mirror, she hopped over to the hand-drier and squatted down under the hot air, turning her head from side to side. Soon she was ready to face the world.

Pushing the window up, Anne perched on the ledge, swung her legs over the sill and eased herself gently to the ground.

• • • • •

Marnie swept into the casualty department, blinking at the sight of the blood-stained adversaries being restrained by policemen, to the hysterical vocal accompaniment of a woman who was herself spattered with blood.

She scanned the waiting area seeking out the familiar blonde head, but of Anne there was no sign. Marnie stepped round the fracas, fighting back the desire to slap the screaming woman hard across the face to shut her up. The staff at the reception desk seemed mesmerised by the spectacle until Marnie planted herself in front of them. They refocused on her and listened to her question.

"I said, have you registered a girl with an injured ankle? Short blonde hair? She may have come in with a police escort ... in the last half hour."

A nurse arrived at the desk and placed a file of notes on the counter top. The receptionist was consulting her papers.

"No. No one with an ankle injury here today, with or without police."

"You're sure of that?" Marnie persisted.

"Yes there was," the nurse said abruptly to the surprise of her colleagues.

"She's gone to use the loo. I took her there myself … not five minutes ago."

"Blonde hair … urchin cut … thin girl … black T-shirt and jeans?"

"That's the one."

"Which loo?"

The nurse pointed. "Down that corridor, second on the left. There's no rush. She could hardly walk. I'll go and see if she needs help in a minute."

Marnie was on the move. "I'll go. You're busy."

She walked calmly round the corner and dived for the door. It came as no surprise that Anne was not there. But had she been there? Both cubicles were empty. Marnie touched the hand drier. Warm. One of the two washbasins was wet. She crossed to the frosted glass window and felt a cool draught at the bottom. It was not fully closed. Yanking it open she looked out onto a small parking area. But if Anne had been there, she was gone.

Calm had returned to the A and E reception area, and Marnie walked quickly through without looking back. The taxi was waiting on double yellow lines opposite the ambulance. Serena and Luther sat grim and wooden with Ralph. Marnie climbed into the front passenger seat and slammed the door.

"It was her. She was the one the police brought in. She's got a damaged ankle."

Ralph stared forward. "I know."

"I think she might've used a trick to … what do you mean, *you know*?"

Ralph thumbed over his shoulder. "She's in the back, under the picnic rug. OK, Colin, let's drive."

· · · · ·

The taxi dropped them outside Serena's house. The street was quiet, a haven of peace after all they had witnessed that morning. Ralph helped Anne from the rear doors. She could now walk reasonably well without assistance. The front door opened before they reached it, and Serena was about to introduce her mother when she realised that ma was distraught, her face wet with tears.

"They killed the boy," she sobbed.

In a state of shock they filed in. The radio was giving live coverage of the turbulent events taking place in the town centre. On the table neatly laid out were plates of sandwiches, bowls of crisps and nuts, bottles of mineral water and fruit juices. Everything remained untouched. Ma left them and went to be with the children playing in the garden. The five sat as if in a trance while the news reports came in.

… now postponed. The prime minister was whisked away by his aides but not before issuing a strongly-worded statement condemning what he described as 'anarchist elements in society that seek only the destruction of everything we in Britain hold dear.' He warned voters of the dangers of turning the country over to any party that relied for support on thugs and hooligans. Garth Brandon, the BFP candidate, retorted that the government was losing control of the country and it needed discipline to ensure that our rights to democratic peaceful protest were not undermined by heavy-handed police tactics.

"Here we go again," Ralph murmured. "The same old story."

"It makes me so mad," Serena snarled with gritted teeth.

A different reporter took up the running.

Witnesses in the racecourse district of the town are saying they saw a gang of rioters attack a black youth with baseball bats. The witnesses, who saw the event from their windows, testified that they saw the boy being beaten on the ground by men who ran off when police officers arrived on the scene. They heard the police stating that the gang had beaten him to death. This has not yet been formally confirmed.

Serena held a hand to her mouth. Anne slumped in a chair. Marnie leaned across to her.

"Is that what happened?"

"I think so ... couldn't see everything. I was lying under a van. I wish I could've done something to gain them more time to get away."

"You were very brave," said Luther. He put a hand on her shoulder.

"No I wasn't. I just couldn't run ... had to think of something on the spot. I was scared stiff."

"No one could've done more than you did, Anne," Marnie said softly.

... but a spokesman for the BFP said there was no evidence or reliable eye witnesses to prove who carried out the attack. He pointed out that some unscrupulous people were using the democratic protests as a smokescreen to cover up gang violence between factions within what he described as immigrant communities. Garth Brandon, the candidate at the centre of the row over police brutality, has demanded protection from the authorities. A government spokesman pointed out that Brandon had his own private army, a point later denied by the BFP leader who insisted that he had no personal bodyguards.

Serena's mother returned unnoticed and began handing round sandwiches to the visitors. She had spent an hour preparing them that morning, and they were delicious. The guests accepted them and ate out of politeness. No one tasted anything.

• • • • •

Donovan walked quickly away from the newspaper offices where he had handed in the film for processing. His head was bent forward and he was deep in thought, a plan forming in his mind. He made his way across town, sometimes forced into taking a long way round to avoid marauding New Force gangs. Eventually he reached the school and, standing on the corner, he watched the comings and goings of the scouts as they prepared lunch in the largest of the tents under the gently waving Union flag.

Biding his time, he waited until all attention was fixed on organising the meal, then he emerged from concealment to cross the road and kneel beside Marnie's Discovery. Pretending to tie his shoe laces, he reached under the front wheel arch and groped for the metal box containing the spare keys. In seconds he was in the driving seat with the engine running. No one seemed to be paying any attention. He engaged first gear and pulled away.

• • • • •

"Accident and Emergency, please."

"One moment."

The delay was more than one moment. Serena was ready to burst when the voice cut in.

"A and E nurses' station." It was an abrupt greeting from a harassed voice.

"I'm phoning to enquire about a boy admitted this morning. He'd been attacked by men with baseball bats."

"Are you a relative?"

"Well no, not actually, but –"

"Sorry we cannot give any information except to members of the family."

"I realise that but these are exceptional circumstances and –"

"We only have exceptional circumstances. I'm sorry I can't help you."

"But the boy may have been killed!" Serena was almost shouting.

"Then you should contact the police with any information you have. I have to go, sorry."

Serena breathed out audibly. Marnie refrained from telling her she had told her so.

"So ..." Luther broke into the silence. "Is there anything we can do this afternoon?"

Ralph reached over and put his plate on Serena's dining table. "Two options, I suppose. We either go home and get on with business as usual, or we stay in town."

"And do what?" Serena sounded as if she wanted an argument.

"That's the question." Ralph kept his voice quiet. "I for one would find it hard to get on with my normal work. I'd be thinking all the time about the riots ... and that poor boy."

"Me too," said Luther.

Serena's eyes blazed. "Well I'm not prepared to just –"

"Serena." Marnie's voice was low but firm. "There's no way we're going back to the centre. Forget it. The best we can do is keep up with what's going on by following the radio reports."

"But –"

"We can't attack New Force. We can't go to the hospital and do any good. That doesn't leave us many other options."

"So you think we should just sit here and twiddle our thumbs while the battle goes on out there?"

"No. I think we should watch and plan ... unless anyone has any better ideas?"

"And worry," Anne joined in.

Ralph smiled across at her. "Good point. We'll all be doing that," he said gently.

They all smiled.

"About anything in particular?" Marnie asked, "Or just a general worry?"

"You all seem to be forgetting Donovan. We don't know what happened to him."

Every smile vanished.

• • • • •

He could not take the risk of going into Knightly St John by the usual roads. Marnie's Discovery was too well-known, and he had no wish to implicate her in any way in his actions. Using the road atlas, Donovan found a cross-country route, hopping from village to village, that would lead him to the top of the field track without going down the high street.

The journey took longer but it was a necessary compromise. He steered for the back of the outbuildings, leaving the track and heading down the hill out of sight of the rooftops of the farmhouse where a builder might spot him. He prayed that no one would be at home and left the car tucked under the trees at the edge of the spinney. Bent double, he hurried through, and hid behind a clump of bushes from where he could observe the boats. They were unoccupied, the docking area deserted.

When something touched his leg he almost cried out. Looking down, he met the steady amber gaze of a sturdy black cat. He put a finger to his lips and spoke softly.

"Not a word, Dolly. OK? Our secret. *Bleib' stumm, Katze!*"

The cat blinked twice and, impressed with her command of German, Donovan set off over the bridge towards *X O 2*. On board in stuffy heat, he went purposefully about his business, first checking that all windows and doors were secure. Tearing off his dirty clothes he quickly showered before changing into a fresh set that he took carefully from the wardrobe. He rummaged in drawers for the things he needed and placed them in his bag. The last items were a light grey cotton sweater that he folded carefully and a red baseball cap that he tucked in beside it. Finally he carried the mountain bike out onto the towpath, probably for the last time, re-set the intruder alarm and locked up.

He rode back to the Discovery, lowered the rear seats to make a cargo platform and loaded in the bike. He carefully laid his shoulder bag on the passenger seat and started the engine. Taking the same route up the hill and out of the village, he was relieved not to meet any other vehicles on his way or pass anyone who might later be able to testify that they had seen either him or Marnie's car that afternoon.

• • • • •

The atmosphere in Serena's dining room made Marnie understand the meaning of the expression, *pent-up frustration*. They sat listening to the local radio reports on the BBC. The station manager had abandoned the usual schedule and thrown everything into the events that were engulfing Northampton. The county town, in its long history, had experienced nothing comparable since the riots in support of the barons against King Henry III in the thirteenth century.

As the afternoon dragged by and the reports came in, the group was on an emotional roller-coaster ride. The good news was that the minority ethnic communities had the wisdom to keep out of harm's way, and the indigenous British population would have nothing to do with the demonstrators, either by joining them or by attacking them and making matters worse. Reports stressed that all involved in smashing shop windows and wrecking bus shelters were outsiders brought in especially to make trouble.

The town held its breath, waiting to see what would be left when the dust eventually settled. The pretty tram shelter on the corner of the racecourse, where Buzz had wanted to hide, was reduced to a battered heap of twisted metal. The statue of a famous Victorian MP had been toppled from its plinth, and the charming Guildhall had been sprayed with racist slogans. The emergency services had their resources stretched to the limit as fires were started all over town. But the line held, courage did not falter, and as the afternoon wore on, hope began to grow that normal life would one day return.

The bad news was that the invading army was fanning out, going from street to street in search of victims. Reports came in that an Asian shop assistant, eighteen years old, had been dragged from her work and only saved from beating and rape by the timely arrival of a carload of policemen. In the almost-deserted market square a stall specialising in sari material had been overturned and set on fire. A similar fate was dealt to a stall that sold West Indian fruit and vegetables, the protesting owner beaten up but dragged to safety by his fellow white stallholders who drove off the attackers.

The most curious report was that a concerted attack had been made on the security CCTV cameras all over the town centre. Every one had had its lens sprayed over with paint so that the police traffic and security centre was blinded in all the areas where riots were taking place.

And predictably Garth Brandon railed at the police and others who were alleged to be perpetrating acts of violence against 'supporters of a democratic political party exercising their right to bring legitimate peaceful manifestations of free speech onto the streets of their own country.'

The group gathered in the dining room consulted their wristwatches so frequently that Serena finally got up and placed a clock in the centre of the table.

"It could be worse," Marnie muttered, while an announcer was explaining yet again why the afternoon's normal programmes had been shelved.

"Thank God so many of the youngsters are out of town," said Luther. "Or thank Serena, I should say."

Marnie sat up in her seat. "Oh, my God!"

"What's up?"

"When they come back … Brandon's lot knows all about the summer scheme. We'll be a sitting target for New Force. All those people … all those races … We've got to stop them going back to the school."

"*Jeez!*" Serena sat, mouth open, staring into disaster.

"How many of the stewards on the coaches have mobile phones?" said Ralph.

"At least one on every bus. That's our policy."

"Do you have the numbers?"

"Not here, but Jackie Brice will have them. So will Greg Roberts at Garfield." Serena got up to go to the phone in the hall. "You'd better make sure your mobiles are working. We've got a load of calls to make."

• • • • •

Donovan stopped a short way from the school and walked to the corner to peer round. Some sort of meeting seemed to be taking place in the large tent, otherwise all was quiet. He climbed back into the Discovery and drove into a parking slot more or less where he had found it. After a quick inspection of the contents of his bag, he jumped out, dragged the mountain bike from the rear and raised the seats to their usual position. With the car keys back in their metal box under the wheel arch, he rode swiftly away, his bag slung over one shoulder.

It was not difficult to locate the epicentre of the rally. The drumming served as a beacon for anyone seeking the heart of the action. Donovan turned away from the racecourse, found a quiet side street not far from where Buzz had been attacked, and padlocked his mountain bike to a rubbish skip out of sight. He looked at the jaunty yellow and black paintwork of the Muddy Fox and wondered if he would ever see it again. He patted the saddle and walked rapidly away without looking back.

• • • • •

Marnie checked her list of numbers, ticked off the last one she had called and pecked out the next one on the mobile.

"Pamela? Is that Pamela Greatorex?"

"It's Pam, yes." The woman sounded in good form. Why not? She had probably had a great day out with the children. "I've only been Pamela to my parents when I was naughty. Who is this?"

"It's Marnie Walker ... from the organising committee."

"Oh, yes. Well, everything's fine with our lot. We did have one incident in –"

"Pam, sorry to cut you off, but we have a situation here."

"A situation?" The first trace of anxiety. "What do you mean?"

"There are riots in Northampton ... big trouble. You mustn't bring the coach back to Garfield. Where are you now?"

"Er ... still on the motorway ... not sure where exactly. Maybe half an hour from home?"

"Right. Here's what you do. Rendezvous at the big sports centre on the western ring road. You know where I mean?"

"Sure."

"We'll see you there and re-route the coaches to collection points around the town. Tell the kids their parents will pick them up. OK?"

"Will do."

Sitting on the hall stairs, Ralph was explaining the arrangements to Greg Roberts, whose scouts would be intercepting and diverting any coaches that could not be contacted and made their way to the school. He knew Greg would have the scouts posted in lookout positions before he could make his next call.

Serena was in the kitchen talking to the manager of the radio station. The purpose of the whole exercise was to keep everyone clear of the town centre. They were gambling on Brandon not wanting to disperse his thugs to locations dotted around the outer suburbs. It was agreed that announcements would be made on air telling parents where their nearest collection point would be. They were asked to spread the word about the new arrangements and to share transport wherever possible.

Luther was in touch with the duty officer at the central police station who was only too glad to know what measures were being taken. There was no spare manpower, but the police would respond as best they could to any call for back-up.

Serena called the group together in the dining room to check progress. Despite the hectic phoning, they were in better spirits from having tasks to achieve. Three coaches had so far not been reached. They would keep trying and if they failed, the scouts would be the safety net, intercepting the buses before they approached the school.

The door opened, and Serena's mother peeped in.

"Can I make you all a cup of tea?"

She was greeted by subdued but manic laughter.

"Ma ... we're gasping."

$$\bullet \quad \bullet \quad \bullet \quad \bullet \quad \bullet$$

The young man walked without hesitation into the huge crowd gathered round the platform. It was made of scaffolding tubes and had been erected so that the BFP van was its backdrop. He moved confidently through the mass of bodies that smelled of sweat and beer and placed himself to one side of the rostrum about ten metres from where the speaker was gesticulating.

Some of the thugs had turned to see who was elbowing his way between them and were surprised at what they saw. This was no skinhead like the hundreds who were thronging the park that sweltering afternoon. He did not even appear mildly warm. And the look he gave the members of New Force was icy cold as he brushed past them.

But for all this arrogant display, no one challenged him. Some even looked apprehensive, for this newcomer had about him an air of menace that matched their own, but was of an entirely different order. A path opened for him as he moved closer to the platform, and space was made so that no one jostled him.

Looking at him they saw a young man dressed like them in black, but immaculately turned out. Over his shoulder he carried a leather bag on a strap. He wore trousers with sharp creases, a freshly-ironed shirt and a brown leather belt with a heavy buckle in the shape of a death's head. What singled the young man out from the rest was the ostentatious red armband with the black swastika on a white circular background, the silver-topped SS dagger in a leather scabbard at his belt and, most surprising of all, the Iron Cross in black and silver at his throat.

The speaker on the dais was warning everyone to be on their guard.

... Britain is under threat from outside and from within. Sixty million people in one small country is enough ... Everyone knows that. Only I – Garth Brandon – and the BFP have the courage to say it openly. I am not advocating sending people back to their 'homelands' ... unless they want to go. But in that case they should receive help to return ...

As the speaker paused for breath, the young man in black clapped loudly so that the applause was taken up around him and spread throughout the crowd.

Brandon raised his hands, waited for the applause to subside and continued, his voice beginning quietly and growing ever louder.

No one should accuse us of intolerance. Our aim is to protect the freedoms for which Britain has always been renowned. It is the immigrants who have come to this country bringing their intolerant views, undermining British values. For many of them, women are second class citizens. How dare anyone accuse the BFP of diminishing half the population of this country! This is not a minor difference of opinion ... this is a clash of cultures on a grand scale!

More applause rang out led by the young man in black. When the clapping died down, Brandon ended his speech, almost shouting, stabbing a finger in the air to stress every word.

The cause of our concern is that this clash of cultures is not between states but within the state. We must not allow it to destroy our sense of justice, freedom and the values that we hold dear. That is why we are here today. That is the heart and soul of our protest.

The crowd went wild. Waving to the mob with both hands, Brandon stepped down from the platform and disappeared from view behind the van. A thunder of applause broke out, fists were thrust skywards amid loud cheering, whistling and chanting, this time with no prompting from the newcomer. When the thugs glanced in his direction, they found that like Brandon he too had vanished.

• • • • •

"I don't care. You can protest all you like, but you're not coming with us. It's not safe."

Marnie was trying to be an irresistible force, but Serena had about her the look of an unmovable object. When her reply came it was in a low voice that would tolerate no argument.

"This is my show, Marnie. I'm not staying home when there's so much at stake."

"Marnie's right," said Luther. "If they see you, there'll be trouble."

"Ever heard of the pot calling the kettle black? I'm the same colour as you are."

Serena grabbed the phone and pressed buttons. By the time she had ordered a cab, resistance had crumbled.

Colin sped the group round the ring road and deposited them at the sports stadium complex. He turned off the clock and agreed to wait until they were ready to return to Garfield Primary to collect their cars. Every coach responded to the change of plan, and Serena's team had little more to do than send them on their way to the new collection points.

Watching the last coach pull out of the car park, Serena sighed and climbed into the cab.

"God knows what they'll make of this added expense at county hall. Well, tough gazungas! I'm past caring."

They set off for the town centre where the cab parked immediately behind Serena's car so that she had only a few paces to walk. She climbed in and drove off quickly. Marnie looked over at the Discovery while Ralph was paying Colin.

"Strange. I thought I'd left it just in *front* of Serena's. Oh well ... that must've been yesterday. My brain's getting addled by this heat."

Anne frowned and half-limped, half-jogged off to get a paper from the corner shop. She was back in seconds, hopping across the road.

"They've got the lot ... a whole spread ... two pages of photos ... definitely

Donovan's. He must've got away safely."

She spread out the evening edition on the bonnet of Marnie's car. Touching the steel bodywork with her hand, she thought for a moment it was warmer than she would have expected. Putting it down to the hot weather, she focused attention on the pictures. The editor had gone to town.

With sombre faces they stared at the images, some violent, others full of pathos. Donovan must have taken serious risks to manage some of these shots. They showed with great clarity the New Force thugs smashing the BMW. The caption underlined that here was irrefutable evidence that the damage was committed by white men, not the black ones condemned by Brandon. Hardest to bear were two pictures of the gang beating Buzz with baseball bats. The caption made no apologies for the explicit nature of the photographs. The paper believed it was important to reveal the true scale of the violence being committed in the name of 'legitimate democratic protest' by the supporters of the BFP. The final picture showed the body of Buzz being lifted into the ambulance on a stretcher.

Anne's head slumped forward onto her chest, silent tears coursing down her face.

"Come on," Marnie said gently. "Let's go home."

Beside her Ralph muttered, "We've all had quite enough shocks for one day."

But he was wrong.

•　•　•　•　•

Donovan walked slowly through the crowd with his head down, away from the centre of everyone's attention. The noise from the clapping, chanting and cheering was thunderous, and he rode it like a surfer on a giant wave. No one paid him the slightest heed as he slipped through the massed ranks of Brandon's supporters.

Glancing over his shoulder to get his bearings, he began altering course to bring himself round to the cluster of vehicles that had formed a protective backdrop to the speaker's platform. Unobtrusively he raised a hand up his arm as if rubbing a sore muscle. He hooked a thumb over the armband and pulled it down, folding it deftly and tucking it into the shoulder-bag.

A few steps further he raised a hand to rub the back of his neck. Simultaneously he unhooked a fastening and lowered the Iron Cross on its ribbon, clutching it in the palm of his hand and dropping it too into the bag. He reached the vehicles that were parked to form a barrier, but his arrival went unchallenged and he eased himself between two of the taller vans. As he did so, he unclipped the scabbard from his belt and pushed the SS dagger in with the rest of his regalia. Last of all, the belt. Donovan simply twisted it over so that the death's head emblem on the buckle was invisible. By the time he emerged from shelter he was just another young man dressed in black, like thousands of others.

Penetrating the encampment, Donovan became aware of hurried activity. A gang was dismantling the speaker's platform, stacking the poles and boxes into the largest of the vans. They seemed uncoordinated as if working without direction. Watching them, it looked as though they did not even know each other. Without checking his stride, Donovan walked quickly towards the platform, wrenched a box free from its position and began lugging it to the van. Through the parked cars he could see a knot of people gathering together behind the main BFP van. Brandon and his cronies? he wondered.

On his second trip to the platform, one of the other workers spoke to him in passing. "You one of the Leicester lot?" It was a gruff low voice. A London accent.

"Coventry," Donovan replied without making eye contact.

He carried a bundle of scaffolding poles and used the time it took to slide them one by one into the van to observe the comings and goings. It would be hard to penetrate Brandon's entourage. But even as he watched them, they began moving off on foot, Brandon's distinctive bald head visible in the middle of the group. When no one was looking his way, Donovan quietly edged between two other vehicles and began moving closer to the enemy, easily falling into step with them as they threaded their way through the cars and away from the racecourse.

• • • • •

Marnie gunned the engine and pointed the Discovery out of town, anxiously looking back at Anne. Beside her on the back seat, Luther handed her a fresh white handkerchief, and she gratefully wiped her eyes and face. When they reached the ring road Marnie switched on the radio. Ralph fiddled with the controls, and eventually located the local channel. Even when he made the connection, they could not understand what they were hearing, a problem made worse by the high level of background noise surrounding a reporter somewhere in town.

... but it is known that there have been inter-faction rivalries for some time as disparate groups argued over tactics. It's still not clear which of these was responsible, and so far no one group has admitted its part in the incident.

The voice of the studio presenter was a contrast in clarity.

Have the police authorities made any statement as yet, Tricia? Is there any chance of an interview with a senior officer?

No one is prepared to go on record for now. I can't even get near enough to put in a request. It's chaos down here. I'm being jostled by ...

The reporter's voice was lost in a hubbub of shouting and wailing sirens.

"What the hell's going on?" said Ralph.

Marnie slowed down. "Oh God ... It must be one of our coaches, I know it. Something dreadful's happened." She turned off the main road and stopped on the outskirts of a village. Switching off the engine, she rested her forehead on the steering wheel. "I feel sick. I couldn't bear it if anything –"

"Hold on, Marnie. They're back."

Sorry about that. We seem to have lost contact with Tricia Ironside outside BFP headquarters. We'll rejoin her as soon as we can establish a connection. For listeners just joining us, we have breaking news that an attempt has been made on the life of the leader of the Britain First Party, Garth Brandon. Reports are coming in that a lone gunman attacked him soon after he arrived back at the secret HQ of the party in the town centre not far from the racecourse.

"What on earth …?" Ralph reached forward to raise the volume and inadvertently turned off the radio. "*Damn it!* Sorry …" He pressed the power button and connected with a different station. Muttering curses, he started fiddling with the controls.

"Someone's tried to bump off Brandon?" Marnie was incredulous. "That's the 'incident' they were talking about?"

"What does it mean … *an attempt has been made?*" Luther asked. "Does that mean it failed?"

A jingle followed by a traffic report blared out of the radio. Ralph struggled to lower the volume.

"*A lone gunman,*" Marnie repeated. "I wonder if they caught him? I hope to God he wasn't black."

Ralph was pressing buttons, and his efforts were rewarded with a cultured American voice explaining about Mozart's sojourn in Chelsea and the *divertimenti* he composed there.

"I think that's Classic fm, Ralph," Marnie suggested.

Without speaking, Anne extended an arm between the front seats and pressed one button with her forefinger.

… whose identity remains a mystery.

"Bingo!" Ralph exclaimed. "Anne, you're a genius."

… and it is not clear how the assailant could have known about the BFP base, which was a closely-guarded secret. Only a handful of Brandon's inner circle of associates knew its location. We are still trying to obtain a statement from the police, but so far no one has been available.

Here's a recap on the dramatic events that have taken place in the past half hour. Garth Brandon appears to have returned to his HQ on foot after addressing a mass rally on the racecourse. As always, he was protected by supporters wearing the distinctive all-black clothing that Brandon himself favoured. It was when he reached the front door that a shot was heard and a man shouted to everyone to get down. More shots were fired and Garth Brandon was hit. The attacker ran off while everyone was on the ground. It's thought that he might have had an accomplice, as he vanished from the scene leaving no trace behind him.

"This is amazing." Marnie sat back, anxious but relieved. "Whoever it was must've been in Brandon's outfit."

"Or part of New Force," Ralph suggested. "If it's true there were rivalries, anything might be possible."

"But you don't kill a colleague over a policy dispute, surely?" said Luther, "Even if you are rivals."

"Who else could get near enough? Who else would be able to get them all to hit the ground like that?"

Marnie stroked her chin. "That must've come from an eye-witness. It sounded authentic."

Luther leaned forward. "Then the eye-witness would surely have known who did it. That's the part I don't understand."

"Perhaps it was just someone who looked like one of them," Anne surmised.

"What do you mean?"

"I dunno … just a thought. Who could get close to Brandon? Luther couldn't. He's the wrong colour. So it might've been a BFP or New Force person ... or someone like that."

"That's logical." Marnie turned on the ignition. "But they'd have to know where to go to find Brandon at his secret HQ. I think it points to an insider ... from a rival faction."

"I rather agree with Marnie," said Ralph. "It would have to be a pretty sophisticated infiltrator for it to be an outsider."

"An undercover police agent?" Luther speculated.

Anne gazed out of the window as Marnie performed a U-turn and drove back to the main road. She was composed again, and Luther took his handkerchief from her lap and tucked it back into his pocket. They travelled in silence, listening as the news reports on the Brandon incident came in, each one regurgitating the same facts. The BBC eventually interviewed a police officer who was only able to confirm the earlier story.

... no word yet from the hospital on the extent of Mr Brandon's injuries, though it is believed he was wounded in the attack.

Thank you, Superintendent. We're now going live to our reporter Lance Macey, at the General Hospital, who I think has some news for us ...

The Discovery was filled with the crackle of static.

"It's all a bit chaotic," Marnie murmured, pulling out to overtake a lorry.

Ralph agreed. "Probably just arrived there in the radio car. They're having to cobble it all together as best they can."

... just made this statement. "Mr Garth Brandon was admitted to the Accident and Emergency department a short while ago. He was suffering from gunshot wounds to the head and neck and was immediately taken to the operating theatre for emergency surgery. Before any treatment could be administered, however, he died without regaining consciousness."

"*Bloody hell!*" Marnie made a supreme effort to keep her attention focused on the road.

"He's *dead!*" Anne exclaimed. "He's really dead. What will happen now?"

Ralph summed it up in one word. "Trouble."

· · · · ·

Back at Glebe Farm, Marnie dashed into the office to phone Serena. Luther was invited to eat with them that evening and went to the cottage to shower and change clothing. Anne was still feeling stunned when she climbed out of the car and slammed the door and she was walking stiffly towards the spinney when autopilot cut in. She remembered she had to note the mileage for her accounting records.

She took the notebook from her back pocket as she opened the driver's door. Despite the air-conditioning, the inside of the car was warm and smelled of hot bodies. It would be a good idea to open the windows to let it cool and freshen up. Marnie had taken her keys so Anne hopped round to the wheel arch and found the spares in their magnetic hiding place. Turning the power on, she pressed the buttons for the electric windows, then read the mileage and added the numbers to the appropriate column of the notebook.

· · · · ·

"Sorry it's only pizza." Marnie was squatting to look through the glass door of the oven in the galley on *Sally Ann*. "I was relieved to find these two in the freezer."

Luther, looking cool and fresh in white T-shirt and cream slacks, was picking up a tray. "I don't think we expected a four-course chicken dinner, Marnie, not after all we've been through today. It'll be good just to sit down and put it all behind us."

It was a day for making false predictions.

Outside, Anne was sitting at the table, tossing a salad. She was resting her foot, which was now less swollen but still ached. Ralph was opening a bottle of red Rioja.

They had barely taken their first mouthful when they heard movement in the spinney. To their collective dismay, Chief Inspector Bartlett and Sergeant Marriner emerged from the trees and approached the table. Something inside Marnie was close to snapping. She took a few deep breaths staring down at her plate before looking up at the visitors.

"Good evening. I'm sorry to interrupt your meal."

Bartlett did not look sorry. He looked grim, and Marnie had the good sense to remain silent.

"What can we do for you, Mr Bartlett?" Ralph sounded as courteous as ever.

"You will have heard about the incident involving Garth Brandon."

"On the radio, yes."

"We're pursuing a number of enquiries, following up some leads ... connections with the deceased."

"Then I'm the person you're looking for," said Ralph.

Marnie made a startled sound. Luther shifted uneasily in his seat. Anne's mouth dropped open.

Ralph continued. "Can we discuss this perhaps tomorrow? We've had rather a tiring day. I appreciate you need to make progress but –"

"Why do you think we need to talk to you, sir?" Bartlett cut in.

"I'm the only one here who's ever met Brandon. I interviewed him for an article I wrote when he was a minister ... saw him several times at meetings. No one else here has ever seen him in person."

Bartlett turned his gaze on Marnie, who was looking tense.

"In fact, it's you I wanted to talk to, Mrs Walker."

She put down her knife and fork. "Surprise, surprise. Although actually I suppose I shouldn't be surprised. You usually come to see me when you're looking for a suspect."

"I really don't want to take up your time, but I do have a couple of questions."

"Fire away." She grimaced. "Sorry. Go ahead."

"Can you tell me where you were this afternoon at around five o'clock."

"I was in Northampton."

"You can prove that?"

Marnie raised her hands indicating Ralph, Anne and Luther.

"Any other witnesses?"

"Serena McDowell, her mother, her children, a Starcabs taxi driver called Colin."

"And earlier in the afternoon, say between noon and four?"

"These four plus a Mrs Battams who lives opposite the racecourse. We saw her in the morning and were then at Serena's house in the Eastern District all afternoon."

Marnie became more relaxed. This was the easiest interview she had ever had with DCI Bartlett.

"Thank you, Mrs Walker."

"Will that be all? Our pizzas are getting cold."

"Just two more questions, or probably three. Did you drive your car out of town at around lunchtime?"

"No. I've already told you. I was at Serena's house all afternoon and in town all day."

"So can you explain why it was spotted on closed-circuit television cameras on the main road at that time of day? Did you lend it to someone, perhaps? Or does anyone else have use of it with your permission?"

Marnie tensed again. "I think you must be mistaken, inspector. Discoverys are not uncommon. Mine was parked all day outside Garfield Primary School."

"And no one could have used it without your knowledge?"

"Definitely not. I think you asked more than two or three questions there. Is that everything?"

"Those counted as only one ... perhaps two, including the supplementaries."

Ralph spoke again. "Mr Bartlett, we've had a very long and exhausting day ..."

"Then one last question and I'll leave you in peace. At least, I hope so. Do you own or know anyone who owns a gun ... a pistol ... 9 mm?"

"No." Marnie's voice was firm.

"You're quite sure?"

"Absolutely certain."

"Then that will be all, thank you."

"I hope you'll find whoever's responsible for the killing," said Ralph.

"We will, sir. That kind of gun shouldn't be hard to trace."

"Oh? I thought guns were becoming more common nowadays, sadly."

"Not this type, sir. This was a Luger. You know the sort?"

"I've seen them in films ... I know roughly what they look like. I didn't realise they were still being made."

"The one in question probably dates from the second world war. It's rare to find one in working order with ammunition these days."

Anne started coughing, and Luther pushed a glass of water towards her. As she sipped she was praying they would not check the surveillance cameras in the hospital.

"You're sure it's that kind?" Ralph asked.

"Oh yes, sir, no doubt about it. They removed three shells from the body. We know exactly what we're looking for."

"So it probably was an inside job," Ralph suggested. "A Luger would be *the* status symbol for a neo-Nazi."

"Possibly, sir. Or it could be *the* trophy for an anti-Nazi. We're keeping all our options open ... as always."

• • • • •

While Ralph showered that night, Marnie walked through the spinney to see Anne in her attic room. She sat on the corner of the bed.

"How did you manage climbing the ladder?"

"Slowly." Anne produced her ankle from under the sheet. "See? It's gone down a lot and it's not too painful any more."

Marnie ran cool fingers lightly over the bruised skin. "What a day it's been! Did you notice Donovan wasn't there?"

Anne's eyes widened. "Wasn't where?"

"On his boat. It's all locked up. Do you think we should worry about him, Anne?"

"How should I know? Sorry ... I mean ... I don't know where he is."

"We know he must've got his film to the newspaper." Marnie chewed her lip. "Those were his photos in the late edition. But where did he go after that?"

Anne shrugged. Marnie looked up at the roof beams. She could see tiny holes where woodworm had been at work.

"He's resourceful, isn't he ... good at taking care of himself. Did you notice if he was credited with the photos?"

Anne shook her head. "There was no name, only the pictures and the captions."

Marnie began to rise. "Ah, well ..."

"Marnie? Do you think the police will come looking for me? I mean ... I was sort of ... in custody when I made a break for it in hospital."

"They hadn't taken your name?"

"No. There was a lot going on ... with Buzz and everything ..."

"And you said they weren't the local force?"

"I think their badges said they came from Leicester."

"Don't worry about it. I expect they had enough on their hands without bothering about one girl in all that crowd ... especially after the murder."

After Marnie left, Anne was about to put out the light when she remembered the car windows. She debated with herself whether she could leave them open all night, but concluded that Marnie would want them closed and the doors locked. London habits died hard, and there were some odd people about these days.

She pulled on her jeans and sandals and crept carefully down the ladder, stepping gently onto the floor with her 'good' foot. Outside it was cooler now, and night was gradually descending. She rummaged by the wheel for the keys and turned them in the ignition to switch on the power. The instrument panel glowed in the darkened barn. While the windows were sliding up, Anne's eyes strayed over the dials and readings. The Discovery was more complicated than her Mini, with an onboard computer and air-conditioning, instruments giving fuel consumption and how far you could go with the diesel remaining in the tank. Even the trip gauge looked high-tech. She stared ... the trip gauge. It mesmerised her.

They had used the Discovery for one trip to Garfield and back. The other journeys had been in the cab. The trip gauge showed more than double the routine mileage ... Had Marnie forgotten to reset it to zero that morning? Anne pulled the notebook from her back pocket, flicked on the interior light and checked the figures for yesterday's total mileage. It tallied. Had they made an extra journey that she had forgotten?

She pondered. Ideas floated through her mind ... Marnie thinking she had left the Discovery in front of Serena's car ... her telling Donovan about the magnetic box and spare keys ... the traffic cameras spotting a Discovery leaving town that afternoon ... the day's mileage. There had been no other trip in the car that she had forgotten. She stared at the glowing instruments and understood.

29

Marnie felt leaden when the alarm woke her on Friday morning and she overslept by half an hour. It was gone seven when she stepped into the shower on *Thyrsis* and felt the jets of the power-spray easing her body into life. Ralph was sitting on the side of the bed trying to persuade his feet into slippers when the mobile rang. He spoke for two minutes with Serena, gratefully agreed to her suggestion and wished her a good morning.

He had the kettle on the hob and was taking cups and plates from a cupboard when Marnie arrived at the entrance to the galley, dabbing her hair with a towel, to announce that the shower was free.

"That was Serena on the phone."

"Oh?"

"She said there was no need for us to come in this morning."

"Why not?"

"She thought it best if we all stayed away and left it to Jackie and the other colleagues to get everything sorted out."

"Did she give any reason?"

"She thought Greg Roberts and his scouts were quite capable of getting the right kids on the right coaches. She thought we should let them get on with it for today."

"What do you think, Ralph?"

"Well ... I think she has a point. And don't forget, George Stubbs is going along with Angela Hemingway and Dorothy Vane-Henderson. It's their turn on duty. No need to go mob-handed."

"But we've got things to talk about ... especially after everything that happened yesterday." Marnie looked out of the window at the still-calm water. Donovan's boat lay at her mooring. But where was Donovan? "I suppose we don't have to go into town to have a talk. We can use the phone or ..."

"Or what?"

"Maybe Serena would like to come here for a change of scene. I frankly feel like a zombie. I wouldn't mind taking it easy for at least part of today."

•　•　•　•　•

Instead of her usual jog, Anne walked slowly through the spinney that morning testing the damaged ankle. The swelling had subsided and only a light bruising remained as evidence of her accident. The constant throbbing had given way to an occasional twinge. She was delighted to see that Ralph had laid breakfast on the table on the bank and gladly accepted his invitation to sit down and let him handle everything.

Marnie was in the saloon making a series of hurried phone calls and she emerged into the early sunshine, smiling and relaxed.

"That's it ... all sorted, more or less. We're staying here this morning, the others are dealing with the coaches at the school ... Serena's coming to join us late morning in Cosgrove. We'll have a sandwich lunch in the pub garden and complete the final arrangements for the fete on Sunday."

"Why Cosgrove?" Ralph asked. "Why not here ... or in *The Two Roses*?"

"Serena's idea. She wanted to meet on what she called 'neutral ground' ... somewhere we'd be less conspicuous. And in view of the numbers involved she didn't want to impose on our hospitality. We're running low on supplies, so I just agreed."

"Who's coming?"

"The three of us plus Luther and Serena. I'm trying to get hold of George, Angela, Dorothy and Ronny."

"You think Luther needs to be involved? With Estelle due back tomorrow, I can't see them getting up much before Monday." Marnie flashed him the heavy eyelids. "She'll probably be jetlagged," he added innocently.

Anne was already pulling the notebook out of her back pocket. "Do I need to draw up an agenda?"

"Nope. Dorothy's in charge. But don't panic ... I'm sure you'll have plenty of lists to write before the day's out. This morning you can take it easy."

Marnie was right ... for at least half an hour.

• • • • •

The day was rapidly warming up, and Anne wanted to change from trainers to cooler sandals after breakfast. Thus it was that she was in her attic room when Bartlett and Marriner returned to Glebe Farm. Marnie called softly up the ladder.

"Visitors, Anne. Can you see them?"

Footsteps overhead as Anne went to the window slit. "What do they want, d'you think?"

"Dunno. Following up from yesterday, I expect."

"What should we do?"

"Not sure ... play for time, maybe."

Marnie was sitting at her desk deeply engrossed in reading correspondence when the door opened. She managed a smile.

"Good morning, gentlemen. You're lucky to catch me. I'm usually on my way to the summer scheme at this time of day."

Bartlett crossed the room and perched on the corner of Anne's desk. "I think we'd need a lot of luck to catch you at any time of day, Mrs Walker."

"What can I do for you?"

"It's your young friend we want to talk to."

"Anne? I think she's down at the boat." She began to rise. "I'll come with you. You'll need me there if you want to question her ... as a minor."

Bartlett rose slowly. "Sorry to disturb you."

"No problem."

While they were searching for Anne at the docking area, Marnie was trying to wheedle out of Bartlett exactly what they wanted to ask her, but he was as forthcoming as a block of wood. All the time, Marnie was hoping that Anne would be preparing herself, getting her story straight for when they tracked her down. Walking back through the spinney, she was regretting that she had lured the detectives away. They were not stupid and could give them a hard time if they suspected this was a run-around. With a sinking feeling in her stomach, convinced she had made a tactical error, Marnie followed Bartlett back into the office, with Marriner behind her.

"Ah ..." Bartlett muttered in satisfaction.

He had stopped in front of Marnie, blocking her view, and her insides turned over. She walked round Bartlett to see Anne by her desk and was amazed.

Anne was sitting on her office chair, bent forward, elbows on her knees, hands dangling down, feet apart, breathing heavily. She was wearing a jogging suit and trainers with a Nike headband and was perspiring visibly. A pink glow in her cheeks, she looked up at the visitors.

"Morning," she breathed. "Phew! That's the last time ... I try and keep up ... with Luther."

Marnie fought to control her face muscles. An Oscar-nomination was definitely on the cards.

"Anne, Mr Bartlett would like to talk to you."

"Oh?" She was taking long deep breaths. "Now ... or ... after I've had my ... shower?"

"Will it take long?" Marnie asked Bartlett. "Perhaps you'd like a cup of coffee while Anne changes?"

"How can I ... help you, Mr Bartlett? I'm sure you don't want ... to be kept waiting."

Bartlett looked unsettled. He frowned. "We had reports that a girl answering to Anne's description had been taken to the general hospital by a police officer for treatment." He sounded as if he did not quite believe what he was saying.

"What for?" Marnie kept a straight face.

" A suspected ... broken ankle."

Marriner coughed quietly in the background. Bartlett's frown deepened. He turned to see Marriner incline his head towards the window. On the other side of the yard, Luther was jogging on the spot as he put the key in the lock to let himself in to the cottage.

"That's me," said Anne, still panting. "Only I think I've got ... a suspected broken ... everything. For exercise ... I'm sticking to tiddlywinks from now on."

Bartlett looked back at Anne. "I thought you said you were following Mr Curtiss. How is it that you're here and he's only just got back?"

"He probably went on as far as ... Newcastle ... after I gave up."

Bartlett moved quickly across the room and knelt beside her, as if he was going to propose. "Can you just show me your ankle, Anne?"

Marnie held her breath.

"Which one is it?" Anne asked evenly. "The broken one, I mean."

"I'd better see them both."

Anne yanked the tabs on her trainers to the sound of Velcro pulling apart. She slipped her feet free and raised them from the floor. Bartlett inspected them closely and stood up. With head bowed, he walked back to stand next to Marriner.

"You can take your shower, Anne. Afterwards, we'd like you to come with us. We're going on a trip to the hospital. Ted, get on to the station and ask Cathy Lamb to join us here."

Marnie offered coffee while Anne took her shower, but they preferred to wait outside, strolling in the spinney.

"That was a turn-up, sir."

"Mm ..."

Marriner wanted to ask Bartlett if he really reckoned it was worth taking Anne to the hospital, but he thought better of it. "You think they might recognise her from yesterday?"

"What do you think, Ted?"

"I was thinking Anne might not be the person we're looking for."

"They gave a perfect description of her."

"With a *broken ankle.*"

"I think you're missing the point, Ted. She obviously doesn't have a broken ankle."

"No, sir. I just ... well, I thought that *was* the point."

In the cubicle at the back of the office barn, Anne lathered herself all over with her Sunday best shower gel. Seeing Luther through the window slit as he powered off on his morning jog had given her the idea. A rapid exercise routine had certainly brought her out in a sweat, and now it was her mind's turn to work at high speed trying to devise a plan. With her distinctive colouring and urchin-cut blonde hair they would surely recognise her at the hospital. What could she do?

Outside, Bartlett was sorting out his own thinking.

"She can't pretend not having a broken ankle. So ... are you with me, Ted?"

Marriner looked doubtful.

"So ..." Bartlett repeated. "Perhaps she was only pretending *yesterday*. She got away, didn't she?"

"Right. I see what you mean, sir. But I thought the report said her ankle was badly swollen and she could only walk with assistance."

"We'll see. The one way to sort this out is to take her there and get them to confirm identification. That'll clinch it."

"We could get them to examine the ankle as well," Marriner suggested.

"No need. Just look at her. With the summer we've been having, kids her age are all tanned. Paleface in there will stand out like a sore thumb ... dead easy to identify."

Anne finished the shower by running it cold over her ankle for as long as she could bear. When she re-appeared in the office she saw Marnie outside in the yard, talking to Bob the foreman. She walked slowly to the fridge in a towelling bathrobe, grabbed a bag of ice cubes and eased herself up the loft ladder. Sitting in front of her mirror, she propped the damaged foot on a pile of magazines with the ice bag resting on it like a saddle, and applied just enough make-up to put a little colour in her cheeks. She had to act quickly to avoid arousing suspicion. The final touch was a dab of make-up on the ankle. She completed the transformation, dressed in a rush and descended the ladder with caution.

Marnie was returning to the office as Anne's feet touched down. A slow smile spread across her face as she saw the result of Anne's efforts. Bartlett and Marriner followed her into the office and stared. Marnie switched off the smile and turned to the men.

"I think that's your colleague arriving. I can hear a car. Will you want me to come with you?"

"No, thanks. That won't be necessary."

• • • • •

Marnie felt her usual protective anxiety, watching the two unmarked police cars set off in convoy, Anne travelling with WDC Cathy Lamb. As they took her away, she waved her fingers reassuringly to Marnie with a tentative smile. Anne was bright and quick-witted but she was outnumbered, and it was always a mistake to underestimate the police. They were not the lumbering plodders of popular fiction.

Her musings were terminated by the phone ringing in the office.

"It's Dorothy, Marnie. I've got good news."

"That's nice to hear. We could use some of that."

"Well, you'll be glad to know that everything is under control for Sunday."

"Sunday," Marnie repeated vaguely.

"The summer fete?"

"Of course." It seemed a lifetime away. Would they survive that long? She tried to sound enthusiastic. "That's great news, Dorothy."

"And I've got a surprise for you. First, though, let me tell you ... we've got a bouncy castle, a giant trampoline, two roundabouts, a brass band, one of those – what do you call them? – DJs for the youngsters, a reggae band, a steel band ..." She was obviously reading from a checklist. "Fourteen stalls, including a tombola, a coconut shy, produce from the W.I. and the Townswomen's' Guild ..."

Dorothy's voice droned on. The town was occupied by an army of neo-fascists, and her team was planning to throw balls to win coconuts. It was Nero and Rome burning all over again. Marnie suddenly registered that a question had been asked, and her attention snapped back.

"Sorry, Dorothy, what was that?"

"Have you seen her on television?"

"I ... don't think I have." A safe reply. "What programme is she in?"

"Well, it's called *Leila Ravenswood* ... because ... that's her name."

"I see." Marnie was lost.

"She used to be in *Eastenders*. Anyway, she's agreed to do the opening. You have to have someone from TV to open everything these days, so that it goes off with a bang."

An alarm bell clanged in Marnie's head. She thought of a minister opening a community centre in Leicester and saw the rag-tag New Force army on the streets throwing petrol-bombs at the police. She thought of the Prime Minister coming to open the business park in Northampton and being forced to withdraw from the ceremony because of the rioting ... rioting that had led to murder.

"Dorothy, are you sure that's a good idea?"

"Why not?" Mrs V-H was not accustomed to having her plans questioned.

"I was just wondering whether it might attract attention from ... undesirable elements."

"*Undesirable* ... oh, you mean those *ghastly* New Force thugs."

"Exactly."

"Marnie, I have to say this to you – and please don't take it the wrong way – but your ... generation ... the people like you, who've grown up with everything politically correct ... you sometimes have a tendency to think that everything has to be achieved somehow without risk. Sometimes you have to stand up and be counted and not back down just because you think there might be trouble."

"But –"

"I'm afraid this is one of those times, Marnie."

"I'm worried about the consequences, Dorothy. People will get hurt if there are more disturbances. More people might even get killed."

"And so it will go on until the time comes when someone stops this nonsense in its tracks. That time is now. We cannot back down."

"Despite the dangers?"

"Despite everything."

• • • • •

Anne did her best to walk into A and E as normally as possible. Each step on her left foot caused a stab of pain to shoot up her leg, but it was bearable. She used the excuse of people coming and going to walk slowly and hoped the swelling would not return.

Bartlett marched them all up to the reception desk, where Anne was horrified to recognise the duty officer. There was nothing for it. The Brave Face was presented with a smile as Bartlett produced his warrant card and introduced the group.

"This is Miss Anne Price. We have reason to believe she was the young woman admitted here yesterday with a broken ... that is, with apparent ankle injuries. We'd like you to tell us if you can identify her."

The woman fixed Anne with a stare before swivelling her eyes round to Bartlett without blinking.

"We didn't *admit* anyone with ankle injuries yesterday, at least not during my hours on duty."

"You were here all afternoon?"

"From two till ten."

"All right, she came here with a police officer who believes he saw her being taken away for treatment by a nurse. Can you remember seeing her?"

Another stare at Anne. The woman pondered. "Yes. Definitely."

Anne felt the waiting room sway. She battled with her expression, desperate to keep cool. Her plan was coming unravelled. This was a disaster. *What could she do?*

"You're quite certain of that?" Bartlett persisted.

"Quite certain."

"You saw this girl yesterday and she was being treated for ankle injuries. Is that correct?"

The woman frowned. The frown turned into a smile and grew into a quiet laugh.

"*That girl?*" She shook her head, grinning all the while. "Not *that* girl. I saw *a girl* with a suspected fracture, but she wasn't admitted and, as far as

I know, she wasn't treated."

"How can you be sure?" Bartlett was highly agitated. "Don't you keep an eye on your patients?"

"Of course, but we can't hold them here against their will. They can come and go as they please."

"Look ... we believe this girl was here yesterday and she absconded from police custody."

"So *you* lost her. Don't you keep an eye on your detainees?"

Bartlett smarted. "Never mind about that. What I'm saying is, I want to see the nurse who took her away for treatment."

"She's not on duty till this evening."

"Then who can identify her?"

"I can."

"You said she wasn't the girl with the ankle injuries."

"Correct." Before Bartlett could object again, she added, "Look at her."

They did as she asked. They saw a clear-eyed young woman in a simple white summer dress with a tiny flower design. She was clean, fresh and wholesome, with neatly brushed shining blonde hair and the merest touch of make-up discreetly applied. There was a hint of perfume in the air.

Bartlett looked grim. "Obviously she wasn't dressed like this when she came in yesterday. She's just had a shower and put on different clothes. But it's the same girl."

"No it isn't."

"How can you be so certain?"

"The girl who came here was one of those far-right types." Bartlett opened his mouth to object, but the woman raised her hand to silence him. "How do I know? *That* girl had a tattoo."

Bartlett gaped. "Where? Nobody said anything about a tattoo."

"On her face ... her forehead. It was a swastika. I saw it clearly. This girl is blonde, that I grant you, and she's had a shower ... fine. But she'd have needed surgery to remove that tattoo. Now if you'll excuse me, I have work to do."

There was an awkward silence as the duty officer turned away to deal with a queue of arrivals. Bartlett stared at Anne's forehead. He blinked several times, and Anne feared he might explode. Instead, he made for the exit, and the others followed in his wake. Just inside the doorway he suddenly stopped and turned to Anne.

"Look ... Anne ... I'm sorry about this. There appears to have been a case of mistaken identity."

"I'm not one of those far-right types, Mr Bartlett," Anne said simply. "I may have the right colouring, but I'm not ..."

Her voice faded and her eyes focused somewhere over his shoulder. They were standing partly blocking the entrance, and people were having to squeeze round them to enter the building. One group was hanging back, and it was on them that Anne's gaze had fallen, four people; a woman and three youths, West Indians. The boys wore multi-coloured berets with dreadlocks visible at the edges. Bartlett was saying something to Anne, but she did not hear him. Her eyes filled with tears.

Leaving Bartlett flat-footed, Anne eased past him and flung her arms round the neck of one of the youths, to his great surprise. He held her lightly while the others in his party looked on in amazement. Anne pulled back.

"Don't you know me? It's Anne. You gave me the Bob Marley stickers, remember?"

Understanding dawned. "Yeah ... yeah, course I remember. How're you doin'?

She wiped tears from her face with her fingertips. "OK. You?"

They performed the shuffle, nodding. The young Rasta indicated the woman beside him. "This is my mum."

"Hallo. I'm Anne." She inclined towards her escort. "This is Det– ... er ... these are my friends, Mr Bartlett, Mr Marriner and Cathy."

It took less than a second for the West Indians to work out that Anne's *friends* were the police.

"Why are you here?" Anne asked quickly, anxious to move away from personalities.

The boy shrugged. "Come to see Buzz."

Bartlett, who was observing this encounter with impatience tempered with curiosity, suddenly found himself holding on to Anne. She had stepped back from the West Indians and almost collapsed into him. He could feel her body shudder as a spasm of emotion ran through her. Steadying herself, she put a hand to her chest.

"Buzz?" she repeated weakly. "He's being kept here?"

Cathy Lamb reached across to support Anne's arm. It was the mother who replied.

"Bertram has come out of intensive care. They've moved him to another room."

Anne's voice was barely audible. "Bertram ... *Buzz* ... he's alive ... I mean, he's all right?"

"Apart from a fractured skull and some other injuries. They say he'll mend."

• • • • •

WDC Cathy Lamb drove Anne home to Glebe Farm. On the way back, she rested her head against the side window with her eyes closed, and they travelled most of the way in silence.

"The police did a good job, getting to Buzz like that after he was attacked."

"Where was that, Anne? Did you see it happen?"

Red warning lights flashed in Anne's brain. She kept her eyes closed and took a few deep breaths.

"It was in the paper ... photos of Buzz being beaten by a New Force gang. They said he'd been killed."

"Right. Buzz is Bertram ... that's his real name?"

"I suppose. I only knew him as Buzz. He was a helper at the summer scheme. I'm so glad ..."

"Good news," said Cathy. She smiled at Anne. "He'll sing reggae again. Did you know him well?"

• • • • •

In the other car Bartlett sat in silence while his sergeant drove to the station. Eventually Marriner spoke.

"That was more than just a convincing performance, sir."

"You reckon?"

"She nearly passed out when those black kids said the boy was alive. Good job you were there to catch her."

"Mm ... You don't think she knows more than she's telling?"

"Marnie Walker and Anne with an 'e' ... you never know with those two, sir. But I don't think she was acting back there."

"No ... maybe not. I told Lamb to see what she could get out of her on the way back, but I doubt she'll get much."

"We've got no evidence, no witnesses ... nothing. No chance of her giving us a lead to what's going on."

Bartlett grunted. "And there's no sign of her in any of the photos in the paper. When we get back, ring up the editor ... find out if they have any shots they didn't use. If they have, check 'em out."

"Yes, sir."

Bartlett ran a hand round his jaw. "I wonder ..."

"Sir?"

"Who took those photos? A bit of luck to have a photographer on the spot at that precise moment ... They're good clear shots ... very professional."

"I'll find out, sir."

"You know, there's a lot about this that doesn't meet the eye. Who trashed that BMW? They weren't black. They were a white gang ... far-right hooligans ... New Force or whatever."

"That car belonged to one of Brandon's lot," Marriner observed. "A rival mob, perhaps?"

"In-fighting, you mean, Ted? Mm ... Like the brown shirts."

"The what?"

"The brown shirts ... the SA ... Hitler's storm troops when he came to power. They were massacred by the SS ... their own side, but deadly rivals."

"That might be the answer to what happened to Brandon, sir ... killed by one of his inner circle who wanted to take his place. Who else could get that close to him?"

Bartlett shook his head. "God knows. It's all a right bloody mess. Here we are, trying to follow up any tiny lead, and the killer's just gone ... vanished."

"Or being protected from within the organisation, sir, if it was an inside job."

• • • • •

At Glebe Farm Anne told her story to Marnie and Ralph. All eyes were moist when she explained about Buzz, and Marnie immediately rang Serena to give her the news of his survival.

Ralph crossed the courtyard and called up to Luther. He signalled from the upstairs window that he was using the phone in the study and would come down as soon as he could. Anne went to switch on the kettle. Ralph hovered outside.

By the time Marnie had finished her call, Anne had coffee ready in the office.

"I knew we should've gone to the school this morning." Marnie was brisk and business-like. She stood in the doorway of the office barn. "There are so many things to sort out with Serena."

Anne handed them each a mug. "We'll see her soon enough. We ought to be leaving as soon as we've finished this."

Marnie sipped her coffee. "Is Luther in the cottage?"

"He's on the phone," said Ralph. "He'll be down in a minute."

"I think I can guess who he's calling."

Right on cue Luther stepped out of the front door.

"Have you spoken to Estelle?" said Marnie. "I've been meaning to ring her."

"No luck. Every time I phone, they say she's out. I've left a message for her to call me back."

"She'll have her hands full. It'll be frantic. We didn't want to change her travel plans yet again."

"I wanted to check the arrival time of her flight tomorrow."

Anne turned to her desk. "I've got a note of it in the file. I can give you a copy, if you want."

Marnie said, "It's today's plans that are concerning me just now. Are you ready to leave for Cosgrove, Luther?"

"Is it time already? I'm struggling to finish a paper for my supervisor … my first assignment for the university. I wanted to get it done before Estelle gets back … keep the weekend clear." He smiled.

"Of course. Then you stick to your plan. We'll fill you in on what we agree when we get back."

"It won't take me much longer… another hour or so. If you go on to Cosgrove, I can walk or jog down as soon as I've finished here. It's only a couple of miles."

• • • • •

Bartlett put the phone down and finished scribbling notes on a pad. Superintendent Harris, who was heading the Brandon investigation, was bogged down in a mass of routine. House-to-house inquiries were underway but revealing nothing. No one could give a description of Brandon's killer, even the eye witnesses to the shooting. A 'fair-haired man in black' was the best they could manage. No one had spotted where he went when he left the scene. Either the killer was very clever, with a car standing by to whisk him away, or the BFP people had hit the deck and kept their eyes shut out of fear for their lives. Probably both.

It irked Bartlett to be stuck out on the periphery of the murder investigation, following up minor leads. He looked down at his notes, desperate to be in at the centre of the action.

One man in black
Fair hair – slight build
4 shots fired
3 hits
Point-blank range
Pistol – 9mm – Luger
No retaliation
No description of killer
Killer vanished
No sound of car – <u>odd</u>
Inside plot?

The more he pondered the facts, the more convinced he became that there was another possibility. Marriner could be right. Only one of Brandon's own people could get so close to their leader. Only they knew Brandon's movements and where the party HQ was situated. Who else would be likely to have a Luger? All the signs pointed to one of them.

Why had no one reacted or tried to stop the killing? Were there dissidents in the group? Bartlett drew a circle round *inside plot*, becoming increasingly convinced this was an assassination from within the party.

Harris was keeping an open mind. He was an experienced officer and played it by the book. He knew that murders were solved by method and painstaking thoroughness. But all the witnesses were telling the same story. They all seemed genuinely stunned. The police knew shock when they saw it, and Brandon's people had been scared out of their wits.

There had been only one sighting from a neighbour living near the scene of the crime, but Harris was inclined to discount it. A woman had seen *a boy on a bicycle* leaving the vicinity just after the shots were fired. He was cycling steadily without undue haste, possibly wearing a light grey sweater and a red baseball cap, with the peak turned to the back. Her impression was that the bicycle was a light colour, maybe white or yellow. Her view of the boy lasted only a few seconds and her last sight of him was when he signalled and turned a corner.

Bartlett had doodled a bike and a baseball cap on his pad. He bit his lip and scratched through the drawings. Someone who has just shot a man dead did not saunter off on a bicycle and make hand signals. Harris was probably right, and in any case there had been no other sightings of the *boy*.

A knock on the door, and Sergeant Marriner stuck his head in.

"Those photos in the paper, sir. They were handed in anonymously to the newspaper office yesterday morning. A roll of film was left in reception for processing, marked urgent. No one remembers who delivered it. There was a whole film, twenty-four exposures. The editor says we can see the others, but they don't show any more than we've already seen in print. No girl with blonde hair anywhere in sight."

"OK."

"Cathy Lamb's here. She's just got back. Do you want a word?"

"Wheel her in, Ted."

As soon as she walked through the door, Bartlett knew Lamb had had no success in pumping Anne for information.

"Nothing?"

"No, sir. She just dozed in the car most of the time. I think she was overcome at finding out the boy was alive. It's all been a bit much for her to take."

Bartlett scowled. "I suppose so. She's not exactly built like a wrestler, that one."

"Oh, but she'll get over it, sir. She's as tough as old boots."

"What do you mean?"

"She was certainly shocked, no doubt about that. But her whole performance today was ... like an act."

"Go on, Cathy. Let's have your *woman's intuition*."

Lamb resisted the urge to kill her boss with a karate chop to the neck. "The clothes, the make-up ... It was like ... *camouflage*. And that perfume

... It was really expensive ... much too sophisticated for a girl of – how old is she? I bet it was Marnie Walker's."

"So what's your point?"

"She got all dressed up ... trying to look like an English rose ... to make an impression. I'm sure of it."

• • • • •

Luther heard movement outside and leaned over from the desk to look down into the courtyard. Marnie and Ralph were leaving the office, both carrying folders. They made their way round the corner of the barn to the Discovery, leaving Anne to lock the office and bring up the rear. She too was carrying a folder, clasping a note pad on top of it in her fingers, and as she turned away from the door she looked up in his direction and their eyes met. Her face lit up in a smile, and slipping the office keys into her jeans pocket, she gave a friendly wave, standing in the sunshine. On impulse Luther blew her a kiss. Anne laughed, wrinkled her nose, gave another wave and jumped in the air before turning to go.

The car doors slammed, and Luther moved to the window, leaning out to watch the Discovery climb the slope up the field track. Silence and peace returned to Glebe Farm. For a few seconds he stood, elbows resting on the window-sill. This was a good place, he thought, good people leading interesting lives. He knew that despite the current troubles, he would always look back with affection on this time in this place with Estelle and, whatever they did in the years ahead, together or not, he would be glad they had shared this experience.

He returned to his seat, conscious now of the hum from the computer, its screen filled with notes as he tried to convert them to coherent flowing prose. He began re-reading his last paragraphs, ready to move on to *Conclusions*.

His eyes strayed to the telephone, and he looked at his watch for the umpteenth time that morning. Estelle would ring soon and tell him how things were progressing in Umbria. He would sit there while she enthused about the landscape, the architecture, the climate, the villa where she was working. It would be her usual over-the-top gushing, and he loved it. A woman of passion and passions. They would make a life together and perhaps one day they would make a home as good as this one.

The phone rang. He seized it quickly. The sound that greeted him was a steady rushing, the background noise of a car on the road.

"Hi Luther! It's Anne. Heard anything from Estelle?"

"Nothing so far."

"Seeing you just now I realised I hadn't given you the time for her flight back tomorrow morning. In case I forget later, she's due to land at 9.45."

"Thanks, Anne. I'll make a note of it."

"I've got the terminal and flight numbers as well in the office."

"That's all right. She's got her car at the airport. She'll be driving straight back ... probably be in time for lunch, if the flight's on time."

"OK. See you later. Hope your paper's going well. Bye!"

• • • • •

They were passing the turn to Yardley Gobion when Anne's mobile began ringing. She read the name on the screen. "Marnie, it's Ronny. Did you invite him to the meeting?"

"Tried to. His line was busy."

Anne pressed the green button. "Hi Ronny. We've been trying to phone you."

"Yeah? When?" He sounded incredulous.

"This morning."

"Well, I've been here."

"Right." Anne waited. It was his call.

He gave in first. "So why were you phoning?"

"We're having a meeting about the fete on Sunday."

"When?"

"Now."

"I'll come down."

"Er ... it's at Cosgrove, at the pub."

"Are you on your way there now? Sounds like you're in the car."

"I'm in Marnie's car. We're almost there. Sorry we missed you."

"Yeah. You seem to have been missing me a lot these days."

"Yes."

"Shall I come on the bike? It'll take me ten minutes or so."

"Sure. That's great."

He disconnected.

"He's coming on his bike," Anne explained. "Is that all right?"

"Of course." Marnie looked at Anne in the rear-view mirror. "Is he OK?"

"He sounded ... not quite OK. I think I've been neglecting him since ... well, just lately."

"I'll tell him I rang a few times but his line was engaged. I thought he might be surfing the Net. Maybe I should've tried harder, but it's been a busy morning."

Ralph turned in his seat with a grin. "I'm sure your charm will win him round, Anne."

"Yeah."

· · · · ·

Luther was able to warp up his closing argument with a series of succinct points. He read his last paragraphs, made some amendments, saved to disk and closed down the computer.

The most direct route to Cosgrove was alongside the canal, and he set off to cross the bridge near the docking area. Picking up the towpath, he glanced briefly in passing at the battleship-grey paintwork of *X O 2*, noting how it contrasted with the colours of *Sally Ann* and *Thyrsis* on the opposite bank. He strode out, relishing the walk ahead of him in the sunshine. Luther measured his pace carefully. It would be anti-social to arrive hot and sweaty for lunch in the garden.

Tomorrow Estelle would be home, and he would take her out for a quiet lunch so that she could tell him all about her trip. Unless she had something else in mind.

There was a hint of a smile on his face as the mobile began ringing at his belt.

• • • • •

They had reached the pub garden when a dark green Range Rover turned into the car park behind them. George climbed out, followed by Margaret Giles, while Dorothy Vane-Henderson waited for him to walk round and open her door.

"Where's Serena?" George asked, kissing Marnie on the cheeks. He had that frisky look in his eye. "Where's my lovely fellow-Jamaican?"

"Coming in her own car. She wanted to be independent in case she got called back to town."

"Then we'd better grab some tables before the lunchtime crowd arrives."

George's haste was unwarranted; the garden was almost empty. It was just on noon, and the lunch period had scarcely begun. While the others pulled two tables together to accommodate their group, Ralph went with Anne into the bar to organise drinks and collect menus. They chose quickly, and Anne was on her way back to rejoin Ralph when she saw Ronny coming down the road. She waited for him to ride in and dismount.

"Hi! That was quick. We're ordering baguettes. What do you fancy?"

He rested the bike against a wall and fitted the lock on the wheels. "Whatever."

"That type's not on the menu." She smiled.

"Ham, then."

"And to drink? We're mostly having spritzers."

"Fine."

She added two ticks to her list. "We've got a big table in the garden. I'll be back in a minute."

She was true to her word, and came out to find Ronny standing where she had left him. She smiled again.

"Marnie's sorry she couldn't get through when she rang … figured you were surfing."

Ronny looked hot from his exertions on the bike. He said nothing, gave a slight nod.

"Will you give me a hand with the drinks? We'll need two trays. There are seven of us."

She turned towards the pub, but Ronny grabbed her arm, moving closer.

"I want to talk to you." His voice was gruff. Anne could feel the warmth radiating from his body.

"OK. But I think we should fetch the drinks first. People are waiting."

Without a word, he released her arm and walked quickly into the building. Anne followed. Ralph was loading glasses of spritzer onto the trays when they arrived and greeted Ronny in friendly fashion. Anne hoped it would calm him down, but he seized one of the trays so forcefully that the glasses clashed together, spilling their contents and all but fell over.

"Steady, old lad," said Ralph easily, stepping back to avoid being splashed. "We can't slurp it out of the tray."

He lifted the tray and gave it carefully to Ronny who muttered an apology and headed for the exit. Anne took the other one. At the table, she distributed glasses while Ronny left, apparently to help fetch the food. Again, Anne set off after him and found him round the corner waiting for her.

"Ronny, look, I'm *sorry*. We did try to contact you but –"

"Not here. Let's walk by the canal."

"We can't. The path's on the other side."

Ronny breathed out loudly in exasperation.

Anne pointed. "There's another part of the garden over there away from the rest. Come on."

• • • • •

Marnie looked at her watch. "Where's Serena got to?"

"You're not worried about her, are you?" said Ralph.

"These days I worry about everything. She should be here by now."

"You could try her mobile."

"Yeah, I will."

Marnie pressed buttons on her phone. A message told her that the number she was calling was not available at that time. She should try later. Ralph tried to sound reassuring.

"She's probably got it switched off because she's driving. You usually do that."

"Do I?"

"Yes. Look, Marnie, let's give her a few more minutes before we have the nervous breakdown, OK?"

"OK."

• • • • •

The other garden was fitted out with children's play equipment, and they sat on a bench provided for parents. The bright colours of the swings and slides seemed to clash with the bleak atmosphere brought in by the two young people.

"Is this OK?" said Anne.

Ronny looked down at the ground. "Why are you leaving me out all the time? You never phone ... never invite me to the summer scheme ... never tell me what's going on. I thought I was supposed to be one of the team ... part of the group ... your ... friend."

"You are," Anne said quietly. "All of those things. It's just that ... everything's been happening so quickly."

"Then why didn't you keep me in the picture?"

"It was difficult. We got caught up in the riots ... attacked by the mob ... I got arrested by the police ... got injured ... taken to hospital ... escaped ... hauled back into town to be identified on suspicion of being a Nazi ..."

Anne glanced sideways at Ronny. His mouth had dropped open. He was staring at her, wide-eyed.

"You *what* ...?"

"Yeah. And you don't get much time to make phone calls while all that's happening."

"When was this?"

"Yesterday and today."

"*Arrested?*"

Anne nodded. "In town yesterday morning."

"And you escaped from gaol?"

"From custody. I didn't get as far as the cells."

"Bloody hell," he murmured. "I had no idea … You got injured?"

"Suspected broken ankle." She lifted her foot from the ground and waggled it slowly. "It's OK now, though … just a sprain."

Ronny knelt down and supported her heel in his hand. In a quick movement he removed the shoe and cradled her foot.

"Is it painful?"

"Throbs a bit now and then, but it's much better than it was."

He caressed it gently. Anne found the warmth of his hands comforting. She was relieved he had become his old self again and had pangs of remorse about his complaint. She closed her eyes and put her head back while the ache was eased from her ankle.

"I'm sorry about what I said, Anne. I didn't know you'd been through all that."

Without opening her eyes Anne said, "Of course, you didn't. How could you? And that was only part of it. We almost got caught by a gang. Well, I did get caught on account of not being able to run."

"*Christ!* So what did they do to you?"

"Nothing, as it happens. I distracted them so they ended up vandalising a car … one of their own people's, but they didn't know that. Then the police arrived and carted me off."

"You said *we*." Ronny was massaging her ankle and the underneath of her foot. "Who else was involved?"

"One of the West Indian boys … remember Buzz? They caught him and … it was horrible. I thought they'd killed him."

Anne's voice was growing softer, the more her foot was soothed. A feeling of lethargy was rolling over her, and she could feel how depleted her energy reserves had become. The strains and tensions of the past weeks were being concentrated in her foot and eased away with each stroke of Ronny's warm hands.

"It must've been awful."

"Mm …"

Anne was aware of voices in the distance, birds singing somewhere nearby, a steady thumping that she recognised as the sound of a boat engine on the canal not far behind them. She felt a slight movement as Ronny shifted his position.

"Don't stop," she murmured. "That's nice."

But Ronny was on the bench beside her again, nearer this time. She felt his arm around her shoulders and his breath on her cheek as he inclined his face towards hers.

"Oh Anne," he whispered in a husky voice. "I wish I could be closer to you."

With her eyes still closed, she smiled. "If you got any closer, you'd be behind me."

"I'm serious." His voice was urgent. "Don't you understand how I feel about you, Anne?"

Eyes suddenly open, she sat up quickly, their cheeks colliding as Ronny moved forward. Anne put a hand to her face. She looked startled. "Sorry, I …"

Ronny stayed where he was, his arm still around her. "No, I'm the one who's sorry, Anne. I just want to –"

Anne put her hand on his chest and pushed gently. "Ronny, please ... We ought to be getting back to the others."

"I thought you liked what I was doing."

"What do you mean?"

"To your ankle ... making it better."

"I did. It was very ... nice ... comforting. But we –"

He pulled away. "I know, I know, I know!"

"Don't be like that, Ronny. We're sitting in a pub garden. Anyone can come here. You can't do that sort of thing in a place like this. It's too open."

"But it wouldn't make any difference where we were, would it? You never let me get close to you. You just treat me like a casual friend. I want to be more than that, but you don't want to. Ever since you met that Donovan character with his fancy boat ... ever since he came on the scene, I've been left out."

"No. That's not true."

"Then promise me there's nothing between you and Donovan."

"You can't expect me to make promises like that."

"No. I can't expect anything. And there's Luther, too. You hardly take your eyes off him ... *Mr Superman*. I thought you and I were ..."

"We're friends, Ronny ... *good* friends."

"*Friends!*" He spat the word out. "I don't want to be *friends*. And don't pretend you don't know what I mean."

"We are friends, Ronny, but that doesn't give you rights over me. You don't own me."

Ronny took his arm away and sat forward, his head in his hands. Anne laid a hand on his back.

"One of my mates at school said he thought you looked ... frigid."

Anne breathed in sharply. They had never spoken like this before. She had known Ronny for more than a year and, although they had never been on intimate terms, never even kissed apart from socially, she realised that he had invested more in their relationship than she had. There had always been something that kept them at a distance: his studying for exams, her job with Marnie. But now she knew there never could be a close relationship because her feelings were not strong enough. Sitting there together, all too aware of her youth and inexperience, Anne struggled to find the words that would make clear how she felt without being hurtful.

"It's a strange way of being a friend," she said evenly, "having that sort of conversation about me with your mates at school. But then I suppose that's what boys talk about. Girls are the same."

"I wasn't having that sort of conversation about you ... it was just something someone said ... making a joke."

"Fine."

"I don't think you're frigid, Anne." He sat up and turned to look at her. "You didn't feel frigid when I was rubbing your foot."

"That's not quite the same thing."

"No. And you'd know all about that. I know it's nothing personal. You'd just prefer sleeping with someone else."

Anne could not stop herself blushing. She felt the crimson surge over her face and she could say nothing. Ronny stared into her eyes and leapt to his feet so suddenly that Anne thought he was going to strike her. She remained where she was without flinching. He turned on his heels and stormed off.

• • • • •

Luther checked his watch. He would soon be there. Round the next bend in the canal and he would be in sight of Solomon's bridge, with its niches and carved stonework.

Now that he was almost at his destination, he increased his stride, looking forward to seeing everybody. He had a spring in his step.

The bridge came into view, and he was mildly surprised to find that he had to cross it to regain the towpath on the opposite bank. His memory had deceived him, but he had only been to this pub once before and he had come with Estelle by car. Sure enough, there was the pub on the other side of the canal. He stopped to think. He would have to retrace his steps to find a way round by following the road from the bridge … It was then that he remembered the pedestrian tunnel *under* the canal.

Luther found the steps leading down from where he was standing and turned to enter the tunnel. As he approached it, he recalled Anne once saying it was her favourite tunnel of all because it looked just like a child's drawing.

There was a smile on his face as he stooped to enter.

• • • • •

As Anne sat for some minutes regaining her composure, a Clio pulled into the car park. Serena got out looking tired and drawn and walked quickly into the pub garden. Anne made a great effort to stir herself and rejoin the group, noticing as she went that Ronny's bike had gone. She had not heard him ride off.

Marnie signalled a space kept free beside her, and Anne took her seat. Of Serena there was no sign.

"Serena's arrived. I just saw her."

Marnie nodded. "She knows we're here … went inside to freshen up." She lowered her voice. "Is everything all right?"

"Ronny's upset because he thought we'd left him out."

"Shall I have a word with him? It's my fault, after all. I'm sure I could put him straight."

"I think he's gone."

"Oh … I'll … pop round and see him when we get back. I'm sorry if I've caused a problem between you. I'll do my best to put it right."

"I'm sure he'd like that. He'll have calmed down by then."

Marnie squeezed her hand. "I'm really sorry."

Anne attempted a smile. "He'll get over it." As an afterthought, she added, "Perhaps I should go and see if there's time to cancel his baguette."

"Or we could keep it for Luther. He should be here soon."

Anne stood up. "I want to go inside anyway. Back in a minute."

Only Marnie watched her as she walked towards the pub. When Anne knew she was out of sight of the garden, she continued past the entrance and reached the narrow side street that sloped down towards the little tunnel. A few minutes walking quietly along the canal towpath would restore her to normality. There was no need to lower her head as she entered the tunnel, but she would have to take care in the middle section where the height was reduced and even she could hit her head. She did not want any unpleasant surprises.

• • • • •

Ronny cycled out of the village at a tearaway pace, powered by rage and guilt. He felt like a fool, bitterly regretting what he had said and done. Wiping his eyes with the back of one hand, he almost collided with a group of mothers and children crossing the road near the green. The bike swayed, and he nearly lost control, fighting to keep it upright as he braked heavily and swerved, while the mothers pulled their infants towards them, calling out after him.

He felt shame and humiliation, knowing that things said and done could not be unsaid or undone. He liked Anne, *really* liked Anne. And now he had been stupid and thoughtless, blurting out ridiculous accusations. *How could he have done that!* He had even repeated what that stupid Gus had said about her at school.

Things would never be the same again. He felt sick, a pain starting to throb over his left eye. It was a mess and a nightmare. Fighting off his misery, he forced himself to focus as he approached the main road. He took the junction steadily, leaving nothing to chance, and rode out fast on the two-mile stretch to home.

The traffic was light and only one lorry overtook him, buffeting him with its bow-wave and causing the bike to tremble in its wake. He was within sight of his turning when he saw the police cars racing in convoy in the opposite direction. There were two white patrol cars with lights flashing, and sandwiched between them was a dark grey Cavalier. He could still hear the sirens wailing in the distance after he had pulled off the main road and headed for Knightly St John.

• • • • •

Anne did not see the shape at first. Watching her footing on the floor in the narrow tunnel, the change of light was confusing, a mixture of shadows around her and a glare from the opening at the far end, twenty metres away. She gave her full attention to planting her feet with care, not daring to risk twisting her ankle on the concrete surface. It would be more than unfortunate if she had to be taken back to casualty, where the sight of her might rekindle memories among the staff. With eyes downcast, she stepped cautiously forward, one hand steadying herself against the wall.

In the centre the roof lining was lower, and she raised her hand to touch it, keeping her balance and checking the headroom. It was when she lifted her eyes briefly to check the distance ahead that she became aware of an unexpected object on the ground in the mouth of the tunnel. Her eyes were adjusting to the brightness of the outside light now just a short way in front of her, and it took a second or two for her to register what it was. Beyond any doubt it was a man.

Her mind went into overdrive. Part of her brain wanted to flee, to run back and fetch the group. The other part wanted desperately to run forward and offer help. She was just moving when a sound reached her ears. Sirens were wailing nearby. Still watching her footfalls, Anne advanced quickly and knelt to examine the man.

Oh no! She gasped and reached out, shaking him, seeing a trickle of blood from his left ear. From some way off she could hear noises, one of them she realised was her own sobbing.

"Luther!" she cried out. *"Luther! Luther! Oh no, please God no!"*

He was lying on his back, eyes closed, lips slightly apart showing the edges of perfect white teeth. Anne was on her knees reaching towards his broad strong shoulders trying to shake him back to consciousness. Absurdly the words uttered by Ronny came into her mind – *Mr Superman* – as she felt the inert muscles through the cotton. Luther's head wobbled as she shook him, but there was no life to revive, no consciousness possible. Anne's head drooped forward onto his chest, and she saw a stain growing on his shirt, where her tears were falling.

Sounds filled her brain, assailing her from all sides, a strange rushing noise of blood pounding in her head, a crunching like tyres on gravel, whining and wailing like mourners at a funeral, voices calling. She thought she was going to pass out and steadied herself against Luther's arm. It was all too hideous that this magnificent man should lie here like a dog at the side of a road. It was all so unfair. Poor Luther ... poor Estelle! A new wave of sadness flooded over her when she remembered Estelle. How would she cope, how could she possibly come to terms with the death of this man she loved above all others, who had given her back her love of life?

Anne was dizzy with shock and pity when she finally disentangled one voice from all the other sounds.

"Stand up and move away from the body."

It was a magnified sound, a man's voice imbued with authority, speaking clearly and slowly. Through her tears, Anne looked up and saw the blurred colours of police cars, white with red stripes, blue flashing lights, and an ambulance in green and yellow chequered livery.

"Stand up and come out of the tunnel. Now."

He means me, Anne thought. *That man is talking to me.* But despite her understanding of the situation, Anne was powerless to move. Her brain was not connecting with the rest of her body, her limbs were not responding. She pitched forward onto Luther's lifeless torso, resting her head on her forearm, exhausted.

The voice again. "You will stand up –"

Abruptly the sound was cut off. Another voice, this one known to her, interrupted the amplified command. She could hear it without the electric megaphone.

"All right Larry, I'll handle this. I know her."

With her eyes still closed, Anne heard footsteps approaching. Sergeant Marriner came to a halt beside her and reached down to take her arm.

"Anne, it's me," he said gently. "Are you hurt? Are you all right to stand up? Let me help you."

With ungainly effort, Anne rose to her feet and clung on to the detective. She was already beyond sobbing. Her grief was numb and silent, her face a river of tears.

"Anne?" Marnie's voice, from the other end of the tunnel. A sound of quickening footsteps. "What's happening?"

"Keep back, Mrs Walker. There's been an accident. Don't come any nearer."

The instructions were ignored, and Marnie hurried to within a few metres of where Anne and the detective were standing.

"Oh my God ... What's happened here?"

"Marnie ... please." Marriner spoke quietly but emphatically, still holding Anne to his chest. "This is almost certainly a crime scene. Keep back."

"Is Anne all right? Does she have to stay here?"

"She appears to have discovered the body."

Marnie focused on the prostrate form. She groaned. Marriner spoke again.

"What are you actually doing here ... at this moment?"

"We're in the pub garden having lunch ... a meeting of our planning group."

"Go back there. I'll bring Anne round."

Marriner turned to issue instructions to the other officers while Marnie retraced her steps, her mind in turmoil.

• • • • •

Minutes later, Marnie sat on a bench in the garden holding Anne in her arms. Both had a traumatised look that Marriner had seen many times before. The others sat in a loose circle in varying degrees of shock. Marriner watched the group while he called to Bartlett on the mobile. Anne needed medical attention; she looked on the point of collapse. Marriner told a uniformed constable to fetch one of the paramedics from the ambulance before it left.

"You must have arrived very quickly," Marnie muttered.

Sergeant Marriner had to strain to catch the words.

"No more than ten minutes at the outside. A three nines call came in for an ambulance. A woman ... anonymous. It sounded suspicious. We were in the area ... got diverted."

"Had the woman seen what happened?"

"She just called in and hung up. Obviously it wasn't you or one of your group."

"Obviously not."

"We're going to need all the help we can get, Marnie."

"Of course. No one left the table in the timeframe you've described. We were all together. We saw and heard nothing."

"Anne left the table," Marriner reminded her.

"Yes, but –"

"Why did she leave? Why was she in the tunnel?"

Marnie put her hand on the back of Anne's head resting against her shoulder.

"She needed a few moments of peace and quiet. She'd had –"

The constable's radio crackled. He announced himself and listened. A disembodied voice could be heard.

"... a suspicious sighting. A boy was seen at the time of the incident cycling away from the scene. Almost ran into a group of mothers and children. The description was of a youth in a light sweater or T-shirt wearing a baseball cap, last seen heading north towards the A508."

The constable spoke. "Sarge, there was a boy on a bike when we were on our way here."

"Did he fit that description?"

"Absolutely."

Marriner stared at Marnie.

She felt uncomfortable. "What's the matter?"

"Boy on a bike," Marriner said softly. "Light sweater, baseball cap ... Could it be ..."

"What's on your mind?" Ralph asked.

Marriner became aware that the whole group was surrounding him. "We had a sighting of a boy on a bike in a baseball cap after the shooting yesterday."

"Sergeant," Ralph began. "There are over half a million people in Northamptonshire. There must be thousands of boys with bikes and baseball caps."

"Ronny would fit that description."

The voice dropped into the conversation like a stone in a pond. Everyone looked at Dorothy Vane-Henderson.

"Ronny who?" Marriner asked her.

"Ronny Cope. He was here not long before you arrived, sergeant."

"And nobody thought to tell me?"

"I was about to, but I got interrupted," said Marnie. "Anyway, we didn't know you were interested in a boy on a bike ... and it hardly mattered ... he wasn't even here when Anne discovered ..."

Marriner's brows creased. "I'll want to know exactly what Anne was doing in that tunnel at that precise time."

Ralph moved closer to speak quietly. "Mr Marriner, he'd had words with Anne and had left in a rush ... a tiff between teenagers ... just one of those things."

"Nevertheless we shall have to check it out, sir. Can someone give us his address?"

While they were talking, the ambulance rolled into the car park and two paramedics got out, walking quickly towards the group. Marriner directed them to Anne and while all attention was focused on the girl, Marnie stood up.

"Just popping to the loo," she muttered quietly. "Won't be a minute."

• • • • •

Ronny threw his bike down on the gravel drive and charged into the house, bounding up the stairs to his room. He slammed the door behind him and stood breathing heavily staring out of the window, seeing nothing.

Outside, his mother was on her knees weeding at the top of the garden, a trug lying beside her on the lawn. The quarter-acre was her pride and joy, with curved borders to the immaculately trimmed grass, mown in neat stripes every week by her husband. It was packed with colours like an impressionist's palette, an exuberant high summer display. She had heard sounds in the house, and knowing that Ronny had returned home, she did not move when she heard the phone ringing.

Ronny was on his way to the shower when the call came. He stopped at the top of the stairs, waiting for the answerphone to cut in. At the sound of Marnie's voice he pursed his lips.

· · · · ·

Marnie was back almost before Marriner realised she had gone. Her hair was combed, and a faint fresh tang of Cologne hung about her.

"I feel a bit more capable of facing the world now," she said to Marriner. The paramedics had taken Anne to a separate table and were kneeling beside her. "This is a dreadful business. Do you think it could've been an accident?"

Marriner looked doubtful. "Did Mr Curtiss seem like the kind of man who could slip in a place like that and accidentally kill himself?"

"What else could it be? I know you don't think Anne – or any of us – was involved. He was a very dear friend ... a lovely man." She took a few deep breaths.

"We're going to follow every lead we can get, Mrs Walker."

"We'll co-operate fully, but I assure you none of us has the slightest idea of what happened."

"You all knew Mr Curtiss was coming to join you?"

"Yes."

"There are seven plates of food on the table."

"We had a ham sandwich for Luther."

"So what about Ronny Cope? What was he going to eat? Or did he just come to have a ... tiff ... with Anne?"

"He was going to stay, but they had a quarrel. I suggested we keep the sandwich for Luther. Actually, Ronny didn't know Luther was coming. I'm sure you'll check that out. You don't seem to miss much."

"It won't be me, Mrs Walker. The DCI was on his way here, but instead he's calling in on Ronny to ask him a few questions."

"Mr Bartlett?"

Marriner nodded. He glanced at Marnie's shoulder bag. "Talking of details ... is your mobile phone in there?"

"My ...? Yes, it should be."

"Aren't you sure? Could you just check. I'd like to see it, please."

Marnie reached in and gave Marriner the phone.

"I'm not very good with these things," Marriner said in a conversational tone. "You're probably much more technically-minded than I am. Do these ones have a way of showing what was the last call you made?"

"Mm ... yes. You can bring up the last ten numbers, I think."

"Can you show me?"

He handed her the phone and moved round to watch over her shoulder. Marnie began scrolling back through the last numbers dialled.

"Not so fast, please. I'd like to make a note of the numbers. Can you tell me whose they are? That last one, for instance, whose is that?"

"It's Serena's mobile."

"When did you call her?"

"Shortly after we arrived here. I wanted to check she was on her way."

"And that's the last time you used the phone?"

"Yes."

"And when did you last speak to Ronny Cope on the phone?"

"That I can't remember for sure. I've rung him several times recently, making arrangements for the summer scheme. My phone bill looks like the National Debt. I rang him twice this morning from the office, but his line was busy."

"And you're sure you haven't spoken to him since?"

"Positive. That's the trouble ..."

"Meaning?"

"I was the cause of the so-called *tiff* with Anne. He thought *she'd* forgotten to invite him, but it was my fault for not persevering. It slipped my mind completely."

"We'll need statements from all your people here, but we can do that later. And I'll probably need a copy of your itemised phone bill in due course."

"OK. I never realised you were so suspicious."

Marriner gave her a weary look. "It's called routine. We have to check everything. It's all in the detail."

"The devil is in the detail," Marnie muttered.

"That's right. I assume this is all your planning group. Apart from Ronny, is everyone else present?"

The simple question hit Marnie like a sledgehammer. Of course everyone was not present. Luther would never be present again. Pain and anguish struck her a double blow as the recollection of Luther's death reared up.

"No." Her voice was choked and dry, barely audible. "Estelle's not here. She's in Italy ... due back tomorrow. God knows how I'm going to break this to her ..."

• • • • •

Carolyn Cope heard a car on the drive and turned off the hose. Moments later the doorbell sounded. She waited to see if Ronny was coming down to answer it. The bell rang again. Adjusting her sunhat from which unruly wisps of hair were visible, she walked round the side of the house and was surprised to find a man and a woman standing at the door.

The man produced a warrant card and introduced himself as DCI Jack Bartlett. His colleague was WDC Cathy Lamb. Mrs Cope ushered them into the garden to sit at the table under the parasol while she went in to tell her son they were waiting to see him. The police officers sat admiring the garden, and could hear Mrs Cope calling up the stairs. After her initial surprise, the police intrusion was made to seem like a regular social visit.

"Ronny's just coming down now. He'll only be a minute or two." She laid a tray with a jug and glasses on the table. "I thought you might like a cool drink while you wait. This is my homemade ginger beer."

"What's keeping your son, Mrs Cope?"

"He was in the shower." She began pouring the drinks.

"At this time of day? That's a little unusual, isn't it?"

"He'd been out on his bike." She lowered her voice as if imparting shameful information that could offend the neighbours. "He was a bit sweaty, I expect."

"That's his bike on the drive?"

"It was. I've just put it in the carport." She rolled her eyes. "You know what boys are like."

She passed Bartlett and Lamb a glass of chilled cloudy liquid. Cathy Lamb grabbed hers as fast as she could without undue haste, dreading that her boss might decline the offer.

"Do you know where he went on his bike, Mrs Cope?"

"To Cosgrove. They were having a meeting of the summer scheme group. He likes to help." The voice lowered again. "And he likes to see Anne, of course. Now you drink up and I'll tell Ronny to get a move on."

When Ronny came out into the garden he looked wary. The detectives stood up, but Mrs Cope thrust a glass of ginger beer into her son's hand and sat him at the table. The expected questioning looked like a quiet chat as they all sat holding their drinks. Bartlett declined the offer of sandwiches and coffee, and Cathy Lamb opened her notebook. The first questions established Ronny's movements, timing and his conversation with Anne at the pub. He answered succinctly and without hesitation. When Bartlett asked about his quarrel with Anne, he looked down at his lap before replying.

"It was stupid, really. It wasn't Anne's fault. They tried to ring me, but our phone was engaged —"

"That must've been me," Mrs Cope interrupted. "I had a long chat with my mother this morning. Dad's recovering from a heart attack, and the doctors have said he needs one of those bypass operations. Mum's worried stiff about it and —"

"I'm sorry to hear that, Mrs Cope, but time is pressing and we're investigating a possible case of murder."

"Oh, my goodness!" she exclaimed, pressing a hand to her cheek.

Ronny jerked upright, splashing ginger beer into his lap. *What?*

Bartlett was watching him closely. "You didn't know, Ronny?"

"Murder? *Christ!* Sorry, mum. Who's been murdered?" Ronny shuddered as he spoke.

"Mr Luther Curtiss was found dead soon after you left Cosgrove. We're treating his death as suspicious."

Ronny closed his eyes and breathed out audibly. "Luther ... I can't believe it. It's ... it's all so ... incredible."

"When did you last see him?"

"When did I ...? Er ... this morning."

"At what time was that?"

"Around eight ... eight-thirty, I suppose."

"Where did you meet him? Can you remember what you said to each other?"

"We didn't actually meet. I just saw Luther out jogging. He came past the house when I was getting up. I saw him from the upstairs landing window. He didn't see me."

"What was he wearing?"

Ronny shrugged and said vaguely, "Jogging gear ... grey, I think."

"Can you tell me where you were yesterday afternoon?"

"Yesterday? I was here ... mostly in the garden. Mum got me helping with the weeding for a bit. Then I sat out reading, listening to music on the walkman."

"That's quite right, Inspector. He did all that flower-bed over there … and dead-headed the roses. He's good at that sort of thing."

"Do you have a red baseball cap, Ronny?"

At each sudden change of tack by Bartlett, Ronny frowned and paused to think. "I expect so. I think I've got a Ferrari one somewhere. That's red."

"You gave that to Tim," Mrs Cope corrected him. To the police officers she said, "That's my youngest. He usually wears it for his paper round."

"Do you have any other bikes?"

Ronny looked puzzled. "No. I have had others in the past."

"Have you ever owned a *yellow* bike?"

"No."

Bartlett glanced at Mrs Cope, but she added nothing. He stood up. Cathy Lamb finished her drink with a smile at Mrs Cope.

Bartlett continued. "Have you spoken to Marnie Walker on the phone this morning?"

Ronny shook his head. "No. I saw her at the pub, but we didn't speak."

"Who rang earlier, then?" asked Mrs Cope. "I heard it when I was in the garden. I thought you answered it."

"No, mum. I was in the shower. I didn't answer the phone."

"Do you have an answering machine?" asked Bartlett.

"Yes."

"Would you mind if we just checked it, Mrs Cope?"

"I'll show you where it is."

There was no light glowing on the machine, no messages recorded. Bartlett rested an index finger on the box for a few thoughtful seconds. He pressed a tab, and the tape compartment flipped open. Extracting the cassette, he held it up. It was fully rewound, and he put it back in place. Finally, with Ronny and his mother looking on impassively, he picked up the receiver and pressed four buttons. 1 – 4 – 7 – 1. A message told him that the last caller had withheld their number.

$$\bullet \quad \bullet \quad \bullet \quad \bullet \quad \bullet$$

The village was small, but sizeable crowds had formed, appearing as if by magic near the pub and at the end of the pedestrian tunnel where Luther had been found. That area was cordoned off and screens erected to enable the scene-of-crime officers to work in privacy. The ambulance had left to be replaced by a plain dark blue van that had reversed off the road down towards the tunnel entrance, where it waited patiently for the police to authorise the removal of Luther's body.

Ralph was unaccustomed to driving the Discovery and he manoeuvred it cautiously past the groups of onlookers who were standing together speaking in muffled voices at the car park exit. Behind him, Marnie sat with Anne, holding her hand.

"Are you sure you want to do this now?" Ralph said to Marnie.

It was Anne who answered. "I want to get it over with. The sooner I do this, the sooner they'll leave me alone."

"And the sooner we can get on with other things," Marnie added. "You're really sure you're feeling up to it?"

"As ready as I'll ever be."

Ralph was puzzled. It was Marnie's custom to try to shelter Anne from difficult situations, but now here they were setting off for the police station to make her statement when she was still looking dazed. This was not Marnie's normal behaviour.

Ralph studied her face in the rear-view mirror. "Do you think you know what happened ... to Luther?"

"Haven't a clue. Try not to drive on the pavement, Ralph."

"*Damn!* Sorry." He straightened the car and kept his eyes on the road. "That business with your mobile ... Bartlett wanting to check the numbers you'd called ..."

"Wanting to see if I'd rung Ronny to warn him."

"Of course. But you had, hadn't you?"

"Not on the mobile. It'd be a give-away. There's a payphone just by the door to the *Ladies*. I used that. No one can find out ... I made sure of it."

Ralph smiled wryly. "You always have everything worked out."

"All I know is we have to get daylight between us and the investigation. We've got a lot on our plate ... the summer scheme ... the fete on Sunday ... worst of all, Estelle coming back tomorrow. And now a possible second murder. Someone's got to contact Luther's family and tell them what's happened. The whole thing's a nightmare. I want to clear the decks. Then Anne can recover from her ordeal."

Ralph concentrated on his driving. Marnie was right. Luther's death would add to their worries and increase the danger surrounding them. He turned onto the main road and accelerated.

• • • • •

DCI Bartlett briefed Superintendent Harris by phone on the Cosgrove situation. DS Marriner was setting up the incident room down the corridor. With all the troubles in town they were short-handed to investigate a second suspicious death that would probably turn into a murder inquiry. WDC Lamb pushed backwards into the room carrying two mugs of tea.

"Do you think it was a blow to the back of the head, sarge?"

"Let's wait for the autopsy report. No point trying to guess. Thanks, Cathy." He took the tea. "I'm gasping."

Cathy sat on the edge of a desk. "It just doesn't add up ... big strong bloke like that. He's hardly likely to trip and fall over. The surface wasn't bumpy."

"There was an irregular bit just at the entrance to the tunnel," Marriner pointed out.

"Even so ... What are the other possibilities? Perhaps he was ambushed ... maybe a New Force gang was lying in wait."

"In a tunnel, in a country village, miles from town ... like trolls ... on the off-chance that some black person would come along?"

"Well someone attacked him, sarge. It could've been racially motivated. Perhaps he was being followed or got mugged and it went wrong."

"Can you seriously imagine any mugger going for a strong fit bloke like that in a confined space? Too big a risk of getting thumped back."

"Well someone attacked him, sarge, and he did fall back and hit his head. They struck him with enough force for the fall to be fatal. I don't think one person could've done it alone."

"Nobody seems to have seen your gang of villains, Cathy. Did they just vanish into thin air?"

"Maybe ..." She stared in front of her. "Maybe they were ... hiding on a boat on the canal."

"Maybe, maybe," Marriner mimicked. "Let's get the evidence together before we jump to conclusions. If the DCI hears you going on like that, he'll go up the wall. Facts and evidence ... that's the way forward."

"May– ... perhaps when Anne comes in and gives me her statement, we'll have some facts and evidence to go on."

Marriner blew on his tea to cool it. "Don't count on it, Cathy."

• • • • •

Serena was on the phone to her colleague, Jackie Brice. There was a crowd of reporters outside the front door and no way that Serena would be leaving the house to meet the returning coaches that evening. Jackie was on the same grade as Serena in the council's hierarchy but she took her orders and accepted Serena's authority – at least on this project – without question. That was how it was. Serena was a leader.

"Leave it to me. I don't think there'll be any problems."

"I hope you're right, Jackie. But things could be hotting up. If anything happens, you phone me, right? I'll come over straight away."

"Sure. Are you OK?"

"How can I answer that? One of my friends has been found dead, my home's under siege by reporters, and I think a TV crew's just arrived on my doorstep. Meanwhile my mother's trying to keep my kids occupied in the garden in the playpool."

"Just ignore the media and keep your head down."

"I don't think it's quite that simple. Any minute there could be riots all over town. If anyone's going to have to say something to keep things calm, it's got to be me."

The doorbell rang.

"Gotta go, Jackie. We'll talk soon."

Serena took a deep breath and opened the front door. The reporters surged forward. Flash bulbs went off like starbursts.

"Hallo, Serena. I'm Clare Saunders from TV News East." Behind her a cameraman was lining up. A microphone like a giant furry caterpillar was extending towards her over the journalist's head. "Any chance of an interview or at least a statement?"

Serena's inner voice told her to keep calm and dignified. "I'm not sure I have much to say, but I'd be glad to help ... if you'd then please leave ... for my children's sake. All this attention is very scary for them."

"We believe you were in Cosgrove when the body of Mr Curtiss was found. Is that correct?"

"Yes. We were having a meeting of the summer scheme organisers ... a working lunch."

"Why Cosgrove? It's a long way out of town."

"Several of our group members live in that area."

"Were you present when the body was discovered?"

"No."

"How well did you know Mr Curtiss?"

"I only met him quite recently … through the summer scheme."

"Would you say you were friends?"

"I'm friends with all the members of the organising group."

"You were photographed with him a few days ago in the local press. You seemed to be on good terms."

"Like I told you … we were friends. He was a good man and a good –"

"Would you describe your relationship as *close*?"

"What do you mean… *close*?" Her eyes blazed. "I'm a married woman with a husband and a family."

"But it has been suggested that you and Mr Curtiss were –"

"Suggested? Who suggested what? What are you talking about?"

"The photo in the paper made it look as if you were more than just –"

"What on *earth* do you mean?" Serena was appalled and could not keep the emotion out of her voice. "This poor man is dead, and you just want to rake up scandal about him. You should be ashamed of yourself, asking questions like that."

"This is a matter of major public interest, Mrs McDowell –"

"It's muck-raking."

"Are you saying –"

"I'm saying nothing more to you. You're a disgrace to your profession. Now get away from my house and leave me alone. You *disgust* me!"

Serena turned and slammed the door behind her. She staggered forward and slumped on the stairs, holding her head. Minutes passed before her rage subsided.

• • • • •

"And you didn't see anyone, Anne, or hear anything that made you suspect there'd been a fight or a struggle in the tunnel when you reached it?"

"Nothing. I was thinking about Ronny going off on his bike, and how upset he was. I was upset, too … not really paying attention to anything else."

Cathy looked down at her notes. "How long was it between Ronny leaving and you going for your walk?"

"Not long … a few minutes."

"Five, ten, fifteen?"

"Maybe five."

"How did Ronny get on with Luther?"

Anne looked surprised at the question. "Fine."

"You're sure about that?"

"Of course. I thought I was just here to give a statement."

Cathy nodded. "Sorry. I was just trying to fill in a few gaps."

Anne looked straight at Cathy. "Ronny admired him … and his family. They were great sportsmen and women, you know. Ronny was impressed."

"I have to ask you this, Anne. Think carefully. Was Luther dead when you found him, to the best of your knowledge? Or did he say anything before he died?"

Anne shook her head. The memory came back. Two tears slid down her face.

Cathy re-read the notes for Anne's statement. She went into the tunnel, saw a body, recognised it, the police arrived. Sergeant Marriner had been right. They had learnt nothing.

• • • • •

The builders were already packing up for the weekend when the Discovery rolled into the yard at Glebe Farm. Mentally exhausted, Anne went to phone her parents and assure them she was all right before having a rest in her attic room. Ralph made his way through the spinney to *Thyrsis* to check messages. Muttering that the day was practically over and she had done virtually no work, Marnie collared Bob the foreman for a quick review of progress on site before settling down to a list of phone calls. Opening the filofax, her heart froze when she saw the first item in the diary for the following day: *Estelle returns from Italy.* She scribbled a note to ask Anne to remind her about the arrival time of her flight.

Time raced by. Wading through the 'jobs to do' list, Marnie was astonished to hear a recorded voice informing her that the Willards Brewery switchboard was now closed, that office hours were eight-thirty till five-thirty, Monday to Friday. Replacing the receiver she looked up at the clock in disbelief. As she did so, the evening newspaper came through the letterbox and hit the doormat.

Marnie's shoulders sagged when she saw the front page. The headline was *Another Murder?* Below a photograph of Luther and Serena laughing together, was the caption *Police treating man's death as suspicious.* Turning to the inside, Marnie found the story continued on page three with a photograph of Serena looking angry by her front door. *Serena McDowell, organiser of the popular summer scheme for children, and a close friend of the deceased man, Luther Curtiss, was 'disgusted' at what had happened.*

The article went on to describe how Luther's body had been found by another member of Serena's 'inner circle' of friends and asked if this could have been a revenge attack following the shooting of BFP leader Garth Brandon the previous day. It ended with an appeal for witnesses who might have seen anyone or anything unusual near the scene of the 'incident'.

A sudden thought leapt into her mind, and Marnie grabbed the phone.

"Knightly Stores, Molly Appleton."

"Molly, it's Marnie. I've just seen the paper."

"Isn't it dreadful, Marnie? Richard and I are totally stunned."

"Yes. I'm thinking about Estelle."

"Oh that poor young woman ..."

"I just wanted to check that you aren't faxing her the newspaper."

"No. Not any more. Wasn't she due back yesterday?"

Marnie sighed with relief. "We had to change plans. She's flying home tomorrow morning."

"Oh dear ... You'll want to break the news to her yourself, I expect."

Not quite how I'd put it, Marnie thought.

30

Oversleeping was becoming a habit. Squinting through one eye, Marnie could see the line of brightness where the curtains joined over the porthole in the sleeping cabin and for the second day in succession she lay soporific for half an hour. Ralph stirred. She wondered if he felt as exhausted as she did. They always slept naked, enjoying the close bodily contact, but for the past two nights they had not made love, fading instead into a sleep that was as disturbed as it was unsatisfying.

Lying on her back with eyes closed, she could feel Ralph's side against her hip, and he turned slightly towards her. If this was the beginning of an advance, she had to admire his fortitude and resolve. But it was followed by the sound of his breathing out in a long sleepy sigh, and he continued to lie inert beside her.

Reality started to seep into her consciousness. There was no need to rush. No coaches would be setting off from Garfield that morning. Shortly, stalls would be set up for the fete; scouts would be mobilised to help with lifting and carrying instead of supervising embarkations and departures. This was the weekend.

And then it struck her. Saturday. Today Estelle was coming home. Marnie made a rapid mental calculation. She would already be at Pisa airport, probably queuing at the check-in, clutching the change of flight confirmation that Anne had faxed her, or waiting in the departure lounge, watching the monitors for boarding information. Was she flicking through a glossy Italian design magazine, ignorant of the dread that awaited her? Or did she know already about Luther? Would European papers carry articles on the death of one man in a tiny tunnel in a little English village? What a bombshell lay ahead of her. Marnie's stomach tightened at the thought that she might have to be the one to break the news.

• • • • •

The police had drafted in every available officer to resume house-to-house enquiries that Saturday morning. DCI Bartlett's station superintendent had long resigned himself to the overtime budget going into freefall that summer. Every house in Cosgrove received at least one visit, with DS Marriner taking charge of the operation.

When Bartlett arrived, they stood on the towpath above the tunnel entrance. Marriner had nothing substantial to report.

"Well some bugger must've seen something, Ted. For crying out loud ..."

"The trouble is, sir, it's a very secluded spot, just there. See how the ground slopes down, with these steep sides and vegetation all round. It's like a funnel. You'd have to be right on the spot to see anything."

Bartlett looked decidedly unhappy. "Have you had replies in all the houses?"

"Not all, sir."

"Ah ... So there's a chance of getting information later on."

"Not really. We've checked. The empty houses are where people are away on holiday. No hope there."

"*Blast!* We'll have to widen our enquiries."

"Sir?" Marriner experienced a feeling approaching panic. There was a caravan park nearby, with hundreds of trailers, maybe thousands. Most of them were occupied now with owners who had just arrived for a weekend in the country. It would be a nightmare to have to comb that lot.

"Check out all the boats on the canal."

Marriner looked glum. "How far do we extend the search, sir?"

Bartlett scowled and pointed south. "That way as far as the Iron Trunk aqueduct. And don't forget that side arm near the lock. North ... go up as far as the next pub. There are some moorings up there."

Could be worse, Marriner thought. He wanted to do a thorough job, but had no expectation that this would reveal anything. His frustration was palpable. It was a relief when Bartlett looked at his watch and announced he had to go. A meeting with Superintendent Harris in Northampton. Walking away, Bartlett suddenly turned and called back over his shoulder.

"When you've done the boats, you'd better get started on that caravan park."

• • • • •

It was a quiet breakfast on *Sally Ann*. The sky was overcast, with a light breeze, and they decided to eat on board. Ralph made the preparations while Marnie went to see how Anne was feeling after yesterday's ordeal. They returned together arm-in-arm through the spinney and paused on the stern deck to look across the water at *X O 2*. There was no yellow mountain bike on the roof; the hatches and doors were shut, the curtains all tightly drawn.

They had only half an ear between them on the radio news programme that was broadcasting quietly in the background.

Ralph took his seat at the table. "This morning we've got to take it easy. We've got two tough days ahead of us, though I'd be surprised if the police let the fete go ahead tomorrow. It could be a major target for troublemakers."

"There could be trouble enough whether the fete goes ahead or not," said Marnie. "New Force don't need an excuse."

"OK, so we've got Estelle returning today and the fete tomorrow. I expect Estelle will have heard about Luther by the time she gets here."

"What time does she get in, Anne?" Marnie asked.

"Nine forty-five."

Marnie looked at the cabin clock. Ten to eight. "If I set off now and made good time, I could probably get to Heathrow to meet her."

Ralph reached across the table and took her hand. He spoke gently. "Marnie, that's a very kind thought, but I think you need to take care not to over-stretch yourself. Estelle's going to be hit hard whatever you or anyone else does. Putting pressure on yourself won't make things any better."

She closed her hand over Ralph's. "Maybe my concern would be an intrusion. And perhaps she'll prefer to go to her flat first rather than drive up."

"I'd come with you if you wanted to go and meet her," said Anne. "But I think Ralph's right. We're all feeling the strain."

Ralph straightened up. "Right. More coffee." He picked up the pot and began pouring.

"Are we expected anywhere today?" Marnie asked.

Anne shook her head. "Mrs V-H said we should leave everything to her army of helpers and the scouts."

"A formidable line-up," said Marnie. "I wonder how the investigations are getting on."

Ralph passed Marnie the milk jug. "There was nothing on the news about Brandon. I think they're no further forward. And all they said about Luther was that inquiries were proceeding."

"Which presumably means the same. Two murders in public places, one with a crowd of witnesses, and no suspects. A mysterious boy seen in the vicinity ... on a bike ... in a baseball cap ... both times. And that's it."

Anne took a piece of toast. "You're not suggesting it was the same person?"

"I'm not suggesting anything. I'm just looking at the facts as we know them."

"Well, one boy on a bike was Ronny. He can't have had anything to do with Luther's death."

"Is that certain?" said Ralph.

"*Ralph!*" Anne looked shocked.

"I'm not suggesting he did. But to the police his actions must seem suspicious. You yourself said he was jealous of Luther ... and Donovan."

Anne was bewildered. "You think the police might suspect Ronny of a double murder, one of them out of jealousy over me?"

Marnie chewed her lip. "Donovan hasn't been seen since ... No ... this is all too far-fetched."

"So what do we know for sure?" Ralph rested a finger on the coffee pot. "Fact: Ronny storms off in a jealous rage. You didn't see where he went after he left you. He nearly runs down a group of women and children ... reliable witnesses. Minutes later, Luther's body is found nearby."

"But –"

Ralph's raised hand cut off Anne's interjection. He put a finger on the milk jug. "Fact: Brandon is shot dead ... surrounded by his own people ... also reliable witnesses ... at a location that was their secret hideout. Shot, mark you ... with an unusual weapon. In both cases a boy on a bike is observed leaving the scene of the crime immediately afterwards."

"I can't believe you're suggesting that Ronny killed Brandon and Luther," said Anne.

"I'm not. I'm simply pointing out what we know for certain about what happened in both cases ... and how it must look to the police."

"You think they could suspect Ronny?"

"Of course they do, as things stand at the moment. What else do they have to go on?"

"But ..."

There was no interruption from Ralph this time. He waited. "But what?"

"Ronny's not like that ... he's not capable of ... it's too ridiculous ..."

"What do you actually think, Ralph?" said Marnie.

"We can't arrive at any conclusions. We only have the reports on the radio. The police will know much more than we do. At least, I hope they do."

"I don't see how the murders can be linked. They can't be racially motivated –"

"On the contrary. They could both easily be racially motivated."

"I mean not if they were committed by the same person. Brandon's white, Luther's black."

"Let's assume two separate murderers, then," said Ralph. "Brandon could've been killed for a political motive. I'd have thought that's highly likely."

"Could he have been shot by a concealed sniper that no one could see?" Anne asked.

"No. We know he was shot at point blank range with a pistol."

"So it must've been someone in his own group," said Marnie.

Ralph nodded slowly. "Which could explain why no one has come forward to identify the killer."

"Like Julius Caesar," Anne said quickly. "We did it in English Lit at school. He was killed by the senators … his own people, but all rivals, jealous of his power."

"That has to be a possibility," Ralph agreed. "Except …"

"What?"

"The police said the group around him were all clearly shocked by what had happened."

"*I'd* be shocked if someone had just been killed beside *me*," said Marnie. "Even if I *was* part of the conspiracy. Being splattered with blood would certainly give me the jitters."

Anne's eyes suddenly filled with tears. "It wasn't like that for Luther."

Marnie put an arm round her shoulders. "Oh Anne … how thoughtless of me to be talking like this …"

"It's all right … really … it's not something we can ignore or forget about. It just brought it back to me."

Ralph took her hands. "Forgive me, Anne. I'm so sorry. I wasn't thinking …"

Marnie kissed Anne on the side of her head. *This would be a day of tears*, she thought.

• • • • •

Bartlett had just reached his office and was checking notes on his desk when a uniformed PC looked round the door.

"Oh, you're back, sir."

"What is it?"

"Just had a message from Pathology. I told them I thought you were probably on your way to attend the autopsy."

"What did they want?"

"If you're not going, could you give them a ring."

Bartlett took the number and dialled. He asked for the pathologist and briefly explained he had to go to a meeting in Northampton. The doctor came straight to the point.

"Our initial examination has thrown up something you'll want to know. Two things to be precise. The deceased had a tiny trace of lipstick on the edge of his lip."

"*Lipstick?*"

"Yes. I gather there was a woman present when your chaps arrived on the scene."

"That's right. Can you tell me anything about it?"

"Not much at the moment. There must be thousands of different sorts. It was red."

"I could use a little more than that." Bartlett's voice was chilly.

The pathologist noticed. "Not all lipstick is red, chief inspector. There are shades of other colours ... pink, mauve, even purple and black."

"All right. I take your point. Is it a bright red?"

"Very ... and glossy."

"Why the hell didn't *we* spot this?"

"Like I said, chief inspector, it was a tiny trace, virtually invisible."

"Did you say there were two things?"

"The deceased had a handkerchief in his pocket."

"So?"

"It was neatly folded, but it's been used. There are marks on it, very faint, traces of something."

"Can you identify it? What colour is it?"

The pathologist paused. "One of my team said she thought it could be ... eye shadow ... a very pale blue."

"Eye shadow? You mean make-up?"

"It's just a guess at this stage."

After disconnecting, Bartlett stood immersed in his thoughts. *Lipstick and make-up.* Luther Curtiss had been in contact with a woman ... unless he was a cross-dresser. He winced and rejected the idea – for the time being. His girlfriend was away in Italy, so who else could it be? He assumed this was no casual greeting. These days a lot of people in what he regarded as the chattering classes had adopted the French habit of kissing on the cheeks. Marnie Walker's crowd would do that sort of thing. But kissing on the lips ... that was something else.

He tried to picture the women in that circle. Anne Price had found the body. She had worn make-up when they took her to the hospital to be identified. Did she wear lipstick? He had no recollection of anything bright, red and glossy. What about Marnie Walker? She was always well-groomed, but somehow understated. There was the horsy woman from Hanford Hall. If she wore lipstick it was probably tweed. And the head teacher from the school? Nothing glossy about her. Then there was Serena McDowell. Yes. Almost everything about her seemed glossy. Bartlett glanced at the clock and grabbed the phone. He rapidly explained to Cathy Lamb about the lipstick trace.

"Cathy, did Anne Price wear lipstick when we took her to the hospital?"

No hesitation. "A pale pink, sir. She couldn't wear red with her colouring."

"Could any of the others?"

Again, an immediate response. "Serena McDowell."

"And eye shadow?"

"Yes, sir. She could and she does ... but not all the time. For work I doubt if she wears much make-up."

"For a social occasion?"

"That would depend. She was wearing some yesterday at the pub."

"You're sure of that?"

"Definite. I had the feeling she was trying to keep her spirits up. Make-up can do that."

"For any other occasion?"

"What do you mean, sir?"

"An assignation ... if she was meeting a lover, for instance?"

A pause. "Yes."

"Are you sure? You hesitated."

"It's just ... she strikes me as being happily married."

"Cathy, don't be naive."

"Well ..."

"What?"

"She was wearing perfume yesterday as well, sir."

"You think that was just to keep her spirits up?"

"Possibly. Or if she was meeting someone ... someone special."

"Cathy, I want you to check out the make-up of all the women in that group. Just say it's routine. Get over to Northampton first and pay a call on Serena McDowell."

"Sir ... she did arrive at the pub after the others had got there."

"I know. Get moving, Cathy."

• • • • •

Marnie sat at her desk staring at the phone, feeling helpless. At the back of the office she could hear the rushing sound of Anne taking a belated shower. An atmosphere of gloomy apprehension hung over their lives. By now Estelle would be seven miles above the ground, racing homewards at over five hundred miles an hour, ignorant of the fact that she was returning to the greatest tragedy of her life. Worse than that, she was basking in the anticipation of being reunited with her lover. Marnie could imagine her preparing to gush all over Luther in her inimitable style. The reality that awaited her would be like the impact of the plane crashing into a mountain. Total devastation.

She reached forward and picked up the receiver, hesitating while the buzz of dialling tone hummed expectantly in her ear. *What am I waiting for?* Marnie knew she had to be the one to break the news. Decisively, she pressed the buttons, rang both numbers in succession and left messages to wait for Estelle on the phone in her London flat and on the mobile answering service.

"Estelle, it's Marnie. I hope you had a good journey back. Please ring me straight away. It's important that I speak to you before you set off. Thanks."

• • • • •

Serena unplugged the telephone at the wall socket. Few people knew her mobile number. Now she could control contact with the outside world. There would be no interviews, no comment. Her last call before disconnecting the phone had been to ask BT to arrange a new number. She was ex-directory from now on.

Even the helpful messages had become nuisance calls. An organisation calling itself *BAN* – Britain Against Nazism – had been pestering her all morning with offers of a 'demonstration of solidarity'. A woman who gave her name as Margo promised huge numbers and a 'strictly-peaceful protest'. If she would just give her agreement, they would do the rest. Tersely Serena told them to stay away, but Margo was very persistent: *Someone has got to stand up to these bastards!*

And there had been a steady flow of abusive messages. It was evident that Serena's number was being circulated among the membership of New Force. The calls ranged from the simply menacing to the now customary death threats and the startlingly obscene. Only the most lurid had provoked a response from Serena: *For someone who doesn't like black people, I'd say that was a highly intimate suggestion. The position you describe could do physical harm to both participants.* She had been quite pleased with that, as an off-the-cuff reaction, but it left a bitter aftertaste.

The decider that led to the unplugging of the phone was a call that came from neither supporters nor enemies – not in the strict sense of the word – but from her own department. Murfitt had phoned. He had actually rung her at home on a Saturday morning! It was a first. His purpose was to warn her that he had been going over the figures; she had spent the *entire allocation* – budget line EYS0036, Events and Activities – *all* of it for the *whole year* on the summer scheme. She found herself coming dangerously close to telling him where to stick budget line EYS0036 when a double beep informed her that another caller was trying to reach her. She had excused herself. *Sorry Lee, gotta go. I've got another death threat waiting to get through. The Nazis must be on overtime this weekend. Or it could be the CID with more questions about the two murder investigations I'm involved in. See you! Bye!*

Sitting on the stairs she scrolled through the address list on the mobile. After the family numbers, the next name to appear was *Curtiss, Luther*. She stared at the name, and her stomach turned over. For a moment she could scarcely breathe. Her head fell forward. Eyes closed.

Oh God, what have I done? What have I done?

Time slipped by. Her breathing settled and her nerves returned to calm. The touch on the knee made her jump, her eyes snapping wide open. With a huge effort she forced the smile into place as she found herself looking into the concerned gaze of her four year-old son.

"What's the matter, mummy? Are you crying?"

"No, sweetie, of course not. Mummy's just having a little rest."

"Why are you on the stairs?" A frown still creased the little brown face.

"Mummy's got phone calls to make. This is her special phoning seat."

"Can we play?"

"*Play?*" The question caught her out. "Play what?" A silly answer.

"You never play any more. It's always nan who comes to play. I want *you* to play."

That's all I need, she thought, *the guilt thing.*

"We'll play soon, sweetie. Mummy's been very busy at work just lately. Nan's gone to the shops. She'll be here soon. Then you can play."

She heard a car draw up outside the house, and her stomach churned. Serena leapt up and ushered Joey into the rear sitting room, telling him to stay there watching TV with his sister until mummy came back. She slipped into the front room and craned sideways to look through the net curtains. Her shoulders relaxed. It was a woman getting out of the car, alone and somehow familiar. By the time the visitor reached the door, Serena was there to open it.

A warrant card was held up for inspection. "DC Cathy Lamb, Mrs McDowell. We've met before. Can I have a word?"

"What can I do for you?"

"Perhaps I could come inside?"

Serena admitted her to the hall.

"Have you found who killed Luther?"

"Our inquiries are still proceeding."

"So you haven't."

"I need your help, please. Would you mind letting me see your make-up?"

"*My make-up?* What for?"

"Please?"

Serena sighed loudly. "Wait here." She turned to mount the stairs, but Lamb held her back.

"*You* wait here, Mrs McDowell. Just tell me where it is. And let's start with your handbag, if you don't mind." The tone was calm but the words were firm.

Serena walked through to the rear of the house and opened the kitchen door. The remains of breakfast were still on the table.

"Sorry for the mess. The phone's been going non-stop since before I got up."

"Nuisance calls?"

"You could say that. I've unplugged it."

"You can get your number changed … go ex-directory."

"I've done that."

"Have you been receiving threats?"

"Of course." She passed her handbag to Lamb. "Help yourself. The rest is on the dressing table in the front bedroom … and there are one or two bits in the bathroom. Do you want coffee?"

"No thanks, better not. I've got to be going soon. I'm afraid I'll have to take a few things."

"What things?"

"I'll show you when I've finished."

Lamb rummaged in the handbag and produced lipstick, eye liner and a comb. She dropped them into a plastic bag and went out. Serena could hear her moving around upstairs as she filled the kettle. By the time Lamb returned, she was pouring water over instant coffee in a cup.

"You look as if you need this. Busy time for you, too, this summer, eh?"

Lamb accepted the offer of a seat and took a gulp of the hot drink. "I'll be a millionaire with all the overtime … if I live long enough to collect it."

"Did you find what you were looking for?"

"I just need these few things. I'll give you a receipt for them."

"Don't bother, I've got plenty more. What do you want them for? Are you going to tell me you just want to eliminate me from your inquiries … or whatever the expression is?"

"Something like that."

Serena stared at her. "No. It's more than that, isn't it?"

"Is your husband in?"

"He's taken my mother shopping. I don't go out if I can help it. You didn't answer my question. And why do you want my husband?"

"We don't answer people's questions as a rule, Mrs McDowell. It's nothing personal. It's our job to *ask* the questions. We don't seem to have seen your husband so far."

"He's got a job to do. He's not involved in any of the summer scheme business. I almost envy him ..."

"What does he do?"

"He works for a pharmaceutical company."

"Do you know where he was yesterday?"

A pause. "I think he had a meeting with an NHS Trust in Oxford. He usually stays on for lunch before going on to his next meeting."

"Do you know where that was?"

Another pause. "Banbury, I think ... yes."

"Do you know what time he left home to go to Oxford?"

"That I don't know. He was here doing paperwork when I left. I needed to collect something from the office before setting off for Cosgrove."

"Was anybody else here at that time?"

"No. The children were out with my mother, buying shoes. Why the interest in my husband? Oh, I was forgetting ... you don't answer questions. Well, let me guess. You want to know his movements in case he needs an alibi."

"We have to ask all sorts of questions. It's the routine."

"Yeah." Serena was past anger or even indignation, all her emotions drained. When she spoke again her voice was weary. "Do you think I would harm Luther? What possible reason could I have? Do you think my husband would become insanely jealous over a photograph in a newspaper?"

Cathy Lamb had answers to those questions, but she simply drank the coffee.

• • • • •

The coffee at the central police station in Northampton was no better than Serena's instant brew. Bartlett had accepted Harris's offer automatically, just as he always refused the coffee from Marnie Walker. It occurred to him that his policy in that regard was faulty.

"Thanks for coming over, Jack. I appreciate you've got a lot on your plate with the Curtiss murder. You are treating it as murder, I presume?"

"Until I get the autopsy report I'm trying to keep an open mind, sir, but there's been a development that makes me think it will probably turn out to be murder ... or manslaughter."

"Development?"

"Forensics have found a trace of lipstick ... a tiny speck on the edge of his lip ... and a handkerchief with traces of what could be eye make-up."

"You think that's significant? He had a girlfriend, didn't he? Couldn't it be hers?"

Bartlett shook his head. "She's in Italy ... due back today."

"On holiday without him?"

"No, a business trip. Alibis from Marnie Walker, Anne Price and the couple who run the village shop in Knightly St John. They've all been in touch with her at her hotel."

"So whose make-up is it? Any ideas?"

"The hot money's on Serena McDowell."

"*Jesus!*"

"And we're checking out Walker and a few others to see if there's a match with their make-up ... or – eventually – their DNA."

"*Christ!*"

"Quite."

"Well, good luck, Jack. You've got a hot potato there. And talking of hot potatoes ..."

"Any developments on the Brandon case, sir?"

Harris pursed his lips. "Between you and me, we've got bugger all. We've questioned every member of Brandon's group who was present. They're all telling the same story. They arrived back at their HQ – the house near the racecourse – all on foot. Just as they reached the door someone yelled, 'Look out, he's got a gun! Hit the deck.' A shot was fired and they all dropped to the ground. Brandon was on his knees apparently when more shots went off. By the time they looked up, Brandon was lying flat out with blood pouring from his wounds. Everyone was at first too stunned to react. Then one of them used his mobile to make a three nines call. Whoever did the shooting was in that group, and in the general confusion, he slipped round the corner and got away."

"How could someone get so near to Brandon when he was supposed to be surrounded by bodyguards ... or at least by his own people?"

"Not that simple. There were men from several groups, not just Brandon's crowd. One or two had come from an outfit in Leicester ... another bloke from Coventry, two or three down from Birmingham ... New Force. They were all dressed in black ... all of them white, of course."

"What about the boy on the bike, sir?"

"Not much to go on ... just a boy on a bike cycling away from the area." Harris shook his head. "I can't imagine a kid carrying out a calculated murder like that."

"The boy was white."

"Yes. No one of any other race could've got that close ... assuming they'd wanted to ... too dangerous ... too conspicuous."

"Is that the official view, then, sir? A rival from inside the far-right block?"

"Well ... it's not completely far-fetched. We know there were tensions between the various groups ... even violence. There were those photos in the press ... New Force yobs smashing the car of one of Brandon's closest supporters."

"You're sure they were New Force, sir?"

"We didn't manage to catch any from New Force as such, but they had just beaten the shit out of some poor black lad who got in their way ... nearly killed him. And the camera cannot lie ... supposedly. But ... there are too many buts in this."

"And you're not totally convinced about the inside job theory, sir. It seemed pretty clear-cut the way you described it."

"That would mean several of them were in on it, Jack. They'd have to be to stand a chance of making it happen."

"I suppose so."

"They were all in a state of shock ... genuine ... not acting. I'm convinced of that."

"So where does that leave us, sir?"

"Up a well-known creek without a paddle."

• • • • •

Marnie's desk had never been so tidy. Alone in the office, with Anne preparing a sandwich lunch on *Sally Ann* and Ralph working in his study on *Thyrsis*, she had been going through all the items in her in-tray and pending-tray for half the morning, wondering why Estelle had not rung, assuming that the flight from Pisa had been delayed, steadily filling the waste-paper basket beside the desk, when the phone rang. But it was not the call she had been expecting.

"Marnie Walker."

"Marnie, it's Molly. I think you'd better come up to the shop."

"Er ... it's not a good time just now, Molly. Estelle's due back this morning and I want to be here when she rings."

"Ah but that's just it ... she's here."

"In the shop?"

"Outside ... sitting in her car ... been there a few minutes. She hasn't moved. I was going to go out and see if she was all right, but Richard said he thought I should ring you first."

"I'll come straight away."

For the first time that day Marnie noticed the weather. A thin veil of clouds was filtering the sunlight and it was cooler than it had been for some time. A merciful respite from the heat. Merciful ... There was not much mercy about, she thought as she steered the Discovery up the track to the village. Marnie braced herself for what was to come.

She drove past the shop, made a three-point turn and pulled up behind Estelle's Golf. Opening the passenger door, she quietly slid into the seat. The engine was running and the radio was playing. It was a chat show, with a studio audience joining in. Marnie pressed the power button to switch it off. In the silence that filled the car, Estelle moved her head slightly towards Marnie, her eyes still staring ahead.

"Estelle," Marnie said gently.

"It was on the news." Estelle's voice came from far off. Incongruously the sun chose that moment to break through the clouds and light up the village. "A mention ... in a list of headlines ... his name ... the police still investigating ... no progress yet ... and then a quick round-up of the weekend weather prospects."

"I'm so sorry, Estelle. I tried to contact you ... left messages ... I didn't want you to find out like this."

"Seeing the village ... I couldn't go any further ... felt paralysed ..."

Marnie put a hand on Estelle's shoulder. "Let me drive you." She had become aware of faces looking out from the shop window and did not want Estelle to remain there, a figure of curiosity, all her emotions on display in the high street. "Let me take you home. Are you able to stand up?"

Marnie got out and walked round to open the driver's door. She reached in, undid the seat belt, took Estelle's arm and helped her out, spotting her handbag and a file of papers in the back. While Estelle steadied herself, Marnie leaned in and took the bag. Pushing the door shut with a knee, she led Estelle to the Discovery and guided her into the seat. Having once received traumatic news herself, Marnie understood that in her state of shock Estelle knew little of what was happening to her and would remember even less. Drawing away from the kerb, Marnie raised a hand to Molly in the window.

By the time they reached Glebe Farm, Marnie was making plans to seek medical help. Neither had spoken. Estelle was stunned, her expression glazed, as if all her feelings had been cauterised. There were no tears, no exaggerated outbursts, none of the outpourings that Marnie had expected. Standing at the passenger door, she paused briefly, looking at Estelle. The face that she had always regarded as attractive in its habitual animation had taken on a new appearance, and Marnie saw for the first time that in repose Estelle was possessed of a remarkable and sombre beauty.

She led her friend across the courtyard and into the cottage that had been their first home, where they had become Estelle and Luther, and would be no more. Her only consolation at this sad return was that Estelle seemed disconnected from her surroundings. The full realisation of what had happened to her would come later. And it would stay with her for always.

Sitting Estelle on the bed, Marnie slipped off her sandals and made to lift her feet off the floor, but Estelle resisted. It was the only sign she had given that she recognised where she was and what was going on around her.

"You need to rest, Estelle. I'm going to phone the doctor."

"No."

"You need help," Marnie insisted gently.

Distressed, Estelle pointed vaguely across the room. "In my bag ... my sleeping pills. That's all I need."

She remained sitting there while Marnie located the box and pressed a tablet out of the foilwrap. After taking the pill with water she settled back on the pillow, lying on top of the duvet. Marnie wondered about helping her to undress, but decided to make as little fuss as possible. She feared breaking through the tranquillity that seemed to be protecting Estelle from the pain that would overwhelm her once the numbness had worn off.

It was strange to be in Estelle's company in that monastic silence. Marnie added more water to the glass from the bathroom washbasin and set it down on the bedside table. Estelle was staring up at the ceiling like a cadaver. Marnie picked up the box of sleeping tablets and put it in her pocket. As an afterthought she went back to the bathroom and checked the wall cabinet for any more pills. There were no others there or in the handbag. Marnie would have felt guilty at this invasion of private space and possessions, but knew she had no choice.

Now Estelle's eyes were closed, and she was breathing steadily. A crunching on the gravel drew Marnie to the small front bed-room that had been Luther's study. She saw Anne hovering in the doorway of the office barn. A tap on the window and Anne looked up, realising at once why Marnie was in the cottage. With a final glance at Estelle, Marnie went quietly downstairs and out into the courtyard.

"Estelle's back?" Anne spoke in a whisper.

"She's lying down. I gave her a sleeping pill."

Anne was alarmed. "She's got *sleeping pills*?"

"No. I've got them."

"Good. How is she?"

"Traumatised."

"Will she be all right?"

"One day … perhaps."

• • • • •

Anne had made simple sandwiches with what she could find in the fridge: cucumber, cheese and tomato, ham with mustard, granary bread. Sparkling water with chunks of ice and lemon and a bowl of strawberries completed the table. It looked and smelled delicious, and all three of them felt sad that they ate without enthusiasm or interest.

"Thanks for making this, Anne. It's wonderful."

A fleeting smile acknowledged Ralph's words.

"Marvellous." Marnie had just returned from checking that Estelle was resting.

"When my wife died I had a course of sleeping pills. They knocked me out for several hours and I felt groggy for most of the next day."

"I suppose it's the right thing to do." Marnie sounded unconvinced. "If she sleeps from now till bedtime and then dozes through the night, perhaps that'll be for the best. It's only putting off the grieving …"

Anne suddenly put a hand to her mouth.

"What is it?" said Marnie.

"Will the police want to question her? She'd never stand it. They wouldn't do that, would they?"

Ralph wiped his lips with a napkin. "I don't see why they should. They'll probably want to search the cottage, though."

"Why?"

Marnie touched her arm. "They always need to find out all they can about a … victim of crime. Don't worry. I'll arrange for Estelle not to be there when they do it."

They ate on without speaking, all three focused on Estelle and her misery. Marnie was planning to spend most of the day in the cottage, trying to concentrate on designs and plans, on hand for Estelle if needed. Ralph would field any phone calls that came in and ensure privacy as far as he was able. Anne dreaded Estelle's eventual and inevitable return to reality and all the pain it would bring. She had seen enough emotion these past weeks to last her a long time. Without warning she suddenly spoke.

"Ronny phoned this morning. He wanted to apologise."

"What for?" Ralph seemed puzzled.

"Because of our argument. He thought he was being left out of things."

"He was really jealous?"

"Yes. I told him he had no need to be." Anne frowned. "That's not true, actually. He was right to be jealous." Marnie and Ralph waited. "So … anyway … he was saying the police had been round to see him. That must've got the curtains twitching in Martyrs Close."

"What happened?" said Marnie.

"They asked all sorts of odd questions … about his bike … other bikes …

baseball caps. It was weird."

"Did he think they treated him as a suspect?"

"He wasn't sure. He didn't understand what was going on. I told him they're always like that."

"Is he worried?"

"Confused. I told him he's got nothing to be concerned about as he's entirely innocent of anything."

Ralph changed tack. "What about Donovan? Have you heard from him lately?"

"No."

"Maybe he's gone back to London. His uncle's funeral must be taking place some time now."

Anne began gathering plates and cutlery from the table. "Coffee?"

Marnie opted to take hers to the cottage to be near Estelle, while Ralph had files to sort out on his computer. Anne was at a loose end.

"Would you like to bring some work or a book and sit in the cottage with me?"

"Thanks, Marnie. Perhaps I'll go for a walk first." She suddenly looked up. "That's funny. I went round to get my sandals from the Mini ... Estelle's car isn't there."

"It's outside the village shop." Marnie explained about Molly's phone call. "I ought to go up and get it some time."

"Why don't I do that? I can walk up and drive it back. I'm sure I can manage it."

"I don't know what I did with the keys. Maybe I left them in it."

"No probs. We've got a spare set in the cupboard in the office. I'll take them from there."

Anne set off, glad to have something useful to do.

• • • • •

Molly Appleton was certain that no harm would come to Estelle's car while it was parked outside the shop, but that did not prevent her from looking at it every few minutes. In normal times she would never have given it another thought. Nothing was ever stolen or damaged in Knightly St John. It would be unthinkable. Thank goodness the old values still prevailed in some small parts of the world. But in these strange times, with undesirables and hooligans running all over the county, people were learning to think the unthinkable.

So it was that she was glad when Marnie rang briefly to let her know that Estelle was sleeping and that Anne was on her way up to collect the car. Minutes later Anne walked into the shop, bought a toasting loaf, potatoes and red peppers, and exited to drive the Golf home.

She dropped the shopping onto the passenger seat and checked the controls. It all looked reasonably clear, and the engine started without fuss. Wondering about the insurance position, she tip-toed the car along the high street while the road was empty and took it gently down the field track on the lookout for any passing rabbits that might crash into her. Without mishap she turned into the garage barn and parked between the Discovery and Ralph's Volvo.

It was while she was closing the door that she spotted the file on the back seat and recognised it as the travel folder that she had given Estelle for the Italian trip. It would contain all the receipts, documents and ticket stubs needed for her travel expenses claim. Glad to be able to relieve Estelle of at least one care, she yanked the back door open and pulled out the folder. Before going over to the cottage she let herself into the office barn and dropped it on her desk. She would tackle it in the morning.

Feeling restless, Anne slowly crossed the threshold out into the sunshine and closed the door behind her. Without thinking, she found her steps leading through the spinney towards the canal. Reaching the bridge, she paused and looked over at Donovan's boat, once regarded with suspicion, now a question mark without an answer. Where was Donovan? What had become of him?

Anne walked down and stood on the towpath, touching the boat's handrail. He had not gone home to see his family, she was sure of that. He would have found some way of letting her know. Or would he? Did she matter that much to him? Only one thing was certain. Standing by Donovan's boat, she heard his voice as clearly as if he was there with her, echoing loudly as if they were standing in a tunnel.

I hate the Nazis to death ... to death ... to death ... to death ...

• • • • •

Marnie met Anne in the entrance to the cottage and ushered her back outside so that they could talk without fear of disturbing Estelle. Even so, she spoke in a hushed tone, walking quietly on the courtyard gravel.

"You were gone a long time. I was beginning to wonder what had become of you. You managed the car all right?"

"No probs. It was fine. How's Estelle?"

"It's uncanny. She's lying there like Sleeping Beauty."

"Only her handsome prince isn't going to come and wake her up," Anne said solemnly.

"No. You'd hardly know she was breathing."

"But she is ..." Anne looked anxious.

"Yes. Don't worry. I only gave her one pill."

"I'm not worrying now." She stopped walking and turned to Marnie. "I've been thinking. That's what I was doing ... I went for a walk by the canal ... needed to get my thoughts straightened out."

"Yes. You're in need of some TLC, too. That was a horrible thing to happen yesterday ... finding Luther like that ... coming on top of your row with Ronny."

Anne said nothing. She closed her eyes for a few seconds, breathing deeply.

"Have you told me everything, Anne?"

"What do you mean?"

"You didn't see anything – or anyone – when you were in the tunnel?"

"Only Luther ... honestly. Marnie, Ronny was nowhere near there. He didn't have time to get round to –"

"Anne, I didn't think he did. I was only wondering ... was Luther – look, I really hate to ask you this – but was he dead when you got there? He didn't say anything before he died?"

"He was definitely dead." Anne's eyes flickered in the direction of the cottage. "No doubt about it. You don't have any ideas, do you, Marnie?"

"No. Do you?"

"Not a clue."

"But you do have an idea about what happened to Brandon, don't you, Anne?"

Anne was knocked off balance by the sudden change of subject. "Why do you say that?"

"Because I know you so well. In all the time we've lived and worked together you've only kept something from me about this Brandon business ... and on one other occasion. I'm right, aren't I?"

Marnie waited patiently. Anne was silent for almost a minute, visions of her night in Garfield Primary school swimming in her mind. She saw Donovan coming back from the shower, the towel round his waist, the smile as he came into the common room, the strange feeling of excitement and apprehension as he slipped into her sleeping bag. She saw the half-open drawer on his boat, the shadow of the pistol – the *Luger* – the box of medals and the Iron Cross. "Yes. You knew about the other thing I kept from you, didn't you?" Marnie nodded. Anne continued. "And you know about Brandon now ... or at least what I think happened."

"Yes. I think so. Anne, listen, your private life will always be your own affair. I've no desire to pry or interfere in personal matters. But I am glad there are no secrets between us."

"No."

"You're not going to do anything about the Brandon affair, are you ... contact the police or anything?"

"Would you?"

Marnie looked her straight in the eye. "Definitely not."

• • • • •

Marnie felt the mobile vibrating in her back pocket; she had switched off the ringing tone to maintain silence in the cottage. Hastily she pushed aside her papers, leapt to her feet and rushed to the front door, pressing the green button as she crossed the threshold. It was Serena.

"I'm starting to think the anti-fascists are as bad as the BFP and New Force. They just will not take no for an answer." She sounded calm but resolute.

"And there's not much you can do to stop them," Marnie sympathised. "What are they planning?"

"God knows ... some counter-demonstration, I expect. I've told them it will only do more harm than good. The media will love it. I wish the whole fete would just disappear ... can't think why I agreed to it in the first place."

Marnie groaned. "I rather recall it was my idea ... at least partly ... my brainwave to involve the voluntary organisations. I suppose it seemed a good idea at the time."

"I'm not blaming you or anyone else, Marnie, but things have moved on – become more dangerous, if that's possible – and we could really do with a break from it all right now."

"Have you spoken with Dorothy, told her how you feel?"

"Of course. Do you know what she said, what she *actually* said? *The lady's not for turning*. I'm serious. She thinks she's another Margaret Thatcher … or even Winston Churchill. What do you think, Marnie? Am I being paranoid?"

"No."

"What does Ralph think about it all? He's always very sensible."

"Last night after we'd gone to bed he said he was worried there could be revenge attacks from both sides … for Brandon's killing and for Luther's."

"Your pillow talk has really suffered." There was no humour in Serena's voice.

"That's about as far as it goes these days," Marnie reflected.

"Yeah … same here."

After disconnecting, Marnie stood in the sunny courtyard, regretting the waste of a beautiful summer spent in conflict and anxiety. Tomorrow would be another fine warm day according to the forecast. She had not told Serena everything Ralph thought about the coming event. Lying in bed the previous night, she and Ralph had remembered the line about the *long hot summer* and *happiness being a warm gun*. Ralph remarked it had been the theme tune of the season and reminded her of another famous – *infamous* – quote, the warning from the politician Enoch Powell years ago:

The streets will run with rivers of blood …

31

Sunday morning dawned bright and clear, and all was calm in the town, at least on the surface. For the police all rest days and leave had been cancelled, and patrols had been doubled ready for a day of anticipated trouble on a big scale. Orders had been given for riot gear to be worn, and reinforcements had been drafted in from neighbouring constabularies.

It was barely light when the call came in. A disturbance in a residential area not far from the town centre, sounds of a scuffle and cries heard in an alley behind Victorian terraced houses. The woman who made the call had sounded alarmed. Had she gone out to check what had happened? Certainly not … not after the repeated police warnings to stay away from trouble. The call was as far as her civic duty was going.

A patrol car had been sent to investigate. The officers left their vehicle blocking one end of the alley and made their way slowly forwards, pressing against each back door, finding every one locked. The only features confronting them were a few wheelie bins and a skip containing builders rubble. As they drew nearer they could see something bundled between the skip and the wall. Approaching with caution they found nothing more sinister than a bicycle, a mountain bike. It was in relatively undamaged condition with no bloodstains or breakages but the paintwork was scratched and scoured. Despite that, it glowed in the shady gap into which it had been squeezed, a bright yellow.

One of the officers leaned forward to read the words printed on the frame. A trail of painted black pawprints led to the title, *Muddy Fox*.

• • • • •

Marnie stood in the doorway of the cottage and yawned. It had been a restless night, and three times she had woken to hear Estelle sobbing. Each time, she had gone to hold and comfort her, each time Estelle had gradually drifted off to sleep again, helped by the residue of sleeping draught in her veins. By some miracle, or probably through sheer mental exhaustion, Marnie too had managed to go back to sleep. Now she stood looking out on the beginning of another fine day, patting her hair, damp from the shower, with a towel as sunlight spread over the courtyard. There was perfect stillness, disturbed only by birdsong, and she paused momentarily trying to enjoy the moment, before returning to make Estelle some breakfast.

Breathing in deeply, she closed her eyes and caught the scent of the roses climbing round the door. So much that was perfect ... but so much tragedy. And the worst could be yet to come.

Opening her eyes, she saw Anne across the courtyard standing by the door to the office barn, a faint smile playing on her lips, an inquisitive raising of the eyebrows. Marnie nodded.

• • • • •

Bartlett was in the office early and immediately rang Superintendent Harris. It was no surprise that Harris was already on the job. He had arranged for his opposite number in Highways Division to keep careful watch on the approach roads to Northampton for any convoys that might be bringing anti-fascist demonstrators to the town in large numbers. Patrol cars had spotted nothing significant, and the motorway cameras had revealed no lines of coaches or even minibuses.

Bartlett was grateful for anything that fell short of disaster. "So far, so good then, sir."

"Not really, Jack. I've been on to Commander Dennison at the Met, their top man on civil disturbances. Apparently these BAN people know every trick in the book."

"Oh? Well they've still got to move large numbers to make a crowd, and when they get going we'll be able to spot them, surely."

"Not necessarily. For starters, they won't all be coming from the same place."

"We knew that, sir."

"And they won't risk travelling in convoys of coaches. They know their history. They know about the pickets whose buses were intercepted during the miners' strike and the same for animal rights demonstrators, etcetera, etcetera. You get the picture?"

"So what'll they do?"

"Easy. They'll travel in individual buses, people-carriers, minibuses, private cars. They'll choose a variety of routes, some of them coming in on minor roads for the last run into the town. Anyone stopped will say they're going shopping or just visiting friends ..."

"Or even going to the summer fete at Garfield School."

"Exactly."

"The cunning sods. They'll be too dispersed for us to catch them, and anyone we try to pick up will accuse us of police harassment. It's a lose-lose situation, sir."

"You've got it, Jack. The only way to defuse this one is to arrest everyone in sight ..."

•　•　•　•　•

Anne did not want to butt in on Marnie's efforts to console Estelle, thinking it best to let her administer TLC by herself for now. When Marnie went back into the cottage, Anne made a mug of coffee in the office kitchen area and sat at her desk to drink it, nibbling a biscuit. She had had a restless night and felt jaded.

Reaching for the coffee, she had been assailed by a yawn and mis-judged her aim, with the result that she nudged the mug and sent the liquid slopping over the brim onto the folder lying in the middle of her desk. She grabbed for a tissue and began mopping it. As a precaution, she quickly opened the flap and pulled out the papers. They were unmarked.

On the top of the collection of bills and receipts, she was looking down at Estelle's signature, a strong, confident flowing hand that seemed to taunt Anne with its irony. It was a Visa card bill for a simple lunch in a trattoria in Assisi. Anne flicked through the pile and saw that Estelle had been as punctilious as always. She read the names of the hotel, the car hire firm and the restaurants and could feel Italian sunshine rising from the paper. The receipt showed that Estelle had eaten *insalata al tonno* with a bottle of San Pellegrino mineral water and rounded off with a cappuccino. When she had signed the bill, Anne could imagine her happy and looking forward to the rest of her life, unaware of the nightmare that awaited her at home.

Anne began automatically putting the receipts in order, spotting her own signature on the fax note confirming the change of flight. The idea struck her that if Estelle had flown back on the day originally planned, perhaps the death of Luther would have been avoided. She felt a lead weight in her stomach. Staring at the fax and its chatty ending – *Hope you're having a good time, See you, Anne* – it felt to her as if she had unwittingly signed Luther's death warrant.

Anne shuddered, hastily pushed the papers back into the folder and closed it. For some minutes she sat with her head in her hands, eyes shut tight, feeling wretched that a simple change of plan could have had such tragic consequences.

The sound of the door opening and a voice speaking to her were in a distant land. Anne opened her eyes and sat up, bringing Marnie into focus, framed in the sunlit doorway.

"Sorry?"

Marnie crossed the floor quickly and knelt beside her. "Are you all right?"

"Fine."

Marnie touched her face. "You've been crying."

Anne pressed her fingers against her damp cheeks. "I didn't realise ... didn't think I had any tears left ... thought I'd used them all up."

"Anne, I can't tell you how sorry I am. It's no wonder you're feeling like this. We've all been under a huge strain."

"It's not that ... well, of course, it is ... but it was ... Estelle's travel expenses." She glanced at the folder. "She was having such a nice interesting time in Italy, never knowing what was going to happen to her

... and Luther ... their whole life together destroyed."

Marnie eased herself back. "Don't worry too much about the travel claim. I'll deal with it."

"No. It's my job."

"Then just add up the bills and let me know the total. I'll write her a cheque and we can forget all about it ... just stick it in the accounts."

"OK."

"Anne, why don't you take the day off ... go home and see your folks? You haven't been back for ages."

Anne shook her head. "No. I'm not leaving. Whatever happens today, I'm going to be here to see it through."

・　・　・　・　・

DC Cathy Lamb was driving Sergeant Marriner in the Cavalier. Bartlett had gone direct to county police headquarters for a senior officers' meeting with the Assistant Chief Constable.

Lamb cruised the streets in the town centre. For early on a summer Sunday morning there were plenty of people about and more traffic than they had expected, but no armies of demonstrators on the move. There were walkers and joggers on the old racecourse. Dogs were charging about in the sunshine, chasing sticks and balls. Everything looked normal, and Lamb began to hope that the opposing forces had had enough after two violent deaths and were pulling back from the brink.

Marriner told her to cut through to the Wellingborough Road and take the turning to Garfield Primary School. In the side streets things were quieter, though they saw several police cars patrolling, a stronger presence than usual. Turning the corner of the school site, they were immediately struck by a stepping up of activity. The playground was a-buzz with people, parked cars and vans with doors and bootlids wide open as goods and provisions were being ferried to stalls in preparation for the big event of the day.

In the middle of the bustle, across the playground, the scouts in their uniforms were assembling in lines, and as Lamb parked the car they saw the boys and young men snap to attention and salute while the union flag rose slowly up the pole to hang limply in the still air. Lamb momentarily held her breath. It was only the routine flag-raising parade, but to her it seemed as if a battle line was being drawn.

・　・　・　・　・

Anne hoped that a stroll through the spinney would help to clear her head. Even among the cool greenery she could feel it would be another hot day. A rustling in the undergrowth announced that Dolly was on her morning prowl, and the cat duly appeared, winding herself between Anne's ankles before falling into step with her on the familiar track to breakfast.

It was a morning of encounters. Anne had gone barely three paces when Ralph marched briskly across her path on his customary walk, cheeks glowing.

"How are you feeling?" he called.

"All right. You?"

"Same. What are your plans for today, Anne?"

A shrug. "To go to the summer fete and help, I suppose. Aren't we all?"

"You don't think it might be wise for you to take it easy ... after what you've been through these past few days?"

"I'll be OK. The last thing I need is to sit around on my own, moping. Better to be doing something with other people."

Ralph refrained from pointing out that the 'other people' might include New Force and the BFP. They reached the end of the spinney, and through the gap between *Sally Ann* and *Thyrsis*, Anne could see *X O 2* still tied up at her mooring.

Ralph turned to go for his shower. "I don't suppose you've heard anything from Donovan lately?"

"Not a word."

⬤ ⬤ ⬤ ⬤ ⬤

The police had cordoned off the alleyway at both ends, blocking it with cars and vans. They had roped off the area around the skip with incident tape and were giving it the full treatment of a crime scene. When Marriner and Lamb reached the barrier a photographer was systematically recording every inch of the site. Scene-of-crime officers in luminous orange jackets were inspecting every cobble at close range, two of them perched on the rim of the skip examining the contents, carefully moving aside plasterboard, broken bricks and strands of ancient electrical wiring.

The officer in charge was a detective sergeant from the town, Martin Croyland, who knew Marriner from way back and filled him in on the situation. Marriner sent a text message to Bartlett's mobile.

A uniformed constable made his way towards them, pointing over his shoulder to the end of the alley.

"Sarge ... reporters from the local rag and the radio station ... want to know what's going on."

"Surprise, surprise."

Marriner was pocketing his phone. "Must have had a tip-off."

Cathy Lamb touched his arm. "More than just a tip-off, I think." She looked up at the windows of the houses backing onto the alley. From several of them faces were peering down. "If I'm not mistaken, one of those people up there is pointing a large camera lens in our direction ... a professional?"

Sergeant Croyland grunted. "We'd better give them something to chew on before they start making up their own stories."

Marriner agreed. "Wild speculation's the last thing we need right now."

"The trouble is, what do we tell'em?"

The answer came immediately; a call from the edge of the skip.

"What is it?"

"I think you'll want to see this, sarge."

The object in question had been uncovered not far below the surface in the middle of the rubbish. It was a baseball cap, filthy, torn and badly crumpled. On the front above the peak was a shield depicting a prancing black horse on a yellow background. Like most Ferrari merchandise, the cap was red.

⬤ ⬤ ⬤ ⬤ ⬤

Anne could not remember the last time she had eaten something and actually tasted it. She went through the motions of having breakfast on *Sally Ann* with Ralph. Marnie joined them while they were listening to the radio news programme.

Ralph looked up. "Is Estelle bearing up?"

"I persuaded her to take fruit juice and a piece of toast and go back to bed. She looks strung out, but at least she's relatively calm now."

"The sleeping pill has probably –"

Ralph was interrupted by Anne suddenly extending a hand across the table. "Listen!"

They all froze.

… are investigating a skip in an alleyway less than half a mile from where Garth Brandon was murdered on Thursday. What is clear is that the police are obviously treating this as a crime scene. We know that they were phoned in the early hours of this morning by a neighbour whose house backs on to the alleyway, and who heard some kind of disturbance. We believe they've found something wedged between a skip and the boundary wall of one of the houses. What they've found is not yet known, but their attention is now focused on the skip itself. Minutes ago there was an increase in activity, one officer calling the others to examine something found in the skip. Was this the moment of discovery?

"That'll be a headline," Ralph muttered.

… are now erecting screens round the skip in an atmosphere of expectancy. We'll keep you informed of developments as they occur, but this is undoubtedly regarded by the police as an important incident. There's no official statement at present, but speculation must be that they have uncovered something very serious. Could it be another victim of the racial violence that has been rife in recent weeks?

"*Damn!*" Marnie exclaimed. "I *hate* it when they do that. Why must they *always* speculate? Don't they realise they're stirring things up … making things worse than they are already?"

Ralph nodded. "I wonder if that's possible … to make things worse than they are already."

He was soon to find out.

• • • • •

The two constables sat in their patrol car in a lay-by on the outer ring road trying to work out if what they were seeing was suspicious. Traffic was flowing steadily and mostly keeping within the speed limit. The problem was that a fair proportion of the vehicles contained three or four passengers.

"Well I think it's not normal. Look at that. Three cars in a row, all of them full."

His companion was unconvinced. "So?"

"So I'm just saying it doesn't look right. We're supposed to be watching out for anything unusual, and I'm saying it's not normal for so many cars to be full."

"It's a summer weekend. People are going out for the day … to do things."

"What things? The football season hasn't started. You don't get crowds for cricket, not cars full of supporters like that."

"Well I think this is daft. How are we supposed to know what's going on if we're not allowed to pull'em over and ask questions? You could be right. They might all be racist activists going to town to make trouble ..."

"Or *anti-racist* activists with the same idea ..."

"Right. But how are we meant to know? Do you see anyone wearing a Ku Klux Klan hood or carrying a red flag? This is *ridiculous*. We ought to be nearer to the centre. Then we could pull over any suspicious cars and check'em out."

"The guv'nor said it'd be too late then. We're supposed to be watching for coachloads of trouble-makers."

"Do you see any coaches?"

"No. So what's your point, Sherlock?"

"My point? Look, whoever we're looking for isn't going to oblige us by travelling in convoys of coaches that we can identify, stop and turn back. If there are activists coming our way, they're not giving us any help to find them. No ... we're dealing with some right clever bastards. That's my point."

• • • • •

After breakfast Marnie took Estelle's notes and sketches over to the cottage and sat in the study reading them. The problems had been handled decisively, and the scheme elaborated with Estelle's customary energy, flair and thoroughness. From time to time Marnie crossed to the other side of the landing to look in on Estelle from the half-open door. She lay on the bed, staring up at the ceiling, a pale shadow of herself.

Convinced that she had moved unnoticed, Marnie was surprised when Estelle spoke. Her voice was clear. "What happens now?"

A good question. Marnie had shied away from thinking about it. Estelle was gazing into the abyss of the rest of her life. The only consolation was that at least she would not be required to perform the identification of Luther's body. Or perhaps she needed to see him one last time to say good-bye.

Estelle interrupted her thoughts. "Marnie?"

"Oh ... well ... I think it's probably best to take one day at a time." A cliché like so many others that sprang to mind on occasions such as this. *Time will heal the pain ... your family and friends will be a great comfort ... you will have the memories of your time together; no one can take those away from you ...*

"There'll be lots of days," Estelle murmured.

"Yes. Can I get you anything?"

"No thanks."

Marnie turned to go.

"What's happening today, Marnie? Is anything planned?"

"There's the summer fete in town at the school this afternoon ... if it goes ahead."

"Are you expecting more trouble?"

"The police are expecting it, yes."

"Because of what happened to Luther?"

"Partly, perhaps."

• • • • •

While two officers carefully lifted out the chunks of rubble, a group of SOCOs sorted through it on the ground beside the skip, examining everything in minute detail. Bartlett had told Marriner and Lamb to stay at the scene in the alleyway, and Marriner watched proceedings with growing impatience. The sun was climbing, and it was hot work, the air filling with dust from mortar, bricks and plasterboard that irritated the eyes and caught the back of the throat. Marriner muttered something under his breath.

"Sorry, sarge?" Lamb asked quietly.

"I said they're bloody slow." He kept his voice low.

"Just being careful, I suppose."

"Yeah, well … If they were our blokes I'd tell 'em to get a move on. They're looking for a body not a fingerprint. And on that material they're not likely to find anything significant at all. They ought to heave out the rubbish and get at what's underneath."

Cathy Lamb did not really want to contemplate what they would find underneath, but she knew her sergeant was right. There were several tonnes of rubble to clear, and the sooner they worked through it, the better.

"Are we staying on here, sarge? I mean … until they find … whatever's there?"

Marriner nodded. "Bartlett will probably come on over once his meeting's finished. He'll put a bomb under them all right."

They jumped back as a lump of masonry was swung through the air to land on the cobbles. It disintegrated on impact, throwing up a cloud of dust and splinters of brick.

"Sorry, sarge," a voice called out from the skip.

Marriner flapped a hand in front of his face to fan away the dust. "How much more is there?"

"Too much. Bloody loads of it."

The other officer swore in the background. DS Croyland moved towards them.

"It's tough that the skip was full up. They're due to take it away on Monday. Just our luck."

"Probably why they chose it," said Marriner.

"*They*," Croyland repeated. "That's what I was thinking. It would've taken a few people a while to bury anything under that lot."

"Obviously."

"I mean … it must've been a gang. That's all I'm saying."

Cathy Lamb nodded. Marriner's eyes narrowed.

"It doesn't add up," he muttered.

"What do you mean? I thought you said …"

Marriner shook his head but did not answer.

"Ted?" said Croyland.

"It's not right, Martin."

"What isn't?"

Marriner walked away. He paced up and down before rejoining them.

"How was this reported?"

"You know how … a three nines call … one of the neighbours …"

"Saying?"

"They heard a noise like a scuffle … a disturbance … thought it was a fight …"

Marriner looked thoughtful. "It doesn't stack up."

Cathy Lamb's mouth opened wide. She understood.

"Why not?" said Croyland.

"Think about it. What scuffle? How long before the neighbour rang in?"

"She said she phoned straight away. She'd heard the Chief Constable on the radio: *report any suspicious incident at once.*"

"And how long before anyone responded?"

"There was a patrol car round the corner on the racecourse. It arrived in a couple o' minutes."

"How long have your blokes been digging?"

Sergeant Croyland pondered. "About a quarter of an ..." Enlightenment dawned. *"Bugger!"*

"Precisely. No one had any time to attack and presumably murder someone – making a noise like a scuffle – bury them in that skip and make a getaway in the time it took your car to arrive."

"So what are you saying?"

"Just that. Whatever the noise was, it wasn't what we've been thinking. It may have been made to attract attention ..."

At that moment a call rang out from the skip. They had found something.

"What is it?" called Croyland.

They peered over the edge. One of the officers was pointing. In amongst the dirt and mess they had uncovered something that was not builder's rubble. Barely visible but still distinct between the bricks and plaster was the tail of a black shirt. They had reached their goal.

"Well done, lads," said Croyland, triumphant.

Cathy Lamb looked at Marriner. He was scowling.

• • • • •

Serena parked in Garfield Road and sat staring at the playground. It looked like a film set for *Henry V*, small colourful tents pitched in a broad semi-circle like the English camp before the Battle of Agincourt. In the middle of the scene, in the title role was the figure of Dorothy Vane-Henderson in lilac twin-set and pearls, marshalling the troops, armed with clipboard and ball-point pen. Around her a small gathering of the general staff was waiting for orders, being sent off one by one to finalise the disposition of forces on the field of glory.

Beyond the central group, scouts were busy fetching and carrying, their green uniforms providing a sense of stability and purpose. On the far side of the school grounds, Serena made out the blue-and-white light-bubbles on the roof of a patrol car, its two occupants standing beside their vehicle, keeping watch.

Swinging her legs out of the car, she made her way towards Mrs Vane-Henderson, catching the crisp words of command as she drew nearer.

"Emily, I want you to make sure Priscilla hasn't put all the tombola prizes out at once. We need to keep a good number out of sight under the stall to fill in the gaps as the day goes on. Above all she must hold some bottles of wine in reserve."

Registering the arrival of Serena, she spoke to another helper who passed her something small and flat. She held out a hand in Serena's direction, and at first Serena thought she should shake it. As she reached forward she realised she was being offered a badge.

"Good morning, Serena. Nice to see you. You'll need to put this on." Her voice was a business-like staccato.

"What is it?"

"It's your official pass. You must wear it at all times."

"What for?"

"Without it you won't be allowed on any of the stalls. With it, you'll be available to help as and when needed."

"I wasn't actually planning to work on any of the –"

"Never mind. *Needs must when the devil drives*, as they say. We might all have to do things above and beyond the call of duty today. Here ... take it."

Serena did as she was told with as good a grace as she could muster, fastening it to her sweatshirt. Her name was printed in black letters beside a red star and a number.

"How are things going?"

"As you can see, everything is under control. But you'll have to excuse me now ... there's still a lot to sort out before we're finally ready for the opening ceremony."

"Opening ceremony?"

"Of course. There's always an official opening and a short speech of welcome from a prominent person."

"Sure. You've got this ... er ... Leila Ravenswood person coming, right? From the TV soap."

Mrs V-H lowered her voice, putting on a brave face. "Not actually. She's cried off. Her agent rang me last night. They consider it too dangerous ... in the circumstances."

"What about *the show must go on* ... and all that stuff?"

Mrs V-H bristled. "No back-bone."

"So which *prominent person* do you have?"

"Me." The tone of voice suggested that it should have been obvious. "Ah ... there's the band arriving. Patricia, will you go and see that they have everything they need. Greg Roberts will assign scouts to carry any instruments and music stands. They're to set up in the middle directly in front of the scouts' main tent by the flagpole."

A middle-aged woman scurried away, and Serena realised she was now dismissed as Mrs V-H turned to another helper with a list of commands. She winced as a shrill squawking sound pierced her eardrums, feedback from the public address system. It wailed out from loudspeakers that were mounted on stands ringing the playground.

Testing, testing, one two three, Mary had a little lamb ...

More deafening feedback. Serena saw another helper rushing towards the tent where the sound expert was coaxing the system into life. Serena guessed he was about to have some strongly-worded feedback from the prominent organiser that would have nothing to do with graphic equalisers. She would personally have liked to suggest something graphic that he could do with his loudspeakers – not to mention Mary and her little lamb – but contented herself with a tour of the grounds.

The scouts were mounting guard on tape barriers they had set up across the playground to cordon off the stalls. Everyone involved in the setting up was sporting a badge, with stars in different colours, no doubt depending on the status of the wearer. She wondered what was the significance of her red star. Ancillary helper? Hanger-on? Liability? It was interesting that for all the brisk confident organising of the event, Mrs V-H had given priority to the question of security.

And to underline the point, a woman without a badge, and armed only with two small children in a double buggy, was being politely but firmly escorted away by scouts, protesting that the children only wanted to look at the cuddly toys on the tombola stall.

Feeling superfluous in the face of this bustling organisation, Serena dug out her mobile. She switched on the phone for the first time that day. Words appeared on the tiny screen: *1 missed call*. She checked the voicemail, listened to a message and rang back.

"Victoria, hi, it's Serena. I got your message. What's up?"

She listened, made appropriate responses and hung up. Without delay she rang a familiar number.

• • • • •

Anne was at a loose end, unable to settle or concentrate, so she fell back on routine and set about tidying the office, starting with her own desk. She was beginning with the papers in her pending tray when Marnie crossed the courtyard and walked in.

Anne looked up. "How's Estelle?"

"Like a wrung-out dish-cloth. It's strange … she just sits there as if all feeling and emotion had been drained out of her."

"She's not got any pills, has she?"

"No. I've checked every cupboard and drawer. There's nothing."

"Her bag?"

"Ditto."

"What are we going to do … I mean about the fete today? What's Estelle going to do? We can't leave her here alone. I can stay with her if you like."

Marnie flopped onto her chair. "I must say I feel undecided. God knows what's going to happen in town today. If it weren't for the complication with Estelle, I know I'd have to be there. Other people are depending on us for support."

A warbling sound emanated from Marnie's desk, and she picked up the mobile. On the screen she read one word: *Serena*.

"Morning, Serena. How are things?"

"Marnie, listen. I've had a call from one of our organising committee, Victoria Leyland. She lives in the middle of town."

"Trouble?"

"You've heard about the skip the police are investigating? Well, her house backs onto the alley. They've found something. They've put screens up, but she's been watching them through binoculars."

"*Binoculars?*"

"Her husband does bird-watching. Anyway, they've found a cap … a red baseball cap."

"A red baseball cap," Marnie muttered. "That sounds familiar."

"And they've uncovered something else. Victoria's not sure what it is, but it's got the police really excited."

"Something buried in the skip?"

"Yes. And there's more. Something is stuck behind the skip."

"Yes, I know. It was mentioned on the radio."

"Victoria says it's something yellow ... looks like a bike."

"A yellow bike ... she's sure of that?"

"It was only a glimpse when they moved a screen to let someone in, but she couldn't think what else it could be. Marnie ... didn't Donovan have a yellow bike?"

"Yes." Marnie noticed the past tense. Serena had already reached conclusions about the situation.

"This could be more trouble, Marnie. What are your plans for today?"

"Er ... that's complicated. Estelle's in a bit of a state ... naturally. I'm not sure what's happening." There was silence at the other end. Serena was waiting. "Look, let me go and see Estelle. I'll try and talk to her. I won't let you down, Serena."

"I know."

They disconnected. Marnie turned to find Anne staring at her.

"What is it? What was that about the baseball cap and the yellow bike?"

"They may have found them in town."

"In that skip?" Anne was turning paler than ever.

"Perhaps Donovan hid them there." Marnie sounded less than convincing.

"Right." Anne sounded less than convinced. She got up and went to turn on the radio, changing the channel from national Radio Four to the local station. Pop music. She turned down the volume but left it running quietly, ready for local news updates. "Serena wants you in town?"

"Yeah."

"So now you're even more torn than before."

"What do you mean?"

"First you had Estelle to worry about, now you're worried about me ... because of the news about the yellow bike."

Marnie let out a long sigh. "I'd better go and see how Estelle's bearing up. It's decision time."

· · · · ·

Bartlett noticed the movement as soon as he began driving across town. People were thronging every pavement like a football crowd. And traffic was inordinately heavy for a Sunday morning. Cars were parked in every side street, every parking space taken. Everyone seemed to be heading in the same direction. There was no speed or sense of urgency, but a steady tide was rolling towards Garfield Road.

He pressed buttons on the mobile phone fitted to the dashboard. It was connected to a speaker, so that when Marriner answered, his voice filled the car.

"What progress, Ted?"

"Slow, sir. The SOCOs have dug down and found a black shirt. It was buried nearly two feet below the surface."

"Is that it?"

"So far."

"What's the thinking?"

Marriner lowered his voice. "The locals think there was a fight and someone's buried under the rubble."

"Is that your opinion?"

"I can't see how anyone had time to bury a body under all that lot and make a getaway before the patrol car arrived ... a couple of minutes later."

"Which means?"

"I'm not really sure, sir. Are you coming over?"

"I'm on my way. The traffic's choc-a-bloc, and half the county seems to be on the streets. What's it like where you are?"

"Can't get much impression down here, but there's a crowd at each end of the alleyway."

"I'll be there as soon as I can. Any developments ... ring me at once."

He was tempted to clamp the blue light on the roof and turn on the siren, but the Chief Constable had ordered a low-key presence for as long as possible. He had the fan on full, and the car was starting to smell of exhaust fumes drawn in from the other traffic. This was one more day that summer when he wished he had air conditioning.

• • • • •

Estelle followed Marnie out of the cottage, and even from where Anne was sitting, going through the accounts, it was obvious they were in heated discussion. It was also clear that Estelle's usual spark of energy was extinguished. Marnie came first through the door.

"I hear what you say, Estelle, but I think you need rest more than anything else. You shouldn't even be out of bed in my opinion."

"I've been in bed forever, Marnie." Her protest was in a dull expressionless voice.

Marnie sat Estelle down at her desk. "You sit here and I'll make coffee."

"Oh –" Anne started to get up. Marnie gestured to her to stay in her seat. "But, Marnie, I haven't washed up the cups yet. I'm disorganised this morning."

"Never mind. I'll do them while the kettle boils. Let's just all relax, OK?"

Anne settled back and smiled faintly across at Estelle. She was on the edge of her emotions and feared that if Estelle asked her about finding Luther, she would flood the office with tears.

"Hi, Anne." She glanced at the papers on Anne's desk. "You keeping the show on the road as usual?"

"Yeah."

"Is that my travel folder you've got there?"

"I took it from the car ... one less thing for you to worry about."

Estelle took a couple of deep breaths, blinking. Anne felt a lump rise in her throat.

"If there's anything you need, Anne, just let me know." Estelle's voice was low and hesitant.

"It's OK, everything's here. I'm just going to total it all up and file it. I'll write a cheque for Marnie to sign."

Grateful to have something to occupy her, Anne finished putting the receipts and slips into chronological order on the desk and opened the spreadsheet program on her computer. In the background Marnie was spooning ground coffee into the pot, and the kettle was humming. Anne chewed her lip. Nothing seemed to be going right for her that morning. Even the simplest of tasks was confusing her.

"Problem?" said Estelle.

"What? ... oh ... no ... I seem to have mixed up your baggage tag and boarding card with the ticket stubs. I'm all fingers and thumbs. What with the change of flight, I've got everything jumbled up. I'll just sort these through."

"I would've done that before giving them to you."

"Don't worry. I'll get it right ... sooner or later."

The smell of fresh coffee wafted across the room, and Marnie brought the tray over to the desks.

"Black without for you, Estelle ... white without for Anne ... black for me." She sat on the corner of Anne's desk. There was an awkward silence.

"I expect you've made plans ..." Estelle began. "It's the summer fete today, isn't it?"

"Well ... yes ... but I'm not sure –"

"You have to be there, Marnie."

"It's not as simple as that."

"You mean I'm a complication."

"You're not a complication."

"But?"

"But ... you are a factor. Of course."

"Is that all? Why don't you just go into town and join in the fun. I'll be all right here. I'm not going to do anything stupid, Marnie, if that's what you're thinking."

"Fun? Estelle, *fun* isn't quite the right word."

"What is?"

"Look ... it's complicated."

"Spell it out. I'm a big girl, I'll understand."

Marnie paused. "Since Brandon was killed, things have gone bad ... much worse than they were before. There could be real danger. And now both sides of the political divide ... extremists ... are threatening trouble ..."

"You mean ... Luther's death has made matters worse?"

Marnie stared into her cup. "It looks that way."

"They're going to need someone with a cool head like you in town today, Marnie. You've got to be there."

"I'm not leaving you, Estelle. The presence – or absence – of one solitary woman isn't going to influence things that much."

"Don't you believe it. It could make all the difference."

Anne carefully clipped the travel receipts and tickets together, slipped them inside the folder and wrote a figure on a yellow post-it note. She stuck it on the flap for Marnie's attention.

"That's decided, then," said Estelle. "You're going into town ... and I'm coming with you."

• • • • •

Bartlett stood looking into the skip, exuding frustration. His impatience had transmitted itself to the SOCOs, who were working faster, heaving rubble out over the side with jerky movements. They had cleared half the contents and were sweating in their all-enveloping tunics. DS Croyland was fretting in the background, aware of Bartlett's greater experience, but worried they might be damaging evidence, compromising a crime scene.

Bartlett stomped back to Marriner and Lamb. "Ridiculous!" he growled. "It'd take a gang of navvies to bury anything that deep. What's been going on here?"

"Beats me," said Marriner. "The neighbour insists she rang as soon as she heard the shouting."

"She described it as like someone calling out for help," Cathy Lamb added.

"Did she say how many voices she heard?"

Marriner pursed his lips. "I'm not sure. Martin talked to her."

Bartlett called to DS Croyland to join them. He repeated his question.

"She just said she heard someone crying out. It sounded as if he was being attacked or chased. Then there was a clattering sound and the shouting stopped suddenly. She made the three nines call straight away."

"Sergeant, what's your assessment of the situation here? Are you assuming someone was attacked, probably murdered and concealed in the skip?"

"It would appear to fit the facts, sir."

"Where's the body?"

Croyland half-turned his head in the direction of the skip. "So far we've recovered some clothing ... a baseball cap and a black shirt."

"Exactly. You think *they* had time to undress the body for some reason as well as hide it?"

"Well ... do you think we should stop searching, sir?"

"That's the point. Now that we've started, we have to go on. Right?"

"Yes, sir." Croyland looked as if his approach was finally being vindicated.

"And that's what we're supposed to be doing."

"Sorry?"

"My assessment," Bartlett began, "is that we've found all there is to be found in that skip."

"But you said –"

"I know what I said. But unless I'm very much mistaken, there isn't a body concealed under that rubbish."

"There wasn't enough time to conceal it," Marriner added.

"No, Ted, there wasn't. This isn't the scene of a murder. It's a smoke screen. For what purpose, I don't know. Or it's possible that it may be a signal of some kind. Either way, we're wasting time here."

• • • • •

Marnie had the local BBC station playing on the car radio to catch news bulletins as they headed towards the town. The intermittent pop music intruded a festive atmosphere in the Discovery that was out of place. Anne was in the back, gazing out over meadows and woods that were basking in brilliant sunshine under a cloudless sky. A heat haze was blurring the horizon. While they travelled they were immune from the temperature, the car's air-conditioning humming along with the music. Estelle was in the front passenger seat, her head tilted back against the restraint, eyes closed. At intervals Marnie shot glances in her direction. She had never known Estelle so quiet.

Ralph had stayed behind, delayed at the last minute by a lengthy phone call from America. He would join them later.

The last bars of *American Pie* faded out, Don McLean describing everyone's feelings on the day the music died, and it was time for a news update. Marnie touched the button to raise the volume.

There are tailbacks reported on the eastbound A45 south of Northampton where a collision has blocked the overtaking lane near the Brackmills junction. Motorists are advised to slow down in good time and are warned to expect delays for at least the next hour.

Otherwise traffic is reported as heavy on all roads into the town, so if you're visiting friends, going to the county cricket ground or wanting to join in the fun at the summer fete at Garfield Primary School, the authorities are advising that you allow plenty of time for your journey.

The latest position on the police investigation in the town centre is that officers are continuing to examine a skip that was the centre of a disturbance in the early hours of this morning. They are not yet prepared to make a formal statement, but it's understood they have recovered some articles of clothing and also a yellow bicycle that appears to have been abandoned.

Meanwhile there's a heavy police presence in town, with officers once again brought in from neighbouring forces. The cause of the extra activity is concern that further trouble will break out following the assassination of Britain First Party leader, Garth Brandon, on Thursday and the suspicious death of Mr Luther Curtiss in Cosgrove on Friday. Police are not saying that one death led to the other at this stage, but neither are they denying that there could be a connection between the two incidents. Common to both cases, however, is the fact that there are few clues as to who carried out the killings and no witnesses able to give an accurate description of the perpetrators.

The Chief Constable has appealed for calm amid mounting tension in the Afro-Caribbean community and the threat of further demonstrations and reprisals from far-right organisations. The one hopeful sign so far is that there have been no sightings of transport bringing potential troublemakers into the area.

At the county ground Northamptonshire are entertaining Yorkshire in the third round of the Benson and Hedges Cup. Play is underway after the home side won the toss and opted to bat. We're going over to the match where Rob Murray is reporting.

Marnie turned down the volume, calculating how to avoid the tailback on the southern by-pass that was her chosen route.

"Take the motorway north when we reach the M1." Anne was speaking from the rear.

Marnie looked in the mirror. "You're reading my thoughts. The motorway, you think?"

"We can go up to the next junction and come in from the west. It's further, but we'll avoid the bottleneck that way. You'll just have to cut through town."

"That makes sense."

"Incidents." This time it was Estelle, her voice quiet and husky.

"Sorry?" Marnie was straining to hear.

Estelle cleared her throat. "He said ... *incidents*." Her eyes were still closed. "A man loses his life – that was full of promise and fulfilment – and they call it an *incident*."

"It's awful, I know," said Marnie. "But to the media everything is probably regarded as an *incident*."

"It makes it sound as if Luther's whole life only happened so he could become an item in a news bulletin." She breathed in deeply and sniffed. "I know the person who did it will relive that moment over and over for the rest of their life."

"If they have any conscience," Marnie added.

· · · · ·

Mrs Vane-Henderson had lost her composure. It was a rare occurrence in a life where order and discipline, especially self-discipline, were watchwords. Now, in the middle of organising the summer fete, she found herself confronted by uncompromising forces brought into play by her own actions.

The improbable first inkling that all was not as it should be came with a cry from the information desk. Jackie Brice, seasoned campaigner that she was, was standing her ground face to face with a group of black youths. Arms were being waved in jerky movements, voices were raised, fingers were being pointed at her.

Thrusting her clipboard at the nearest helper with a brusque *Hold the fort*, Mrs V-H marched across the playground, chin held high, elbows pumping. No one got in her way. She arrived at the same time as Greg Roberts, the scout master.

"What's going on?"

The Voice of Authority brought the argument to a sudden halt for some seconds. Then everyone started talking at once.

"Dorothy, I have tried to explain to these young men –"

"We're not taking this shit, no way –"

"You said this was a fete for everyone, and we've got a right to be here. We want a stand too –"

"A community event, you said it was, and we're the community as much as anyone else, so –"

"Where's Serena? We want to talk to her. We thought she was in charge here –"

Rapid movement followed by the shrill and piercing blast on the whistle took everyone by surprise, including Greg Roberts, whose whistle it was. Mrs V-H had turned swiftly towards him, yanked the whistle from his breast pocket and produced a sound that would have brought a Wembley Cup Final to an end. Greg jumped. Everyone within ten metres winced at the interminable piercing noise. All movement stopped across the playground.

Mrs V-H pointed at Jackie Brice. "You go first ... while the rest of us listen." She enunciated every word through clenched teeth, glaring at the youths. "... without a sound."

"These lads came onto the playground demanding a stall. They had no security badges so the scouts asked them to leave until the fete was officially opened."

"Asked them *politely*," Greg added, quickly closing his mouth at A Look from Mrs V-H.

"Is that it?"

Jackie nodded. "Yes. Your instructions were very clear, Dorothy , and –"

"Yes, all right. I get the picture." She turned to the gang of youths. "Well?"

They all began again simultaneously. Mrs V-H raised the whistle towards her lips and silence instantly fell on the group.

She pointed at the nearest boy, who seemed to be the ringleader. "You ... what's your name?"

"Winston."

Mrs V-H look startled. "Er ... well ... Winston ... can you speak for your friends?"

"You know the score. It's like Jackie said. We want a stall to put up our sh– ... our stuff. We just get here and the scouts start hustling us out. We didn't do nothin' wrong ... we been here every day on the playscheme ... you know we have ..."

"Buzz nearly got himself killed by them thugs," another interjected, only to be silenced by a raised finger from Mrs V-H.

"And what is your ... er ... *stuff*?"

They began unrolling banners in the cheerful warm colours of the Jamaican flag, some of them bearing smiling portraits of Bob Marley. One boy held up a ghetto blaster, a box of tapes and CDs swinging from his shoulder.

"I tried to explain we didn't have any spare stalls, "Jackie Brice began. "But they wouldn't take no for an answer."

"No isn't an answer," Winston said firmly. "No way. We came here to join in, and now you're saying we got no rights. We live here, man. We all went to this school when we was kids. Did you?"

"That's not quite the point ... Winston." Mrs V-H seemed to have difficulty addressing him by his name.

"Then what is the point?" Behind him, the others were murmuring agreement.

"Dorothy, may I have a word with you?" It was a quiet voice. No one had noticed Serena arriving unobtrusively on the edge of the group.

"Not just now, Serena, I'm talking to these young men."

"Dorothy, just a word ... please."

"In a minute." Mrs V-H spoke with emphasis. "As you can see, I'm dealing with a situation here."

Serena raised her voice. "And you're not dealing with it very well."

All sound stopped. Every eye turned first towards Serena, then to Dorothy for her reaction. It was a simple response. Her mouth opened and no words came out. Serena moved forward, took her by the elbow and walked her a few steps away, speaking to her in a whisper.

"*What* are you doing, Dorothy?"

"*Doing?* I'm trying to organise the summer fete so that everything runs smoothly ... as my events always do."

"And do you have plans for unexpected eventualities ... like the local community wanting to be involved in their own event?

"Serena, there is only a limited number of stalls. Have you *any* idea how much effort goes in to getting all this kind of ..." Her voice tailed off. "Stupid thing to say ... sorry ... of course you have. The summer scheme's your work, and it's a brilliant success. I just meant –"

"I know what you meant, Dorothy, but the key to that success is involving all the community. Come on, let's find some space for these boys and their music."

They turned back to the others, but the damage had been done. The boys were gone, taking their banners, their tapes and CDs and their goodwill with them.

"Winston," Dorothy muttered under her breath.

• • • • •

A horn sounded impatiently, and Marnie knew she was in the wrong. She had gone through the lights on amber, only to find herself blocking the oncoming lanes as she tried to make a right turn. The traffic in front of her had come to an abrupt halt with the Discovery straddling the highway. She raised a hand in a feeble gesture of guilt. She could almost hear the comments from the other cars around her about women drivers – especially the four-wheel-drive brigade – and she guessed that most of them were not sitting cocooned in air-conditioned comfort like her.

"I shouldn't have done that," she murmured.

Estelle opened her eyes and stared at the packed ranks of the other vehicles. "What day is it?" She sounded bewildered.

"Sunday."

"Why all the traffic?"

"That's what they were talking about on the radio. I must admit, I never expected it to be like this."

"It can't be normal."

Anne chimed in from behind them. "Some of the traffic may be coming this way to avoid the hold-up on the by-pass, like us."

"True," Marnie agreed.

"They said there was a heavy police presence, too," said Estelle. "I wonder ..."

"What?"

"Have you noticed how many cars are full? That isn't usual."

She was right. And more to the point, most of them were full of men. All three sat up in their seats and studied the other cars. Marnie was able to ease the Discovery forward by a length, clearing the lanes just as the lights turned back to red. She tried not to think of the bad feeling she had generated among her fellow drivers, and concentrated instead on trying to identify potential trouble.

"There's a sticker in the back window of that car there," said Anne, indicating a Mondeo ahead of them. "Some kind of slogan."

As they focused on it, they became aware that the four occupants were Asians. It occurred to all of them at the same time that this might be part of a backlash against the far right.

"Can you read what's on the sticker?" said Estelle.

"Not from here."

The cars began rolling forward, bringing them closer to the Mondeo. Marnie strained against the seatbelt, her chin over the steering wheel. Breathing out audibly with relief, she settled back in the seat.

"False alarm. It reads: *Cricket – watch Yorkshire.*"

"They've probably driven down from Bradford or somewhere for the match," Estelle said.

They were now rolling steadily but slowly. There were crowds of people thronging the pavements on both sides, heading towards the town centre, nearly all of them men. It reminded her of the time she had ill-advisedly driven across north London on Cup Final day, through streets clogged by battalions of Arsenal and Manchester United fans. Staring at the cars beside her, she was aware that her interest was being returned. The passengers, white men this time, in a Peugeot that was slowly edging past them were smiling up at her. In normal circumstances she would have ignored their attentions, but wanting to create a friendlier atmosphere than she had managed so far in the town traffic, she smiled back briefly before returning to watching the road ahead.

"Did you see those men smiling at you, Marnie?" Anne asked from behind her.

"Yes. I thought it was an improvement on the drivers back at the traffic lights."

"Take another look. They're going past now."

The Peugeot was picking up speed. Marnie glanced sideways. It looked clean and shiny, fairly new. Her gaze fell on the number-plate; sure enough, it was that year's model. Then she spotted the rear bumper. In the middle, positioned with care and pride, was a sticker, the flag of the Confederate States of America, much loved by segregationists and the Ku Klux Klan.

"Great. So now I'm big buddies with the redneck right."

At the next set of traffic lights Marnie made sure she did not over-run and rolled obediently to a stop in the front rank. The Peugeot had sped on its way, to her relief. Estelle closed her eyes again and leaned back. In the rearview mirror Marnie could see Anne observing their surroundings with intense interest, her head turning from side to side.

"What is it, Anne?"

"Just looking."

She was not just looking. Marnie followed her example, closely watching the people crossing the road. There was something about them. They were mostly walking in small groups, many with bags over their shoulders as if carrying provisions for a picnic. But this was no holiday crowd. The lights changed to red and amber, and Marnie eased forward. Initially the marchers showed no inclination to stop walking. Suddenly men were holding back the tide, spreading their arms at the kerbside, stopping others from continuing against the pedestrian red light.

"Oh God," Marnie murmured.

In her mind she saw another crowd of pedestrians in another city, black leather jackets, black jeans, heavy boots, the banners of an army on the move. She remembered Leicester all those weeks ago on the day of the riots, the first time she had encountered the massed ranks of New Force heading into action.

Behind her, a horn sounded impatiently.

• • • • •

"There's a parking space over there …" DCI Bartlett shifted in his seat. "If we can ever get round this corner."

"Where, sir?" Cathy Lamb was at the wheel of the grey Cavalier. They had opted to travel together in one car.

"Where that van pulled out, behind the white estate car."

"I see it. We're stuck for the moment, sir, until the traffic moves forward."

"This is where they were all coming," Marriner observed. "Look at them. There must be hundreds …"

"Quite a few are families come for the fete," said Lamb. "They're not all troublemakers. I can see children in amongst them."

Bartlett pointed. "I hope to God they've got reinforcements here. There are clusters of black youths down there. It's only a matter of time before they make contact with the far-right mob."

Even from their position at the end of the road, they could see that the main school site was already full to overflowing, with crowds extending into the side streets, and more and more people arriving by the second.

"Oh damn!" Marriner was shaking his head. "Just our luck. There's another car coming up the road. It's going to get that parking space."

"I'll pull up onto the pavement when we get off the main road, sarge. No one's going to give us a ticket."

Bartlett groaned. "Typical."

"What is, sir?" said Marriner.

"Don't you recognise the car that's pinching our space … dark blue Discovery … haven't you seen it somewhere before? Marnie Walker … I might've known it …"

• • • • •

Dorothy Vane-Henderson was telling her team of acolytes that she thought the turnout was encouraging. Serena, who had noted the large number of young white males on one side of the grounds and young blacks on the other, wondered if Mrs V-H inhabited a parallel universe. In her role as 'prominent person' she had just emerged from the school where she had changed, refreshed make-up and tidied her hair in the staff cloakroom in readiness for appearing at the microphone to perform the official opening.

Her concession to the informal ethos of modern times was that she was not wearing a hat or gloves. Serena had urged her to follow the dress code appropriate to the occasion, which she described as 'cool casual'. Mrs V-H stood ready for action in a pale blue summer dress with a Liberty floral pattern and a single row of pearls. Beside her, Serena waited wearing a loose silk tunic comprising a scooped top and flared trousers in the shade of cream that made her skin glow.

Marnie, Estelle and Anne pushed their way through the crowd and were admitted into the cordoned-off enclosure by the scouts who required no official badges to recognise the trio.

"It's going to be a big success." Dorothy beamed at them. Her eyes fell on Estelle, and she touched her arm. "So brave of you to be here, my dear. Stiff upper lip."

Serena was studying the crowd. "It's certainly a big turn-out. Let's just hope they're holidaymakers out for some harmless fun. We could do with a break."

"Something else gone wrong?" asked Marnie.

Serena rolled her eyes discreetly towards Dorothy. "We've had a slight altercation with some of our younger friends. They weren't allowed to install a DJ with reggae music, so they walked out in a huff."

Marnie pulled a face. "No chance of getting them back?"

"It was all my fault," Dorothy interjected. "I was too bound up in sorting out the last-minute details. I wish we could persuade them somehow to return to the fold."

Anne suddenly stood up on tip-toe, staring into the distance. "I can see Otis and Louis. They're over there near the shop. There's a bunch of them."

"Is Winston there?"

"Er … yes … and Rodney … and a few others."

Dorothy sighed, looking at her watch.

"When do you open the fete?" said Marnie.

"At noon. Ten minutes."

"Otis has got his ghetto-blaster, "said Anne. "I bet he'd do his stuff if we asked him. Shall I go and see?"

"What do you think, Marnie?" Dorothy took her arm. "I always think a band goes down well at the start … creates the right sort of atmosphere. Perhaps we could have the … er … reggae music, is it called? … once the fete is in full swing … to jazz it up a little. Wouldn't that be a good compromise?"

"I suppose so, especially as you've got the band in place now."

Marnie turned to Anne. But Anne had gone, threading her way through the crowd, that was growing increasingly impatient and uncomfortable in the hot sun.

Marnie felt uneasy. "Estelle, did you see where Anne went? She was standing beside you a moment ago."

Estelle looked as if she was finding it hard to focus. "What? Oh … I think she muttered something and went off to see somebody." She breathed in deeply. "Look … is there anywhere I can go for a breather. I'm feeling a bit –"

"Have a seat over there, dear," said Dorothy. "Jackie, take Estelle and sit her down by the information desk." She lowered her voice. "She's a bit peaky … hardly surprising … she's putting up a very brave front."

Meanwhile, Marnie was scanning the multitude and thought she caught sight of Anne's blonde head in the distance, making slow progress towards the black boys. Unaware of her approach, they were moving along the pavement away from her. Marnie was far from reassured at locating Anne; she was nearing a group of young white men with closely shaven heads and black T-shirts.

• • • • •

Cathy Lamb made the turn into the side street and eased the Cavalier between the pedestrians walking on the road. Like everyone else, she was only inching forward and trying to contain her impatience.

"Try not to kill more than about a dozen, Cathy," Marriner said cheerily.

"It looks bad when you file your report ... spoils the Chief Constable's statistics."

"Women and children first, sarge?" Cathy replied.

"Just park the bloody car." Bartlett was fuming in the back. "We can save the double act for the Christmas party ... assuming we survive that long."

"Yes, sir." Cathy would have rolled her eyes, but she knew Bartlett could see them in the rear-view mirror.

Trying not to alarm the crowd, she opened the window, attached the blue lamp to the roof and signalled her intention to ease the car onto the pavement. The throng parted at the sight of the flashing police lamp, and she was able to bump up the kerb to bring the car to a halt with two wheels on the edge.

"Good thinking," said Bartlett. "But don't leave the lamp on the roof. Some yob's bound to pinch it as a trophy."

When they were out of the car, Bartlett decided they would stay together as a group, working their way to the back of the crowd so as to gain the best view of the whole proceedings. Initially they made good progress, with people knowing they were police officers giving them room to pass. But within a minute they were absorbed into the mass and had to fend for themselves, each of them wishing they were wearing lighter clothing.

• • • • •

Anne had the impression that the further she penetrated into the crowd, the further away the black boys were going. Otis had the ghetto-blaster on his shoulder, and it was a good marker to aim at, but it seemed to be receding at a quicker rate than she could manage. Desperate measures, she decided. The aim was to get to the boys, not make friends with the crowd. There was nothing for it but to put her head down and barge through. For the first few steps it worked well and the mass parted. But when she raised her head to check on range and bearings, she had a surprise. It was like wading into a pack of alligators. On lunch break. The faces glaring at her showed real hatred, that turned to curiosity and finally recognition.

"Goin' somewhere? In a hurry are yer?"

They closed ranks around her. Too terrified to speak, she looked from one to another. Skinheads all, in black T-shirts and heavy boots. She could smell their sweat and wondered if they could smell her fear. She had butted her way into the centre of a New Force gang.

"Where's your boyfriend, nigger-lover?" A low, ugly growl.

"I don't know what you mean." It was a lame reply, but the best she could do.

"We done 'im in, din't we?" Another snarling voice.

"*Shut up!*" the first one snapped.

Anne tried arrogance. "Excuse me, I want to get past."

Arrogance was obviously not flavour of the month. Two of the thugs grabbed her elbows, their fingers digging into the bones so that she gasped in agony. *Why wasn't anybody helping her out of this mess?* The people nearest to the group were pressing forward, no one paying attention to the undesirables who had formed into a bunch at the back of the crowd. Anne took a deep breath to scream blue bloody murder, but a hand clamped itself over her mouth, an odour like engine grease filling her nostrils, rough fingers tightly pinching her narrow jaw. All her upper body was contorted with pain. She wanted to bite the hand, but moving her mouth was impossible. Tears came into her eyes. Her head was going to explode.

• • • • •

Marnie was feeling highly uneasy. Anne had been gone for several minutes and had not been seen since she plunged into the crowd. Greg Roberts was showing Dorothy Vane-Henderson which button to press on the microphone to make it work. Behind them, Estelle was sitting by the information desk looking blank and desolate. Serena was twitching with impatience, her breath a series of short audible exhalations. She took Mrs V-H by the elbow.

"Dorothy, why don't we get started now? It's near enough time. What are you waiting for ... the noonday gun?"

Dorothy looked at her watch and sighed. "Oh well ... yes ... I suppose it is almost time."

"And it *is* very hot," Serena added.

Dorothy turned to the scout master. "Everything clear, Greg? When I finish my speech of welcome, I'll nod in your direction and you'll get the band to strike up. OK?"

"Fine."

"Good. Then let's get started."

Dorothy stepped up to the microphone. There was a short whistle from the loudspeakers that quietened the spectators. Heads craned forward to see who was going to speak. A rumour had been running through the crowd that the fete was to be opened by a star from a television soap opera, and a frisson of disappointment rippled across the playground as Dorothy stood at the microphone.

"Ladies and gentlemen ... and children, of course, welcome to the Garfield summer fete. It is a pleasure to see you all here on this beautiful day. Thank you so much for coming. Before I declare the fete open, I would like to thank my fellow committee-members for all their ..."

Dorothy droned on in predictable fashion. Serena nudged Marnie and spoke softly into her ear.

"Did you see that? Right over there at the back near the corner shop ... some sort of disturbance ... police were involved."

A police van was parked near the corner, and Marnie could see blue uniforms around it. Beyond the sound from the loudspeakers she thought she could hear the wail of an ambulance approaching. Her stomach turned over in panic. *Where the hell was Anne?*

Dorothy was in full swing.

"... and without their tireless dedication, none of this would have been possible ..."

Serena stood on tip-toe. "Look, Marnie ... over there ..."

"Is it Anne?"

"No, but I can see that ghetto-blaster. That's where she was going, right? To get the boys back."

Marnie frowned. "But they weren't right over there. Oh God ..."

"What?"

"She was heading towards the back where the police are."

• • • • •

They began dragging her away, and still no one seemed to take the slightest notice. In the middle of the gang she was probably invisible to the outside world.

"You're not gettin' away this time, bitch. We got plans for you."

Anne knew that round the corner was an alleyway. Once they got her into it, she had no chance of getting out in one piece. She made a huge effort to wrench herself free. Result: the hand squeezed tighter round her face, the fingers dug deeper into her arms, a fist crashed into her stomach. She almost gagged as the breath was knocked out of her body.

For a second the grip over her mouth loosened as reflexes made her double up, retching and gasping, vision blurred, her head spinning. Close to collapse, instinct told her to fight for survival. She yelled, but the sound was cut off by the hand tightening again. She was certain that to feel more pain was impossible. She was wrong. From behind, a hand gripped the back of her neck like the pincers of a giant crab. It squeezed. Her whole body went rigid. A bolt of lightning flashed up and down her spine, and blinding lights exploded in her head. She was on the brink of passing out, all resistance crushed. Whatever they had in mind for her, it was going to happen.

Bizarrely she saw the face of Donovan floating in the air, heard the crack of a pistol, smelled cordite, saw blood spurting. But she knew it was an illusion, knew for certain that he had suffered the same fate they were planning for her. Probably with one slight difference; being a girl offered an extra dimension. She did not care any more, no longer inhabited her body but was merely a spectator. Vision returned. They had almost reached the corner. Two minutes at most and they would be in the alleyway. At the turning they stopped. Some kind of blockage was barring the way. For a millisecond Anne hoped for an intervention that would save her. Too bad. She heard a woman's voice somewhere in another world.

"Stop that!"

"*Sod off!*" A hand brushed the woman aside as if swotting a fly. Light reflected from a knife blade.

Anne prayed the woman would have the sense to get out of their way. It was too late to help her now. Over the shoulders of the gang she could see the top of her head. The grip on Anne's mouth and arms eased at this new distraction. The ringleader turned his attention on the woman, who was trying to help when everyone else passed by. The situation called for a do-or-die effort. Anne arched her back and kicked out with both feet, trying to hit the ringleader in the back and at least give the woman time to get away. She missed. But one foot caught him in the back of the knee, and he went down off balance, listing to one side, performing a strange bob-curtsy. At that moment the woman raised her arm in a curious Nazi-style salute. But the hand kept moving, rigid and fast, straight fingers flying like a rocket till they connected with the gang leader's exposed throat. His eyes bulged, mouth opened and his tongue spilled out with a croaking sound. He pitched forward and fell to his knees out of Anne's sight. There was an ominous crack as his head struck the pavement.

"Police!" yelled the woman.

"Where?" said the thug nearest to her, releasing Anne's mouth to grab at the attacker.

Instead of retreating, the woman moved forward, risking the all-enveloping grasp of her opponent. The unexpected reaction seemed to unsettle him and in hesitating he lost the initiative. The woman smashed her knee into his groin, and the thug buckled up. Feeling the pressure ease on her neck, Anne took her cue from the woman and remembered a judo lesson from long ago. She stamped down on the instep of her oppressor and heard him grunt with pain. One of her arms was released by a thug wanting to take his chance with the woman, and Anne rammed her freed elbow hard behind her. Another grunt.

All this movement gave Anne a clear view of her rescuer for the first time. It was Cathy Lamb. And suddenly she was not alone. Bartlett and Marriner raced up to join her with a pack of uniformed officers, each brandishing a truncheon. Anne pulled clear of the skinheads and was caught by Lamb, the two of them holding on to each other, both shaking. They were dimly aware that the New Force gang were not offering resistance. The ringleader appeared barely conscious, lying on his side in a foetal position with blood pouring from his head. The other victim of Lamb's assault was on his knees, clutching his groin, throwing up in the gutter.

"You all right, Cathy?" Marriner put his hands on their shoulders. "Anne?"

Anne tried to nod and regretted it. Lamb smiled weakly.

While handcuffs were being fastened and the gang led away, Bartlett came over.

"I told you not to charge off like that, Lamb. Someone might've got hurt." He looked at the two injured thugs and smiled. "They were lucky we were here to protect'em. Well done."

Lamb was breathing heavily. "I'm glad all that martial arts training wasn't wasted. And what about Anne here, sir? That was a pretty impressive performance."

Bartlett put an arm around Anne. She was bent forward, her hands on her knees. Through the thin T-shirt he could feel how slightly-built she was.

"You were brilliant. You made all the difference, you know that?"

"Where did you learn that technique?" Marriner asked.

Anne looked up, gasping. "We did it at school ... self-defence for girls ... I got a B for the practical."

The officers were smiling when Bartlett's mobile began to ring.

• • • • •

"And so, ladies and gentlemen ... and children, of course, it gives me great pleasure to declare the Garfield summer fete open."

A half-hearted cheer and a desultory round of applause went up from the crowd as Dorothy nodded at Greg. He signalled to the bandmaster, and the air was assailed by the blast of music. Suddenly all was festive. The long wait was forgotten, the spectators became participants and the holiday atmosphere was underway. The scouts removed the tape barriers and stood down from their posts as the crowd surged forward to reach the stands.

Marnie immediately made to take off into the throng, but Serena held her back.

"Where are you *going*?"

"I've got to find Anne."

"Not a good idea, Marnie."

"What are you talking about I've got –"

"Listen." Serena cocked her head to one side. "You hear that noise? You know what it is."

Over the sound of the band, another noise was growing. From one side of the grounds a chant was swelling, a deep ugly growl. *New Force ... New Force ... New Force ... New Force ...*

"You can't just waltz off into that lot, Marnie."

"But Anne –"

"She's a resourceful girl. She'll have taken shelter somewhere. Marnie, *think!*"

Punctuating the chants they could hear shouts and screams from the people who had come for the fete. Children were crying. Ice creams lay abandoned on the dusty ground. Parents were running with their children, shielding their heads with their hands, scooping up the smallest in their arms and rushing about, desperate to find refuge from the battle that would erupt at any moment.

Marnie turned to Dorothy and Greg. "Get the school open. People can shelter in there. *Hurry!*"

Greg needed no second telling. He turned to his lieutenants, firing off instructions. In seconds they were speeding away to spread the word among the other scouts. Dorothy's helpers were likewise spurred into action, joining Marnie and Serena in herding the nearest families towards the school entrance doors. Parents began stumbling in to claim the sanctuary of the building.

Aside from this frenzied action Estelle stood, her back against the wall, devoid of all feeling, as if disconnected from everything that was going on. The rising noise of the chanting, the unfurling of New Force banners, bricks, stones and bottles flying through the air, the whiff of smoke bombs. Police men and women, some in yellow jerkins, some in riot gear, others in shirtsleeves were forcing their way between the would-be combatants. All of this mayhem was beyond her grasp, and she leaned back letting it wash over her like a drowning person who has given up all hope of survival.

Out of the crowd Bartlett and Marriner appeared, dragging Cathy Lamb between them.

"Good idea ..." Bartlett gasped. "... getting them in the school ... shelter ... Ted, Cathy, see what you can do to help round people up."

"Can your officers keep the two sides apart?" said Serena.

"God knows. I've called up reinforcements, but ..." He shrugged. "It's a big town. This isn't the only disturbance. Those bastards are clever. There are incidents all over the place. Stop one and another happens somewhere else."

"Did you see Anne?" Marnie looked worried. "She went off looking for some black boys."

"She didn't find them. Some of those thugs found her."

"What happened?" Marnie was on the verge of panic. "Where is she?"

"She was just behind us. We rescued her – well, it was Cathy who did it – but Anne gave as good as she got."

"And?"

"We arrested them ... all of them."

"And Anne's all right?"

"A bit shaken, but she got through."

"Where is she now?"

"Can't be far behind."

Marnie peered into the crowd, her unease mounting. "You didn't bring her with you?"

"She was literally just behind us."

They all scanned the playground. Clusters of parents and children were still streaming away from the conflict towards the safety of the school. But of Anne there was no sighting.

"Where *is* that girl?" Marnie muttered through clenched teeth.

Serena touched her arm. "Marnie, don't worry. Just be patient. She'll be fine. Anne's sensible. She wouldn't take any risks."

• • • • •

Anne plunged through the ranks of New Force, praying that her blonde hair would be her passport and that no one else would recognise her. She had been following in the wake of her police rescuers when a cacophony of sounds made her hesitate. All around her the skinheads were chanting the war-cry in their habitual low growl, but somewhere beyond them a different sound was straining to be heard. She stopped, scarcely aware of the thugs dodging about, hurling stones and empty beer cans towards the police and the young blacks beyond them.

The new sound was music. It was lilting and rhythmic with a compelling beat. *Reggae!* Otis and his ghetto-blaster were putting up resistance with the only means they had against the raucous barking of New Force.

Idiots! she murmured to herself. *They'll be a target for every missile New Force can throw. They're sitting ducks.*

Without hesitation she resumed pushing her way through the mob, grateful for once that they were surging forward at random like the rabble they were. At once she realised her task was virtually impossible. In front of her she could see police helmets, an impenetrable wall – so far – a barrier between the opposing sides. She looked desperately about her and had a moment of inspiration.

Away to the right, mounted on the pavement, she saw a rostrum where a TV crew were filming. By chance they were more or less in line with the police cordon, raised up like the umpire in a tennis match. She immediately veered off, setting her sights on the camera around which a space had been left. New Force wanted all the publicity they could get. They thrived on it. Even without Garth Brandon, they would use it to allege police intimidation and brutality.

Anne reached the rostrum and edged her way round the crew who were preoccupied with their work. A radio reporter was speaking breathlessly into a microphone, with a sound engineer behind him holding a recording machine. Anne smiled reassuringly as they glanced at her. They saw a thin girl trying to escape the crush. No one tried to stop her. Trying to look like a gofer, she moved steadily along the fronts of the houses before seizing her chance and sprinting the last few metres into the ranks of the black youths.

At the first hostile stares she called out, "It's me – Anne – I'm trying to get to Otis and Winston."

It worked. Some recognised her from the summer scheme, others decided she was no threat and left her to go on her way. It was easy to find Otis. She just followed the sound, all the while amazed at the numbers who had assembled to resist New Force, amazed to see white faces in amongst the brown and black. *Who were these people?*

· · · · ·

Cathy Lamb reported back to DCI Bartlett. She had checked the *refugees* in the school. None seemed to be in need of medical attention, though most were shaken, many of the children in distress. Bartlett had told her to look out especially for anyone who might be connected with New Force. An infiltrator could cause havoc.

Bartlett received her report while pressing buttons on his mobile. He grunted an acknowledgement and began speaking into the phone, turning and walking a few steps away. Lamb sidled up to Sergeant Marriner.

"The boss looks worried. I've never seen him look so ... rattled before."

"Small wonder," said Marriner. "Look at all this. We've got to have back-up. It's ridiculous to expect two dozen officers to keep this lot apart. Most of our blokes haven't even got proper equipment."

"And several of our 'blokes' are women," Lamb observed.

"That too," Marriner agreed.

Bartlett came back, shaking his head. "Half a dozen ... the Super says they can't spare any more. *Shit!*"

"Half a dozen? Blimey, sir. Where is everybody?"

"Everywhere else. I tried to explain that this is definitely the main action, what they've been aiming at all along. But there are ... co*mpeting pressures*, he called it."

Marriner half turned his head. "Here's something."

A siren was getting nearer, soon distinguishable as two sirens. Bartlett prayed for two people carriers filled with trained officers in full riot gear, preferably armed with assault rifles, shields, stun grenades and tear gas. The vehicles turned the corner and slid to a halt. Ford Sierras from Highways division. Traffic cops. Bartlett groaned.

From each car three officers leapt out, all wearing dayglo yellow jackets, all looking nervous as hell. Marriner waved them over. Bartlett and his two colleagues watched them pushing their way towards the school. Marnie and Serena had turned their attention away from the crowds to watch the reinforcements, hoping this was only the first batch to arrive.

"*Jesus ...*" Bartlett looked grim.

As they came nearer, half of them looked as if they were no more than kids.

· · · · ·

"Turn that thing off!" Anne stood in front of Otis who was taller and broader by a mile. "*Please.*"

"Can't hear you," he said, cocking his head towards the ghetto-blaster mounted on his shoulder.

Anne reached for the switches but he swayed away and she grabbed the air. The group of friends – *her* friends – surrounded her. Gone was the easy-going manner, the slouch and shuffle that had been their trademark. They looked hardened, underlined by a deep sadness.

"You're a target for missiles while you hold that thing and have that music playing. Don't you see?"

As if to strengthen her argument a beer can flew past their heads.

"Don't *you* see, Anne?" It was Winston, Buzz's brother. He took her shoulders and turned her round gently. "Look. Don't you see that?"

The banners of New force were waving like a crowd at a football match. Even while they were watching, three or four bricks flew through the air to land among the anti-Nazi demonstrators. Another smoke bomb exploded close to the thin blue and yellow lines of police officers.

Anne spun back. "I can see a lot of well-meaning people being goaded into a fight they can't win ... a load of people who'll get *injured* ... some even *killed.*"

"We've got no choice."

"Yes you *have*. Stop now ... go *away* ... leave here ... New Force will have no one to fight ... no publicity. You're playing into their hands. *Surely* you can see that?"

The black boys stared at her. She pleaded with her eyes.

"I don't think you understand, Anne. We're not well-meaning ... not being goaded. We came ready to fight ... all of us."

Anne was exasperated. "*No!* Fighting won't get you *anywhere*. You can't beat these thugs that way. You're playing *their* game ... that's what they *want.*"

"You really don't get it, do you? Let me spell it out for you, Anne. Those bastards killed Luther. That's why we're here ... for revenge."

• • • • •

The TV camera operator was doing cutaways. She was taking shots of the crowds, the police, the cluster of organisers gathered at the school entrance, faces of parents looking out from the windows, snippets that the editor at the studio would insert to convey the atmosphere when compiling the report for the evening news. This would get a slot on the national programme as well as more detailed local coverage. Because the media forces were divided over several locations, the small crew were left to their own devices without a producer on hand to direct them. She was looking for anything that would provide visual interest, following the old dictum of her craft that the best pictures told a story. Suddenly she found it.

In amongst the mass of protesters there was movement. She homed in, twisting the grip to adjust the telephoto lens, at the same time altering the focus. The image in the viewfinder blurred, steadied and sharpened. A blonde head was threading its way through the crowd that was mainly a mass of black and brown. It looked like a girl, pale and slightly-built, vulnerable but somehow determined. She made erratic progress, cutting through the ranks of demonstrators like a small boat through rough water. Nearing the police cordon, the head changed tack and took a new course until it reached the school building where it disappeared, only to re-emerge round the back of the stands, moving quickly through the scout camp to join the organisers and the small band of plain clothes police who were trying – vainly – to direct operations.

• • • • •

Bartlett was on the mobile again. The Chief Constable was demanding situation reports from senior staff all over the town, a chance to state his case that Bartlett was not going to let pass. Forcing himself to speak calmly, Bartlett described the scene unfolding, the confrontation that would grow to become a pitched battle at any minute, the families taking shelter in the school, the mounting violence. Above all, he stressed that he could not be held responsible if there were casualties among participants, bystanders or police officers struggling to keep the hostile factions apart. Marnie and Serena strained to catch as much of what he said as possible.

"… and I'm not exaggerating when I say this is a desperate situation, sir … it's started already … both sides … blacks, yes, but they've been joined by some outfit calling themselves BAN, according to their flags … several hundred on each side … we've got no more than thirty officers separating them … it couldn't be more urgent … thank you, sir. Right."

When Bartlett disconnected, Marriner was at his side. "Any joy, sir?

"God, I hope so. At least he listened. There's live coverage, apparently, on radio and TV."

"Did he offer to send reinforcements?"

"*Still reviewing the situation* … better than a flat *no*, I suppose."

"This *has* to be the main action. He's got to understand that."

"I told him, Ted, OK?"

"*Anne!*"

The cry made the policemen turn abruptly. It was Marnie who had exclaimed. Anne leapt out from behind the nearest stall and rushed towards the group. She was breathless but unharmed. Marnie hugged her.

"How did you get through?" Bartlett asked.

Anne stepped back and pointed over her shoulder, gasping. "Round the TV crew … through the demonstrators … round the police … through the scout camp."

"No one challenged you?" The DCI was incredulous.

"No." Anne was matter-of-fact.

Bartlett sighed. "So much for keeping order …"

"What were you *doing*?" said Marnie. "I was worried *sick*."

Anne agreed. "So was I. But I heard the reggae music – Otis and his bloomin' ghetto-blaster – saw everyone around me trying to hit him with bricks and stuff …"

"You were in with New Force?" Bartlett again.

"Right in the middle." She turned to Marnie. "So I got through to Otis and the others –"

"You had no trouble with New Force?" Bartlett incredulous again.

"They've taken me for one of them before ... I mean, look at me ... I'm not exactly Black Power, am I?"

"What about the other side?"

"They let me through. A lot of them know me, anyway."

"So no trouble with them ... and no trouble getting through the police line?"

Anne reflected. "I think I must be invisible."

"Or slippery as hell," Bartlett suggested.

"Probably."

All the while the chanting was growing louder, and Otis's music was blaring at full blast. New Force were beginning a new tactic, pulling back and rushing the police lines. It looked like a well-practised manoeuvre. Each time they withdrew, a hail of missiles rained down on anti-Nazis, blacks and police alike. It was the classic assault pattern: bombardment followed by an infantry charge. Both sides seemed to be growing, and the banners and flags were multiplying like standards on an ancient battlefield. The anti-Nazis were now picking up bricks and beer cans from the ground, hurling them back at the enemy.

The situation was growing uglier by the minute, but Bartlett feared further escalation. It was not long in coming. They had seen it all before, and no one was surprised.

New Force retreated from the police line and this time as they turned, more missiles arced through the air. Marnie gripped Anne round the shoulders and held her close as if worried that she might slip away again and never return. Serena raised a hand to shield her eyes from the sun, tracking the new missiles on their flight path. These ones looked distinct from the others. They had a different shape and seemed to flicker in their trajectory.

"Oh no ..." Marnie recognised them at once.

"What are they?" said Serena.

"Molotov cocktails," Marnie muttered. "Petrol bombs."

The crowd on the anti-Nazi side cried out in fear, and there was a rush to avoid the new threat, like crops blown about by a sudden storm. Petrol bombs landed among them, with a sound of breaking glass, exploding into flame. People stumbled and fell in their haste to get clear. The smell of burning fuel drifted on the air.

"Chief Inspector!" Dorothy Vane-Henderson, punctilious as ever. "Chief Inspector, where are your reinforcements?"

Bartlett's eyes strayed to the small band of late arrivals who were joining the wall with the rest of their colleagues. Dorothy's outrage subsided.

"That's it?" she said in disbelief. "Those skinny boys?"

Bartlett nodded.

Mrs V-H glared at him. "Should I speak to the Chief Constable?"

"He knows."

Serena grabbed Bartlett's sleeve. "The loudspeaker system's still working. I could appeal to our side to withdraw before it's too late."

Bartlett wondered briefly who *our side* were. Meanwhile more petrol bombs were in flight. The reply was a volley of bricks and stones from, presumably, *our side*.

"You don't think it's too late already?" he said.

• • • • •

The TV camera operator zoomed out. Having missed a shot of the petrol bombs flying through the air, she went for a wide angle to give the general picture. It made spectacular viewing: multiple fires, the surging crowd, flames and smoke, shouts and screams. And all the while, the menacing low chanting from the aggressors.

The anti-Nazi side – BAN – were impressive. They had expected fire bombs and dodged them without panicking. The operator zoomed in through the flames, group shots with the telephoto lens, making it appear that they were practically engulfed in the fire.

New Force were impressive too. She had seen riots before, but this bunch, for all their rag-tag appearance, knew what they were doing. Football hooligans just charged about at random. New Force were different. They had a guiding vision, moving from one tactic to another. At that point they were raising the stakes, no longer charging the police cordon, leaving just enough in the front line to maintain position, while the petrol bombers lobbed over their heads from the rear.

The radio reporter was giving a continuous commentary from the shelter of the raised camera platform. The operator pulled smoothly out to wide angle, locked it there and looked down at her assistant, standing behind her holding the cables. She signalled a question: could they get closer in on the action? He looked horrified and raised his middle finger. A petrol bomb exploded barely five metres from their position. The assistant tapped his forehead. She had to agree.

Returning to the job in hand, she bent towards the viewfinder and panned across the whole scene, hunting for the best images. Away over by the school entrance there seemed to be an animated discussion involving the police and the fete organisers. She lingered on the group for about ten seconds before focusing on one solitary figure, a woman she did not recognise, who had been standing with her back to the wall and who, while the camera was trained in that direction, slid down the wall to the ground. The operator twisted the grip and zoomed in, carefully keeping the woman in focus, sitting with head bent to her knees, a picture of defeat and dejection. The editor would use that. The human angle.

• • • • •

From the corner of her eye Marnie saw that Estelle had slumped to the ground. She went over and knelt beside her, putting an arm on her shoulder. That image would be seen in a million homes in the evening's regional news programme. It would feature in newspaper reports all over the country. Compassion in the midst of conflict.

Anne knelt on the other side, her mind filled with anxiety. She turned to look towards the riot and had the first inkling of what was going to happen. It was inevitable. Only two people at the scene of the battle knew how it was going to end, and she was one of them.

• • • • •

The sound engineer had set up a microphone to catch *wild sound*, background to the recorded images. The camera operator was enjoying the freedom to select the pictures and the angles and was sending a continuous stream of clear steady images. Because of the deaths of Brandon and Luther the event was going out live like a major sporting occasion.

As another clutch of petrol bombs rained down on the anti-Nazi ranks, an angry cry went up. The operator panned slowly across the scene. She had been concentrating for some minutes on New Force, capturing the group at the rear preparing the incendiary missiles – petrol-filled milk bottles – using lighters to ignite fuel-soaked rags tied round the neck, the classic *Molotov cocktail*, that could knock out a tank at close quarters.

The scene gradually changed as the operator slowly brought the panning shot to a halt. Pleased that there had been no juddering to spoil the image, she snatched a glance over the top of the camera to select her next view like a gunner looking for a new target. The best prospect was where two or three 'bombs' had fallen close together. This new tactic had caused near-panic among their opponents, who stumbled into one another trying to avoid the flames. *What next?* the camera operator asked herself.

Pulling in to give a closer grouping, she looked for a reaction shot from the crowd. One man tripped and went down, rising a moment later with blood pouring from a gashed hand. By now there was broken glass from the bottles all over the ground. The injured man was hustled away by his comrades, tracked by the watchful camera.

The operator wanted a smooth transition to a new subject, and a movement beyond the wounded man caught her attention. At first she was disappointed. The response to the latest assault seemed to be nothing more than the unfurling of new banners. But as she studied the action, she looked again. *Could it be?* She zoomed in tighter, but too many bodies were blocking her view. Although the picture was not as good as she would have wished, she kept the camera aimed at the same part of the crowd, just in case.

She wanted to be sure her eyes had not deceived her.

• • • • •

"I am *not* going to give in to intimidation!" Dorothy was defiant. "It would be the worst *possible* signal to those ... *barbarians*."

Bartlett was trying to persuade the organisers to leave the scene and take refuge in the school with the families. Dorothy was appealing for someone with a motor-cycle to take her to see the Chief Constable *at once*.

"Mrs Frightfully-Frightfully is back in Winston Churchill mode again," Anne observed neutrally.

Marnie glanced up from Estelle. "God help us."

"I wish He would."

"Don't count on it."

In an effort to appease Mrs V-H, Bartlett took out his mobile and pressed the buttons to redial the last caller. He asked for the Chief Constable, which at least succeeded in getting Dorothy's full attention. While he waited to be connected, a group of scouts arrived with the man whose hand was bleeding profusely. On Greg's instructions they took him into the school for treatment.

Dorothy gave them the name of the W.I. member trained in first aid, but would not leave Bartlett's side. He half expected her to make a grab at the phone.

When he was finally put through, Bartlett began by telling his chief he feared a bloodbath. It was a good start. Dorothy clearly approved. She hovered over him while he rattled off his assessment of the situation. As he spoke, more bombs were bursting in the playground and in the street. Bartlett's report was brief, pithy and relied heavily on Anglo-Saxon. He ended with: "It's only a matter of time before we'll have people frying down here." Dorothy liked that.

Bartlett listened to the Chief Constable's reply, raised his eyebrows and disconnected.

"Well?" said Dorothy. Her tone made it clear that backing down was not an option.

Bartlett looked bemused.

"Well?" she repeated, more loudly.

"Well ..." he began. "I've never heard the Chief Constable blaspheme before ... him, a Methodist lay preacher and all ..."

"Hardly surprising," said Dorothy.

"Really?"

"I don't suppose he's ever had one of his subordinates tell him to ... *get off his arse and do something* before."

Bartlett blinked. He had surprised himself.

Marnie came over and joined them, leaving Anne with Estelle. "So when does the Seventh Cavalry arrive?"

"That depends," said Bartlett, "on how keen they are to reach the Little Big Horn, assuming they can get through."

More petrol bombs. The prospect of more casualties.

Bartlett grimaced. "It looks like Enoch Powell could be proved right, after all ..."

• • • • •

It was a few minutes later when they noticed the music had stopped abruptly. Anne leapt to her feet and scanned the crowd. She was still craning her neck when Otis was carried into their midst. He had been hit by a brick and was barely conscious. His clothes showed signs of burning.

"Oh you silly boy," she said as gently as she could. "I tried to tell you, but you wouldn't listen to me."

He attempted to focus on her. "My ghetto-blaster ..." he murmured.

Anne wiped blood from his eyebrows and shook her head wearily. Greg moved in.

"He needs attention, Anne. You can talk to him later."

She touched Otis lightly on the cheek and stepped aside.

"Your lads are going to be busy," she said.

Greg pointed the way, and the scouts took Otis off to be patched up. "Yes, well ... we're not equipped to cope with a full-scale battle. This is a shambles ... and it's going to get worse, I reckon."

At that moment Marnie's mobile rang. It was Ralph. Anne watched her while she spoke.

"Where are you? ... Roadblocks? ... So you're stuck on the by-pass? ...

Don't worry, there's nothing you – or anybody – can do here ... No, we're OK, for now at any rate ... No, no one's been seriously hurt ... I wouldn't put money on it, Ralph. Things aren't looking good ... The fete? It's more like a battleground ... How do you know? ... On the radio? Well, it's true ..."

A sudden noise made her snap round. "What on *earth* ... what the devil's going on?" Even Ralph heard it. "I'm not sure. Look, Ralph, I think I'd better hang up ... Sure, yes I promise I'll keep you posted."

Anne was at her side. "Was that what I think it was?"

"What else could it be?" said Dorothy.

"Are you sure?"

"Of course. I've lived in the country all my life. I know a gunshot when I hear it."

Slowly, Estelle looked up.

• • • • •

The operator jerked the camera and swore under her breath. The shot had taken her by surprise. She had seen what looked like a banner being unfurled, but an odd shape had aroused her suspicions. Then she had lost it in the crowd. Could it have been a rifle of some kind?

The surging of the demonstrators made it hard to relocate that particular group through the viewfinder, and she was sweeping their ranks when the shot rang out. A moment's silence from the rioters, while the noise echoed off the buildings. Shouts from the police. A snarl from New Force. A cheer from the other side.

The operator felt a tap on her leg. Her assistant was pointing. And there it was. As quickly as she could without wobbling, she homed in on the weapon. A man was waving it in the air. A double-barrelled shotgun. Even as she sharpened the focus, the gun disappeared into the crowd

• • • • •

"*Christ!*" Bartlett raced to the information desk and jumped up. He knew he had seen something, but it had vanished in an instant. He shielded his eyes from the sun and peered into the anti-Nazi crowd but banners were waving defiantly in the smoke, obscuring his view.

Marriner ran towards him. "Sir! For God's sake!"

"Did you spot it, Ted?" Bartlett shouted.

"Somewhere in the middle. Sir, *please*, for Chrissake get down from there!"

Bartlett jumped from the table but not for his own safety. He was hitting buttons on the phone before his feet touched the ground, demanding the Chief Constable again.

What happened next was as horrifying as it was sudden. New Force retaliated. One of their bombers hurled a missile high into the air. It mesmerised the onlookers as it sped skywards, but not everyone was taken by surprise. It was still on its upward trajectory when the second shot was fired. Whoever had the gun was an experienced marksman. The petrol-filled bottle shattered like a clay pigeon at a snap-shoot. Glass flew in all directions. A fireball erupted sending blazing fuel back and down into the packed ranks below it.

The incident lasted only a few seconds, but in that moment the tide turned. New Force had lost the initiative. They had taken the main impact of the blast. Looking up to cheer their missile on its way, many of them had been hit in the face and eyes by pieces of the disintegrated bottle. Others were caught in the spray of ignited petrol. Everywhere on their side was panic, yelling and screaming.

A roar went up from their enemies. The banners of the anti-Nazis were raised on high as they surged forward against the police line. A new chant filled the air.

"Lu-ther! Lu-ther! Lu-ther!"

New Force were trying to fall back but there were too many of them in the confined space. The police were faltering in their battle to hold off the advance. The noise from the anti-Nazis was swelling.

"Lu-ther! Lu-ther! Lu-ther!"

The TV crew had hit the ground when the missile exploded. The operator, knocked off balance, had fallen from her position, but she scrambled back to her feet and seized the camera, widening the angle over the battlefield. The opposing forces were restricted in the confined space in front of the school and its grounds. There was nowhere to run. It would be a fight to the end.

"Lu-ther!" The chant went on. "Lu-ther!" Ever louder. "Lu-ther!"

At the school entrance the fete organisers had frozen, powerless to influence the disaster that was unfolding before their eyes. Marnie was wracking her brain for an idea, any step they could take to halt the impending carnage. Anne moved beside Marnie who put an arm round her. Greg was staring, his mouth open. Recovering his presence of mind, he signalled to the scouts to withdraw into the school. Even Dorothy looked resigned to the inevitability of the outcome.

"Lu-ther!" The anti-Nazis were surging forward again. "Lu-ther! Lu-ther!"

Serena moved quickly, grabbing Bartlett's arm.

"I could speak to them …" Her voice was urgent but trembling "… get our side to hold back, if your officers could push against that lot."

Bartlett shook his head. "No one's going to listen. All we can do is hold on and hope for reinforcements."

"But I could plead with them to back off … while there's still time."

"Listen to them! They wouldn't even hear you."

"I can use the microphone," she yelled.

"You'd be wasting your time."

Serena put her hands to her face. "I can't bear this. People are going to get killed out there … and we're just standing by doing nothing."

"Listen to me, woman!" Bartlett shouted in her face and spoke through clenched teeth. "I am trying to get back-up here. That is not *doing nothing*. We can't work *miracles*, but we are professionals. Leave things to us and don't interfere."

Serena staggered back as if he had struck her. Marnie removed her arm from Anne and went to Serena, taking her by the shoulders. Serena collapsed sobbing into her arms.

Another push from the crowd. "Lu-ther! Lu-ther! Lu-ther!"

There were no more fire bombs from New Force, the risk being too great, but bricks and stones had begun flying again, albeit haphazardly. Without the mass of New Force to bolster them from behind, the police were buckling under the pressure.

"It's just a matter of time now." Dorothy spoke as if from far off.

"This is a nightmare," said Marnie. "We're helpless."

She looked over her shoulder, still cradling Serena, to check that Anne was safe. For her part, Anne was worrying about the effect of the battle on Estelle. She was turning to go to her when Estelle picked herself up from the ground. Her languor had gone. For the first time since her return she looked as if she knew where she was and what she was doing. She took a step forward, stopped and saw Anne staring at her. Their eyes met. A grim smile crossed Estelle's face. Anne was suddenly desolate, knowing what was to come.

Estelle began walking rapidly towards the battle. With an expression of bewilderment, Marnie released Serena and moved to intercept her.

"Estelle!" She tried to take her arm, but Estelle twisted away. "What are you doing?"

Estelle raised a hand as if to ward Marnie off. "Don't try and stop me."

"You don't realise what's happening. It's dangerous here. Come on, let me take you into the school. It's safer there."

"Nowhere's safe for me, Marnie. Not any more."

Marnie had the firm impression that Estelle had become deranged. "I don't understand you."

Estelle turned her head. "Anne will explain. She knows."

Marnie looked towards Anne who was standing alone where Estelle had left her, a picture of misery. "What does she know?"

But when Marnie looked back, Estelle had gone.

• • • • •

The camera operator wiped sweat from her forehead and was surprised to see blood on her hand. There was no time to dwell on it; there was too much to do. She stretched forward and peered in at the lens. Thanking God that it was undamaged, she returned to her work.

So many possibilities presented themselves. The police line, becoming ragged under the strain of holding back the surging crowd; the banners waving; the defiant ranks of New Force reduced to throwing stones, but not retreating. She filmed them all, quickly scanning the field of action for the best shots to show the battleground.

Movement among the group of organisers caught her eye. The scouts were falling back in an orderly retreat, their leader signalling them to take cover. The police officer back on the ground after leaping onto the table was locked in heated discussion with the black woman who looked like a model.

She was on the point of altering the shot when a lone woman – the one who had been slumped against the wall – detached herself from the others and walked calmly into the melee. It was a startling image. The operator zoomed in, praying she would not lose sight of her. The woman did not hesitate. Raising both arms in the air she strode on, oblivious to the danger, pushing herself to the front of the anti-Nazi demonstrators. Their chant filled the air.

"Lu-ther! Lu-ther! Lu-ther!"

Still she plunged on, turning to face the onslaught. The hands did not waver and made tracking her all the easier. Looking up from the viewfinder she could see New Force trying to rally. More stones and bricks were hurled high. When she put her eye back to the viewfinder, the woman had disappeared under the shower of missiles.

· · · · ·

It was Sergeant Marriner who moved first. He raced into the crowd as soon as he saw Estelle go down. Cathy Lamb charged after him, ignoring Bartlett's shouts to get back. They shouted *Police! Police!* as they ran. Cursing under his breath, Bartlett set off in pursuit with Marnie at his heels.

Anne rushed forward, but Serena grabbed her and held her fast.

"Let me go!"

"No, Anne. It's no good."

"But I've got to –"

"Look!" Serena turned Anne to face the crowd. "It's all right."

The group was returning, all of them shaken but uninjured. As they drew nearer Anne could see that Marriner was carrying Estelle, who seemed to be struggling in his arms. The side of her head was covered in blood, her face the colour of chalk.

It had been a lightning strike. Marriner had dived in and seized Estelle where she had fallen while all around were reeling under the missiles. A brick had caught her a glancing blow and knocked her to the ground. A direct hit would have killed her.

The demonstrators were regrouping, undeterred by the battering they had received. Nothing was going to stop them in their lust for revenge.

"Lu-ther! Lu-ther!" The war cry echoed across the battlefield. "Lu-ther!"

Estelle slipped from Marriner's arms and stood shakily, gasping and unsteady. The others surrounded her, fearing she might even now try to rush back into the action. There was a manic tension about her that they could all sense.

Bartlett planted himself firmly in front of her. "Don't even think about it."

Estelle nodded, eyes cast down, swallowing and breathing heavily. She winced with pain and put a hand to her head.

"I'll take her inside," Marnie offered. "There's nothing anyone can do here."

She took Estelle gently by the arm and began leading her away. To everyone's surprise, Estelle let herself be guided by Marnie. Anne fell into step beside them. They had walked only a few paces when Estelle stopped. Marnie waited patiently.

"We'll just take it easy," she said.

Behind them another roar went up and the chanting resumed.

"Lu-ther!"

Estelle turned towards Marnie and spoke quietly. "You've got to let me do one more thing."

"No way."

"I promise I won't try to go back there." Her voice was weak but determined. "That was a waste of time."

"It was worse than that. Estelle, you need medical attention. And that's what you're going to get. Now."

"Just one last thing, Marnie. Trust me. Please."

"After what you just did —"

"No. I mean it, Marnie. I have to do this. You mustn't stop me. Ask Anne. She'll explain everything. It's our last chance. I can't have all these people's lives in my hands and do nothing."

Marnie faltered. "What — what's Anne got to do with it?"

"*Please!*"

Estelle backed away. Marnie looked at Anne who was staring into the depths of Hell, immobile.

"What's going on?"

Anne said nothing.

"Do you understand this, Anne?" Marnie insisted.

Anne nodded slowly, not taking her eyes off Estelle. To Marnie's surprise she did not attempt to run back to the riot. Calmly, she took the microphone from its stand and walked a few paces to the information desk where Bartlett had stood. She sat on the desk, swung her legs up and got to her feet.

On the far side of the area a TV camera zoomed in on her and, seeing the microphone, the assistant adjusted the settings on his recorder.

Some of the crowd glanced in Estelle's direction, noticing the blood that had now spread down the right side of her shirt. Over the sound of the chanting a solitary amplified voice rang out.

"Listen to me!" A blast of feedback. Estelle moved the microphone from her mouth. "Listen! All of you listen!"

Many in the anti-Nazi ranks recognised her from the summer scheme. The chanting diminished but the surging continued.

"Listen to what I say! Listen!"

It was becoming a mantra. The persistent tone of voice was slowly winning their attention.

"Listen to me! Luther was ... my partner. He was my boyfriend ... my whole life. Everything I had depended on him. All my future. Absolutely everything."

Some demonstrators were beginning to think this was going to be the signal for their final push. More of them listened.

"You want revenge for Luther!" Estelle intoned.

A cheer went up.

"You can have your revenge!"

Marnie turned to Anne, alarmed. "What's she playing at? What the Hell is this?"

Anne nodded towards Estelle. "The truth. It's all quite simple, really. The devil was in the detail. ..."

Marnie frowned.

Estelle raised her free hand in the air. "If you want revenge ... you can take it! I know who killed Luther!" She took a deep breath and screamed into the microphone. "I know who killed Luther!"

A deafening blast of feedback shrieked from every speaker in the grounds like a howl of anguished ghosts wailing. There was a stirring on both sides of the divide. The police turned their heads to look up at Estelle. In a million homes people stopped what they were doing to stare at their TV screens.

"You can take your revenge ..." Estelle put a hand to her chest, "... on me!"

The incipient cheer turned into a moan of doubt, turning to puzzlement, to disbelief. Even New Force grew quieter.

"I killed Luther!" Estelle's voice was firm and steady.

Shouts of *No!* rose from all over the anti-Nazi side of the crowd.

"I killed Luther. It was my fault he died." She pointed towards New Force. "They didn't do it. It was me. I destroyed him ... I destroyed myself ... I ..."

She swayed, tottered and fell. If it had not been for Marnie's fast reflexes, she would have hit the ground head first. Kneeling, Marnie held Estelle's limp body in her arms, unaware of the tears falling down her own cheeks. She felt Anne touch her shoulder at the moment when the first sound of the sirens reached her ears.

32

Marnie felt something close to her face and was instantly awake, eyes wide open. The sudden wakening made her momentarily dizzy, and it took a second or two to focus. A little longer to remember where she was.

She had been trying to hide. Pursuers had chased her down a long dark alley. It had been night. They had caught her against a brick wall at the furthest end that was too high to climb. There had been no way out. She was trapped like a rat in a sewer pipe.

Slowly she turned her head. Ralph was hovering over her. He kissed her on the cheek.

"Good morning." He spoke quietly. "Did you manage to get some sleep?"

"What?"

"You don't look very rested. Can I get you something? The hospital canteen produces quite drinkable coffee."

The hospital. Of course. It all came back. She had travelled in the ambulance with Estelle who had been rushed into Accident and Emergency unconscious, her head still bleeding after being hit by the brick. They had taken her straight to Radiology for X-rays, and eventually admitted her to the Intensive Therapy Unit. Marnie and Anne had sat with her till too exhausted to stay awake, and the doctors had offered accommodation for the night in guest rooms.

"Where's Anne?"

"In the next room ... still sleeping."

"What about Estelle?"

"Not much change. The nurse said she had a hairline fracture of the skull."

Marnie got up on one elbow. "Will she be all right?"

Ralph shrugged. "She looks worse than you do."

"That bad? I feel shattered."

"You look wonderful ... wonderful but ... shattered. I've brought you both some clothes. There's a shower next door ... down the corridor, first right."

"Sounds good. I'll give it a whirl."

"Oh ... I forgot to bring your dressing gown."

Marnie was wearing only pants. "No problem. I can hop along like this. They've seen it all before."

Anne came into the room while Marnie was gone. She was yawning, still wearing yesterday's clothes. Ralph hugged her.

Anne kissed him on the cheek. "I've been to see Estelle. The nurse said you were here ... said you'd brought some clothes."

"Yes."

"I'm not a very good advert for the hospital. I fell asleep like this."

Her T-shirt and jeans were dirty, crumpled and stained with Estelle's blood.

"I'd never have known," said Ralph. "How are you feeling?"

"Actually, I'm quite hungry. Ravenous, in fact. I could eat a horse."

"You're vegetarian."

"You're pedantic." She yawned.

• • • • •

In the canteen only a few groups of nurses and ancillary staff were having a break. They found a table by the window and breakfasted on orange juice, coffee and toast. The showers and change of clothes had done wonders.

Marnie sipped the coffee. Ralph had been right; it was drinkable. "I'm amazed I just crashed out like that."

"Nervous exhaustion. You'd been through the mill. You'd been through Hell."

"I don't want too many more days like that one," Anne muttered.

Marnie touched her hand. "No. I wish you hadn't been there at all." Suddenly she picked up a thread that had been bothering her subconsciously since the riot. "Anne, what was all that business about *Anne will understand ... Anne will explain it all ...?*"

Anne hesitated. "Oh ... well, it was – you know – about Luther ... and what happened ..."

"You *knew*?"

"Yes."

"How did you know?"

"Well, I sort of guessed, really. But it was the only thing that made sense."

"That's more than you're doing," Marnie said gently. "Can you spell it out for us?"

Anne stirred her coffee. "It was like Mr Crawford said ..."

"*Rex*? Our *accountant*? What's he got to do with it?"

"What did he say?" said Ralph.

"*The devil is in the detail.*"

"Go on."

"I was putting Estelle's receipts together for her expenses claim – to save her having to worry about it – and it didn't add up ... I mean it didn't make sense. The return flight number was wrong."

"And you spotted a detail like that ... in spite of everything?"

"Yeah. Remember, I'd altered her flight back ... had to confirm it by fax. The date and flight number had both changed. I'd got her a booking on the

359

flight that only comes back on Saturdays. Her boarding card showed the original flight number for the Friday plane. I just glanced at it when I was stapling it to the receipt and I saw that number. Naturally I looked for the changed one – with the *right* number – then I realised I was holding an actual ticket stub – from a *boarding card* – with the original number."

Marnie said reflectively, "She came back a day early."

"Yes. It was the only explanation possible. She must have changed it herself in Italy ... got the plane back on Friday morning."

"But why?"

Anne shrugged. "Dunno."

"Anne," Ralph began, "why did Estelle think you knew about Luther ... what she'd done?"

"She was there in the office with me when I was clipping the receipts together ... when I realised she must've changed the flight. She saw I was confused at first ... then I worked it out."

"Did you in fact understand the implications ... suspect she'd been involved in Luther's death?"

"Well no, not straight away. I was just going to query why the ticket was wrong when Estelle looked at me. She looked so ... haunted, and ..."

"And you knew," said Marnie.

"It made me wonder. It's not the first thing you think about, is it? I mean, that the person sitting opposite you – your *friend* – has actually *killed* her boyfriend. You look for other possibilities."

"But?"

"It was the way she looked at me. That's when I knew she'd been involved somehow."

"When you discovered Luther in the tunnel," Ralph said, "did you see anything there to link Estelle with his death?"

"No. It was only when I saw the airline ticket afterwards."

"No other ... actual evidence that she'd been there?"

"Nothing I could see. Nothing at all."

"What do we do about this?" said Marnie.

Ralph sat back and folded his arms. "Good question. No one else is likely to spot the different flight number – or understand its significance. Who else will see the ticket?"

"Our accountants, eventually. They won't realise what it means."

"*The devil is in the detail*," Ralph reminded her.

"Sure, but they won't do the accounts till some time next year. The date will mean nothing to them. They'll only want to check the figures add up."

"So who else will know about this?"

"You're forgetting something, aren't you?" Anne said. "Estelle did actually *confess* ... in public ... in front of dozens of police officers ... not to mention thousands of rioters ... and a TV crew. She told the world she'd killed him."

"Mmm ..." Ralph made a non-committal sound. "After she'd just been struck on the head by a brick that fractured her skull. Not the most reliable testimony, perhaps."

Marnie looked doubtful. "You think we could argue she was somehow ... deranged ... or just did what she did ... confessed ... to stop the fighting?"

"It's a possibility ... in the absence of any proof ... any evidence that's likely to be brought forward."

"But –"

"Did she?" Marnie cut across Anne's interjection. "I mean, did she in fact stop the fighting? What happened?"

"You were there, Marnie, both of you. I was stuck in a jam on the by-pass … remember?"

"But we went off in the ambulance. My mind was on other things. There was all that blood … I thought Estelle was going to die. I think I saw police vans, but … I dunno … it was nothing but chaos and confusion. Didn't you hear anything on the car radio?"

"The reports kept hopping about. It was all very unclear. Then the police began waving us on … shepherding us away from the town. I had to watch where I was going in that crush."

"But Marnie –"

Before Anne could continue, Ralph raised a finger from the tabletop and pointed towards the entrance. They turned to see DCI Bartlett and DS Marriner in the doorway, scanning the canteen. The detectives spotted them and came over.

Bartlett looked more friendly than usual. "Good morning. We'd like to talk to you. Perhaps somewhere private?"

"I think these two deserve their breakfast, don't you?" said Ralph. "Why don't you join us?"

They pulled up chairs. Bartlett sat down while Marriner went to the servery. Marnie got in first.

"What's happening on the summer scheme, do you know?"

Bartlett frowned. "It's been stopped while the school area is cleaned up after the … riot. I believe they're hoping to restart it next week."

"We were just talking about the riot. What happened after we left in the ambulance?"

"It ended pretty quickly. A load of our blokes – in full riot gear – arrived on the scene as you were pulling away. They piled into the New Force side who took one look at their weapons and equipment and decided the game was up. Their opponents backed off and just melted away."

"No cause for revenge after Estelle had spoken like that."

"Presumably not. Talking of whom … the medics say your friend's still unconscious and has a fractured skull."

"So what can we do for you?" said Ralph. "You said you wanted to talk to us."

"There's not much we can add to what you know already." Marnie picked up her coffee cup. "You were there, after all."

"Of course. No, it's not about Estelle. We can only wait till she comes round and hear what she has to say. It's the other matter that concerns me this morning."

"Other matter?"

"What the newspapers are calling the *body in the skip*."

Anne dropped her knife onto the plate. It clattered and fell to the floor. "*Body?* You found a body?"

"Well, no, that's just it. Everything seemed to point to there being a body in that skip, but there wasn't one … only some clothes."

"What clothes?"

"We found a black shirt and a red baseball cap … buried in amongst builders' rubble. And a bicycle … a mountain bike … yellow. Familiar?"

Anne bent down to retrieve her knife. She seemed to have some difficulty in picking it up.

"Why should it be?" said Marnie. "Ah … wait a minute … Weren't you looking for someone on a bike wearing a red cap in connection with the Brandon killing?"

"That was a line of enquiry we were following."

"And also when you were investigating Luther's death," Ralph added.

Anne re-emerged from under the table and laid the knife beside her plate.

"Correct," said Bartlett.

Ralph passed his knife to Anne while still looking at Bartlett. "You're keeping an open mind on that?"

"Until we've had a chance to speak to Miss Greenwood we're keeping every option open."

Marnie was looking puzzled. "So how can we help you with the skip business?"

"Are you missing anybody from your group of … colleagues … associates?"

"We're not the ones who wear the black shirts, inspector."

Sergeant Marriner returned with a tray, placed cups and biscuits on the table and sat down.

"And we don't possess a bicycle between us," Marnie continued. "Or a baseball cap, for that matter."

Ralph shuddered. "Heaven forbid!"

"What about you, Anne?" Bartlett turned suddenly to face her.

"What about me?"

"Do any of those things mean anything to you?"

She shrugged. "I've seen enough black shirts lately to put me off them for life. Yes, I've seen plenty of baseball caps, too … and mountain bikes. They're all the rage."

"Not much to go on," said Ralph.

The detectives drank their coffee.

Bartlett ran a finger over his lips. "There was one other thing. We found part of a strap of some sort … leather. Does that mean anything to any of you?"

"We've probably all got belts made of leather," said Marnie.

"This has been identified as more the kind of strap fitted to shoulder bags."

Marnie bent down and lifted her own bag by its strap, holding it up for inspection before lowering it again.

"Very nice too," Bartlett observed. "But the one we found was sturdier … thicker … more masculine, if you know what I mean."

"I don't mean to be unhelpful," said Ralph, "but most men don't carry shoulder bags … at least not in this country."

"Precisely. So one who did would be easier to spot."

"I don't possess one. An old-fashioned briefcase – rather battered – is more in my line."

"What about you, Anne? You're very quiet."

"I'm not very masculine."

Bartlett smiled. "I meant, do you know anyone who might have such a thing?"

Before Anne could reply, Marnie said, "Mr Bartlett, we live in a very conventional English village. There aren't any trendies with continental-style accessories knocking about in Knightly St John. I could check out George Stubbs, if you like."

Marriner grinned. "We have to check every possibility, Mrs Walker. You know how we work by now."

"Yes. But I can't say I understand why you think we might know anything about some unidentified person – someone you can't trace – whose possessions have turned up in a rubbish skip in Northampton."

"What's it all about?" said Ralph. "Why can't those items just be old clothes that have been discarded?"

"That's what we're trying to work out, sir. Someone took the trouble to make sure they came to our attention."

"And you expected to find a body? Seems far-fetched to me."

"We think we were being *led* to expect to find a body."

"This is too subtle for me, inspector. I'm just a humble professor of economics at Oxford."

Marnie said, "Are you saying you think there was a body but that it's vanished?"

"Maybe."

"For what purpose, do you think?"

Neither detective spoke.

"Perhaps someone wanted to lure you away from the action?" Ralph suggested.

"Or it could've been a sign," said Marnie. "A warning, perhaps. Maybe they removed the body because bodies contain clues ... evidence that could be traced back to their killers."

Anne stared into her cup.

• • • • •

The hours passed slowly, sitting at Estelle's bedside while the nurses and doctors adjusted drips and made alterations to the machines that were regulating her survival. Intensive care was well-named. Every few minutes someone came to check readings and settings. Every alteration was noted on charts and forms. The specialist staff conferred in groups huddled round the equipment that was keeping her alive.

After a time Marnie asked what was happening. The head of the unit told her they were monitoring Estelle's condition closely. It was possible they would need to operate if haemorrhaging occurred in the brain. So far she seemed not to be in danger, but things could change rapidly. How soon she might come out of the coma was anybody's guess.

An hour later her eyelids began to flicker. The staff became animated, carried out more adjustments, ushered Marnie, Ralph and Anne out of the way. After ten minutes Marnie was allowed back with warnings not to stay long and not to tire Estelle with too much talk.

Surprisingly, it was Estelle who was able to do the talking. Her voice was quiet and husky, but her mind was clear.

"The nurse said I had a hairline fracture of the skull ... from a brick ..."

"Yes, but you're going to be all right," Marnie whispered.

"You think so? It aches like hell. She said you caught me when I fell ... another blow on the head could've finished me off."

"Don't think about it. Just get better."

"Did I tell everyone about ... Luther ... or did I just dream that?"

"You said it to stop the fighting ... and it worked."

"Good. But it was the truth."

"Estelle, you were travelling that day. We all know that."

"You're hopeless at lying, Marnie." She closed her eyes and took several shallow breaths. "Anne will tell you. I changed my flight back. I couldn't wait to get home to sort it all out. I was desperate."

"But you didn't know where Luther would be on Friday at that time. How could you?"

"When I was approaching Knightly I rang him on the mobile ... he said he was on his way to Cosgrove. I turned off and waited for him by the tunnel."

"Just take it gently, Estelle. Don't over-tire yourself."

Estelle ignored the warning. "There was no one there to see me."

"Did you have an argument?"

"Yes. I was so jealous of Luther and Serena ... I'd seen the photos in the press ... Molly was faxing the articles every day."

"Serena's a happily-married woman with a super husband and lovely children."

"I know, but the papers made them look like ... an item."

"They weren't."

"I'd missed him so much and he just seemed to want to talk about Serena ... how marvellous she'd been. I'd lost someone before ... it nearly destroyed me then. It was Luther who brought me back from the brink, but I could see it happening all over again. Something inside me just snapped."

"It was an accident," said Marnie. "It wasn't your fault."

"He went to put his arms round me. I was ready to be persuaded there was nothing between him and Serena."

"That's absolutely right."

"But I still felt angry ... hadn't got it out of my system. I yelled at him. I pushed him away – just to hold him off. He stepped back ... I think he caught his heel on something ... he slipped backwards, hit his head on brickwork at the side of the path. I thought he was just knocked out. I rang for help and ran away."

"Why?"

"I was in a state ... almost hysterical. It never occurred to me anyone might get into trouble. When I'd calmed down I realised I'd been a fool. I went back ... saw the ambulance, the police, people looking on. No one paid any attention to me. I decided I'd go and see Luther in hospital and make it up. Then I heard about him on the radio in the car ... that he was dead."

Tears rolled down Estelle's cheeks. Marnie reached for a tissue and wiped her face.

"You need to rest."

"Ironic, isn't it, Marnie? A big strong guy like Luther ... a small woman like me. One unlucky fall and it kills him. A brick cracks my skull and I'm alive."

• • • • •

Marnie parked the Discovery opposite Serena's house. She was pulling the door handle when Ralph took her arm.

"Will you tell Serena about Estelle ... what she did ... and why?"

"I don't know. Why rake up problems? We have enough already."

"Sometimes it's best to tell the truth," said Anne. "It's going to come out anyway, eventually."

It was Serena's husband Rod, quiet, serious and dignified, who answered the doorbell. He showed them into the living room. A minute later he returned with Serena. As always she looked as if ready for a photoshoot, but her expression betrayed her anxiety.

"What's happened to Estelle?"

"She's conscious ... out of danger ... desperately unhappy."

Rod put an arm round his wife.

"Was it true?" said Serena, "what she said about Luther?"

"Yes."

"I had hoped she was only saying that to defuse the situation."

"Me too. But they had a minor row. It was just a tragic accident."

"Why were they having a row? She'd only just got back from her trip."

Marnie glanced at Rod. "It was just a silly misunderstanding about some private matter."

Rod shook his head slowly. "A fine man like that ... someone we all admired. It's very sad."

"And very brave of Estelle," Serena added. "What she said made our side back down. It was because of her courage and honesty that major bloodshed was averted ... you realise that."

"Bartlett said the arrival of police reinforcements played a part, too," said Marnie.

"He's right. But it could still have been a full-scale battle. I felt really proud of Estelle ... and of our community ... how mature they were when they knew the truth."

"Tell the truth and shame the devil," Anne muttered. They all looked at her. "That's what my gran always used to say."

• • • • •

It was a sombre homecoming. They had hardly spoken in the car all the way back from Northampton. Even the turn off the main road on the last mile into the village did not seem to raise their spirits. Marnie looked over her shoulder at Anne.

"Are you OK back there?"

"Yes, thanks."

"You haven't said much all day."

"I've been thinking about things."

"We've all got a lot on our minds," said Ralph. "And we're probably down on blood sugar. We've hardly eaten a thing since breakfast."

"I'll do something with pasta," said Marnie. "That'll revive us, and it won't take long. All right with you, Anne?"

"Fine. I'll help."

"Anne, don't fret about things. With any luck Estelle won't be charged. I don't think Bartlett will find any actual evidence against her."

"I was thinking about something else."

"Oh?"

There was no reply from the back seat.

"What is it, Anne?"

The car drove in to the high street, past the village shop.

"I was wondering … what became of Donovan."

"I must admit …" Ralph stopped himself in mid-sentence.

Anne continued it for him. "You thought he was murdered and his clothes dumped in the skip as a warning … but they didn't leave his body in case it could be traced back to his killers."

"Oh, Anne …" Marnie forced her concentration back to driving. "Let's talk about it when we get home. It's not far now."

She would be able to comfort Anne and try to reassure her once they were back at Glebe Farm. It would be easier to make her feel better in their own surroundings. She hoped the sight of the farm complex would lift their morale as it always did. But it was not to be.

Reaching the bottom of the field track where the ground levelled out, her heart sank. Parked outside the office barn stood the grey Cavalier of DCI Bartlett.

The Chief Inspector and his sergeant were sitting in the office when Marnie pushed the door open. Bartlett gave his version of a smile when they walked in.

"How did you get in?" said Marnie. "We left the office locked. Has there been a break-in?"

"Only by us," said Marriner. "We know the place so well, we even know where you keep the spare key hidden."

"Are you going to run true to form and turn down my offer of coffee?"

"Yes." Bartlett looked serious. Then his expression softened. "I for one would prefer a cup of tea … if that's on offer too."

Anne went straight to the kitchen area and filled the kettle, glad to have something to occupy her hands.

Bartlett came straight to the point. "We've been able to speak with Miss Greenwood. They gave us five minutes, and we're going back tomorrow."

Marnie sat down. "I hope you're bearing in mind the condition she was in when she spoke at the microphone."

"A fractured skull would hardly help her think properly," Ralph added.

"She wasn't able to tell us very much," Bartlett admitted.

"There's nothing we can add to what she said." Marnie hoped she had deflected any further questioning in that direction. "We were all together at the pub when the … incident took place. And Anne didn't arrive on the scene till some time later."

"Quite so," Bartlett agreed.

Anne was tinkling tea cups in the background, laying a tray.

Marnie continued. "We're assuming it was about Estelle that you came to see us."

"I think you've worked out why we're here, Mrs Walker. We certainly don't suspect you … or your friends here .. of any part in what took place."

"Makes a pleasant change," said Marnie.

"That's what we were thinking."

"Can you use what Estelle said as a confession?" Ralph asked. "I would've thought her statement would be highly questionable in the circumstances."

Bartlett looked at Marnie. "I'm sure your lawyer – Mr Broadbent, isn't it? – would wish to stress the mitigating nature of the *circumstances*."

"I expect he would ... and rightly."

Anne brought the tray from the kitchen and set it down on her desk where she began pouring tea. Marnie went to help her and gave out the cups and a plate of biscuits.

"Are you intending to charge her, chief inspector?"

"Good question, Mrs Walker. How we proceed rather depends on whether we believe her or not. She could've just made it up to stop the riot. But I expect you've thought of that."

"Presumably if she says nothing more you wouldn't have anything to charge her with?"

"It would be difficult under the law as it currently stands to take matters further ... *if* she refused to co-operate."

Anne moved between the visitors with a bowl of sugar. Both detectives took a few lumps. She stood in front of Bartlett.

"Estelle was telling the truth when she confessed." Her voice was quiet but it seized the attention of everyone in the room.

Bartlett was quick to regain his composure. "You have evidence of this? You saw something in the tunnel?"

"No. But I know she wasn't lying. She changed her flight and came back a day early to see him. That's how she could be there."

Bartlett's eyes narrowed. "You have proof that she changed her flight?"

"Ticket and boarding card ..." She nodded towards her desk. "In the blue folder."

"Why are you doing this, Anne?"

"Because if it doesn't get told, no one will believe her story. People will think she was only making it up as an excuse to stop the fighting. Then there'll be more trouble. She wouldn't want that ... not after all she's been through."

"You realise people might think you're betraying her?" said Bartlett.

"I don't think so. And it doesn't matter. You have to fight the enemy with the truth. A friend of mine made me see that."

Bartlett sipped his tea. Marriner watched Anne intensely. She turned and sat at her desk. Marnie and Ralph said nothing, trading glances as they tried to make sense of what Anne was doing.

"Now listen to me." Bartlett put down his cup. "Anne, you did the right thing. Don't be in any doubt that we would've found out about her coming back a day early when we checked her movements ... airline manifests ... security camera images ... credit card records. And what you didn't know is we also have a trace of lipstick that I believe we'll establish by DNA testing came from Estelle."

"So you had all the proof you needed all the time," said Marnie.

"That isn't really the point."

"I thought you thrived on facts and hard evidence. That's what you've told me in the past."

"Of course. But we also have to take the circumstances into account. What Estelle did yesterday was a brave thing, and it helped prevent a major catastrophe. By voluntarily helping us with our enquiries – yes, I know you've heard that phrase before – she ... and you, Anne ... have given us the full picture. I shall be reporting everything to the Crown Prosecution Service ... including the circumstances."

"Will you be urging them to bring Estelle to trial?" said Ralph.

"That's for the CPS to decide. But I think it's clear that what happened was almost certainly an accident."

"A reasonable assumption, given the way they felt about each other ... that was clear to everyone who knew them."

"Still ... it can only be an assumption. We'll get more details when Estelle can make a full statement."

"But even then you won't have verifiable evidence," said Marnie.

"No," Bartlett conceded. "Only Estelle will ever know what really happened in the tunnel."

"A lot will depend on how you present the facts..." Ralph checked himself. "... how you interpret the details."

Bartlett pulled a face. "Well ... would anyone seriously believe that a woman like Estelle would be capable of overpowering a strong, athletic man like Mr Curtiss? I think that's doubtful." He stood up. "Thank you for the tea. We'll show ourselves out. We know the way."

"What about the Brandon killing?" Ralph asked. "Are you any further forward?"

Bartlett shook his head. "Between ourselves ... a total blank. This has not been a good week for our crime statistics."

After the detectives had left, Anne sat with her head in her hands. Ralph crossed the room and knelt down beside her, holding her gently. Marnie breathed out audibly. She walked over, squatted down and hugged them both.

"I could use a brandy," said Ralph.

"Make it two," Marnie agreed.

"Three." Anne spoke without looking up.

"Mm?" Marnie was surprised.

"Doubles," Anne added. "For medicinal purposes ..."

Ralph walked to the medicine cabinet and took out a bottle. "Anne, remind me never to play poker with you."

Marnie kissed the top of Anne's head. "For once I agree with Bartlett. You did the right thing."

Ralph returned carrying three glasses. "What was that about *fighting the enemy with the truth?*"

"It was Donovan, wasn't it?" said Marnie.

"Yes. Something I'll never forget."

33

On the following day, Anne awoke feeling calm and rested, but strangely empty. She had slept soundly but had no recollection of going to bed the previous night. It was a morning of new beginnings. Everything needed recharging.

The sound of footsteps in the courtyard drew her to the window slit. Marnie was opening the front door of Estelle's cottage. She would be tidying her things, the first step in Estelle's gradual withdrawal from Glebe Farm and out of their lives.

Anne pulled on jeans and a sweatshirt and left the barn to go through the spinney to prepare breakfast on *Sally Ann*. It was her first walk along that path since setting off for the riot. She expected to meet Dolly, but the sturdy black cat did not intercept her. Probably on mouse patrol. It was early morning, though too late for the dawn chorus. Anne's walk through the sunlit trees was accompanied by silence.

Leaving the spinney she found the two narrowboats lying comfortably at their moorings. *Thyrsis* looked unoccupied. Anne knew Ralph would be striding up the hill, taking his morning exercise. Suddenly her eyes were drawn to movement on the roof of *Sally Ann*. On the hatch cover above the entrance door Dolly was skitting about. Anne groaned inwardly. It looked as if the cat had taken a mouse up there and was toying with it, patting it with one paw then the other. Anne quickened her pace to try and save the poor creature.

Her attention fixed on the cat and her mind on rescue, Anne was surprised to see that Dolly's plaything was not an animal. Dolly made a stab at the flower as Anne picked it up. Stroking Dolly's head, Anne was musing on why and how the cat had carried it up to the hatch cover when she realised what she was holding. It was a single white rose.

She snapped her head round so fast she almost had vertigo. Across the still water of the canal, the mooring of *X O 2* was empty. Donovan's boat had gone. Anne sniffed the rose ... *die weiße Rose*. It looked suspiciously like those that Marnie had planted in the farm garden.

They had all been wrong. The clothes found in the skip had not been a sign from their enemies, a warning to opponents. They had been a smokescreen. Donovan had covered his tracks. Quickly Anne jumped onto the bank and raced towards the bridge. But no boat was visible in any direction. She was still clutching the white rose. A smile crept slowly across her face.

Postscript

In cottage number two Marnie had finished gathering Estelle's Umbria papers together, as always admiring the quality and thoroughness of her work. She checked the desk but it was empty. As she slid open the bottom drawer and was making to close it, she heard something rustle inside. Bending down she looked in and found a bundle of papers at the back, letters addressed to Estelle in Luther's firm confident handwriting.

Marnie was turning her eyes away when she noticed something protruding from underneath them. She moved the bundle aside with a finger. It was a Valentine card. She could not help reading the inscription on the front. *To the Most Perfect Man in the World.*

Marnie covered it with the letters, pushed the whole collection to the back and closed the drawer.

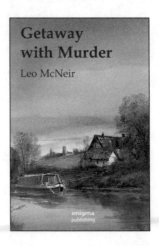

Getaway with Murder

Leo McNeir

Marnie Walker is an interior designer with a passion for boats, in particular her sister's boat Sally Ann, that she borrowed a year ago for an extended trip on the Grand Union Canal during the summer. While on her travels, Marnie had discovered a derelict farmhouse in a Northamptonshire village.

A year later, wishing to set up her own company, she finds herself buying the farm to restore it as an investment and a base, aided and abetted by her sister Beth and her friend, Anne with an 'e'. But she does not reckon with the tensions underlying the peace and tranquillity of her new home. All is going well until Marnie finds herself embroiled in not one unsolved murder but two, separated by almost 350 years.

The old feuds of the Civil War period seem to be fermenting again in a village becoming torn apart by factions. It is only a matter of time before something sinister emerges to shatter the calm of the countryside, and Marnie herself is dragged into the ancient conflict with terrifying results.

"... is destined to become a classic of crime fiction."
Canal and Riverboat

" ... the story has many fascinating twists – great holiday reading."
Inland Waterways Association

Available from enigma publishing: ISBN 0 9524052 6 1

Visit the author's website at www.leomcneir.com

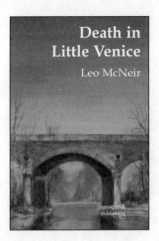

Death in Little Venice

Leo McNeir

A winter's afternoon on a deserted stretch of canal in Regent's park, and the discovery of a body under the 'blow-up' bridge, the body of a famous MP. A nasty shock for Marnie Walker, but more surprises lie in wait for her. Why do the police try to link her with the murder victim? Who is going to great lengths to try to eliminate her? Why should anyone want to destroy her if she really knows nothing?

Marnie finds herself pursued by unseen predators, who seem to know her every move, read her every thought. Out of her depth in a world of political intrigue and treachery, she is thrown together with the dead man's best friend, ally and fellow MP in an attempt to get to the bottom of the mystery. But the police appear to regard them both as suspects, despite every effort they make to clear their names. Neither Marnie's guile, nor the MP's connections can shake off their pursuers on both sides of the law.

In the heart of London's Little Venice, in the idyllic setting of her canalside Northamptonshire home and in the corridors of power at Westminster, there seems to be no escape. Sooner or later someone else could become a second victim, and the pursuers have Marnie firmly in their sights.

"Political intrigue in the corridors of power at Westminster and alongside the canals add spice to the story and flashes of humour combine to make this a most enjoyable whodunit."   *Waterways World*

"His are the only books our reviewer read twice, just for the fun of it."
Canal and Riverboat

Available from enigma publishing: ISBN 0 9524052 7 X

Visit the author's website at www.leomcneir.com

Kiss and Tell

Leo McNeir

Marnie Walker has a successful and growing business, a home in idyllic surroundings and a boat on the Grand Union Canal, sharing all these with Ralph her lover and Anne her closest friend. Life does not get much better than hers, until one day a stranger arrives on the scene, a fugitive with a shameful past, hounded by the media, accused of hypocrisy and depravity. But is he as guilty as everyone believes? If so, why does Marnie feel drawn to help him?

Keeping barely a step ahead of their pursuers, they try desperately to fight back, from rural Northamptonshire to London's Docklands and Little Venice. The situation becomes more desperate and heartbreaking at every turn as the strain takes its toll. How can anyone stand up to the power of the press? It seems a hopeless cause, but Marnie is not one to back down from a challenge.

In the midst of this conflict other hazards emerge. A violent mugger is on the loose in their community. Marnie's ex-husband comes back into her life. The complications pile up, and no one can escape the tragic consequences that threaten to blow Marnie's world apart.

And nothing is quite what it seems ...

"... these books are sure-fire hits." *Waterways World*

"A lot of action for your money!" *Canal and Riverboat*

Available from enigma publishing: ISBN 0 9531742 1 2

Visit the author's website at www.leomcneir.com